D0648272

an International Treasury of MYSTERY & SUSPENSE

an International Treasury of MYSTERY & SUSPENSE

Selected and with an Introduction
by MARIE R. RENO

Doubleday & Co., Inc.
Garden City, New York

Copyright © 1983 by Nelson Doubleday, Inc.
Library of Congress Cataloging in Publication Data
Main entry under title:

An International treasury of mystery & suspense.

1. Detective and mystery stories. I. Reno, Marie R.
PN6120.95.D45T58   1983   808.83'872

ISBN: 0-385-18532-4
Library of Congress Catalog Card Number 82-45400

All Rights Reserved
Printed in the United States of America

Design by Jeanette Portelli

ACKNOWLEDGMENTS

Grateful acknowledgment is made to the following for permission to reprint their copyrighted material:

"Red Wind" from THE SIMPLE ART OF MURDER by Raymond Chandler. Copyright 1950 by Raymond Chandler. Reprinted by permission of Houghton Mifflin Company.

MURDER ON THE ORIENT EXPRESS by Agatha Christie. Copyright 1933 by Agatha Christie. Copyright renewed 1961 by Agatha Christie Mallowan. Reprinted by permission of Dodd, Mead & Company, Inc.

"Lamb to the Slaughter" from SOMEONE LIKE YOU by Roald Dahl. Copyright 1953 by Roald Dahl. Reprinted by permission of Alfred A. Knopf, Inc.

"The Fat Man" by Isak Dinesen from CARNIVAL: ENTERTAINMENTS AND POSTHUMOUS TALES. Copyright © 1975 by Rungstedlundfonden. Copyright © 1977 by The University of Chicago. Reprinted by permission of The University of Chicago Press.

"Not After Midnight" from DON'T LOOK NOW by Daphne du Maurier. Copyright © 1971 by Daphne du Maurier. Reprinted by permission of Doubleday & Company, Inc. and Curtis Brown, Ltd.

"For Your Eyes Only" from FOR YOUR EYES ONLY by Ian Fleming. Copyright © 1959, 1960 by Glidrose Productions Ltd. Reprinted by permission of Viking Penguin Inc. and Jonathan Cape Ltd.

"Africa Emergent" from SELECTED STORIES by Nadine Gordimer. Copyright © 1971, 1975 by Nadine Gordimer. Reprinted by permission of Viking Penguin Inc. and Russell & Volkening, Inc.

"The Gatewood Caper" from THE BIG KNOCKOVER: SELECTED STORIES AND SHORT NOVELS OF DASHIELL HAMMETT edited by Lillian Hellman. Copyright © 1966 by Lillian Hellman. Reprinted by permission of Random House, Inc.

"Great-Aunt Allie's Flypapers" by P. D. James from VERDICT OF THIRTEEN edited by Julian Symons. Copyright © 1978 by Faber & Faber, Ltd., Publishers. Reprinted by permission of Harper & Row Publishers, Inc. and International Creative Management, Inc.

"Time and Time Again" from THE NINE MILE WALK by Harry Kemelman. Copyright 1947 by The American Mercury, Inc. Reprinted by permission of the author and the author's agents, Scott Meredith Literary Agency, Inc., 845 Third Avenue, New York, New York 10022.

"Strawberry Spring" from NIGHT SHIFT by Stephen King. Copyright © 1976, 1977, 1978 by Stephen King. Reprinted by permission of Doubleday & Company, Inc.

"Wild Goose Chase" by Ross Macdonald from THE NAME IS ARCHER. Copyright © 1954 by Kenneth Millar. Reprinted by permission of Harold Ober Associates Incorporated.

"The Prognosis for This Patient Is Horrible" by Berton Roueché as it originally appeared in *The New Yorker*. Copyright © 1982 by Berton Roueché. Reprinted by permission of *The New Yorker*.

"The Image in the Mirror" from HANGMAN'S HOLIDAY by Dorothy Sayers. Copyright 1933 by Dorothy Leigh Sayers Fleming. Reprinted by permission of Harper & Row Publishers, Inc. and David Higham Associates Limited.

"The Most Obstinate Customer in the World" by Georges Simenon from MAIGRET'S CHRISTMAS. English translation by Jean Stewart. Copyright © 1976 by Georges Simenon. Reprinted by permission of Harcourt Brace Jovanovich, Inc.

"The Affair of the Twisted Scarf" from CURTAINS FOR THREE (under the title "Disguise for Murder") by Rex Stout. Copyright 1950 by Rex Stout. Copyright © renewed 1978 by Pola Stout, Barbara Selleck, and Rebecca Bradbury. Reprinted by permission of Viking Penguin Inc.

"Wisp of Wool and Disk of Silver" by Arthur W. Upfield. First published in Ellery Queen's Mystery Magazine. Copyright © 1979 by Davis Publications, Inc. Reprinted by permission of the publisher.

"The Man Who Liked Dickens" from A HANDFUL OF DUST by Evelyn Waugh. Copyright 1934, © 1962 by Evelyn Waugh. Reprinted by permission of Little, Brown and Company and A. D. Peters & Company Ltd.

INTRODUCTION

The Landscape of Suspense

MARIE R. RENO

An English country house, a body in the library, a whole platoon of suspicious characters, and a brilliant sleuth unraveling all their tangled motives—these are the classic (and sometimes the clichéd) elements of the traditional detective story.

Tradition has its place, but mystery writers have long since broken out of this confining pattern, and the varied landscape of suspense now encompasses the whole world. The novel and novellas and short stories gathered here range the globe, touching down on six continents, thirteen countries, and sixteen towns and cities. Written over a period of the past sixty years, they provide fascinating glimpses of our changing manners and mores and are themselves a journey through time as well as distance.

Take, for instance, the three California stories with their prototypal private eyes—Raymond Chandler's Philip Marlowe, Dashiell Hammett's Continental Op, and Ross Macdonald's Lew Archer. All three detectives maintain a somewhat wary relationship with the local police, but Marlowe in the 1930s almost casually accepts a kind of police corruption and brutality that a modern reader finds alien—and shocking. Marlowe didn't approve either, I hasten to add, but his reactions are so mild that we realize he expects nothing better—brutality is routine. Our modern raised consciousness about civil rights makes Chandler's Los Angeles seem as foreign to us as . . . South Africa is today. There, in "Africa Emergent," Nadine Gordimer plays with a terrible irony in her story of a young black man, a sculptor, who can redeem himself in the eyes of his friends only by going to prison for a nameless crime, or perhaps no crime at all. Who will ever know? It's part South Africa and part pure Kafka.

Evelyn Waugh enfolds us in a different kind of horror, taking us to Brazil to meet "The Man Who Liked Dickens." Whatever the heat of the Amazon jungle, we suffer a chill that persists long after the story has ended.

Horror is Stephen King's forte, too, as fear stalks a New England college campus during a recent "strawberry spring." King's novels, from *Carrie* to *Cujo,* always bring on the shivers, but he is equally adept with the *frisson* of a short story.

Like Stephen King, Harry Kemelman favors a New England setting, but his is a more cerebral form of mystery, both in his classic Rabbi novels and in his Nicky Welt short stories. Professor Welt, with his deductive reasoning and logical analysis, is clearly identifiable as one of the many spiritual descendants of the master sleuth, Sherlock Holmes.

Claiming a similar kinship is Rex Stout's Nero Wolfe, aided as always by the faithful Archie Goodwin. And, as expected, while Archie does all the legwork, at risk of life and limb, Wolfe hovers over his orchids, having deduced who the murderer is from one telltale clue.

The ghost of Conan Doyle haunts every mystery writer, of course, and Sherlock Holmes's early feats of detection still dazzle us when echoed by the modern masters. Still, it is altogether startling to observe Isak Dinesen (in a rare excursion into the mystery field) proving the guilt of a killer by a ruse that takes us straight back to the most quotable dialogue in all the Holmes canon:

"Is there any point to which you would wish to draw my attention?"
"To the curious incident of the dog in the night-time."
"The dog did nothing in the night-time."
"That was the curious incident."

In most murder mysteries the suspense comes from the chase and from the discovery of clues identifying the killer, with the reader cheering on the gallant detective in his pursuit of truth and justice. But the next three stories turn this formula inside out, each with a particular charm and sometimes with a rough justice that satisfies the reader, if not the strict structures of the law.

Roald Dahl, equally famed for his wickedly ironic short stories and his delightful children's books (*Charlie and the Chocolate Factory*), is at the top of his form when he leads astray the ravenous forces of the law in "Lamb to the Slaughter."

P. D. James takes a different tack. In "Great-Aunt Allie's Fly-papers," we watch Chief Inspector Dalgliesh painstakingly unravel a long-ago murder while the unsuspecting culprit . . . But to reveal any more would be to commit another kind of crime.

Arthur W. Upfield also turns the usual formula upside down, revealing at the beginning exactly how a "perfect" crime is to be committed. "I never fail," declares Detective Inspector Napoleon Bonaparte, who is thoroughly at home in the harsh Australian outback of "Wisp of Wool and Disk of Silver." Half aboriginal and completely endearing, "Bony" is the star of a whole series of Upfield novels, but this is his only appearance in a short story.

Daphne du Maurier, whose novels and short stories have delighted a generation of readers and served as the basis of many successful movies (most memorably *Rebecca* and *The Birds*), turns to the novella form in "Not After Midnight"—with skin-prickling results. Who would have thought that on a Mediterranean holiday, with the sea sparkling, the island of Crete baking in the sun . . .

The sun is shining in Georges Simenon's Paris, too, which is a newsworthy event all by itself. Inspector Maigret, who is usually found caught in a drizzle, sniffling with a winter cold, for once can celebrate the joys of spring, the chestnuts in blossom on the Boulevard Saint-Germain. In such a season it is no wonder that Maigret finds it suspicious that a man should linger all day long in a dim café—"The Most Obstinate Customer in the World."

Sunny Crete, sunny Paris, and, in "For Your Eyes Only," sunny Jamaica, too. The island looks like a picture postcard, but Ian Fleming is not writing a travel brochure; with the first rattle of guns we know that James Bond is on the way—from London to Ottawa to Echo Lake, Vermont. One should not be surprised that on this journey he meets a beautiful girl—although the fact that she is stalking human prey with a bow and arrow gives pause even to the celebrated Mr. Bond.

With this quick tour of the globe, we return to the two most familiar landscapes for suspense, England and the United States.

The stylized world of Dorothy Sayers, England in the 1920s, contrasts sharply with the real world of violence in America today. However, Berton Roueché is every bit as masterful in creating suspense in his true tale of a crime in Nebraska as Miss Sayers was in posing puzzles for Peter Wimsey in London between World Wars I and II. Surely even debonair Lord Peter, who had a shrewd mind and a surprisingly practical streak, would have been impressed by the way a crime can be solved today—with all the resources of the medical laboratory combined with solid old-fashioned police work.

Having ranged the world and sampled the highly varied styles of suspense, we return to the most traditional of all forms, with the incomparable Agatha Christie at full throttle. Assembling her characters from Asia, Europe, and the United States, proceeding from Syria to Turkey to Yugoslavia, she has created her own international treasury in one star-studded novel. *Murder on the Orient Express* has all the best ingredients—the discovery of a body on a snowbound train, a carriage full of glamorous suspects, and one brilliant sleuth, none other than Hercule Poirot. If in his pursuit of truth and justice Poirot finds those two worthy goals in conflict, that only goes to show that Dame Agatha knew how to invert the classic mystery formula as well as anyone else. After all, she virtually invented it.

Happy reading, and happy travels.

Marie R. Reno

Contents

INTRODUCTION:

The Landscape of Suspense   *Marie R. Reno*   vii

CALIFORNIA PRIVATE EYES, PAST AND PRESENT

Red Wind   *Raymond Chandler*   3
The Gatewood Caper   *Dashiell Hammett*   45
Wild Goose Chase   *Ross Macdonald*   60

IRONY AND TERROR—SOUTH AFRICA, BRAZIL, NEW ENGLAND

Africa Emergent   *Nadine Gordimer*   85
The Man Who Liked Dickens   *Evelyn Waugh*   97
Strawberry Spring   *Stephen King*   111

HEIRS OF SHERLOCK HOLMES—NEW ENGLAND, NEW YORK, NORWAY

Time and Time Again   *Harry Kemelman*   123
The Affair of the Twisted Scarf   *Rex Stout*   135
The Fat Man   *Isak Dinesen*   179

VARIATIONS ON THE CLASSIC FORM OF MYSTERIES—FROM LONDON TO AUSTRALIA

Lamb to the Slaughter   *Roald Dahl*   189
Great-Aunt Allie's Flypapers   *P. D. James*   198
Wisp of Wool and Disk of Silver   *Arthur W. Upfield*   217

SUSPENSE IN SUNNY CLIMES—CRETE, PARIS, JAMAICA

Not After Midnight   *Daphne du Maurier*   231
The Most Obstinate Customer in the World   *Georges Simenon*   268
For Your Eyes Only   *Ian Fleming*   299

CRIME SOLVING, STYLIZED PAST AND TRUE-LIFE PRESENT—ENGLAND AND AMERICA

The Image in the Mirror   *Dorothy Sayers*   333
The Prognosis for This Patient Is Horrible   *Berton Roueché*   354

AN INTERNATIONAL TOUR DE FORCE, WITH A CAST FROM THREE CONTINENTS ON A SNOWBOUND TRAIN

Murder on the Orient Express   *Agatha Christie*   369

CALIFORNIA PRIVATE EYES

PAST AND PRESENT

Red Wind

RAYMOND CHANDLER

1

There was a desert wind blowing that night. It was one of those hot dry Santa Anas that come down through the mountain passes and curl your hair and make your nerves jump and your skin itch. On nights like that every booze party ends in a fight. Meek little wives feel the edge of the carving knife and study their husbands' necks. Anything can happen. You can even get a full glass of beer at a cocktail lounge.

I was getting one in a flossy new place across the street from the apartment house where I lived. It had been open about a week and it wasn't doing any business. The kid behind the bar was in his early twenties and looked as if he had never had a drink in his life.

There was only one other customer, a souse on a bar stool with his back to the door. He had a pile of dimes stacked neatly in front of him, about two dollars' worth. He was drinking straight rye in small glasses and he was all by himself in a world of his own.

I sat farther along the bar and got my glass of beer and said: "You sure cut the clouds off them, buddy. I will say that for you."

"We just opened up," the kid said. "We got to build up trade. Been in before, haven't you, mister?"

"Uh-huh."

"Live around here?"

"In the Berglund Apartments across the street," I said. "And the name is Philip Marlowe."

"Thanks, mister. Mine's Lew Petrolle." He leaned close to me across the polished dark bar. "Know that guy?"

"No."

"He ought to go home, kind of. I ought to call a taxi and send him home. He's doing his next week's drinking too soon."

"A night like this," I said. "Let him alone."

"It's not good for him," the kid said, scowling at me.

"Rye!" the drunk croaked, without looking up. He snapped his fingers so as not to disturb his piles of dimes by banging on the bar.

The kid looked at me and shrugged. "Should I?"

"Whose stomach is it? Not mine."

The kid poured him another straight rye and I think he doctored it with water down behind the bar because when he came up with it he looked as guilty as if he'd kicked his grandmother. The drunk paid no attention. He lifted coins off his pile with the exact care of a crack surgeon operating on a brain tumor.

The kid came back and put more beer in my glass. Outside the wind howled. Every once in a while it blew the stained-glass door open a few inches. It was a heavy door.

The kid said: "I don't like drunks in the first place and in the second place I don't like them getting drunk in here, and in the third place I don't like them in the first place."

"Warner Brothers could use that," I said.

"They did."

Just then we had another customer. A car squeaked to a stop outside and the swinging door came open. A fellow came in who looked a little in a hurry. He held the door and ranged the place quickly with flat, shiny, dark eyes. He was well set up, dark, good-looking in a narrow-faced, tight-lipped way. His clothes were dark and a white handkerchief peeped coyly from his pocket and he looked cool as well as under a tension of some sort. I guessed it was the hot wind. I felt a bit the same myself only not cool.

He looked at the drunk's back. The drunk was playing checkers with his empty glasses. The new customer looked at me, then he looked along the line of half-booths at the other side of the place. They were all empty. He came on in—down past where the drunk sat swaying and muttering to himself—and spoke to the bar kid.

"Seen a lady in here, buddy? Tall, pretty, brown hair, in a print bolero jacket over a blue crêpe silk dress. Wearing a wide-brimmed straw hat with a velvet band." He had a tight voice I didn't like.

"No, sir. Nobody like that's been in," the bar kid said.

"Thanks. Straight Scotch. Make it fast, will you?"

The kid gave it to him and the fellow paid and put the drink down in a gulp and started to go out. He took three or four steps and stopped, facing the drunk. The drunk was grinning. He swept a gun from somewhere so fast that it was just a blur coming out. He held it steady and he didn't look any drunker than I was. The tall dark guy stood quite still and then his head jerked back a little and then he was still again.

A car tore by outside. The drunk's gun was a .22 target automatic, with a large front sight. It made a couple of hard snaps and a little smoke curled—very little.

"So long, Waldo," the drunk said.

Then he put the gun on the barman and me.

The dark guy took a week to fall down. He stumbled, caught himself, waved one arm, stumbled again. His hat fell off, and then he hit the floor with his face. After he hit it he might have been poured concrete for all the fuss he made.

The drunk slid down off the stool and scooped his dimes into a pocket and slid towards the door. He turned sideways, holding the gun across his body. I didn't have a gun. I hadn't thought I needed one to buy a glass of beer. The kid behind the bar didn't move or make the slightest sound.

The drunk felt the door lightly with his shoulder, keeping his eyes on us, then pushed through it backwards. When it was wide a hard gust of air slammed in and lifted the hair of the man on the floor. The drunk said: "Poor Waldo. I bet I made his nose bleed."

The door swung shut. I started to rush it—from long practice in doing the wrong thing. In this case it didn't matter. The car outside let out a roar and when I got onto the sidewalk it was flicking a red smear of taillight around the nearby corner. I got its license number the way I got my first million.

There were people and cars up and down the block as usual. Nobody acted as if a gun had gone off. The wind was making enough noise to make the hard quick rap of .22 ammunition sound like a slammed door, even if anyone heard it. I went back into the cocktail bar.

The kid hadn't moved, even yet. He just stood with his hands flat on the bar, leaning over a little and looking down at the dark guy's back. The dark guy hadn't moved either. I bent down and felt his neck artery. He wouldn't move—ever.

The kid's face had as much expression as a cut of round steak and was about the same color. His eyes were more angry than shocked.

I lit a cigarette and blew smoke at the ceiling and said shortly: "Get on the phone."

"Maybe he's not dead," the kid said.

"When they use a twenty-two that means they don't make mistakes. Where's the phone?"

"I don't have one. I got enough expenses without that. Boy, can I kick eight hundred bucks in the face!"

"You own this place?"

"I did till this happened."

He pulled his white coat off and his apron and came around the inner end of the bar. "I'm locking this door," he said, taking keys out.

He went out, swung the door to and jiggled the lock from the outside until the bolt clicked into place. I bent down and rolled Waldo over. At first I couldn't even see where the shots went in. Then I could. A couple of tiny holes in his coat, over his heart. There was a little blood on his shirt.

The drunk was everything you could ask—as a killer.

The prowl-car boys came in about eight minutes. The kid, Lew Petrolle, was back behind the bar by then. He had his white coat on again and he was counting his money in the register and putting it in his pocket and making notes in a little book.

I sat at the edge of one of the half-booths and smoked cigarettes and watched Waldo's face get deader and deader. I wondered who the girl in the print coat was, why Waldo had left the engine of his car running outside, why he was in a hurry, whether the drunk had been waiting for him or just happened to be there.

The prowl-car boys came in perspiring. They were the usual large size and one of them had a flower stuck under his cap and his cap on a bit crooked. When he saw the dead man he got rid of the flower and leaned down to feel Waldo's pulse.

"Seems to be dead," he said, and rolled him around a little more. "Oh yeah, I see where they went in. Nice clean work. You two see him get it?"

I said yes. The kid behind the bar said nothing. I told them about it, that the killer seemed to have left in Waldo's car.

The cop yanked Waldo's wallet out, went through it rapidly and whistled. "Plenty jack and no driver's license." He put the wallet away. "O.K., we didn't touch him, see? Just a chance we could find did he have a car and put it on the air."

"The hell you didn't touch him," Lew Petrolle said.

The cop gave him one of those looks. "O.K., pal," he said softly. "We touched him."

The kid picked up a clean highball glass and began to polish it. He polished it all the rest of the time we were there.

In another minute a homicide fast-wagon sirened up and screeched to a stop outside the door and four men came in, two dicks, a photographer and a laboratory man. I didn't know either of the dicks. You can be in the detecting business a long time and not know all the men on a big city force.

One of them was a short, smooth, dark, quiet, smiling man, with curly black hair and soft intelligent eyes. The other was big, raw-boned, long-jawed, with a veined nose and glassy eyes. He looked like a heavy drinker. He looked tough, but he looked as if he thought he was a little tougher than he was. He shooed me into the last booth against the wall and his partner got the kid up front and the bluecoats went out. The fingerprint man and photographer set about their work.

A medical examiner came, stayed just long enough to get sore because there was no phone for him to call the morgue wagon.

The short dick emptied Waldo's pockets and then emptied his wallet and dumped everything into a large handkerchief on a booth table. I saw a lot of currency, keys, cigarettes, another handkerchief, very little else.

The big dick pushed me back into the end of the half-booth. "Give," he said. "I'm Copernik, Detective Lieutenant."

I put my wallet in front of him. He looked at it, went through it, tossed it back, made a note in a book.

"Philip Marlowe, huh? A shamus. You here on business?"

"Drinking business," I said. "I live just across the street in the Berglund."

"Know this kid up front?"

"I've been in here once since he opened up."

"See anything funny about him now?"

"No."

"Takes it too light for a young fellow, don't he? Never mind answering. Just tell the story."

I told it—three times. Once for him to get the outline, once for him to get the details and once for him to see if I had it too pat. At the end he said: "This dame interests me. And the killer called the guy Waldo, yet didn't seem to be anyways sure he would be in. I mean, if Waldo wasn't sure the dame would be here, nobody could be sure Waldo would be here."

"That's pretty deep," I said.

He studied me. I wasn't smiling. "Sounds like a grudge job, don't it? Don't sound planned. No getaway except by accident. A guy don't leave his car unlocked much in this town. And the killer works in front of two good witnesses. I don't like that."

"I don't like being a witness," I said. "The pay's too low."

He grinned. His teeth had a freckled look. "Was the killer drunk really?"

"With that shooting? No."

"Me too. Well, it's a simple job. The guy will have a record and he's left plenty prints. Even if we don't have his mug here we'll make him in hours. He had something on Waldo, but he wasn't meeting Waldo tonight. Waldo just dropped in to ask about a dame he had a date with and had missed connections on. It's a hot night and this wind would kill a girl's face. She'd be apt to drop in somewhere to wait. So the killer feeds Waldo two in the right place and scrams and don't worry about you boys at all. It's that simple."

"Yeah," I said.

"It's so simple it stinks," Copernik said.

He took his felt hat off and tousled up his ratty blond hair and leaned his head on his hands. He had a long mean horse face. He got a handkerchief out and mopped it, and the back of his neck and the back of his hands. He got a comb out and combed his hair—he looked worse with it combed—and put his hat back on.

"I was just thinking," I said.

"Yeah? What?"

"This Waldo knew just how the girl was dressed. So he must already have been with her tonight."

"So what? Maybe he had to go to the can. And when he came back she's gone. Maybe she changed her mind about him."

"That's right," I said.

But that wasn't what I was thinking at all. I was thinking that Waldo had described the girl's clothes in a way the ordinary man wouldn't know how to describe them. Printed bolero jacket over blue crêpe silk dress. I didn't even know what a bolero jacket was. And I might have said blue dress or even blue silk dress, but never blue crêpe silk dress.

After a while two men came with a basket. Lew Petrolle was still polishing his glass and talking to the short dark dick.

We all went down to headquarters.

Lew Petrolle was all right when they checked on him. His father had a grape ranch near Antioch in Contra Costa County. He had given Lew a thousand dollars to go into business and Lew had opened the cocktail bar, neon sign and all, on eight hundred flat.

They let him go and told him to keep the bar closed until they were sure they didn't want to do any more printing. He shook hands all around and grinned and said he guessed the killing would be good for business after all, because nobody believed a newspaper account of anything and people would come to him for the story and buy drinks while he was telling it.

"There's a guy won't ever do any worrying," Copernik said, when he was gone. "Over anybody else."

"Poor Waldo," I said. "The prints any good?"

"Kind of smudged," Copernik said sourly. "But we'll get a classification and teletype it to Washington some time tonight. If it don't click, you'll be in for a day on the steel picture racks downstairs."

I shook hands with him and his partner, whose name was Ybarra, and left. They didn't know who Waldo was yet either. Nothing in his pockets told.

2

I got back to my street about 9 P.M. I looked up and down the block before I went into the Berglund. The cocktail bar was farther down on the other side, dark, with a nose or two against the glass, but no real crowd. People had seen the law and the morgue wagon, but they didn't know what had happened. Except the boys playing pinball games in the drugstore on the corner. They know everything, except how to hold a job.

The wind was still blowing, oven-hot, swirling dust and torn paper up against the walls.

I went into the lobby of the apartment house and rode the automatic elevator up to the fourth floor. I unwound the doors and stepped out and there was a tall girl standing there waiting for the car.

She had brown wavy hair under a wide-brimmed straw hat with a velvet band and loose bow. She had wide blue eyes and eyelashes that didn't quite reach her chin. She wore a blue dress that might have been crêpe silk, simple in lines but not missing any curves. Over it she wore what might have been a print bolero jacket.

I said: "Is that a bolero jacket?"

She gave me a distant glance and made a motion as if to brush a cobweb out of the way.

"Yes. Would you mind—I'm rather in a hurry. I'd like—"

I didn't move. I blocked her off from the elevator. We stared at each other and she flushed very slowly.

"Better not go out on the street in those clothes," I said.

"Why, how dare you—"

The elevator clanked and started down again. I didn't know what she was going to say. Her voice lacked the edgy twang of a beer-parlor frill. It had a soft light sound, like spring rain.

"It's not a make," I said. "You're in trouble. If they come to this floor in the elevator, you have just that much time to get off the hall. First take off the hat and jacket—and snap it up!"

She didn't move. Her face seemed to whiten a little behind the not-too-heavy make-up.

"Cops," I said, "are looking for you. In those clothes. Give me the chance and I'll tell you why."

She turned her head swiftly and looked back along the corridor. With her looks I didn't blame her for trying one more bluff.

"You're impertinent, whoever you are. I'm Mrs. Leroy in Apartment Thirty-one. I can assure—"

"That you're on the wrong floor," I said. "This is the fourth." The elevator had stopped down below. The sound of doors being wrenched open came up the shaft.

"Off!" I rapped. "Now!"

She switched her hat off and slipped out of the bolero jacket, fast. I grabbed them and wadded them into a mess under my arm. I took her elbow and turned her and we were going down the hall.

"I live in Forty-two. The front one across from yours, just a floor up. Take your choice. Once again—I'm not on the make."

She smoothed her hair with that quick gesture, like a bird preening itself. Ten thousand years of practice behind it.

"Mine," she said, and tucked her bag under her arm and strode down the hall fast. The elevator stopped at the floor below. She stopped when it stopped. She turned and faced me.

"The stairs are back by the elevator shaft," I said gently.

"I don't have an apartment," she said.

"I didn't think you had."

"Are they searching for me?"

"Yes, but they won't start gouging the block stone by stone before tomorrow. And then only if they don't make Waldo."

She stared at me. "Waldo?"

"Oh, you don't know Waldo," I said.

She shook her head slowly. The elevator started down in the shaft again. Panic flicked in her blue eyes like a ripple on water.

"No," she said breathlessly, "but take me out of this hall."

We were almost at my door. I jammed the key in and shook the lock around and heaved the door inward. I reached in far enough to switch lights on. She went in past me like a wave. Sandalwood floated on the air, very faint.

I shut the door, threw my hat into a chair and watched her stroll over to a card table on which I had a chess problem set out that I couldn't solve. Once inside, with the door locked, her panic had left her.

"So you're a chess player," she said, in that guarded tone, as if she had come to look at my etchings. I wished she had.

We both stood still then and listened to the distant clang of elevator doors and then steps—going the other way.

I grinned, but with strain, not pleasure, went out into the kitchenette and started to fumble with a couple of glasses and then realized I still had her hat and bolero jacket under my arm. I went into the dressing room behind the wall bed and stuffed them into a drawer, went back out to the kitchenette, dug out some extra-fine Scotch and made a couple of highballs.

When I went in with the drinks she had a gun in her hand. It was a small automatic with a pearl grip. It jumped up at me and her eyes were full of horror.

I stopped, with a glass in each hand, and said: "Maybe this hot wind has got you crazy too. I'm a private detective. I'll prove it if you let me."

She nodded slightly and her face was white. I went over slowly and put a glass down beside her, and went back and set mine down and got a card out that had no bent corners. She was sitting down, smoothing one blue knee with her left hand, and holding the gun on the other. I put the card down beside her drink and sat with mine.

"Never let a guy get that close to you," I said. "Not if you mean business. And your safety catch is on."

She flashed her eyes down, shivered, and put the gun back in her bag. She drank half the drink without stopping, put the glass down hard and picked the card up.

"I don't give many people that liquor," I said. "I can't afford to."

Her lips curled. "I supposed you would want money."

"Huh?"

She didn't say anything. Her hand was close to her bag again.

"Don't forget the safety catch," I said. Her hand stopped. I went on: "This fellow I called Waldo is quite tall, say five-eleven, slim, dark, brown eyes with a lot of glitter. Nose and mouth too thin. Dark suit, white handkerchief showing, and in a hurry to find you. Am I getting anywhere?"

She took her glass again. "So that's Waldo," she said. "Well, what about him?" Her voice seemed to have a slight liquor edge now.

"Well, a funny thing. There's a cocktail bar across the street . . . Say, where have you been all evening?"

"Sitting in my car," she said coldly, "most of the time."

"Didn't you see a fuss across the street up the block?"

Her eyes tried to say no and missed. Her lips said: "I knew there was some kind of disturbance. I saw policemen and red searchlights. I supposed someone had been hurt."

"Someone was. And this Waldo was looking for you before that. In the cocktail bar. He described you and your clothes."

Her eyes were set like rivets now and had the same amount of expression. Her mouth began to tremble and kept on trembling.

"I was in there," I said, "talking to the kid that runs it. There was nobody in there but a drunk on a stool and the kid and myself. The drunk wasn't paying any attention to anything. Then Waldo came in and asked about you and we said no, we hadn't seen you and he started to leave."

I sipped my drink. I like an effect as well as the next fellow. Her eyes ate me.

"Just started to leave. Then this drunk that wasn't paying any attention to anyone called him Waldo and took a gun out. He shot him twice"—I snapped my fingers twice—"like that. Dead."

She fooled me. She laughed in my face. "So my husband hired you to spy on me," she said. "I might have known the whole thing was an act. You and your Waldo."

I gawked at her.

"I never thought of him as jealous," she snapped. "Not of a man who had been our chauffeur anyhow. A little about Stan, of course—that's natural. But Joseph Coates—"

I made motions in the air. "Lady, one of us has this book open at the wrong page," I grunted. "I don't know anybody named Stan or Joseph Coates. So help me, I didn't even know you had a chauffeur. People around here don't run to them. As for husbands—yeah, we do have a husband once in a while. Not often enough."

She shook her head slowly and her hand stayed near her bag and her blue eyes had glitters in them.

"Not good enough, Mr. Marlowe. No, not nearly good enough. I know you private detectives. You're all rotten. You tricked me into your apartment, if it is your apartment. More likely it's the apartment of some horrible man who will swear anything for a few dollars. Now you're trying to scare me. So you can blackmail me—as well as get money from my husband. All right," she said breathlessly, "how much do I have to pay?"

I put my empty glass aside and leaned back. "Pardon me if I light a cigarette," I said. "My nerves are frayed."

I lit it while she watched me without enough fear for any real guilt to be under it. "So Joseph Coates is his name," I said. "The guy that killed him in the cocktail bar called him Waldo."

She smiled a bit disgustedly, but almost tolerantly. "Don't stall. How much?"

"Why were you trying to meet this Joseph Coates?"

"I was going to buy something he stole from me, of course. Something that's valuable in the ordinary way too. Almost fifteen thousand dollars. The man I loved gave it to me. He's dead. There! He's dead! He died in a burning plane. Now, go back and tell my husband that, you slimy little rat!"

"I'm not little and I'm not a rat," I said.

"You're still slimy. And don't bother about telling my husband. I'll tell him myself. He probably knows anyway."

I grinned. "That's smart. Just what was I supposed to find out?"

She grabbed her glass and finished what was left of her drink. "So he thinks I'm meeting Joseph. Well, perhaps I was. But not to make love. Not with a chauffeur. Not with a bum I picked off the front step and gave a job to. I don't have to dig down that far, if I want to play around."

"Lady," I said, "you don't indeed."

"Now, I'm going," she said. "You just try and stop me." She snatched the pearl-handled gun out of her bag. I didn't move.

"Why, you nasty little string of nothing," she stormed. "How do I know you're a private detective at all? You might be a crook. This card you gave me doesn't mean anything. Anybody can have cards printed."

"Sure," I said. "And I suppose I'm smart enough to live here two years because you were going to move in today so I could blackmail you for not meeting a man named Joseph Coates who was bumped off across the street under the name of Waldo. Have you got the money to buy this something that cost fifteen grand?"

"Oh! You think you'll hold me up, I suppose!"

"Oh!" I mimicked her. "I'm a stick-up artist now, am I? Lady, will you please either put that gun away or take the safety catch off? It hurts my professional feelings to see a nice gun made a monkey of that way."

"You're a full portion of what I don't like," she said. "Get out of my way."

I didn't move. She didn't move. We were both sitting down—and not even close to each other.

"Let me in on one secret before you go," I pleaded. "What in hell did you take the apartment down on the floor below for? Just to meet a guy down on the street?"

"Stop being silly," she snapped. "I didn't. I lied. It's his apartment."

"Joseph Coates'?"

She nodded sharply.

"Does my description of Waldo sound like Joseph Coates?"

She nodded sharply again.

"All right. That's one fact learned at last. Don't you realize Waldo described your clothes before he was shot—when he was looking for you —that the description was passed on to the police—that the police don't know who Waldo is—and are looking for somebody in those clothes to help tell them? Don't you get that much?"

The gun suddenly started to shake in her hand. She looked down at it, sort of vacantly, slowly put it back in her bag.

"I'm a fool," she whispered, "to be even talking to you." She stared at me for a long time, then pulled in a deep breath. "He told me where he was staying. He didn't seem afraid. I guess blackmailers are like that. He was to meet me on the street, but I was late. It was full of police when I got here. So I went back and sat in my car for a while. Then I came up to Joseph's apartment and knocked. Then I went back to my car and waited again. I came up here three times in all. The last time I walked up a flight to take the elevator. I had already been seen twice on the third floor. I met you. That's all."

"You said something about a husband," I grunted. "Where is he?"

"He's at a meeting."

"Oh, a meeting," I said, nastily.

"My husband's a very important man. He has lots of meetings. He's a hydroelectric engineer. He's been all over the world. I'd have you know—"

"Skip it," I said. "I'll take him to lunch some day and have him tell me himself. Whatever Joseph had on you is dead stock now. Like Joseph."

"He's really dead?" she whispered. "Really?"

"He's dead," I said. "Dead, dead, dead. Lady, he's dead."

She believed it at last. I hadn't thought she ever would somehow. In the silence, the elevator stopped at my floor.

I heard steps coming down the hall. We all have hunches. I put my finger to my lips. She didn't move now. Her face had a frozen look. Her big blue eyes were as black as the shadows below them. The hot wind boomed against the shut windows. Windows have to be shut when a Santa Ana blows, heat or no heat.

The steps that came down the hall were the casual ordinary steps of one man. But they stopped outside my door, and somebody knocked.

I pointed to the dressing room behind the wall bed. She stood up without a sound, her bag clenched against her side. I pointed again, to her glass. She lifted it swiftly, slid across the carpet, through the door, drew the door quietly shut after her.

I didn't know just what I was going to all this trouble for.

The knocking sounded again. The backs of my hands were wet. I creaked my chair and stood up and made a loud yawning sound. Then I went over and opened the door—without a gun. That was a mistake.

3

I didn't know him at first. Perhaps for the opposite reason Waldo hadn't seemed to know him. He'd had a hat on all the time over at the cocktail bar and he didn't have one on now. His hair ended completely and exactly where his hat would start. Above that line was hard white sweatless skin almost as glaring as scar tissue. He wasn't just twenty years older. He was a different man.

But I knew the gun he was holding, the .22 target automatic with the big front sight. And I knew his eyes. Bright, brittle, shallow eyes like the eyes of a lizard.

He was alone. He put the gun against my face very lightly and said between his teeth: "Yeah, me. Let's go on in."

I backed in just far enough and stopped. Just the way he would want me to, so he could shut the door without moving much. I knew from his eyes that he would want me to do just that.

I wasn't scared. I was paralyzed.

When he had the door shut he backed me some more, slowly, until there was something against the back of my legs. His eyes looked into mine.

"That's a card table," he said. "Some goon here plays chess. You?"

I swallowed. "I don't exactly play it. I just fool around."

"That means two," he said with a kind of hoarse softness, as if some cop had hit him across the windpipe with a blackjack once, in a third-degree session.

"It's a problem," I said. "Not a game. Look at the pieces."

"I wouldn't know."

"Well, I'm alone," I said, and my voice shook just enough.

"It don't make any difference," he said. "I'm washed up anyway. Some nose puts the bulls on me tomorrow, next week, what the hell? I just didn't like your map, pal. And that smug-faced pansy in the bar coat that played left tackle for Fordham or something. To hell with guys like you guys."

I didn't speak or move. The big front sight raked my cheek lightly, almost caressingly. The man smiled.

"It's kind of good business too," he said. "Just in case. An old con like me don't make good prints, all I got against me is two witnesses. The hell with it."

"What did Waldo do to you?" I tried to make it sound as if I wanted to know, instead of just not wanting to shake too hard.

"Stooled on a bank job in Michigan and got me four years. Got himself a nolle prosse. Four years in Michigan ain't no summer cruise. They make you be good in them lifer states."

"How'd you know he'd come in there?" I croaked.

"I didn't. Oh yeah, I was lookin' for him. I was wanting to see him all right. I got a flash of him on the street night before last but I lost him. Up to then I wasn't lookin' for him. Then I was. A cute guy, Waldo. How is he?"

"Dead," I said.

"I'm still good," he chuckled. "Drunk or sober. Well, that don't make no doughnuts for me now. They make me downtown yet?"

I didn't answer him quick enough. He jabbed the gun into my throat and I choked and almost grabbed for it by instinct.

"Naw," he cautioned me softly. "Naw. You ain't that dumb."

I put my hands back, down at my sides, open, the palms towards him. He would want them that way. He hadn't touched me, except with the gun. He didn't seem to care whether I might have one too. He wouldn't—if he just meant the one thing.

He didn't seem to care very much about anything, coming back on that block. Perhaps the hot wind did something to him. It was booming against my shut windows like the surf under a pier.

"They got prints," I said. "I don't know how good."

"They'll be good enough—but not for teletype work. Take 'em airmail time to Washington and back to check 'em right. Tell me why I came here, pal."

"You heard the kid and me talking in the bar. I told him my name, where I lived."

"That's how, pal. I said why." He smiled at me. It was a lousy smile to be the last one you might see.

"Skip it," I said. "The hangman won't ask you to guess why he's there."

"Say, you're tough at that. After you, I visit that kid. I tailed him home from headquarters, but I figure you're the guy to put the bee on first. I tail him home from the city hall, in the rent car Waldo had. From headquarters, pal. Them funny dicks. You can sit in their laps and they don't know you. Start runnin' for a streetcar and they open up with machine guns and bump two pedestrians, a hacker asleep in his cab, and an old scrubwoman on the second floor workin' a mop. And they miss the guy they're after. Them funny lousy dicks."

He twisted the gun muzzle in my neck. His eyes looked madder than before.

"I got time," he said. "Waldo's rent car don't get a report right away. And they don't make Waldo very soon. I know Waldo. Smart he was. A smooth boy, Waldo."

"I'm going to vomit," I said, "if you don't take that gun out of my throat."

He smiled and moved the gun down to my heart. "This about right? Say when."

I must have spoken louder than I meant to. The door of the dressing-room by the wall bed showed a crack of darkness. Then an inch. Then four inches. I saw eyes, but didn't look at them. I stared hard into the bald-headed man's eyes. Very hard. I didn't want him to take his eyes off mine.

"Scared?" he asked softly.

I leaned against his gun and began to shake. I thought he would enjoy seeing me shake. The girl came out through the door. She had her gun in her hand again. I was sorry as hell for her. She'd try to make the door—or scream. Either way it would be curtains—for both of us.

"Well, don't take all night about it," I bleated. My voice sounded far away, like a voice on a radio on the other side of a street.

"I like this, pal," he smiled. "I'm like that."

The girl floated in the air, somewhere behind him. Nothing was ever more soundless than the way she moved. It wouldn't do any good though. He wouldn't fool around with her at all. I had known him all my life but I had been looking into his eyes for only five minutes.

"Suppose I yell," I said.

"Yeah, suppose you yell. Go ahead and yell," he said with his killer's smile.

She didn't go near the door. She was right behind him.

"Well—here's where I yell," I said.

As if that was the cue, she jabbed the little gun hard into his short ribs, without a single sound.

He had to react. It was like a knee reflex. His mouth snapped open and both his arms jumped out from his sides and he arched his back just a little. The gun was pointing at my right eye.

I sank and kneed him with all my strength, in the groin.

His chin came down and I hit it. I hit it as if I was driving the last spike on the first transcontinental railroad. I can still feel it when I flex my knuckles.

His gun raked the side of my face but it didn't go off. He was already limp. He writhed down gasping, his left side against the floor. I kicked his right shoulder—hard. The gun jumped away from him, skidded on the carpet, under a chair. I heard the chessmen tinkling on the floor behind me somewhere.

The girl stood over him, looking down. Then her wide dark horrified eyes came up and fastened on mine.

"That buys me," I said. "Anything I have is yours—now and forever."

She didn't hear me. Her eyes were strained open so hard that the whites showed under the vivid blue iris. She backed quickly to the door with her little gun up, felt behind her for the knob and twisted it. She pulled the door open and slipped out.

The door shut.

She was bareheaded and without her bolero jacket.

She had only the gun, and the safety catch on that was still set so that she couldn't fire it.

It was silent in the room then, in spite of the wind. Then I heard him gasping on the floor. His face had a greenish pallor. I moved behind him and pawed him for more guns, and didn't find any. I got a pair of store cuffs out of my desk and pulled his arms in front of him and snapped them on his wrists. They would hold if he didn't shake them too hard.

His eyes measured me for a coffin, in spite of their suffering. He lay in the middle of the floor, still on his left side, a twisted, wizened, bald-headed little guy with drawn-back lips and teeth spotted with cheap silver fillings. His mouth looked like a black pit and his breath came in little waves, choked, stopped, came on again, limping.

I went into the dressing room and opened the drawer of the chest. Her hat and jacket lay there on my shirts. I put them underneath, at the back, and smoothed the shirts over them. Then I went out to the kitchenette and poured a stiff jolt of whiskey and put it down and stood a moment listening to the hot wind howl against the window glass. A garage door banged, and a power-line wire with too much play between the insulators thumped the side of the building with a sound like somebody beating a carpet.

The drink worked on me. I went back into the living room and opened a window. The guy on the floor hadn't smelled her sandalwood, but somebody else might.

I shut the window again, wiped the palms of my hands and used the phone to dial headquarters.

Copernik was still there. His smart-aleck voice said: "Yeah? Marlowe? Don't tell me. I bet you got an idea."

"Make that killer yet?"

"We're not saying, Marlowe. Sorry as all hell and so on. You know how it is."

"O.K. I don't care who he is. Just come and get him off the floor of my apartment."

"Holy Christ!" Then his voice hushed and went down low. "Wait a minute, now. Wait a minute." A long way off I seemed to hear a door shut. Then his voice again. "Shoot," he said softly.

"Handcuffed," I said. "All yours. I had to knee him, but he'll be all right. He came here to eliminate a witness."

Another pause. The voice was full of honey. "Now listen, boy, who else is in this with you?"

"Who else? Nobody. Just me."

"Keep it that way, boy. All quiet. O.K.?"

"Think I want all the bums in the neighborhood in here sightseeing?"

"Take it easy, boy. Easy. Just sit tight and sit still. I'm practically there. No touch nothing. Get me?"

"Yeah." I gave him the address and apartment number again to save him time.

I could see his big bony face glisten. I got the .22 target gun from under the chair and sat holding it until feet hit the hallway outside my door and knuckles did a quiet tattoo on the door panel.

Copernik was alone. He filled the doorway quickly, pushed me back into the room with a tight grin and shut the door. He stood with his back to it, his hand under the left side of his coat. A big hard bony man with flat cruel eyes.

He lowered them slowly and looked at the man on the floor. The man's neck was twitching a little. His eyes moved in short stabs—sick eyes.

"Sure it's the guy?" Copernik's voice was hoarse.

"Positive. Where's Ybarra?"

"Oh, he was busy." He didn't look at me when he said that. "Those your cuffs?"

"Yeah."

"Key."

I tossed it to him. He went down swiftly on one knee beside the killer and took my cuffs off his wrists, tossed them to one side. He got his own off his hip, twisted the bald man's hands behind him and snapped the cuffs on.

"All right, you bastard," the killer said tonelessly.

Copernik grinned and balled his fist and hit the handcuffed man in the mouth a terrific blow. His head snapped back almost enough to break his neck. Blood dribbled from the lower corner of his mouth.

"Get a towel," Copernik ordered.

I got a hand towel and gave it to him. He stuffed it between the handcuffed man's teeth, viciously, stood up and rubbed his bony fingers through his ratty blond hair.

"All right. Tell it."

I told it—leaving the girl out completely. It sounded a little funny. Copernik watched me, said nothing. He rubbed the side of his veined nose. Then he got his comb out and worked on his hair just as he had done earlier in the evening, in the cocktail bar.

I went over and gave him the gun. He looked at it casually, dropped it into his side pocket. His eyes had something in them and his face moved in a hard bright grin.

I bent down and began picking up my chessmen and dropping them into the box. I put the box on the mantel, straightened out a leg of the card table, played around for a while. All the time Copernik watched me. I wanted him to think something out.

At last he came out with it. "This guy uses a twenty-two," he said. "He uses it because he's good enough to get by with that much gun. That means he's good. He knocks at your door, pokes that gat in your belly, walks you back into the room, says he's here to close your mouth for keeps—and yet you take him. You not having any gun. You take him alone. You're kind of good yourself, pal."

"Listen," I said, and looked at the floor. I picked up another chessman and twisted it between my fingers. "I was doing a chess problem," I said. "Trying to forget things."

"You got something on your mind, pal," Copernik said softly. "You wouldn't try to fool an old copper, would you, boy?"

"It's a swell pinch and I'm giving it to you," I said. "What the hell more do you want?"

The man on the floor made a vague sound behind the towel. His bald head glistened with sweat.

"What's the matter, pal? You been up to something?" Copernik almost whispered.

I looked at him quickly, looked away again. "All right," I said. "You know damn well I couldn't take him alone. He had the gun on me and he shoots where he looks."

Copernik closed one eye and squinted at me amiably with the other. "Go on, pal. I kind of thought of that too."

I shuffled around a little more, to make it look good. I said, slowly:

"There was a kid here who pulled a job over in Boyle Heights, a heist job. It didn't take. A two-bit service station stick-up. I know his family. He's not really bad. He was here trying to beg train money off me. When the knock came he sneaked in—there."

I pointed at the wall bed and the door beside. Copernik's head swiveled slowly, swiveled back. His eyes winked again. "And this kid had a gun," he said.

I nodded. "And he got behind him. That takes guts, Copernik. You've got to give the kid a break. You've got to let him stay out of it."

"Tag out for this kid?" Copernik asked softly.

"Not yet, he says. He's scared there will be."

Copernik smiled. "I'm a homicide man," he said. "I wouldn't know—or care."

I pointed down at the gagged and handcuffed man on the floor. "You took him, didn't you?" I said gently.

Copernik kept on smiling. A big whitish tongue came out and massaged his thick lower lip. "How'd I do it?" he whispered.

"Get the slugs out of Waldo?"

"Sure. Long twenty-two's. One smashed a rib, one good."

"You're a careful guy. You don't miss any angles. You know anything about me? You dropped in on me to see what guns I had."

Copernik got up and went down on one knee again beside the killer. "Can you hear me, guy?" he asked with his face close to the face of the man on the floor.

The man made some vague sound. Copernik stood up and yawned. "Who the hell cares what he says? Go on, pal."

"You wouldn't expect to find I had anything, but you wanted to look around my place. And while you were mousing around in there"—I pointed to the dressing room—"and me not saying anything, being a little sore, maybe, a knock came on the door. So he came in. So after a while you sneaked out and took him."

"Ah," Copernik grinned widely, with as many teeth as a horse. "You're on, pal. I socked him and I kneed him and I took him. You didn't have no gun and the guy swiveled on me pretty sharp and I left-hooked him down the backstairs. O.K.?"

"O.K.," I said.

"You'll tell it like that downtown?"

"Yeah," I said.

"I'll protect you, pal. Treat me right and I'll always play ball. Forget about that kid. Let me know if he needs a break."

He came over and held out his hand. I shook it. It was as clammy as a dead fish. Clammy hands and the people who own them make me sick.

"There's just one thing," I said. "This partner of yours—Ybarra. Won't he be a bit sore you didn't bring him along on this?"

Copernik tousled his hair and wiped his hatband with a large yellowish silk handkerchief.

"That guinea?" he sneered. "To hell with him!" He came close to me and breathed in my face. "No mistakes, pal—about that story of ours."

His breath was bad. It would be.

4

There were just five of us in the chief-of-detective's office when Copernik laid it before them. A stenographer, the chief, Copernik, myself, Ybarra. Ybarra sat on a chair tilted against the side wall. His hat was down over his eyes but their softness loomed underneath, and the small still smile hung at the corners of the clean-cut Latin lips. He didn't look directly at Copernik. Copernik didn't look at him at all.

Outside in the corridor there had been photos of Copernik shaking hands with me, Copernik with his hat on straight and his gun in his hand and a stern, purposeful look on his face.

They said they knew who Waldo was, but they wouldn't tell me. I didn't believe they knew, because the chief-of-detectives had a morgue photo of Waldo on his desk. A beautiful job, his hair combed, his tie straight, the light hitting his eyes just right to make them glisten. Nobody would have known it was a photo of a dead man with two bullet holes in his heart. He looked like a dance-hall sheik making up his mind whether to take the blonde or the redhead.

It was about midnight when I got home. The apartment door was locked and while I was fumbling for my keys a low voice spoke to me out of the darkness.

All it said was: "Please!" but I knew it. I turned and looked at a dark Cadillac coupe parked just off the loading zone. It had no lights. Light from the street touched the brightness of a woman's eyes.

I went over there. "You're a darn fool," I said.

She said: "Get in."

I climbed in and she started the car and drove it a block and a half along Franklin and turned down Kingsley Drive. The hot wind still burned and blustered. A radio lilted from an open, sheltered side window of an apartment house. There were a lot of parked cars but she found a vacant space behind a small brand-new Packard cabriolet that had the dealer's sticker on the windshield glass. After she'd jockeyed us up to the curb she leaned back in the corner with her gloved hands on the wheel.

She was all in black now, or dark brown, with a small foolish hat. I smelled the sandalwood in her perfume.

"I wasn't very nice to you, was I?" she said.

"All you did was save my life."

"What happened?"

"I called the law and fed a few lies to a cop I don't like and gave him all the credit for the pinch and that was that. That guy you took away from me was the man who killed Waldo."

"You mean—you didn't tell them about me?"

"Lady," I said again, "all you did was save my life. What else do you want done? I'm ready, willing, and I'll try to be able."

She didn't say anything, or move.

"Nobody learned who you are from me," I said. "Incidentally, I don't know myself."

"I'm Mrs. Frank C. Barsaly, Two-twelve Fremont Place, Olympia Two-four-five-nine-six. Is that what you wanted?"

"Thanks," I mumbled, and rolled a dry unlit cigarette around in my fingers. "Why did you come back?" Then I snapped the fingers of my left hand. "The hat and jacket," I said. "I'll go up and get them."

"It's more than that," she said. "I want my pearls." I might have jumped a little. It seemed as if there had been enough without pearls.

A car tore by down the street going twice as fast as it should. A thin bitter cloud of dust lifted in the street lights and whirled and vanished. The girl ran the window up quickly against it.

"All right," I said. "Tell me about the pearls. We have had a murder and a mystery woman and a mad killer and a heroic rescue and a police detective framed into making a false report. Now we will have pearls. All right—feed it to me."

"I was to buy them for five thousand dollars. From the man you call Waldo and I call Joseph Coates. He should have had them."

"No pearls," I said. "I saw what came out of his pockets. A lot of money, but no pearls."

"Could they be hidden in his apartment?"

"Yes," I said. "So far as I know he could have had them hidden anywhere in California except in his pockets. How's Mr. Barsaly this hot night?"

"He's still downtown at his meeting. Otherwise I couldn't have come."

"Well, you could have brought him," I said. "He could have sat in the rumble seat."

"Oh, I don't know," she said. "Frank weighs two hundred pounds and he's pretty solid. I don't think he would like to sit in the rumble seat, Mr. Marlowe."

"What the hell are we talking about anyway?"

She didn't answer. Her gloved hands tapped lightly, provokingly on the rim of the slender wheel. I threw the unlit cigarette out the window, turned a little and took hold of her.

When I let go of her, she pulled as far away from me as she could against the side of the car and rubbed the back of her glove against her mouth. I sat quite still.

We didn't speak for some time. Then she said very slowly: "I meant you to do that. But I wasn't always that way. It's only been since Stan Phillips was killed in his plane. If it hadn't been for that, I'd be Mrs. Phillips now. Stan gave me the pearls. They cost fifteen thousand dollars, he said once. White pearls, forty-one of them, the largest about a third of an inch across. I don't know how many grains. I never had them appraised or showed them to a jeweler, so I don't know those things. But I loved them on Stan's account. I loved Stan. The way you do just the one time. Can you understand?"

"What's your first name?" I asked.

"Lola."

"Go on talking, Lola." I got another dry cigarette out of my pocket and fumbled it between my fingers just to give them something to do.

"They had a simple silver clasp in the shape of a two-bladed propeller. There was one small diamond where the boss would be. I told Frank they were store pearls I had bought myself. He didn't know the difference. It's not so easy to tell, I dare say. You see—Frank is pretty jealous."

In the darkness she came closer to me and her side touched my side. But I didn't move this time. The wind howled and the trees shook. I kept on rolling the cigarette around in my fingers.

"I suppose you've read that story," she said. "About the wife and the real pearls and her telling her husband they were false?"

"I've read it," I said. "Maugham."

"I hired Joseph. My husband was in Argentina at the time. I was pretty lonely."

"*You* should be lonely," I said.

"Joseph and I went driving a good deal. Sometimes we had a drink or two together. But that's all. I don't go around—"

"You told him about the pearls," I said. "And when your two hundred pounds of beef came back from Argentina and kicked him out—he took the pearls, because he knew they were real. And then offered them back to you for five grand."

"Yes," she said simply. "Of course I didn't want to go to the police. And of course in the circumstance Joseph wasn't afraid of my knowing where he lived."

"Poor Waldo," I said. "I feel kind of sorry for him. It was a hell of a time to run into an old friend that had a down on you."

I struck a match on my shoe sole and lit the cigarette. The tobacco was so dry from the hot wind that it burned like grass. The girl sat quietly beside me, her hands on the wheel again.

"Hell with women—these fliers," I said. "And you're still in love with him, or think you are. Where did you keep the pearls?"

"In a Russian malachite jewelry box on my dressing table. With some other costume jewelry. I had to, if I ever wanted to wear them."

"And they were worth fifteen grand. And you think Joseph might have hidden them in his apartment. Thirty-one, wasn't it?"

"Yes," she said. "I guess it's a lot to ask."

I opened the door and got out of the car. "I've been paid," I said. "I'll go look. The doors in my apartment are not every obstinate. The cops will find out where Waldo lived when they publish his photo, but not tonight, I guess."

"It's awfully sweet of you," she said. "Shall I wait here?"

I stood with a foot on the running board, leaning in, looking at her. I didn't answer her question. I just stood there looking in at the shine of her eyes. Then I shut the car door and walked up the street towards Franklin.

Even with the wind shriveling my face I could still smell the sandalwood in her hair. And feel her lips.

I unlocked the Berglund door, walked through the silent lobby to the elevator, and rode up to Three. Then I soft-footed along the silent corridor and peered down at the sill of Apartment 31. No light. I rapped—the old light, confidential tattoo of the bootlegger with the big smile and the extra-deep hip pockets. No answer. I took the piece of thick hard celluloid that pretended to be a window over the driver's license in my wallet, and eased it between the lock and the jamb, leaning hard on the knob, pushing it toward the hinges. The edge of the celluloid caught the slope of the spring lock and snapped it back with a small brittle sound, like an icicle breaking. The door yielded and I went into near darkness. Street light filtered in and touched a high spot here and there.

I shut the door and snapped the light on and just stood. There was a queer smell in the air. I made it in a moment—the smell of dark-cured tobacco. I prowled over to a smoking stand by the window and looked down at four brown butts—Mexican or South American cigarettes.

Upstairs, on my floor, feet hit the carpet and somebody went into a bathroom. I heard the toilet flush. I went into the bathroom of Apartment 31. A little rubbish, nothing, no place to hide anything. The kitchenette was a longer job, but I only half searched. I knew there were no pearls in that apartment. I knew Waldo had been on his way out and that he was in a hurry and that something was riding him when he turned and took two bullets from an old friend.

I went back to the living room and swung the wall bed and looked past its mirror side into the dressing room for signs of still current occupancy. Swinging the bed farther I was no longer looking for pearls. I was looking at a man.

He was small, middle-aged, iron-gray at the temples, with a very dark skin, dressed in a fawn-colored suit with a wine-colored tie. His neat little brown hands hung limply by his sides. His small feet, in pointed polished shoes, pointed almost at the floor.

He was hanging by a belt around his neck from the metal top of the bed. His tongue stuck out farther than I thought it possible for a tongue to stick out.

He swung a little and I didn't like that, so I pulled the bed shut and he nestled quietly between the two clamped pillows. I didn't touch him yet. I didn't have to touch him to know that he would be cold as ice.

I went around him into the dressing room and used my handkerchief on drawer knobs. The place was stripped clean except for the light litter of a man living alone.

I came out of there and began on the man. No wallet. Waldo would have taken that and ditched it. A flat box of cigarettes, half full, stamped in gold: "Louis Tapia y Cia, Calle de Paysandú, 19, Montevideo." Matches from the Spezia Club. An under-arm holster of dark-grained leather and in it a 9-millimeter Mauser.

The Mauser made him a professional, so I didn't feel so badly. But not a very good professional, or bare hands would not have finished him, with the Mauser—a gun you can blast through a wall with—undrawn in his shoulder holster.

I made a little sense of it, not much. Four of the brown cigarettes had been smoked, so there had been either waiting or discussion. Somewhere along the line Waldo had got the little man by the throat and held him in just the right way to make him pass out in a matter of seconds. The Mauser had been less useful to him than a toothpick. Then Waldo had hung him up by the strap, probably dead already. That would account for haste, cleaning out the apartment, for Waldo's anxiety about the girl. It would account for the car left unlocked outside the cocktail bar.

That is, it would account for these things if Waldo had killed him, if this was really Waldo's apartment—if I wasn't just being kidded.

I examined some more pockets. In the left trouser one I found a gold penknife, some silver. In the left hip pocket a handkerchief, folded, scented. On the right hip another, unfolded but clean. In the right leg pocket four or five tissue handkerchiefs. A clean little guy. He didn't like to blow his nose on his handkerchief. Under these there was a small new keytainer holding four new keys—car keys. Stamped in gold on the keytainer was: Compliments of R. K. Vogelsang, Inc. "The Packard House."

I put everything as I had found it, swung the bed back, used my handkerchief on knobs and other projections, and flat surfaces, killed the light and poked my nose out the door. The hall was empty. I went down to the street and around the corner to Kingsley Drive. The Cadillac hadn't moved.

I opened the car door and leaned on it. She didn't seem to have moved, either. It was hard to see any expression on her face. Hard to see anything but her eyes and chin, but not hard to smell the sandalwood.

"That perfume," I said, "would drive a deacon nuts . . . no pearls."

"Well, thanks for trying," she said in a low, soft vibrant voice. "I guess I can stand it. Shall I . . . Do we . . . Or . . . ?"

"You go on home now," I said. "And whatever happens, you never saw me before. Whatever happens. Just as you may never see me again."

"I'd hate that."

"Good luck, Lola." I shut the car door and stepped back.

The lights blazed on, the motor turned over. Against the wind at the corner the big coupe made a slow contemptuous turn and was gone. I stood there by the vacant space at the curb where it had been.

It was quite dark there now. Windows had become blanks in the apartment where the radio sounded. I stood looking at the back of a Packard cabriolet which seemed to be brand new. I had seen it before—before I went upstairs, in the same place, in front of Lola's car. Parked, dark, silent, with a blue sticker pasted to the right-hand corner of the shiny windshield.

And in my mind I was looking at something else, a set of brand-new car keys in a keytainer stamped: "The Packard House," upstairs, in a dead man's pocket.

I went up to the front of the cabriolet and put a small pocket flash on the blue slip. It was the same dealer all right. Written in ink below his name and slogan was a name and address—Eugénie Kolchenko, 5315 Arvieda Street, West Los Angeles.

It was crazy. I went back up to Apartment 31, jimmied the door as I had done before, stepped in behind the wall bed and took the keytainer from the trousers pocket of the neat brown dangling corpse. I was back down on the street beside the cabriolet in five minutes. The keys fitted.

5

It was a small house, near a canyon rim out beyond Sawtelle, with a circle of writhing eucalyptus trees in front of it. Beyond that, on the other side of the street, one of those parties was going on where they come out and smash bottles on the sidewalk with a whoop like Yale making a touchdown against Princeton.

There was a wire fence at my number and some rose trees, and a flagged walk and a garage that was wide open and had no car in it. There was no car in front of the house either. I rang the bell. There was a long wait, then the door opened rather suddenly.

I wasn't the man she had been expecting. I could see it in her glittering kohl-rimmed eyes. Then I couldn't see anything in them. She just stood and looked at me, a long, lean, hungry brunette, with rouged cheekbones, thick black hair parted in the middle, a mouth made for three-decker sandwiches, coral-and-gold pajamas, sandals—and gilded toenails. Under her ear lobes a couple of miniature temple bells gonged lightly in the breeze. She made a slow disdainful motion with a cigarette in a holder as long as a baseball bat.

"We-el, what ees it, little man? You want sometheeng? You are lost from the bee-ootiful party across the street, hein?"

"Ha-ha," I said. "Quite a party, isn't it? No, I just brought your car home. Lost it, didn't you?"

Across the street somebody had delirium tremens in the front yard and a mixed quartet tore what was left of the night into small strips and did what they could to make the strips miserable. While this was going on the exotic brunette didn't move more than one eyelash.

She wasn't beautiful, she wasn't even pretty, but she looked as if things would happen where she was.

"You have said what?" she got out, at last, in a voice as silky as a burnt crust of toast.

"Your car." I pointed over my shoulder and kept my eyes on her. She was the type that uses a knife.

The long cigarette holder dropped very slowly to her side and the cigarette fell out of it. I stamped it out, and that put me in the hall. She backed away from me and I shut the door.

The hall was like the long hall of a railroad flat. Lamps glowed pinkly in iron brackets. There was a bead curtain at the end, a tiger skin on the floor. The place went with her.

"You're Miss Kolchenko?" I asked, not getting any more action.

"Ye-es. I am Mees Kolchenko. What the 'ell you want?"

She was looking at me now as if I had come to wash the windows, but at an inconvenient time.

I got a card out with my left hand, held it out to her. She read it in my hand, moving her head just enough. "A detective?" she breathed.

"Yeah."

She said something in a spitting language. Then in English: "Come in! Thees damn wind dry up my skeen like so much teesue paper."

"We're in," I said. "I just shut the door. Snap out of it, Nazimova. Who was he? The little guy?"

Beyond the bead curtain a man coughed. She jumped as if she had been stuck with an oyster fork. Then she tried to smile. It wasn't very successful.

"A reward," she said softly. "You weel wait 'ere? Ten dollars it is fair to pay, no?"

"No," I said.

I reached a finger towards her slowly and added: "He's dead."

She jumped about three feet and let out a yell.

A chair creaked harshly. Feet pounded beyond the bead curtain, a large hand plunged into view and snatched it aside, and a big hard-looking blond man was with us. He had a purple robe over his pajamas, his right hand held something in his robe pocket. He stood quite still as soon as he was through the curtain, his feet planted solidly, his jaw out, his colorless eyes like gray ice. He looked like a man who would be hard to take out on an off-tackle play.

"What's the matter, honey?" He had a solid, burring voice, with just the right sappy tone to belong to a guy who would go for a woman with gilded toenails.

"I came about Miss Kolchenko's car," I said.

"Well, you could take your hat off," he said. "Just for a light workout."

I took it off and apologized.

"O.K.," he said, and kept his right hand shoved down hard in the purple pocket. "So you came about Miss Kolchenko's car. Take it from there."

I pushed past the woman and went closer to him. She shrank back against the wall and flattened her palms against it. Camille in a high-school play. The long holder lay empty at her toes.

When I was six feet from the big man he said easily: "I can hear you from there. Just take it easy. I've got a gun in this pocket and I've had to learn to use one. Now about the car?"

"The man who borrowed it couldn't bring it," I said, and pushed the card I was still holding towards his face. He barely glanced at it. He looked back at me.

"So what?" he said.

"Are you always this tough?" I asked. "Or only when you have your pajamas on?"

"So why couldn't he bring it himself?" he asked. "And skip the mushy talk."

The dark woman made a stuffed sound at my elbow.

"It's all right, honeybunch," the man said. "I'll handle this. Go on."

She slid past both of us and flicked through the bead curtain.

I waited a little while. The big man didn't move a muscle. He didn't look any more bothered than a toad in the sun.

"He couldn't bring it because somebody bumped him off," I said. "Let's see you handle that."

"Yeah?" he said. "Did you bring him with you to prove it?"

"No," I said. "But if you put your tie and crush hat on, I'll take you down and show you."

"Who the hell did you say you were, now?"

"I didn't say. I thought maybe you could read." I held the card at him some more.

"Oh, that's right," he said. "Philip Marlowe, Private Investigator. Well, well. So I should go with you to look at who, why?"

"Maybe he stole the car," I said.

The big man nodded. "That's a thought. Maybe he did. Who?"

"The little brown guy who had the keys to it in his pocket, and had it parked around the corner from the Berglund Apartments."

He thought that over, without any apparent embarrassment. "You've got something there," he said. "Not much. But a little. I guess this must be the night of the Police Smoker. So you're doing all their work for them."

"Huh?"

"The card says private detective to me," he said. "Have you got some cops outside that were too shy to come in?"

"No, I'm alone."

He grinned. The grin showed white ridges in his tanned skin. "So you find somebody dead and take some keys and find a car and come riding out here—all alone. No cops. Am I right?"

"Correct."

He sighed. "Let's go inside," he said. He yanked the bead curtain aside and made an opening for me to go through. "It might be you have an idea I ought to hear."

I went past him and he turned, keeping his heavy pocket towards me. I hadn't noticed until I got quite close that there were beads of sweat on his face. It might have been the hot wind but I didn't think so.

We were in the living room of the house.

We sat down and looked at each other across a dark floor, on which a few Navajo rugs and a few dark Turkish rugs made a decorating combination with some well-used overstuffed furniture. There was a fireplace, a small baby grand, a Chinese screen, a tall Chinese lantern on a teakwood pedestal, and gold net curtains against lattice windows. The windows to the south were open. A fruit tree with a whitewashed trunk whipped about outside the screen, adding its bit to the noise from across the street.

The big man eased back into a brocaded chair and put his slippered feet on a footstool. He kept his right hand where it had been since I met him—on his gun.

The brunette hung around in the shadows and a bottle gurgled and her temple bells gonged in her ears.

"It's all right, honeybunch," the man said. "It's all under control. Somebody bumped somebody off and this lad thinks we're interested. Just sit down and relax."

The girl tilted her head and poured half a tumbler of whiskey down her throat. She sighed, said, "Goddam," in a casual voice, and curled up on a davenport. It took all of the davenport. She had plenty of legs. Her gilded toenails winked at me from the shadowy corner where she kept herself quiet from then on.

I got a cigarette out without being shot at, lit it and went into my story. It wasn't all true, but some of it was. I told them about the Berglund Apartments and that I had lived there and that Waldo was living there in Apartment 31 on the floor below mine and that I had been keeping an eye on him for business reasons.

"Waldo what?" the blond man put in. "And what business reasons?"

"Mister," I said, "have you no secrets?" He reddened slightly.

I told him about the cocktail lounge across the street from the Berglund and what had happened there. I didn't tell him about the printed bolero jacket or the girl who had worn it. I left her out of the story altogether.

"It was an undercover job—from my angle," I said. "If you know what I mean." He reddened again, bit his teeth. I went on: "I got back from the city hall without telling anybody I knew Waldo. In due time, when I decided they couldn't find out where he lived that night, I took the liberty of examining his apartment."

"Looking for what?" the big man said thickly.

"For some letters. I might mention in passing there was nothing there at all—except a dead man. Strangled and hanging by a belt to the top of the wall bed—well out of sight. A small man, about forty-five, Mexican or South American, well-dressed in a fawn-colored——"

"That's enough," the big man said. "I'll bite, Marlowe. Was it a blackmail job you were on?"

"Yeah. The funny part was this little brown man had plenty of gun under his arm."

"He wouldn't have five hundred bucks in twenties in his pocket, of course? Or are you saying?"

"He wouldn't. But Waldo had over seven hundred in currency when he was killed in the cocktail bar."

"Looks like I underrated this Waldo," the big man said calmly. "He took my guy and his pay-off money, gun and all. Waldo have a gun?"

"Not on him."

"Get us a drink, honeybunch," the big man said. "Yes, I certainly did sell this Waldo person shorter than a bargain-counter shirt."

The brunette unwound her legs and made two drinks with soda and ice. She took herself another gill without trimmings, wound herself back on the davenport. Her big glittering black eyes watched me solemnly.

"Well, here's how," the big man said, lifting his glass in salute. "I haven't murdered anybody, but I've got a divorce suit on my hands from now on. You haven't murdered anybody, the way you tell it, but you laid an egg down at police headquarters. What the hell! Life's a lot of trouble, any way you look at it. I've still got honeybunch here. She's a white Russian I met in Shanghai. She's safe as a vault and she looks as if she could cut your throat for a nickel. That's what I like about her. You get the glamor without the risk."

"You talk damn foolish," the girl spat at him.

"You look O.K. to me," the big man went on ignoring her. "That is, for a keyhole peeper. Is there an out?"

"Yeah. But it will cost a little money."

"I expected that. How much?"

"Say another five hundred."

"Goddam, thees hot wind make me dry like the ashes of love," the Russian girl said bitterly.

"Five hundred might do," the blond man said. "What do I get for it?"

"If I swing it—you get left out of the story. If I don't—you don't pay."

He thought it over. His face looked lined and tired now. The small beads of sweat twinkled in his short blond hair.

"This murder will make you talk," he grumbled. "The second one, I mean. And I don't have what I was going to buy. And if it's a hush, I'd rather buy it direct."

"Who was the little brown man?" I asked.

"Name's Leon Valesanos, a Uruguayan. Another of my importations. I'm in a business that takes me a lot of places. He was working in the Spezzia Club in Chiseltown—you know, the strip of Sunset next to Beverly Hills. Working on roulette, I think. I gave him the five hundred to go down to this—this Waldo—and buy back some bills for stuff Miss Kolchenko had charged to my account and delivered here. That wasn't bright, was it? I had them in my briefcase and this Waldo got a chance to steal them. What's your hunch about what happened?"

I sipped my drink and looked at him down my nose. "Your Uruguayan pal probably talked curt and Waldo didn't listen good. Then the little guy thought maybe that Mauser might help his argument—and Waldo was too quick for him. I wouldn't say Waldo was a killer—not by intention. A blackmailer seldom is. Maybe he lost his temper and maybe he just held on to the little guy's neck too long. Then he had to take it on the lam. But he had another date, with more money coming up. And he worked the neighborhood looking for the party. And accidentally he ran into a pal who was hostile enough and drunk enough to blow him down."

"There's a hell of a lot of coincidence in all this business," the big man said.

"It's the hot wind," I grinned. "Everybody's screwy tonight."

"For the five hundred you guarantee nothing? If I don't get my cover-up, you don't get your dough. Is that it?"

"That's it," I said, smiling at him.

"Screwy is right," he said, and drained his highball. "I'm taking you up on it."

"There are just two things," I said softly, leaning forward in my chair. "Waldo had a getaway car parked outside the cocktail bar where he was killed, unlocked with the motor running. The killer took it. There's always the chance of a kickback from that direction. You see, all Waldo's stuff must have been in that car."

"Including my bills, and your letters."

"Yeah. But the police are reasonable about things like that—unless you're good for a lot of publicity. If you're not, I think I can eat some stale dog downtown and get by. If you are—that's the second thing. What did you say your name was?"

The answer was a long time coming. When it came I didn't get as much kick out of it as I thought I would. All at once it was too logical.

"Frank C. Barsaly," he said.

After a while the Russian girl called me a taxi. When I left, the party across the street was doing all that a party could do. I noticed the walls of the house were still standing. That seemed a pity.

6

When I unlocked the glass entrance door of the Berglund I smelled policeman. I looked at my wrist watch. It was nearly 3 A.M. In the dark corner of the lobby a man dozed in a chair with a newspaper over his face. Large feet stretched out before him. A corner of the paper lifted an inch, dropped again. The man made no other movement.

I went on along the hall to the elevator and rode up to my floor. I soft-footed along the hallway, unlocked my door, pushed it wide and reached in for the light switch.

A chain switch tinkled and light glared from a standing lamp by the easy chair, beyond the card table on which my chessmen were still scattered.

Copernik sat there with a stiff unpleasant grin on his face. The short dark man, Ybarra, sat across the room from him, on my left, silent, half smiling as usual.

Copernik showed more of his big yellow horse teeth and said: "Hi. Long time no see. Been out with the girls?"

I shut the door and took my hat off and wiped the back of my neck slowly, over and over again. Copernik went on grinning. Ybarra looked at nothing with his soft dark eyes.

"Take a seat, pal," Copernik drawled. "Make yourself to home. We got pow-wow to make. Boy, do I hate this night sleuthing. Did you know you were low on hooch?"

"I could have guessed it," I said. I leaned against the wall.

Copernik kept on grinning. "I always did hate private dicks," he said, "but I never had a chance to twist one like I got tonight."

He reached down lazily beside his chair and picked up a printed bolero jacket, tossed it on the card table. He reached down again and put a wide-brimmed hat beside it.

"I bet you look cuter than all hell with these on," he said.

I took hold of a straight chair, twisted it around and straddled it, leaned my folded arms on the chair and looked at Copernik.

He got up very slowly—with an elaborate slowness, walked across the room and stood in front of me smoothing his coat down. Then he lifted his open right hand and hit me across the face with it—hard. It stung but I didn't move.

Ybarra looked at the wall, looked at the floor, looked at nothing.

"Shame on you, pal," Copernik said lazily. "The way you was taking care of this nice exclusive merchandise. Wadded down behind your old shirts. You punk peepers always did make me sick."

He stood there over me for a moment. I didn't move or speak. I looked into his glazed drinker's eyes. He doubled a fist at his side, then shrugged and turned and went back to the chair.

"O.K.," he said. "The rest will keep. Where did you get these things?"

"They belong to a lady."

"Do tell. They belong to a lady. Ain't you the light-hearted bastard! I'll tell you what lady they belong to. They belong to the lady a guy named Waldo asked about in a bar across the street—about two minutes before he got shot kind of dead. Or would that have slipped your mind?"

I didn't say anything.

"You was curious about her yourself," Copernik sneered on. "But you were smart, pal. You fooled me."

"That wouldn't make me smart," I said.

His face twisted suddenly and he started to get up. Ybarra laughed, suddenly and softly, almost under his breath. Copernik's eyes swung on him, hung there. Then he faced me again, bland-eyed.

"The guinea likes you," he said. "He thinks you're good."

The smile left Ybarra's face, but no expression took its place. No expression at all.

Copernik said: "You knew who the dame was all the time. You knew who Waldo was and where he lived. Right across the hall a floor below you. You knew this Waldo person had bumped a guy off and started to lam, only this broad came into his plans somewhere and he was anxious to meet up with her before he went away. Only he never got the chance. A heist guy from back East named Al Tessilore took care of that by taking care of Waldo. So you met the gal and hid her clothes and sent her on her way and kept your trap glued. That's the way guys like you make your beans. Am I right?"

"Yeah," I said. "Except that I only knew these things very recently. Who was Waldo?"

Copernik bared his teeth at me. Red spots burned high on his sallow cheeks. Ybarra, looking down at the floor, said very softly: "Waldo Ratigan. We got him from Washington by teletype. He was a two-bit porch climber with a few small terms on him. He drove a car in a bank stickup job in Detroit. He turned the gang in later and got a nolle prosse. One of the gang was this Al Tessilore. He hasn't talked a word, but we think the meeting across the street was purely accidental."

Ybarra spoke in the soft quiet modulated voice of a man for whom sounds have a meaning. I said: "Thanks, Ybarra. Can I smoke—or would Copernik kick it out of my mouth?"

Ybarra smiled suddenly. "You may smoke, sure," he said.

"The guinea likes you all right," Copernik jeered. "You never know what a guinea will like, do you?"

I lit a cigarette. Ybarra looked at Copernik and said very softly: "The word guinea—you overwork it. I don't like it so well applied to me."

"The hell with what you like, guinea."

Ybarra smiled a little more. "You are making a mistake," he said. He took a pocket nail file out and began to use it, looking down.

Copernik blared: "I smelled something rotten on you from the start, Marlowe. So when we make these two mugs, Ybarra and me think we'll drift over and dabble a few more words with you. I bring one of Waldo's morgue photos—nice work, the light just right in his eyes, his tie all straight and a white handkerchief showing just right in his pocket. Nice work. So on the way up, just as a matter of routine, we rout out the manager here and let him lamp it. And he knows the guy. He's here as A. B. Hummel, Apartment Thirty-one. So we go in there and find a stiff. Then we go round and round with that. Nobody knows him yet, but he's got some swell finger bruises under that strap and I hear they fit Waldo's fingers very nicely."

"That's something," I said. "I thought maybe I murdered him."

Copernik stared at me a long time. His face had stopped grinning and was just a hard brutal face now. "Yeah. We got something else even," he said. "We got Waldo's getaway car—and what Waldo had in it to take with him."

I blew cigarette smoke jerkily. The wind pounded the shut windows. The air in the room was foul.

"Oh, we're bright boys," Copernik sneered. "We never figured you with that much guts. Take a look at this."

He plunged his bony hand into his coat pocket and drew something up slowly over the edge of the card table, drew it along the green top and left it there stretched out, gleaming. A string of white pearls with a clasp like a two-bladed propeller. They shimmered softly in the thick smoky air.

Lola Barsaly's pearls. The pearls the flier had given her. The guy who was dead, the guy she still loved.

I stared at them, but I didn't move. After a long moment Copernik said almost gravely: "Nice, ain't they? Would you feel like telling us a story about now, Mis-ter Marlowe?"

I stood up and pushed the chair from under me, walked slowly across the room and stood looking down at the pearls. The largest was perhaps a third of an inch across. They were pure white, iridescent, with a mellow softness. I lifted them slowly off the card table from beside her clothes. They felt heavy, smooth, fine.

"Nice," I said. "A lot of the trouble was about these. Yeah, I'll talk now. They must be worth a lot of money."

Ybarra laughed behind me. It was a very gentle laugh. "About a hundred dollars," he said. "They're good phonies—but they're phony."

I lifted the pearls again. Copernik's glassy eyes gloated at me. "How do you tell?" I asked.

"I know pearls," Ybarra said. "These are good stuff, the kind women very often have made on purpose, as a kind of insurance. But they are slick like glass. Real pearls are gritty between the edges of the teeth. Try."

I put two or three of them between my teeth and moved my teeth back and forth, then sideways. Not quite biting them. The beads were hard and slick.

"Yes. They are very good," Ybarra said. "Several even have little waves and flat spots, as real pearls might have."

"Would they cost fifteen grand—if they were real?" I asked.

"Sí. Probably. That's hard to say. It depends on a lot of things."

"This Waldo wasn't so bad," I said.

Copernik stood up quickly, but I didn't see him swing. I was still looking down at the pearls. His fist caught me on the side of the face, against the molars. I tasted blood at once. I staggered back and made it look like a worse blow than it was.

"Sit down and talk, you bastard!" Copernik almost whispered.

I sat down and used a handkerchief to pat my cheek. I licked at the cut inside my mouth. Then I got up again and went over and picked up the cigarette he had knocked out of my mouth. I crushed it out in a tray and sat down again.

Ybarra filed at his nails and held one up against the lamp. There were beads of sweat on Copernik's eyebrows, at the inner ends.

"You found the beads in Waldo's car," I said, looking at Ybarra. "Find any papers?"

He shook his head without looking up.

"I'd believe you," I said. "Here it is. I never saw Waldo until he stepped into the cocktail bar tonight and asked about the girl. I knew nothing I didn't tell. When I got home and stepped out of the elevator this girl, in the printed bolero jacket and the wide hat and the blue silk crêpe dress—all as he had described them—was waiting for the elevator, here on my floor. And she looked like a nice girl."

Copernik laughed jeeringly. It didn't make any difference to me. I had him cold. All he had to do was know that. He was going to know it now, very soon.

"I knew what she was up against as a police witness," I said. "And I suspected there was something else to it. But I didn't suspect for a minute that there was anything wrong with her. She was just a nice girl in a jam—and she didn't even know she was in a jam. I got her in here. She pulled a gun on me. But she didn't mean to use it."

Copernik sat up very suddenly and he began to lick his lips. His face had a stony look now. A look like wet gray stone. He didn't make a sound.

"Waldo had been her chauffeur," I went on. "His name was then Joseph Coates. Her name is Mrs. Frank C. Barsaly. Her husband is a big hydroelectric engineer. Some guy gave her the pearls once and she told her husband they were just store pearls. Waldo got wise somehow there was a romance behind them and when Barsaly came home from South America and fired him, because he was too good-looking, he lifted the pearls."

Ybarra lifted his head suddenly and his teeth flashed. "You mean he didn't know they were phony?"

"I thought he fenced the real ones and had imitations fixed up," I said.

Ybarra nodded. "It's possible."

"He lifted something else," I said. "Some stuff from Barsaly's briefcase that showed he was keeping a woman—out in Brentwood. He was blackmailing wife and husband both, without either knowing about the other. Get it so far?"

"I get it," Copernik said harshly, between his tight lips. His face was still wet gray stone. "Get the hell on with it."

"Waldo wasn't afraid of them," I said. "He didn't conceal where he lived. That was foolish, but it saved a lot of finagling, if he was willing to risk it. The girl came down here tonight with five grand to buy back her pearls. She didn't find Waldo. She came here to look for him and walked up a floor before she went back down. A woman's idea of being cagey. So I met her. So I brought her in here. So she was in that dressing room when Al Tessilore visited me to rub out a witness." I pointed to the dressing-room door. "So she came out with her little gun and stuck it in his back and saved my life," I said.

Copernik didn't move. There was something horrible in his face now. Ybarra slipped his nail file into a small leather case and slowly tucked it into his pocket.

"Is that all?" he said gently.

I nodded. "Except that she told me where Waldo's apartment was and I went in there and looked for the pearls. I found the dead man. In his pocket I found new car keys in a case from a Packard agency. And down on the street I found the Packard and took it to where it came from. Barsaly's kept woman. Barsaly had sent a friend from the Spezzia Club down to buy something and he had tried to buy it with his gun instead of the money Barsaly gave him. And Waldo beat him to the punch."

"Is that all?" Ybarra said softly.

"That's all," I said, licking the torn place on the inside of my cheek.

Ybarra said slowly: "What do you want?"

Copernik's face convulsed and he slapped his long hard thigh. "This guy's good," he jeered. "He falls for a stray broad and breaks every law in the book and you ask him what does he want? I'll give him what he wants, guinea!"

Ybarra turned his head slowly and looked at him. "I don't think you will," he said. "I think you'll give him a clean bill of health and anything else he wants. He's giving you a lesson in police work."

Copernik didn't move or make a sound for a long minute. None of us moved. Then Copernik leaned forward and his coat fell open. The butt of his service gun looked out of his underarm holster.

"So what do you want?" he asked me.

"What's on the card table there. The jacket and hat and the phony pearls. And some names kept away from the papers. Is that too much?"

"Yeah—it's too much," Copernik said almost gently. He swayed sideways and his gun jumped neatly into his hand. He rested his forearm on his thigh and pointed the gun at my stomach.

"I like better that you get a slug in the guts resisting arrest," he said. "I like that better, because of a report I made out on Al Tessilore's arrest and how I made the pinch. Because of some photos of me that are in the morning sheets going out about now. I like it better that you don't live long enough to laugh about that baby."

My mouth felt suddenly hot and dry. Far off I heard the wind booming. It seemed like the sound of guns.

Ybarra moved his feet on the floor and said coldly: "You've got a couple of cases all solved, policeman. All you do for it is leave some junk here and keep some names from the papers. Which means from the D.A. If he gets them anyway, too bad for you."

Copernik said: "I like the other way." The blue gun in his hand was like a rock. "And God help you, if you don't back me up on it."

Ybarra said: "If the woman is brought out into the open, you'll be a liar on a police report and a chisler on your own partner. In a week they won't even speak your name at Headquarters. The taste of it would make them sick."

The hammer clicked back on Copernik's gun and I watched his big finger slide in farther around the trigger.

Ybarra stood up. The gun jumped at him. He said: "We'll see how yellow a guinea is. I'm telling you to put that gun up, Sam."

He started to move. He moved four even steps. Copernik was a man without a breath of movement, a stone man.

Ybarra took one more step and quite suddenly the gun began to shake.

Ybarra spoke evenly: "Put it up, Sam. If you keep your head everything lies the way it is. If you don't—you're gone."

He took one more step. Copernik's mouth opened wide and made a gasping sound and then he sagged in the chair as if he had been hit on the head. His eyelids dropped.

Ybarra jerked the gun out of his hand with a movement so quick it was no movement at all. He stepped back quickly, held the gun low at his side.

"It's the hot wind, Sam. Let's forget it," he said in the same even, almost dainty voice.

Copernik's shoulders sagged lower and he put his face in his hands. "O.K.," he said between his fingers.

Ybarra went softly across the room and opened the door. He looked at me with lazy, half-closed eyes. "I'd do a lot for a woman who saved my life, too," he said. "I'm eating this dish, but as a cop you can't expect me to like it."

I said: "The little man in the bed is called Leon Valesanos. He was a croupier at the Spezzia Club."

"Thanks," Ybarra said. "Let's go, Sam."

Copernik got up heavily and walked across the room and out of the open door and out of my sight. Ybarra stepped through the door after him and started to close it.

I said: "Wait a minute."

He turned his head slowly, his left hand on the door, the blue gun hanging down close to his right side.

"I'm not in this for money," I said. "The Barsalys live at Two-twelve Fremont Place. You can take the pearls to her. If Barsaly's name stays out of the paper, I get five *C's*. It goes to the Police Fund. I'm not so damn smart as you think. It just happened that way—and you had a heel for a partner."

Ybarra looked across the room at the pearls on the card table. His eyes glistened. "You take them," he said. "The five hundred's O.K. I think the fund has it coming."

He shut the door quietly and in a moment I heard the elevator doors clang.

7

I opened a window and stuck my head out into the wind and watched the squad car tool off down the block. The wind blew in hard and I let it blow. A picture fell off the wall and two chessmen rolled off the card table. The material of Lola Barsaly's bolero jacket lifted and shook.

I went out to the kitchenette and drank some Scotch and went back into the living room and called her—late as it was.

She answered the phone herself, very quickly, with no sleep in her voice.

"Marlowe," I said. "O.K. your end?"

"Yes . . . yes," she said. "I'm alone."

"I found something," I said. "Or rather the police did. But your dark boy gypped you. I have a string of pearls. They're not real. He sold the real ones, I guess, and made you up a string of ringers, with your clasp."

She was silent for a long time. Then, a little faintly: "The police found them?"

"In Waldo's car. But they're not telling. We have a deal. Look at the papers in the morning and you'll be able to figure out why."

"There doesn't seem to be anything more to say," she said. "Can I have the clasp?"

"Yes. Can you meet me tomorrow at four in the Club Esquire bar?"

"You're really rather sweet," she said in a dragged out voice. "I can. Frank is still at his meeting."

"Those meetings—they take it out of a guy," I said. We said good-bye.

I called a West Los Angeles number. He was still there, with the Russian girl.

"You can send me a check for five hundred in the morning," I told him. "Made out to the Police Relief Fund, if you want to. Because that's where it's going."

Copernik made the third page of the morning papers with two photos and a nice half-column. The little brown man in Apartment 31 didn't make the paper at all. The Apartment House Association has a good lobby too.

I went out after breakfast and the wind was all gone. It was soft, cool, a little foggy. The sky was close and comfortable and gray. I rode down to the boulevard and picked out the best jewelry store on it and laid a string of pearls on a black velvet mat under a daylight-blue lamp. A man in a wing collar and striped trousers looked down at them languidly.

"How good?" I asked.

"I'm sorry, sir. We don't make appraisals. I can give you the name of an appraiser."

"Don't kid me," I said. "They're Dutch."

He focused the light a little and leaned down and toyed with a few inches of the string.

"I want a string just like them, fitted to that clasp, and in a hurry," I added.

"How, like them?" He didn't look up. "And they're not Dutch. They're Bohemian."

"O.K., can you duplicate them?"

He shook his head and pushed the velvet pad away as if it soiled him. "In three months, perhaps. We don't blow glass like that in this country. If you wanted them matched—three months at least. And this house would not do that sort of thing at all."

"It must be swell to be that snooty," I said. I put a card under his black sleeve. "Give me a name that will—and not in three months—and maybe not exactly like them."

He shrugged, went away with the card, came back in five minutes and handed it back to me. There was something written on the back.

The old Levantine had a shop on Melrose, a junk shop with everything in the window from a folding baby carriage to a French horn, from a mother-of-pearl lorgnette in a faded plush case to one of those

.44 Special Single Action six-shooters they still make for Western peace officers whose grandfathers were tough.

The old Levantine wore a skull cap and two pairs of glasses and a full beard. He studied my pearls, shook his head sadly, and said: "For twenty dollars, almost so good. Not so good, you understand. Not so good glass."

"How like will they look?"

He spread his firm strong hands. "I am telling you the truth," he said. "They would not fool a baby."

"Make them up," I said. "With this clasp. And I want the others back, too, of course."

"Yah. Two o'clock," he said.

Leon Valesanos, the little brown man from Uruguay, made the afternoon papers. He had been found hanging in an unnamed apartment. The police were investigating.

At four o'clock I walked into the long cool bar of the Club Esquire and prowled along the row of booths until I found one where a woman sat alone. She wore a hat like a shallow soup plate with a very wide edge, a brown tailor-made suit with a severe mannish shirt and tie.

I sat down beside her and slipped a parcel along the seat. "You don't open that," I said. "In fact you can slip it into the incinerator as is, if you want to."

She looked at me with dark tired eyes. Her fingers twisted a thin glass that smelled of peppermint. "Thanks." Her face was very pale.

I ordered a highball and the waiter went away. "Read the papers?"

"Yes."

"You understand now about this fellow Copernik who stole your act? That's why they won't change the story or bring you into it."

"It doesn't matter now," she said. "Thank you, all the same. Please— please show them to me."

I pulled the string of pearls out of the loosely wrapped tissue paper in my pocket and slid them across to her. The silver propeller clasp winked in the light of the wall bracket. The little diamond winked. The pearls were as dull as white soap. They didn't even match in size.

"You were right," she said tonelessly. "They are not my pearls."

The waiter came with my drink and she put her bag on them deftly. When he was gone she fingered them slowly once more, dropped them into the bag and gave me a dry mirthless smile.

I stood there a moment with a hand hard on the table.

"As you said—I'll keep the clasp."

I said slowly: "You don't know anything about me. You saved my life last night and we had a moment, but it was just a moment. You still don't know anything about me. There's a detective downtown named Ybarra, a Mexican of the nice sort, who was on the job when the pearls were found in Waldo's suitcase. That is in case you would like to make sure—"

She said: "Don't be silly. It's all finished. It was a memory. I'm too young to nurse memories. It may be for the best. I loved Stan Phillips—but he's gone—long gone."

I stared at her, didn't say anything.

She added quietly: "This morning my husband told me something I hadn't known. We are to separate. So I have very little to laugh about today."

"I'm sorry," I said lamely. "There's nothing to say. I may see you sometime. Maybe not. I don't move much in your circle. Good luck."

I stood up. We looked at each other for a moment. "You haven't touched your drink," she said.

"You drink it. That peppermint stuff will just make you sick."

I stood there a moment with a hand on the table.

"If anybody ever bothers you," I said, "let me know."

I went out of the bar without looking back at her, got into my car and drove west on Sunset and down all the way to the Coast Highway. Everywhere along the way gardens were full of withered and blackened leaves and flowers which the hot wind had burned.

But the ocean looked cool and languid and just the same as ever. I drove on almost to Malibu and then parked and went and sat on a big rock that was inside somebody's wire fence. It was about half-tide and coming in. The air smelled of kelp. I watched the water for a while and then I pulled a string of Bohemian glass imitation pearls out of my pocket and cut the knot at one end and slipped the pearls off one by one.

When I had them all loose in my left hand I held them like that for a while and thought. There wasn't really anything to think about. I was sure.

"To the memory of Mr. Stan Phillips," I said aloud. "Just another four-flusher."

I flipped her pearls out into the water one by one at the floating seagulls.

They made little splashes and the seagulls rose off the water and swooped at the splashes.

The Gatewood Caper

DASHIELL HAMMETT

Harvey Gatewood had issued orders that I was to be admitted as soon as I arrived, so it took me only a little less than fifteen minutes to thread my way past the doorkeepers, office boys, and secretaries who filled up most of the space between the Gatewood Lumber Corporation's front door and the president's private office. His office was large, all mahogany and bronze and green plush, with a mahogany desk as big as a bed in the center of the floor.

Gatewood, leaning across the desk, began to bark at me as soon as the obsequious clerk who had bowed me in bowed himself out.

"My daughter was kidnaped last night! I want the gang that did it if it takes every cent I got!"

"Tell me about it," I suggested.

But he wanted results, it seemed, and not questions, and so I wasted nearly an hour getting information that he could have given me in fifteen minutes.

He was a big bruiser of a man, something over 200 pounds of hard red flesh, and a czar from the top of his bullet head to the toes of his shoes that would have been at least number twelves if they hadn't been made to measure.

He had made his several millions by sandbagging everybody that stood in his way, and the rage he was burning up with now didn't make him any easier to deal with.

His wicked jaw was sticking out like a knob of granite and his eyes were filmed with blood—he was in a lovely frame of mind. For a while it looked as if the Continental Detective Agency was going to lose a client, because I'd made up my mind that he was going to tell me all I wanted to know, or I'd chuck the job.

But finally I got the story out of him.

His daughter Audrey had left their house on Clay Street at about 7 o'clock the preceding evening, telling her maid that she was going for a walk. She had not returned that night—though Gatewood had not known that until after he had read the letter that came this morning.

The letter had been from someone who said that she had been kidnaped. It demanded $50,000 for her release, and instructed Gatewood to get the money ready in hundred-dollar bills—so that there would be no delay when he was told the manner in which the money was to be paid over to his daughter's captors. As proof that the demand was not a hoax, a lock of the girl's hair, a ring she always wore, and a brief note from her, asking her father to comply with the demands, had been enclosed.

Gatewood had received the letter at his office and had telephoned to his house immediately. He had been told that the girl's bed had not been slept in the previous night and that none of the servants had seen her since she started out for her walk. He had then notified the police, turning the letter over to them, and a few minutes later he had decided to employ private detectives also.

"Now," he burst out, after I had wormed these things out of him, and he had told me that he knew nothing of his daughter's associates or habits, "go ahead and do something! I'm not paying you to sit around and talk about it!"

"What are you going to do?" I asked.

"Me? I'm going to put those——behind bars if it takes every cent I've got in the world!"

"Sure! But first you get that $50,000 ready, so you can give it to them when they ask for it."

He clicked his jaw shut and thrust his face into mine.

"I've never been clubbed into doing anything in my life! And I'm too old to start now!" he said. "I'm going to call these people's bluff!"

"That's going to make it lovely for your daughter. But, aside from what it'll do to her, it's the wrong play. Fifty thousand isn't a whole lot to you, and paying it over will give us two chances that we haven't got now. One when the payment is made—a chance either to nab whoever comes for it or get a line on them. And the other when your daughter is returned. No matter how careful they are, it's a cinch she'll be able to tell us something that will help us grab them."

He shook his head angrily, and I was tired of arguing with him. So I left, hoping he'd see the wisdom of the course I had advised before it was too late.

At the Gatewood residence I found butlers, second men, chauffeurs, cooks, maids, upstairs girls, downstairs girls, and a raft of miscellaneous flunkies—he had enough servants to run a hotel.

What they told me amounted to this: the girl had not received a phone call, note by messenger or telegram—the time-honored devices for luring a victim out to a murder or abduction—before she left the house. She had told her maid that she would be back within an hour or two; but the maid had not been alarmed when her mistress failed to return all that night.

Audrey was the only child, and since her mother's death she had come and gone to suit herself. She and her father didn't hit it off very well together—their natures were too much alike, I gathered—and he never knew where she was. There was nothing unusual about her remaining away all night. She seldom bothered to leave word when she was going to stay overnight with friends.

She was nineteen years old, but looked several years older, about five feet five inches tall, and slender. She had blue eyes, brown hair—very thick and long—was pale and very nervous. Her photographs, of which I took a handful, showed that her eyes were large, her nose small and regular and her chin pointed.

She was not beautiful, but in the one photograph where a smile had wiped off the sullenness of her mouth, she was at least pretty.

When she left the house she was wearing a light tweed skirt and jacket with a London tailor's label in them, a buff silk shirtwaist with stripes a shade darker, brown wool stockings, low-heeled brown oxfords, and an untrimmed gray felt hat.

I went up to her rooms—she had three on the third floor—and looked through all her stuff. I found nearly a bushel of photographs of men, boys, and girls; and a great stack of letters of varying degrees of intimacy, signed with a wide assortment of names and nicknames. I made notes of all the addresses I found.

Nothing in her rooms seemed to have any bearing on her abduction, but there was a chance that one of the names and addresses might be of someone who had served as a decoy. Also, some of her friends might be able to tell us something of value.

I dropped in at the Agency and distributed the names and addresses among the three operatives who were idle, sending them out to see what they could dig up.

Then I reached the police detectives who were working on the case—O'Gar and Thode—by telephone, and went down to the Hall of Justice to meet them. Lusk, a post office inspector, was also there. We turned the job around and around, looking at it from every angle, but not getting very far. We were all agreed, however, that we couldn't take a chance on any publicity, or work in the open, until the girl was safe.

They had had a worse time with Gatewood than I—he had wanted to put the whole thing in the newspapers, with the offer of a reward, photographs and all. Of course, Gatewood was right in claiming that this was the most effective way of catching the kidnapers—but it would have been tough on his daughter if her captors happened to be persons of sufficiently hardened character. And kidnapers as a rule aren't lambs.

I looked at the letter they had sent. It was printed with pencil on ruled paper of the kind that is sold in pads by every stationery dealer in the world. The envelope was just as common, also addressed in pencil, and postmarked *San Francisco, September 20, 9* P.M. That was the night she had been seized.

The letter read:

Sir:

We have your charming daughter and place a value of $50,000 upon her. You will get the money ready in $100 bills at once so there will be no delay when we tell you how it is to be paid over to us.

We beg to assure you that things will go badly with your daughter should you not do as you are told, or should you bring the police into this matter, or should you do anything foolish.

$50,000 is only a small fraction of what you stole while we were living in mud and blood in France for you, and we mean to get that much or else!

Three.

A peculiar note in several ways. They are usually written with a great pretense of partial illiterateness. Almost always there's an attempt to lead suspicion astray. Perhaps the ex-service stuff was there for that purpose—or perhaps not.

Then there was a postscript:

We know someone who will buy her even after we are through with her—in case you won't listen to reason.

The letter from the girl was written jerkily on the same kind of paper, apparently with the same pencil.

Daddy—

    Please do as they ask! I am so afraid—

Audrey

A door at the other end of the room opened, and a head came through.

"O'Gar! Thode! Gatewood just called up. Get up to his office right away!"

The four of us tumbled out of the Hall of Justice and into a police car.

Gatewood was pacing his office like a maniac when we pushed aside enough hirelings to get to him. His face was hot with blood and his eyes had an insane glare in them.

"She just phoned me!" he cried thickly, when he saw us.

It took a minute or two to get him calm enough to tell us about it.

"She called me on the phone. Said, 'Oh, Daddy! Do something! I can't stand this—they're killing me!' I asked her if she knew where she was, and she said, 'No, but I can see Twin Peaks from here. There's three men and a woman, and—' And then I heard a man curse, and a sound as if he had struck her, and the phone went dead. I tried to get central to give me the number, but she couldn't! It's a damned outrage the way the telephone system is run. We pay enough for service, God knows, and we . . ."

O'Gar scratched his head and turned away from Gatewood. "In sight of Twin Peaks! There are hundreds of houses that are!"

Gatewood meanwhile had finished denouncing the telephone company and was pounding on his desk with a paperweight to attract our attention.

"Have you people done anything at all?" he demanded.

I answered him with another question: "Have you got the money ready?"

"No," he said, "I won't be held up by anybody!"

But he said it mechanically, without his usual conviction—the talk with his daughter had shaken him out of some of his stubbornness. He was thinking of her safety a little now instead of only his own fighting spirit.

We went at him hammer and tongs for a few minutes, and after a while he sent a clerk out for the money.

We split up the field then. Thode was to take some men from headquarters and see what he could find in the Twin Peaks end of town; but we weren't very optimistic over the prospects there—the territory was too large.

Lusk and O'Gar were to carefully mark the bills that the clerk brought from the bank, and then stick as close to Gatewood as they could without attracting attention. I was to go out to Gatewood's house and stay there.

The abductors had plainly instructed Gatewood to get the money ready immediately so that they could arrange to get it on short notice—not giving him time to communicate with anyone or make plans.

Gatewood was to get hold of the newspapers, give them the whole story, with the $10,000 reward he was offering for the abductors' capture, to be published as soon as the girl was safe—so we would get the help of publicity at the earliest possible moment without jeopardizing the girl.

The police in all the neighboring towns had already been notified—that had been done before the girl's phone message had assured us that she was held in San Francisco.

Nothing happened at the Gatewood residence all that evening. Harvey Gatewood came home early; and after dinner he paced his library floor and drank whiskey until bedtime, demanding every few minutes that we, the detectives in the case, do something besides sit around like a lot of damned mummies. O'Gar, Lusk, and Thode were out in the street, keeping an eye on the house and neighborhood.

At midnight Harvey Gatewood went to bed. I declined a bed in favor of the library couch, which I dragged over beside the telephone, an extension of which was in Gatewood's bedroom.

At 2:30 the telephone bell rang. I listened in while Gatewood talked from his bed.

A man's voice, crisp and curt: "Gatewood?"

"Yes."

"Got the dough?"

"Yes."

Gatewood's voice was thick and blurred—I could imagine the boiling that was going on inside him.

"Good!" came the brisk voice. "Put a piece of paper around it and leave the house with it, right away! Walk down Clay Street, keeping on the same side as your house. Don't walk too fast and keep walking. If everything's all right, and there's no elbows tagging along, somebody'll come up to you between your house and the waterfront. They'll have a handkerchief up to their face for a second, and then they'll let it fall to the ground.

"When you see that, you'll lay the money on the pavement, turn around, and walk back to your house. If the money isn't marked, and you don't try any fancy tricks, you'll get your daughter back in an hour or two. If you try to pull anything—remember what we wrote you! Got it straight?"

Gatewood sputtered something that was meant for an affirmative, and the telephone clicked silent.

I didn't waste any of my precious time tracing the call—it would be from a public telephone, I knew—but yelled up the stairs to Gatewood, "You do as you were told, and don't try any foolishness!"

Then I ran out into the early morning air to find the police detectives and the post office inspector.

They had been joined by two plainclothesmen, and had two automobiles waiting. I told them what the situation was, and we laid hurried plans.

O'Gar was to drive in one of the cars down Sacramento Street, and Thode, in the other, down Washington Street. These streets parallel Clay, one on each side. They were to drive slowly, keeping pace with Gatewood, and stopping at each cross street to see that he passed.

When he failed to cross within a reasonable time they were to turn up to Clay Street—and their actions from then on would have to be guided by chance and their own wits.

Lusk was to wander along a block or two ahead of Gatewood, on the opposite side of the street, pretending to be mildly intoxicated.

I was to shadow Gatewood down the street, with one of the plainclothesmen behind me. The other plainclothesman was to turn in a call at headquarters for every available man to be sent to City Street. They would arrive too late, of course, and as likely as not it would take them some time to find us; but we had no way of knowing what was going to turn up before the night was over.

Our plan was sketchy enough, but it was the best we could do—we were afraid to grab whoever got the money from Gatewood. The girl's talk with her father that afternoon had sounded too much as if her captors were desperate for us to take any chances on going after them roughshod until she was out of their hands.

We had hardly finished our plans when Gatewood, wearing a heavy overcoat, left his house and turned down the street.

Farther down, Lusk, weaving along, talking to himself, was almost invisible in the shadows. There was no one else in sight. That meant that I had to give Gatewood at least two blocks' lead, so that the man who came for the money wouldn't tumble to me. One of the plainclothesmen was half a block behind me, on the other side of the street.

We walked two blocks down, and then a chunky man in a derby hat came into sight. He passed Gatewood, passed me, went on.

Three blocks more.

A touring car, large, black, powerfully engined and with lowered curtains, came from the rear, passed us, went on. Possibly a scout. I scrawled its license number down on my pad without taking my hand out of my overcoat pocket.

Another three blocks.

A policeman passed, strolling in ignorance of the game being played under his nose; and then a taxicab with a single male passenger. I wrote down its license number.

Four blocks with no one in sight of me but Gatewood—I couldn't see Lusk any more.

Just ahead of Gatewood a man stepped out of a black doorway, turned around, called up to a window for someone to come down and open the door for him.

We went on.

Coming from nowhere, a woman stood on the sidewalk fifty feet ahead of Gatewood, a handkerchief to her face. It fluttered to the pavement.

Gatewood stopped, standing stiff-legged. I could see his right hand come up, lifting the side of the overcoat in which it was pocketed—and I knew his hand was gripped around a pistol.

For perhaps half a minute he stood like a statue. Then his left hand came out of his pocket, and the bundle of money fell to the sidewalk in front of him, where it made a bright blur in the darkness. Gatewood turned abruptly, and began to retrace his steps homeward.

The woman had recovered her handkerchief. Now she ran to the bundle, picked it up, and scuttled to the black mouth of an alley a few feet distant—a rather tall woman, bent, and in dark clothes from head to feet.

In the black mouth of the alley she vanished.

I had been compelled to slow up while Gatewood and the woman stood facing each other, and I was more than a block away now. As soon as the woman disappeared, I took a chance and started pounding my rubber soles against the pavement.

The alley was empty when I reached it.

It ran all the way through to the next street, but I knew that the woman couldn't have reached the other end before I got to this one. I carry a lot of weight these days, but I can still step a block or two in good time. Along both sides of the alley were the rears of apartment buildings, each with its back door looking blankly, secretively, at me.

The plainclothesman who had been trailing behind me came up, then O'Gar and Thode in their cars, and soon, Lusk. O'Gar and Thode rode off immediately to wind through the neighboring streets, hunting for the woman. Lusk and the plainclothesman each planted himself on a corner from which two of the streets enclosing the block could be watched.

I went through the alley, hunting vainly for an unlocked door, an open window, a fire escape that would show recent use—any of the signs that a hurried departure from the alley might leave.

Nothing!

O'Gar came back shortly with some reinforcements from head-quarters that he had picked up, and Gatewood.

Gatewood was burning.

"Bungled the damn thing again! I won't pay your agency a nickel, and I'll see that some of these so-called detectives get put back in a uniform and set to walking beats!"

"What'd the woman look like?" I asked him.

"I don't know! I thought you were hanging around to take care of her! She was old and bent, kind of, I guess, but I couldn't see her face for her veil. I don't know! What the hell were you men doing? It's a damned outrage the way . . ."

I finally got him quieted down and took him home, leaving the city men to keep the neighborhood under surveillance. There were fourteen or fifteen of them on the job now, and every shadow held at least one.

The girl would head for home as soon as she was released and I wanted to be there to pump her. There was an excellent chance of catching her abductors before they got very far, if she could tell us anything at all about them.

Home, Gatewood went up against the whiskey bottle again, while I kept one ear cocked at the telephone and the other at the front door. O'Gar or Thode phoned every half-hour or so to ask if we'd heard from the girl.

They had still found nothing.

At 9 o'clock they, with Lusk, arrived at the house. The woman in black had turned out to be a man and got away.

In the rear of one of the apartment buildings that touched the alley— just a foot or so within the back door—they found a woman's skirt, long coat, hat and veil—all black. Investigating the occupants of the house, they had learned that an apartment had been rented to a young man named Leighton three days before.

Leighton was not home, when they went up to his apartment. His rooms held a lot of cold cigarette butts, an empty bottle, and nothing else that had not been there when he rented it.

The inference was clear; he had rented the apartment so that he might have access to the building. Wearing women's clothes over his own, he had gone out of the back door—leaving it unlatched behind him

—to meet Gatewood. Then he had run back into the building, discarded his disguise and hurried through the building, out the front door, and away before we had our feeble net around the block—perhaps dodging into dark doorways here and there to avoid O'Gar and Thode in their cars.

Leighton, it seemed, was a man of about thirty, slender, about five feet eight or nine inches tall, with dark hair and eyes; rather good-looking, and well-dressed on the two occasions when people living in the building had seen him, in a brown suit and a light brown felt hat.

There was no possibility, according to both of the detectives and the post office inspector, that the girl might have been held, even temporarily, in Leighton's apartment.

Ten o'clock came, and no word from the girl.

Gatewood had lost his domineering bullheadedness by now and was breaking up. The suspense was getting him, and the liquor he had put away wasn't helping him. I didn't like him either personally or by reputation, but this morning I felt sorry for him.

I talked to the Agency over the phone and got the reports of the operatives who had been looking up Audrey's friends. The last person to see her had been an Agnes Dangerfield, who had seen her walking down Market Street near Sixth, alone, on the night of her abduction—some time between 8:15 and 8:45. Audrey had been too far away from the Dangerfield girl to speak to her.

For the rest, the boys had learned nothing except that Audrey was a wild, spoiled youngster who hadn't shown any great care in selecting her friends—just the sort of girl who could easily fall into the hands of a mob of highbinders.

Noon struck. No sign of the girl. We told the newspapers to turn loose the story, with the added developments of the past few hours.

Gatewood was broken; he sat with his head in his hands, looking at nothing. Just before I left to follow a hunch I had, he looked up at me, and I'd never have recognized him if I hadn't seen the change take place.

"What do you think is keeping her away?" he asked.

I didn't have the heart to tell him what I had every reason to suspect, now that the money had been paid and she had failed to show up. So I stalled with some vague assurances and left.

I caught a cab and dropped off in the shopping district. I visited the five largest department stores, going to all the women's wear departments from shoes to hats, and trying to learn if a man—perhaps one answering Leighton's description—had been buying clothes in the past couple days that would fit Audrey Gatewood.

Failing to get any results, I turned the rest of the local stores over to one of the boys from the Agency, and went across the bay to canvass the Oakland stores.

At the first one I got action. A man who might easily have been Leighton had been in the day before, buying clothes of Audrey's size. He had bought lots of them, everything from lingerie to a coat, and—my luck was hitting on all cylinders—had had his purchases delivered to T. Offord, at an address on Fourteenth Street.

At the Fourteenth Street address, an apartment house, I found Mr. and Mrs. Theodore Offord's names in the vestibule for Apartment 202.

I had just found the apartment number when the front door opened and a stout, middle-aged woman in a gingham housedress came out. She looked at me a bit curiously, so I asked, "Do you know where I can find the superintendent?"

"I'm the superintendent," she said.

I handed her a card and stepped indoors with her. "I'm from the bonding department of the North American Casualty Company"—a repetition of the lie that was printed on the card I had given her—"and a bond for Mr. Offord has been applied for. Is he all right so far as you know?" With the slightly apologetic air of one going through with a necessary but not too important formality.

"A bond? That's funny! He is going away tomorrow."

"Well, I can't say what the bond is for," I said lightly. "We investigators just get the names and addresses. It may be for his present employer, or perhaps the man he is going to work for has applied for it. Or some firms have us look up prospective employees before they hire them, just to be safe."

"Mr. Offord, so far as I know, is a very nice young man," she said, "but he has been here only a week."

"Not staying long, then?"

"No. They came here from Denver, intending to stay, but the low altitude doesn't agree with Mrs. Offord, so they are going back."

"Are you sure they came from Denver?"

"Well," she said, "they told me they did."

"How many of them are there?"

"Only the two of them; they're young people."

"Well, how do they impress you?" I asked, trying to get over the impression that I thought her a woman of shrewd judgment.

"They seem to be a very nice young couple. You'd hardly know they were in their apartment most of the time, they're so quiet. I'm sorry they can't stay."

"Do they go out much?"

"I really don't know. They have their keys, and unless I should happen to pass them going in or out I'd never see them."

"Then, as a matter of fact you couldn't say whether they stayed away all night some nights or not. Could you?"

She eyed me doubtfully—I was stepping way over my pretext now, but I didn't think it mattered—and shook her head. "No, I couldn't say."

"They have many visitors?"

"I don't know. Mr. Offord is not—"

She broke off as a man came in quietly from the street, brushed past me, and started to mount the steps to the second floor.

"Oh, dear!" she whispered. "I hope he didn't hear me talking about him. That's Mr. Offord."

A slender man in brown, with a light brown hat—Leighton, perhaps.

I hadn't seen anything of him except his back, nor he anything except mine. I watched him as he climbed the stairs. If he had heard the woman mention his name he would use the turn at the head of the stairs to sneak a look at me.

He did.

I kept my face stolid, but I knew him.

He was "Penny" Quayle, a con man who had been active in the east four or five years before.

His face was as expressionless as mine. But he knew me.

A door on the second floor shut. I left the woman and started for the stairs.

"I think I'll go up and talk to him," I told her.

Coming silently to the door of Apartment 202, I listened. Not a sound. This was no time for hesitation. I pressed the bell-button.

As close together as the tapping of three keys under the fingers of an expert typist, but a thousand times more vicious, came three pistol shots. And waist-high in the door of Apartment 202 were three bullet holes.

The three bullets would have been in my fat carcass if I hadn't learned years ago to stand to one side of strange doors when making uninvited calls.

Inside the apartment sounded a man's voice, sharp, commanding. "Cut it, kid! For God's sake, not that!"

A woman's voice, shrill, spiteful, screaming blasphemies.

Two more bullets came through the door.

"Stop! No! No!" The man's voice had a note of fear in it now.

The woman's voice, cursing hotly. A scuffle. A shot that didn't hit the door.

I hurled my foot against the door, near the knob, and the lock broke away.

On the floor of the room, a man—Quayle—and a woman were tussling. He was bending over her, holding her wrists, trying to keep her down. A smoking pistol was in one of her hands. I got to it in a jump and tore it loose.

"That's enough!" I called to them when I was planted. "Get up and receive company."

Quayle released his antagonist's wrists, whereupon she struck at his eyes with curved, sharp-nailed fingers, tearing his cheek open. He scrambled away from her on hands and knees, and both of them got to their feet.

He sat down on a chair immediately, panting and wiping his bleeding cheek with a handkerchief.

She stood, hands on hips, in the center of the room, glaring at me. "I suppose," she spat, "you think you've raised hell!"

I laughed—I could afford to.

"If your father is in his right mind," I told her, "he'll do it with a razor strap when he gets you home again. A fine joke you picked out to play on him!"

"If *you'd* been tied to him as long as I have and had been bullied and held down as much, I guess *you'd* do most anything to get enough money so that you could go away and live your own life."

I didn't say anything to that. Remembering some of the business methods Harvey Gatewood had used—particularly some of his war contracts that the Department of Justice was still investigating—I suppose the worst that could be said about Audrey was that she was her father's own daughter.

"How'd you rap to it?" Quayle asked me, politely.

"Several ways," I said. "First, one of Audrey's friends saw her on Market Street between 8:15 and 8:45 the night she disappeared, and your letter to Gatewood was postmarked 9 P.M. Pretty fast work. You should have waited awhile before mailing it. I suppose she dropped it in the post office on her way over here?"

Quayle nodded.

"Then second," I went on, "there was that phone call of hers. She knew it took anywhere from ten to fifteen minutes to get her father on the wire at the office. If she had gotten to a phone while imprisoned, time would have been so valuable that she'd have told her story to the first person she got hold of—the switchboard operator, most likely. So that made it look as if, besides wanting to throw out that Twin Peaks line, she wanted to stir the old man out of his bullheadedness.

"When she failed to show up after the money was paid, I figured it was a sure bet that she had kidnaped herself. I knew that if she came back home after faking this thing, we'd find out before we'd talked to her very long—and I figured she knew that too and would stay away.

"The rest was easy—I got some good breaks. We knew a man was working with her after we found the woman's clothes you left behind, and I took a chance on there being no one else in it. Then I figured she'd need clothes—she couldn't have taken any from home without tipping her mitt—and there was an even chance that she hadn't laid in a stock beforehand. She's got too many girl friends of the sort that do a lot of shopping to make it safe for her to have risked showing herself in stores. Maybe, then, the man would buy what she needed. And it turned out that he did, and that he was too lazy to carry away his purchases, or perhaps there were too many of them, and so he had them sent out. That's the story."

Quayle nodded again.

"I was damned careless," he said, and then, jerking a contemptuous thumb toward the girl, "But what can you expect? She's had a skinful of hop ever since we started. Took all my time and attention keeping her from running wild and gumming the works. Just now was a sample—I told her you were coming up and she goes crazy and tries to add your corpse to the wreckage!"

The Gatewood reunion took place in the office of the captain of inspectors on the second floor of the Oakland City Hall, and it was a merry little party.

For over an hour it was a tossup whether Harvey Gatewood would die of apoplexy, strangle his daughter or send her off to the state reformatory until she was of age. But Audrey licked him. Besides being a chip off the old block, she was young enough to be careless of consequences, while her father, for all his bullheadedness, had had some caution hammered into him.

The card she beat him with was a threat of spilling everything she knew about him to the newspapers, and at least one of the San Francisco papers had been trying to get his scalp for years.

I don't know what she had on him, and I don't think he was any too sure himself; but with his war contracts still being investigated by the Department of Justice, he couldn't afford to take a chance. There was no doubt at all that she would have done as she threatened.

And so, together, they left for home, sweating hate for each other from every pore.

We took Quayle upstairs and put him in a cell, but he was too experienced to let that worry him. He knew that if the girl was to be spared, he himself couldn't very easily be convicted of anything.

I was glad it was over. It had been a tough caper.

Wild Goose Chase

ROSS MACDONALD

The plane turned in towards the shoreline and began to lose altitude. Mountains detached themselves from the blue distance. Then there was a city between the sea and the mountains, a little city made of sugar cubes. The cubes increased in size. Cars crawled like colored beetles between the buildings, and matchstick figures hustled jerkily along the white morning pavements. A few minutes later I was one of them.

The woman who had telephoned me was waiting at the airport, as she had promised. She climbed out of her Cadillac when I appeared at the entrance to the waiting room, and took a few tentative steps towards me. In spite of her height and her blondeness, the dark harlequin glasses she wore gave her an oddly Oriental look.

"You must be Mr. Archer."

I said I was, and waited for her to complete the exchange of names—she hadn't given me her name on the telephone. All she had given me, in fact, was an urgent request to catch the first plane north, and assurances that I would be paid for my time.

She sensed what I was waiting for. "I'm sorry to be so mysterious. I really can't afford to tell you my name. I'm taking quite a risk in coming here at all."

I looked her over carefully, trying to decide whether this was another wild goose chase. Although she was well-groomed in a sharkskin suit, her hair and face were slightly disarranged, as if a storm had struck her a glancing blow. She took off her glasses to wipe them. I could see that the storm was inside of her, roiling the blue-green color of her eyes.

"What's the problem?" I said.

She stood wavering between me and her car, beaten by surges of sound from the airfield where my plane was about to take off again. Behind her, in the Cadillac's front seat, a little girl with the coloring of a Dresden doll was sitting as still as one. The woman glanced at the child and moved farther away from the car:

"I don't want Janie to hear. She's only three and a half but she understands a great deal." She took a deep gasping breath, like a swimmer about to dive. "There's a man on trial for murder here. They claim he murdered his wife."

"Glenway Cave?"

Her whole body moved with surprise. "You know him?"

"No, I've been following the trial in the papers."

"Then you know he's testifying today. He's probably on the witness stand right now." Her voice was somber, as if she could see the courtroom in her mind's eye.

"Is Mr. Cave a friend of yours?"

She bit her lip. "Let's say that I'm an interested observer."

"And you don't believe he's guilty."

"Did I say that?"

"By implication. You said they *claim* he murdered his wife."

"You have an alert ear, haven't you? Anyway, what I believe doesn't matter. It's what the jury believes. Do you think they'll acquit him?"

"It's hard to form an opinion without attending the trial. But the average jury has a prejudice against the idea of blowing off your wife's head with a twelve-gauge shotgun. I'd say he stands a good chance of going to the gas chamber."

"The gas chamber." Her nostrils dilated, and she paled, as if she had caught a whiff of the fatal stuff. "Do you seriously think there's any danger of that?"

"They've built a powerful case against him. Motive. Opportunity. Weapon."

"What motive?"

"His wife was wealthy, wasn't she? I understand Cave isn't. They were alone in the house; the housekeeping couple were away for the weekend. The shotgun belonged to Cave, and according to the chemical test his driving gloves were used to fire it."

"You *have* been following the trial."

"As well as I could from Los Angeles. Of course you get distortions in the newspapers. It makes a better story if he looks guilty."

"He isn't guilty," she said in a quiet voice.

"Do you know that, or merely hope it?"

She pressed one hand across her mouth. The fingernails were bitten down to the quick. "We won't go into that."

"Do you know who murdered Ruth Cave?"

"No. Of course not."

"Am I supposed to try and find out who did?"

"Wouldn't that be very difficult, since it happened so long ago? Anyway, it doesn't really matter to me. I barely knew the woman." Her thoughts veered back to Cave. "Won't a great deal depend on the impression he makes on the witness stand?"

"It usually does in a murder trial."

"You've seen a lot of them, haven't you?"

"Too many. I take it I'm going to see another."

"Yes." She spoke sharply and definitely, leaning forward. "I don't dare go myself. I want you to observe the jurors, see how Glen—how Mr. Cave's testimony affects them. And tell me if you think he's going to get off."

"What if I can't tell?"

"You'll have to give me a yes or no." Her breast nudged my arm. She was too intent on what she was saying to notice. "I've made up my mind to go by your decision."

"Go where?" I said.

"To hell if necessary—if his life is really in danger."

"I'll do my best. Where shall I get in touch with you?"

"I'll get in touch with you. I've made a reservation for you at the Rubio Inn. Right now I'll drop you at the courthouse. Oh, yes—the money." She opened her leather handbag, and I caught the gleam of a blue revolver at the bottom of the bag. "How much?"

"A hundred dollars will do."

A few bills changed hands, and we went to the car. She indicated the right rear door. I went around to the left so that I could read the white slip on the steering column. But the leatherette holder was empty.

The little girl stood up in the front seat and leaned over the back of it to look at me. "Hello. Are you my daddy?" Her eyes were as blue and candid as the sky.

Before I could answer, her mother said: "Now Janie, you know he isn't your daddy. This is Mr. Archer."

"Where is my daddy?"

"In Pasadena, darling. You know that. Sit down, Janie, and be still."

The little girl slid down out of my sight. The engine roared in anger.

It was ten minutes past eleven by the clock on the courthouse tower. Superior Court was on the second floor. I slid into one of the vacant seats in the back row of the spectators' section. Several old ladies turned to glare at me, as though I had interrupted a church service.

The trial was more like an ancient tribal ceremony in a grotto. Red draperies were drawn over the lofty windows. The air was dim with human exhalations. Black iron fixtures suspended from the ceiling shed a wan light on the judge's gray head, and on the man on the witness stand.

I recognized Glenway Cave from his newspaper pictures. He was a big handsome man in his early thirties who had once been bigger and handsomer. Four months in jail waiting for trial had pared him down to the bone. His eyes were pressed deep into hollow sockets. His double-breasted gabardine suit hung loosely on his shoulders. He looked like a suitable victim for the ceremony.

A broad-backed man with a straw-colored crewcut was bent over the stenograph, talking in an inaudible voice to the court reporter. Harvey, chief attorney for the defense. I had met Rod Harvey several times in the course of my work, which was one reason why I had followed the trial so closely.

The judge chopped the air with his hatchet face: "Proceed with your examination, Mr. Harvey."

Harvey raised his clipped blond head and addressed the witness: "Mr. Cave, we were attempting to establish the reason behind your—ah —misunderstanding with your wife. Did you and Mrs. Cave have words on the evening of May nineteenth?"

"We did. I've already told you that." Cave's voice was shallow, with high-pitched overtones.

"What was the nature of the conversation?"

"It was more of an argument than a conversation."

"But a purely verbal argument?" Harvey sounded as if his own witness had taken him by surprise.

A sharp-faced man spoke up from the prosecution end of the attorneys' table. "Objection. The question is leading—not to say *mis*leading."

"Sustained. The question will be stricken."

Harvey shrugged his heavy tweed shoulders. "Tell us just what was said then, Mr. Cave. Beginning at the beginning."

Cave moved uncomfortably, passing the palm of one hand over his eyes. "I can't recall it *verbatim*. It was quite an emotional scene—"

Harvey cut him off. "Tell us in your own words what you and Mrs. Cave were talking about."

"The future," Cave said. "Our future. Ruth was planning to leave me for another man."

An insect-buzzing rose from the spectators. I looked along the row where I was sitting. A couple of seats to my right, a young woman with artificial violets at her waist was leaning forward, her bright dark eyes intent on Cave's face. She seemed out of place among the frowsy old furies who surrounded her. Her head was striking, small and boyishly chic, its fine bony structure emphasized by a short haircut. She turned, and her brown eyes met mine. They were tragic and opaque.

The D.A.'s voice rose above the buzzing. "I object to this testimony.

The witness is deliberately blackening the dead woman's reputation, without corroborative evidence of any kind, in a cowardly attempt to save his own neck."

He glanced sideways at the jury. Their faces were stony. Cave's was as white as marble. Harvey's was mottled red. He said, "This is an essential part of the case for the defense. A great deal has been made of Mr. Cave's sudden departure from home on the day of his wife's death. I am establishing the reason for it."

"We know the reason," the D.A. said in a carrying undertone.

Harvey looked up mutely at the judge, whose frown fitted the lines in his face like an old glove.

"Objection overruled. The prosecution will refrain from making unworthy comments. In any case, the jury will disregard them."

But the D.A. looked pleased with himself. He had made his point, and the jury would remember. Their twenty-four eyes, half of them female, and predominantly old, were fixed on Cave in uniform disapproval.

Harvey spoke in a voice thickened by emotion. "Did your wife say who the man was that she planned to leave you for?"

"No. She didn't."

"Do you know who it was?"

"No. The whole thing was a bolt from the blue to me. I don't believe Ruth intended to tell me what she had on her mind. It just slipped out, after we started fighting." He caught himself up short. "Verbally fighting, I mean."

"What started this verbal argument?"

"Nothing important. Money trouble. I wanted to buy a Ferrari, and Ruth couldn't see any sense in it."

"A Ferrari motor car?"

"A racing car, yes. I asked her for the money. She said that she was tired of giving me money. I said that I was equally tired of taking it from her. Then it came out that she was going to leave me for somebody else." One side of Cave's mouth lifted in a sardonic smile. "Somebody who would love her for herself."

"When did she plan to leave you?"

"As soon as she could get ready to go to Nevada. I told her to go ahead, that she was free to go whenever and wherever she wanted to go, with anybody that suited her."

"And what did you do then?"

"I packed a few clothes and drove away in my car."

"What time did you leave the house?"

"I don't know exactly."

"Was it dark when you went?"

"It was getting dark, but I didn't have to use my headlights right away. It couldn't have been later than eight o'clock."

"And Mrs. Cave was alive and well when you left?"

"Certainly she was."

"Was your parting friendly?"

"Friendly enough. She said good-bye and offered me some money. Which I didn't take, incidentally. I didn't take much of anything, except for bare essentials. I even left most of my clothes behind."

"Why did you do that?"

"Because she bought them for me. They belonged to her. I thought perhaps her new man might have a use for them."

"I see."

Harvey's voice was hoarse and unsteady. He turned away from Cave, and I could see that his face was flushed, either with anger or impatience. He said without looking at the prisoner, "Did the things you left behind include a gun?"

"Yes. A twelve-gauge double-barreled shotgun. I used it for shooting rabbits, mostly, in the hills behind the house."

"Was it loaded?"

"I believe so. I usually kept it loaded."

"Where did you leave your shotgun?"

"In the garage. I kept it there. Ruth didn't like to have a gun in the house. She had a phobia—"

Harvey cut in quickly. "Did you also leave a pair of driving gloves, the gloves on the table here marked by the prosecution as Exhibit J?"

"I did. They were in the garage, too."

"And the garage door—was it open or closed?"

"I left it open, I think. In any case, we never kept it locked."

"Mr. Cave," Harvey said in a deep voice, "did you kill your wife with the shotgun before you drove away?"

"I did not." In contrast with Harvey's, Cave's voice was high and thin and unconvincing.

"After you left around eight o'clock, did you return to the house again that night?"

"I did not. I haven't been back since, as a matter of fact. I was arrested in Los Angeles the following day."

"Where did you spend the night—that is, after eight o'clock?"

"With a friend."

The courtroom began to buzz again.

"What friend?" Harvey barked. He suddenly sounded like a prosecutor cross-examining a hostile witness.

Cave moved his mouth to speak, and hesitated. He licked his dry lips. "I prefer not to say."

"Why do you prefer not to say?"

"Because it was a woman. I don't want to involve her in this mess."

Harvey swung away from the witness abruptly and looked up at the judge. The judge admonished the jury not to discuss the case with anyone, and adjourned the trial until two o'clock.

I watched the jurors file out. Not one of them looked at Glenway Cave. They had seen enough of him.

Harvey was the last man to leave the well of the courtroom. I waited for him at the little swinging gate which divided it from the spectators' section. He finished packing his briefcase and came towards me, carrying the case as if it was weighted.

"Mr. Harvey, can you give me a minute?"

He started to brush me off with a weary gesture, then recognized my face. "Lew Archer? What brings you here?"

"It's what I want to talk to you about."

"This case?"

I nodded. "Are you going to get him off?"

"Naturally I am. He's innocent." But his voice echoed hollowly in the empty room and he regarded me doubtfully. "You wouldn't be snooping around for the prosecution?"

"Not this time. The person who hired me believes that Cave is innocent. Just as you do."

"A woman?"

"You're jumping to conclusions, aren't you?"

"When the sex isn't indicated, it's usually a woman. Who is she, Archer?"

"I wish I knew."

"Come on now." His square pink hand rested on my arm. "You don't accept anonymous clients any more than I do."

"This one is an exception. All I know about her is that she's anxious to see Cave get off."

"So are we all." His bland smile tightened. "Look, we can't talk here. Walk over to the office with me. I'll have a couple of sandwiches sent up."

He shifted his hand to my elbow and propelled me towards the door. The dark-eyed woman with the artificial violets at her waist was waiting in the corridor. Her opaque gaze passed over me and rested possessively on Harvey.

"Surprise." Her voice was low and throaty to match her boyish look. "You're taking me to lunch."

"I'm pretty busy, Rhea. And I thought you were going to stay home today."

"I tried to. Honestly. But my mind kept wandering off to the court-house, so I finally up and followed it." She moved towards him with a queer awkwardness, as if she was embarrassingly conscious of her body, and his. "Aren't you glad to see me, darling?"

"Of course I'm glad to see you," he said, his tone denying the words.

"Then take me to lunch." Her white-gloved hand stroked his lapel. "I made a reservation at the club. It will do you good to get out in the air."

"I told you I'm busy, Rhea. Mr. Archer and I have something to dis-cuss."

"Bring Mr. Archer along. I won't get in the way. I promise." She turned to me with a flashing white smile. "Since my husband seems to have forgotten his manners, I'm Rhea Harvey."

She offered me her hand, and Harvey told her who I was. Shrugging his shoulders resignedly, he led the way outside to his bronze converti-ble. We turned towards the sea, which glimmered at the foot of the town like a fallen piece of sky.

"How do you think it's going, Rod?" she said.

"I suppose it could have been worse. He could have got up in front of the judge and jury and confessed."

"Did it strike you as that bad?"

"I'm afraid it was pretty bad." Harvey leaned forward over the wheel in order to look around his wife at me. "Were you in on the debacle, Archer?"

"Part of it. He's either very honest or very stupid."

Harvey snorted. "Glen's not stupid. The trouble is, he simply doesn't care. He pays no attention to my advice. I had to stand there and ask the questions, and I didn't know what crazy answers he was going to come up with. He seems to take a masochistic pleasure in wrecking his own chances."

"It could be his conscience working on him," I said.

His steely blue glance raked my face and returned to the road. "It could be, but it isn't. And I'm not speaking simply as his attorney. I've known Glen Cave for a long time. We were roommates in college. Hell, I introduced him to his wife."

"That doesn't make him incapable of murder."

"Sure, any man is capable of murder. That's not my point. My point is that Glen is a sharp customer. If he had decided to kill Ruth for her money, he wouldn't do it that way. He wouldn't use his own gun. In fact, I doubt very much that he'd use a gun at all. Glen isn't that obvious."

"Unless it was a passional crime. Jealousy can make a man lose his sophistication."

"Not Glen. He wasn't in love with Ruth—never has been. He's got about as much sexual passion as a flea." His voice was edged with contempt. "Anyway, this tale of his about another man is probably malarkey."

"Are you sure, Rod?"

He turned on his wife almost savagely. "No, I'm not sure. I'm not sure about anything. Glen isn't confiding in me, and I don't see how I can defend him if he goes on this way. I wish to God he hadn't forced me into this. He knows as well as I do that trial work isn't my forte. I advised him to get an attorney experienced in this sort of thing, and he wouldn't listen. He said if I wouldn't take on his case that he'd defend himself. And he flunked out of law school in his second year. What could I do?"

He stamped the accelerator, cutting in and out of the noon traffic on the ocean boulevard. Palm trees fled by like thin old wild-haired madmen racing along the edge of the quicksilver sea.

The beach club stood at the end of the boulevard, a white U-shaped building whose glass doors opened "For Members and Guests Only." Its inner court contained a swimming pool and an alfresco dining space dotted with umbrella tables. Breeze-swept and sluiced with sunlight, it was the antithesis of the dim courtroom where Cave's fate would be decided. But the shadow of the courtroom fell across our luncheon and leeched the color and flavor from the food.

Harvey pushed away his salmon salad, which he had barely disturbed, and gulped a second Martini. He called the waiter to order a third. His wife inhibited him with a barely perceptible shake of her head. The waiter slid away.

"This woman," I said, "the woman he spent the night with. Who is she?"

"Glen told me hardly anything more than he told the court." Harvey paused, half gagged by a lawyer's instinctive reluctance to give away information, then forced himself to go on. "It seems he went straight from home to her house on the night of the shooting. He spent the night with her, from about eight-thirty until the following morning. Or so he claims."

"Haven't you checked his story?"

"How? He refused to say anything that might enable me to find her or identify her. It's just another example of the obstacles he's put in my way, trying to defend him."

"Is this woman so important to his defense?"

"Crucial. Ruth was shot sometime around midnight. The p.m. established that through the stomach contents. And at that time, if he's telling the truth, Glen was with a witness. Yet he won't let me try to locate her, or have her subpoenaed. It took me hours of hammering at him to get him to testify about her at all, and I'm not sure that wasn't a mistake. That miserable jury—" His voice trailed off. He was back in court fighting his uphill battle against the prejudices of a small elderly city.

And I was back on the pavement in front of the airport, listening to a woman's urgent whisper: *You'll have to give me a yes or no. I've made up my mind to go by your decision.*

Harvey was looking away across the captive water, fishnetted under elastic strands of light. Under the clear September sun I could see the spikes of gray in his hair, the deep small scars of strain around his mouth.

"If I could only lay my hands on the woman." He seemed to be speaking to himself, until he looked at me from the corners of his eyes. "Who do *you* suppose she is?"

"How would I know?"

He leaned across the table confidentially. "Why be so cagey, Archer? I've let down my hair."

"This particular hair doesn't belong to me."

I regretted the words before I had finished speaking them.

Harvey said, "When will you see her?"

"You're jumping to conclusions again."

"If I'm wrong, I'm sorry. If I'm right, give her a message for me. Tell her that Glen—I hate to have to say this, but he's in jeopardy. If she likes him well enough to—"

"Please, Rod." Rhea Harvey seemed genuinely offended. "There's no need to be coarse."

I said, "I'd like to talk to Cave before I do anything. I don't know that it's the same woman. Even if it is, he may have reasons of his own for keeping her under wraps."

"You can probably have a few minutes with him in the courtroom." He looked at his wristwatch and pushed his chair back violently. "We better get going. It's twenty to two now."

We went along the side of the pool, back toward the entrance. As we entered the vestibule, a woman was just coming in from the boulevard.

She held the heavy plate-glass door for the little flaxen-haired girl who was trailing after her.

Then she glanced up and saw me. Her dark harlequin glasses flashed in the light reflected from the pool. Her face became disorganized behind the glasses. She turned on her heel and started out, but not before the child had smiled at me and said: "Hello. Are you coming for a ride?" Then she trotted out after her mother.

Harvey looked quizzically at his wife. "What's the matter with the Kilpatrick woman?"

"She must be drunk. She didn't even recognize us."

"You know her, Mrs. Harvey?"

"As well as I care to." Her eyes took on a set, glazed expression—the look of congealed virtue faced with its opposite. "I haven't seen Janet Kilpatrick for months. She hasn't been showing herself in public much since her divorce."

Harvey edged closer and gripped my arm. "Would Mrs. Kilpatrick be the woman we were talking about?"

"Hardly."

"They seemed to know you."

I improvised. "I met them on the Daylight one day last month, coming down from Frisco. She got plastered, and I guess she didn't want to recall the occasion."

That seemed to satisfy him. But when I excused myself, on the grounds that I thought I'd stay for a swim in the pool, his blue ironic glance informed me that he wasn't taken in.

The receptionist had inch-long scarlet fingernails and an air of contemptuous formality. Yes, Mrs. Kilpatrick was a member of the club. No, she wasn't allowed to give out members' addresses. She admitted grudgingly that there was a pay telephone in the bar.

The barroom was deserted except for the bartender, a slim white-coated man with emotional Mediterranean eyes. I found Mrs. Janet Kilpatrick in the telephone directory: her address was 1201 Coast Highway. I called a taxi, and ordered a beer from the bartender.

He was more communicative than the receptionist. Sure, he knew Glenway Cave. Every bartender in town knew Glenway Cave. The guy was sitting at this very bar the afternoon of the same day he murdered his wife.

"You think he murdered her?"

"Everybody else thinks so. They don't spend all that money on a trial unless they got the goods on them. Anyway, look at the motive he had."

"You mean the man she was running around with?"

"I mean two million bucks." He had a delayed reaction. "What man is that?"

"Cave said in court this morning that his wife was going to divorce him and marry somebody else."

"He did, eh? You a newspaperman by any chance?"

"A kind of one." I subscribed to several newspapers.

"Well, you can tell the world that that's a lot of baloney. I've seen quite a bit of Mrs. Cave around the club. She had her own little circle, see, and you can take it from me she never even looked at other guys. *He* was always the one with the roving eye. What can you expect, when a young fellow marries a lady that much older than him?" His faint accent lent flavor to the question. "The very day of the murder he was making a fast play for another dame, right here in front of me."

"Who was she?"

"I wouldn't want to name names. She was pretty far gone that afternoon, hardly knew what she was doing. And the poor lady's got enough trouble as it is. Take it from me."

I didn't press him. A minute later a horn tooted in the street.

A few miles south of the city limits a blacktop lane led down from the highway to Mrs. Kilpatrick's house. It was a big old-fashioned redwood cottage set among trees and flowers above a bone-white beach. The Cadillac was parked beside the vine-grown verandah, like something in a four-color advertisement. I asked my driver to wait, and knocked on the front door.

A small rectangular window was set into the door. It slid open, and a green eye gleamed like a flawed emerald through the aperture.

"You," she said in a low voice. "You shouldn't have come here."

"I have some questions for you, Mrs. Kilpatrick. And maybe a couple of answers. May I come in?"

She sighed audibly. "If you must." She unlocked the door and stood back to let me enter. "You will be quiet, won't you? I've just put Janie to bed for her afternoon nap."

There was a white silk scarf draped over her right hand, and under the silk a shape which contrasted oddly with her motherly concern—the shape of a small hand gun.

"You'd better put that thing away. You don't need it, do you?"

Her hand moved jerkily. The scarf fell from the gun and drifted to the floor. It was a small blue revolver. She looked at it as if it had somehow forced its way into her fist, and put it down on the telephone table.

"I'm sorry. I didn't know who was at the door. I've been so worried and frightened—"

"Who did you think it was?"

"Frank, perhaps, or one of his men. He's been trying to take Janie away from me. He claims I'm not a fit mother. And maybe I'm not," she added in the neutral tones of despair. "But Frank is worse."

"Frank is your husband?"

"My ex-husband. I got a divorce last year and the court gave me custody of Janie. Frank has been fighting the custody order ever since. Janie's grandmother left her a trust fund, you see. That's all Frank cares about. But I'm her mother."

"I think I see what it's all about," I said. "Correct me if I'm wrong. Cave spent the night with you—the night he was supposed to have shot his wife. But you don't want to testify at his trial. It would give your ex-husband legal ammunition to use in the custody fight for Janie."

"You're not wrong." She lowered her eyes, not so much in shame as in submission to the facts. "We got talking in the bar at the club that afternoon. I hardly knew him, but I—well, I was attracted to him. He asked if he could come and see me that night. I was feeling lonely, very low and lonely. I'd had a good deal to drink. I let him come."

"What time did he arrive?"

"Shortly after eight."

"And he stayed all night?"

"Yes. He couldn't have killed Ruth Cave. He was with me. You can understand why I've been quietly going crazy since they arrested him—sitting at home and biting on my nails and wondering what under heaven I should do." Her eyes came up like green searchlights under her fair brow. "What *shall* I do, Mr. Archer?"

"Sit tight for a while yet. The trial will last a few more days. And he may be acquitted."

"But you don't think he will be, do you?"

"It's hard to say. He didn't do too well on the stand this morning. On the other hand, the averages are with him, as he seems to realize. Very few innocent men are convicted of murder."

"He didn't mention me on the stand?"

"He said he was with a woman, no names mentioned. Are you two in love with each other, Mrs. Kilpatrick?"

"No, nothing like that. I was simply feeling sorry for myself that night. I needed some attention from a man. He was a piece of flotsam and I was a piece of jetsam and we were washed together in the dark. He did get rather—emotional at one point, and said that he would like to marry me. I reminded him that he had a wife."

"What did he say to that?"

"He said his wife wouldn't live forever. But I didn't take him seriously. I haven't even seen him since that night. No, I'm not in love with him. If I let him die, though, for something I know he didn't do—I couldn't go on living with myself." She added, with a bitter grimace, "It's hard enough as it is."

"But you do want to go on living."

"Not particularly. I have to because Janie needs me."

"Then stay at home and keep your doors locked. It wasn't smart to go to the club today."

"I know. I needed a drink badly. I'm out of liquor, and it was the nearest place. Then I saw you and I panicked."

"Stay panicked. Remember if Cave didn't commit that murder, somebody else did—and framed him for it. Somebody who is still at large. What do you drink, by the way?"

"Anything. Scotch, mostly."

"Can you hold out for a couple of hours?"

"If I have to." She smiled, and her smile was charming. "You're very thoughtful."

When I got back to the courtroom, the trial was temporarily stalled. The jury had been sent out, and Harvey and the D.A. were arguing in front of the judge's bench. Cave was sitting by himself at the far end of the long attorneys' table. A sheriff's deputy with a gun on his thigh stood a few feet behind him, between the red-draped windows.

Assuming a self-important legal look, I marched through the swinging gate into the well of the courtroom and took the empty chair beside Cave. He looked up from the typed transcript he was reading. In spite of his prison pallor he was a good-looking man. He had a boyish look about him and the kind of curly brown hair that women are supposed to love to run their fingers through. But his mouth was tight, his eyes dark and piercing.

Before I could introduce myself, he said, "You the detective Rod told me about?"

"Yes. Name is Archer."

"You're wasting your time, Mr. Archer, there's nothing you can do for me." His voice was a dull monotone, as if the cross-examination had rolled over his emotions and left them flat.

"It can't be that bad, Cave."

"I didn't say it was bad. I'm doing perfectly well, and I know what I'm doing."

I held my tongue. It wouldn't do to tell him that his own lawyer had lost confidence in his case. Harvey's voice rose sharp and strained above the courtroom mutter, maintaining that certain questions were irrelevant and immaterial.

Cave leaned towards me and his voice sank lower. "You've been in touch with her?"

"She brought me into the case."

"That was a rash thing for her to do, under the circumstances. Or don't you know the circumstances?"

"I understand that if she testifies she risks losing her child."

"Exactly. Why do you think I haven't had her called? Go back and tell her that I'm grateful for her concern but I don't need her help. They can't convict an innocent man. I didn't shoot my wife, and I don't need an alibi to prove it."

I looked at him, admiring his composure. The armpits of his gabardine suit were dark with sweat. A fine tremor was running through him.

"Do you know who did shoot her, Cave?"

"I have an opinion. We won't go into it."

"Her new man?"

"We won't go into it," he repeated, and buried his aquiline nose in the transcript.

The judge ordered the bailiff to bring in the jury. Harvey sat down beside me, looking disgruntled, and Cave returned to the witness stand.

What followed was moral slaughter. The D.A. forced Cave to admit that he hadn't had gainful employment since his release from the army, that his sole occupations were amateur tennis and amateur acting, and that he had no means of his own. He had been completely dependent on his wife's money since their marriage in 1946, and had used some of it to take extended trips in the company of other women.

The prosecutor turned his back on Cave in histrionic disgust. "And you're the man who dares to impugn the morals of your dead wife, the woman who gave you everything."

Harvey objected. The judge instructed the D.A. to rephrase his "question."

The D.A. nodded, and turned on Cave. "Did you say this morning that there was another man in Mrs. Cave's life?"

"I said it. It was true."

"Do you have anything to confirm that story?"

"No."

"Who is this unknown vague figure of a man?"

"I don't know. All I know is what Ruth told me."

"She isn't here to deny it, is she? Tell us frankly now, Mr. Cave, didn't you invent this man? Didn't you make him up?"

Cave's forehead was shining with sweat. He took a handkerchief out of his breast pocket and wiped his forehead, then his mouth. Above the white fabric masking his lower face, he looked past the D.A. and across the well of the courtroom. There was silence for a long moment.

Then Cave said mildly, "No, I didn't invent him."

"Does this man exist outside your fertile brain?"

"He does."

"Where? In what guise? Who is he?"

"I don't know," Cave said on a rising note. "If you want to know, why don't you try and find him? You have plenty of detectives at your disposal."

"Detectives can't find a man who doesn't exist. Or a woman either, Mr. Cave."

The D.A. caught the angry eye of the judge, who adjourned the trial until the following morning. I bought a fifth of scotch at a downtown liquor store, caught a taxi at the railroad station, and rode south out of town to Mrs. Kilpatrick's house.

When I knocked on the door of the redwood cottage, someone fumbled the inside knob. I pushed the door open. The flaxen-haired child looked up at me, her face streaked with half-dried tears.

"Mummy won't wake up."

I saw the red smudge on her knee, and ran in past her. Janet Kilpatrick was prone on the floor of the hallway, her bright hair dragging in a pool of blood. I lifted her head and saw the hole in her temple. It had stopped bleeding.

Her little blue revolver lay on the floor near her lax hand. One shot had been fired from the cylinder.

The child touched my back. "Is Mummy sick?"

"Yes, Janie. She's sick."

"Get the doctor," she said with pathetic wisdom.

"Wasn't he here?"

"I don't know. I was taking my nap."

"Was anybody here, Janie?"

"Somebody was here. Mummy was talking to somebody. Then there was a big bang and I came downstairs and Mummy wouldn't wake up."

"Was it a man?"

She shook her head.

"A woman, Janie?"

The same mute shake of her head. I took her by the hand and led her outside to the cab. The dazzling postcard scene outside made death seem unreal. I asked the driver to tell the child a story, any story so long as it was cheerful. Then I went back into the grim hallway and used the telephone.

I called the sheriff's office first. My second call was to Frank Kilpatrick in Pasadena. A manservant summoned him to the telephone. I told him who I was and where I was and who was lying dead on the floor behind me.

"How dreadful!" He had an Ivy League accent, somewhat withered by the coastal sun. "Do you suppose that Janet took her own life? She's often threatened to."

"No," I said, "I don't suppose she took her own life. Your wife was murdered."

"What a tragic thing!"

"Why take it so hard, Kilpatrick? You've got the two things you wanted—your daughter, and you're rid of your wife."

It was a cruel thing to say, but I was feeling cruel. I made my third call in person, after the sheriff's men had finished with me.

The sun had fallen into the sea by then. The western side of the sky was scrawled with a childish finger-painting of colored cirrus clouds. Twilight flowed like iron-stained water between the downtown buildings. There were lights on the second floor of the California-Spanish building where Harvey had his offices.

Harvey answered my knock. He was in shirtsleeves and his tie was awry. He had a sheaf of papers in his hand. His breath was sour in my nostrils.

"What is it, Archer?"

"You tell me, lover-boy."

"And what is that supposed to mean?"

"You were the one Ruth Cave wanted to marry. You were going to divorce your respective mates and build a new life together—with her money."

He stepped backward into the office, a big disordered man who looked queerly out of place among the white-leather and black-iron furniture, against the limed-oak paneling. I followed him in. An automatic door closer shushed behind me.

"What in hell is this? Ruth and I were good friends and I handled her business for her—that's all there was to it."

"Don't try to kid me, Harvey. I'm not your wife, and I'm not your judge . . . I went to see Janet Kilpatrick a couple of hours ago."

"Whatever she said, it's a lie."

"She didn't say a word, Harvey. I found her dead."

His eyes grew small and metallic, like nailheads in the putty of his face. "Dead? What happened to her?"

"She was shot with her own gun. By somebody she let into the house, somebody she wasn't afraid of."

"Why? It makes no sense."

"She was Cave's alibi, and she was on the verge of volunteering as a witness. You know that, Harvey—you were the only one who did know, outside of Cave and me."

"I didn't shoot her. I had no reason to. Why would I want to see my client convicted?"

"No, you didn't shoot her. You were in court at the time that she was shot—the world's best alibi."

"Then why are you harassing me?"

"I want the truth about you and Mrs. Cave."

Harvey looked down at the papers in his hand, as if they might suggest a line to take, an evasion, a way out. Suddenly his hands came together and crushed the papers into a misshapen ball.

"All right, I'll tell you. Ruth was in love with me. I was—fond of her. Neither of us was happily married. We were going to go away together and start over. After we got divorces, of course."

"Uh-huh. All very legal."

"You don't have to take that tone. A man has a right to his own life."

"Not when he's already committed his life."

"We won't discuss it. Haven't I suffered enough? How do you think I felt when Ruth was killed?"

"Pretty bad, I guess. There went two million dollars."

He looked at me between narrowed lids, in a fierce extremity of hatred. But all that came out of his mouth was a weak denial. "At any rate, you can see I didn't kill her. I didn't kill either of them."

"Who did?"

"I have no idea. If I did, I'd have had Glen out of jail long ago."

"Does Glen know?"

"Not to my knowledge."

"But he knew that you and his wife had plans?"

"I suppose he did—I've suspected it all along."

"Didn't it strike you as odd that he asked you to defend him, under the circumstances?"

"Odd, yes. It's been terrible for me, the most terrible ordeal."

Maybe that was Cave's intention, I thought, to punish Harvey for stealing his wife. I said, "Did anybody besides you know that Janet Kilpatrick was the woman? Did you discuss it with anybody?"

He looked at the thick pale carpeting between his feet. I could hear an electric clock somewhere in the silent offices, whirring like the thoughts in Harvey's head. Finally he said, "Of course not," in a voice that was like a crow cawing.

He walked with an old man's gait into his private office. I followed and saw him open a desk drawer. A heavy automatic appeared in his hand. But he didn't point it at me. He pushed it down inside the front of his trousers and put on his suit jacket.

"Give it to me, Harvey. Two dead women are enough."

"You know then?"

"You just told me. Give me that gun."

He gave it to me. His face was remarkably smooth and blank. He turned his face away from me and covered it with his hands. His entire body hiccuped with dry grief. He was like an overgrown child who had lived on fairy tales for a long time and now couldn't stomach reality.

The telephone on the desk chirred. Harvey pulled himself together and answered it.

"Sorry, I've been busy, preparing for re-direct . . . Yes, I'm finished now . . . Of course I'm all right. I'm coming home right away."

He hung up and said, "That was my wife."

She was waiting for him at the front door of his house. The posture of waiting became her narrow, sexless body, and I wondered how many years she had been waiting.

"You're so thoughtless, Rod," she chided him. "Why didn't you tell me you were bringing a guest for dinner?" She turned to me in awkward graciousness. "Not that you're not welcome, Mr. Archer."

Then our silence bore in on her. It pushed her back into the high white Colonial hallway. She took up another pose and lit a cigarette with a little golden lighter shaped like a lipstick. Her hands were steady, but I could see the sharp edges of fear behind the careful expression on her face.

"You both look so solemn. Is something wrong?"

"Everything is wrong, Rhea."

"Why, didn't the trial go well this afternoon?"

"The trial is going fine. Tomorrow I'm going to ask for a directed acquittal. What's more, I'm going to get it. I have new evidence."

"Isn't that grand?" she said in a bright and interested tone. "Where on earth did you dig up the new evidence?"

"In my own backyard. All these months I've been so preoccupied trying to cover up my own sordid little secret that it never occurred to me that you might have secrets, too."

"What do you mean?"

"You weren't at the trial this afternoon. Where were you? What were you doing?"

"Errands—I had some errands. I'm sorry, I didn't realize you— wanted me to be there."

Harvey moved towards her, a threat of violence in the set of his shoulders. She backed against a closed white door. I stepped between them and said harshly, "We know exactly where you were, Mrs. Harvey. You went to see Janet Kilpatrick. You talked your way into her house, picked up a gun from the table in the hall, and shot her with it. Didn't you?"

The flesh of her face was no more than a stretched membrane.

"I swear, I had no intention—All I intended to do was talk to her. But when I saw that she realized, that she *knew*—"

"Knew what, Mrs. Harvey?"

"That I was the one who killed Ruth. I must have given myself away, by what I said to her. She looked at me, and I saw that she knew. I saw it in her eyes."

"So you shot her?"

"Yes. I'm sorry." She didn't seem to be fearful or ashamed. The face she turned on her husband looked starved, and her mouth moved over her words as if they were giving her bitter nourishment. "But I'm not sorry for the other one, for Ruth. You shouldn't have done it to me, Rod. I warned you, remember? I warned you when I caught you with Anne that if you ever did it to me again—I would kill the woman. You should have taken me seriously."

"Yes," he said drearily. "I guess I should have."

"I warned Ruth, too, when I learned about the two of you."

"How did you find out about it, Mrs. Harvey?"

"The usual way—an anonymous telephone call. Some friend of mine, I suppose."

"Or your worst enemy. Do you know who it was?"

"No. I didn't recognize the voice. I was still in bed, and the telephone call woke me up. He said—it was a man—he said that Rod was going to divorce me, and he told me why. I went to Ruth that very morning—Rod was out of town—and I asked her if it was true. She admitted it was. I told her flatly I'd kill her unless she gave you up, Rod. She laughed at me. She called me a crazy woman."

"She was right."

"Was she? If I'm insane, I know what's driven me to it. I could bear the thought of the other ones. But not her! What made you take up with *her*, Rod—what made you want to marry that gray-haired old woman? She wasn't even attractive, she wasn't nearly as attractive as I am."

"She was well-heeled," I said.

Harvey said nothing.

Rhea Harvey dictated and signed a full confession that night. Her husband wasn't in court the following morning. The D.A. himself moved for a directed acquittal, and Cave was free by noon. He took a taxi directly from the courthouse to the home of his late wife. I followed him in a second taxi. I still wasn't satisfied.

The lawns around the big country house had grown knee-high and had withered in the summer sun. The gardens were overgrown with rank flowers and ranker weeds. Cave stood in the drive for a while after he dismissed his taxi, looking around the estate he had inherited. Finally he mounted the front steps.

I called him from the gate. "Wait a minute, Cave."

He descended the steps reluctantly and waited for me, a black scowl twisting his eyebrows and disfiguring his mouth. But they were smooth and straight before I reached him.

"What do you want?"

"I was just wondering how it feels."

He smiled with boyish charm. "To be a free man? It feels wonderful. I guess I owe you my gratitude, at that. As a matter of fact, I was planning to send you a check."

"Save yourself the trouble. I'd send it back."

"Whatever you say, old man." He spread his hands disarmingly. "Is there something else I can do for you?"

"Yes. You can satisfy my curiosity. All I want from you is a yes or no." The words set up an echo in my head, an echo of Janet Kilpatrick's voice. "Two women have died and a third is on her way to prison or the state hospital. I want to hear you admit your responsibility."

"Responsibility? I don't understand."

"I'll spell it out for you. The quarrel you had with your wife didn't occur on the nineteenth, the night she was murdered. It came earlier, maybe the night before. And she told you who the man was."

"She didn't have to tell me. I've known Rod Harvey for years, and all about him."

"Then you must have known that Rhea Harvey was insanely jealous of her husband. You thought of a way to put her jealousy to work for you. It was you who telephoned her that morning. You disguised your voice, and told her what her husband and your wife were planning to do. She came to this house and threatened your wife. No doubt you overheard the conversation. Seeing that your plan was working, you left your loaded shotgun where Rhea Harvey could easily find it and went down to the beach club to establish an alibi. You had a long wait at the club, and later at Janet Kilpatrick's house, but you finally got what you were waiting for."

"They also serve who only stand and wait."

"Does it seem so funny to you, Cave? You're guilty of conspiracy to commit murder."

"I'm not guilty of anything, old man. Even if I were, there's nothing you could possibly do about it. You heard the court acquit me this morning, and there's a little rule of law involving double jeopardy."

"You were taking quite a risk, weren't you?"

"Not so much of a risk. Rhea's a very unstable woman, and she had to break down eventually, one way or the other."

"Is that why you asked Harvey to defend you, to keep the pressure on Rhea?"

"That was part of it." A sudden fury of hatred went through him, transfiguring his face. "Mostly I wanted to see him suffer."

"What are you going to do now, Cave?"

"Nothing. I plan to take it easy. I've earned a rest. Why?"

"A pretty good woman was killed yesterday on account of you. For all I know you planned that killing the same way you planned the other. In any case, you could have prevented it."

He saw the mayhem in my eyes and backed away. "Take it easy, Archer. Janet was no great loss to the world, after all."

My fist smashed his nervous smile and drove the words down his throat. He crawled away from me, scrambled to his feet and ran, jumping over flowerbeds and disappearing around the corner of the house. I let him go.

A short time later I heard that Cave had been killed in a highway accident near Palm Springs. He was driving a new Ferrari at the time.

IRONY AND TERROR

SOUTH AFRICA
BRAZIL
NEW ENGLAND

Africa Emergent

NADINE GORDIMER

He's in prison now, so I'm not going to mention his name. It mightn't be a good thing, you understand.—Perhaps you think you understand too well; but don't be quick to jump to conclusions from five or six thousand miles away: if you lived here, you'd understand something else—friends know that shows of loyalty are all right for children holding hands in the school playground; for us they're luxuries, not important and maybe dangerous. If I said, I was a friend of so-and-so, a black man awaiting trial for treason, what good would it do him? And, who knows, it might draw just that decisive bit more attention to me. *He*'d be the first to agree.

Not that one feels that if they haven't got enough in my dossier already, this would make any difference; and not that he really was such a friend. But that's something else you won't understand; everything is ambiguous, here. We hardly know, by now, what we can do and what we can't do; it's difficult to say, goaded in on oneself by laws and doubts and rebellion and caution and—not least—self-disgust, what is or is not a friendship. I'm talking about black and white, of course. If you stay with it, boy, on the white side in the country clubs and garden suburbs if you're white, and on the black side in the locations and beerhalls if you're black, none of this applies, and you can go all the way to your segregated cemetery in peace. But neither he nor I did.

I began mixing with blacks out of what is known as an outraged sense of justice, plus strong curiosity, when I was a student. There were two ways—one was through the white students' voluntary service organization, a kibbutz-type junket where white boys and girls went into rural areas and camped while they built school classrooms for African children. A few coloured and African students from their segregated universities used to come along too, and there was the novelty, not without value, of dossing down alongside them at night, although we knew we were likely to be harbouring Special Branch spies among our willing workers, and we dared not make a pass at the coloured or black girls. The other way—less hard on the hands—was to go drinking with the jazz musicians and journalists, painters and would-be poets and actors who gravitated towards whites partly because such people naturally feel they can make free of the world, and partly because they found an encouragement and appreciation there that was sweet to them. I tried the V.S.O. briefly, but the other way suited me better; anyway, I didn't see why I should help this Government by doing the work it ought to be doing for the welfare of black children.

I'm an architect and the way I was usefully drawn into the black scene was literally that: I designed sets for a mixed-colour drama group got together by a white director. Perhaps there's no urban human group as intimate, in the end, as a company of this kind, and the colour problem made us even closer. I don't mean what *you* mean, the how-do-I-feel-about-that-black-skin stuff; I mean the daily exasperation of getting round, or over, or on top of the colour-bar laws that plagued our productions and our lives. We had to remember to write out "passes" at night, so that our actors could get home without being arrested for being out after the curfew for blacks, we had to spend hours at the Bantu Affairs Department trying to arrange local residence permits for actors who were being "endorsed out" of town back to the villages to which, "ethnically," apparently, they belonged although they'd never set eyes on them, and we had to decide which of us could play the sycophant well enough to persuade the Bantu Commissioner to allow the show to go on the road from one Group Area, designated by colour, to another, or to talk some town clerk into getting his council to agree to the use of a "white" public hall by a mixed cast. The black actors' lives were in our hands, because they were black and we were white, and could, must, intercede for them. Don't think this made everything love and light between us; in fact it caused endless huffs and rows. A white woman who'd worked like a slave acting as P.R.O.-cum-wardrobe-mistress hasn't spoken to me for years because I made her lend her little car to one of the chaps who'd worked until after the last train went back to the location, and then he kept it the whole weekend and she couldn't get hold of him because, of course, location houses rarely have telephones and once a black man has disappeared among those warrens you won't find him till he chooses to surface in the white town again. And when this one did surface, he was biting, to me, about white bitches' "patronage" of people they secretly still thought of as "boys." Yet our arguments, resentments and misunderstandings were not only as much part of the intimacy of this group as the good times, the parties and the love-making we had, but were more—the defining part, because we'd got close enough to admit argument, resentment and misunderstanding between us.

He was one of this little crowd, for a time. He was a dispatch clerk and then a "manager" and chucker-out at a black dance club. In his spare time he took a small part in our productions now and then, and made himself generally handy; in the end it was discovered that what he really was good at was front-of-house arrangements. His tubby charm (he was a large young man and a cheerful dresser) was just the right thing to deal with the unexpected moods of our location audiences when we went on tour—sometimes they came stiffly encased in their church-going best and seemed to feel it was vulgar to laugh or respond to what was going on, on stage; in other places they rushed the doors, tried to get in without paying, and were dominated by a *tsotsi,* street urchin, element who didn't want to hear anything but themselves. He was the particular friend—the other, passive half—of a particular friend of mine, Elias Nkomo.

And here I stop short. How shall I talk about Elias? I've never even learnt, in five years, how to think about him.

Elias was a sculptor. He had one of those jobs—messenger "boy" or some such—that literate young black men can aspire to in a small gold-mining and industrial town outside Johannesburg. Somebody said he was talented, somebody sent him to me—at the beginning, the way for every black man to find himself seems inescapably to lead through a white man. Again, how can I say what his work was like? He came by train to the black people's section of Johannesburg central station, carrying a bulky object wrapped in that morning's newspaper. He was slight, round-headed, tiny-eared, dunly dressed, and with a frown of effort between his eyes, but his face unfolded to a wide, apologetic yet confident smile when he realized that the white man in a waiting car must be me—the meeting had been arranged. I took him back to my "place" (he always called people's homes that) and he unwrapped the newspaper. What was there was nothing like the clumps of diorite or sandstone you have seen in galleries in New York, London or Johannesburg, marked "Africa Emergency," "Spirit of the Ancestors."

What was there was a goat, or goat-like creature, in the way that a centaur is a horse-like, man-like creature, carved out of streaky knotted wood. It was delightful (I wanted to put out my hand to touch it), it was moving in its somehow concrete diachrony, beast-man, coarse wood-fine workmanship, and there was also something exposed about it (one would withdraw the hand, after all).

I asked him whether he knew Picasso's goats. He had heard of

Picasso but never seen any of his work. I showed him a photograph of the famous bronze goat in Picasso's own house; thereafter all his beasts had sex organs as joyful as Picasso's goat's udder, but that was the only "influence" that ever took, with him. As I say, a white man always intercedes in some way, with a man like Elias; mine was to keep him from those art-loving ladies with galleries who wanted to promote him, and those white painters and sculptors who were willing to have him work under their tutelage. I gave him an old garage (well, that means I took my car out of it) and left him alone, with plenty of chunks of wood.

But Elias didn't like the loneliness of work. That garage never became his "place." Perhaps when you've lived in an overcrowded yard all your life the counter-stimulus of distraction becomes necessary to create a tension of concentration. No—well all I really mean is that he liked company. At first he came only at weekends, and then, as he began to sell some of his work, he gave up the messenger job and moved in more or less permanently—we fixed up the "place" together, putting in a ceiling and connecting water and so on. It was illegal for him to live there in a white suburb, of course, but such laws breed complementary evasions in people like Elias and me and the white building inspector didn't turn a hair of suspicion when I said that I was converting the garage as a flat for my wife's mother. It was better for Elias once he'd moved in; there was always some friend of his sharing his bed, not to mention the girls who did; sometimes the girls were shy little things almost of the kitchenmaid variety, who called my wife "madam" when they happened to bump into her, crossing the garden, sometimes they were the bewigged and painted actresses from the group who sat smoking and gossiping with my wife while she fed the baby.

And *he* was there more often than anyone—the plump and cheerful front-of-house manager; he was married, but as happens with our sex, an old friendship was a more important factor in his life than a wife and kids—if that's a characteristic of black men, then I must be black under the skin, myself. Elias had become very involved in the theatre group, anyway like *him;* Elias made some beautiful *papier mâché* gods for a play by a Nigerian that we did—"spirit of the ancestors" at once amusing and frightening—and once when we needed a singer he surprisingly turned out to have a voice that could phrase a madrigal as easily as whatever the forerunner of Soul was called—I forget now, but it blared hour after hour from the garage when he was working. Elias seemed to like best to work when the other one was around; *he* would sit with his fat boy's legs rolled out before him, flexing his toes in his fashionable shoes, dusting down the lapels of the latest thing in jackets, as he changed the records and kept up a monologue contentedly punctuated by those soft growls and sighs of agreement, those sudden squeezes of almost silent laughter—responses possible only in an African language—that came from Elias as he chiselled and chipped. For they spoke in their own tongue, and I have never known what it was they talked about.

In spite of my efforts to let him alone, inevitably Elias was "taken up" (hadn't I started the process myself, with that garage?) and a gallery announced itself his agent. He walked about at the opening of his one-man show in a purple turtle-necked sweater I think his best friend must have made him buy, laughing a little, softly, at himself, more embarrassed than pleased. An art critic wrote about his transcendental values and plastic modality, and he said, "Christ, man, does he dig it or doesn't he?" while we toasted his success in brandy chased with beer—brandy isn't a rich man's sip in South Africa, it's made here and it's what people use to get drunk on.

He earned quite a bit of money that year. Then the gallery-owner and the art critic forgot him in the discovery of yet another interpreter of the African soul, and he was poor again, but he had acquired a patroness who, although she lived far away, did not forget him. She was, as you might have thought, an American lady, very old and wealthy according to South African legend but probably simply a middle-aged widow with comfortable stock holdings and a desire to get in on the cultural ground floor of some form of art collecting not yet overcrowded. She had bought some of his work while a tourist in Johannesburg. Perhaps she did have academic connections with the art world; in any case, it was she who got a foundation to offer Elias Nkomo a scholarship to study in America.

I could understand that he wanted to go simply in order to go: to see the world outside. But I couldn't believe that at this stage he wanted or could make use of formal art-school disciplines. As I said to him at the time, I'm only an architect, but I've had experience of the academic and even, God help us, the frenziedly non-academic approach in the best schools, and it's not for people who have, to fall back on the jargon, found themselves.

I remember he said, smiling, "You think I've found myself?"

And I said, "But you've never been lost, man. That very first goat wrapped in newspaper was your goat."

But later, when he was refused a passport and the issue of his going abroad was much on our minds, we talked again. He wanted to go because he felt he needed some kind of general education, general cultural background that he'd missed, in his six years at the location school.

"Since I've been at your place I've been reading a lot of your books. And man, I know nothing. I'm as ignorant as that kid of yours there in the pram. Right, I've picked up a bit of politics, a few art terms here and there—I can wag my head and say 'plastic values' all right, eh? But man, what do I know about life? What do I know about how it all works? How do I know *how* I do the work I do? Why we live and die? —If I carry on here I might as well be carving walking sticks," he added. I knew what he meant: there are old men, all over Africa, who make a living squatting at a decent distance from tourist hotels, carving fancy walking sticks from local wood, only one step in sophistication below the "Africa Emergent" school of sculptors so rapturously acclaimed by gallery owners. We both laughed at this, and following the line of thought suggested to me by his question to himself: "How do I know how I do the work I do?", I asked him whether in fact there was any sort of traditional skill in his family. As I imagined, there was not—he was an urban slum kid, brought up opposite a municipal beerhall among paraffin-tin utensils and abandoned motor-car bodies which, perhaps curiously, had failed to bring out a Duchamp in him but from which, on the contrary, he had sprung, full-blown, as a classical expressionist. Although there were no rural walking-stick carvers in his ancestry, he did tell me something I had no idea would have been part of the experience of a location childhood—he had been sent, in his teens, to a tribal initiation school in the bush and been circumcised according to rite. He described the experience vividly.

Once all attempts to get him a passport had failed, Elias's desire to go to America became something else, of course: an obsessive resentment against confinement itself. Inevitably, he was given no reason for the refusal. The official answer was the usual one—that it was "not in the public interest" to reveal the reason for such things. Was it because "they" had got to know he was "living like a white man"? (Theory put to me by one of the black actors in the group.) Was it because a critic had dutifully described his work as expressive of the "agony of the emergent African soul"? Nobody knew. Nobody ever knows. It is enough to be black; blacks are meant to stay put, in their own ethnically-apportioned streets in their own segregated areas, in those parts of South Africa where the government says they belong. Yet—the whole way our lives are manœuvred, as I say, is an unanswered question— Elias's best friend suddenly got a passport. I hadn't even realized that *he* had been offered a scholarship or a study grant or something, too; *he* was invited to go to New York to study production and the latest acting techniques (it was the time of the Method rather than Grotowski). And *he* got a passport, "first try" as Elias said with ungrudging pleasure and admiration; when someone black got a passport, then, there was a collective sense of pleasure in having outwitted we didn't quite know what. So they went together, *he* on his passport, and Elias Nkomo on an exit permit.

An exit permit is a one-way ticket, anyway. When you are granted one at your request but at the government's pleasure, you sign an undertaking that you will never return to South Africa or its mandatory territory, South West Africa. You pledge this with signature and thumbprint. Elias Nkomo never came back. At first he wrote (and he wrote quite often) enthusiastically about the world outside that he had gained, and he seemed to be enjoying some kind of small vogue, not so much as a sculptor as a genuine, real live African Negro who was sophisticated enough to be asked to comment on this and that: the beauty of American women, life in Harlem or Watts, Black Power as seen through the eyes, etc. He sent cuttings from *Ebony* and even from *The New York Times Magazine*. He said that a girl at *Life* was trying to get them to run a piece on his work; his work?—well, he hadn't settled down to anything new, yet, but the art centre was a really swinging place, Christ, the things people were doing, there! There were silences, naturally; we forgot about him and he forgot about us for weeks on end. Then the local papers picked up the sort of news they are alert to from all over the world. Elias Nkomo had spoken at an anti-apartheid rally. Elias Nkomo, in West African robes, was on the platform with Stokely Carmichael. "Well, why not? He hasn't got to worry about keeping his hands clean for the time when he comes back home, has he?"—My wife was bitter in his defence. Yes, but I was wondering about his work— "Will they leave him alone to work?" I didn't write to him, but it was as if my silence were read by him: a few months later I received a cutting from some university art magazine devoting a number to Africa, and there was a photograph of one of Elias's wood sculptures, with his handwriting along the margin of the page—*I know you don't think much of people who don't turn out new stuff but some people here seem to think this old thing of mine is good*. It was the sort of wry remark that, spoken aloud to me in the room, would have made us both laugh. I smiled, and meant to write. But within two weeks Elias was dead. He drowned himself early one morning in the river of the New England town were the art school was.

It was like the refusal of the passport; none of us knew why. In the usual arrogance one has in the face of such happenings, I even felt guilty about the letter. Perhaps, if one were thousands of miles from one's own "place," in some sort of a bad way, just a small thing like a letter, a word of encouragement from someone who had hurt by being rather niggardly with encouragement in the past . . . ? And what pathetic arrogance, at that! As if the wisp of a letter, written by someone between other preoccupations, and in substance an encouraging lie (how splendid that your old work is receiving recognition in some piddling little magazine) could be anything round which the hand of a man going down for the second time might close.

Because before Elias went under in that river he must have been deep in forlorn horrors about which I knew nothing, nothing. When people commit suicide they do so apparently out of some sudden self-knowledge that those of us, the living, do not have the will to acquire. That's what's meant by despair, isn't it—what they have come to know? And that's what one means when one says in extenuation of oneself, *I knew so little about him, really*. I knew Elias only in the self that he had presented at my "place"; why, how out of place it had been, once, when he happened to mention that as a boy he had spent weeks in the bush with his circumcision group! Of course we—his friends—decided out of the facts we knew and our political and personal attitudes, why he had died: and perhaps it is true that he was sick to death, in the real sense of the phrase that has been forgotten, sick unto death with homesickness for the native land that had shut him out for ever and that he was forced to conjure up for himself in the parody of "native" dress that had nothing to do with his part of the continent, and the shame that a new kind of black platform-solidarity forced him to feel for his old dependence, in South Africa, on the friendship of white people. It was the South African government who killed him, it was culture shock—but perhaps neither our political bitterness nor our glibness with fashionable phrases can come near what combination of forces, within and without, led him to the fatal baptism of that early morning. *It is not in the private interest that this should be revealed.* Elias never came home. That's all.

But his best friend did, towards the end of that year.

He came to see me after he had been in the country some weeks—I'd heard he was back. The theatre group had broken up; it seemed to be that, chiefly, he'd come to talk to me about: he wanted to know if there was any money left in the kitty for him to start up a small theatrical venture of his own, he was eager to use the know-how (his phrase) he'd learned in the States. He was really plump now and he wore the most extraordinary clothes. A Liberace jacket. Plastic boots. An Afro wig that looked as if it had been made out of a bit of karakul from South West Africa. I teased him about it—we were at least good enough friends for that—asking him if he'd really been with the guerrillas instead of Off-Broadway? (There was a trial on at home, at the time, of South African political refugees who had tried to infiltrate through South West Africa.) And felt slightly ashamed of my patronage of his taste when he said with such good humour, "It's just a fun thing, man, isn't it great?" I was too cowardly to bring the talk round to the point: Elias. And when it couldn't be avoided, I said the usual platitudes and he shook his head at them—"Hell, man," and we fell silent. Then he told me that that was how he had got back—because Elias was dead, on the unused portion of Elias's air ticket. *His* study grant hadn't included travel expenses and he'd had to pay his own way over. So he'd had only a one-way ticket, but Elias's scholarship had included a return fare to the student's place of origin. It had been difficult to get the airline to agree to the transfer; he'd had to go to the scholarship foundation people, but they'd been very decent about fixing it for him.

He had told me all this so guilelessly that I was one of the people who became angrily indignant when the rumour began to go around that he was a police agent: who else would have the cold nerve to come back on a dead man's ticket, a dead man who couldn't ever have used that portion of the ticket himself, because he had taken an exit permit? And who could believe the story, anyway? Obviously, *he* had to find some way of explaining why he, a black man like any other, could travel freely back and forth between South Africa and other countries. He had a passport, hadn't he? Well, there you were. Why should *he* get a passport? What black man these days had a passport?

Yes, I was angry, and defended him, by proof of the innocence of the very naïveté with which—a black man, yes, and therefore used to the necessity of salvaging from disaster all his life, unable to afford the nice squeamishness of white men's delicacy—he took over Elias's air ticket because he was alive and needed it, as he might have taken up Elias's coat against the cold. I refused to avoid him, the way some members of the remnant of our group made it clear they did now, and I remained stony-faced outside the complicity of those knowing half-smiles that accompanied the mention of his name. We had never been close friends, of course, but he would turn up from time to time. He could not find theatrical work and had a job as a travelling salesman in the locations. He took to bringing three or four small boys along when he visited us; they were very subdued and whisperingly well-behaved and well-dressed in miniature suits—our barefoot children stared at them in awe. They were his children plus the children of the family he was living with, we gathered. He and I talked mostly about his difficulties—his old car was unreliable, his wife had left him, his commissions were low, and he could have taken up an offer to join a Chicago repertory company if he could have raised the fare to go back to America—while my wife fed ice-cream and cake to the silent children, or my children dutifully placed them one by one on the garden swing. We had begun to be able to talk about Elias's death. He had told me how, in the weeks before he died, Elias would get the wrong way on the moving stairway going down in the subway in New York and keep walking, walking up. "I thought he was foolin' around, man, you know? Jus' climbin' those stairs and goin' noplace?"

He clung nostalgically to the American idiom; no African talks about "noplace" when he means "nowhere." But he had abandoned the Afro wig and when we got talking about Elias he would hold his big, well-shaped head with its fine, shaven covering of his own wool propped between his hands as if in an effort to think more clearly about something that would never come clear; I felt suddenly at one with him in that gesture, and would say, "Go on." He would remember another example of how Elias had been "acting funny" before he died. It was on one of those afternoon visits that he said, "And I don't think I ever told you about the business with the students at the college? How that last weekend—before he did it, I mean—he went around and invited everybody to a party, I dunno, a kind of feast he said it was. Some of them said he said a barbecue—you know what that is, same as a *braaivleis,* eh? But one of the others told me afterwards that he'd told them he was going to give them a real African feast, he was going to show them how the country people do it here at home when somebody gets married or there's a funeral or so. He wanted to know where he could buy a goat."

"A goat?"

"That's right. A live goat. He wanted to kill and roast a goat for them, on the campus."

It was round about this time that *he* asked me for a loan. I think that was behind the idea of bringing those pretty, dressed-up children along with him when he visited; he wanted firmly to set the background of his obligations and responsibilities before touching me for money. It was rather a substantial sum, for someone of my resources. But he couldn't carry on his job without a new car, and he'd just got the opportunity to acquire a really good second-hand buy. I gave him the money in spite of —because of, perhaps—new rumours that were going around then that, in a police raid on the house of the family with whom he had been living, every adult except himself who was present on that night had been arrested on the charge of attending a meeting of a banned political organization. His friends were acquitted on the charge simply through the defence lawyer's skill at showing the *agent provocateur,* on whose evidence the charge was based, to be an unreliable witness—that is to say, a liar. But the friends were promptly served with personal banning orders, anyway, which meant among other things that their movements were restricted and they were not allowed to attend gatherings.

He was the only one who remained, significantly, it seemed impossible to ignore, free. And yet his friends let him stay on in the house; it was a mystery to us whites—and some blacks, too. But then so much becomes a mystery where trust becomes a commodity on sale to the police. Whatever my little show of defiance over the loan, during the last year or two we have reached the stage where if a man is black, literate, has "political" friends and white friends, *and* a passport, he must be considered a police spy. I was sick with myself—that was why I gave him the money—but I believed it, too. There's only one way for a man like that to prove himself, so far as we're concerned: he must be in prison.

Well, *he* was at large. A little subdued over the fate of his friends, about which he talked guilelessly as he had about the appropriation of Elias's air ticket, harassed as usual about money, poor devil, but generally cheerful. Yet our friendship, that really had begun to become one since Elias's death, waned rapidly. It was the money that did it. Of course, he was afraid I'd ask him to begin paying back and so he stopped coming to my "place," he stopped the visits with the beautifully dressed and well-behaved black infants. I received a typed letter from him, once, solemnly thanking me for my kind cooperation, etc., as if I were some business firm, and assuring me that in a few months he hoped to be in a position, etc. I scrawled a note in reply, saying of course I darned well hoped he was going to pay the money he owed, sometime, but why, for God's sake, in the meantime, did this mean we had to carry on as if we'd quarrelled? Damn it all, he didn't have to treat me as if I had some nasty disease, just because of a few rands.

But I didn't see him again. I've become too busy with my own work—the building boom of the last few years, you know; I've had the contract for several shopping malls and a big cultural centre—to do any work for the old theatre group in its sporadic comings-to-life. I don't think he had much to do with it anymore, either; I heard he was doing quite well as a salesman and was thinking of marrying again. There was even a—yet another—rumour, that he was actually building a house in Dube, which is the nearest to a solid bourgeois suburb a black can get in these black dormitories outside the white man's city, if you can be considered to be a bourgeois without having freehold. I didn't need the money, by then, but you know how it is with money—I felt faintly resentful about the debt anyway, because it looked as if now *he* could have paid it back just as well as *I* could say I didn't need it. As for the friendship, he'd shown me the worth of that. It's become something the white man must buy just as he must buy the cooperation of police stool-pigeons. Elias has been dead five years; we live in our situation as of now, as the legal phrase goes; one falls back on legal phrases as other forms of expression become too risky.

And then, two hundred and seventy-seven days ago, there was a new rumour, and this time it was confirmed, this time it was no rumour. *He* was fetched from his room one night and imprisoned. That's perfectly legal, here; it's the hundred-and-eighty-day Detention Act. At least, because he was something of a personality, with many friends and contacts in particular among both black and white journalists, the fact has become public. If people are humble, or of no particular interest to the small world of white liberals, they are sometimes in detention for many months before this is known outside the eyewitness of whoever happened to be standing by, in house or street, when they were taken away by the police. But at least we all know where *he* is: in prison. They say that charges of treason are being prepared against him and various others who were detained at the same time, and still others who have been detained for even longer—three hundred and seventy-one days, three hundred and ten days—the figures, once finally released, are always as precise as this—and that soon, soon they will be brought to trial for whatever it is that we do not know they have done, for when people are imprisoned under the Detention Act no one is told why and there are no charges. There are suppositions among us, of course. Was he a double agent, as it were, using his *laissez-passer* as a police spy in order to further his real work as an underground African nationalist? Was he just unlucky in his choice of friends? Did he suffer from a dangerous sense of loyalty in place of any strong convictions of his own? Was it all due to some personal, unguessed-at bond it's none of our business to speculate about? Heaven knows—those police-spy rumours aside—nobody could have looked more unlikely to be a political activist than that cheerful young man, second-string, always ready to jump up and turn over the record, fond of Liberace jackets and aspiring to play Le Roi Jones Off-Broadway.

But as I say, we know where he is now; inside. In solitary most of the time—they say, those who've also been inside. Two hundred and seventy-seven days he's been there.

And so we white friends can purge ourselves of the shame of rumours. We can be pure again. We are satisfied at last. He's in prison. He's proved himself, hasn't he?

The Man Who
Liked Dickens

EVELYN WAUGH

Although Mr. McMaster had lived in Amazonas for nearly sixty years, no one except a few families of Shiriana Indians was aware of his existence. His house stood in a small savannah, one of those little patches of sand and grass that crop up occasionally in that neighborhood, three miles or so across, bounded on all sides by forest.

The stream which watered it was not marked on any map; it ran through rapids, always dangerous and at most seasons of the year impassable, to join the upper waters of the River Uraricuera, whose course, though boldly delineated in every school atlas, is still largely conjectural. None of the inhabitants of the district, except Mr. McMaster, had ever heard of the republic of Colombia, Venezuela, Brazil or Bolivia, each of whom had at one time or another claimed its possession.

Mr. McMaster's house was larger than those of his neighbours, but similar in character—a palm-thatch roof, breast-high walls of mud and wattle, and a mud floor. He owned a dozen or so head of puny cattle which grazed in the savannah, a plantation of cassava, some banana and mango trees, a dog, and, unique in the neighbourhood, a single-barrelled, breech-loading shotgun. The few commodities which he employed from the outside world came to him through a long succession of traders, passed from hand to hand, bartered for in a dozen languages at the extreme end of one of the longest threads in the web of commerce that spreads from Manáos into the remote fastness of the forest.

One day, while Mr. McMaster was engaged in filling some cartridges, a Shiriana came to him with the news that a white man was approaching through the forest, alone and very sick. He closed the cartridge and loaded his gun with it, put those that were finished into his pocket and set out in the direction indicated.

The man was already clear of the bush when Mr. McMaster reached him, sitting on the ground, clearly in a bad way. He was without hat or boots, and his clothes were so torn that it was only by the dampness of his body that they adhered to it; his feet were cut and grossly swollen, every exposed surface of skin was scarred by insect and bat bites; his eyes were wild with fever. He was talking to himself in delirium, but stopped when Mr. McMaster approached and addressed him in English.

"I'm tired," the man said; then: "Can't go on any farther. My name is Henty and I'm tired. Anderson died. That was a long time ago. I expect you think I'm very odd."

"I think you are ill, my friend."

"Just tired. It must be several months since I had anything to eat."

Mr. McMaster hoisted him to his feet and, supporting him by the arm, led him across the hummocks of grass towards the farm.

"It is a very short way. When we get there I will give you something to make you better."

"Jolly kind of you." Presently he said: "I say, you speak English. I'm English, too. My name is Henty."

"Well, Mr. Henty, you aren't to bother about anything more. You're ill and you've had a rough journey. I'll take care of you."

They went very slowly, but at length reached the house.

"Lie there in the hammock. I will fetch something for you."

Mr. McMaster went into the back room of the house and dragged a tin canister from under a heap of skins. It was full of a mixture of dried leaf and bark. He took a handful and went outside to the fire. When he returned he put one hand behind Henty's head and held up the concoction of herbs in a calabash for him to drink. He sipped, shuddering slightly at the bitterness. At last he finished it. Mr. McMaster threw out the dregs on the floor. Henty lay back in the hammock sobbing quietly. Soon he fell into a deep sleep.

"Ill-fated" was the epithet applied by the Press to the Anderson expedition to the Parima and upper Uraricuera region of Brazil. Every stage of the enterprise from the preliminary arrangements in London to its tragic dissolution in Amazonas was attacked by misfortune. It was due to one of the early setbacks that Paul Henty became connected with it.

He was not by nature an explorer; an even-tempered, good-looking young man of fastidious tastes and enviable possessions, unintellectual, but appreciative of fine architecture and the ballet, well-traveled in the more accessible parts of the world, a collector though not a connoisseur, popular among hostesses, revered by his aunts. He was married to a lady of exceptional charm and beauty, and it was she who upset the good order of his life by confessing her affection for another man for the second time in the eight years of their marriage. The first occasion had been a short-lived infatuation with a tennis professional, the second was a captain in the Coldstream Guards, and more serious.

Henty's first thought under the shock of this revelation was to go out and dine alone. He was a member of four clubs, but at three of them he was liable to meet his wife's lover. Accordingly he chose one which he rarely frequented, a semi-intellectual company composed of publishers, barristers, and men of scholarship awaiting election to the Athenæum.

Here, after dinner, he fell into conversation with Professor Anderson and first heard of the proposed expedition to Brazil. The particular misfortune that was retarding arrangements at the moment was defalcation of the secretary with two-thirds of the expedition's capital. The principals were ready—Professor Anderson, Dr. Simmons the anthropologist, Mr. Necher the biologist, Mr. Brough the surveyor, wireless operator and mechanic—the scientific and sporting apparatus was packed up in crates ready to be embarked, the necessary facilities had been stamped and signed by the proper authorities but unless twelve hundred pounds was forthcoming the whole thing would have to be abandoned.

Henty, as has been suggested, was a man of comfortable means; the expedition would last from nine months to a year; he could shut his country house—his wife, he reflected, would want to remain in London near her young man—and cover more than the sum required. There was a glamour about the whole journey which might, he felt, move even his wife's sympathies. There and then, over the club fire he decided to accompany Professor Anderson.

When he went home that evening he announced to his wife: "I have decided what I shall do."

"Yes, darling?"

"You are certain that you no longer love me?"

"*Darling,* you *know,* I *adore* you."

"But you are certain you love this guardsman, Tony whatever-his-name-is, more?"

"Oh, yes, *ever* so much more. Quite a different thing altogether."

"Very well, then. I do not propose to do anything about a divorce for a year. You shall have time to think it over. I am leaving next week for the Uraricuera."

"Golly, where's that?"

"I am not perfectly sure. Somewhere in Brazil, I think. It is unexplored. I shall be away a year."

"But darling, how ordinary! Like people in books—big game, I mean, and all that."

"You have obviously already discovered that I am a very ordinary person."

"Now, Paul, don't be disagreeable—oh, there's the telephone. It's probably Tony. If it is, d'you mind terribly if I talk to him alone for a bit?"

But in the ten days of preparation that followed she showed greater tenderness, putting off her soldier twice in order to accompany Henty to the shops where he was choosing his equipment and insisting on his purchasing a worsted cummerbund. On his last evening she gave a supper-party for him at the Embassy to which she allowed him to ask any of his friends he liked; he could think of no one except Professor Anderson, who looked oddly dressed, danced tirelessly and was something of a failure with everyone. Next day Mrs. Henty came with her husband to the boat train and presented him with a pale blue, extravagantly soft blanket, in a suède case of the same colour furnished with a zip fastener and monogram. She kissed him good-bye and said, "Take care of yourself in wherever it is."

Had she gone as far as Southampton she might have witnessed two dramatic passages. Mr. Brough got no farther than the gangway before he was arrested for a debt—a matter of £32; the publicity given to the dangers of the expedition was responsible for the action. Henty settled the account.

The second difficulty was not to be overcome so easily. Mr. Necher's mother was on the ship before them; she carried a missionary journal in which she had just read an account of the Brazilian forests. Nothing would induce her to permit her son's departure; she would remain on board until he came ashore with her. If necessary, she would sail with him, but go into those forests alone he should not. All argument was unavailing with the resolute old lady who eventually, five minutes before the time of embarkation, bore her son off in triumph, leaving the company without a biologist.

Nor was Mr. Brough's adherence long maintained. The ship in which they were travelling was a cruising liner taking passengers on a round voyage. Mr. Brough had not been on board a week and had scarcely accustomed himself to the motion of the ship before he was engaged to be married; he was still engaged, although to a different lady, when they reached Manáos and refused all inducements to proceed farther, borrowing his return fare from Henty and arriving back in Southampton engaged to the lady of his first choice, whom he immediately married.

In Brazil the officials to whom their credentials were addressed were all out of power. While Henty and Professor Anderson negotiated with the new administrators, Dr. Simmons proceeded up river to Boa Vista where he established a base camp with the greater part of the stores. These were instantly commandeered by the revolutionary garrison, and he himself imprisoned for some days and subjected to various humiliations which so enraged him that, when released, he made promptly for the coast, stopping at Manáos only long enough to inform his colleagues that he insisted on leaving his case personally before the central authorities at Rio.

Thus while they were still a month's journey from the start of their labours, Henty and Professor Anderson found themselves alone and deprived of the greater part of their supplies. The ignominy of immediate return was not to be borne. For a short time they considered the advisability of going into hiding for six months in Madeira or Tenerife, but even there detection seemed probable; there had been too many photographs in the illustrated papers before they left London. Accordingly, in low spirits, the two explorers at last set out alone for the Uraricuera with little hope of accomplishing anything of any value to anyone.

For seven weeks they paddled through green, humid tunnels of forest. They took a few snapshots of naked, misanthropic Indians, bottled some snakes and later lost them when their canoe capsized in the rapids; they overtaxed their digestions, imbibing nauseous intoxicants at native galas; they were robbed of the last of their sugar by a Guianese prospector. Finally, Professor Anderson fell ill with malignant malaria, chattered feebly for some days in his hammock, lapsed into coma and died, leaving Henty alone with a dozen Maku oarsmen, none of whom spoke a word of any language known to him. They reversed their course and drifted down stream with a minimum of provisions and no mutual confidence.

One day, a week or so after Professor Anderson's death, Henty awoke to find that his boys and his canoe had disappeared during the night, leaving him with only his hammock and pyjamas some two or three hundred miles from the nearest Brazilian habitation. Nature forbade him to remain where he was although there seemed little purpose in moving. He set himself to follow the course of the stream, at first in the hope of meeting a canoe. But presently the whole forest became peopled for him with frantic apparitions, for no conscious reason at all. He plodded on, now wading in the water, now scrambling through the bush.

Vaguely at the back of his mind he had always believed that the jungle was a place full of food, that there was danger of snakes and savages and wild beasts, but not of starvation. But now he observed that this was far from being the case. The jungle consisted solely of immense tree trunks, embedded in a tangle of thorn and vine rope, all far from nutritious. On the first day he suffered hideously. Later he seemed anæsthetized and was chiefly embarrassed by the behavior of the inhabitants who came out to meet him in footmen's livery, carrying his dinner, and then irresponsibly disappeared or raised the covers of their dishes and revealed live tortoises. Many people who knew him in London appeared and ran round him with derisive cries, asking him questions to which he could not possibly know the answer. His wife came, too, and he was pleased to see her, assuming that she had got tired of her guardsman and was there to fetch him back, but she soon disappeared, like all the others.

It was then that he remembered that it was imperative for him to reach Manáos; he redoubled his energy, stumbling against boulders in the stream and getting caught up among the vines. "But I mustn't waste my breath," he reflected. Then he forgot that, too, and was conscious of nothing more until he found himself lying in a hammock in Mr. McMaster's house.

His recovery was slow. At first, days of lucidity alternated with delirium; then his temperature dropped and he was conscious even when most ill. The days of fever grew less frequent, finally occurring in the normal system of the tropics between long periods of comparative health. Mr. McMaster dosed him regularly with herbal remedies.

"It's very nasty," said Henty, "but it does do good."

"There is medicine for everything in the forest," said Mr. McMaster; "to make you well and to make you ill. My mother was an Indian and she taught me many of them. I have learned others from time to time from my wives. There are plants to cure you and give you fever, to kill you and send you mad, to keep away snakes, to intoxicate fish so that you can pick them out of the water with your hands like fruit from a tree. There are medicines even I do not know. They say that it is possible to bring dead people to life after they have begun to stink, but I have not seen it done."

"But surely you are English?"

"My father was—at least a Barbadian. He came to British Guiana as a missionary. He was married to a white woman but he left her in Guiana to look for gold. Then he took my mother. The Shiriana women are ugly but very devoted. I have had many. Most of the men and women living in this savannah are my children. That is why they obey—for that reason and because I have the gun. My father lived to a great age. It is not twenty years since he died. He was a man of education. Can you read?"

"Yes, of course."

"It is not everyone who is so fortunate. I cannot."

Henty laughed apologetically. "But I suppose you haven't much opportunity here."

"Oh, yes, that is just it. I have a great many books. I will show you when you are better. Until five years ago there was an Englishman—at least a black man, but he was well educated in Georgetown. He died. He used to read to me every day until he died. You shall read to me when you are better."

"I shall be delighted to."

"Yes, you shall read to me," Mr. McMaster repeated, nodding over the calabash.

During the early days of his convalescence Henty had little conversation with his host; he lay in the hammock staring up at the thatched roof and thinking about his wife, rehearsing over and over again different incidents in their life together, including her affairs with the tennis professional and the soldier. The days, exactly twelve hours each, passed without distinction. Mr. McMaster retired to sleep at sundown, leaving a little lamp burning—a hand-woven wick drooping from a pot of beef fat—to keep away vampire bats.

The first time that Henty left the house Mr. McMaster took him for a little stroll around the farm.

"I will show you the black man's grave," he said, leading him to a mound between the mango trees. "He was very kind to me. Every afternoon until he died, for two hours, he used to read to me. I think I will put up a cross—to commemorate his death and your arrival—a pretty idea. Do you believe in God?"

"I've never really thought about it much."

"You are perfectly right. I have thought about it a *great* deal and I still do not know . . . Dickens did."

"I suppose so."

"Oh yes, it is apparent in all his books. You will see."

That afternoon Mr. McMaster began the construction of a headpiece for the negro's grave. He worked with a large spokeshave in a wood so hard that it grated and rang like metal.

At last when Henty had passed six or seven consecutive days without fever, Mr. McMaster said, "Now I think you are well enough to see the books."

At one end of the hut there was a kind of loft formed by a rough platform erected up in the eaves of the roof. Mr. McMaster propped a ladder against it and mounted. Henty followed, still unsteady after his illness. Mr. McMaster sat on the platform and Henty stood at the top of the ladder looking over. There was a heap of small bundles there, tied up with rag, palm leaf and raw hide.

"It has been hard to keep out the worms and ants. Two are practically destroyed. But there is an oil the Indians know how to make that is useful."

He unwrapped the nearest parcel and handed down a calf-bound book. It was an early American edition of *Bleak House*.

"It does not matter which we take first."

"You are fond of Dickens?"

"Why, yes, of course. More than fond, far more. You see, they are the only books I have ever heard. My father used to read them and then later the black man . . . and now you. I have heard them all several times by now but I never get tired; there is always more to be learned and noticed, so many characters, so many changes of scene, so many words. . . . I have all Dickens's books except those that the ants devoured. It takes a long time to read them all—more than two years."

"Well," said Henty lightly, "they will well last out my visit."

"Oh, I hope not. It is delightful to start again. Each time I think I find more to enjoy and admire."

They took down the first volume of *Bleak House* and that afternoon Henty had his first reading.

He had always rather enjoyed reading aloud and in the first year of marriage had shared several books in this way with his wife, until one day, in one of her rare moments of confidence, she remarked that it was torture to her. Sometimes after that he had thought it might be agreeable to have children to read to. But Mr. McMaster was a unique audience.

The old man sat astride his hammock opposite Henty, fixing him throughout with his eyes, and following the words, soundlessly, with his lips. Often when a new character was introduced he would say, "Repeat the name, I have forgotten him," or, "Yes, yes, I remember her well. She dies, poor woman." He would frequently interrupt with questions; not as Henty would have imagined about the circumstances of the story —such things as the procedure of the Lord Chancellor's Court or the social conventions of the time, though they must have been unintelligible, did not concern him—but always about the characters. "Now, why does she say that? Does she really mean it? Did she feel faint because of the heat of the fire or of something in that paper?" He laughed loudly at all the jokes and at some passages which did not seem humorous to Henty, asking him to repeat them two or three times; and later at the description of the sufferings of the outcasts in "Tom-all-alone" tears ran down his cheeks into his beard. His comments on the story were usually simple. "I think that Dedlock is a very proud man," or, "Mrs. Jellyby does not take enough care of her children." Henty enjoyed the readings almost as much as he did.

At the end of the first day the old man said, "You read beautifully, with a far better accent than the black man. And you explain better. It is almost as though my father were here again." And always at the end of a session he thanked his guest courteously. "I enjoyed that very much. It was an extremely distressing chapter. But, if I remember rightly, it will all turn out well."

By the time that they were well into the second volume, however, the novelty of the old man's delight had begun to wane, and Henty was feeling strong enough to be restless. He touched more than once on the subject of his departure, asking about canoes and rains and the possibility of finding guides. But Mr. McMaster seemed obtuse and paid no attention to these hints.

One day, running his thumb through the pages of *Bleak House* that remained to be read, Henty said, "We still have a lot to get through. I hope I shall be able to finish it before I go."

"Oh, yes," said Mr. McMaster. "Do not disturb yourself about that. You will have time to finish it, my friend."

For the first time Henty noticed something slightly menacing in his host's manner. That evening at supper, a brief meal of farine and dried beef eaten just before sundown, Henty renewed the subject.

"You know, Mr. McMaster, the time has come when I must be thinking about getting back to civilization. I have already imposed myself on your hospitality for too long."

Mr. McMaster bent over his plate, crunching mouthfuls of farine, but made no reply.

"How soon do you think I shall be able to get a boat? . . . I said how soon do you think I shall be able to get a boat? I appreciate all your kindness to me more than I can say, but . . ."

"My friend, any kindness I may have shown is amply repaid by your reading of Dickens. Do not let us mention the subject again."

"Well, I'm very glad you have enjoyed it. I have, too. But I really must be thinking of getting back . . ."

"Yes," said Mr. McMaster. "The black man was like that. He thought of it all the time. But he died here . . ."

Twice during the next day Henty opened the subject but his host was evasive. Finally he said, "Forgive me, Mr. McMaster, but I really must press the point. When can I get a boat?"

"There is no boat."

"Well, the Indians can build one."

"You must wait for the rains. There is not enough water in the river now."

"How long will that be?"

"A month . . . two months . . ."

They had finished *Bleak House* and were nearing the end of *Dombey and Son* when the rain came.

"Now it is time to make preparations to go."

"Oh, that is impossible. The Indians will not make a boat during the rainy season—it is one of their superstitions."

"You might have told me."

"Did I not mention it? I forgot."

Next morning Henty went out alone while his host was busy, and, looking as aimless as he could, strolled across the savannah to the group of Indian houses. There were four or five Shirianas sitting in one of the doorways. They did not look up as he approached them. He addressed them in the few words of Maku he had acquired during the journey but they made no sign whether they understood him or not. Then he drew a sketch of a canoe in the sand, he went through some vague motions of carpentry, pointed from them to him, then made motions of giving something to them and scratched out the outlines of a gun and a hat and a few other recognizable articles of trade. One of the women giggled, but no one gave any sign of comprehension, and he went away unsatisfied.

At their midday meal Mr. McMaster said: "Mr. Henty, the Indians tell me that you have been trying to speak with them. It is easier that you say anything you wish through me. You realize, do you not, that they would do nothing without my authority. They regard themselves, quite rightly in most cases, as my children."

"Well, as a matter of fact, I was asking them about a canoe."

"So they gave me to understand . . . and now if you have finished your meal perhaps we might have another chapter. I am quite absorbed in the book."

They finished *Dombey and Son;* nearly a year had passed since Henty had left England, and his gloomy foreboding of permanent exile became suddenly acute when, between the pages of *Martin Chuzzlewit,* he found a document written in pencil in irregular characters.

Year 1919.

I James McMaster of Brazil do swear to Barnabas Washington of Georgetown that if he finish this book in fact Martin Chuzzlewit I will let him go away back as soon as finished.

There followed a heavy pencil *X*, and after it: *Mr. McMaster made this mark signed Barnabas Washington.*

"Mr. McMaster," said Henty, "I must speak frankly. You saved my life, and when I get back to civilization I will reward you to the best of my ability. I will give you anything within reason. But at present you are keeping me here against my will. I demand to be released."

"But, my friend, what is keeping you? You are under no restraint. Go when you like."

"You know very well that I can't get away without your help."

"In that case you must humour an old man. Read me another chapter."

"Mr. McMaster, I swear by anything you like that when I get to Manáos I will find someone to take my place. I will pay a man to read to you all day."

"But I have no need of another man. You read so well."

"I have read for the last time."

"I hope not," said Mr. McMaster politely.

That evening at supper only one plate of dried meat and farine was brought in and Mr. McMaster ate alone. Henty lay without speaking, staring at the thatch.

Next day at noon a single plate was put before Mr. McMaster, but with it lay his gun, cocked, on his knee, as he ate. Henty resumed the reading of *Martin Chuzzlewit* where it had been interrupted.

Weeks passed hopelessly. They read *Nicholas Nickleby* and *Little Dorrit* and *Oliver Twist*. Then a stranger arrived in the savannah, a half-caste prospector, one of that lonely order of men who wander for a lifetime through the forests, tracing the little streams, sifting the gravel and, ounce by ounce, filling the little leather sack of gold dust, more often than not dying of exposure and starvation with five hundred dollars' worth of gold hung round their necks. Mr. McMaster was vexed at his arrival, gave him farine and *passo* and sent him on his journey within an hour of his arrival, but in that hour Henty had time to scribble his name on a slip of paper and put it into the man's hand.

From now on there was hope. The days followed their unvarying routine: coffee at sunrise, a morning of inaction while Mr. McMaster pottered about on the business of the farm, farine and *passo* at noon, Dickens in the afternoon, farine and *passo* and sometimes some fruit for supper, silence from sunset to dawn with the small wick glowing in the beef fat and the palm thatch overhead dimly discernible; but Henty lived in quiet confidence and expectation.

Some time, this year or the next, the prospector would arrive at a Brazilian village with news of his discovery. The disasters to the Ander-

son expedition would not have passed unnoticed. Henty could imagine
the headlines that must have appeared in the popular Press; even now
probably there were search parties working over the country he had
crossed; any day English voices might sound over the savannah and a
dozen friendly adventurers come crashing through the bush. Even as he
was reading, while his lips mechanically followed the printed pages, his
mind wandered away from his eager, crazy host opposite, and he began
to narrate to himself incidents of his home-coming—the gradual re-en-
counters with civilization; he shaved and bought new clothes at Manáos,
telegraphed for money, received wires of congratulation; he enjoyed the
leisurely river journey to Belem, the big liner to Europe; savoured good
claret and fresh meat and spring vegetables; he was shy at meeting his
wife and uncertain how to address . . . *"Darling,* you've been much
longer than you said. I quite thought you were lost. . . ."

And then Mr. McMaster interrupted. "May I trouble you to read that
passage again? It is one I particularly enjoy."

The weeks passed; there was no sign of rescue, but Henty endured
the day for hope of what might happen on the morrow; he even felt a
slight stirring of cordiality towards his gaoler and was therefore quite
willing to join him when, one evening after a long conference with an
Indian neighbour, he proposed a celebration.

"It is one of the local feast days," he explained, "and they have been
making *piwari.* You may not like it, but you should try some. We will
go across to this man's home to-night."

Accordingly after supper they joined a party of Indians that were assembled round the fire in one of the huts at the other side of the savannah. They were singing in an apathetic, monotonous manner and passing a large calabash of liquid from mouth to mouth. Separate bowls
were brought for Henty and Mr. MacMaster, and they were given ham-
mocks to sit in.

"You must drink it all without lowering the cup. That is the eti-
quette."

Henty gulped the dark liquid, trying not to taste it. But it was not unpleasant, hard and muddy on the palate like most of the beverages he
had been offered in Brazil, but with a flavour of honey and brown
bread. He leant back in the hammock feeling unusually contented. Perhaps at that very moment the search party was in camp a few hours'
journey from them. Meanwhile he was warm and drowsy. The cadence
of song rose and fell interminably, liturgically. Another calabash of *piwari* was offered him and he handed it back empty. He lay full length
watching the play of shadows on the thatch as the Shirianas began to

dance. Then he shut his eyes and thought of England and his wife and fell asleep.

He awoke, still in the Indian hut, with the impression that he had outslept his usual hour. By the position of the sun he knew it was late afternoon. No one else was about. He looked for his watch and found to his surprise that it was not on his wrist. He had left it in the house, he supposed, before coming to the party.

"I must have been tight last night," he reflected. "Treacherous drink, that." He had a headache and feared a recurrence of fever. He found when he set his feet to the ground that he stood with difficulty; his walk was unsteady and his mind confused as it had been during the first weeks of his convalescence. On the way across the savannah he was obliged to stop more than once, shutting his eyes and breathing deeply. When he reached the house he found Mr. McMaster sitting there.

"Ah, my friend, you are late for the reading this afternoon. There is scarcely another half-hour of light. How do you feel?"

"Rotten. That drink doesn't seem to agree with me."

"I will give you something to make you better. The forest has remedies for everything; to make you awake and to make you sleep."

"You haven't seen my watch anywhere?"

"You have missed it?"

"Yes. I thought I was wearing it. I say, I've never slept so long."

"Not since you were a baby. Do you know how long? Two days."

"Nonsense. I can't have."

"Yes, indeed. It is a long time. It is a pity because you missed our guests."

"Guests?"

"Why, yes. I have been quite gay while you were asleep. Three men from outside. Englishmen. It is a pity you missed them. A pity for them, too, as they particularly wished to see you. But what could I do? You were so sound asleep. They had come all the way to find you, so—I thought you would not mind—as you could not greet them yourself I gave them a little souvenir, your watch. They wanted something to take home to your wife who is offering a great reward for news of you. They were very pleased with it. And they took some photographs of the little cross I put up to commemorate your coming. They were pleased with that, too. They were very easily pleased. But I do not suppose they will visit us again, our life here is so retired . . . no pleasures except reading . . . I do not suppose we shall ever have visitors again . . . well, well, I will get you some medicine to make you feel better. Your head aches, does it not. . . . We will not have any Dickens to-day . . . but tomorrow, and the day after that, and the day after that. Let us read *Little Dorrit* again. There are passages in that book I can never hear without the temptation to weep."

Strawberry Spring

STEPHEN KING

Springheel Jack . . .

I saw those two words in the paper this morning and my God, how they take me back. All that was eight years ago, almost to the day. Once, while it was going on, I saw myself on nationwide TV—the Walter Cronkite Report. Just a hurrying face in the general background behind the reporter, but my folks picked me out right away. They called long-distance. My dad wanted my analysis of the situation; he was all bluff and hearty and man-to-man. My mother just wanted me to come home. But I didn't want to come home. I was enchanted.

Enchanted by that dark and mist-blown strawberry spring, and by the shadow of violent death that walked through it on those nights eight years ago. The shadow of Springheel Jack.

In New England they call it a strawberry spring. No one knows why; it's just a phrase the old-timers use. They say it happens once every eight or ten years. What happened at New Sharon Teachers' College that particular strawberry spring . . . there may be a cycle for that, too, but if anyone has figured it out, they've never said.

At New Sharon, the strawberry spring began on March 16, 1968. The coldest winter in twenty years broke on that day. It rained and you could smell the sea twenty miles west of the beaches. The snow, which had been thirty-five inches deep in places, began to melt and the campus walks ran with slush. The Winter Carnival snow sculptures, which had been kept sharp and clearcut for two months by the subzero temperatures, at last began to sag and slouch. The caricature of Lyndon Johnson in front of the Tep fraternity house cried melted tears. The dove in front of Prashner Hall lost its frozen feathers and its plywood skeleton showed sadly through in places.

And when night came the fog came with it, moving silent and white along the narrow college avenues and thoroughfares. The pines on the

mall poked through it like counting fingers and it drifted, slow as cigarette smoke, under the little bridge down by the Civil War cannons. It
made things seem out of joint, strange, magical. The unwary traveler
would step out of the juke-thumping, brightly lit confusion of the
Grinder, expecting the hard clear starriness of winter to clutch him . . .
and instead he would suddenly find himself in a silent, muffled world of
white drifting fog, the only sound his own footsteps and the soft drip of
water from the ancient gutters. You half expected to see Gollum or
Frodo and Sam go hurrying past, or to turn and see that the Grinder
was gone, vanished, replaced by a foggy panorama of moors and yew
trees and perhaps a Druid-circle or a sparkling fairy ring.

The jukebox played "Love Is Blue" that year. It played "Hey, Jude"
endlessly, endlessly. It played "Scarborough Fair."

And at ten minutes after eleven on that night a junior named John
Dancey on his way back to his dormitory began screaming into the fog,
dropping books on and between the sprawled legs of the dead girl lying
in a shadowy corner of the Animal Sciences parking lot, her throat cut
from ear to ear but her eyes open and almost seeming to sparkle as if
she had just successfully pulled off the funniest joke of her young life—
Dancey, an education major and a speech minor, screamed and
screamed and screamed.

The next day was overcast and sullen, and we went to classes with
questions eager in our mouths—who? why? when do you think they'll
get him? And always the final thrilled question: Did you know her? Did
you know her?

Yes, I had an art class with her.

Yes, one of my roommate's friends dated her last term.

*Yes, she asked me for a light once in the Grinder. She was at the next
table.*

Yes,

Yes, I

Yes . . . yes . . . oh yes, I

We all knew her. Her name was Gale Cerman (pronounced Kerr-
man), and she was an art major. She wore granny glasses and had a
good figure. She was well liked but her roommates had hated her. She
had never gone out much even though she was one of the most promis-
cuous girls on campus. She was ugly but cute. She had been a vivacious
girl who talked little and smiled seldom. She had been pregnant and she
had had leukemia. She was a lesbian who had been murdered by her
boyfriend. It was strawberry spring, and on the morning of March 17
we all knew Gale Cerman.

Half a dozen State Police cars crawled onto the campus, most of them parked in front of Judith Franklin Hall, where the German girl had lived. On my way past there to my ten o'clock class I was asked to show my student ID. I was clever. I showed him the one without the fangs.

"Do you carry a knife?" the policeman asked cunningly.

"Is it about Gale German?" I asked, after I told him that the most lethal thing on my person was a rabbit's-foot key chain.

"What makes you ask?" he pounced.

I was five minutes late to class.

It was strawberry spring and no one walked by themselves through the half-academical, half-fantastical campus that night. The fog had come again, smelling of the sea, quiet and deep.

Around nine o'clock my roommate burst into our room, where I had been busting my brains on a Milton essay since seven. "They caught him," he said. "I heard it over at the Grinder."

"From who?"

"I don't know. Some guy. Her boyfriend did it. His name is Carl Amalara."

I settled back, relieved and disappointed. With a name like that it had to be true. A lethal and sordid little crime of passion.

"Okay," I said. "That's good."

He left the room to spread the news down the hall. I reread my Milton essay, couldn't figure out what I had been trying to say, tore it up and started again.

It was in the papers the next day. There was an incongruously neat picture of Amalara—probably a high-school graduation picture—and it showed a rather sad-looking boy with an olive complexion and dark eyes and pockmarks on his nose. The boy had not confessed yet, but the evidence against him was strong. He and Gale German had argued a great deal in the last month or so, and had broken up the week before. Amalara's roomie said he had been "despondent." In a footlocker under his bed, police had found a seven-inch hunting knife from L. L. Bean's and a picture of the girl that had apparently been cut up with a pair of shears.

Beside Amalara's picture was one of Gale German. It blurrily showed a dog, a peeling lawn flamingo, and a rather mousy blond girl wearing spectacles. An uncomfortable smile had turned her lips up and her eyes were squinted. One hand was on the dog's head. It was true then. It had to be true.

The fog came again that night, not on little cat's feet but in an improper silent sprawl. I walked that night. I had a headache and I walked for air, smelling the wet, misty smell of the spring that was slowly wiping away the reluctant snow, leaving lifeless patches of last year's grass bare and uncovered, like the head of a sighing old grandmother.

For me, that was one of the most beautiful nights I can remember. The people I passed under the haloed streetlights were murmuring shadows, and all of them seemed to be lovers, walking with hands and eyes linked. The melting snow dripped and ran, dripped and ran, and from every dark storm drain the sound of the sea drifted up, a dark winter sea now strongly ebbing.

I walked until nearly midnight, until I was thoroughly mildewed, and I passed many shadows, heard many footfalls clicking dreamily off down the winding paths. Who is to say that one of those shadows was not the man or the thing that came to be known as Springheel Jack? Not I, for I passed many shadows but in the fog I saw no faces.

The next morning the clamor in the hall woke me. I blundered out to see who had been drafted, combing my hair with both hands and running the fuzzy caterpillar that had craftily replaced my tongue across the dry roof of my mouth.

"He got another one," someone said to me, his face pallid with excitement. "They had to let him go."

"Why go?"

"Amalara!" someone else said gleefully. "He was sitting in jail when it happened."

"When what happened?" I asked patiently. Sooner or later I would get it. I was sure of that.

"The guy killed somebody else last night. And now they're hunting all over for it."

"For what?"

The pallid face wavered in front of me again. "Her head. Whoever killed her took her head with him."

New Sharon isn't a big school now, and was even smaller then—the kind of institution the public relations people chummily refer to as a "community college." And it really was like a small community, at least in those days; between you and your friends, you probably had at least a nodding acquaintance with everybody else and their friends. Gale Cerman had been the type of girl you just nodded to, thinking vaguely that you had seen her around.

We all knew Ann Bray. She had been the first runner-up in the Miss New England pageant the year before, her talent performance consisting of twirling a flaming baton to the tune of "Hey, Look Me Over." She was brainy, too; until the time of her death she had been editor of the school newspaper (a once-weekly rag with a lot of political cartoons and bombastic letters), a member of the student dramatics society, and president of the National Service Sorority, New Sharon Branch. In the hot, fierce bubblings of my freshman youth I had submitted a column idea to the paper and asked for a date—turned down on both counts.

And now she was dead . . . worse than dead.

I walked to my afternoon classes like everybody else, nodding to people I knew and saying hi with a little more force than usual, as if that would make up for the close way I studied their faces. Which was the same way they were studying mine. There was someone dark among us, as dark as the path which twisted across the mall or wound among the hundred-year-old oaks on the quad in back of the gymnasium. As dark as the hulking Civil War cannons seen through a drifting membrane of fog. We looked into each other's faces and tried to read the darkness behind one of them.

This time the police arrested no one. The blue beetles patrolled the campus ceaselessly on the foggy spring nights of the eighteenth, nineteenth, and twentieth, and spotlights stabbed into dark nooks and crannies with erratic eagerness. The administration imposed a mandatory nine o'clock curfew. A foolhardy couple discovered necking in the landscaped bushes north of the Tate Alumni Building were taken to the New Sharon police station and grilled unmercifully for three hours.

There was a hysterical false alarm on the twentieth when a boy was found unconscious in the same parking lot where the body of Gale Cerman had been found. A gibbering campus cop loaded him into the back of his cruiser and put a map of the county over his face without bothering to hunt for a pulse and started toward the local hospital, siren wailing across the deserted campus like a seminar of banshees.

Halfway there the corpse in the back seat had risen and asked hollowly, "Where the hell am I?" The cop shrieked and ran off the road. The corpse turned out to be an undergrad named Donald Morris who had been in bed the last two days with a pretty lively case of flu—was it Asian that year? I can't remember. Anyway, he fainted in the parking lot on his way to the Grinder for a bowl of soup and some toast.

The days continued warm and overcast. People clustered in small groups that had a tendency to break up and re-form with surprising speed. Looking at the same set of faces for too long gave you funny ideas about some of them. And the speed with which rumors swept from one end of the campus to the other began to approach the speed of light; a well-liked history professor had been overheard laughing and weeping down by the small bridge; Gale Cerman had left a cryptic two-word message written in her own blood on the blacktop of the Animal Sciences parking lot; both murders were actually political crimes, ritual murders that had been performed by an offshoot of the SDS to protest the war. This was really laughable. The New Sharon SDS had seven members. One fair-sized offshoot would have bankrupted the whole organization. This fact brought an even more sinister embellishment from the campus right-wingers: outside agitators. So during those queer, warm days we all kept our eyes peeled for them.

The press, always fickle, ignored the strong resemblance our murderer bore to Jack the Ripper and dug further back—all the way to 1819. Ann Bray had been found on a soggy path of ground some twelve feet from the nearest sidewalk, and yet there were no footprints, not even her own. An enterprising New Hampshire newsman with a passion for the arcane christened the killer Springheel Jack, after the infamous Dr. John Hawkins of Bristol, who did five of his wives to death with odd pharmaceutical knickknacks. And the name, probably because of that soggy yet unmarked ground, stuck.

On the twenty-first it rained again, and the mall and quadrangle became quagmires. The police announced that they were salting plainclothes detectives, men and women, about, and took half the police cars off duty.

The campus newspaper published a strongly indignant, if slightly incoherent, editorial protesting this. The upshot of it seemed to be that, with all sorts of cops masquerading as students, it would be impossible to tell a real outside agitator from a false one.

Twilight came and the fog with it, drifting up the tree-lined avenues slowly, almost thoughtfully, blotting out the buildings one by one. It was soft, insubstantial stuff, but somehow implacable and frightening. Springheel Jack was a man, no one seemed to doubt that, but the fog was his accomplice and it was female . . . or so it seemed to me. It was as if our little school was caught between them, squeezed in some crazy lovers' embrace, part of a marriage that had been consummated in blood. I sat and smoked and watched the lights come on in the growing darkness and wondered if it was all over. My roommate came in and shut the door quietly behind him.

"It's going to snow soon," he said.

I turned around and looked at him. "Does the radio say that?"

"No," he said. "Who needs a weatherman? Have you ever heard of strawberry spring?"

"Maybe," I said. "A long time ago. Something grandmothers talk about, isn't it?"

He stood beside me, looking out at the creeping dark.

"Strawberry spring is like Indian summer," he said, "only much more rare. You get a good Indian summer in this part of the country once every two or three years. A spell of weather like we've been having is supposed to come only every eight or ten. It's a false spring, a lying spring, like Indian summer is a false summer. My own grandmother used to say strawberry spring means the worst norther of the winter is still on the way—and the longer this lasts, the harder the storm."

"Folk tales," I said. "Never believe a word." I looked at him. "But I'm nervous. Are you?"

He smiled benevolently and stole one of my cigarettes from the open pack on the window ledge. "I suspect everyone but me and thee," he said, and then the smile faded a little. "And sometimes I wonder about thee. Want to go over to the Union and shoot some eight-ball? I'll spot you ten."

"Trig prelim next week. I'm going to settle down with a magic marker and a hot pile of notes."

For a long time after he was gone, I could only look out the window. And even after I had opened my book and started in, part of me was still out there, walking in the shadows where something dark was now in charge.

That night Adelle Parkins was killed. Six police cars and seventeen collegiate-looking plainclothesmen (eight of them were women imported all the way from Boston) patrolled the campus. But Springheel Jack killed her just the same, going unerringly for one of our own. The false spring, the lying spring, aided and abetted him—he killed her and left her propped behind the wheel of her 1964 Dodge to be found the next morning and they found part of her in the back seat and part of her in the trunk. And written in blood on the windshield—this time fact instead of rumor—were two words: HA! HA!

The campus went slightly mad after that; all of us and none of us had known Adelle Parkins. She was one of those nameless, harried women who worked the break-back shift in the Grinder from six to eleven at night, facing hordes of hamburger-happy students on study break from the library across the way. She must have had it relatively easy those last three foggy nights of her life; the curfew was being rigidly observed, and after nine the Grinder's only patrons were hungry cops and happy janitors—the empty buildings had improved their habitual bad temper considerably.

There is little left to tell. The police, as prone to hysteria as any of us and driven against the wall, arrested an innocuous homosexual sociology graduate student named Hanson Gray, who claimed he "could not remember" where he had spent several of the lethal evenings. They charged him, arraigned him, and let him go to scamper hurriedly back to his native New Hampshire town after the last unspeakable night of strawberry spring when Marsha Curran was slaughtered on the mall.

Why she had been out and alone is forever beyond knowing—she was a fat, sadly pretty thing who lived in an apartment in town with three other girls. She had slipped on campus as silently and as easily as Springheel Jack himself. What brought her? Perhaps her need was as deep and as ungovernable as her killer's, and just as far beyond understanding. Maybe a need for one desperate and passionate romance with the warm night, the warm fog, the smell of the sea, and the cold knife.

That was on the twenty-third. On the twenty-fourth the president of the college announced that spring break would be moved up a week, and we scattered, not joyfully but like frightened sheep before a storm, leaving the campus empty and haunted by the police and one dark specter.

I had my own car on campus, and I took six people downstate with me, their luggage crammed in helter-skelter. It wasn't a pleasant ride. For all any of us knew, Springheel Jack might have been in the car with us.

That night the thermometer dropped fifteen degrees, and the whole northern New England area was belted by a shrieking norther that began in sleet and ended in a foot of snow. The usual number of old duffers had heart attacks shoveling it away—and then, like magic, it was April. Clean showers and starry nights.

They called it strawberry spring, God knows why, and it's an evil, lying time that only once comes every eight or ten years. Springheel Jack left with the fog, and by early June, campus conversation had turned to a series of draft protests and a sit-in at the building where a well-known napalm manufacturer was holding job interviews. By June, the subject of Springheel Jack was almost unanimously avoided—at least aloud. I suspect there were many who turned it over and over privately, looking for the one crack in the seamless egg of madness that would make sense of it all.

That was the year I graduated, and the next year was the year I married. A good job in a local publishing house. In 1971 we had a child, and now he's almost school age. A fine and questing boy with my eyes and her mouth.

Then, today's paper.

Of course I knew it was here. I knew it yesterday morning when I got up and heard the mysterious sound of snowmelt running down the gutters, and smelled the salt tang of the ocean from our front porch, nine miles from the nearest beach. I knew strawberry spring had come again when I started home from work last night and had to turn on my headlights against the mist that was already beginning to creep out of the fields and hollows, blurring the lines of the buildings and putting fairy haloes around the streetlamps.

This morning's paper says a girl was killed on the New Sharon campus near the Civil War cannons. She was killed last night and found in a melting snowbank. She was not . . . she was not all there.

My wife is upset. She wants to know where I was last night. I can't tell her because I don't remember. I remember starting home from work, and I remember putting my headlights on to search my way through the lovely creeping fog, but that's all I remember.

I've been thinking about that foggy night when I had a headache and walked for air and passed all the lovely shadows without shape or substance. And I've been thinking about the trunk of my car—such an ugly word, *trunk*—and wondering why in the world I should be afraid to open it.

I can hear my wife as I write this, in the next room, crying. She thinks I was with another woman last night.

And oh dear God, I think so too.

HEIRS OF
SHERLOCK HOLMES

NEW ENGLAND
NEW YORK
NORWAY

Time and Time Again

HARRY KEMELMAN

Although it was more than two years since I had left the Law Faculty to become County Attorney, I still maintained some connection with the university. I still had the privileges of the gymnasium and the library and I still kept up my membership in the Faculty Club. I dropped in there occasionally for a game of billiards, and about once a month I dined there, usually with Nicholas Welt.

We had finished dinner, Nicky and I, and had repaired to the Commons Room for a game of chess, only to find that all the tables were in use. So we joined the group in front of the fire where there was always interminable talk about such highly scholarly matters as to whether there was any likelihood of favorable action by the trustees on an increase in salary schedules—there wasn't—or whether you got more miles per gallon with a Chevrolet than you got with a Ford.

This evening as we joined the group, the talk was about Professor Rollins' paper in the *Quarterly Journal of Psychic Research* which no one had read but on which everyone had an opinion. The title of the paper was something like "Modifications in the Sprague Method of Analysis of Extra-Sensory Experimentation Data," but the academic mind with its faculty for generalization had quickly gone beyond the paper and Rollins' theories to a discussion on whether there was anything in "this business of the supernatural," with burly Professor Lionel Graham, Associate in Physics, asserting that "of course, there couldn't be when you considered the type of people who went in for it, gypsies and what not." And gentle, absent-minded Roscoe Summers, Professor of Archaeology, maintaining doggedly that you couldn't always tell by that and that he had heard stories from people whose judgment he respected that made you pause and think a bit.

To which Professor Graham retorted, "That's just the trouble. It's always something that happened to somebody else. Or better still, something that somebody told you that happened to somebody *he* knew." Then catching sight of us, he said, "Isn't that right, Nicky? Did you ever hear about anything supernatural as having happened to somebody you yourself knew well and whose word and opinion you could rely on?"

Nicky's lined, gnomelike face relaxed in a frosty little smile. "I'm afraid that's how I get most of my information," he said. "I mean through hearing about it at third or fourth hand."

Dr. Chisholm, the young instructor in English Composition, had been trying to get a word in and now he succeeded. "I had a case last summer. I mean I was there and witnessed something that was either supernatural or was a most remarkable coincidence."

"Something on the stage, or was it a seance in a dark room?" asked Graham with a sneer.

"Neither," said Chisholm defiantly. "I saw a man cursed and he died of it." He caught sight of a pompous little man with a shining bald head and he called out, "Professor Rollins, won't you join us? I'm sure you'd be interested in a little incident I was about to tell."

Professor Rollins, the author of the paper in the *Quarterly,* approached and the men sitting on the red leather divan moved over respectfully to make room for him. But he seemed to sense that he was being asked to listen as an expert and he selected a straight-backed chair as being more in keeping with the judicial role he was to play.

I spent my summer vacation (Chisholm began) in a little village on the Maine coast. It was not a regular summer resort and there was little to do all day long except sit on the rocks and watch the gulls as they swooped above the water. But I had worked hard all year and it was precisely what I wanted.

The center of the town was inland, clustered about the little railroad depot, and I was fortunate in getting a room way out at the end of town near the water. My host was a man named Doble, a widower in his forties, a decent quiet man who was good company when I wanted company and who did not obtrude when I just wanted to sit and daydream. He did a little farming and had some chickens; he had a boat and some lobster pots; and for the rest, he'd make a little money at various odd jobs. He didn't work by the day but would contract for the whole job, which put him a cut above the ordinary odd jobman, I suppose.

Ours was the last house on the road and our nearest neighbor was about a hundred yards away. It was a large nineteenth century mansion, set back from the road, and decorated with the traditional fretsaw trim

and numerous turrets and gables. It was owned and occupied by Cyrus
Cartwright, the president of the local bank and the richest man in town.

He was a brisk, eager sort of man, like the advertisement for a correspondence course in salesmanship, the type of man who carries two
watches and is always glancing at his wristwatch and then checking it
against his pocket watch.

(Chisholm warmed as he described Cyrus Cartwright, the result of
the natural antipathy of a man who spends his summer watching sea
gulls for the type of man who weighs out his life in small minutes. Now
he smiled disarmingly and shrugged his shoulders.)

I saw him only once. I had come in town with Doble and before
going home, he stopped in at the bank to see if Cartwright was still interested in making some change in the electric wiring system in his
house which they had talked about some months ago. It was typical of
Doble that he should only now be coming around to make further inquiry about it.

Cartwright glanced at the radium dial of his wristwatch and then
tugged at his watch chain and drew out his pocket watch, squeezing it
out of its protective chamois covering. He mistook my interest in the ritual for interest in the watch itself and held it out so that I could see it,
explaining with some condescension that it was a repeater, a five-minute
repeater he was at some pains to point out, and then proceeded to dem-
onstrate it by pressing a catch so that I could hear it tinkle the hour and
then in a different key tinkle once for every five-minute interval after
the hour.

I made some comparison between the man who carries two watches
and the man who wears both a belt and suspenders. But though he realized I was joking, he said with some severity, "Time is money, sir, and I
like to know just where I am with both. So I keep accurate books and
accurate watches."

Having put me in my place, he turned to Doble and said crisply, "I
don't think I'll bother with it, Doble. It was Jack's idea having the extra
light and switch in the hallway and now that he's gone into the service, I
don't think I'll need it. When it gets dark, I go to bed."

Once again he glanced at his wristwatch, checked its accuracy against
his pocket watch as before, and then he smiled at us, a short, meaning-
less, businessman's smile of dismissal.

As I say, I saw him only that once, but I heard a great deal about
him. You know how it is, you hear a man's name mentioned for the first
time and then it seems to pop up again and again in the next few days.

According to Doble, Cartwright was a tight-fisted old skinflint who had remained a bachelor, probably to save the expense of supporting a wife.

When I pointed out that paying a housekeeper to come in every day was almost as expensive as keeping a wife, and that in addition he had brought up his nephew Jack, Doble retorted that nobody but Mrs. Knox would take the job of Cartwright's housekeeper and that she took it only because no one else would take her. She was almost stone deaf and general opinion was that her wages were small indeed.

"As for Jack," he went on, "the old man never let him see a penny more than he actually needed. He never had a dime in his pocket, and when he'd go into town of an evening, he'd just have to hang around—usually didn't even have the price of a movie. Nice young fellow too," he added reflectively.

"He could have got a job and left," I suggested.

"I suppose he could've," Doble said slowly, "but he's the old man's heir, you see, and I guess he figured it was kind of politic, as you might say, to hang around doing any little jobs at the bank that the old man might ask of him."

I was not too favorably impressed with the young man's character from Doble's description, but I changed my mind when he came down a few days later on furlough.

He turned out to be a decent chap, quiet and reserved, but with a quick and imaginative mind. We grew quite close in those few days and saw a great deal of each other. We went fishing off the rocks, or lazed around in the sun a good deal talking of all sorts of things, or shot at chips in the water with an old rifle that he had.

He kept his gun and fishing rod over at our house. And that gives some indication of the character of Cyrus Cartwright and of Jack's relations with him. He explained that his uncle knew that he wasn't doing anything during this week of furlough and didn't really expect him to, but if he saw him with the fishing rod, that traditional symbol of idleness, it would seem as though he were flaunting his indolence in his face. As for the gun, Cyrus Cartwright considered shooting at any target that could not subsequently be eaten as an extravagant waste of money for shells.

Jack came over every evening to play cribbage or perhaps to sit on the porch and sip at a glass of beer and argue about some book he had read at my suggestion. Sometimes he spoke about his uncle and in discussing him, he was not bitter—ironic, rather.

On one occasion he explained, "My uncle is a good man according to his lights. He likes money because it gives him a sense of accomplishment to have more than anyone else in town. But that alone doesn't make him a hard person to live with. What does make him difficult is that everything is set in a rigid routine, a senseless routine, and his household has to conform to it. After dinner, he sits and reads his paper until it gets dark. Then he looks at his wristwatch and shakes his head a little as though he didn't believe it was that late. Then he takes his pocket watch out and checks the wristwatch against it. But of course, even that doesn't satisfy him. So he goes into the dining room where he has an electric clock and he sets both watches by that.

"When he's got all timepieces perfectly synchronized, he says, 'Well, it's getting late,' and he goes upstairs to his room. In about fifteen minutes he calls to me and I go up to find him already in bed.

"'I forgot to fix the windows,' he says. So I open them an inch at the top and an inch at the bottom. It takes a bit of doing because if I should open them a quarter of an inch too wide, he says he'll catch his death of cold, and if it is short of an inch, he's sure he'll smother. But finally I get them adjusted just right and he says, 'My watch, would you mind, Jack?' So I get his pocket watch that he had put on the bureau while undressing and I put it on the night table near his bed.

"As far back as I can remember, I've had to do that little chore. I am sure he insists on it so as to fix our relations in my mind. While I was away, he must have remembered to do it for himself, but the first day I got back I had to do it."

(Chisholm looked from one to the other of us as if to make sure that we all understood the characters and their relations with each other. I nodded encouragingly and he continued.)

Jack was scheduled to leave Sunday morning and naturally we expected to see him Saturday, but he did not show up during the day. He came over in the evening after dinner, however, and he was hot and angry.

"The hottest day of the summer," he exclaimed, "and today of all days my uncle suddenly finds a bunch of errands for me to do. I've been all over the county and I couldn't even take the car. I'll bet you fellows were lying out on the beach all day. How about going in for a dip right now?"

Well, of course, we had been in and out of the water all day long, but it was still hot and muggy, and besides we could see that he wanted very much to go, so we agreed. We took some beer down and we didn't bother with bathing suits since it was already quite dark. After a while, however, it began to get chilly. It had clouded up and the air was oppressive as though a storm were impending. So we got dressed again and went back to our house.

The atmosphere had a charged, electric quality about it, and whether it was that or because he was leaving the following day, Jack was unusually quiet and conversation lagged. Around half past eleven, he rose and stretched and said he thought he ought to be going.

"It's been good meeting you," he said. "I didn't look forward to this furlough particularly, but now I'm sure I'm going to look back on it."

We shook hands and he started for the door. Then he remembered about his fishing rod and his rifle and came back for them. He seemed reluctant to leave us, and Doble, understanding, said, "We might as well walk down with you, Jack."

He nodded gratefully and all three of us strolled out into the darkness. We walked along slowly, Jack with his fishing rod over one shoulder and his gun over the other.

I offered to carry the gun, but he shook his head and handed me the rod instead. I took it and walked on in silence until we reached the gate of his uncle's house. Perhaps he misinterpreted my silence and felt that he had been ungracious, for he said, "I'm a lot more used to carrying a rifle than you are." And then lest I take his remark as a reflection on my not being in the service, he hurried on with, "I'm kind of fond of this gun. I've had it a long time and had a lot of fun with it."

He patted the stock affectionately like a boy with a dog and then he nestled the butt against his shoulder and sighted along the barrel.

"Better not, Jack," said Doble with a grin. "You'll wake your uncle."

"Damn my uncle," he retorted lightly, and before we could stop him, he pulled the trigger.

In that silence, the crack of the rifle was like a thunderclap. I suppose we all expected one of the windows to fly up and the irate voice of old Cartwright to demand what was going on. In any case, instinctively, like three small boys, we all ducked down behind the fence where we could not be seen. We waited several minutes, afraid to talk lest we be overheard. But when nothing happened, we straightened up slowly and Doble said, "You better get to bed, Jack. I think maybe you've had a little too much beer."

"Maybe I ought at that," Jack answered and eased the gate open.

Then he turned and whispered, "Say, do you fellows mind waiting a minute? I think I may have locked the door and I haven't a key."

We nodded and watched as he hurried down the path to the house. Just before he reached the door, however, he hesitated, stopped, and then turned and came hurrying back to us.

"Could you put me up for the night, Doble?" he asked in a whisper.

"Why sure, Jack. Was the door locked?"

He didn't answer immediately and we started down the road to our house. We had gone about halfway when he said, "I didn't check to see if the door was locked or not."

"I noticed that," I remarked.

There was another silence and then as we mounted the porch steps, the moon, which had been hidden by clouds, suddenly broke through and I saw that he was deathly pale.

"What's the matter, Jack?" I asked quickly.

He shook his head and did not answer. I put my hand on his arm and asked again, "Are you all right?"

He nodded and tried to smile.

"I've—I've— Something funny happened to me," he said. "Did you mean what you said the other day about believing in spirits?"

At first I could not think what he was referring to, and then I remembered having argued—not too seriously—for belief in the supernatural during a discussion of William Blake's *Marriage of Heaven and Hell*, which I had lent him.

I shrugged my shoulders noncommittally, wondering what he was getting at.

He smiled wanly. "I didn't really have too much beer," he said and looked at me for confirmation.

"No, I don't think you did," I said quietly.

"Look," he went on, "I'm cold sober. And I was sober a few minutes ago when I started for my uncle's house. But as I came near the door, I felt something like a cushion of air building up against me to block my progress. And then, just before I reached the door, it became so strong that I could not go on. It was like a wall in front of me. But it was something more than an inanimate wall. It did not merely block me, but seemed to be pushing me back as though it had a will and intelligence like a strong man. It frightened me and I turned back. I'm still frightened."

"Your uncle—" I began.

"Damn my uncle!" he said vehemently. "I hope he falls and breaks his neck."

Just then Doble's kitchen clock chimed twelve. The brassy ring, coming just as he finished, seemed to stamp the curse with fateful approval.

It made us all a little uncomfortable. We didn't seem to feel like talking, and after a while we went to bed.

We were awakened the next morning early by someone pounding on the door. Doble slipped his trousers on and I managed to get into my bathrobe. We reached the front door about the same time. It was Mrs. Knox, Cartwright's housekeeper, and she was in a state of considerable excitement.

"Mister Cartwright's dead!" she shouted to us. "There's been an accident."

Since she was deaf, it was no use to question her. We motioned her to wait while we put on our shoes. Then we followed her back to the house. The front door was open as she had left it when she had hurried over to us. And from the doorway we could see the figure of Cyrus Cartwright in an old-fashioned nightgown, lying at the foot of the stairs, his head in a sticky pool of blood.

He was dead all right, and looking up we could see the bit of rumpled carpeting at the head of the stairs which had probably tripped him up and catapulted him down the long staircase.

He had died as he had lived, for in his right hand he still clutched his precious pocket watch. The watch he was wearing on his wrist, however, had smashed when he fell and it gave us the time of his death. The hands pointed to just before twelve, the exact time as near as I could judge, that Jack had uttered his curse!

There was a minute of appreciative silence after Chisholm finished. I could see that no one's opinion had been changed materially by the story. Those who had been skeptical were scornful now and those who were inclined to believe, were triumphant, but we all turned to Professor Rollins to see what he thought and he was nodding his head portentously.

Nicky, however, was the first to speak. "And the pocket watch," he said, "had that stopped, too?"

"No, that was ticking away merrily," Chisholm replied. "I guess his hand must have cushioned it when he fell. It had probably been badly jarred though, because it was running almost an hour ahead."

Nicky nodded grimly.

"What about Jack? How did he take it?" I asked.

Chisholm considered for a moment. "He was upset naturally, not so much over his uncle's death, I fancy, since he did not care for him very much, but because of the fact that it confirmed his fears of the night before that some supernatural influence was present." He smiled sadly. "I did not see him much after that. He had got his leave extended, but he was busy with his uncle's affairs. When finally he went back to the Army, he promised to write, but he never did. Just last week, however, I got a letter from Doble. He writes me occasionally—just the usual gossip of the town. In his letter he mentions that Jack Cartwright crashed in his first solo flight."

"Ah." Professor Rollins showed interest. "I don't mind admitting that I rather expected something like that."

"You expected Jack to die?" Chisholm asked in amazement.

Rollins nodded vigorously. "This was truly a supernatural manifestation. I haven't the slightest doubt about it. For one thing, Jack felt the supernatural forces. And the curse, followed almost immediately by its fulfillment even to the manner of death, that is most significant. Now, of course we know very little of these things, but we suspect that they follow a definite pattern. Certain types of supernatural forces have what might be called an ironic bent, a sort of perverted sense of humor. To be sure, when Jack uttered his fervent wish that his uncle fall and break his neck, he was speaking as a result of a momentary exasperation, but it is the nature of evil or mischievous forces to grant just such wishes. We meet with it again and again in folklore and fairy tales, which are probably the cryptic or symbolic expression of the wisdom of the folk. The pattern is familiar to you all, I am sure, from the stories of your childhood. The wicked character is granted three wishes by a fairy, only to waste them through wishes that are just such common expressions of exasperation as Jack used. You see, when supernatural forces are present, a mere wish, fervently expressed, may serve to focus them, as it were. And that is what happened at the Cartwright house that fateful evening."

He held up a forefinger to ward off the questions that leaped to our minds.

"There is another element in the pattern," he went on soberly, "and that is that whenever a person does profit materially through the use of evil supernatural forces, even though unintentionally on his part, sooner or later, they turn on him and destroy him. I have no doubt that Jack's death was just as much the result of supernatural forces as was the death of his uncle."

Professor Graham muttered something that sounded like "Rubbish."

Dana Rollins, who could have gone on indefinitely I suppose, stopped abruptly and glared.

But Professor Graham was not one to be silenced by a look. "The young man died as a result of a plane crash. Well, so did thousands of others. Had they all been granted three wishes by a wicked fairy? Poppycock! The young man died because he went up in a plane. That's reason enough. As for the old man, he tumbled down the stairs and cracked his skull or broke his neck, whichever it was. You say his nephew's curse must have been uttered about the same time. Well, even granting that by some miracle Doble's kitchen clock was synchronized to Cartwright's watches, that would still be nothing more than a coincidence. The chances are that the young man uttered that same wish hundreds of times. It was only natural: he was his heir and besides, he didn't like him. Now on one of those hundreds of times, it actually happened. There's nothing supernatural in that—not even anything out of the ordinary. It makes a good story, young man, but it doesn't prove anything."

"And Jack's sensing of a supernatural force," asked Chisholm icily, "is that just another coincidence?"

Graham shrugged his massive shoulders. "That was probably just an excuse not to go home. He was probably afraid he'd get a dressing down from his uncle for shooting off his rifle in the middle of the night. What do you think, Nicky?"

Nicky's little blue eyes glittered. "I rather think," he said, "that the young man was not so much afraid of his uncle asking him about the rifle as he was that he would ask him what time it was."

We all laughed at Nicky's joke. But Professor Graham was not to be put off.

"Seriously, Nicky," he urged.

"Well then, seriously," said Nicky with a smile as though he were indulging a bright but impetuous freshman, "I think you're quite right in calling the young man's death an accident. Parenthetically, I might point out that Dr. Chisholm did not suggest that it was anything else. As for the uncle's death, I cannot agree with you that it was merely coincidence."

Professor Rollins pursed his lips and appeared to be considering Nicky's cavalier dismissal of half his theory, but it was obvious that he was pleased at his support for the other half. I could not help reflecting how Nicky automatically assumed control over any group that he found himself in. He had a way of treating people, even his colleagues on the faculty, as though they were immature schoolboys. And curiously, people fell into this role that he assigned to them.

Professor Graham, however, was not yet satisfied. "But dammit all, Nicky," he insisted, "a man trips on a bit of carpet and falls downstairs. What is there unusual about that?"

"In the first place, I think it is unusual that he should go downstairs at all," said Nicky. "Why do you suppose he did?"

Professor Graham looked at him in aggrieved surprise like a student who has just been asked what he considers an unfair question.

"How should I know why he went downstairs?" he said. "I suppose he couldn't sleep and wanted a snack, or maybe a book to read."

"And took his pocket watch with him?"

"Well, according to Chisholm he was always checking his wristwatch against it."

Nicky shook his head. "When you're wearing two watches, it's almost impossible not to check the other after you've glanced at the one, just as we automatically glance at our watches when we pass the clock in the jeweler's window even though we might have set it by the radio only a minute or two before. But for Cyrus Cartwright to take his pocket watch downstairs with him when he had a watch on his wrist is something else again. I can think of only one reason for it."

"And what's that?" asked Chisholm curiously.

"To see what time it was on the electric clock."

I could understand something of Graham's exasperation as he exclaimed, "But dammit, Nicky, the man had two watches. Why would he want to go downstairs to see the time?"

"Because in this case, two watches were not as good as one," said Nicky quietly.

I tried to understand. Did he mean that the supernatural force that had manifested itself to Jack Cartwright that night and had prevented him from entering the house had somehow tampered with the watches?

"What was wrong with them?" I asked.

"They disagreed."

Then he leaned back in his chair and looked about him with an air of having explained everything. There was a short silence and as he scanned our faces, his expression of satisfaction changed to one of annoyance.

"Don't you see yet what happened?" he demanded. "When you wake up in the middle of the night, the first thing you do is look at the clock on the mantelpiece or your watch on the night table in order to orient yourself. That's precisely what Cyrus Cartwright did. He woke up and glancing at his wristwatch he saw that it was a quarter to twelve, say. Then quite automatically he reached for his pocket watch on the night table. He pressed the catch and the chiming mechanism tinkled twelve and then went on to tinkle half or three quarters past. He had set the watches only a few hours before and both of them were going, and yet one was about an hour faster than the other. Which was right? What time was it? I fancy he tried the repeater again and again and then tried to dismiss the problem from his mind until morning. But after tossing about for a few minutes, he realized that if he hoped to get back to sleep that night, he would have to go downstairs to see what time it really was." Nicky turned to Chisholm. "You see, the jar from the fall would not have moved the watch ahead. A blow will either stop the movement or it might speed up or slow down the escapement for a few seconds. But a watch with hands so loose that a jar will move them would be useless as a timepiece. Hence, the watch must have been moved ahead sometime before the fall. Cyrus Cartwright would not do it, which means that his nephew must have, probably while transferring the watch from the bureau to the night table."

"You mean accidentally?" asked Chisholm. "Or to annoy his uncle?"

Nicky's little blue eyes glittered. "Not to annoy him," he said, "to murder him!"

He smiled pleasantly at our stupefaction. "Oh yes, no doubt about it," he assured us. "After arranging the windows to his uncle's satisfaction and placing the watch on the night table, Jack bade his uncle a courteous good night. And on his way out, he stopped just long enough to rumple or double over the bit of carpet at the head of the stairs. There was no light in the hallway, remember."

"But—but I don't understand. I don't see—I mean, how did he know that his uncle was going to wake up in the middle of the night?" Chisholm finally managed.

"Firing off his rifle under his uncle's windows insured that, I fancy," Nicky replied. He smiled. "And now you can understand, I trust, why he could not enter his uncle's house that night. He was afraid that his uncle, awake now, would hear him come in and instead of venturing downstairs, would simply call down to him to ask what time it was."

This time we did not laugh.

The silence that followed was suddenly broken by the chiming of the chapel clock. Subconsciously, we glanced at our watches, and then realizing what we were doing, we all laughed.

"Quite," said Nicky.

The Affair of the Twisted Scarf

REX STOUT

My problems hit a new high that day. What I really felt like doing was to go out for a walk but I wasn't quite desperate enough for that. So I merely beat it down to the office, shutting the door from the hall behind me, and went and sat at my desk with my feet up, leaned back and closed my eyes, and took a couple of deep breaths.

I had made two mistakes. When Bill McNab, garden editor of the *Gazette,* had suggested to Nero Wolfe that the members of the Manhattan Flower Club be invited to drop in some afternoon to look at the orchids, I should have fought it.

And when the date had been set and the invitations sent, and Wolfe had arranged that Fritz and Saul should do the receiving at the front door and I should stay up in the plant-rooms with him and Theodore, mingling with the guests, if I had had an ounce of brains I would have put my foot down. But I hadn't, and as a result I had been up there a good hour and a half, grinning around and acting pleased and happy. . . . "No, sir, that's not a brasso, it's a laelia." . . . "Quite all right, madam—your sleeve happened to hook it. It'll bloom again next year."

It wouldn't have been so bad if there had been something for the eyes. It was understood that the Manhattan Flower Club was choosy about whom it took in, but obviously its standards were totally different from mine. The men were just men; okay as men go. But the women! It was a darned good thing they had picked on flowers to love, because flowers don't have to love back.

There had, in fact, been one—just one. I had got a glimpse of her at the other end of the crowded aisle as I went through the door into the cool-room. From ten paces off she looked absolutely promising, and when I had maneuvered close enough to make her an offer to answer questions if she had any, there was simply no doubt about it—no doubt at all.

The first quick, slanting glance she gave me said plainly that she could tell the difference between a flower and a man, but she just smiled and shook her head, and moved on with her companions, an older female and two males. Later, I had made another try and got another brush-off, and still later, too long later, feeling that the grin might freeze on me for good if I didn't take a recess, I went AWOL by worming my way to the far end of the warm-room and sidling on out.

All the way down the three flights of stairs new guests were coming up, though it was then four o'clock. Nero Wolfe's old brownstone house on West 35th Street had seen no such throng as that within my memory, which is long and good. One flight down, I stopped off at my bedroom for a pack of cigarettes; and another flight down, I detoured to make sure the door of Wolfe's bedroom was locked.

In the main hall downstairs I halted a moment to watch Fritz Brenner, busy at the door with both departures and arrivals, and to see Saul Panzer emerge from the front room, which was being used as a cloakroom, with someone's hat and topcoat. Then, as aforesaid, I entered the office, shutting the door from the hall behind me, went and sat at my desk with my feet up, leaned back and closed my eyes, and took some deep breaths.

I had been there maybe eight or ten minutes, and was getting relaxed and a little less bitter, when the door opened and she came in. Her companions were not along. By the time she had closed the door and turned to me I had got to my feet, with a friendly leer, and had begun, "I was just sitting here thinking—"

The look on her face stopped me. There was nothing wrong with it basically, but something had got it out of kilter. She headed for me, got halfway, jerked to a stop, sank into one of the yellow chairs, and squeaked, "Could I have a drink?"

"Sure thing," I said. I went to the cupboard and got a hooker of old whiskey. Her hand was shaking as she took the glass, but she didn't spill any, and she got it down in two swallows.

"Did I need that!"

"More?"

She shook her head. Her bright brown eyes were moist, from the whiskey, as she gave me a full, straight look with her head tilted up.

"You're Archie Goodwin," she stated.

I nodded. "And you're the Queen of Egypt?"

"I'm a baboon," she declared. "I don't know how they ever taught me to talk." She looked around for something to put the glass on, and I moved a step and reached for it. "Look at my hand shake," she complained.

She kept her hand out, looking at it, so I took it in mine and gave it some friendly but gentle pressure. "You do seem a little upset," I conceded.

She jerked the hand away. "I want to see Nero Wolfe. I want to see him right away, before I change my mind." She was gazing up at me, with the moist brown eyes. "I'm in a fix now, all right! I've made up my mind. I'm going to get Nero Wolfe to get me out of this somehow."

I told her it couldn't be done until the party was over.

She looked around. "Are people coming in here?"

I told her no.

"May I have another drink, please?"

I told her she should give the first one time to settle, and instead of arguing she arose and helped herself. I sat down and frowned at her. Her line sounded fairly screwy for a member of the Manhattan Flower Club, or even for a daughter of one. She came back to her chair, sat, and met my eyes. Looking at her straight like that could have been a nice way to pass the time if there had been any chance for a meeting of minds.

"I could tell you," she said.

"Many people have," I said modestly.

"I'm going to."

"Good. Shoot."

"Okay. I'm a crook."

"It doesn't show," I objected. "What do you do—cheat at Canasta?"

"I didn't say I'm a cheat." She cleared her throat for the hoarseness. "I said I'm a crook. Remind me some day to tell you the story of my life—how my husband got killed in the war and I broke through the gate. Don't I sound interesting?"

"You sure do. What's your line—orchid-stealing?"

"No. I wouldn't be small and I wouldn't be dirty— That's what I used to think, but once you start it's not so easy. You meet people and you get involved. Two years ago four of us took over a hundred grand from a certain rich woman with a rich husband. I can tell you about that one, even names, because she couldn't move, anyhow."

I nodded. "Blackmailers' customers seldom can. What—?"

"I'm not a blackmailer!"

"Excuse me. Mr. Wolfe often says I jump to conclusions."

"You did that time." She was still indignant. "A blackmailer's not a crook; he's a snake! Not that it really matters. What's wrong with being a crook is the other crooks—they make it dirty whether you like it or not. It makes a coward of you, too—that's the worst. I had a friend once—as close as a crook ever comes to having a friend—and a man killed her, strangled her. If I had told what I knew about it they could have caught him, but I was afraid to go to the cops, so he's still loose. And she was my friend! That's getting down toward the bottom. Isn't it?"

"Fairly low," I agreed, eying her. "Of course, I don't know you any too well. I don't know how you react to two stiff drinks. Maybe your hobby is stringing private detectives."

She simply ignored it. "I realized long ago," she went on, as if it were a one-way conversation, "that I had made a mistake. About a year ago I decided to break loose. A good way to do it would have been to talk to someone the way I'm talking to you now, but I didn't have sense enough to see that."

I nodded. "Yeah, I know."

"So I kept putting it off. We got a good one in December and I went to Florida for a vacation, but down there I met a man with a lead, and we followed it up here just a week ago. That's what I'm working on now. That's what brought me here today. This man—" She stopped abruptly.

"Well?" I invited her.

She looked dead serious, not more serious, but a different kind. "I'm not putting anything on him," she declared. "I don't owe him anything, and I don't like him. But this is strictly about me and no one else—only, I had to explain why I'm here. I wish to heaven I'd never come!"

There was no question about that coming from her heart, unless she had done a lot of rehearsing in front of a mirror.

"It got you this talk with me," I reminded her.

She was looking straight through me and beyond. "If only I hadn't come! If only I hadn't seen him!"

She leaned toward me for emphasis. "I'm either too smart or not smart enough; that's my trouble. I should have looked away from him, turned away quick, when I realized I knew who he was, before he turned and saw it in my eyes. But I was so shocked I couldn't help it! I stood there staring at him, thinking I wouldn't have recognized him if he hadn't had a hat on, and then he looked at me and saw what was happening. But it was too late.

"I know how to manage my face with nearly anybody, anywhere, but that was too much for me. It showed so plain that Mrs. Orwin asked me what was the matter with me, and I had to try to pull myself together. Then, seeing Nero Wolfe gave me the idea of telling him; only of course

I couldn't right there with the crowd. Then I saw you going out, and as soon as I could break away I came down to find you."

She tried smiling at me, but it didn't work so good. "Now I feel somewhat better," she said hopefully.

I nodded. "That's good whiskey. Is it a secret who you recognized?"

"No. I'm going to tell Nero Wolfe."

"You decided to tell me." I flipped a hand. "Suit yourself. Whoever you tell, what's the good?"

"Why—then he can't do anything to me."

"Why not?"

"Because he wouldn't dare. Nero Wolfe will tell him that I've told about him, so that if anything happened to me he would know it was him, and he'd know who he is—I mean, Nero Wolfe would know—and so would you."

"We would if we had his name and address." I was studying her. "He must be quite a specimen, to scare you that bad. And speaking of names, what's yours?"

She made a little noise that could have been meant for a laugh. "Do you like Marjorie?"

"Not bad. What are you using now?"

She hesitated, frowning.

"For Pete's sake," I protested, "you're not in a vacuum, and I'm a detective. They took the names down at the door."

"Cynthia Brown," she said.

"That's Mrs. Orwin you came with?"

"Yes."

"She's the current customer? The lead you picked up in Florida?"

"Yes. But that's—" She gestured. "That's finished. I'm through."

"I know. There's just one thing you haven't told me, though. Who was it you recognized?"

She turned her head for a glance at the door and then turned it still farther to look behind her.

"Can anyone hear us?" she asked.

"Nope. That other door goes to the front room—today, the cloak-room. Anyhow, this room's soundproofed."

She glanced at the hall door again, returned to me, and lowered her voice: "This has to be done the way I say."

"Sure; why not?"

"I wasn't being honest with you."

"I wouldn't expect it from a crook. Start over."

"I mean . . ." She used the teeth on the lip again. "I mean I'm not just scared about myself. I'm scared, all right, but I don't just want

Nero Wolfe for what I said. I want him to get him for murder, but he
has to keep me out of it. I don't want to have anything to do with any
cops—not now I don't, especially. If he won't do it that way—Do you
think he will?"

I was feeling a faint tingle at the base of my spine. I only get that on
special occasions, but this was unquestionably something special. I gave
her a hard look and didn't let the tingle get into my voice: "He might,
for you, if you pay him. What kind of evidence have you got? Any?"

"I saw him."

"You mean today?"

"I mean I saw him then." She had her hands clasped tight. "I told
you—I had a friend. I stopped in at her apartment that afternoon. I was
just leaving—Doris was inside, in the bathroom—and as I got near the
entrance door I heard a key turning in the lock, from the outside. I
stopped, and the door came open and a man came in. When he saw me
he just stood and stared. I had never met Doris's bank account, and I
knew she didn't want me to. And since he had a key I supposed of
course it was him, making an unexpected call; so I mumbled something
about Doris being in the bathroom and went past him, through the door
and on out."

She paused. Her clasped hands loosened and then tightened again.

"I'm burning my bridges," she said, "but I can deny all this if I have
to. I went and kept a cocktail date, and then phoned Doris's number to
ask if our dinner date was still on, considering the visit of the bank account. There was no answer, so I went back to her apartment and rang
the bell, and there was no answer to that, either. It was a self-service-
elevator place, no doorman or hallman, so there was no one to ask anything.

"Her maid found her body the next morning. The papers said she
had been killed the day before. That man killed her. There wasn't a
word about him—no one had seen him enter or leave. And I didn't open
my mouth! I was a rotten coward!"

"And today, all of a sudden, there he is, looking at orchids?"

"Yes."

"Are you sure he knows you recognized him?"

"Yes. He looked straight at me, and his eyes—"

She was stopped by the house phone buzzing. Stepping to my desk, I
picked it up and asked it, "Well?"

Nero Wolfe's voice, peevish, came: "Archie!"

"Yes, sir."

"What the devil are you doing? Come back up here!"

"Pretty soon. I'm talking with a prospective client—"

"This is no time for clients! Come at once!"

The connection went. He had slammed it down. I hung up and went back to the prospective client: "Mr. Wolfe wants me upstairs. Do you want to wait here?"

"Yes."

"If Mrs. Orwin asks about you?"

"I didn't feel well and went home."

"Okay. It shouldn't be long—the invitations said two thirty to five. If you want a drink, help yourself. . . . What name does this murderer use when he goes to look at orchids?"

She looked blank.

I got impatient: "What's his name? This bird you recognized."

"I don't know."

"Describe him."

She thought it over a little, gazing at me, and then shook her head. "Not now. I want to see what Nero Wolfe says first."

She must have seen something in my eyes, or thought she did, for suddenly she came up out of her chair and moved to me and put a hand on my arm. "That's all I mean," she said earnestly. "It's not you—I know you're all right. I might as well tell you—you'd never want any part of me anyhow—this is the first time in years, I don't know how long, that I've talked to a man straight—you know, just human. I—" She stopped for a word, and a little color showed in her cheeks. "I've enjoyed it very much."

"Good. Me, too. Call me Archie. I've got to go, but describe him."

But she hadn't enjoyed it that much. "Not until Nero Wolfe says he'll do it," she said firmly.

I had to leave it at that, knowing as I did that in three more minutes Wolfe might have a fit. Out in the hall I had the notion of passing the word to Saul and Fritz to give departing guests a good look, but rejected it because (a) they weren't there, both of them presumably being busy in the cloakroom, (b) he might have departed already, and (c) I had by no means swallowed a single word of Cynthia's story, let alone the whole works.

Up in the plant-rooms there were plenty left. When I came into Wolfe's range he darted me a glance of cold fury, and I turned on the grin. Anyway, it was a quarter to five, and if they took the hint on the invitation it wouldn't last much longer.

They didn't take the hint on the dot, but it didn't bother me because my mind was occupied. I was now really interested in them—or at least one of them, if he had actually been there and hadn't gone home.

First, there was a chore to get done. I found the three Cynthia had been with, a female and two males.

"Mrs. Orwin?" I asked politely.

She nodded at me and said, "Yes?" Not quite tall enough, but plenty plump enough, with a round, full face and narrow little eyes that might have been better if they had been wide open. She struck me as a lead worth following.

"I'm Archie Goodwin," I said. "I work here."

I would have gone on if I had known how, but I needed a lead myself.

Luckily one of the males horned in. "My sister?" he inquired anxiously.

So it was a brother-and-sister act. As far as looks went he wasn't a bad brother at all. Older than me maybe, but not much. He was tall and straight, with a strong mouth and jaw and keen gray eyes. "My sister?" he repeated.

"I guess so. You are—?"

"Colonel Brown. Percy Brown."

"Yeah." I switched back to Mrs. Orwin: "Miss Brown asked me to tell you that she went home. I gave her a little drink and it seemed to help, but she decided to leave. She asked me to apologize for her."

"She's perfectly healthy," the colonel asserted. He sounded a little hurt.

"Is she all right?" Mrs. Orwin asked.

"For her," the other male put in, "you should have made it three drinks. Or just hand her the bottle."

His tone was mean and his face was mean, and anyhow that was no way to talk in front of the help in a strange house, meaning me. He was a bit younger than Brown, but he already looked enough like Mrs. Orwin, especially the eyes, to make it more than a guess that they were mother and son.

That point was settled when she commanded him, "Be quiet, Gene!" She turned to the colonel: "Perhaps you should go and see about her?"

He shook his head, with a fond but manly smile at her. "It's not necessary, Mimi. Really."

"She's all right," I assured them, and pushed off, thinking there were a lot of names in this world that could stand a reshuffle. Calling that overweight, narrow-eyed, pearl-and-mink proprietor Mimi was a paradox.

I moved around among the guests, being gracious. Fully aware that I was not equipped with a Geiger counter that would flash a signal if and when I established contact with a strangler, the fact remained that I had been known to have hunches. It would be something for my scrapbook if I picked the killer of Doris Hatten.

Cynthia Brown hadn't given me the Hatten, only the Doris, but with the context that was enough. At the time it had happened, some five months ago, early in October, the papers had given it a big play, of course. She had been strangled with her own scarf, of white silk with the Declaration of Independence printed on it, in her cozy fifth-floor apartment in the West Seventies, and the scarf had been left around her neck, knotted at the back.

The cops had never got within a mile of charging anyone, and Sergeant Purley Stebbins of Homicide had told me that they had never even found out who was paying the rent.

I kept on the go through the plant-rooms, leaving all switches open for a hunch. Some of them were plainly preposterous, but with everyone else I made an opportunity to exchange some words, full face and close up. That took time, and it was no help to my current and chronic campaign for a raise in wages, since it was the women, not the men, that Wolfe wanted off his neck. I stuck at it, anyhow. It was true that if Cynthia was on the level, we would soon have specifications, but I had had that tingle at the bottom of my spine and I was stubborn.

As I say, it took time, and meanwhile five o'clock came and went and the crowd thinned out. Going on five-thirty, the remaining groups seemed to get the idea all at once that time was up and made for the entrance to the stairs.

I was in the moderate-room when it happened, and the first thing I knew I was alone there, except for a guy at the north bench studying a row of dowianas. He didn't interest me, as I had already canvassed him and crossed him off as the wrong type for a strangler; but as I glanced his way he suddenly bent forward to pick up a pot with a flowering plant, and as he did so I felt my back stiffening. The stiffening was a reflex, but I knew what had caused it; the way his fingers closed around the pot, especially the thumbs. No matter how careful you are of other people's property, you don't pick up a five-inch pot as if you were going to squeeze the life out of it.

I made my way around to him. When I got there he was holding the pot so that the flowers were only a few inches from his eyes.

"Nice flower," I said brightly.

He nodded.

He leaned to put the pot back, still choking it. I swiveled my head. The only people in sight, beyond the glass partition between us and the cool-room, were Nero Wolfe and a small group of guests, among whom were the Orwin trio and Bill McNab, the garden editor of the *Gazette*.

As I turned my head back to my man he straightened up, pivoted on his heel, and marched off without a word.

I followed him out to the landing and down the three flights of stairs. Along the main hall I was courteous enough not to step on his heel, but a lengthened stride would have reached it. The hall was next to empty. A woman, ready for the street in a caracul coat, was standing there, and Saul Panzer was posted near the front door with nothing to do.

I followed my man on into the front room, now the cloakroom, where Fritz Brenner was helping a guest on with his coat. Of course, the racks were practically bare, and with one glance my man saw his property and went to get it. I stepped forward to help, but he ignored me without even bothering to shake his head. I was beginning to feel hurt.

When he emerged into the hall I was beside him, and as he moved to the front door I spoke: "Excuse me, but we're checking guests out as well as in. Your name, please?"

"Ridiculous," he said curtly, and reached for the knob, pulled the door open, and crossed the sill.

Saul, knowing I must have had a reason for wanting to check him out, was at my elbow, and we stood watching his back as he descended the seven steps of the stoop.

"Tail?" Saul muttered to me.

I shook my head and was parting my lips to mutter something back, when a sound came from behind us that made us both whirl around—a screech from a woman, not loud but full of feeling. As we whirled, Fritz and the guest he had been serving came out of the front room, and all four of us saw the woman in the caracul coat come running out of the office into the hall. She kept coming, gasping something, and the guest, making a noise like an alarmed male, moved to meet her. I moved faster, needing about eight jumps to the office door and two inside. There I stopped.

Of course, I knew the thing on the floor was Cynthia, but only because I had left her in there in those clothes. With the face blue and contorted, the tongue halfway out and the eyes popping, it could have been almost anybody. I knelt down and slipped my hand inside her dress front, kept it there ten seconds, and felt nothing.

Saul's voice came from behind: "I'm here."

I got up and went to the phone on my desk and started dialing, telling Saul "No one leaves. We'll keep what we've got. Have the door open for Doc Vollmer." After only two whirs the nurse answered and put Vollmer on, and I snapped it at him: "Doc, Archie Goodwin. Come on the run. Strangled woman. . . . Yeah, strangled."

I pushed the phone back, reached for the house phone, and buzzed the plant-rooms, and after a wait had Wolfe's irritated bark in my ear: "Yes?"

"I'm in the office. You'd better come down. That prospective client I mentioned is here on the floor strangled. I think she's done, but I've sent for Vollmer."

"Is this flummery?" he roared.

"No, sir. Come down and look at her and then ask me."

The connection went. He had slammed it down. I got a sheet of thin tissue paper from a drawer, tore off a corner, and placed it carefully over Cynthia's mouth and nostrils.

Voices had been sounding from the hall. Now one of them entered the office. Its owner was the guest who had been in the cloakroom with Fritz when the screech came. He was a chunky, broad-shouldered guy with sharp, domineering dark eyes and arms like a gorilla's. His voice was going strong as he started toward me from the door, but it stopped when he had come far enough to get a good look at the object on the floor.

"Oh, no!" he said huskily.

"Yes, sir," I agreed.

"How did it happen?"

"Don't know."

"Who is it?"

"Don't know."

He made his eyes come away from it and up until they met mine, and I gave him an A for control. It really was a sight.

"The man at the door won't let us leave," he stated.

"No, sir. You can see why."

"I certainly can." His eyes stayed with me, however. "But we know nothing about it. My name is Carlisle, Homer N. Carlisle. I am the executive vice-president of the North American Foods Company. My wife was merely acting under impulse; she wanted to see the office of Nero Wolfe, and she opened the door and entered. She's sorry she did, and so am I. We have an appointment, and there's no reason why we should be detained."

"I'm sorry, too," I told him, "but for one thing if for nothing else; your wife discovered the body. We're stuck worse than you are, with a corpse here in our office. So I guess—Hello, Doc."

Vollmer, entering and nodding at me on the fly, was panting a little as he set his black case on the floor and knelt beside it. His house was down the street and he had had only two hundred yards to trot, but he was taking on weight. As he opened the case and got out the stethoscope, Homer Carlisle stood and watched with his lips pressed tight, and I did likewise until I heard the sound of Wolfe's elevator.

Crossing to the door and into the hall, I surveyed the terrain. Toward the front, Saul and Fritz were calming down the woman in the caracul coat, now Mrs. Carlisle to me. Nero Wolfe and Mrs. Mimi Orwin were emerging from the elevator. Four guests were coming down the stairs: Gene Orwin, Colonel Percy Brown, Bill McNab, and a middle-aged male with a mop of black hair. I stayed by the office door to block the quartet on the stairs.

As Wolfe headed for me, Mrs. Carlisle darted to him and grabbed his arm: "I only wanted to see your office! I want to go! I'm not—"

As she pulled at him and sputtered, I noted a detail: the caracul coat was unfastened, and the ends of a silk scarf, figured and gaily colored, were flying loose. Since at least half of the female guests had sported scarfs, I mention it only to be honest and admit that I had got touchy on that subject.

Wolfe, who had already been too close to too many women that day to suit him, tried to jerk away, but she hung on. She was the big-boned, flat-chested, athletic type, and it could have been quite a tussle, with him weighing twice as much as her and four times as big around, if Saul hadn't rescued him by coming in between and prying her loose. That didn't stop her tongue, but Wolfe ignored it and came on toward me: "Has Dr. Vollmer come?"

"Yes, sir."

The executive vice-president emerged from the office, talking: "Mr. Wolfe, my name is Homer N. Carlisle and I insist—"

"Shut up," Wolfe growled. On the sill of the door to the office, he faced the audience. "Flower lovers," he said with bitter scorn. "You told me, Mr. McNab, a distinguished group of sincere and devoted gardeners. Pfui! . . . Saul!"

"Yes, sir."

"Put them all in the dining-room and keep them there. Let no one touch anything around this door, especially the knob . . . Archie, come with me."

He wheeled and entered the office. Following, I used my foot to swing the door neatly shut, leaving no crack but not latching it. When I turned, Vollmer was standing, facing Wolfe's scowl.

"Well?" Wolfe demanded.

"Dead," Vollmer told him. "With asphyxiation from strangling."

"How long ago?"

"I don't know, but not more than an hour or two. Two hours at the outside, probably less."

Wolfe looked at the thing on the floor with no change in his scowl, and back at Doc. "Finger marks?"

"No. A constricting band of something with pressure below the hyoid bone. Not a stiff or narrow band; something soft, like a strip of cloth— say, a scarf."

Wolfe switched to me: "You didn't notify the police?"

"No, sir." I glanced at Vollmer and back. "I need a word."

"I suppose so." He spoke to Doc: "If you will leave us for a moment? The front room?"

Vollmer hesitated, uncomfortable. "As a doctor called to a violent death I'd catch the devil. Of course, I could say—"

"Then go to a corner and cover your ears."

He did so. He went to the farthest corner, the angle made by the partition of the bathroom, pressed his palms to his ears, and stood facing us. I addressed Wolfe with a lowered voice:

"I was here and she came in. She was either scared good or putting on a very fine act. Apparently, it wasn't an act, and I now think I should have alerted Saul and Fritz, but it doesn't matter what I now think. Last October a woman named Doris Hatten was killed, strangled, in her apartment. No one got elected. Remember?"

"Yes."

"She said she was a friend of Doris Hatten's and was at her apartment that day, and saw the man that did the strangling, and that he was here this afternoon. She said he was aware that she had recognized him —that's why she was scared—and she wanted to get you to help by telling him that we were wise and he'd better lay off. No wonder I didn't gulp it down. I realize that you dislike complications and therefore might want me to scratch this out, but at the end she touched a soft spot by saying that she had enjoyed my company, so I prefer to open up to the cops."

"Then do so. Confound it!"

I went to the phone and started dialing WAtkins 9-8241. Doc Vollmer came out of his corner. Wolfe was pathetic. He moved around behind his desk and lowered himself into his own oversized custom-made number; but there smack in front of him was the object on the floor, so after a moment he made a face, got back onto his feet, grunted like an outraged boar, went across to the other side of the room, to the shelves, and inspected the backbones of books.

But even that pitiful diversion got interrupted. As I finished with my phone call and hung up, sudden sounds of commotion came from the hall. Dashing across, getting fingernails on the edge of the door and pulling it open, I saw trouble. A group was gathered in the open doorway of the dining-room, which was across the hall. Saul Panzer went bounding past me toward the front.

At the front door, Colonel Percy Brown was stiff-arming Fritz Brenner with one hand and reaching for the doorknob with the other. Fritz, who is chef and housekeeper, is not supposed to double in acrobatics, but he did fine. Dropping to the floor, he grabbed the colonel's ankles and jerked his feet out from under him.

Then I was there, and Saul, with his gun out; and there, with us, was the guest with the mop of black hair.

"You fool," I told the colonel as he sat up. "If you'd got outdoors Saul would have winged you."

"Guilt," said the black-haired guest emphatically. "The compression got unbearable and he exploded. I'm a psychiatrist."

"Good for you." I took his elbow and turned him. "Go back in and watch all of 'em. With that wall mirror you can include yourself."

"This is illegal," stated Colonel Brown, who had scrambled to his feet.

Saul herded them to the rear.

Fritz got hold of my sleeve: "Archie, I've got to ask Mr. Wolfe about dinner."

"Nuts," I said savagely. "By dinner-time this place will be more crowded than it was this afternoon."

"But he has to eat; you know that."

"Nuts," I said. I patted him on the shoulder. "Excuse my manners, Fritz; I'm upset. I've just strangled a young woman."

"Phooey," he said scornfully.

"I might as well have," I declared.

The doorbell rang. It was the first consignment of cops.

In my opinion, Inspector Cramer made a mistake. It is true that in a room where a murder has occurred the city scientists may shoot the works. And they do. But, except in rare circumstances, the job shouldn't take all week, and in the case of our office a couple of hours should have been ample. In fact, it was. By eight o'clock the scientists were through. But Cramer, like a sap, gave the order to seal it up until further notice, in Wolfe's hearing. He knew that Wolfe spent at least three hundred evenings a year in there, and that was why he did it.

It was a mistake. If he hadn't made it, Wolfe might have called his attention to a certain fact as soon as Wolfe saw it himself, and Cramer would have been saved a lot of trouble.

The two of them got the fact at the same time, from me. We were in the dining-room—this was shortly after the scientists had got busy in the office, and the guests, under guard, had been shunted to the front room

—and I was relating my conversation with Cynthia Brown. Whatever else my years as Wolfe's assistant may have done for me or to me, they have practically turned me into a tape recorder. I gave them the real thing, word for word. When I finished, Cramer had a slew of questions, but Wolfe not a one. Maybe he had already focused on the fact above referred to, but neither Cramer nor I had.

Cramer called a recess on the questions to take steps. He called men in and gave orders. Colonel Brown was to be photographed and finger-printed, and headquarters records were to be checked for him and Cynthia. The file on the murder of Doris Hatten was to be brought to him at once. The lab reports were to be rushed. Saul Panzer and Fritz Brenner were to be brought in.

They came. Fritz stood like a soldier at attention, grim and grave. Saul, only five feet seven, with the sharpest eyes and one of the biggest noses I have ever seen, in his unpressed brown suit and his necktie crooked—he stood like Saul, not slouching and not stiff. Of course, Cramer knew both of them.

"You and Fritz were in the hall all afternoon?"

Saul nodded. "The hall and the front room, yes."

"Who did you see enter or leave the office?"

"I saw Archie go in about four o'clock—I was just coming out of the front room with someone's hat and coat. I saw Mrs. Carlisle come out just after she screamed. In between those two I saw no one either enter or leave. We were busy most of the time, either in the hall or the front room."

Cramer grunted. "How about you, Fritz?"

"I saw no one." Fritz spoke louder than usual. "I would like to say something."

"Go ahead."

"I think a great deal of all this disturbance is unnecessary. My duties here are of the household and not professional, but I cannot help hearing what reaches my ears. Many times Mr. Wolfe has found the answer to problems that were too much for you. This happened here in his own house, and I think it should be left entirely to him."

I yooped, "Fritz, I didn't know you had it in you!"

Cramer was goggling at him. "Wolfe told you to say that, huh?"

"Bah." Wolfe was contemptuous. "It can't be helped, Fritz. Have we plenty of ham and sturgeon?"

"Yes, sir."

"Later, probably. For the guests in the front room, but not the police. . . . Are you through with them, Mr. Cramer?"

"No." Cramer went back to Saul: "How'd you check the guests in?"

"I had a list of the members of the Manhattan Flower Club. They had to show their membership cards. I checked on the list those who came. If they brought a wife or husband, or any other guest, I took the names."

"Then you have a record of everybody?"

"Yes."

"About how many names?"

"Two hundred and nineteen."

"This place wouldn't hold that many."

Saul nodded. "They came and went. There wasn't more than a hundred or so at any one time."

"That's a help." Cramer was getting more and more disgusted, and I didn't blame him. "Goodwin says he was there at the door with you when that woman screamed and came running out of the office, but that you hadn't seen her enter the office. Why not?"

"We had our backs turned. We were watching a man who had just left. Archie had asked him for his name and he had said that was ridiculous. If you want it, his name is Malcolm Vedder."

"How do you know?"

"I had checked him in with the rest."

Cramer stared. "Are you telling me that you could fit that many names to that many faces after seeing them once?"

Saul's shoulders went slightly up and down. "There's more to people than faces. I might go wrong on a few, but not many."

Cramer spoke to a dick standing by the door: "You heard that name, Levy—Malcolm Vedder. Tell Stebbins to check it on that list and send a man to bring him in."

Cramer returned to Saul: "Put it this way: Say I sit you here with that list, and a man or woman is brought in—"

"I could tell you positively whether the person had been here or not, especially if he was wearing the same clothes and hadn't been disguised. On fitting him to his name I might go wrong in a few cases, but I doubt it."

"I don't believe you."

"Mr. Wolfe does," Saul said complacently. "Archie does. I have developed my faculties."

"You sure have. All right; that's all for now. Stick around."

Saul and Fritz went. Wolfe, in his own chair at the end of the dining table, where ordinarily, at this hour, he sat for a quite different purpose, heaved a deep sigh and closed his eyes. I, seated beside Cramer at the side of the table which put us facing the door to the hall, was beginning to appreciate the problem we were up against.

"Goodwin's story," Cramer growled. "I mean her story. What do you think?"

Wolfe's eyes came open a little. "What followed seems to support it. I doubt if she would have arranged for that"—he flipped a hand in the direction of the office across the hall—"just to corroborate a tale. I accept it."

"Yeah. I don't need to remind you that I know you well and I know Goodwin well. So I wonder how much chance there is that in a day or so you'll suddenly remember that she had been here before, or one or more of the others had, and you've got a client, and there was something leading up to this."

"Bosh," Wolfe said dryly. "Even if it were like that—and it isn't—you would be wasting time, since you know us."

A dick came to relay a phone call from a deputy commissioner. Another dick came in to say that Homer Carlisle was raising the roof in the front room. Meanwhile, Wolfe sat with his eyes shut, but I got an idea of his state of mind from the fact that intermittently his forefinger was making little circles on the polished top of the table.

Cramer looked at him. "What do you know," he asked abruptly, "about the killing of that Doris Hatten?"

"Newspaper accounts," Wolfe muttered. "And what Mr. Stebbins has told Mr. Goodwin, casually."

"Casual is right." Cramer got out a cigar, conveyed it to his mouth, and sank his teeth in it. He never lit one. "Those houses with self-service elevators are worse than walk-ups for a checking job. No one ever sees anyone coming or going. Even so, the man who paid the rent for that apartment was lucky. He may have been clever and careful, but also he was lucky never to have anybody see him enough to give a description of him."

"Possibly Miss Hatten paid the rent herself."

"Sure," Cramer conceded, "she paid it all right, but where did she get it from? No, it was that kind of a set-up. She had only been living there two months, and when we found out how well the man who paid for it had kept himself covered, we decided that maybe he had installed her there just for that purpose. That was why we gave it all we had. Another reason was that the papers started hinting that we knew who he was and that he was such a big shot we were sitting on the lid."

Cramer shifted his cigar one tooth over to the left. "That kind of thing used to get me sore, but what the heck; for newspapers that's just routine. Big shot or not, he didn't need us to do any covering for him—he did too good a job himself. Now, if we're to take it the way this Cynthia Brown gave it to Goodwin, it was the man who paid the rent. I would hate to tell you what I think of the fact that Goodwin sat there in your office and was told he was right here on these premises, and all he did was—"

"You're irritated," I said charitably. "Not that he *was* on the premises, that he *had* been. Also, I was taking it with salt. Also, she was saving specifications for Mr. Wolfe. Also—"

"Also, I know you. How many of these two hundred and nineteen people were men?"

"I would say a little over half."

"Then how do *you* like it?"

"I hate it."

Wolfe grunted. "Judging from your attitude, Mr. Cramer, something that has occurred to me has not occurred to you."

"Naturally. You're a genius. What is it?"

"Something that Mr. Goodwin told us. I want to consider it a little."

"We could consider it together."

"Later. Those people in the front room are my guests. Can't you dispose of them?"

"One of your guests," Cramer rasped, "was a beaut, all right." He spoke to the dick by the door: "Bring in that woman—what's her name? Carlisle."

Mrs. Homer N. Carlisle came in with all her belongings: her caracul coat, her gaily colored scarf, and her husband. Perhaps I should say that her husband brought her. As soon as he was through the door he strode across to the dining table and delivered a harangue.

At the first opening Cramer, controlling himself, said he was sorry and asked them to sit down.

Mrs. Carlisle did. Mr. Carlisle didn't.

"We're nearly two hours late now," he stated. "I know you have your duty to perform, but citizens have a few rights left, thank God. Our presence here is purely adventitious. I warn you that if my name is published in connection with this miserable affair, I'll make trouble. Why should we be detained? What if we had left five or ten minutes earlier, as others did?"

"That's not quite logical," Cramer objected. "No matter when you left, it would have been the same if your wife had acted the same. She discovered the body."

"By accident!"

"May I say something, Homer?" the wife put in.

"It depends on what you say."

"Oh," Cramer said significantly.

"What do you mean, oh?" Carlisle demanded.

"I mean that I sent for your wife, not you, but you came with her, and that tells me why. You wanted to see to it that she wasn't indiscreet."

"What's she got to be indiscreet about?"

"I don't know. Apparently you do. If she hasn't, why don't you sit down and relax?"

"I would, sir," Wolfe advised him. "You came in here angry, and you blundered. An angry man is a jackass."

It was a struggle for the executive vice-president, but he made it.

Cramer went to the wife: "You wanted to say something, Mrs. Carlisle?"

"Only that I'm sorry." Her bony hands, the fingers twined, were on the table before her. "For the trouble I've caused."

"I wouldn't say you caused it exactly—except for yourself and your husband." Cramer was mild. "The woman was dead, whether you went in there or not. But if only as a matter of form, it was essential for me to see you, since you discovered the body. That's all there is to it as far as I know."

"How could there be anything else?" Carlisle blurted.

Cramer ignored him. "Goodwin, here, saw you standing in the hall not more than two minutes, probably less, prior to the moment you screamed and ran out of the office. How long had you then been downstairs?"

"We had just come down. I was waiting for my husband to get his things."

"Had you been downstairs before that?"

"No—only when we came in."

"What time did you arrive?"

"A little after three, I think."

"Were you and your husband together all the time?"

"Of course. Well—you know how it is . . . He would want to look longer at something, and I would—"

"Certainly we were," Carlisle said irritably. "You can see why I made that remark about it depending on what she said. She has a habit of being vague."

"I'm not actually vague," she protested. "It's just that everything is relative. Who would have thought my wish to see Nero Wolfe's office would link me with a crime?"

Carlisle exploded. "Hear that? *Link!*"

"Why did you want to see Wolfe's office?" Cramer inquired.

"Why, to see the globe."

I gawked at her. I had supposed that naturally she would say it was curiosity about the office of a great and famous detective. Apparently, Cramer reacted the same as me.

"The globe?" he demanded.

"Yes, I had read about it, and I wanted to see how it looked. I thought a globe that size, three feet in diameter, would be fantastic in an ordinary room—Oh!"

"Oh, what?"

"I didn't see it!"

Cramer nodded. "You saw something else, instead. By the way, I forgot to ask—Did you know her?"

"You mean—her?"

"We had never known her or seen her or heard of her," the husband declared.

"Had you, Mrs. Carlisle?"

"No."

"Of course. She wasn't a member of this flower club. Are you a member?"

"My husband is."

"We both are," Carlisle stated. "Vague again. It's a joint membership. Isn't this about enough?"

"Plenty," Cramer conceded. "Thank you, both of you. We won't bother you again unless we have to. . . . Levy, pass them out."

When the door had closed behind them Cramer glared at me and then at Wolfe. "This is sure a sweet one," he said grimly. "Say it's within the range of possibility that Carlisle is it, and the way it stands right now, why not? So we look into him. We check back on him for six months, and try doing it without getting roars out of him—a man like that in his position. However, it can be done—by three or four men in two or three weeks. Multiply that by what? How many men were here?"

"Around a hundred and twenty," I told him. "But you'll find that at least half of them are disqualified one way or another. As I told you, I took a survey. Say sixty."

"All right, multiply it by sixty. Do you care for it?"

"No," I said.

"Neither do I." Cramer took the cigar from his mouth. "Of course," he said sarcastically, "when she sat in there telling you about him the situation was different. You wanted her to enjoy being with you. You couldn't reach for the phone and tell us you had a self-confessed crook who could put a quick finger on a murderer and let us come and take over. No! You had to save it for a fee for Wolfe!"

"Don't be vulgar," I said severely.

"You had to go upstairs and make a survey! You had to—Well?"

Lieutenant Rowcliff had opened the door and entered. There were some city employees I liked, some I admired, some I had no feeling about, some I could have done without easy—and one whose ears I was going to twist some day. That was Rowcliff. He was tall, strong, handsome, and a pain in the neck.

"We're all through in there, sir," he said importantly. "We've covered everything. Nothing is being taken away, and it is all in order. We were especially careful with the contents of the drawers of Wolfe's desk, and also we—"

"My desk!" Wolfe roared.

"Yes, your desk," Rowcliff said precisely, smirking.

The blood was rushing into Wolfe's face.

"She was killed there," Cramer said gruffly. "Did you get anything at all?"

"I don't think so," Rowcliff admitted. "Of course, the prints have to be sorted, and there'll be lab reports. How do we leave it?"

"Seal it up and we'll see tomorrow. You stay here and keep a photographer. The others can go. Tell Stebbins to send that woman in—Mrs. Irwin."

"Orwin, sir."

"Wait a minute," I objected. "Seal what up? The office?"

"Certainly," Rowcliff sneered.

I said firmly, to Cramer, not to him, "You don't mean it. We work there. We live there. All our stuff is there."

"Go ahead, Lieutenant," Cramer told Rowcliff, and he wheeled and went.

I was full of both feelings and words, but I knew they had to be held in. This was far and away the worst Cramer had ever pulled. It was up to Wolfe. I looked at him. He was white with fury, and his mouth was pressed to so tight a line that there were no lips.

"It's routine," Cramer said aggressively.

Wolfe said icily, "That's a lie. It is not routine."

"It's *my* routine—in a case like this. Your office is not just an office. It's the place where more fancy tricks have been played than any other spot in New York. When a woman is murdered there, soon after a talk with Goodwin, for which we have no word but his—I say sealing it is routine."

Wolfe's head came forward an inch, his chin out. "No, Mr. Cramer. I'll tell you what it is. It is the malefic spite of a sullen little soul and a crabbed and envious mind. It is the childish rancor of a primacy too often challenged and offended. It is the feeble wiggle—"

The door came open to let Mrs. Orwin in.

With Mrs. Carlisle, the husband had come along. With Mrs. Orwin, it was the son. His expression and manner were so different I would hardly have known him. Upstairs his tone had been mean and his face had been mean. Now his narrow little eyes were working overtime to look frank and cordial.

He leaned across the table at Cramer, extending a hand: "Inspector Cramer? I've been hearing about you for years! I'm Eugene Orwin." He glanced at his right. "I've already had the pleasure of meeting Mr. Wolfe and Mr. Goodwin—earlier today, before this terrible thing happened. It *is* terrible."

"Yes," Cramer agreed. "Sit down."

"I will in a moment. I do better with words standing up. I would like to make a statement on behalf of my mother and myself, and I hope you'll permit it. I'm a member of the bar. My mother is not feeling well. At the request of your men she went in with me to identify the body of Miss Brown, and it was a bad shock, and we've been detained now more than two hours."

His mother's appearance corroborated him. Sitting with her head propped on a hand and her eyes closed, obviously she didn't care as much about the impression they made on the inspector as her son did.

"A statement would be welcome," Cramer told him, "if it's relevant."

"I thought so," Gene said approvingly. "So many people have an entirely wrong idea of police methods! Of course, you know that Miss Brown came here today as my mother's guest, and therefore it might be supposed that my mother knows her. But actually she doesn't."

"Go ahead."

Gene glanced at the shorthand dick. "If it's taken down I would like to go over it when convenient."

"You may."

"Then here are the facts: In January my mother was in Florida. You meet all kinds in Florida. My mother met a man who called himself Colonel Percy Brown—a British colonel in the reserve, he said. Later on, he introduced his sister Cynthia to her. My mother saw a great deal of them. My father is dead, and the estate, a rather large one, is in her control. She lent Brown some money, not much—that was just an opener."

Mrs. Orwin's head jerked up. "It was only five thousand dollars and I didn't promise him anything," she said wearily.

"All right, Mother." Gene patted her shoulder. "A week ago she returned to New York and they came along. The first time I met them I thought they were impostors. They weren't very free with family details, but from them and Mother, chiefly Mother, I got enough to inquire about, and sent a cable to London. I got a reply Saturday and another one this morning and there was more than enough to confirm my suspicion, but not nearly enough to put it up to my mother. When she likes people she can be very stubborn about them.

"I was thinking it over, what step to take next. Meanwhile, I thought it best not to let them be alone with her if I could help it. That's why I came here with them today—my mother is a member of that flower club —I'm no gardener myself—"

He turned a palm up. "That's what brought me here. My mother came to see the orchids, and she invited Brown and his sister to come, simply because she is goodhearted. But actually she knows nothing about them."

He put his hands on the table and leaned on them, forward at Cramer. "I'm going to be quite frank, Inspector. Under the circumstances, I can't see that it would serve any useful purpose to let it be published that that woman came here with my mother. I want to make it perfectly clear that we have no desire to evade our responsibility as citizens. But how would it help to get my mother's name in the headlines?"

"Names in headlines aren't what I'm after," Cramer told him, "but I don't run the newspapers. If they've already got it I can't stop them. I'd like to say I appreciate your frankness. So you only met Miss Brown a week ago?"

Cramer had plenty of questions for both mother and son. It was in the middle of them that Wolfe passed me a slip of paper on which he had scribbled:

"Tell Fritz to bring sandwiches and coffee for you and me. Also for those left in the front room. No one else. Of course, Saul and Theodore."

I left the room, found Fritz in the kitchen, delivered the message, and returned.

Gene stayed cooperative to the end, and Mrs. Orwin tried, though it was an effort. They said they had been together all the time, which I happened to know wasn't so, having seen them separated at least twice during the afternoon, and Cramer did too, since I had told him.

They said a lot of other things, among them that they hadn't left the plant-rooms between their arrival and their departure with Wolfe; that they had stayed until most of the others were gone because Mrs. Orwin wanted to persuade Wolfe to sell her some plants; that Colonel Brown had wandered off by himself once or twice; that they had been only mildly concerned about Cynthia's absence, because of assurances from Colonel Brown and me; and so on.

Before they left, Gene made another try for a commitment to keep his mother's name out of it, and Cramer promised to do his best.

Fritz had brought trays for Wolfe and me, and we were making headway with them. In the silence that followed the departure of the Orwins, Wolfe could plainly be heard chewing a mouthful of mixed salad.

Cramer sat frowning at us. He turned his head: "Levy! Get that Colonel Brown in."

"Yes, sir. That man you wanted—Vedder—he's here."

"Then I'll take him first."

Up in the plant-room, Malcolm Vedder had caught my eye by the way he picked up a flowerpot and held it. As he took a chair across the dining table from Cramer and me, I still thought he was worth another good look, but after his answer to Cramer's third question I relaxed and concentrated on my sandwiches. He was an actor and had had parts in three Broadway plays. Of course, that explained it. No actor would pick up a flowerpot just normally, like you or me. He would have to dramatize it some way, and Vedder had happened to choose a way that looked to me like fingers closing around a throat.

Now he was dramatizing this by being wrought-up and indignant.

"Typical!" he told Cramer, his eyes flashing and his voice throaty with feeling. "Typical of police clumsiness! Pulling *me* into this!"

"Yeah," Cramer said sympathetically. "It'll be tough for an actor, having your picture in the paper. You a member of this flower club?"

No, Vedder said, he wasn't. He had come with a friend, a Mrs. Beauchamp, and when she had left to keep an appointment he had remained to look at more orchids. They had arrived about three-thirty and he had remained in the plant-rooms continuously until leaving.

Cramer went through all the regulation questions, and got all the expected negatives, until he suddenly asked, "Did you know Doris Hatten?"

Vedder frowned. "Who?"

"Doris Hatten. She was also—"

"Ah!" Vedder cried. "She was also strangled! I remember!"

"Right."

Vedder made fists of his hands, rested them on the table, and leaned forward. "You know," he said tensely, "that's the worst of all, strangling —especially a woman."

"Did you know Doris Hatten?"

"Othello," Vedder said in a deep, resonant tone. His eyes lifted to

Cramer and his voice lifted, too: "No, I didn't know her; I only read about her." He shuddered all over, and then, abruptly, he was out of his chair and on his feet. "I only came here to look at orchids!"

He ran his fingers through his hair, turned, and made for the door.

Levy looked at Cramer with his brows raised, and Cramer shook his head.

The next one in was Bill McNab, garden editor of the *Gazette*.

"I can't tell you how much I regret this, Mr. Wolfe," he said miserably.

"Don't try," Wolfe growled.

"What a terrible thing! I wouldn't have dreamed such a thing could happen—the Manhattan Flower Club! Of course, she wasn't a member, but that only makes it worse, in a way." McNab turned to Cramer: "I'm responsible for this."

"You are?"

"Yes, it was my idea. I persuaded Mr. Wolfe to arrange it. He let me word the invitations. And I was congratulating myself on the great success! Then this! What can I do?"

"Sit down a minute," Cramer invited him.

McNab varied the monotony on one detail, at least. He admitted that he had left the plant-rooms three times during the afternoon, once to accompany a departing guest down to the ground floor, and twice to go down alone to check on who had come and who hadn't. Aside from that, he was more of the same. By now it was beginning to seem not only futile, but silly to spend time on seven or eight of them merely because they happened to be the last to go and so were at hand. Also, it was something new to me from a technical standpoint. I had never seen one stack up like that.

Any precinct dick knows that every question you ask of everybody is aimed at one of the three targets: motive, means, and opportunity. In this case there were no questions to ask, because those were already answered. Motive: the guy had followed her downstairs, knowing she had recognized him, had seen her enter Wolfe's office and thought she was doing exactly what she was doing, getting set to tell Wolfe, and had decided to prevent that the quickest and best way he knew. Means: any piece of cloth, even his handkerchief, would do. Opportunity: he was there—all of them on Saul's list were.

So, if you wanted to learn who strangled Cynthia Brown, first you had to find out who had strangled Doris Hatten.

As soon as Bill McNab had been sent on his way, Colonel Percy Brown was brought in. Brown was not exactly at ease, but he had himself well in hand. You would never have picked him for a con man, and neither would I. His mouth and jaw were strong and attractive, and as he sat down he leveled his keen gray eyes at Cramer and kept them there. He wasn't interested in Wolfe or me. He said his name was Colonel Percy Brown, and Cramer asked him which army he was a colonel in.

"I think," Brown said in a cool, even tone, "it will save time if I state my position: I will answer fully and freely all questions that relate to what I saw, heard, or did since I arrived here this afternoon. Answers to any other questions will have to wait until I consult my attorney."

Cramer nodded. "I expected that. The trouble is I'm pretty sure I don't give a hoot what you saw or heard this afternoon. We'll come back to that. I want to put something up to you. As you see, I'm not even wanting to know why you tried to break away before we got here."

"I merely wanted to phone—"

"Forget it. On information received, I think it's like this: The woman who called herself Cynthia Brown, murdered here today, was not your sister. You met her in Florida six or eight weeks ago. She went in with you on an operation of which Mrs. Orwin was the subject, and you introduced her to Mrs. Orwin as your sister. You two came to New York with Mrs. Orwin a week ago, with the operation well under way. As far as I'm concerned, that is only background. Otherwise, I'm not interested in it. My work is homicide.

"For me," Cramer went on, "the point is that for quite a period you have been closely connected with this Miss Brown, associating with her in a confidential operation. You must have had many intimate conversations with her. You were having her with you as your sister, and she wasn't, and she's been murdered. We could give you a merry time on that score alone.

"But I wanted to give you a chance first," Cramer continued. "For two months you've been on intimate terms with Cynthia Brown. She certainly must have mentioned that a friend of hers named Doris Hatten was murdered—strangled last October. Cynthia Brown had information about the murderer which she kept to herself. If she had come out with it she'd be alive now. She must have told you all about it. Now you can tell me. If you do, we can nail him for what he did here today, and it might even make things a little smoother for you. Well?"

Brown had pursed his lips. They straightened out again, and his hand came up for a finger to scratch his cheek.

"I'm sorry I can't help."

"Do you expect me to believe that during all those weeks she never mentioned the murder of her friend Doris Hatten?"

"I'm sorry I can't help." Brown's tone was firm and final.

Cramer said, "Okay. We'll move on to this afternoon. Do you remember a moment when something about Cynthia Brown's appearance —some movement she made or the expression on her face—caused Mrs. Orwin to ask her what was the matter with her?"

A crease was showing on Brown's forehead. "I'm sorry. I don't believe I do," he stated.

"I'm asking you to try. Try hard."

Silence. Brown pursed his lips and the crease in his forehead deepened. Finally he said, "I may not have been right there at the moment. In those aisles—in a crowd like that—we weren't rubbing elbows continuously."

"You do remember when she excused herself because she wasn't feeling well?"

"Yes, of course."

"Well, this moment I'm asking about came shortly before that. She exchanged looks with some man nearby, and it was her reaction to that that made Mrs. Orwin ask her what was the matter. What I'm interested in is that exchange of looks."

"I didn't see it."

Cramer banged his fist on the table so hard the trays danced. "Levy! Take him out and tell Stebbins to send him down and lock him up. Material witness. Put more men on him—he's got a record somewhere. Find it!"

As the door closed behind them, Cramer turned and said, "Gather up, Murphy. We're leaving."

Levy came back in and Cramer addressed him: "We're leaving. Tell Stebbins one man out front will be enough—No, I'll tell him—"

"There's one more, sir. His name is Nicholson Morley. He's a psychiatrist."

"Let him go. This is getting to be a joke."

Cramer looked at Wolfe. Wolfe looked back at him.

"A while ago," Cramer rasped, "you said something had occurred to you."

"Did I?" Wolfe inquired coldly.

Their eyes went on clashing until Cramer broke the connection by turning to go. I restrained an impulse to knock their heads together. They were both being childish. If Wolfe really had something, anything at all, he knew Cramer would gladly trade the seals on the office door for it, sight unseen. And Cramer knew he could make the deal himself with nothing to lose. But they were both too sore and stubborn to show any horse sense.

Cramer had circled the end of the table on his way out when Levy reentered to report: "That man Morley insists on seeing you. He says it's vital."

Cramer halted, glowering. "What is he, a screwball?"

"I don't know, sir. He may be."

"Oh, bring him in."

This was my first really good look at the middle-aged male with the mop of black hair. His quick-darting eyes were fully as black as his hair.

Cramer nodded impatiently. "You have something to say, Dr. Morley?"

"I have. Something vital."

"Let's hear it."

Morley got better settled in his chair. "First, I assume that no arrest has been made. Is that correct?"

"Yes—if you mean an arrest with a charge of murder."

"Have you a definite object of suspicion, with or without evidence in support?"

"If you mean am I ready to name the murderer, no. Are you?"

"I think I may be."

Cramer's chin went up. "Well? I'm in charge here."

Dr. Morley smiled. "Not quite so fast. The suggestion I have to offer is sound only with certain assumptions." He placed the tip of his right forefinger on the tip of his left little finger. "One: that you have no idea who committed this murder, and apparently you haven't." He moved over a finger. "Two: that this was not a commonplace crime with a commonplace discoverable motive." To the middle finger. "Three: that nothing is known to discredit the hypothesis that this girl was strangled by the man who strangled Doris Hatten . . . May I make those assumptions?"

"You can try. Why do you want to?"

Morley shook his head. "Not that I want to. That if I am permitted to, I have a suggestion. I wish to make it clear that I have great respect for the competence of the police, within proper limits. If the man who murdered Doris Hatten had been vulnerable to police techniques and resources, he would almost certainly have been caught. But he wasn't. You failed. Why?

"Because he was out of bounds for you. Because your exploration of motive is restricted by your preconceptions." Morley's black eyes gleamed. "You're a layman, so I won't use technical terms. The most powerful motives on earth are motives of the personality, which cannot be exposed by any purely objective investigation. If the personality is twisted, distorted, as it is with a psychotic, then the motives are twisted, too. As a psychiatrist I was deeply interested in the published reports on the murder of Doris Hatten—especially the detail that she was strangled with her own scarf. When your efforts to find the culprit ended in complete failure, I would have been glad to come forward with a suggestion, but I was as helpless as you."

"Get down to it," Cramer muttered.

"Yes." Morley put his elbows on the table and paired all his fingertips. "Now, today. On the basis of the assumptions I began with, it is a tenable theory, worthy to be tested, that this was the same man. If so, it is no longer a question of finding him among thousands or millions; it's a mere hundred or so, and I am willing to contribute my services." The black eyes flashed. "I admit that for a psychiatrist this is a rare opportunity. Nothing could be more dramatic than a psychosis exploding into murder. All you have to do is to have them brought to my office, one at a time—"

"Wait a minute," Cramer put in. "Are you suggesting that we deliver everyone that was here today to your office for you to work on?"

"No, not everyone, only the men. When I have finished I may have nothing that can be used as evidence, but there's an excellent chance that I can tell you who the strangler is—"

"Excuse me," Cramer said. He was on his feet. "Sorry to cut you off, Doctor, but I must get downtown." He was on his way. "I'm afraid your suggestion wouldn't work—I'll let you know—"

He went, and Levy and Murphy with him.

Dr. Morley pivoted his head to watch them go, kept it that way a moment, and then he arose and walked out without a word.

"Twenty minutes to ten," I announced.

Wolfe muttered, "Go look at the office door."

"I just did, as I let Morley out. It's sealed. Malefic spite. But this isn't a bad room to sit in," I said brightly.

"Pfui! I want to ask you something."

"Shoot."

"I want your opinion of this. Assume that we accept without reservation the story Miss Brown told you. Assume also that the man she had recognized, knowing she had recognized him, followed her downstairs and saw her enter the office; that he surmised she intended to consult me; that he postponed joining her in the office, either because he knew you were in there with her or for some other reason; that he saw you come out and go upstairs; that he took an opportunity to enter the office unobserved, got her off guard, killed her, got out unobserved, and returned upstairs."

"I'll take it that way."

"Very well. Then we have significant indications of his character. Consider it. He has killed her and is back upstairs, knowing that she was in the office talking with you for some time. He would like to know what she said to you. Specifically, he would like to know whether she told you about him, and, if so, how much. Had she or had she not named or described him in his current guise? With that question unanswered, would a man of his character, as indicated, *leave the house?* Or would he prefer the challenge and risk of remaining until the body had been discovered, to see what you would do? And I, too, of course, after you had talked with me, and the police?"

"Yeah." I chewed my lip. There was a long silence. "So that's how your mind's working. I could offer a guess."

"I prefer a calculation to a guess. For that, a basis is needed, and we have it. We know the situation as we have assumed it, and we know something of his character."

"Okay," I conceded, "a calculation. The answer I get, he would stick around until the body was found, and if he did, then he is one of the bunch Cramer has been talking with. So that's what occurred to you, huh?"

"No. By no means. That's a different matter. This is merely a tentative calculation for a starting point. If it is sound, I *know* who the murderer is."

I gave him a look. Sometimes I can tell how much he is putting on and sometimes I can't tell. I decided to buy it.

"That's interesting," I said admiringly. "If you want me to get him on the phone I'll have to use the one in the kitchen."

"I want to test the calculation."

"So do I."

"But that's a difficulty. The best I have in mind, the only one I can contrive to my satisfaction—only you can make it. And in doing so you would have to expose yourself to great personal risk."

"For Pete's sake!" I gawked at him. "This is a brand-new one. The errands you've sent me on! Since when have you flinched or faltered in the face of danger to me?"

"This danger is extreme."

"Let's hear the test."

"Very well." He turned a hand over. "Is that old typewriter of yours in working order?"

"Fair."

"Bring it down here, and some sheets of blank paper—any kind. I'll need a blank envelope."

"I have some."

"Bring one. Also the telephone book, Manhattan, from my room."

When I returned to the dining-room and was placing the typewriter in position on the table, Wolfe spoke: "No, bring it here. I'll use it myself."

I lifted my brows at him. "A page will take you an hour."

"It won't be a page. Put a sheet of paper in it."

I did so, got the paper squared, lifted the machine, and put it in front of him. He sat and frowned at it for a long minute, and then started pecking. I turned my back on him to make it easier to withhold remarks about his two-finger technique, and passed the time by trying to figure his rate. All at once he pulled the paper out.

"I think that will do," he said.

I took it and read what he had typed:

"She told me enough this afternoon so that I know who to send this to, and more. I have kept it to myself because I haven't decided what is the right thing to do. I would like to have a talk with you first, and if you will phone me tomorrow, Tuesday, between nine o'clock and noon, we can make an appointment; please don't put it off or I will have to decide myself."

I read it over three times. I looked at Wolfe. He had put an envelope in the typewriter and was consulting the phone book. He began pecking, addressing the envelope. I waited until he had finished and rolled the envelope out.

"Just like this?" I asked. "No name or initials signed?"

"No."

"I admit it's nifty," I admitted. "We could forget the calculation and send this to every guy on that list and wait to see who phoned."

"I prefer to send it only to one person—the one indicated by your report of that conversation. That will test the calculation."

"And save postage." I glanced at the paper. "The extreme danger, I suppose, is that I'll get strangled."

"I don't want to minimize the risk of this, Archie."

"Neither do I. I'll have to borrow a gun from Saul—ours are in the office. . . . May I have that envelope? I'll have to go to Times Square to mail it."

"Yes. Before you do so, copy that note. Keep Saul here in the morning. If and when the phone call comes you will have to use your wits to arrange the appointment advantageously."

"Right. The envelope, please."

He handed it to me.

That Tuesday morning I was kept busy from eight o'clock on by the phone and the doorbell. After nine, Saul was there to help, but not with the phone, because the orders were that I was to answer all calls. They were mostly from newspapers, but there were a couple from Homicide and a few scattered ones. I took them on the extension in the kitchen.

Every time I lifted the thing and told the transmitter, "Nero Wolfe's office, Archie Goodwin speaking," my pulse went up a notch, and then had to level off again. I had one argument, with a bozo in the District Attorney's office who had the strange idea that he could order me to report for an interview at eleven-thirty sharp, which ended by my agreeing to call later to fix an hour.

A little before eleven I was in the kitchen with Saul, who, at Wolfe's direction, had been briefed to date, when the phone rang.

"Nero Wolfe's office, Archie Goodwin speaking."

"Mr. Goodwin?"

"Right."

"You sent me a note."

My hand wanted to grip the phone the way Vedder had gripped the flowerpot, but I wouldn't let it.

"Did I? What about?"

"You suggested that we make an appointment. Are you in a position to discuss it?"

"Sure. I'm alone and no extensions are on. But I don't recognize your voice. Who is this?"

"I have two voices. This is the other one. Have you made a decision yet?"

"No. I was waiting to hear from you."

"That's wise, I think. I'm willing to discuss the matter. Are you free this evening?"

"I can wiggle free."

"With a car to drive?"

"Yeah, I have a car."

"Drive to a lunchroom at the north-east corner of Fifty-first Street and Eleventh Avenue. Get there at eight o'clock. Park your car on Fifty-first Street, but not at the corner. You will be alone, of course. Go in the lunchroom and order something to eat. I won't be there, but you will get a message. You'll be there at eight?"

"Yes. I still don't recognize your voice. I don't think you're the person I sent the note to."

"I am. It's good, isn't it?"

The connection went. I hung up, told Fritz he could answer calls now, and hotfooted it to the stairs and up three flights.

Wolfe was in the cool-room. When I told him about the call he merely nodded.

"That call," he said, "validates our assumption and verifies our calculation, but that's all. Has anyone come to take those seals off?"

I told him no. "I asked Stebbins about it and he said he'd ask Cramer."

"Don't ask again," he snapped. "We'll go down to my room."

If the strangler had been in Wolfe's house the rest of that day he would have felt honored—or anyway he should. Even during Wolfe's afternoon hours in the plant-rooms, from four to six, his mind was on my appointment, as was proved by the crop of new slants and ideas that poured out of him when he came down to the kitchen. Except for a trip to Leonard Street to answer an hour's worth of questions by an assistant district attorney, my day was devoted to it, too. My most useful errand—though at the time it struck me as a waste of time and money—was one made to Doc Vollmer for a prescription and then to a drugstore, under instructions from Wolfe.

When I got back from the D.A.'s office Saul and I got in the sedan and went for a reconnaissance. We didn't stop at 51st Street and 11th Avenue but drove past it four times. The main idea was to find a place for Saul. He and Wolfe both insisted that he had to be there.

We finally settled for a filling station across the street from the lunchroom. Saul was to have a taxi drive in there at eight o'clock, and stay in the passenger's seat while the driver tried to get his carburetor adjusted. There were so many contingencies to be agreed on that if it had been anyone but Saul I wouldn't have expected him to remember more than half. For instance, in case I left the lunchroom and got in my car and drove off, Saul was not to follow unless I cranked my window down.

Trying to provide for contingencies was okay, in a way, but actually it was strictly up to me, since I had to let the other guy make the rules. And with the other guy making the rules no one gets very far, not even Nero Wolfe arranging for contingencies ahead of time.

Saul left before I did, to find a taxi driver that he liked the looks of. When I went to the hall for my hat and raincoat, Wolfe came along.

"I still don't like the idea," he insisted, "of your having that thing in your pocket. I think you should slip it inside your sock."

"I don't." I was putting the raincoat on. "If I get frisked, a sock is as easy to feel as a pocket."

"You're sure that gun is loaded?"

"I never saw you so anxious. Next you'll be telling me to put on my rubbers."

He even opened the door for me.

It wasn't actually raining, merely trying to make up its mind, but after a couple of blocks I reached to switch on the windshield wiper. As I turned uptown on 10th Avenue the dash clock said 7:47; as I turned left on 51st Street it had only got to 7:51. At that time of day in that district there was plenty of space, and I rolled to the curb and stopped about twenty yards short of the corner, stopped the engine and turned the window down for a good view of the filling station across the street. There was no taxi there. At 7:59 a taxi pulled in and stopped by the pumps, and the driver got out and lifted the hood and started peering. I put my window up, locked the doors, and entered the lunchroom.

There was one hash slinger behind the counter and five customers scattered along on the stools. I picked a stool that left me elbowroom, sat, and ordered ice cream and coffee. The counterman served me and I took my time. At 8:12 the ice cream was gone and my cup empty, and I ordered a refill.

I had about got to the end of that, too, when a male entered, looked along the line, came straight to me, and asked me what my name was. I told him, and he handed me a folded piece of paper and turned to go. He was barely old enough for high school and I made no effort to hold him, thinking that the bird I had a date with was not likely to be an absolute sap. Unfolding the paper, I saw, neatly printed in pencil:

"Go to your car and get a note under the windshield wiper. Sit in the car to read it."

I paid what I owed, walked to my car and got the note as I was told, unlocked the car and got in, turned on the light, and read, in the same print:

"Make no signal of any kind. Follow instructions precisely. Turn right on 11th Ave. and go slowly to 56th St. Turn right on 56th and go to 9th Ave. Turn right on 9th Ave. Right again on 45th. Left on 11th Ave. Left on 38th. Right on 7th Ave. Right on 27th St. Park on 27th between 9th and 10th Aves. Go to No. 814 and tap five times on the door. Give the man who opens the door this note and the other one. He will tell you where to go."

I didn't like it much, but I had to admit it was a handy arrangement for seeing to it that I went to the conference unattached.

It had now decided to rain. Starting the engine, I could see dimly through the misty window that Saul's taxi driver was still monkeying with his carburetor, but of course I had to resist the impulse to crank the window down to wave so-long. Keeping the instructions in my left hand, I rolled to the corner, waited for the light to change, and turned right on 11th Avenue.

Since I had not been forbidden to keep my eyes open I did so, and as I stopped at 52nd for the red light I saw a black or dark-blue sedan pull away from the curb behind me and creep in my direction. I took it for granted that that was my chaperon.

The guy in the sedan was not the strangler, as I soon learned. On 27th Street there was space smack in front of Number 814, and I saw no reason why I shouldn't use it. The sedan went to the curb right behind me. After locking my car I stood on the sidewalk a moment, but my chaperon just sat tight, so I kept to the instructions, mounted the steps to the stoop of the rundown old brownstone, entered the vestibule, and knocked five times on the door. Through the glass panel the dimly-lit hall looked empty. As I peered in, I heard footsteps behind and turned. It was my chaperon.

"Well, we got here," I said cheerfully.

"You almost lost me at one light," he said. "Give me them notes."

I handed them to him—all the evidence I had. As he unfolded them for a look, I took him in. He was around my age and height, skinny but with muscles, with outstanding ears and a purple mole on his right jaw.

"They look like it," he said, and stuffed the notes in a pocket. From another pocket he produced a key, unlocked the door, and pushed it open. "Follow me."

As we ascended two flights, with him in front, it would have been a cinch for me to reach and take a gun off his hip if there had been one there, but there wasn't. He may have preferred a shoulder holster, like me. The stair steps were bare, worn wood, the walls had needed plaster since at least Pearl Harbor, and the smell was a mixture I wouldn't want to analyze. On the second landing he went down the hall to a door at the rear and signaled me through.

There was another man there, but still it wasn't my date—anyway, I hoped not. It would be an overstatement to say the room was furnished, but I admit there was a table, a bed, and three chairs, one of them upholstered. The man, who was lying on the bed, pushed himself up as we entered, and as he swung around to sit, his feet barely reached the floor. He had shoulders and a torso like a heavyweight wrestler, and legs like an underweight jockey. His puffed eyes blinked in the light from the unshaded bulb as if he had been asleep.

"That him?" he demanded.

Skinny said it was.

The wrestler-jockey, W-J for short, got up and went to the table, picked up a ball of thick cord. "Take off your hat and coat and sit there." He pointed to one of the straight chairs.

"Hold it," Skinny commanded him. "I haven't explained yet." He faced me: "The idea is simple. This man that's coming to see you don't want any trouble. He just wants to talk. So we tie you in that chair and leave you, and he comes and you have a talk, and after he leaves we come back and cut you loose, and out you go. Is that plain enough?"

I grinned at him. "It sure is, brother. It's too plain. What if I won't sit down?"

"Then he don't come and you don't have a talk."

"What if I walk out now?"

"Go ahead. We get paid anyhow. If you want to see this guy there's only one way: We tie you in the chair."

"We get more if we tie him," W-J objected. "Let me persuade him."

"Lay off," Skinny commanded.

"I don't want any trouble either," I stated. "How about this? I sit in the chair and you fix the cord to look right, but so I'm free to move in case of fire. There's a hundred bucks in the wallet in my breast pocket. Before you leave, you help yourselves."

"A lousy C?" W-J sneered. "Shut up and sit down."

"He had his choice," Skinny said reprovingly.

I did, indeed. It was a swell illustration of how much good it does to try to consider contingencies in advance. In all our discussions that day none of us had put the question, what to do if a pair of smooks offered me my pick of being tied in a chair or going home to bed. As far as I could see, standing there looking them over, that was all there was to it, and it was too early to go home to bed.

"Okay," I told them, "but don't overdo it. I know my way around, and I can find you if I care enough."

They unrolled the cord, cutting pieces off, and went to work. W-J tied my left wrist to the rear left leg of the chair, while Skinny did the right. They wanted to do my ankles the same way, to the bottoms of the front legs of the chair, but I claimed I would get cramps sitting like that. It would be just as good to tie my ankles together. They discussed it, and I had my way. Skinny made a final inspection of the knots and then went over me. He took the gun from my shoulder holster and tossed it on the bed, made sure I didn't have another one, and left the room.

W-J picked up the gun, and scowled at it. "These things," he muttered. "They make more trouble." He went to the table and put the gun down on it. Then he crossed to the bed and stretched out on it.

"How long do we have to wait?" I asked.

"Not long. I wasn't to bed last night." He closed his eyes.

He got no nap. His barrel chest couldn't have gone up and down more than a dozen times before the door opened and Skinny came in.

With him was a man in a gray pinstripe suit and a dark-gray homburg, with a gray topcoat over his arm. He had gloves on. W-J got off the bed and onto his toothpick legs. Skinny stood by the open door. The man put his hat and coat on the bed, came and took a look at my fastenings, and told Skinny, "All right; I'll come for you." The two rummies departed, shutting the door. The man stood facing me.

He smiled. "Would you have known me?"

"Not from Adam," I said, both to humor him and because it was true.

I wouldn't want to exaggerate how brave I am. It wasn't that I was too fearless to be impressed by the fact that I was thoroughly tied up and the strangler was standing there smiling at me; I was simply astounded. It was an amazing disguise. The two main changes were the eyebrows and eyelashes; these eyes had bushy brows and long, thick lashes, whereas yesterday's guest hadn't had much of either one. The real change was from the inside. I had seen no smile on the face of yesterday's guest, but if I had it wouldn't have been like this one. The hair made a difference too, of course, parted on the side and slicked down.

He pulled the other straight chair around and sat. I admired the way he moved. That in itself could have been a dead giveaway, but the movements fitted the get-up to a T.

"So she told you about me?" he said.

It was the voice he had used on the phone. It was actually different, pitched lower, for one thing, but with it, as with the face and movements, the big change was from the inside. The voice was stretched tight, and the palms of his gloved hands were pressed against his knee-caps with the fingers straight out.

I said, "Yes," and added conversationally, "When you saw her go in the office why didn't you follow her in?"

"I had seen you leave, upstairs, and I suspected you were in there."

"Why didn't she scream or fight?"

"I talked to her. I talked a little first." His head gave a quick jerk, as if a fly were bothering him and his hands were too occupied to attend to it. "What did she tell you?"

"About that day at Doris Hatten's apartment—you coming in and her going out. And of course her recognizing you there yesterday."

"She is dead. There is no evidence. You can't prove anything."

I grinned. "Then you're wasting a lot of time and energy and the best disguise I ever saw. Why didn't you just toss my note in the waste-basket? . . . Let me answer. You didn't dare. In getting evidence, knowing exactly what and who to look for makes all the difference. You knew I knew."

"And you haven't told the police?"

"No."

"Nor Nero Wolfe?"

"No."

"Why not?"

I shrugged. "I may not put it very well," I said, "because this is the first time I have ever talked with my hands and feet tied, and I find it cramps my style. But it strikes me as the kind of coincidence that doesn't happen very often. I'm fed up with the detective business, and I'd like to quit. I have something that's worth a good deal to you—say, fifty thousand dollars. It can be arranged so that you get what you pay for. I'll go the limit on that, but it has to be closed quick. If you don't buy, I'm going to have a tough time explaining why I didn't remember sooner what she told me. Twenty-four hours from now is the absolute limit."

"It couldn't be arranged so I could get what I paid for."

"Sure, it could. If you don't want me on your neck the rest of your life, believe me, I don't want you on mine, either."

"I suppose you don't. I suppose I'll have to pay."

There was a sudden noise in his throat as if he had started to choke. He stood up. "You're working your hand loose," he said huskily, and moved toward me.

It might have been guessed from his voice, thick and husky from the blood rushing to his head, but it was plain as day in his eyes, suddenly fixed and glassy, like a blind man's eyes. Evidently he had come there fully intending to kill me, and had now worked himself up to it.

"Hold it!" I snapped at him.

He halted, muttering, "You're getting your hand loose," and moved again, passing me to get behind.

I jerked my body and the chair violently aside and around, and had him in front of me again.

"No good," I told him. "They only went down one flight. I heard 'em. It's no good, anyway. I've got another note for you—from Nero Wolfe—here in my breast pocket. Help yourself, but stay in front of me."

He was only two steps from me, but it took him four small, slow ones. His gloved hand went inside my coat to the breast pocket, and came out with a folded slip of yellow paper. From the way his eyes looked, I doubted if he would be able to read, but apparently he was. I watched his face as he took it in, in Wolfe's precise handwriting:

"If Mr. Goodwin is not home by midnight the information given him by Cynthia Brown will be communicated to the police, and I shall see that they act immediately. NERO WOLFE."

He looked at me, and slowly his eyes changed. No longer glassy, they began to let light in. Before, he had just been going to kill me. Now, he hated me.

I got voluble: "So it's no good, see? He did it this way because if you had known I had told him, you would have sat tight. He figured that you would think you could handle me, and I admit you tried your best. He wants fifty thousand dollars by tomorrow at six o'clock, no later. You say it can't be arranged so you'll get what you pay for, but we say it can and it's up to you. You say we have no evidence, but we can get it—don't think we can't. As for me, I wouldn't advise you even to pull my hair. It would make him sore at you, and he's not sore now, he just wants fifty thousand bucks."

He had started to tremble, and knew it, and was trying to stop.

"Maybe," I conceded, "you can't get that much that quick. In that case he'll take your I.O.U.—you can write it on the back of that note he sent you. My pen's here in my vest pocket. He'll be reasonable."

"I'm not such a fool," he said harshly.

"Who said you were?" I was sharp and urgent, and thought I had loosened him. "Use your head, that's all. We've either got you cornered or we haven't. If we haven't, what are you doing here? If we have, a little thing like your name signed to an I.O.U. won't make it any worse. He won't press you too hard. Here, get my pen, right here."

I still think I had loosened him. It was in his eyes and the way he stood, sagging a little. If my hands had been free, so I could have got the pen myself, and uncapped it and put it between his fingers, I would have had him. I had him to the point of writing and signing, but not to the point of taking my pen out of my pocket. But, of course, if my hands had been free I wouldn't have been bothering about an I.O.U. and a pen.

So he slipped from under. He shook his head, and his shoulders stiffened. The hate that filled his eyes was in his voice, too: "You said twenty-four hours. That gives me tomorrow. I'll have to decide. Tell Nero Wolfe I'll decide."

He crossed to the door and pulled it open. He went out, closing the door, and I heard his steps descending the stairs; but he hadn't taken his hat and coat, and I nearly cracked my temples trying to use my brain. I hadn't got far when there were steps on the stairs again, coming up, and in they came, all three of them.

My host spoke to Skinny: "What time does your watch say?"

Skinny glanced at his wrist. "Nine thirty-two."

"At half-past ten untie his left hand. Leave him like that and go. It will take him five minutes or more to get his other hand and his feet free. Have you any objection to that?"

"Nah. He's got nothing on us."

The strangler took a roll of bills from his pocket, having a little difficulty on account of his gloves, peeled off two twenties, went to the table with them, and gave them a good rub on both sides with his handkerchief.

He held the bills out to Skinny. "I've got the agreed amount, as you know. This extra is so you won't get impatient and leave before half-past ten."

"Don't take it!" I called sharply.

Skinny, the bills in his hand, turned. "What's the matter—they got germs?"

"No, but they're peanuts, you sap! He's worth ten grand to you! As is!"

"Nonsense," the strangler said scornfully, and started for the bed to get his hat and coat.

"Gimme my twenty," W-J demanded.

Skinny stood with his head cocked, regarding me. He looked faintly interested but skeptical, and I saw it would take more than words. As the strangler picked up his hat and coat and turned, I jerked my body violently to the left, and over I went, chair and all. I have no idea how I got across the floor to the door. I couldn't simply roll, on account of the chair; I couldn't crawl without hands; and I didn't even try to jump. But I made it, and not slow, and was there down on my right side, the chair against the door and me against the chair, before any of them snapped out of it enough to reach me.

"You think," I yapped at Skinny, "it's just a job? Let him go and you'll find out! Do you want his name? Mrs. Carlisle—*Mrs.* Homer N. Carlisle. Do you want her address?"

The strangler, on his way to me, stopped and froze. He—or I should say, she—stood stiff as a bar of steel, the long-lashed eyes aimed at me.

"Missus?" Skinny demanded incredulously. "Did you say 'Missus'?"

"Yes. She's a woman. I'm tied up, but you've got her. I'm helpless, so you can have her. You might give me a cut of the ten grand." The strangler made a movement. "Watch her!"

W-J, who had started for me and stopped, turned to face her. I had banged my head and it hurt. Skinny stepped up to her, jerked both sides of her double-breasted coat open, released them, and backed up a step.

"It could be a woman," he said.

"We can find that out easy enough." W-J moved. "Dumb as I am, I can tell *that*."

"Go ahead," I urged. "That will check her and me both. Go ahead!"

W-J got to her and put out a hand.

She shrank away and screamed, "Don't touch me!"

"I'll be—" W-J said wonderingly.

"What's this gag," Skinny demanded, "about ten grand?"

"It's a long story," I told him, "but it's there if you want it. If you'll cut me in for a third, it's a cinch. If she gets out of here and gets safe home, we can't touch her. All we have to do is connect her as she is—here now, disguised—with Mrs. Homer N. Carlisle, which is what she'll be when she gets home. If we do that we've got her shirt. As she is here now, she's red-hot. As she is at home, you couldn't even get in."

"So what?" Skinny asked. "I didn't bring my camera."

"I've got something better. Get me loose and I'll show you."

Skinny didn't like that. He eyed me a moment and turned for a look at the others. Mrs. Carlisle was backed against the bed, and W-J stood studying her with his fists on his hips.

Skinny returned to me. "I'll do it. Maybe. What is it?"

I snapped, "At least, put me right side up. These cords are eating my wrists."

He came and got the back of the chair with one hand and my arm with the other, and I clamped my feet to the floor to give us leverage. He was stronger than he looked. Upright on the chair again, I was still blocking the door.

"Get a bottle," I told him, "out of my right-hand coat pocket. . . . No, here; the coat I've got on. I hope it didn't break."

He fished it out. It was intact. He held it to the light to read the label. "What is it?"

"Silver nitrate. It makes a black, indelible mark on most things, including skin. Pull up her pants leg and mark her with it."

"Then what?"

"Let her go. We'll have her. With the three of us able to explain how and when she got marked, she's sunk."

"How come you've got this stuff?"

"I was hoping for a chance to mark her myself."

"How much will it hurt her?"

"Not at all. Put some on me—anywhere you like, as long as it doesn't show."

He studied the label again. I watched his face, hoping he wouldn't ask if the mark would be permanent, because I didn't know what answer would suit him, and I had to sell him.

"A woman," he muttered. "A woman!"

"Yeah," I said sympathetically. "She sure made a monkey of you."

He swiveled his head and called, "Hey!"

W-J turned.

Skinny commanded him, "Pin her up! Don't hurt her."

W-J reached for her. But, as he did so, all of a sudden she was neither man nor woman, but a cyclone. Her first leap, away from his reaching hand, was sidewise, and by the time he had realized he didn't have her she had got to the table and grabbed the gun. He made for her, and she pulled the trigger, and down he went, tumbling right at her feet. By that time Skinny was almost to her, and she whirled and blazed away again. He kept going, and from the force of the blow on my left shoulder I might have calculated, if I had been in a mood for calculating, that the bullet had not gone through Skinny before it hit me. She pulled the trigger a third time, but by then Skinny had her wrist and was breaking her arm.

"She got me!" W-J was yelling indignantly. "She got me in the leg!"

Skinny had her down on her knees. "Come and cut me loose," I called to him, "and go find a phone."

Except for my wrists and ankles and shoulder and head, I felt fine.

"I hope you're satisfied," Inspector Cramer said sourly. "You and Goodwin have got your pictures in the paper again. You got no fee, but a lot of free publicity. I got my nose wiped."

Wolfe grunted comfortably.

The whole squad had been busy with chores: visiting W-J at the hospital; conversing with Mr. and Mrs. Carlisle at the D.A.'s office; starting to round up circumstantial evidence to show that Mr. Carlisle had furnished the necessary for Doris Hatten's rent and Mrs. Carlisle knew it; pestering Skinny; and other items. I had been glad to testify that Skinny, whose name was Herbert Marvel, was one-hundred-proof.

"What I chiefly came for," Cramer went on, "was to let you know that I realize there's nothing I can do. I know Cynthia Brown described her to Goodwin, and probably gave him her name, too, and Goodwin told you. And you wanted to hog it. I suppose you thought you could pry a fee out of somebody. Both of you suppressed evidence." He gestured. "Okay, I can't prove it. But I know it, and I want you to know I know it. And I'm not going to forget it."

"The trouble is," Wolfe murmured, "that if you can't prove you're right, and of course you can't, neither can I prove you're wrong."

"I would gladly try. How?"

Cramer leaned forward. "Like this: If she hadn't been described to Goodwin, how did you pick her for him to send that blackmail note to?"

Wolfe shrugged. "It was a calculation, as I told you. I concluded that the murderer was among those who remained until the body had been discovered. It was worth testing. If there had been no phone call in response to Mr. Goodwin's note, the calculation would have been discredited and I would—"

"Yeah, but why her?"

"There were only two women who remained. Obviously, it couldn't have been Mrs. Orwin; with her physique she would be hard put to pass as a man. Besides, she is a widow, and it was a sound presumption that Doris Hatten had been killed by a jealous wife, who—"

"But why a woman? Why not a man?"

"Oh, that." Wolfe picked up a glass of beer and drained it with more deliberation than usual. He was having a swell time. "I told you in my dining-room"—he pointed a finger—"that something had occurred to me and I wanted to consider it. Later, I would have been glad to tell you about it if you had not acted so irresponsibly and spitefully in sealing up this office. That made me doubt if you were capable of proceeding properly on any suggestion from me, so I decided to proceed, myself.

"What had occurred to me was simply this, that Miss Brown had told Mr. Goodwin that *she wouldn't have recognized 'him' if he hadn't had a hat on!* She used the masculine pronoun, naturally, throughout that conversation, because it had been a man who had called at Doris Hatten's apartment that October day, and he was fixed in her mind as a man. But it was in my plant-rooms that she had seen him that afternoon—*and no man wore his hat up there!* The men left their hats downstairs. Besides, I was there and saw them. *But nearly all the women had hats on.*"

Wolfe upturned a palm. "So it was a woman."

Cramer eyed him. "I don't believe it," he said flatly.

"You have a record of Mr. Goodwin's report of that conversation."

"I still wouldn't believe it."

"There were other little items." Wolfe wiggled a finger. "For example: The strangler of Doris Hatten had a key to the door. But surely the provider, who had so carefully avoided revealment, would not have marched in at an unexpected hour to risk encountering strangers. And who so likely to have found an opportunity, or contrived one, to secure a duplicate key as that provider's jealous wife?"

"Talk all day. I still don't believe it."

Well, I thought to myself, observing Wolfe's smirk and for once completely approving of it, Cramer the office-sealer has his choice of believing it or not.

As for me, I had no choice.

The Fat Man

ISAK DINESEN

On one November evening a horrible crime was committed in Oslo, the capital of Norway. A child was murdered in an uninhabited house on the outskirts of the town.

The newspapers brought long and detailed accounts of the murder. In the short, raw November days people stood in the street outside the house and stared up at it. The victim had been a workman's child, resentment of ancient wrongs stirred in the minds of the crowd.

The police had got but one single clue. A shopkeeper in the street told them that as he was closing up his shop on the evening of the murder he saw the murdered child walk by, her hand in the hand of a fat man.

The police had arrested some tramps and vagabonds and shady persons, but such people as a rule are not fat. So they looked elsewhere, among tradesmen and clerks of the neighborhood. Fat men were stared at in the streets. But the murderer had not been found.

In this same month of November a young student named Kristoffer Lovunden in Oslo was cramming for his examination. He had come down to the town from the north of Norway, where it is day half the year and night the other half and where people are different from other Norwegians. In a world of stone and concrete Kristoffer was sick with longing for the hills and the salt sea.

His people up in Norland were poor and could have no idea of what it cost to live in Oslo, he did not want to worry them for money. To be able to finish his studies he had taken a job as bartender at the Grand Hotel, and worked there every night from eight o'clock till midnight. He was a good-looking boy with gentle and polite manners, conscientious in the performance of his duties, and he did well as a bartender. He was abstinent himself, but took a kind of scientific interest in the composition of other people's drinks.

In this way he managed to keep alive and to go on with his lessons.

But he got too little sleep and too little time for ordinary human intercourse. He read no books outside his textbooks, and not even the newspapers, so that he did not know what was happening in the world around him. He was aware himself that this was not a healthy life, but the more he disliked it the harder he worked to get it over.

In the bar he was always tired, and he sometimes fell asleep standing up, with open eyes. The brilliant light and the noises made his head swim. But as he walked home from the Grand Hotel after midnight the cold air revived him so that he entered his small room wide awake. This he knew to be a dangerous hour. If now a thing caught his mind it would stick in it with unnatural vividness and keep him from sleep, and he would be no good for his books the next day. He had promised himself not to read at this time, and while he undressed to go to bed he closed his eyes.

All the same, one night his glance fell on a newspaper wrapped round a sausage that he had brought home with him. Here he read of the murder. The paper was two days old, people would have been talking about the crime around him all the time, but he had not heard what they said. The paper was torn, the ends of the lines were missing, he had to make them up from his own imagination. After that the thing would not leave him. The words "a fat man" set his mind running from one to another of the fat men he had ever known till at last it stopped at one of them.

There was an elegant fat gentleman who often visited the bar. Kristoffer knew him to be a writer, a poet of a particular, refined, half-mystical school. Kristoffer had read a few of his poems and had himself been fascinated by their queer, exquisite choice of words and symbols. They seemed to be filled with the colors of old precious stained glass. He often wrote about medieval legends and mysteries. This winter the theater was doing a play by him named *The Werewolf,* which was in parts macabre, according to its subject, but more remarkable still for its strange beauty and sweetness. The man's appearance too was striking. He was fat, with wavy dark hair, a large white face, a small red mouth, and curiously pale eyes. Kristoffer had been told that he had lived much abroad. It was the habit of this man to sit with his back to the bar, developing his exotic theories to a circle of young admirers. His name was Oswald Senjen.

Now the poet's picture took hold of the student. All night he seemed to see the big face close to his, with all kinds of expressions. He drank much cold water but was as hot as before. This fat man of the Grand Hotel, he thought, was the fat man of the newspaper.

It did not occur to him, in the morning, to play the part of a detective. If he went to the police they would send him away, since he had no facts whatever, no argument or reason even, to put before them. The fat man would have an alibi. He and his friends would laugh, they would think him mad or they would be indignant and complain to the manager of the hotel, and Kristoffer would lose his job.

So for three weeks the odd drama was played between the two actors only: the grave young bartender behind the bar and the smiling poet before it. The one was trying hard all the time to get out of it, the other knew nothing about it. Only once did the parties look each other in the face.

A few nights after Kristoffer had read about the murder, Oswald Senjen came into the bar with a friend. Kristoffer had no wish to spy upon them—it was against his own will that he moved to the side of the bar where they sat.

They were discussing fiction and reality. The friend held that to a poet the two must be one, and that therefore his existence must be mysteriously happy. The poet contradicted him. A poet's mission in life, he said, was to make others confound fiction with reality in order to render them, for an hour, mysteriously happy. But he himself must, more carefully than the crowd, hold the two apart. "Not as far as enjoyment of them is concerned," he added, "I enjoy fiction, I enjoy reality too. But I am happy because I have an unfailing instinct for distinguishing one from the other. I know fiction where I meet it. I know reality where I meet it."

This fragment of conversation stuck in Kristoffer's mind, he went over it many times. He himself had often before pondered on the idea of happiness and tried to find out whether such a thing really existed. He had asked himself if anybody was happy and, if so, who was happy. The two men at the bar had repeated the word more than once—they were probably happy. The fat man, who knew reality when he saw it, had said that he was happy.

Kristoffer remembered the shopkeeper's evidence. The face of the little girl Mattea, he had explained, when she passed him in the rainy street, had looked happy, as if, he said, she had been promised something, or was looking forward to something, and was skipping along toward it. Kristoffer thought: "And the man by her side?" Would his face have had an expression of happiness as well? Would he too have been looking forward to something? The shopkeeper had not had time to look the man in the face, he had seen only his back.

Night after night Kristoffer watched the fat man. At first he felt it to be a grim jest of fate that he must have this man with him wherever he went, while the man himself should hardly be aware of his existence.

But after a time he began to believe that his unceasing observation had an effect on the observed, and that he was somehow changing under it. He grew fatter and whiter, his eyes grew paler. At moments he was as absent-minded as Kristoffer himself. His pleasing flow of speech would run slower, with sudden unneeded pauses, as if the skilled talker could not find his words.

If Oswald Senjen stayed in the bar till it closed, Kristoffer would slip out while he was being helped into his furred coat in the hall, and wait for him outside. Most often Oswald Senjen's large car would be there, and he would get into it and glide off. But twice he slowly walked along the street, and Kristoffer followed him. The boy felt himself to be a mean, wild figure in the town and the night, sneaking after a man who had done him no harm, and about whom he knew nothing, and he hated the figure who was dragging him after it. The first time it seemed to him that the fat man turned his head a little to one side and the other as if to make sure that there was nobody close behind him. But the second time he walked on looking straight ahead, and Kristoffer then wondered if that first slight nervous movement had not been a creation of his own imagination.

One evening in the bar the poet turned in his deep chair and looked at the bartender.

Toward the end of November Kristoffer suddenly remembered that his examination was to begin within a week. He was dismayed and seized with pangs of conscience, he thought of his future and of his people up in Norland. The deep fear within him grew stronger. He must shake off his obsession or he would be ruined by it.

At this time an unexpected thing happened. One evening Oswald Senjen got up to leave early, his friends tried to hold him back but he would not stay. "Nay," he said, "I want a rest. I want to rest." When he had gone, one of his friends said: "He was looking bad tonight. He is much changed. Surely he has got something the matter with him." One of the others answered: "It is that old matter from when he was out in China. But he ought to look after himself. Tonight one might think that he would not last till the end of the year."

As Kristoffer listened to these assertions from an outside and real world he felt a sudden, profound relief. To this world the man himself, at least, was a reality. People talked about him.

"It might be a good thing," he thought, "it might be a way out if I could talk about the whole matter to somebody else."

He did not choose a fellow student for his confidant. He could imagine the kind of discussion this would bring about and his mind shrank from it. He turned for help to a simple soul, a boy two or three years younger than himself, who washed up at the bar and who was named Hjalmar.

Hjalmar was born and bred in Oslo, he knew all that could be known about the town and very little about anything outside it. He and Kristoffer had always been on friendly terms, and Hjalmar enjoyed a short chat with Kristoffer in the scullery, after working hours, because he knew that Kristoffer would not interrupt him. Hjalmar was a revolutionary spirit, and would hold forth on the worthless rich customers of the bar, who rolled home in big cars with gorgeous women with red lips and nails, while underpaid sailors hauled tarred ropes, and tired laborers led their plowhorses to the stable. Kristoffer wished that he would not do so, for at such times his nostalgia for boats and tar, and for the smell of a sweaty horse, grew so strong that it became a physical pain. And the deadly horror that he felt at the idea of driving home with one of the women Hjalmar described proved to him that his nervous system was out of order.

As soon as Kristoffer mentioned the murder to Hjalmar he found that the scullery boy knew everything about it. Hjalmar had his pockets filled with newspaper cuttings, from which he read reports of the crime and of the arrests, and angry letters about the slowness of the police.

Kristoffer was uncertain how to explain his theory to Hjalmar. In the end he said: "Do you know, Hjalmar, I believe that the fat gentleman in the bar is the murderer." Hjalmar stared at him, his mouth open. The next moment he had caught the idea, and his eyes shone.

After a short while Hjalmar proposed that they should go to the police, or again to a private detective. It took Kristoffer some time to convince his friend, as he had convinced himself, that their case was too weak, and that people would think them mad.

Then Hjalmar, more eager even than before, decided that they must be detectives themselves.

To Kristoffer it was a strange experience, both steadying and alarming, to face his own nightmare in the sharp white light of the scullery, and to hear it discussed by another live person. He felt that he was holding on to the scullery boy like a drowning man to a swimmer; every moment he feared to drag his rescuer down with him, into the dark sea of madness.

The next evening Hjalmar told Kristoffer that they would find some scheme by which to surprise the murderer and make him give himself away.

Kristoffer listened to his various suggestions for some time, then smiled a little. He said: "Hjalmar, thou art even such a man . . ." He stopped. "Nay," he said, "you will not know this piece, Hjalmar. But let me go on a little, all the same—!

> I have heard
> that guilty creatures sitting at a play
> have by the very cunning of the scene
> been struck so to the soul that presently
> they have proclaim'd their malefactions.
> For murder, though it have no tongue, will speak.

"I understand that very well," said Hjalmar.

"Do you, Hjalmar?" asked Kristoffer. "Then I shall tell you one thing more:

> the play's the thing
> wherein we'll catch the conscience of the king.

"Where have you got that from?" asked Hjalmar. "From a play called *Hamlet*," said Kristoffer. "And how do you mean to go and do it?" asked Hjalmar again. Kristoffer was silent for some time.

"Look here, Hjalmar," he said at last, "you told me that you have got a sister."

"Yes," said Hjalmar, "I have got five of them."

"But you have got one sister of nine," said Kristoffer, "the same age as Mattea?"

"Yes," said Hjalmar.

"And she has got," Kristoffer went on, "a school mackintosh with a hood to it, like the one Mattea had on that night?"

"Yes," said Hjalmar.

Kristoffer began to tremble. There was something blasphemous in the comedy which they meant to act. He could not have gone on with it if he had not felt that somehow his reason hung upon it.

"Listen, Hjalmar," he said, "we will choose an evening when the man is in the bar. Then make your little sister put on her mackintosh, and make one of your big sisters bring her here. Tell her to walk straight from the door, through all the room, up to the bar, to me, and to give me something—a letter or what you will. I shall give her a shilling for doing it, and she will take it from the counter when she has put the letter there. Then tell her to walk back again, through the room."

"Yes," said Hjalmar.

"If the manager complains," Kristoffer added after a while, "we will explain that it was all a misunderstanding."

"Yes," said Hjalmar.

"I myself," said Kristoffer, "must stay at the bar. I shall not see his face, for he generally sits with his back to me, talking to people. But you will leave the washing up for a short time, and go round and keep guard by the door. You will watch his face from there."

"There will be no need to watch his face," said Hjalmar, "he will scream or faint, or jump up and run away, you know."

"You must never tell your sister, Hjalmar," said Kristoffer, "why we made her come here."

"No, no," said Hjalmar.

On the evening decided upon for the experiment, Hjalmar was silent, set on his purpose. But Kristoffer was in two minds. Once or twice he came near to giving up the whole thing. But if he did so, and even if he could make Hjalmar understand and forgive—what would become of himself afterwards?

Oswald Senjen was in his chair in his usual position, with his back to the bar. Kristoffer was behind the bar, Hjalmar was at the swinging door of the hall, to receive his sister.

Through the glass door Kristoffer saw the child arrive in the hall, accompanied by an elder sister with a red feather in her hat, for in these winter months people did not let children walk alone in the streets at night. At the same time he became aware of something in the room that he had not noticed before. "I can never, till tonight," he told himself, "have been quite awake in this place, or I should have noticed it." To each side of the glass door there was a tall looking glass, in which he could see the faces turned away from him. In both of them he now saw Oswald Senjen's face.

The little girl in her mackintosh and hood had some difficulty opening the door, and was assisted by her brother. She walked straight up to the bar, neither fast nor slow, placed the letter on the counter, and collected her shilling. As she did so she lifted her small pale face in the hood slightly, and gave her brother's friend a little pert, gentle grin of acquittal—now that the matter was done with. Then she turned and walked back and out of the door, neither fast nor slow.

"Was it right?" she asked her brother who had been waiting for her by the door. Hjalmar nodded, but the child was puzzled at the expression of his face and looked at her big sister for an explanation. Hjalmar remained in the hall till he had seen the two girls disappear in the rainy street. Then the porter asked him what he was doing there, and he ran round to the back entrance and to his tub and glasses.

The next guest who ordered a drink at the bar looked at the bartender and said: "Hello, are you ill?" The bartender did not answer a word. He did not say a word either when, an hour later, as the bar closed, he joined his friend in the scullery.

"Well, Kristoffer," said Hjalmar, "he did not scream or faint, did he?"

"No," said Kristoffer.

Hjalmar waited a little. "If it is him," he said, "he is tough."

Kristoffer stood quite still for a long time, looking at the glasses. At last he said: "Do you know why he did not scream or faint?"

"No," said Hjalmar, "why was it?"

Kristoffer said: "Because he saw the only thing he expected to see. The only thing he ever sees now. All the other men in the bar gave some sign of surprise at the sight of a little girl in a mackintosh walking in here. I watched the fat man's face in the mirror, and saw that he looked straight at her as she came in, and that his eyes followed her as she walked out, but that his face did not change at all."

"What?" said Hjalmar. After a few moments he repeated very low: "What?"

"Yes, it is so," said Kristoffer. "A little girl in a mackintosh is the only thing he sees wherever he looks. She has been with him here in the bar before. And in the streets. And in his own house. For three weeks."

There was a long silence.

"Are we to go to the police now, Kristoffer?" Hjalmar asked.

"We need not go to the police," said Kristoffer. "We need not do anything in the matter. You and I are too heavy, or too grown up, for that. Mattea does it as it ought to be done. It is her small light step that has followed close on his own all the time. She looks at him, just as your sister looked at me, an hour ago. He wanted rest, he said. She will get it for him before the end of the year."

VARIATIONS
ON THE
CLASSIC FORM
OF MYSTERIES

FROM LONDON
TO AUSTRALIA

Lamb to the Slaughter

ROALD DAHL

The room was warm and clean, the curtains drawn, the two table lamps alight—hers and the one by the empty chair opposite. On the sideboard behind her, two tall glasses, soda water, whisky. Fresh ice cubes in the Thermos bucket.

Mary Maloney was waiting for her husband to come home from work.

Now and again she would glance up at the clock, but without anxiety, merely to please herself with the thought that each minute gone by made it nearer the time when he would come. There was a slow smiling air about her, and about everything she did. The drop of the head as she bent over her sewing was curiously tranquil. Her skin—for this was her sixth month with child—had acquired a wonderful translucent quality, the mouth was soft, and the eyes, with their new placid look, seemed larger, darker than before.

When the clock said ten minutes to five, she began to listen, and a few moments later, punctually as always she heard the tyres on the gravel outside, and the car door slamming, the footsteps passing the window, the key turning in the lock. She laid aside her sewing, stood up, and went forward to kiss him as he came in.

"Hullo, darling," she said.

"Hullo," he answered.

She took his coat and hung it in the closet. Then she walked over and made the drinks, a strongish one for him, a weak one for herself; and soon she was back again in her chair with the sewing, and he in the other, opposite, holding the tall glass with both his hands, rocking it so the ice cubes tinkled against the side.

For her, this was always a blissful time of day. She knew he didn't want to speak much until the first drink was finished, and she, on her side, was content to sit quietly, enjoying his company after the long hours alone in the house. She loved to luxuriate in the presence of this man, and to feel—almost as a sunbather feels the sun—that warm male glow that came out of him to her when they were alone together. She loved him for the way he sat loosely in a chair, for the way he came in a door, or moved slowly across the room with long strides. She loved the intent, far look in his eyes when they rested on her, the funny shape of the mouth, and especially, the way he remained silent about his tiredness, sitting still with himself until the whisky had taken some of it away.

"Tired, darling?"

"Yes," he said. "I'm tired." And as he spoke, he did an unusual thing. He lifted his glass and drained it in one swallow although there was still half of it, at least half of it, left. She wasn't really watching him but she knew what he had done because she heard the ice cubes falling back against the bottom of the empty glass when he lowered his arm. He paused a moment, leaning forward in the chair, then he got up and went slowly over to fetch himself another.

"I'll get it!" she cried, jumping up.

"Sit down," he said.

When he came back, she noticed that the new drink was dark amber with the quantity of whisky in it.

"Darling, shall I get your slippers?"

"No."

She watched him as he began to sip the dark yellow drink, and she could see little oily swirls in the liquid because it was so strong.

"I think it's a shame," she said, "that when a policeman gets to be as senior as you, they keep him walking about on his feet all day long."

He didn't answer, so she bent her head again and went on with her sewing; but each time he lifted the drink to his lips, she heard the ice cubes clicking against the side of the glass.

"Darling," she said. "Would you like me to get you some cheese? I haven't made any supper because it's Thursday."

"No," he said.

"If you're too tired to eat out," she went on, "it's still not too late. There's plenty of meat and stuff in the freezer, and you can have it right here and not even move out of the chair."

Her eyes waited on him for an answer, a smile, a little nod, but he made no sign.

"Anyway," she went on, "I'll get you some cheese and crackers first."

"I don't want it," he said.

She moved uneasily in her chair, the large eyes still watching his face. "But you *must* have supper. I can easily do it here. I'd like to do it. We can have lamb chops. Or pork. Anything you want. Everything's in the freezer."

"Forget it," he said.

"But, darling, you *must* eat! I'll fix it anyway, and then you can have it or not, as you like."

She stood up and placed her sewing on the table by the lamp.

"Sit down," he said. "Just for a minute, sit down."

It wasn't till then that she began to get frightened.

"Go on," he said. "Sit down."

She lowered herself back slowly into the chair, watching him all the time with those large, bewildered eyes. He had finished the second drink and was staring down into the glass, frowning.

"Listen," he said, "I've got something to tell you."

"What is it, darling? What's the matter?"

He had become absolutely motionless, and he kept his head down so that the light from the lamp beside him fell across the upper part of his face, leaving the chin and mouth in shadow. She noticed there was a little muscle moving near the corner of his left eye.

"This is going to be a bit of a shock to you, I'm afraid," he said. "But I've thought about it a good deal and I've decided the only thing to do is tell you right away. I hope you won't blame me too much."

And he told her. It didn't take long, four or five minutes at most, and she sat very still through it all, watching him with a kind of dazed horror as he went further and further away from her with each word.

"So there it is," he added. "And I know it's kind of a bad time to be telling you, but there simply wasn't any other way. Of course I'll give you money and see you're looked after. But there needn't really be any fuss. I hope not anyway. It wouldn't be very good for my job."

Her first instinct was not to believe any of it, to reject it all. It occurred to her that perhaps he hadn't even spoken, that she herself had imagined the whole thing. Maybe, if she went about her business and acted as though she hadn't been listening, then later, when she sort of woke up again, she might find none of it had ever happened.

"I'll get the supper," she managed to whisper, and this time he didn't stop her.

When she walked across the room she couldn't feel her feet touching the floor. She couldn't feel anything at all—except a slight nausea and a desire to vomit. Everything was automatic now—down the stairs to the cellar, the light switch, the deep freeze, the hand inside the cabinet taking hold of the first object it met. She lifted it out, and looked at it. It was wrapped in paper, so she took off the paper and looked at it again.

A leg of lamb.

All right then, they would have lamb for supper. She carried it up-stairs, holding the thin bone-end of it with both her hands, and as she went through the living-room, she saw him standing over by the window with his back to her, and she stopped.

"For God's sake," he said, hearing her, but not turning round. "Don't make supper for me. I'm going out."

At that point, Mary Maloney simply walked up behind him and with-out any pause she swung the big frozen leg of lamb high in the air and brought it down as hard as she could on the back of his head.

She might just as well have hit him with a steel club.

She stepped back a pace, waiting, and the funny thing was that he remained standing there for at least four or five seconds, gently swaying. Then he crashed to the carpet.

The violence of the crash, the noise, the small table overturning, helped bring her out of the shock. She came out slowly, feeling cold and surprised, and she stood for a while blinking at the body, still holding the ridiculous piece of meat tight with both hands.

All right, she told herself. So I've killed him.

It was extraordinary, now, how clear her mind became all of a sud-den. She began thinking very fast. As the wife of a detective, she knew quite well what the penalty would be. That was fine. It made no difference to her. In fact, it would be a relief. On the other hand, what about the child? What were the laws about murderers with unborn chil-dren? Did they kill them both—mother and child? Or did they wait until the tenth month? What did they do?

Mary Maloney didn't know. And she certainly wasn't prepared to take a chance.

She carried the meat into the kitchen, placed it in a pan, turned the oven on high, and shoved it inside. Then she washed her hands and ran upstairs to the bedroom. She sat down before the mirror, tidied her face, touched up her lips and face. She tried a smile. It came out rather peculiar. She tried again.

"Hullo Sam," she said brightly, aloud.

The voice sounded peculiar too.

"I want some potatoes please, Sam. Yes, and I think a can of peas."

That was better. Both the smile and the voice were coming out better now. She rehearsed it several times more. Then she ran downstairs, took her coat, went out the back door, down the garden, into the street.

It wasn't six o'clock yet and the lights were still on in the grocery shop.

"Hullo Sam," she said brightly, smiling at the man behind the counter.

"Why, good evening, Mrs. Maloney. How're *you?*"

"I want some potatoes please, Sam. Yes, and I think a can of peas."

The man turned and reached up behind him on the shelf for the peas.

"Patrick's decided he's tired and doesn't want to eat out tonight," she told him. "We usually go out Thursdays, you know, and now he's caught me without any vegetables in the house."

"Then how about meat, Mrs. Maloney?"

"No, I've got meat, thanks. I got a nice leg of lamb, from the freezer."

"Oh."

"I don't much like cooking it frozen, Sam, but I'm taking a chance on it this time. You think it'll be all right?"

"Personally," the grocer said, "I don't believe it makes any difference. You want these Idaho potatoes?"

"Oh yes, that'll be fine. Two of those."

"Anything else?" The grocer cocked his head on one side, looking at her pleasantly. "How about afterwards? What you going to give him for afterwards?"

"Well—what would you suggest, Sam?"

The man glanced around his shop. "How about a nice big slice of cheesecake? I know he likes that."

"Perfect," she said. "He loves it."

And when it was all wrapped and she had paid, she put on her brightest smile and said, "Thank you, Sam. Good night."

"Good night, Mrs. Maloney. And thank *you.*"

And now, she told herself as she hurried back, all she was doing now, she was returning home to her husband and he was waiting for his supper; and she must cook it good, and make it as tasty as possible because the poor man was tired; and if, when she entered the house, she happened to find anything unusual, or tragic, or terrible, then naturally it would be a shock and she'd become frantic with grief and horror. Mind you, she wasn't *expecting* to find anything. She was just going home with the vegetables. Mrs. Patrick Maloney going home with the vegetables on Thursday evening to cook supper for her husband.

That's the way, she told herself. Do everything right and natural. Keep things absolutely natural and there'll be no need for any acting at all.

Therefore, when she entered the kitchen by the back door, she was humming a little tune to herself and smiling.

"Patrick!" she called. "How are you, darling?"

She put the parcel down on the table and went through into the living-room; and when she saw him lying there on the floor with his legs doubled up and one arm twisted back underneath his body, it really was rather a shock. All the old love and longing for him welled up inside her, and she ran over to him, knelt down beside him, and began to cry her heart out. It was easy. No acting was necessary.

A few minutes later she got up and went to the phone. She knew the number of the police station, and when the man at the other end answered, she cried to him, "Quick! Come quick! Patrick's dead!"

"Who's speaking?"

"Mrs. Maloney. Mrs. Patrick Maloney."

"You mean Patrick Maloney's dead?"

"I think so," she sobbed. "He's lying on the floor and I think he's dead."

"Be right over," the man said.

The car came very quickly, and when she opened the front door, two policemen walked in. She knew them both—she knew nearly all the men at that precinct—and she fell right into Jack Noonan's arms, weeping hysterically. He put her gently into a chair, then went over to join the other one, who was called O'Malley, kneeling by the body.

"Is he dead?" she cried.

"I'm afraid he is. What happened?"

Briefly, she told her story about going out to the grocer and coming back to find him on the floor. While she was talking, crying and talking, Noonan discovered a small patch of congealed blood on the dead man's head. He showed it to O'Malley who got up at once and hurried to the phone.

Soon, other men began to come into the house. First a doctor, then two detectives, one of whom she knew by name. Later, a police photographer arrived and took pictures, and a man who knew about fingerprints. There was a great deal of whispering and muttering beside the corpse, and the detectives kept asking her a lot of questions. But they always treated her kindly. She told her story again, this time right from the beginning, when Patrick had come in, and she was sewing, and he was tired, so tired he hadn't wanted to go out for supper. She told how she'd put the meat in the oven—"it's there now, cooking"—and how she'd slipped out to the grocer for vegetables, and come back to find him lying on the floor.

"Which grocer?" one of the detectives asked.

She told him, and he turned and whispered something to the other detective who immediately went outside into the street.

In fifteen minutes he was back with a page of notes and there was more whispering, and through her sobbing she heard a few of the whispered phrases—". . . acted quite normal . . . very cheerful . . . wanted to give him a good supper . . . peas . . . cheesecake . . . impossible that she . . ."

After a while, the photographer and the doctor departed and two other men came in and took the corpse away on a stretcher. Then the fingerprint man went away. The two detectives remained, and so did the two policemen. They were exceptionally nice to her, and Jack Noonan asked if she wouldn't rather go somewhere else, to her sister's house perhaps, or to his own wife who would take care of her and put her up for the night.

No, she said. She didn't feel she could move even a yard at the moment. Would they mind awfully if she stayed just where she was until she felt better? She didn't feel too good at the moment, she really didn't.

Then hadn't she better lie down on the bed? Jack Noonan asked.

No, she said, she'd like to stay right where she was, in this chair. A little later perhaps, when she felt better, she would move.

So they left her there while they went about their business, searching the house. Occasionally one of the detectives asked her another question. Sometimes Jack Noonan spoke to her gently as he passed by. Her husband, he told her, had been killed by a blow on the back of the head administered with a heavy blunt instrument, almost certainly a large piece of metal. They were looking for the weapon. The murderer may have taken it with him, but on the other hand he may've thrown it away or hidden it somewhere on the premises.

"It's the old story," he said. "Get the weapon, and you've got the man."

Later, one of the detectives came up and sat beside her. Did she know, he asked, of anything in the house that could've been used as the weapon? Would she mind having a look around to see if anything was missing—a very big spanner, for example, or a heavy metal vase.

They didn't have any heavy metal vases, she said.

"Or a big spanner?"

She didn't think they had a big spanner. But there might be some things like that in the garage.

The search went on. She knew that there were other policemen in the garden all around the house. She could hear their footsteps on the gravel outside, and sometimes she saw the flash of a torch through a chink in the curtains. It began to get late, nearly nine she noticed by the clock on the mantel. The four men searching the rooms seemed to be growing weary, a trifle exasperated.

"Jack," she said, the next time Sergeant Noonan went by. "Would you mind giving me a drink?"

"Sure I'll give you a drink. You mean this whisky?"

"Yes, please. But just a small one. It might make me feel better."

He handed her the glass.

"Why don't you have one yourself," she said. "You must be awfully tired. Please do. You've been very good to me."

"Well," he answered. "It's not strictly allowed, but I might take just a drop to keep me going."

One by one the others came in and were persuaded to take a little nip of whisky. They stood around rather awkwardly with the drinks in their hands, uncomfortable in her presence, trying to say consoling things to her. Sergeant Noonan wandered into the kitchen, came out quickly and said, "Look, Mrs. Maloney. You know that oven of yours is still on, and the meat still inside."

"Oh *dear* me!" she cried. "So it is!"

"I better turn it off for you, hadn't I?"

"Will you do that, Jack? Thank you so much."

When the sergeant returned the second time, she looked at him with her large, dark eyes. "Jack Noonan," she said.

"Yes?"

"Would you do me a small favour—you and these others?"

"We can try, Mrs. Maloney."

"Well," she said. "Here you all are, and good friends of dear Patrick's too, and helping to catch the man who killed him. You must be terribly hungry by now because it's long past your supper time, and I know Patrick would never forgive me, God bless his soul, if I allowed you to remain in his house without offering you decent hospitality. Why don't you eat up that lamb that's in the oven? It'll be cooked just right by now."

"Wouldn't dream of it," Sergeant Noonan said.

"Please," she begged. "Please eat it. Personally I couldn't touch a thing, certainly not what's been in the house when he was here. But it's all right for you. It'd be a favour to me if you'd eat it up. Then you can go on with your work again afterwards."

There was a good deal of hesitating among the four policemen, but they were clearly hungry, and in the end they were persuaded to go into the kitchen and help themselves. The woman stayed where she was, listening to them through the open door, and she could hear them speaking among themselves, their voices thick and sloppy because their mouths were full of meat.

"Have some more, Charlie?"

"No. Better not finish it."

"She *wants* us to finish it. She said so. Be doing her a favour."

"Okay then. Give me some more."

"That's the hell of a big club the guy must've used to hit poor Patrick," one of them was saying. "The doc says his skull was smashed all to pieces just like from a sledge-hammer."

"That's why it ought to be easy to find."

"Exactly what I say."

"Whoever done it, they're not going to be carrying a thing like that around with them longer than they need."

One of them belched.

"Personally, I think it's right here on the premises."

"Probably right under our very noses. What you think, Jack?"

And in the other room, Mary Maloney began to giggle.

Great-Aunt Allie's Flypapers

P. D. JAMES

"You see, my dear Adam," explained the Canon gently as he walked with Chief Superintendent Dalgliesh under the vicarage elms, "useful as the legacy would be to us, I wouldn't feel happy in accepting it if Great-Aunt Allie came by her money in the first place by wrongful means."

What the Canon meant was that he and his wife wouldn't be happy to inherit Great-Aunt Allie's fifty thousand pounds or so if, sixty-seven years earlier, she had poisoned her elderly husband with arsenic in order to get it. As Great-Aunt Allie had been accused and acquitted of just that charge in a 1902 trial which, for her Hampshire neighbours, had rivalled the Coronation as a public spectacle, the Canon's scruples were not altogether irrelevant. Admittedly, thought Dalgliesh, most people, faced with the prospect of fifty thousand pounds, would be happy to subscribe to the commonly accepted convention that once an English court has pronounced its verdict, the final truth of the matter has been established once and for all. There may possibly be a higher judicature in the next world, but hardly in this. And so Hubert Boxdale might normally have been happy to believe. But faced with the prospect of an unexpected fortune, his scrupulous conscience was troubled. The gentle but obstinate voice went on:

"Apart from the moral principle of accepting tainted money, it wouldn't bring us happiness. I often think of the poor woman driven restlessly around Europe in her search for peace, of that lonely life and unhappy death."

Dalgliesh recalled that Great-Aunt Allie had moved in a predictable progress with her retinue of servants, current lover and general hangers-on from one luxury Riviera hotel to the next, with stays in Paris or Rome as the mood suited her. He was not sure that this orderly program of comfort and entertainment could be described as being restlessly driven around Europe or that the old lady had been primarily in search of peace. She had died, he recalled, by falling overboard from a millionaire's yacht during a rather wild party given by him to celebrate her eighty-eighth birthday. It was perhaps not an edifying death by the Canon's standards, but he doubted whether she had, in fact, been unhappy at the time. Great-Aunt Allie (it was impossible to think of her by any other name), if she had been capable of coherent thought, would probably have pronounced it a very good way to go. But this was hardly a point of view he could put to his companion.

Canon Hubert Boxdale was Superintendent Adam Dalgliesh's godfather. Dalgliesh's father had been his Oxford contemporary and lifelong friend. He had been an admirable godfather, affectionate, uncensorious, genuinely concerned. In Dalgliesh's childhood he had been mindful of birthdays and imaginative about a small boy's preoccupations and desires. Dalgliesh was very fond of him and privately thought him one of the few really good men he had known. It was only surprising that the Canon had managed to live to seventy-one in a carnivorous world in which gentleness, humility and unworldliness are hardly conducive to survival, let alone success. But his goodness had in some sense protected him. Faced with such manifest innocence, even those who exploited him, and they were not a few, extended some of the protection and compassion they might show to the slightly subnormal.

"Poor old darling," his daily woman would say, pocketing pay for six hours when she had worked five and helping herself to a couple of eggs from his refrigerator. "He's really not fit to be let out alone." It had surprised the then young and slightly priggish Detective Constable Dalgliesh to realize that the Canon knew perfectly well about the hours and the eggs, but thought that Mrs. Copthorne with five children and an indolent husband needed both more than he did. He also knew that if he started paying for five hours, she would promptly work only four and extract another two eggs and that this small and only dishonesty was somehow necessary to her self-esteem. He was good. But he was not a fool.

He and his wife were, of course, poor. But they were not unhappy; indeed, it was a word impossible to associate with the Canon. The death of his two sons in the 1939 war had saddened but not destroyed him. But he had anxieties. His wife was suffering from disseminated sclerosis and was finding it increasingly hard to manage. There were comforts and appliances which she would need. He was now, belatedly, about to retire and his pension would be small. The legacy would enable them both to live in comfort for the rest of their lives and would also, Dalgliesh had no doubt, give them the pleasure of doing more for their various lame dogs. Really, he thought, the Canon was an almost embarrass-ingly deserving candidate for a modest fortune. Why couldn't the dear silly old noodle take the cash and stop worrying? He said cunningly:

"She was found not guilty, you know, by an English jury, and it all happened nearly seventy years ago. Couldn't you bring yourself to ac-cept their verdict?"

But the Canon's scrupulous mind was impervious to such sly innu-endos. Dalgliesh told himself that he should have remembered what, as a small boy, he had discovered about Uncle Hubert's conscience; that it operated as a warning bell and that, unlike most people, he never pre-tended that it hadn't sounded or that he hadn't heard it or that, having heard it, something must be wrong with the mechanism.

"Oh, I did accept it while she was alive. We never met, you know. I didn't wish to force myself on her. After all, she was a wealthy woman. Our ways of life were very different. But I usually wrote briefly at Christmas and she sent a card in reply. I wanted to keep some contact in case, one day, she might want someone to turn to and would re-member that I am a priest."

And why should she want a priest? thought Dalgliesh. To clear her conscience? Was that what the dear old boy had in mind? So he must have had doubts from the beginning. But of course he had! Dalgliesh knew something of the story, and the general feeling of the family and friends was that Great-Aunt Allie had been extremely lucky to escape the gallows. His own father's view, expressed with reticence, reluctance and compassion, had not in essentials differed from that given by a local reporter at the time:

"How on earth did she expect to get away with it? Damn lucky to es-cape topping, if you ask me."

"The news of the legacy came as a complete surprise?" asked Dal-gliesh.

"Indeed, yes. We never met except at that first and only Christmas six weeks after her marriage, when my grandfather died. We always talk of her as Great-Aunt Allie, but in fact, as you know, she married my grandfather. But it seemed impossible to think of her as a step-grand-mother. There was the usual family gathering at Colebrook Croft at the time and I was there with my parents and my twin sisters. I was only four and the twins were barely eight months old. I can remember noth-ing of my grandfather or of his wife. After the murder—if one has to use that dreadful word—my mother returned home with us children, leaving my father to cope with the police, the solicitors and the newsmen. It was a terrible time for him. I don't think I was even told that Grandfa-ther was dead until about a year later. My old nurse, who had been given Christmas as a holiday to visit her own family, told me that soon after my return home, I asked her if Grandfather was now young and beautiful for always. She, poor woman, took it as a sign of infant prognostication and piety. Poor Nellie was sadly superstitious and sentimental, I'm afraid. But I knew nothing of Grandfather's death at the time and certainly can recall nothing of the visit or of my new step-grandmother. Mercifully, I was little more than a baby when the murder was done."

"She was a music hall artiste, wasn't she?" asked Dalgliesh.

"Yes, and a very talented one. My grandfather met her when she was working with a partner in a hall in Cannes. He had gone to the south of France with a manservant for his health. I understand that she extracted a gold watch from his chain and when he claimed it, told him that he was English, had recently suffered from a stomach ailment, had two sons and a daughter and was about to have a wonderful surprise. It was all correct except that his only daughter had died in childbirth, leaving him a granddaughter, Marguerite Goddard."

"And all easily guessable from his voice and appearance," said Dalgliesh. "I suppose the surprise was the marriage?"

"It was certainly a surprise, and a most unpleasant one, for the family. It is easy to deplore the snobbishness and the conventions of another age, and indeed there was much in Edwardian England to deplore. But it was not a propitious marriage. I think of the difference in background, education and way of life, the lack of common interest. And there was this great disparity of age. My grandfather had married a girl just three months younger than his own granddaughter. I cannot wonder that the family were concerned; that they felt that the union could not in the end contribute to the contentment or happiness of either party."

And that was putting it charitably, thought Dalgliesh. The marriage certainly hadn't contributed to their happiness. From the point of view of the family, it had been a disaster. He recalled hearing of an incident when the local vicar and his wife, a couple who had actually dined at Colebrook Croft on the night of the murder, first called on the bride. Apparently old Augustus Boxdale had introduced her by saying:

"Meet the prettiest little variety artiste in the business. Took a gold watch and note case off me without any trouble. Would have had the elastic out of my pants if I hadn't watched out. Anyway, she stole my heart, didn't you, sweetheart?" All this accompanied by a hearty slap on the rump and a squeal of delight from the lady, who had promptly demonstrated her skill by extracting the Reverend Venables's bunch of keys from his left ear.

Dalgliesh thought it tactful not to remind the Canon of this story.

"What do you wish me to do, sir?" he inquired.

"It's asking a great deal, I know, when you're so busy at the Yard. But if I had your assurance that you believed in Aunt Allie's innocence, I should feel happy about accepting the bequest. I wondered if it would be possible for you to see the records of the trial. Perhaps it would give you a clue. You're so clever at this sort of thing."

He spoke with no intention to flatter but with an innocent wonder at the peculiar avocations of men. Dalgliesh was, indeed, very clever at this sort of thing. A dozen or so men at present occupying security wings in Her Majesty's prisons could testify to Chief Superintendent Dalgliesh's cleverness, as indeed could a handful of others walking free whose defending counsel had been in their way as clever as Chief Superintendent Dalgliesh. But to reexamine a case over sixty years old seemed to require clairvoyance rather than cleverness. The trial judge and both learned counsel had been dead for over fifty years. Two world wars had taken their toll. Four reigns had passed. It was probable that of those who had slept under the roof of Colebrook Croft on that fateful Boxing Day night of 1901, only the Canon still survived.

But the old man was troubled and had sought his help. And Dalgliesh, with nearly a week's leave due to him, had the time to give it.

"I'll see what I can do," he promised.

The transcript of a trial which had taken place sixty-seven years ago took time and trouble to obtain even for a chief superintendent of the Metropolitan Police. It provided little potential comfort for the Canon. Mr. Justice Medlock had summed up with that avuncular simplicity with which he was wont to address juries, regarding them, apparently, as a panel of well-intentioned but cretinous children. But the salient facts could have been comprehended by any intelligent child. Part of the summing up set them out with admirable lucidity:

And so, gentlemen of the jury, we come to the evening of 26 December. Mr. Augustus Boxdale, who had perhaps indulged a little unwisely on Christmas Day and at luncheon, had retired to rest in his dressing room at three o'clock, suffering from a slight recurrence of the digestive trouble which had afflicted him for most of his life. You have heard that he had taken luncheon with members of his family and ate nothing which they, too, did not eat. You may feel that you can acquit that luncheon of anything worse than overrichness. Mr. Boxdale, as was his habit, did not take afternoon tea.

Dinner was served at 8 P.M. promptly, as was the custom at Colebrook Croft. Members of the jury, you must be very clear who was present at that meal. There was the accused, Mrs. Augustus Boxdale; there was her husband's elder son, Captain Maurice Boxdale, with his wife; the younger son, the Reverend Edward Boxdale, with his wife; the deceased's granddaughter, Miss Marguerite Goddard, and there were two neighbours, the Reverend and Mrs. Henry Venables.

You have heard how the accused took only the first course at dinner, which was ragout of beef, and then left the dining room, saying that she wished to sit with her husband. That was about eight-twenty. Shortly after nine o'clock, she rang for the parlour-maid, Mary Huddy, and ordered a basin of gruel to be brought up to Mr. Boxdale. You have heard that the deceased was fond of gruel, and indeed, as prepared by Mrs. Muncie, the cook, it sounds a most nourishing and comforting dish for an elderly gentleman of weak digestion.

You have heard Mrs. Muncie describe how she prepared the gruel, according to Mrs. Beeton's admirable recipe, in the presence of Mary Huddy, in case, as she said, "The master should take a fancy to it when I'm not at hand and you have to make it." After the gruel had been prepared, Mrs. Muncie tasted it with a spoon and Mary Huddy carried it upstairs to the main bedroom, together with a small jug of water in case it should be too strong. As she reached the door, Mrs. Boxdale came out, her hands full of stockings and underclothes. She has told you that she was on her way to the bathroom to wash them through. She asked the girl to put the basin of gruel on the washstand to cool and Mary Huddy did so in her presence. Miss Huddy has told you that, at the time, she noticed the bowl of flypapers soaking in water and she knew that this solution was one used by Mrs. Boxdale as a cosmetic wash. Indeed, all the women who spent that evening in the house, with the exception of Mrs. Venables, have told you that they knew that it was Mrs. Boxdale's practice to prepare this solution of flypapers.

Mary Huddy and the accused left the bedroom together and you have heard the evidence of Mrs. Muncie that Miss Huddy returned to the kitchen after an absence of only a few minutes. Shortly after nine o'clock, the ladies left the dining room and entered the drawing room to take coffee. At nine-fifteen, Miss Goddard excused herself to the company and said that she would go to see if her grandfather needed anything. The time is established precisely because the clock struck the quarter hour as she left and Mrs. Venables commented on the sweetness of its chime. You have also heard Mrs. Venables's evidence and the evidence of Mrs. Maurice Boxdale and Mrs. Edward Boxdale that none of the ladies left the drawing room during the evening, and Mr. Venables has testified that the three gentlemen remained together until Miss Goddard appeared about three quarters of an hour later to inform them that her grandfather had become very ill and to request that the doctor be sent for immediately.

Miss Goddard has told you that when she entered her grandfather's room, he was just beginning his gruel and was grumbling about its taste. She got the impression that this was merely a protest at being deprived of his dinner rather than that he genuinely considered that there was something wrong with the gruel. At any rate, he finished most of it and appeared to enjoy it despite his grumbles.

You have heard Miss Goddard describe how, after her grandfather had had as much as he wanted of the gruel, she took the bowl next door and left it on the washstand. She then returned to her grandfather's bedroom and Mr. Boxdale, his wife and his granddaughter played three-handed whist for about three quarters of an hour.

At ten o'clock, Mr. Augustus Boxdale complained of feeling very ill. He suffered from griping pains in the stomach, from sickness and from looseness of the bowel. As soon as the symptoms began, Miss Goddard went downstairs to let her uncles know that her grandfather was worse and to ask that Dr. Eversley should be sent for urgently. Dr. Eversley has given you his evidence. He arrived at Colebrook Croft at 10:30 P.M., when he found his patient very distressed and weak. He treated the symptoms and gave what relief he could, but Mr. Augustus Boxdale died shortly before midnight.

Gentlemen of the jury, you have heard Marguerite Goddard describe how, as her grandfather's paroxysms increased in intensity, she remembered the gruel and wondered whether it could have disagreed with him in some way. She mentioned this possibility to her elder uncle, Captain Maurice Boxdale. Captain Boxdale has told you how he at once handed the bowl with its residue of gruel to Dr. Eversley with the request that the doctor should lock it in a cupboard in the library, seal the lock and himself keep the key. You have heard how the contents of the bowl were later analyzed and with what result.

An extraordinary precaution for the gallant captain to have taken, thought Dalgliesh, and a most perspicacious young woman. Was it by chance or by design that the bowl hadn't been taken down to be washed as soon as the old man had finished with it? Why was it, he wondered, that Marguerite Goddard hadn't rung for the parlourmaid and requested her to remove it? Miss Goddard appeared the only other suspect. He wished that he knew more about her.

But except for the main protagonists, the characters in the drama did not emerge very clearly from the trial report. Why, indeed, should they? The accusatorial legal system is designed to answer one question. Is the accused guilty beyond reasonable doubt of the crime charged? Exploration of the nuances of personality, interesting speculation and common gossip have no place in the witness box. Was it really possible after nearly seventy years that these dry bones could live?

The two Boxdale brothers came out as very dull fellows indeed. They and their estimable and respectable sloping-bosomed wives had sat at dinner in full view of each other from eight until nearly nine o'clock (a substantial meal, that dinner) and had said so in the witness box in more or less identical words. The bosoms of the ladies might have been heaving with far from estimable emotions of dislike, envy, embarrassment or resentment of the interloper. If so, they didn't choose to tell the court. But the two brothers and their wives were clearly innocent, even if it had been possible to conceive of the guilt of gentlefolk so respected, so eminently respectable. Even their impeccable alibis for the period after dinner had a nice touch of social and sexual distinction. The Reverend Henry Venables had vouched for the gentlemen; his good wife for the ladies.

Besides, what motive had they? They could no longer gain financially by the old man's death. If anything, it was in their interests to keep him alive in the hope that disillusionment with his marriage or a return to relative sanity might occur to cause him to change his will.

And the rest of the witnesses gave no help. Dalgliesh read all their testimony carefully. The pathologist's evidence. The doctor's evidence. The evidence of Allegra Boxdale's visit to the village store, where, from among the clutter of pots and pans, ointments and liniments, it had been possible to find a dozen flypapers for a customer even in the depth of an English winter. The evidence of the cook. The evidence of the parlourmaid. The remarkably lucid and confident evidence of the granddaughter. There was nothing in any of it which could cause him to give the Canon the assurance for which he hoped.

It was then that he remembered Aubrey Glatt. Glatt was a wealthy amateur criminologist who had made a study of all the notable Victorian and Edwardian poison cases. He was not interested in anything earlier or later, being as obsessively wedded to his period as any serious historian, which indeed he had some claim to call himself. He lived in a Georgian house in Winchester—his affection for the Victorian and Edwardian age did not extend to its architecture—and was only three miles from Colebrook Croft. A visit to the London Library disclosed that he hadn't written a book on the case, but it was improbable that he had totally neglected a crime so close at hand and so in period. Dalgliesh had occasionally helped him with technical details of police procedure. Glatt, in response to a telephone call, was happy to return the favour with the offer of afternoon tea and information.

Tea was served in his elegant drawing room by a parlourmaid in goffered cap with streamers. Dalgliesh wondered what wage Glatt paid her to persuade her to wear it. She looked as if she could have played a role in any of his favourite Victorian dramas, and Dalgliesh had an uncomfortable thought that arsenic might be dispensed with the cucumber sandwiches.

Glatt nibbled away and was expansive.

"It's interesting that you should have taken this sudden and, if I may say so, somewhat inexplicable interest in the Boxdale murder. I got out my notebook on the case only yesterday. Colebrook Croft is being demolished to make way for a new housing estate and I thought I might visit it for the last time. The family, of course, hasn't lived there since the 1914–18 war. Architecturally it's completely undistinguished, but one hates to see it go. We might motor over after tea if you are agreeable.

"I never completed my book on the case, you know. I planned a work entitled *The Colebrook Croft Mystery, or Who Killed Augustus Boxdale?* But alas, the answer was all too obvious."

"No real mystery?" suggested Dalgliesh.

"Who else could it have been but the bride? She was born Allegra Porter, incidentally. Allegra. An extraordinary name. Do you suppose her mother could have been thinking of Byron? I imagine not. There's a picture of Allie on page two of the notebook, by the way, taken in Cannes on her wedding day. I call it 'Beauty and the Beast.'"

The photograph had scarcely faded and Great-Aunt Allie smiled plainly at Dalgliesh across nearly seventy years. Her broad face with its wide mouth and rather snub nose was framed by two wings of dark hair swept high and topped, in the fashion of the day, by an immense flowered hat. The features were too coarse for real beauty, but the eyes were magnificent, deep-set and well-spaced; the chin was round and determined. Beside this vital young Amazon poor Augustus Boxdale, smiling fatuously at the camera and clutching his bride's arm as if for support, was but a frail and pathetic beast. Their pose was unfortunate. She looked as if she were about to fling him over her shoulder.

Glatt shrugged. "The face of a murderess? I've known less likely ones. Her counsel suggested, of course, that the old man had poisoned his own gruel during the short time she left it on the washstand to cool while she visited the bathroom. But why should he? All the evidence suggests that he was in a state of postnuptial euphoria, poor senile old booby. Our Augustus was in no hurry to leave this world, particularly by such an agonizing means. Besides, I doubt whether he even knew the gruel was there. He was in bed next door in his dressing room, remember."

Dalgliesh asked, "What about Marguerite Goddard? There's no evidence about the exact time when she entered the bedroom."

"I thought you'd get on to that. She could have arrived while her step-grandmother was in the bathroom, poisoned the gruel, hidden herself either in the main bedroom or elsewhere until it had been taken in to Augustus, then joined her grandfather and his bride as if she had just come upstairs. It's possible, I admit. But is it likely? She was less inconvenienced than any of the family by her grandfather's second marriage. Her mother was Augustus Boxdale's eldest child and married, very young, a wealthy patent medicine manufacturer. She died in childbirth and the husband only survived her by a year. Marguerite Goddard was an heiress. She was also most advantageously engaged to Captain the Honourable John Brize-Lacey. It was quite a catch for a Boxdale—or a Goddard. Marguerite Goddard, young, beautiful, secure in the possession of the Goddard fortune, not to mention the Goddard emeralds and the eldest son of a lord, was hardly a serious suspect. In my view defence counsel—that was Roland Gort Lloyd—was wise to leave her strictly alone."

"It was a memorable defence, I believe."

"Magnificent. There's no doubt Allegra Boxdale owed her life to Gort Lloyd. I know that concluding speech by heart:

" 'Gentlemen of the jury, I beseech you in the sacred name of justice to consider what you are at. It is your responsibility and yours alone to decide the fate of this young woman. She stands before you now, young, vibrant, glowing with health, the years stretching before her with their promise and their hopes. It is in your power to cut off all this as you might top a nettle with one swish of your cane. To condemn her to the slow torture of those last waiting weeks; to that last dreadful walk; to heap calumny on her name; to desecrate those few happy weeks of marriage with the man who loved her so greatly; to cast her into the final darkness of an ignominious grave.'

"Pause for dramatic effect. Then the crescendo in that magnificent voice. 'And on what evidence, gentlemen? I ask you.' Another pause. Then the thunder. 'On what evidence?' "

"A powerful defence," said Dalgliesh. "But I wonder how it would go down with a modern judge and jury."

"Well, it went down very effectively with that 1902 jury. Of course, the abolition of capital punishment has rather cramped the more histrionic style. I'm not sure that the reference to topping nettles was in the best of taste. But the jury got the message. They decided that, on the whole, they preferred not to have the responsibility of sending the accused to the gallows. They were out six hours reaching their verdict and it was greeted with some applause. If any of those worthy citizens had been asked to wager five pounds of their own good money on her innocence, I suspect that it would have been a different matter. Allegra Boxdale had helped him, of course. The Criminal Evidence Act, passed three years earlier, enabled him to put her in the witness box. She wasn't an actress of a kind for nothing. Somehow she managed to persuade the jury that she had genuinely loved the old man."

"Perhaps she had," suggested Dalgliesh. "I don't suppose there had been much kindness in her life. And he was kind."

"No doubt. No doubt. But love!" Glatt was impatient. "My dear Dalgliesh? He was a singularly ugly old man of sixty-nine. She was an attractive girl of twenty-one!"

Dalgliesh doubted whether love, that iconoclastic passion, was susceptible to this kind of simple arithmetic, but he didn't argue. Glatt went on:

"And the prosecution couldn't suggest any other romantic attachment. The police got in touch with her previous partner, of course. He was discovered to be a bald, undersized little man, sharp as a weasel, with a buxom uxorious wife and five children. He had moved down the coast after the partnership broke up and was now working with a new girl. He said regretfully that she was coming along nicely, thank you, gentlemen, but would never be a patch on Allie, and that if Allie got her neck out of the noose and ever wanted a job, she knew where to come. It was obvious even to the most suspicious policeman that his interest was purely professional. As he said, what was a grain or two of arsenic between friends?

"The Boxdales had no luck after the trial. Captain Maurice Boxdale was killed in 1916, leaving no children, and the Reverend Edward lost his wife and their twin daughters in the 1918 influenza epidemic. He survived until 1932. The boy Hubert may still be alive, but I doubt it. That family were a sickly lot.

"My greatest achievement, incidentally, was in tracing Marguerite Goddard. I hadn't realized that she was still alive. She never married Brize-Lacey or, indeed, anyone else. He distinguished himself in the 1914–18 war, came successfully through, and eventually married an eminently suitable young woman, the sister of a brother officer. He inherited the title in 1925 and died in 1953. But Marguerite Goddard may be alive now, for all I know. She may even be living in the same modest Bournemouth hotel where I found her. Not that my efforts in tracing her were rewarded. She absolutely refused to see me. That's the note that she sent out to me, by the way."

It was meticulously pasted into the notebook in its chronological order and carefully annotated. Aubrey Glatt was a natural researcher; Dalgliesh couldn't help wondering whether this passion for accuracy might not have been more rewardingly spent than in the careful documentation of murder.

The note was written in an elegant upright hand, the strokes black and very thin but unwavering.

Miss Goddard presents her compliments to Mr. Aubrey Glatt. She did not murder her grandfather and has neither the time nor the inclination to gratify his curiosity by discussing the person who did.

Aubrey Glatt said, "After that extremely disobliging note I felt there was really no point in going on with the book."

Glatt's passion for Edwardian England extended to more than its murders and they drove to Colebrook Croft, high above the green Hampshire lanes, in an elegant 1910 Daimler. Aubrey wore a thin tweed coat and deerstalker hat and looked, Dalgliesh thought, rather like a Sherlock Holmes, with himself as attendant Watson.

"We are only just in time, my dear Dalgliesh," he said when they arrived. "The engines of destruction are assembled. That ball on a chain looks like the eyeball of God, ready to strike. Let us make our number with the attendant artisans. You as a guardian of the law will have no wish to trespass."

The work of demolition had not yet begun, but the inside of the house had been stripped and plundered. The great rooms echoed to their footsteps like gaunt and deserted barracks after the final retreat. They moved from room to room, Glatt mourning the forgotten glories of an age he had been born thirty years too late to enjoy, Dalgliesh with his mind on more immediate and practical concerns.

The design of the house was simple and formalized. The second floor, on which were most of the main bedrooms, had a long corridor running the whole length of the façade. The master bedroom was at the southern end, with two large windows giving a distant view of Winchester Cathedral tower. A communicating door led to a small dressing room.

The main corridor had a row of four identical large windows. The curtain rods and rings had been removed, but the ornate carved pelmets were still in place. Here must have hung pairs of heavy curtains giving cover to anyone who wished to slip out of view. And Dalgliesh noted with interest that one of the windows was exactly opposite the door of the main bedroom. By the time they had left Colebrook Croft and Glatt had dropped him at Winchester station, Dalgliesh was beginning to formulate a theory.

His next move was to trace Marguerite Goddard if she was still alive. It took him nearly a week of weary searching, a frustrating trail along the south coast from hotel to hotel. Almost everywhere his inquiries were met with defensive hostility. It was the usual story of a very old lady who had become more demanding, arrogant and eccentric as her health and fortune had waned; an unwelcome embarrassment to manager and fellow guests alike. The hotels were all modest, a few almost sordid. What, he wondered, had become of the Goddard fortune? From the last landlady he learned that Miss Goddard had become ill, really very sick indeed, and had been removed six months previously to the local district general hospital. And it was there that he found her.

The ward sister was surprisingly young, a petite, dark-haired girl with a tired face and challenging eyes.

"Miss Goddard is very ill. We've put her in one of the side wards. Are you a relative? If so, you're the first one who has bothered to call and you're lucky to be in time. When she is delirious she seems to expect a Captain Brize-Lacey to call. You're not he, by any chance?"

"Captain Brize-Lacey will not be calling. No, I'm not a relative. She doesn't even know me. But I would like to visit her if she's well enough and is willing to see me. Could you please give her this note?"

He couldn't force himself on a defenceless and dying woman. She still had the right to say no. He was afraid she would refuse him. And if she did, he might never learn the truth. He thought for a second and then wrote four words on the back page of his diary, signed them, tore out the page, folded it and handed it to the sister.

She was back very shortly.

"She'll see you. She's weak, of course, and very old, but she's perfectly lucid now. Only please don't tire her."

"I'll try not to stay too long."

The girl laughed. "Don't worry. She'll throw you out soon enough if she gets bored. The chaplain and the Red Cross librarian have a terrible time with her. Third door on the left. There's a stool to sit on under the bed. We ring a bell at the end of visiting time."

She bustled off, leaving him to find his own way. The corridor was very quiet. At the far end he could glimpse through the open door of the main ward the regimented rows of beds, each with its pale-blue coverlet; the bright glow of flowers on the over-bed tables; and the laden visitors making their way in pairs to each bedside. There was a faint buzz of welcome, the hum of conversation. But no one was visiting the side wards. Here in the silence of the aseptic corridor Dalgliesh could smell death.

The woman propped high against the pillows in the third room on the left no longer looked human. She lay rigidly, her long arms disposed like sticks on the coverlet. This was a skeleton clothed with a thin membrane of flesh, beneath whose yellow transparency the tendons and veins were plainly visible as if in an anatomist's model. She was nearly bald, and the high-domed skull under its spare down of hair was as brittle and vulnerable as a child's. Only the eyes still held life, burning in their deep sockets with an animal vitality. And when she spoke her voice was distinctive and unwavering, evoking as her appearance never could the memory of imperious youth.

She took up his note and read aloud four words:

" 'It was the child.' You are right, of course. The four-year-old Hubert Boxdale killed his grandfather. You sign this note 'Adam Dalgliesh.' There was no Dalgliesh connected with the case."

"I am a detective of the Metropolitan Police. But I'm not here in any official capacity. I have known about this case for a number of years from a dear friend. I have a natural curiosity to learn the truth. And I have formed a theory."

"And now, like that Aubrey Glatt, you want to write a book?"

"No. I shall tell no one. You have my promise."

Her voice was ironic. "Thank you. I am a dying woman, Mr. Dalgliesh. I tell you that not to invite your sympathy, which it would be an impertinence for you to offer and which I neither want nor require, but to explain why it no longer matters to me what you say or do. But I, too, have a natural curiosity. Your note, cleverly, was intended to provoke it. I should like to know how you discovered the truth."

Dalgliesh drew the visitor's stool from under the bed and sat down beside her. She did not look at him. The skeleton hands, still holding his note, did not move.

"Everyone in Colebrook Croft who could have killed Augustus Boxdale was accounted for, except the one person whom nobody considered, the small boy. He was an intelligent, articulate and lonely child. He was almost certainly left to his own devices. His nurse did not accompany the family to Colebrook Croft and the servants who were there had the extra work of Christmas and the care of the delicate twin girls. The boy spent much time with his grandfather and the new bride. She, too, was lonely and disregarded. He could have trotted around with her as she went about her various activities. He could have watched her making her arsenical face wash and when he asked, as a child will, what it was for, could have been told: 'To make me young and beautiful.' He loved his grandfather, but he must have known that the old man was neither young nor beautiful. Suppose he woke up on that Boxing Day night overfed and excited after the Christmas festivities. Suppose he went to Allegra Boxdale's room in search of comfort and companionship and saw there the basin of gruel and the arsenical mixture together on the washstand. Suppose he decided that here was something he could do for his grandfather."

The voice from the bed said quietly:

"And suppose someone stood unnoticed in the doorway and watched him."

"So you were behind the window curtains on the landing, looking through the open door?"

"Of course. He knelt on the chair, two chubby hands clasping the bowl of poison, pouring it with infinite care into his grandfather's gruel. I watched while he replaced the linen cloth over the basin, got down from his chair, replaced it with careful art against the wall and trotted out into the corridor back to the nursery. About three seconds later Allegra came out of the bathroom and I watched while she carried the gruel in to my grandfather. A second later I went into the main bedroom. The bowl of poison had been a little heavy for Hubert's small hands to manage and I saw that a small pool had been spilt on the polished top of the washstand. I mopped it up with my handkerchief. Then I poured some of the water from the jug into the poison bowl to bring up the level. It only took a couple of seconds and I was ready to join Allegra and my grandfather in the bedroom and sit with him while he ate his gruel.

"I watched him die without pity and without remorse. I think I hated them both equally. The grandfather who had adored, petted and indulged me all through my childhood had deteriorated into this disgusting old lecher, unable to keep his hands off his woman even when I was in the room. He had rejected his family, jeopardized my engagement, made our name a laughingstock in the county, and for a woman my grandmother wouldn't have employed as a kitchen maid. I wanted them both dead. And they were both going to die. But it would be by other hands than mine. I could deceive myself that it wasn't my doing."

Dalgliesh asked, "When did she find out?"

"She guessed that evening. When my grandfather's agony began, she went outside for the jug of water. She wanted a cool cloth for his head.

It was then that she noticed that the level of water in the jug had fallen and that a small pool of liquid on the washstand had been mopped up. I should have realized that she would have seen that pool. She had been trained to register every detail; it was almost subconscious with her. She thought at the time that Mary Huddy had spilt some of the water when she set down the tray and the gruel. But who but I could have mopped it up? And why?"

"And when did she face you with the truth?"

"Not until after the trial. Allegra had magnificent courage. She knew what was at stake. But she also knew what she stood to gain. She gambled with her life for a fortune."

And then Dalgliesh understood what had happened to the Goddard inheritance.

"So she made you pay."

"Of course. Every penny. The Goddard fortune, the Goddard emeralds. She lived in luxury for sixty-seven years on my money. She ate and dressed on my money. When she moved with her lovers from hotel to hotel, it was on my money. She paid them with my money. And if she has left anything, which I doubt, it is my money. My grandfather left very little. He had been senile for years. Money ran through his fingers like sand."

"And your engagement?"

"It was broken, you could say, by mutual consent. A marriage, Mr. Dalgliesh, is like any other legal contract. It is most successful when both parties are convinced they have a bargain. Captain Brize-Lacey was sufficiently discouraged by the scandal of a murder in the family. He was a proud and highly conventional man. But that alone might have been accepted with the Goddard fortune and the Goddard emeralds to deodorize the bad smell. But the marriage couldn't have succeeded if he had discovered that he had married socially beneath him, into a family with a major scandal and no compensating fortune."

Dalgliesh said, "Once you had begun to pay, you had no choice but to go on. I see that. But why did you pay? She could hardly have told her story. It would have meant involving the child."

"Oh, no! That wasn't her plan at all. She never meant to involve the child. She was a sentimental woman and she was fond of Hubert. She intended to accuse me of murder outright. Then, if I decided to tell the truth, how would it help me? How could I admit that I had watched Hubert, actually watched a child barely four years old preparing an agonizing death for his grandfather without speaking a word to stop him? I could hardly claim that I hadn't understood the implication of what I had seen. After all, I wiped up the spilt liquid, I topped up the bowl. She had nothing to lose, remember, neither life nor reputation. They couldn't try her twice. That's why she waited until after the trial. It made her secure forever. But what of me? In the circles in which I moved, reputation was everything. She needed only to breathe the story in the ears of a few servants and I was finished. The truth can be remarkably tenacious. But it wasn't only reputation. I paid because I was in dread of the gallows."

Dalgliesh asked, "But could she ever prove it?"

Suddenly she looked at him and gave an eerie screech of laughter. It tore at her throat until he thought the taut tendons would snap.

"Of course she could! You fool! Don't you understand? She took my handkerchief, the one I used to mop up the arsenic mixture. That was her profession, remember. Sometime during that evening, perhaps when we were all crowding around the bed, two soft plump fingers insinuated themselves between the satin of my evening dress and my flesh and extracted that stained and damning piece of linen."

She stretched out feebly toward the bedside locker. Dalgliesh saw what she wanted and pulled open the drawer. There on the top was a small square of very fine linen with a border of hand-stitched lace. He took it up. In the corner was her monogram, delicately embroidered. And half of the handkerchief was still stiff and stained with brown.

She said, "She left instructions with her solicitors that this was to be returned to me after her death. She always knew where I was. She made it her business to know. You see, it could be said that she had a life interest in me. But now she's dead. And I shall soon follow. You may have the handkerchief, Mr. Dalgliesh. It can be of no further use to either of us now."

Dalgliesh put it in his pocket without speaking. As soon as possible he would see that it was burned. But there was something else he had to say. "Is there anything you would wish me to do? Is there anyone you want told, or to tell? Would you care to see a priest?"

Again there was that uncanny screech of laughter, but it was softer now.

"There's nothing I can say to a priest. I only regret what I did because it wasn't successful. That is hardly the proper frame of mind for a good confession. But I bear her no ill will. No envy, malice or uncharitableness. She won; I lost. One should be a good loser. But I don't want any priest telling me about penance. I've paid, Mr. Dalgliesh. For sixty-seven years I've paid. Great-Aunt Allie and her flypapers! She had me caught by the wings all the rest of my life."

She lay back as if suddenly exhausted. There was silence for a moment. Then she said with sudden vigour:

"I believe your visit has done me good. I would be obliged if you would make it convenient to return each afternoon for the next three days. I shan't trouble you after that."

Dalgliesh extended his leave with some difficulty and stayed at a local inn. He saw her each afternoon. They never spoke again of the murder. And when he came punctually at 2 P.M. on the fourth day, it was to be told that Miss Goddard had died peacefully in the night, with apparently no trouble to anyone. She was, as she had said, a good loser.

A week later, Dalgliesh reported to the Canon.

"I was able to see a man who has made a detailed study of the case. He had already done most of the work for me. I have read the transcript of the trial and visited Colebrook Croft. And I have seen one other person closely connected with the case but who is now dead. I know you will want me to respect confidences and to say no more than I need."

It sounded pompous and minatory, but he couldn't help that. The Canon murmured his quiet assurance. Thank God he wasn't a man to question. Where he trusted, he trusted absolutely. If Dalgliesh gave his word, there would be no more questioning. But he was anxious. Suspense hung around them. Dalgliesh went on quickly:

"As a result, I can give you my word that the verdict was a just verdict and that not one penny of your grandfather's fortune is coming to you through anyone's wrongdoing."

He turned his face away and gazed out the vicarage window at the sweet green coolness of the summer's day so that he did not have to watch the Canon's happiness and relief. There was a silence. The old man was probably giving thanks in his own way. Then he was aware that his godfather was speaking. Something was being said about gratitude, about the time he had given up to the investigation.

"Please don't misunderstand me, Adam. But when the formalities have been completed, I should like to donate something to a charity named by you, one close to your heart."

Dalgliesh smiled. His contributions to charity were impersonal; a quarterly obligation discharged by banker's order. The Canon obviously regarded charities as so many old clothes; all were friends, but some fitted better and were more affectionately regarded than others.

Then inspiration came.

"It's good of you to suggest it, sir. I rather liked what I learned about Great-Aunt Allie. It would be pleasant to give something in her name.

Isn't there a society for the assistance of retired and indigent vaudeville artistes, conjurers and so on?"

The Canon, predictably, knew that there was and could name it.

Dalgliesh said, "Then I think, Canon, that Great-Aunt Allie would agree that a donation to them would be entirely appropriate."

Wisp of Wool and Disk of Silver

ARTHUR W. UPFIELD

It was Sunday. The heat drove the blowflies to roost under the low staging that supported the iron tank outside the kitchen door. The small flies, apparently created solely for the purpose of drowning themselves in the eyes of man and beast, were not noticed by the man lying on the rough bunk set up under the veranda roof. He was reading a mystery story.

The house was of board, and iron-roofed. Nearby were other buildings: a blacksmith's shop, a truck shed, and a junk house. Beyond them a windmill raised water to a reservoir tank on high stilts, which in turn fed a long line of troughing. This was the outstation at the back of Reefer's Find.

Reefer's Find was a cattle ranch. It was not a large station for Australia—a mere half-million acres within its boundary fence. The outstation was forty-odd miles from the main homestead, and that isn't far in Australia.

Only one rider lived at the outstation—Harry Larkin, who was, this hot Sunday afternoon, reading a mystery story. He had been quartered there for more than a year, and every night at seven o'clock, the boss at the homestead telephoned to give orders for the following day and to be sure he was still alive and kicking. Usually, Larkin spoke to a man face to face about twice a month.

Larkin might have talked to a man more often had he wished. His nearest neighbor lived nine miles away in a small stockman's hut on the next property, and once they had often met at the boundary by prearrangement. But then Larkin's neighbor, whose name was William Reynolds, was a difficult man, according to Larkin, and the meetings stopped.

On all sides of this small homestead the land stretched flat to the horizon. Had it not been for the scanty, narrow-leafed mulga and the sick-looking sandalwood trees, plus the mirage which turned a salt bush into a Jack's beanstalk and a tree into a telegraph pole stuck on a bald man's head, the horizon would have been as distant as that of the ocean.

A man came stalking through the mirage, the blanket roll on his back making him look like a ship standing on its bowsprit. The lethargic dogs were not aware of the visitor until he was about ten yards from the veranda. So engrossed was Larkin that even the barking of his dogs failed to distract his attention, and the stranger actually reached the edge of the veranda floor and spoke before Larkin was aware of him.

"He, he! Good day, mate! Flamin' hot today, ain't it?"

Larkin swung his legs off the bunk and sat up. What he saw was not usual in this part of Australia—a sundowner, a bush waif who tramps from north to south or from east to west, never working, cadging rations from the far-flung homesteads and having the ability of the camel to do without water, or find it. Sometimes Old Man Sun tricked one of them, and then the vast bushland took him and never gave up the cloth-tattered skeleton.

"Good day," Larkin said, to add with ludicrous inanity, "Traveling?"

"Yes, mate. Makin' down south." The derelict slipped the swag off his shoulder and sat on it. "What place is this?"

Larkin told him.

"Mind me camping here tonight, mate? Wouldn't be in the way. Wouldn't be here in the mornin', either."

"You can camp over in the shed," Larkin said. "And if you pinch anything, I'll track you and belt the guts out of you."

A vacuous grin spread over the dust-grimed, bewhiskered face.

"Me, mate? I wouldn't pinch nothin'. Could do with a pinch of tea, and a bit of flour. He, he! Pinch—I mean a fistful of tea and sugar, mate."

Five minutes of this bird would send a man crazy. Larkin entered the kitchen, found an empty tin, and poured into it an equal quantity of tea and sugar. He scooped flour from a sack into a brown paper bag, and wrapped a chunk of salt meat in an old newspaper. On going out to the sundowner, anger surged in him at the sight of the man standing by the bunk and looking through his mystery story.

"He, he! Detective yarn!" said the sundowner. "I give 'em away years ago. A bloke does a killing and leaves the clues for the detectives to find. They're all the same. Why in 'ell don't a bloke write about a bloke who kills another bloke and gets away with it? I could kill a bloke and leave no clues."

"You could," sneered Larkin.

"'Course. Easy. You only gotta use your brain—like me."

Larkin handed over the rations and edged the visitor off his veranda. The fellow was batty, all right, but harmless as they all are.

"How would you kill a man and leave no clues?" he asked.

"Well, I tell you it's easy." The derelict pushed the rations into a dirty gunny sack and again sat down on his swag. "You see, mate, it's this way. In real life the murderer can't do away with the body. Even doctors and things like that make a hell of a mess of doing away with a corpse. In fact, they don't do away with it, mate. They leave parts and bits of it all over the scenery, and then what happens? Why, a detective comes along and he says, 'Cripes, someone's been and done a murder! Ah! Watch me track the bloke what done it.' If you're gonna commit a murder, you must be able to do away with the body. Having done that, well, who's gonna prove anythink? Tell me that, mate."

"You tell me," urged Larkin, and tossed his depleted tobacco plug to the visitor. The sundowner gnawed from the plug, almost hit a dog in the eye with a spit, gulped, and settled to the details of the perfect murder.

"Well, mate, it's like this. Once you done away with the body, complete, there ain't nothing left to say that the body ever was alive to be killed. Now, supposin' I wanted to do you in. I don't, mate, don't think that, but I's plenty of time to work things out. Supposin' I wanted to do you in. Well, me and you is out ridin' and I takes me chance and shoots you stone-dead. I chooses to do the killin' where there's plenty of dead wood. Then I gathers the dead wood and drags your body onto it and fires the wood. Next day, when the ashes are cold, I goes back with a sieve and dolly pot. That's all I wants then.

"I takes out your burned bones and I crushes 'em to dust in the dolly pot. Then I goes through the ashes with the sieve, getting out all the small bones and putting them through the dolly pot. The dust I empties out from the dolly pot for the wind to take. All the metal bits, such as buttons and boot sprigs, I puts in me pocket and carries back to the homestead where I throws 'em down the well or covers 'em with sulphuric acid.

"Almost sure to be a dolly pot here, by the look of the place. Almost sure to be a sieve. Almost sure to be a jar of sulphuric acid for solderin' work. Everythin' on tap, like. And just in case the million-to-one chance comes off that someone might come across the fire site and wonder, sort of, I'd shoot a coupler kangaroos, skin 'em, and burn the carcasses on top of the old ashes. You know, to keep the blowies from breeding."

Harry Larkin looked at the sundowner, and through him. A prospector's dolly pot, a sieve, a quantity of sulphuric acid to dissolve the metal parts. Yes, they were all here. Given time a man could commit the perfect murder. Time! Two days would be long enough.

The sundowner stood up. "Good day, mate. Don't mind me. He, he! Flamin' hot, ain't it? Be cool down south. Well, I'll be movin'."

Larkin watched him depart. The bush waif did not stop at the shed to camp for the night. He went on to the windmill and sprawled over the drinking trough to drink. He filled his rusty billy-can, Larkin watching until the mirage to the southward drowned him.

The perfect murder, with aids as common as household remedies. The perfect scene, this land without limits where even a man and his nearest neighbor are separated by nine miles. A prospector's dolly pot, a sieve, and a pint of soldering acid. Simple! It was as simple as being kicked to death in a stockyard jammed with mules.

"William Reynolds vanished three months ago, and repeated searches have failed to find even his body."

Mounted Constable Evans sat stiffly erect in the chair behind the littered desk in the Police Station at Wondong. Opposite him lounged a slight dark-complexioned man having a straight nose, a high forehead, and intensely blue eyes. There was no doubt that Evans was a policeman. None would guess that the dark man with the blue eyes was Detective Inspector Napoleon Bonaparte.

"The man's relatives have been bothering Headquarters about William Reynolds, which is why I am here," explained Bonaparte, faintly apologetic. "I have read your reports, and find them clear and concise. There is no doubt in the Official Mind that, assisted by your black tracker, you have done everything possible to locate Reynolds or his dead body. I may succeed where you and the black tracker failed because I am peculiarly equipped with gifts bequeathed to me by my white father and my aboriginal mother. In me are combined the white man's reasoning powers and the black man's perceptions and bushcraft. Therefore, should I succeed there would be no reflection on your efficiency or the powers of your tracker. Between what a tracker sees and what you have been trained to reason, there is a bridge. There is no such bridge between those divided powers in me. Which is why I never fail."

Having put Constable Evans in a more cooperative frame of mind, Bony rolled a cigarette and relaxed.

"Thank you, sir," Evans said and rose to accompany Bony to the locality map which hung on the wall. "Here's the township of Wondong. Here is the homestead of Morley Downs cattle station. And here, fifteen miles on from the homestead, is the stockman's hut where William Reynolds lived and worked.

"There's no telephonic communication between the hut and the homestead. Once every month the people at the homestead trucked rations to Reynolds. And once every week, every Monday morning, a stockman from the homestead would meet Reynolds midway between homestead and hut to give Reynolds his mail, and orders, and have a yarn with him over a billy of tea."

"And then one Monday, Reynolds didn't turn up," Bony added, as they resumed their chairs at the desk.

"That Monday the homestead man waited four hours for Reynolds," continued Evans. "The following day the station manager ran out in his car to Reynolds' hut. He found the ashes on the open hearth stone-cold, the two chained dogs nearly dead of thirst, and that Reynolds hadn't been at the hut since the day it had rained, three days previously.

"The manager drove back to the homestead and organized all his men in a search party. They found Reynolds' horse running with several others. The horse was still saddled and bridled. They rode the country for two days, and then I went out with my tracker to join in. We kept up the search for a week, and the tracker's opinion was that Reynolds might have been riding the back boundary fence when he was parted from the horse. Beyond that the tracker was vague, and I don't wonder at it for two reasons. One, the rain had wiped out tracks visible to white eyes, and two, there were other horses in the same paddock. Horse tracks swamped with rain are indistinguishable one from another."

"How large is that paddock?" asked Bony.

"Approximately two hundred square miles."

Bony rose and again studied the wall map.

"On the far side of the fence is this place named Reefer's Find," he pointed out. "Assuming that Reynolds had been thrown from his horse and injured, might he not have tried to reach the outstation of Reefer's Find which, I see, is about three miles from the fence whereas Reynolds' hut is six or seven?"

"We thought of that possibility, and we scoured the country on the Reefer's Find side of the boundary fence," Evans replied. "There's a stockman named Larkin at the Reefer's Find outstation. He joined in the search. The tracker, who had memorized Reynolds' footprints, found on the earth floor of the hut's veranda, couldn't spot any of his tracks on Reefer's Find country, and the boundary fence, of course, did not permit Reynolds' horse into that country. The blasted rain beat the tracker. It beat all of us."

"Hm. Did you know this Reynolds?"

"Yes. He came to town twice on a bit of a bender. Good type. Good horseman. Good bushman. The horse he rode that day was not a tricky animal. What do Headquarters know of him, sir?"

"Only that he never failed to write regularly to his mother, and that he had spent four years in the Army from which he was discharged following a head wound."

"Head wound! He might have suffered from amnesia. He could have left his horse and walked away—anywhere—walked until he dropped and died from thirst or starvation."

"It's possible. What is the character of the man Larkin?"

"Average, I think. He told me that he and Reynolds had met when both happened to be riding that boundary fence, the last time being several months before Reynolds vanished."

"How many people besides Larkin at the outstation?"

"No one else excepting when they're mustering for fats."

The conversation waned while Bony rolled another cigarette.

"Could you run me out to Morley Downs homestead?" he asked.

"Yes, of course," assented Evans.

"Then kindly telephone the manager and let me talk to him."

Two hundred square miles is a fairly large tract of country in which to find clues leading to the fate of a lost man, and three months is an appreciable period of time to elapse after a man is reported as lost.

The rider who replaced Reynolds' successor was blue-eyed and dark-skinned, and at the end of two weeks of incessant reading he was familiar with every acre, and had read every word on this large page of the Book of the Bush.

By now Bony was convinced that Reynolds hadn't died in that paddock. Lost or injured men had crept into a hollow log to die, their remains found many years afterward, but in this country there were no trees large enough for a man to crawl into. Men had perished and their bodies had been covered with wind-blown sand, and after many years the wind had removed the sand to reveal the skeleton. In Reynolds' case the search for him had been begun within a week of his disappearance, when eleven men plus a policeman selected for his job because of his bushcraft, and a black tracker selected from among the aborigines who are the best sleuths in the world, had gone over and over the 200 square miles.

Bony knew that, of the searchers, the black tracker would be the most proficient. He knew, too, just how the mind of that aborigine would work when taken to the stockman's hut and put on the job. Firstly, he would see the lost man's bootprints left on the dry earth beneath the veranda roof. Thereafter he would ride crouched forward above his horse's mane and keep his eyes directed to the ground at a point a few feet beyond the animal's nose. He would look for a horse's tracks and a man's tracks, knowing that nothing passes over the ground without leaving evidence, and that even half an inch of rain will not always obliterate the evidence left, perhaps, in the shelter of a tree.

That was all the black tracker could be expected to do. He would not reason that the lost man might have climbed a tree and there cut his own throat, or that he might have wanted to vanish and so had climbed over one of the fences into the adjacent paddock; or had, when suffering from amnesia, or the madness brought about by solitude, walked away beyond the rim of the earth.

The first clue found by Bonaparte was a wisp of wool dyed brown. It was caught by a barb of the top wire of the division fence between the two cattle stations. It was about an inch in length and might well have come from a man's sock when he had climbed over the fence.

It was most unlikely that any one of the searchers for William Reynolds would have climbed the fence. They were all mounted, and when they scoured the neighboring country, they would have passed through the gate about a mile from this tiny piece of flotsam. Whether or not the wisp of wool had been detached from Reynolds' sock at the time of his disappearance, its importance in this case was that it led the investigator to the second clue.

The vital attribute shared by the aboriginal tracker with Napoleon Bonaparte was patience. To both, Time was of no consequence once they set out on the hunt.

On the twenty-ninth day of his investigation Bony came on the site of a large fire. It was approximately a mile distant from the outstation of Reefer's Find, and from a point nearby, the buildings could be seen magnified and distorted by the mirage. The fire had burned after the last rainfall—the one recorded immediately following the disappearance of Reynolds—and the trails made by dead tree branches when dragged together still remained sharp on the ground.

The obvious purpose of the fire had been to consume the carcase of a calf, for amid the mound of white ash protruded the skull and bones of the animal. The wind had played with the ash, scattering it thinly all about the original ash mound.

Question: "Why had Larkin burned the carcase of the calf?" Cattlemen never do such a thing unless a beast dies close to their camp. In parts of the continent, carcases are always burned to keep down the blowfly pest, but out here in the interior, never. There was a possible answer, however, in the mentality of the man who lived nearby, the man who lived alone and could be expected to do anything unusual, even burning all the carcases of animals which perished in his domain. That answer would be proved correct if other fire sites were discovered offering the same evidence.

At daybreak the next morning Bony was perched high in a sandalwood tree. There he watched Larkin ride out on his day's work, and when assured that the man was out of the way, he slid to the ground and examined the ashes and the burned bones, using his hands and his fingers as a sieve.

Other than the bones of the calf, he found nothing but a soft-nosed bullet. Under the ashes, near the edge of the splayed-out mass, he found an indentation on the ground, circular and about six inches in diameter. The bullet and the mark were the second and third clues, the third being the imprint of a prospector's dolly pot.

"Do your men shoot calves in the paddocks for any reason?" Bony asked the manager, who had driven out to his hut with rations. The manager was big and tough, grizzled and shrewd.

"No, of course not, unless a calf has been injured in some way and is helpless. Have you found any of our calves shot?"

"None of yours. How do your stockmen obtain their meat supply?"

"We kill at the homestead and distribute fortnightly a little fresh meat and a quantity of salted beef."

"D'you think the man over on Reefer's Find would be similarly supplied by his employer?"

"Yes, I think so. I could find out from the owner of Reefer's Find."

"Please do. You have been most helpful, and I do appreciate it. In my role of cattleman it wouldn't do to have another rider stationed with me, and I would be grateful if you consented to drive out here in the evening for the next three days. Should I not be here, then wait until eight o'clock before taking from the tea tin over there on the shelf a sealed envelope addressed to you. Act on the enclosed instructions."

"Very well, I'll do that."

"Thanks. Would you care to undertake a little inquiry for me?"

"Certainly."

"Then talk guardedly to those men you sent to meet Reynolds every Monday and ascertain from them the relationship which existed between Reynolds and Harry Larkin. As is often the case with lonely men stationed near the boundary fence of two properties, according to Larkin he and Reynolds used to meet now and then by arrangement. They may have quarreled. Have you ever met Larkin?"

"On several occasions, yes," replied the manager.

"And your impressions of him? As a man?"

"I thought him intelligent. Inclined to be morose, of course, but then men who live alone often are. You are not thinking that—?"

"I'm thinking that Reynolds is not in your country. Had he been still on your property, I would have found him dead or alive. When I set out to find a missing man, I find him. I shall find Reynolds, eventually—if there is anything of him to find."

On the third evening that the manager went out to the little hut, Bony showed him a small and slightly convex disk of silver. It was weathered and in one place cracked. It bore the initials J.M.M.

"I found that in the vicinity of the site of a large fire," Bony said. "It might establish that William Reynolds is no longer alive."

Although Harry Larkin was supremely confident, he was not quite happy. He had not acted without looking at the problem from all angles and without having earnestly sought the answer to the question: "If I shoot him dead, burn the body on a good fire, go through the ashes for the bones which I pound to dust in a dolly pot, and for the metal bits and pieces which I dissolve in sulphuric acid, how can I be caught?" The answer was plain.

He had carried through the sundowner's method of utterly destroying the body of the murder victim, and to avoid the million-to-one chance of anyone coming across the ashes of the fire and being made suspicious, he had shot a calf as kangaroos were scarce.

Yes, he was confident, and confident that he was justified in being confident. Nothing remained of Bill Reynolds, damn him, save a little grayish dust which was floating around somewhere.

The slight unhappiness was caused by a strange visitation, signs of which he had first discovered when returning home from his work one afternoon. On the ground near the blacksmith's shop he found a strange set of boot tracks which were not older than two days. He followed these tracks backward to the house, and then forward until he lost them in the scrub.

Nothing in the house was touched, as far as he could see, and nothing had been taken from the blacksmith's shop, or interfered with. The dolly pot was still in the corner into which he had dropped it after its last employment, and the crowbar was still leaning against the anvil. On the shelf was the acid jar. There was no acid in it. He had used it to dissolve, partially, buttons and the metal band around a pipestem and boot sprigs. The residue of those metal objects he had dropped into a hole in a tree eleven miles away.

It was very strange. A normal visitor, finding the occupier away, would have left a note at the house. Had the visitor been black, he would not have left any tracks, if bent on mischief.

The next day Larkin rode out to the boundary fence and on the way he visited the site of his fire. There he found the plain evidence that someone had moved the bones of the animal and had delved among the ashes still remaining from the action of the wind.

Thus he was not happy, but still supremely confident. They could not tack anything onto him. They couldn't even prove that Reynolds was dead. How could they when there was nothing of him left?

It was again Sunday, and Larkin was washing his clothes at the outside fire when the sound of horses' hoofs led him to see two men approaching. His lips vanished into a mere line, and his mind went over all the answers he would give if the police ever did call on him. One of the men he did not know. The other was Mounted Constable Evans.

They dismounted, anchoring their horses by merely dropping the reins to the ground. Larkin searched their faces and wondered who was the slim half-caste with, for a half-caste, the singularly blue eyes.

"Good day," Larkin greeted them.

"Good day, Larkin," replied Constable Evans, and appeared to give his trousers a hitch. His voice was affable, and Larkin was astonished when, after an abrupt and somewhat violent movement, he found himself handcuffed.

"Going to take you in for the murder of William Reynolds," Evans announced. "This is Detective Inspector Napoleon Bonaparte."

"You must be balmy—or I am," Larkin said.

Evans countered with: "You are. Come on over to the house. A car will be here in about half an hour."

The three men entered the kitchen where Larkin was told to sit down.

"I haven't done anything to Reynolds, or anyone else," asserted Larkin, and for the first time the slight man with the brilliant blue eyes spoke.

"While we are waiting, I'll tell you all about it, Larkin. I'll tell it so clearly that you will believe I was watching you all the time. You used to meet Reynolds at the boundary fence gate, and the two of you would indulge in a spot of gambling—generally at poker. Then one day you cheated and there was a fight in which you were thrashed.

"You knew what day of the week Reynolds would ride that boundary fence and you waited for him on your side. You held him up and made him climb over the fence while you covered him with your .32 high-power Savage rifle. You made him walk to a place within a mile of here, where there was plenty of dry wood, and there you shot him and burned his body.

"The next day you returned with a dolly pot and a sieve. You put all the bones through the dolly pot, and then you sieved all the ashes for metal objects in Reynolds' clothes and burned them up with sulphuric acid. Very neat. The perfect crime, you must agree."

"If I done all that, which I didn't, yes," Larkin did agree.

"Well, assuming that not you but another did all I have outlined, why did the murderer shoot and burn the carcase of a calf on the same fire site?"

"You tell me," said Larkin.

"Good. I'll even do that. You shot Reynolds and you disposed of his body, as I've related. Having killed him, you immediately dragged wood together and burned the body, keeping the fire going for several hours. Now, the next day, or the day after that, it rained, and that rainfall fixed your actions like words printed in a book. You went through the ashes for Reynolds' bones before it rained, and you shot the calf and lit the second fire after it rained. You dropped the calf at least two hundred yards from the scene of the murder, and you carried the carcase on your back over those two hundred yards. The additional weight impressed your boot prints on the ground much deeper than when you walk about normally, and although the rain washed out many of your boot prints, it did not remove your prints made when carrying the dead calf. You didn't shoot the calf, eh?"

"No, of course I didn't," came the sneering reply. "I burned the carcase of a calf that died. I keep my camp clean. Enough blowflies about as it is."

"But you burned the calf's carcase a full mile away from your camp. However, you shot the calf, and you shot it to burn the carcase in order to prevent possible curiosity. You should have gone through the ashes after you burned the carcase of the calf and retrieved the bullet fired from your own rifle."

Bony smiled, and Larkin glared.

Constable Evans said, "Keep your hands on the table, Larkin."

"You know, Larkin, you murderers often make me tired," Bony went on. "You think up a good idea, and then fall down executing it.

"You thought up a good one by dollying the bones and sieving the ashes for the metal objects on a man's clothes and in his boots, and then —why go and spoil it by shooting a calf and burning the carcase on the same fire site? It wasn't necessary. Having pounded Reynolds' bones to ash and scattered the ash to the four corners, and having retrieved from the ashes remaining evidence that a human body had been destroyed, there was no necessity to burn a carcase. It wouldn't have mattered how suspicious anyone became. Your biggest mistake was burning that calf. That act connects you with that fire."

"Yes, well, what of it?" Larkin almost snarled. "I got a bit lonely livin' here alone for months, and one day I sorta got fed up. I seen the calf, and I up with me rifle and took a pot shot at it."

"It won't do," Bony said, shaking his head. "Having taken a pot shot at the calf, accidentally killing it, why take a dolly pot to the place where you burned the carcase? You did carry a dolly pot, the one in the blacksmith's shop, to the scene of the fire, for the imprint of the dolly pot on the ground is still plain in two places."

"Pretty good tale, I must say," said Larkin. "You still can't prove that Bill Reynolds is dead."

"No?" Bony's dark face registered a bland smile, but his eyes were like blue opals. "When I found a wisp of brown wool attached to the boundary fence, I was confident that Reynolds had climbed it, merely because I was sure his body was not on his side of the fence. You made him walk to the place where you shot him, and then you saw the calf and the other cattle in the distance, and you shot the calf and carried it to the fire.

"I have enough to put you in the dock, Larkin—and one other little thing which is going to make certain you'll hang. Reynolds was in the Army during the war. He was discharged following a head wound. The surgeon who operated on Reynolds was a specialist in trepanning. The surgeon always scratched his initials on the silver plate he inserted into the skull of a patient. He has it on record that he operated on William Reynolds, and he will swear that the plate came from the head of William Reynolds, and will also swear that the plate could not have been detached from Reynolds' head without great violence."

"It wasn't in the ashes," gasped Larkin, and then realized his slip.

"No, it wasn't in the ashes, Larkin," Bony agreed. "You see, when you shot him at close quarters, probably through the forehead, the expanding bullet took away a portion of the poor fellow's head—and the trepanning plate. I found the plate lodged in a sandalwood tree growing about thirty feet from where you burned the body."

Larkin glared across the table at Bony, his eyes freezing as he realized that the trap had indeed sprung on him. Bony was again smiling. He said, as though comfortingly, "Don't fret, Larkin. If you had not made all those silly mistakes, you would have made others equally fatal. Strangely enough, the act of homicide always throws a man off balance. If it were not so, I would find life rather boring."

SUSPENSE IN
SUNNY CLIMES

CRETE
PARIS
JAMAICA

Not After Midnight

DAPHNE DU MAURIER

I am a schoolmaster by profession. Or was. I handed in my resignation to the headmaster before the end of the summer term in order to forestall inevitable dismissal. The reason I gave was true enough—ill-health, caused by a wretched bug picked up on holiday in Crete, which might necessitate a stay in hospital of several weeks, various injections, etc. I did not specify the nature of the bug. He knew, though, and so did the rest of the staff. And the boys. My complaint is universal, and has been so through the ages, an excuse for jest and hilarious laughter from earliest times, until one of us oversteps the mark and becomes a menace to society. Then we are given the boot. The passer-by averts his gaze, and we are left to crawl out of the ditch alone, or stay there and die.

If I am bitter, it is because the bug I caught was picked up in all innocence. Fellow-sufferers of my complaint can plead predisposition, poor heredity, family trouble, excess of the good life, and, throwing themselves on a psychoanalyst's couch, spill out the rotten beans within and so effect a cure. I can do none of this. The doctor to whom I endeavoured to explain what had happened listened with a superior smile, and then murmured something about emotionally destructive identification coupled with repressed guilt, and put me on a course of pills. They might have helped me if I had taken them. Instead I threw them down the drain and became more deeply imbued with the poison that seeped through me, made worse, of course, by the fatal recognition of my condition by the youngsters I had believed to be my friends, who nudged one another when I came into class, or, with stifled laughter, bent their loathsome little heads over their desks—until the moment arrived when I knew I could not continue, and took the decision to knock on the headmaster's door.

Well, that's over, done with, finished. Before I take myself to hospital or, alternatively, blot out memory, which is a second possibility, I want to establish what happened in the first place. So that, whatever becomes of me, this paper will be found, and the reader can make up his mind whether, as the doctor suggested, some want of inner balance made me an easy victim to superstitious fear, or whether, as I myself believe, my downfall was caused by an age-old magic, insidious, evil, its origins lost in the dawn of history. Suffice to say that he who first made the magic deemed himself immortal, and with unholy joy infected others, sowing in his heirs, throughout the world and down the centuries, the seeds of self-destruction.

To return to the present. The time was April, the Easter holidays. I had been to Greece twice before, but never Crete. I taught classics to the boys at the preparatory school, but my reason for visiting Crete was not to explore the sites of Knossos or Phaestus but to indulge a personal hobby. I have a minor talent for painting in oils, and this I find all-absorbing, whether on free days or in the school holidays. My work has been praised by one or two friends in the art world, and my ambition was to collect enough paintings to give a small exhibition. Even if none of them sold, the holding of a private show would be a happy achievement.

Here, briefly, a word about my personal life. I am a bachelor. Age forty-nine. Parents dead. Educated Sherborne and Brasenose, Oxford. Profession, as you already know, schoolmaster. I play cricket and golf, badminton, and rather poor bridge. Interests, apart from teaching, art, as I have already said, and occasional travel, when I can afford it. Vices, up to the present, literally none. Which is not being self-complacent, but the truth is my life has been uneventful by any standard. Nor has this bothered me. I am probably a dull man. Emotionally I have had no complications. I was engaged to a pretty girl, a neighbour, when I was twenty-five, but she married somebody else. It hurt at the time, but the wound healed in less than a year. One fault, if fault it is, I have always had, which perhaps accounts for my hitherto monotonous life. This is an aversion to becoming involved with people. Friends I possess, but at a distance. Once involved, trouble occurs, and too often disaster follows.

I set out for Crete in the Easter holidays with no encumbrance but a fair-sized suitcase and my painting gear. A travel agent had recommended a hotel overlooking the Gulf of Mirabello on the eastern coast, after I had told him I was not interested in archaeological sights but wanted to paint. I was shown a brochure which seemed to meet my requirements. A pleasantly situated hotel close to the sea, and chalets by the water's edge where one slept and breakfasted. Clientele well-to-do, and although I count myself no snob I cannot abide paper-bags and orange-peel. A couple of pictures painted the previous winter—a view of

St. Paul's Cathedral under snow, and another one of Hampstead Heath, both sold to an obliging female cousin—would pay for my journey, and I permitted myself an added indulgence, though it was really a necessity —the hiring of a small Volkswagen on arrival at the airport of Herak- leion.

The flight, with an overnight stop in Athens, was pleasant and une- ventful, the forty-odd miles' drive to my destination somewhat tedious, for being a cautious driver I took it slowly, and the twisting road, once I reached the hills, was decidedly hazardous. Cars passed me, or swerved towards me, hooting loudly. Also, it was very hot, and I was hungry. The sight of the blue Gulf of Mirabello and the splendid mountains to the east acted as a spur to sagging spirits, and once I arrived at the hotel, set delightfully in its own grounds, with lunch served to me on the terrace despite the fact that it was after two in the afternoon—how different from England!—I was ready to relax and inspect my quarters. Disappointment followed. The young porter led me down a garden path flagged on either side by brilliant geraniums to a small chalet bunched in by neighbours on either side, and overlooking, not the sea, but a part of the garden laid out for mini-golf. My next-door neighbours, an obvi- ously English mother and her brood, smiled in welcome from their bal- cony, which was strewn with bathing-suits drying under the sun. Two middle-aged men were engaged in mini-golf. I might have been in Maid- enhead.

"This won't do," I said, turning to my escort. "I have come here to paint. I must have a view of the sea."

He shrugged his shoulders, murmuring something about the chalets beside the sea being fully booked. It was not his fault, of course. I made him trek back to the hotel with me, and addressed myself to the clerk at the reception desk.

"There has been some mistake," I said. "I asked for a chalet over- looking the sea, and privacy above all."

The clerk smiled, apologised, began ruffling papers, and the inevita- ble excuses followed. My travel agent had not specifically booked a chalet overlooking the sea. These were in great demand, and were fully booked. Perhaps in a few days there might be some cancellations, one never could tell, in the meantime he was sure I would be very comfort- able in the chalet that had been allotted to me. All the furnishings were the same, my breakfast would be served me, etc., etc.

I was adamant. I would not be fobbed off with the English family and the mini-golf. Not after having flown all those miles at considerable expense. I was bored by the whole affair, tired, and considerably an- noyed.

"I am a professor of art," I told the clerk. "I have been commissioned to execute several paintings while I am here, and it is essential that I should have a view of the sea, and neighbours who will not disturb me."

(My passport states my occupation as professor. It sounds better than schoolmaster or teacher, and usually arouses respect in the attitude of reception clerks.)

The clerk seemed genuinely concerned, and repeated his apologies. He turned again to the sheaf of papers before him. Exasperated, I strode across the spacious hall and looked out of the door on to the terrace down to the sea.

"I cannot believe," I said, "that every chalet is taken. It's too early in the season. In summer, perhaps, but not now." I waved my hand towards the western side of the bay. "That group over there," I said, "down by the water's edge. Do you mean to say every single one of them is booked?"

He shook his head and smiled. "We do not usually open these until mid-season. Also, they are more expensive. They have a bath as well as a shower."

"How much more expensive?" I hedged.

He told me. I made a quick calculation. I could afford it if I cut down on all other expenses. Had my evening meal in the hotel, and went without lunch. No extras in the bar, not even mineral water.

"Then there is no problem," I said grandly. "I will willingly pay more for privacy. And, if you have no objection, I should like to choose the chalet which would suit me best. I'll walk down to the sea now and then come back for the key, and your porter can bring my things."

I gave him no time to reply, but turned on my heel and went out on to the terrace. It paid to be firm. One moment's hesitation, and he would have fobbed me off with the stuffy chalet overlooking the mini-golf. I could imagine the consequences. The chattering children on the balcony next door, the possibly effusive mother, and the middle-aged golfers urging me to have a game. I could not have borne it.

I walked down through the garden to the sea, and as I did so my spirits rose. For this, of course, was what had been so highly coloured on the agent's brochure, and why I had flown so many miles. No exaggeration, either. Little white-washed dwellings, discreetly set apart from one another, the sea washing the rocks below. There was a beach, from which people doubtless swam in high season, but no one was on it now, and, even if they should intrude, the chalets themselves were well to the left, inviolate, private. I peered at each in turn, mounting the steps, standing on the balconies. The clerk must have been telling the truth about none of them being let before full season, for all had their windows shuttered. Except one. And directly I mounted the steps and stood on the balcony, I knew that it must be mine. This was the view I had imagined. The sea beneath me, lapping the rocks, the bay widening into the gulf itself, and beyond the mountains. It was perfect. The chalets to the east of the hotel, which was out of sight anyway, could be ignored. One, close to a neck of land, stood on its own like a solitary outpost with a landing-stage below, but this would only enhance my picture when I came to paint it. The rest were mercifully hidden by rising ground. I turned, and looked through the open windows to the bedroom within. Plain white-washed walls, a stone floor, a comfortable divan bed with rugs upon it. A bedside table with a lamp and telephone. But for these last it had all the simplicity of a monk's cell, and I wished for nothing more.

I wondered why this chalet, and none of its neighbours, was unshuttered, and stepping inside I heard from the bathroom beyond the sound of running water. Not further disappointment, and the place booked after all? I put my head round the open door, and saw that it was a little Greek maid swabbing the bathroom floor. She seemed startled at the sight of me. I gestured, pointed, said, "Is this taken?" She did not understand, but answered me in Greek. Then she seized her cloth and pail and, plainly terrified, brushed past me to the entrance, leaving her work unfinished.

I went back into the bedroom and picked up the telephone, and in a moment the smooth voice of the reception clerk answered.

"This is Mr. Grey," I told him. "Mr. Timothy Grey. I was speaking to you just now about changing my chalet."

"Yes, Mr. Grey," he replied. He sounded puzzled. "Where are you speaking from?"

"Hold on a minute," I said. I put down the receiver and crossed the room to the balcony. The number was above the open door. It was sixty-two. I went back to the telephone. "I'm speaking from the chalet I have chosen," I said. "It happened to be open—one of the maids was cleaning the bathroom, and I'm afraid I scared her away. This chalet is ideal for my purpose. It is number sixty-two."

He did not answer immediately, and when he did he sounded doubtful. "Number sixty-two?" he repeated. And then, after a moment's hesitation, "I am not sure if it is available."

"Oh, for heaven's sake . . ." I began, exasperated, and I heard him talking in Greek to someone beside him at the desk. The conversation went back and forth between them; there was obviously some difficulty, which made me all the more determined.

"Are you there?" I said. "What's the trouble?"

More hurried whispers, and then he spoke to me again. "No trouble, Mr. Grey. It is just that we feel you might be more comfortable in number fifty-seven, which is a little nearer to the hotel."

"Nonsense," I said, "I prefer the view from here. What's wrong with number sixty-two? Doesn't the plumbing work?"

"Certainly the plumbing works," he assured me, while the whispering started again. "There is nothing wrong with the chalet. If you have made up your mind I will send down the porter with your luggage and the key."

He rang off, possibly to finish his discussion with the whisperer at his side. Perhaps they were going to step up the price. If they did, I would have further argument. The chalet was no different from its empty neighbours, but the position, dead centre to sea and mountains, was all I had dreamed and more. I stood on the balcony, looking out across the sea and smiling. What a prospect, what a place! I would unpack and have a swim, then put up my easel and do a preliminary sketch before starting serious work in the morning.

I heard voices, and saw the little maid staring at me from halfway up the garden path, cloth and pail still in hand. Then, as the young porter advanced downhill bearing my suitcase and painting gear, she must have realised that I was to be the occupant of number sixty-two, for she stopped him midway, and another whispered conversation began. I had evidently caused a break in the smooth routine of the hotel. A few moments later they climbed the steps to the chalet together, the porter to set down my luggage, the maid doubtless to finish her swabbing of the bathroom floor. I had no desire to be on awkward terms with either of them, and, smiling cheerfully, placed coins in both their hands.

"Lovely view," I said loudly, pointing to the sea. "Must go for a swim," and made breast-stroke gestures to show my intent, hoping for the ready smile of the native Greek, usually so responsive to goodwill.

The porter evaded my eyes and bowed gravely, accepting the tip nevertheless. As for the little maid, distress was evident in her face, and, forgetting about the bathroom floor, she hurried after him. I could hear them talking as they walked up the garden path together to the hotel.

Well, it was not my problem. Staff and management must sort out their troubles between them. I had got what I wanted, and that was all that concerned me. I unpacked and made myself at home. Then, slipping on bathing-trunks, I stepped down to the ledge of rock beneath the balcony, and ventured a toe into the water. It was surprisingly chill, despite the hot sun that had been upon it all day. Never mind. I must prove my mettle, if only to myself. I took the plunge and gasped, and being a cautious swimmer at the best of times, especially in strange waters, swam round and round in circles rather like a sea-lion pup in a zoological pool.

Refreshing, undoubtedly, but a few minutes were enough, and as I climbed out again on to the rocks I saw that the porter and the little maid had been watching me all the time from behind a flowering bush up the garden path. I hoped I had not lost face. And anyway, why the interest? People must be swimming every day from the other chalets. The bathing-suits on the various balconies proved it. I dried myself on the balcony, observing how the sun, now in the western sky behind my chalet, made dappled patterns on the water. Fishing-boats were returning to the little harbour port a few miles distant, the chug-chug engines making a pleasing sound.

I dressed, taking the precaution of having a hot bath, for the first swim of the year is always numbing, and then set up my easel and became absorbed. This was why I was here, and nothing else mattered. I worked for a couple of hours, and as the light failed, and the colour of the sea deepened and the mountains turned a softer purple blue, I rejoiced to think that tomorrow I should be able to seize this after-glow in paint instead of charcoal, and the picture would begin to come alive.

It was time to stop. I stacked away my gear, and before changing for dinner and drawing the shutters—doubtless there were mosquitoes, and I had no wish to be bitten—watched a motor-boat with gently purring engine draw in softly to the eastward point with the landing-stage away to my right. Three people aboard, fishing enthusiasts no doubt, a woman amongst them. One man, a local, probably, made the boat fast, and stepped on the landing-stage to help the woman ashore. Then all three stared in my direction, and the second man, who had been standing in the stern, put up a pair of binoculars and fixed them on me. He held them steady for several minutes, focussing, no doubt, on every detail of my personal appearance, which is unremarkable enough, heaven knows, and would have continued had I not suddenly become annoyed and withdrawn into the bedroom, slamming the shutters too. How rude can you get, I asked myself? Then I remembered that these western chalets were all unoccupied, and mine was the first to open for the season. Possibly this was the reason for the intense interest I appeared to cause, beginning with members of the hotel staff and now embracing guests as well. Interest would soon fade. I was neither pop star nor millionaire. And my painting efforts, however pleasing to myself, were hardly likely to draw a fascinated crowd.

Punctually at eight o'clock I walked up the garden path to the hotel and presented myself in the dining-room for dinner. It was moderately full and I was allotted a table in the corner, suitable to my single status, close to the screen dividing the service entrance from the kitchens. Never mind. I preferred this position to the centre of the room, where I could tell immediately that the hotel clientele were on what my mother used to describe as an "all fellows to football" basis.

I enjoyed my dinner, treated myself—despite my de luxe chalet—to half a bottle of domestic wine, and was peeling an orange when an almighty crash from the far end of the room disturbed us all. Waiters hurried to the scene. Heads turned, mine amongst them. A hoarse American voice, hailing from the Deep South, called loudly, "For God's sake clear up this God-darn mess!" It came from a square-shouldered man of middle age whose face was so swollen and blistered by exposure to the sun that he looked as if he had been stung by a million bees. His eyes were sunk into his head, which was bald on top, with a grizzled thatch on either side, and the pink crown had the appearance of being tightly stretched, like the skin of a sausage about to burst. A pair of enormous ears the size of clams gave further distortion to his appearance, while a drooping wisp of moustache did nothing to hide the protruding underlip, thick as blubber and about as moist. I have seldom set eyes on a more unattractive individual. A woman, I suppose his wife, sat beside him, stiff and bolt upright, apparently unmoved by the debris on the floor, which appeared to consist chiefly of bottles. She was likewise middle-aged, with a mop of tow-coloured hair turning white, and a face as sunburnt as her husband's, but mahogany brown instead of red.

"Let's get the hell out of here and go to the bar!" The hoarse strains echoed across the room. The guests at the other tables turned discreetly back to their own dinners, and I must have been the only one to watch the unsteady exit of the bee-stung spouse and his wife—I could see the deaf-aid in her ear, hence possibly her husband's rasping tones—as he literally rolled past me to the bar, a lurching vessel in the wake of his steady partner. I silently commended the efficiency of the hotel staff, who made short work of clearing the wreckage.

The dining-room emptied. "Coffee in the bar, sir," murmured my waiter. Fearing a crush and loud chatter, I hesitated before entering, for the camaraderie of hotel bars has always bored me, but I hate going without my after-dinner coffee. I need not have worried. The bar was empty, apart from the white-coated server behind the bar, and the American sitting at a table with his wife. Neither of them was speaking. There were three empty beer bottles already on the table before him. Greek music played softly from some lair behind the bar. I sat myself on a stool and ordered coffee.

The bar-tender, who spoke excellent English, asked if I had spent a pleasant day. I told him yes, I had had a good flight, found the road from Herakleion hazardous, and my first swim rather cold. He explained that it was still early in the year. "In any case," I told him, "I have come to paint, and swimming will take second place. I have a chalet right on the water-front, number sixty-two, and the view from the balcony is perfect."

Rather odd. He was polishing a glass, and his expression changed. He seemed about to say something, then evidently thought better of it, and continued with his work.

"Turn that God-damn record off!"

The hoarse, imperious summons filled the empty room. The bar-man made at once for the gramophone in the corner and adjusted the switch. A moment later the summons rang forth again.

"Bring me another bottle of beer!"

Now, had I been the bar-tender I should have turned to the man and, like a parent to a child, insisted that he say please. Instead, the brute was promptly served, and I was just downing my coffee when the voice from the table echoed through the room once more.

"Hi, you there, chalet number sixty-two. You're not superstitious?"

I turned on my stool. He was staring at me, glass in hand. His wife looked straight in front of her. Perhaps she had removed her deaf-aid. Remembering the maxim that one must humour madmen and drunks, I replied courteously enough.

"No," I said, "I'm not superstitious. Should I be?"

He began to laugh, his scarlet face creasing into a hundred lines.

"Well, God-darn it, I would be," he answered. "The fellow from that chalet was drowned only two weeks ago. Missing for two days, and then his body brought up in a net by a local fisherman, half-eaten by octopuses."

He began to shake with laughter, slapping his hand on his knee. I turned away in disgust, and raised my eyebrows in enquiry to the bar-tender.

"An unfortunate accident," he murmured. "Mr. Gordon was such a nice gentleman. Interested in archaeology. It was very warm the night he disappeared, and he must have gone swimming after dinner. Of course the police were called. We were all most distressed here at the hotel. You understand, sir, we don't talk about it much. It would be bad for business. But I do assure you the bathing is perfectly safe. This is the first accident we have ever had."

"Oh, quite," I said.

Nevertheless, it was rather off-putting, the fact that the poor chap had been the last to use my chalet. However, it was not as though he had died in the bed. And I was not superstitious. I understood now why the staff had been reluctant to let the chalet again so soon, and why the little maid had been upset.

"I tell you one thing," boomed the revolting voice. "Don't go swimming after midnight, or the octopuses will get you too." This statement was followed by another outburst of laughter. Then he said, "Come on, Maud. We're for bed," and I heard him noisily shove the table aside.

I breathed more easily when the room was clear and we were alone. "What an impossible man," I said. "Can't the management get rid of him?"

The bar-tender shrugged. "Business is business. What can they do? The Stolls have plenty of money. This is their second season here, and they arrived when we opened in March. They seem to be crazy about the place. It's only this year, though, that Mr. Stoll has become such a heavy drinker. He'll kill himself if he goes on at this rate. It's always like this, night after night. Yet his day must be healthy enough. Out at sea fishing from early morning until sundown."

"I dare say more bottles go over the side than he catches fish," I observed.

"Could be," the bar-tender agreed. "He never brings his fish to the hotel. The boatman takes them home, I dare say."

"I feel sorry for the wife."

The bar-tender shrugged. "She's the one with the money," he replied sotto voce, for a couple of guests had just entered the bar, "and I don't think Mr. Stoll has it all his own way. Being deaf may be convenient to her at times. But she never leaves his side, I'll grant her that. Goes fishing with him every day. . . . Yes, gentlemen, what can I get for you?"

He turned to his new customers and I made my escape. The cliché that it takes all sorts to make a world passed through my head. Thank heaven it was not my world, and Mr. Stoll and his deaf wife could burn themselves black under the sun all day at sea as far as I was concerned, and break beer bottles every evening into the bargain. In any event, they were not neighbours. Number sixty-two may have had the unfortunate victim of a drowning accident for its last occupant, but at least this had ensured privacy for its present tenant.

I walked down the garden path to my abode. It was a clear starlit night. The air was balmy, and sweet with the scent of the flowering shrubs planted thickly in the red earth. Standing on my balcony, I looked out across the sea towards the distant shrouded mountains and the harbour lights from the little fishing port. To my right winked the lights of the other chalets, giving a pleasing, almost fairy impression, like a clever backcloth on a stage. Truly a wonderful spot, and I blessed the travel agent who had recommended it.

I let myself in through my shuttered doorway and turned on the bed-side lamp. The room looked welcoming and snug; I could not have been better housed. I undressed, and before getting into bed remembered I had left a book I wanted to glance at on the balcony. I opened the shutters and picked it up from the deck-chair where I had thrown it, and once more, before turning in, glanced out at the open sea. Most of the fairy lights had been extinguished, but the chalet that stood on its own on the extreme point still had its light burning on the balcony. The boat, tied to the landing-stage, bore a riding-light. Seconds later I saw something moving close to my rocks. It was the snorkel of an under-water swimmer. I could see the narrow pipe, like a minute periscope, move steadily across the still, dark surface of the sea. Then it disappeared to the far left out of sight. I drew my shutters and went inside.

I don't know why it was, but the sight of that moving object was somehow disconcerting. It made me think of the unfortunate man who had been drowned during a midnight swim. My predecessor. He, too, perhaps, had sallied forth one balmy evening such as this, intent on under-water exploration, and by so doing lost his life. One would imagine the unhappy accident would scare off other hotel visitors from swimming alone at night. I made a firm decision never to bathe except in broad daylight, and—chicken-hearted, maybe—well within my depth.

I read a few pages of my book, then, feeling ready for sleep, turned to switch out my light. In doing so I clumsily bumped the telephone, which fell to the floor. I bent over, picked it up, luckily no damage done, and saw that the small drawer that was part of the fixture had fallen open. It contained a scrap of paper, or rather a card, with the name Charles Gordon upon it, and an address in Bloomsbury. Surely Gordon had been the name of my predecessor? The little maid, when she cleaned the room, had not thought to open the drawer. I turned the card over. There was something scrawled on the other side, the words "Not after midnight." And then, maybe as an afterthought, the figure thirty-eight. I replaced the card in the drawer and switched off the light. Perhaps I was overtired after the journey, but it was well past two before I finally got off to sleep. I lay awake for no rhyme or reason, listening to the water lapping against the rocks beneath my balcony.

I painted solidly for three days, never quitting my chalet except for the morning swim and my evening meal at the hotel. Nobody bothered me. An obliging waiter brought my breakfast, from which I saved rolls for midday lunch, the little maid made my bed and did her chores without disturbing me, and when I had finished my impressionistic scene on the afternoon of the third day I felt quite certain it was one of the best things I had ever done. It would take pride of place in the planned exhibition of my work. Well-satisfied, I could now relax, and I determined to explore along the coast the following day, and discover another view to whip up inspiration. The weather was glorious. Warm as a good English June. And the best thing about the whole site was the total absence of neighbours. The other guests kept to their side of the domain, and, apart from bows and nods from adjoining tables as one entered the dining-room for dinner, no one attempted to strike up acquaintance. I also took good care to drink my coffee in the bar before the obnoxious Mr. Stoll had left his table.

I realised now that it was his boat which lay anchored off the point. They were away too early in the morning for me to watch their departure, but I used to spot them returning in the late afternoon; his square, hunched form was easily recognisable, and the occasional hoarse shout to the man in charge of the boat as they came to the landing-stage. Theirs, too, was the isolated chalet on the point, and I wondered if he had picked it purposely in order to soak himself into oblivion out of sight and earshot of his nearest neighbours. Well, good luck to him, as long as he did not obtrude his offensive presence upon me.

Feeling the need of gentle exercise, I decided to spend the rest of the afternoon taking a stroll to the eastern side of the hotel grounds. Once again I congratulated myself on having escaped the cluster of chalets in this populated quarter. Mini-golf and tennis were in full swing, and the little beach was crowded with sprawling bodies on every available patch of sand. But soon the murmur of the world was behind me, and, screened and safe behind the flowering shrubs, I found myself on the point near to the landing-stage. The boat was not yet at its mooring, nor even in sight out in the gulf. A sudden temptation to peep at the unpleasant Mr. Stoll's chalet swept upon me. I crept up the little path, feeling as furtive as a burglar on the prowl, and stared up at the shuttered windows. It was no different from its fellows, or mine for that matter, except for a tell-tale heap of bottles lying on a corner of the balcony. Brute . . . Then something else caught my eye. A pair of frog-feet, and a snorkel. Surely, with all that liquor inside him, he did not venture his carcass under water? Perhaps he sent the local Greek whom he employed as crew to seek for crabs. I remembered the snorkel on my first evening, close to the rocks, and the riding-light in the boat.

I moved away, for I thought I could hear someone coming down the path and did not want to be caught prying, but before doing so I glanced up at the number of the chalet. It was thirty-eight. The figure had no particular significance for me then, but later on, changing for dinner, I picked up the tie-pin I had placed on my bedside table, and on sudden impulse opened the drawer beneath the telephone to look at my predecessor's card again. Yes, I thought so. The scrawled figure *was* thirty-eight. Pure coincidence, of course, and yet . . . "Not after midnight." The words suddenly had meaning. Stoll had warned me about swimming late on my first evening. Had he warned Gordon too? And Gordon had jotted down the warning on this card with Stoll's chalet number underneath? It made sense, but obviously poor Gordon had disregarded the advice. And so, apparently, did one of the occupants of chalet thirty-eight.

I finished changing, and instead of replacing the card in the telephone drawer put it in my wallet. I had an uneasy feeling that it was my duty to hand it in to the reception desk in case it threw any light on my unfortunate predecessor's demise. I toyed with the thought through dinner, but came to no decision. The point was, I might become involved. And as far as I knew the case was closed. There was little point in my suddenly coming forward with a calling-card lying forgotten in a drawer that probably had no significance at all.

It so happened that the people seated to the right of me in the dining-room appeared to have gone, and the Stolls' table in the corner now came into view without my being obliged to turn my head. I could watch them without making it too obvious, and I was struck by the fact that he never once addressed a word to her. They made an odd contrast. She, stiff as a ramrod, prim-looking, austere, forking her food to her mouth like a Sunday school teacher on an outing, and he, more scarlet than ever, like a great swollen sausage, pushing aside most of what the waiter placed before him after the first mouthful, and reaching out a pudgy, hairy hand to an ever-emptying glass.

I finished my dinner and went through to the bar to drink my coffee. I was early, and had the place to myself. The bar-tender and I exchanged the usual pleasantries and then, after an allusion to the weather, I jerked my head in the direction of the dining-room.

"I noticed our friend Mr. Stoll and his lady spent the whole day at sea as usual," I said.

The bar-tender shrugged. "Day after day, it never varies," he replied, "and mostly in the same direction, westward out of the bay into the gulf. It can be squally, too, at times, but they don't seem to care."

"I don't know how she puts up with him," I said. "I watched them at dinner—he didn't speak to her at all. I wonder what the other guests make of him."

"They keep well clear, sir. You saw how it was for yourself. If he ever does open his mouth it's only to be rude. And the same goes for the staff. The girls dare not go in to clean the chalet until he's out of the way. And the smell!" He grimaced, and leant forward confidentially. "The girls say he brews his own beer. He lights the fire in the chimney, and has a pot standing, filled with rotting grain, like some sort of pig-swill! Oh, yes, he drinks it right enough. Imagine the state of his liver, after what he consumes at dinner and afterwards here in the bar!"

"I suppose," I said, "that's why he keeps his balcony light on so late at night. Drinking pig-swill until the small hours. Tell me, which of the hotel visitors is it who goes under-water swimming?"

The bar-tender looked surprised. "No one, to my knowledge. Not since the accident, anyway. Poor Mr. Gordon liked a night swim, at least so we supposed. He was one of the few visitors who ever talked to Mr. Stoll, now I think of it. They had quite a conversation here one evening in the bar."

"Indeed?"

"Not about swimming, though, or fishing either. They were discussing antiquities. There's a fine little museum here in the village, you know, but it's closed at present for repairs. Mr. Gordon had some connection with the British Museum in London."

"I wouldn't have thought," I said, "that would interest friend Stoll."

"Ah," said the bar-tender, "you'd be surprised. Mr. Stoll is no fool. Last year he and Mrs. Stoll used to take the car and visit all the famous sites, Knossos, Mallia, and other places not so well-known. This year it's quite different. It's the boat and fishing every day."

"And Mr. Gordon," I pursued, "did he ever go fishing with them?"

"No, sir. Not to my knowledge. He hired a car, like you, and explored the district. He was writing a book, he told me, on archaeological finds in eastern Crete, and their connection with Greek mythology."

"Mythology?"

"Yes, I understood him to tell Mr. Stoll it was mythology, but it was all above my head, you can imagine, nor did I hear much of the conversation—we were busy that evening in the bar. Mr. Gordon was a quiet sort of gentleman, rather after your own style, if you'll excuse me, sir, seeming very interested in what they were discussing, all to do with the old gods. They were at it for over an hour."

H'm . . . I thought of the card in my wallet. Should I, or should I not, hand it over to the reception clerk at the desk? I said goodnight to the bar-tender and went back through the dining-room to the hall. The Stolls had just left their table and were walking ahead of me. I hung back until the way was clear, surprised that they had turned their backs upon the bar and were making for the hall. I stood by the rack of post-cards, to give myself an excuse for loitering, but out of their range of vision, and watched Mrs. Stoll take her coat from a hook in the lobby near the entrance, while her unpleasant husband visited the cloakroom, and then the pair of them walked out of the front door, which led direct to the car-park. They must be going for a drive. With Stoll at the wheel in his condition?

I hesitated. The reception clerk was on the telephone. It wasn't the moment to hand over the card. Some impulse, like that of a small boy playing detective, made me walk to my own car, and when Stoll's tail-light was out of sight—he was driving a Mercedes—I followed in his wake. There was only the one road, and he was heading east towards the village and the harbour lights. I lost him, inevitably, on reaching the little port, for, instinctively making for the quayside opposite what appeared to be a main café, I thought he must have done the same. I parked the Volkswagen, and looked around me. No sign of the Mercedes. Just a sprinkling of other tourists like myself, and local inhabitants, strolling, or drinking in front of the café.

Oh well, forget it, I'd sit and enjoy the scene, have a lemonade. I must have sat there for over half-an-hour, savouring what is known as "local colour," amused by the passing crowd, Greek families taking the air, pretty, self-conscious girls eyeing the youths, who appeared to stick together, practising a form of segregation, a bearded Orthodox priest who smoked incessantly at the table next to me, playing some game of dice with a couple of very old men, and of course the familiar bunch of hippies from my own country, considerably longer-haired than anybody else, dirtier, and making far more noise. When they switched on a transistor and squatted on the cobbled stones behind me, I felt it was time to move.

I paid for my lemonade, and strolled to the end of the quay and back —the line upon line of fishing-boats would be colourful by day, and possibly the scene worth painting—and then I crossed the street, my eye caught by a glint of water inland, where a side road appeared to end in a cul-de-sac. This must be the feature mentioned in the guidebook as the Bottomless Pool, much frequented and photographed by tourists in the high season. It was larger than I had expected, quite a sizeable lake, the water full of scum and floating debris, and I did not envy those who had the temerity to use the diving-board at the further end of it by day.

Then I saw the Mercedes. It was drawn-up opposite a dimly-lit café, and there was no mistaking the hunched figure at the table, beer bottles before him, the upright lady at his side, but to my surprise, and I may add disgust, he was not imbibing alone but appeared to be sharing his after-dinner carousal with a crowd of raucous fishermen at the adjoining table.

Clamour and laughter filled the air. They were evidently mocking him, Greek courtesy forgotten in their cups, while strains of song burst forth from some younger member of the clan, and suddenly he put out his hand and swept the empty bottles from his table on to the pavement, with the inevitable crash of broken glass and the accompanying cheers of his companions. I expected the local police to appear at any moment and break up the party, but there was no sign of authority. I did not care what happened to Stoll—a night in gaol might sober him up—but it was a wretched business for his wife. However, it wasn't my affair, and I was turning to go back to the quay when he staggered to his feet, applauded by the fishermen, and, lifting the remaining bottle from his table, swung it over his head. Then, with amazing dexterity for one in his condition, he pitched it like a discus-thrower into the lake. It must have missed me by a couple of feet, and he saw me duck. This was too much. I advanced towards him, livid with rage.

"What the hell are you playing at?" I shouted.

He stood before me, swaying on his feet. The laughter from the café ceased as his cronies watched with interest. I expected a flood of abuse, but Stoll's swollen face creased into a grin, and he lurched forward and patted me on the arm.

"Know something?" he said. "If you hadn't been in the way I could have lobbed it into the centre of the God-damn pool. Which is more than any of those fellows could. Not a pure-blooded Cretan amongst them. They're all of them God-damn Turks."

I tried to shake him off, but he clung on to me with the effusive affection of the habitual drunkard who has suddenly found, or imagines he has found, a life-long friend.

"You're from the hotel, aren't you?" he hiccoughed. "Don't deny it, buddy boy, I've got a good eye for faces. You're the fellow who paints all day on his God-damn porch. Well, I admire you for it. Know a bit about art myself. I might even buy your picture."

His bonhomie was offensive, his attempt at patronage intolerable.

"I'm sorry," I said stiffly, "the picture is not for sale."

"Oh, come off it," he retorted. "You artists are all the same. Play hard to get until someone offers 'em a darn good price. Take Charlie Gordon now . . ." He broke off, peering slyly into my face. "Hang on, you didn't meet Charlie Gordon, did you?"

"No," I said shortly, "he was before my time."

"That's right, that's right," he agreed, "poor fellow's dead. Drowned in the bay there, right under your rocks. At least, that's where they found him."

His slit eyes were practically closed in his swollen face, but I knew he was watching for my reaction.

"Yes," I said, "so I understand. He wasn't an artist."

"An artist?" Stoll repeated the word after me, then burst into a guffaw of laughter. "No, he was a connoisseur, and I guess that means the same God-damn thing to a chap like me. Charlie Gordon, connoisseur. Well, it didn't do him much good in the end, did it?"

"No," I said, "obviously not."

He was making an effort to pull himself together, and, still rocking on his feet, he fumbled for a packet of cigarettes and a lighter. He lit one for himself, then offered me the packet. I shook my head, telling him I did not smoke. Then, greatly daring, I observed, "I don't drink either."

"Good for you," he answered astonishingly, "neither do I. The beer they sell you here is all piss anyway, and the wine is poison." He looked over his shoulder to the group at the café, and with a conspiratorial wink dragged me to the wall beside the pool.

"I told you all those bastards are Turks, and so they are," he said, "wine-drinking, coffee-drinking Turks. They haven't brewed the right stuff here for over five thousand years. They knew how to do it then."

I remembered what the bar-tender had told me about the pig-swill in his chalet. "Is that so?" I enquired.

He winked again, and then his slit eyes widened, and I noticed that they were naturally bulbous and protuberant, a discoloured muddy brown with the whites red-flecked. "Know something?" he whispered hoarsely. "The scholars have got it all wrong. It was beer the Cretans drank here in the mountains, brewed from spruce and ivy, long before wine. Wine was discovered centuries later by the God-damn Greeks."

He steadied himself, one hand on the wall, the other on my arm. Then he leant forward and was sick into the pool. I was very nearly sick myself.

"That's better," he said, "gets rid of the poison. Doesn't do to have poison in the system. Tell you what, we'll go back to the hotel and you shall come along and have a night-cap at our chalet. I've taken a fancy to you, Mr. What's-your-name. You've got the right ideas. Don't drink, don't smoke, and you paint pictures. What's your job?"

It was impossible to shake myself clear, and I was forced to let him tow me across the road. Luckily the group at the café had now dispersed, disappointed, no doubt, because we had not come to blows, and

Mrs. Stoll had climbed into the Mercedes and was sitting in the passenger seat in front.

"Don't take any notice of her," he said. "She's stone-deaf unless you bawl at her. Plenty of room at the back."

"Thank you," I said, "I've got my own car on the quay."

"Suit yourself," he answered. "Well, come on, tell me, Mr. Artist, what's your job? An Academician?"

I could have left it at that, but some pompous strain in me made me tell the truth, in the foolish hope that he would then consider me too dull to cultivate.

"I'm a teacher," I said, "in a boys' preparatory school."

He stopped in his tracks, his wet mouth open wide in a delighted grin. "Oh, my God," he shouted, "that's rich, that's really rich. A God-damn tutor, a nurse to babes and sucklings. You're one of us, my buddy, you're one of us. And you've the nerve to tell me you've never brewed spruce and ivy!"

He was raving mad, of course, but at least this sudden burst of hilarity had made him free my arm, and he went on ahead of me to his car, shaking his head from side to side, his legs bearing his cumbersome body in a curious jog-trot, one-two . . . one-two . . . like a clumsy horse.

I watched him climb into the car beside his wife, and then I moved swiftly away, to make for the safety of the quayside, but he had turned his car with surprising agility, and had caught up with me before I reached the corner of the street. He thrust his head out of the window, smiling still.

"Come and call on us, Mr. Tutor, any time you like. You'll always find a welcome. Tell him so, Maud. Can't you see the fellow's shy?"

His bawling word of command echoed through the street. Strolling passers-by looked in our direction. The stiff, impassive face of Mrs. Stoll peered over her husband's shoulder. She seemed quite unperturbed, as if nothing was wrong, as if driving in a foreign village beside a drunken husband was the most usual pastime in the world.

"Good evening," she said in a voice without any expression. "Pleased to meet you, Mr. Tutor. Do call on us. Not after midnight. Chalet thirty-eight . . ."

Stoll waved his hand, and the car went roaring up the street to cover the few kilometres to the hotel.

It would not be true to say the encounter cast a blight on my holiday and put me off the place. A half-truth, perhaps. I was angry and disgusted, but only with the Stolls. I awoke refreshed after a good night's sleep to another brilliant day, and nothing seems so bad in the morning. I had only the one problem, which was to avoid Stoll and his equally half-witted wife. They were out in their boat all day, so this was easy. By dining early I could escape them in the dining-room. They never walked about the grounds, and meeting them face to face in the garden was not likely. If I happened to be on my balcony when they returned from fishing in the evening, and he turned his field-glasses in my direction, I would promptly disappear inside my chalet. In any event, with luck, he might have forgotten my existence, or, if that was too much to hope for, the memory of our evening's conversation might have passed from his mind. The episode had been unpleasant, even, in a curious sense, alarming, but I was not going to let it spoil the time that remained to me. I had come here to paint and relax, and was determined to go on doing so.

The boat had left its landing-stage by the time I came on to my balcony to have breakfast, and I intended to carry out my plan of exploring the coast with my painting gear, and once absorbed in my hobby could forget all about them. And I would not pass on to the management poor Gordon's scribbled card. I guessed now what had happened. The poor devil, without realising where his conversation in the bar would lead him, had been intrigued by Stoll's smattering of mythology and nonsense about ancient Crete, and, as an archaeologist, had thought further conversation might prove fruitful. He had accepted an invitation to visit chalet thirty-eight—the uncanny similarity of the words on the card and those spoken by Mrs. Stoll still haunted me—though why he had chosen to swim across the bay instead of walking the slightly longer way by the rock path was a mystery. A touch of bravado, perhaps? Who knows? Once in Stoll's chalet he had been induced, poor victim, to drink some of the hell-brew offered by his host, which must have knocked all sense and judgement out of him, and when he took to the water once again, the carousal over, what followed was bound to happen. I only hoped he had been too far gone to panic, and sank instantly. Stoll had never come forward to give the facts, and that was that. Indeed, my theory of what had happened was based on intuition alone, coincidental scraps that appeared to fit, and prejudice. It was time to dismiss the whole thing from my mind and concentrate on the day ahead.

Or rather, days. My exploration along the coast westward, in the opposite direction from the harbour, proved even more successful than I had anticipated. I followed the winding road to the left of the hotel, and having climbed for several kilometres descended again from the hills to sea level, where the land on my right suddenly flattened out to what seemed to be a great stretch of dried marsh, sun-baked, putty-coloured, the dazzling blue sea affording a splendid contrast as it lapped the stretch of land on either side. Driving closer I saw that it was not marsh at all but salt-flats, with narrow causeways running between them, the flats themselves contained by walls intersected by dykes to allow the sea-water to drain, leaving the salt behind. Here and there were the ruins of abandoned windmills, their rounded walls like castle keeps, and in a rough patch of ground a few hundred yards distant, and close to the sea, was a small church—I could see the minute cross on the roof shining in the sun. Then the salt-flats ended abruptly, and the land rose once more to form the long, narrow isthmus of Spinalongha beyond.

I bumped the Volkswagen down to the track leading to the flats. The place was quite deserted. This, I decided, after viewing the scene from every angle, would be my pitch for the next few days. The ruined church in the foreground, the abandoned windmills beyond, the salt-flats on the left, and blue water rippling to the shore of the peninsula on my right.

I set up my easel, planted my battered felt hat on my head, and forgot everything but the scene before me. Those three days on the salt-flats—for I repeated the expedition on successive days—were the high-spot of my holiday. Solitude and peace were absolute. I never saw a single soul. The occasional car wound its way along the coast road in the distance and then vanished. I broke off for sandwiches and lemonade, which I'd brought with me, and then, when the sun was hottest, rested by the ruined windmill. I returned to the hotel in the cool of the evening, had an early dinner, and then retired to my chalet to read until bedtime. A hermit at his prayers could not have wished for greater seclusion.

The fourth day, having completed two separate paintings from different angles, yet loath to leave my chosen territory, which had now become a personal stamping ground, I stacked my gear in the car and struck off on foot to the rising terrain of the peninsula, with the idea of choosing a new site for the following day. Height might give an added advantage. I toiled up the hill, fanning myself with my hat, for it was extremely hot, and was surprised when I reached the summit to find how narrow was the peninsula, no more than a long neck of land with the sea immediately below me. Not the calm water that washed the salt-flats I had left behind, but the curling crests of the outer gulf itself, whipped by a northerly wind that nearly blew my hat out of my hand. A genius might have caught those varying shades on canvas—turquoise blending into Aegean blue with wine-deep shadows beneath—but not an amateur like myself. Besides, I could hardly stand upright. Canvas and easel would have instantly blown away.

I climbed downwards towards a clump of broom affording shelter, where I could rest for a few minutes and watch that curling sea, and it was then that I saw the boat. It was moored close to a small inlet where the land curved and the water was comparatively smooth. There was no mistaking the craft: it was theirs all right. The Greek they employed as crew was seated in the bows, with a fishing-line over the side, but from his lounging attitude the fishing did not seem to be serious, and I judged he was taking his siesta. He was the only occupant of the boat. I glanced directly beneath me to the spit of sand along the shore, and saw there was a rough stone building, more or less ruined, built against the cliff-face, possibly used at one time as a shelter for sheep or goats. There was a haversack and a picnic-basket lying by the entrance, and a coat. The Stolls must have landed earlier from the boat, although nosing the bows of the craft on to the shore must have been hazardous in the running sea, and were now taking their ease out of the wind. Perhaps Stoll was even brewing his peculiar mixture of spruce and ivy, with some goat-dung added for good measure, and this lonely spot on the isthmus of Spinalongha was his "still."

Suddenly the fellow in the boat sat up, and winding in his line he moved to the stern and stood there, watching the water. I saw something move, a form beneath the surface, and then the form itself emerged, head-piece, goggles, rubber suiting, aqualung and all. Then it was hidden from me by the Greek bending to assist the swimmer to remove his top-gear, and my attention was diverted to the ruined shelter on the shore. Something was standing in the entrance. I say "something" because, doubtless owing to a trick of light, it had at first the shaggy appearance of a colt standing on its hind legs. Legs and even rump were covered with hair, and then I realised that it was Stoll himself, naked, his arms and chest as hairy as the rest of him. Only his swollen scarlet face proclaimed him for the man he was, with the enormous ears like saucers standing out from either side of his bald head. I had never in all my life seen a more revolting sight. He came out into the sunlight and looked towards the boat, and then, as if well-pleased with himself and his world, strutted forward, pacing up and down the spit of sand before the ruined shelter with that curious movement I had noticed earlier in the village, not the rolling gait of a drunken man but a stumping jog-trot, arms akimbo, his chest thrust forward, his backside prominent behind him.

The swimmer, having discarded goggles and aqualung, was now coming into the beach with long leisurely strokes, still wearing flippers—I could see them thrash the surface like a giant fish. Then, flippers cast aside on the sand, the swimmer stood up, and despite the disguise of the rubber suiting I saw, with astonishment, that it was Mrs. Stoll. She was carrying some sort of bag around her neck, and, advancing up the sand to meet her strutting husband, she lifted it over her head and gave it to him. I did not hear them exchange a word, and they went together to the hut and disappeared inside. As for the Greek, he had gone once more to the bows of the boat to resume his idle fishing.

I lay down under cover of the broom and waited. I would give them twenty minutes, half-an-hour, perhaps, then make my way back to the salt-flats and my car. As it happened, I did not have to wait so long. It was barely ten minutes before I heard a shout below me on the beach, and peering through the broom I saw that they were both standing on the spit of sand, haversack, picnic-basket, and flippers in hand, and Stoll himself dressed. The Greek was already starting the engine, and immediately afterwards he began to pull up the anchor. Then he steered the boat slowly inshore, touching it beside a ledge of rock where the Stolls had installed themselves. They climbed aboard, and in another moment the Greek had turned the boat and it was heading out to sea away from the sheltered inlet and into the gulf. Then it rounded the point and was out of my sight.

Curiosity was too much for me. I scrambled down the cliff on to the sand and made straight for the ruined shelter. As I thought, it had been a haven for goats; the mudded floor reeked, and their droppings were everywhere. In a corner, though, a clearing had been made, and there were planks of wood, forming a sort of shelf. The inevitable beer bottles were stacked beneath this, but whether they had contained the local brew or Stoll's own poison I could not tell. The shelf itself held odds and ends of pottery, as though someone had been digging in a rubbish dump and had turned up broken pieces of discarded household junk. There was no earth upon them, though; they were scaled with barnacles, and some of them were damp, and it suddenly occurred to me that these were what archaeologists call "sherds," and came from the seabed. Mrs. Stoll had been exploring, and exploring under water, whether for shells or for something of greater interest I did not know, and these pieces scattered here were throw-outs, of no use, and so neither she nor her husband had bothered to remove them. I am no judge of these things, and after looking around me, and finding nothing of further interest, I left the ruin.

The move was a fatal one. As I turned to climb the cliff I heard the throb of an engine, and the boat had returned once more, to cruise along the shore, so I judged from its position. All three heads were turned in my direction, and inevitably the squat figure in the stern had field-glasses poised. He would have no difficulty, I feared, in distinguishing who it was that had just left the ruined shelter and was struggling up the cliff to the hill above.

I did not look back but went on climbing, my hat pulled down well over my brows in the vain hope that it might afford some sort of concealment. After all, I might have been any tourist who had happened to be at that particular spot at that particular time. Nevertheless, I feared recognition was inevitable. I tramped back to the car on the salt-flats, tired, breathless, and thoroughly irritated. I wished I had never decided to explore the farther side of the peninsula. The Stolls would think I had been spying upon them, which indeed was true. My pleasure in the day was spoilt. I decided to pack it in and go back to the hotel. Luck was against me, though, for I had hardly turned on to the track leading from the marsh to the road when I noticed that one of my tyres was flat. By the time I had put on the spare wheel—for I am ham-fisted at all mechanical jobs—forty minutes had gone by.

My disgruntled mood did not improve, when at last I reached the hotel, to see that the Stolls had beaten me to it. Their boat was already at its moorings beside the landing-stage, and Stoll himself was sitting on his balcony with field-glasses trained upon my chalet. I stumped up the steps feeling as self-conscious as someone under a television camera and went into my quarters, closing the shutters behind me. I was taking a bath when the telephone rang.

"Yes?" Towel round the middle, dripping hands, it could not have rung at a more inconvenient moment.

"That you, Mr. Tutor-boy?"

The rasping, wheezing voice was unmistakable. He did not sound drunk, though.

"This is Timothy Grey," I replied stiffly.

"Grey or Black, it's all the same to me," he said. His tone was unpleasant, hostile. "You were out on Spinalongha this afternoon. Correct?"

"I was walking on the peninsula," I told him. "I don't know why you should be interested."

"Oh, stuff it up," he answered, "you can't fool me. You're just like the other fellow. You're nothing but a God-damn spy. Well, let me tell you this. The wreck was clean-picked centuries ago."

"I don't know what you're talking about," I said. "What wreck?"

There was a moment's pause. He muttered something under his breath, whether to himself or to his wife I could not tell, but when he resumed speaking his tone had moderated, something of pseudo-bonhomie had returned.

"O.K. . . . O.K. . . . Tutor-boy," he said. "We won't argue the point. Let us say you and I share an interest. Schoolmasters, university professors, college lecturers, we're all alike under the skin, and above it too sometimes." His low chuckle was offensive. "Don't panic, I won't give you away," he continued. "I've taken a fancy to you, as I told you the other night. You want something for your God-darn school museum, correct? Something you can show the pretty lads and your colleagues too? Fine. Agreed. I've got just the thing. You call round here later this evening, and I'll make you a present of it. I don't want your God-damn money . . ." He broke off, chuckling again, and Mrs. Stoll must have made some remark, for he added, "That's right, that's right. We'll have a cosy little party, just the three of us. My wife's taken quite a fancy to you too."

The towel round my middle slipped to the floor, leaving me naked. I felt vulnerable for no reason at all. And the patronising, insinuating voice infuriated me.

"Mr. Stoll," I said, "I'm not a collector for schools, colleges, or museums. I'm not interested in antiquities. I am here on holiday to paint, for my own pleasure, and quite frankly I have no intention of calling upon you or any other visitor at the hotel. Good evening."

I slammed down the receiver and went back to the bathroom. Infernal impudence. Loathsome man. The question was, would he now leave me alone, or would he keep his glasses trained on my balcony until he saw me go up to the hotel for dinner, and then follow me, wife in tow, to the dining-room? Surely he would not dare to resume the conversation in front of waiters and guests? If I guessed his intentions aright, he wanted to buy my silence by fobbing me off with some gift. Those day-long fishing expeditions of his were a mask for under-water exploration—hence his allusion to a wreck—during which he hoped to find, possibly had found already, objects of value that he intended to smuggle out of Crete. Doubtless he had succeeded in doing this the preceding year, and the Greek boatman would be well-paid for holding his tongue. This season, however, it had not worked to plan. My unfortunate predecessor at chalet sixty-two, Charles Gordon, himself an expert in antiquities, had grown suspicious. Stoll's allusion—"You're like the other fellow. Nothing but a God-damn spy"—made this plain. What if Gordon had received an invitation to chalet thirty-eight, not to drink the spurious beer but to inspect Stoll's collection and be offered a bribe for keeping silent? Had he refused, threatening to expose Stoll? Did he really drown accidentally, or had Stoll's wife followed him down into the water in her rubber suit and mask and flippers, and then, once beneath the surface . . . ?

My imagination was running away with me. I had no proof of anything. All I knew was that nothing in the world would get me to Stoll's chalet, and indeed, if he attempted to pester me again, I should have to tell the whole story to the management.

I changed for dinner, then opened my shutters a fraction and stood behind them, looking out towards his chalet. The light shone on his balcony, for it was already dusk, but he himself had disappeared. I stepped outside, locking the shutters behind me, and walked up the garden to the hotel. I was just about to go through to the reception hall from the terrace when I saw Stoll and his wife sitting on a couple of chairs inside, guarding, as it were, the passage-way to lounge and dining-room. If I wanted to eat I had to pass them. Right, I thought. You can sit there all evening waiting. I went back along the terrace, and circling the hotel by the kitchens, went round to the car-park and got into the Volkswagen. I would have dinner down in the village, and damn the extra expense. I drove off in a fury, found an obscure taverna well away from the harbour itself, and instead of the three-course hotel meal I had been looking forward to on my *en pension* terms—for I was hungry after my day in the open and meagre sandwiches on the salt-flats—I was obliged to content myself with an omelette, an orange, and a cup of coffee.

It was after ten when I arrived back in the hotel. I parked the car, and, skirting the kitchen quarters once again, made my way furtively down the garden path to my chalet, letting myself in through the shutters like a thief. The light was still shining on Stoll's balcony, and by this time he was doubtless deep in his cups. If there was any trouble with him the next day I would definitely go to the management.

I undressed and lay reading in bed until after midnight, then, feeling sleepy, switched out my light and went across the room to open the shutters, for the air felt stuffy and close. I stood for a moment looking out across the bay. The chalet lights were all extinguished except for one. Stoll's, of course. His balcony light cast a yellow streak on the water beside his landing-stage. The water rippled, yet there was no wind. Then I saw it. I mean, the snorkel. The little pipe was caught an instant in the yellow gleam, but before I lost it I knew that it was heading in a direct course for the rocks beneath my chalet. I waited. Nothing happened, there was no sound, no further ripples on the water. Perhaps she did this every evening. Perhaps it was routine, and while I was lying on my bed reading, oblivious of the world outside, she had been treading water close to the rocks. The thought was discomforting, to say the least of it, that regularly after midnight she left her besotted husband

asleep over his hell-brew of spruce and ivy and came herself, his under-
water partner, in her black-seal rubber suit, her mask, her flippers, to
spy upon chalet sixty-two. And on this night in particular, after the telephone conversation and my refusal to visit them, coupled with my new
theory as to the fate of my predecessor, her presence in my immediate
vicinity was more than ominous, it was threatening.

   Suddenly, out of the dark stillness to my right, the snorkel-pipe was
caught in a finger-thread of light from my own balcony. Now it was almost immediately below me. I panicked, turned, and fled inside my
room, closing the shutters fast. I switched off the balcony light and
stood against the wall between my bedroom and bathroom, listening.
The soft air filtered through the shutters beside me. It seemed an eter-
nity before the sound I expected, dreaded, came to my ears. A kind of
swishing movement from the balcony, a fumbling of hands, and heavy
breathing. I could see nothing from where I stood against the wall, but
the sounds came through the chinks in the shutters, and I knew she was
there. I knew she was holding on to the hasp, and the water was dripping from the skin-tight rubber suit, and that even if I shouted "What
do you want?" she would not hear. No deaf-aids under water, no mechanical device for soundless ears. Whatever she did by night must be
done by sight, by touch.

   She began to rattle on the shutters. I took no notice. She rattled
again. Then she found the bell, and the shrill summons pierced the air
above my head with all the intensity of a dentist's drill upon a nerve.
She rang three times. Then silence. No more rattling of the shutters. No
more breathing. She might yet be crouching on the balcony, the water
dripping from the black rubber suit, waiting for me to lose patience, to
emerge.

   I crept away from the wall and sat down on the bed. There was not a
sound from the balcony. Boldly I switched on my bedside light, half-ex-
pecting the rattling of the shutters to begin again, or the sharp ping of
the bell. Nothing happened, though. I looked at my watch. It was half-
past twelve. I sat there hunched on my bed, my mind that had been so
heavy with sleep now horribly awake, full of foreboding, my dread of
that sleek black figure increasing minute by minute so that all sense and
reason seemed to desert me, and my dread was the more intense and
irrational because the figure in the rubber suit was female. What did she
want?

   I sat there for an hour or more until reason took possession once
again. She must have gone. I got up from the bed and went to the shutters and listened. There wasn't a sound. Only the lapping of water beneath the rocks. Gently, very gently, I opened the hasp and peered

through the shutters. Nobody was there. I opened them wider and stepped on to the balcony. I looked out across the bay, and there was no longer any light shining from the balcony of number thirty-eight. The little pool of water beneath my shutters was evidence enough of the figure that had stood there an hour ago, and the wet footmarks leading down the steps towards the rocks suggested she had gone the way she came. I breathed a sigh of relief. Now I could sleep in peace.

It was only then that I saw the object at my feet, lying close to the shutter's base. I bent and picked it up. It was a small package, wrapped in some sort of waterproof cloth. I took it inside and examined it, sitting on the bed. Foolish suspicions of plastic bombs came to my mind, but surely a journey under water would neutralize the lethal effect? The package was sewn about with twine, criss-crossed. It felt quite light. I remembered the old classical proverb, "Beware of the Greeks when they bear gifts." But the Stolls were not Greeks, and, whatever lost Atlantis they might have plundered, explosives did not form part of the treasure-trove of that vanished continent.

I cut the twine with a pair of nail-scissors, then unthreaded it piece by piece and unfolded the waterproof wrapping. A layer of finely-meshed net concealed the object within, and, this unravelled, the final token itself lay in my open hand. It was a small jug, reddish in colour, with a handle on either side for safe holding. I had seen this sort of object before—the correct name, I believe, is rhyton—displayed behind glass cases in museums. The body of the jug had been shaped cunningly and brilliantly into a man's face, with upstanding ears like scallop-shells, while protruding eyes and bulbous nose stood out above the leering, open mouth, the moustache drooping to the rounded beard that formed the base. At the top, between the handles, were the upright figures of three strutting men, their faces similar to that upon the jug, but here human resemblance ended, for they had neither hands nor feet but hooves, and from each of their hairy rumps extended a horse's tail.

I turned the object over. The same face leered at me from the other side. The same three figures strutted at the top. There was no crack, no blemish that I could see, except a faint mark on the lip. I looked inside the jug and saw a note lying on the bottom. The opening was too small for my hand, so I shook it out. The note was a plain white card, with words typed upon it. It read: "Silenos, earth-born satyr, half-horse, half-man, who, unable to distinguish truth from falsehood, reared Dionysus, god of intoxication, as a girl in a Cretan cave, then became his drunken tutor and companion."

That was all. Nothing more. I put the note back inside the jug, and the jug on the table at the far end of the room. Even then the lewd, mocking face leered back at me, and the three strutting figures of the horse-men stood out in bold relief across the top. I was too weary to wrap it up again. I covered it with my jacket and climbed back into bed. In the morning I would cope with the labourious task of packing it up and getting my waiter to take it across to chalet thirty-eight. Stoll could keep his rhyton—heaven knew what the value might be—and good luck to him. I wanted no part of it.

Exhausted, I fell asleep, but, oh God, to no oblivion. The dreams which came, and from which I struggled to awaken, but in vain, belonged to some other unknown world horribly intermingled with my own. Term had started, but the school in which I taught was on a mountain top hemmed in by forest, though the school buildings were the same and the classroom was my own. My boys, all of them familiar faces, lads I knew, wore vine-leaves in their hair, and had a strange, unearthly beauty both endearing and corrupt. They ran towards me, smiling, and I put my arms about them, and the pleasure they gave me was insidious and sweet, never before experienced, never before imagined, the man who pranced in their midst and played with them was not myself, not the self I knew, but a demon shadow emerging from a jug, strutting in his conceit as Stoll had done upon the spit of sand at Spinalongha.

I awoke after what seemed like centuries of time, and indeed broad daylight seeped through the shutters, and it was a quarter to ten. My head was throbbing. I felt sick, exhausted. I rang for coffee, and looked out across the bay. The boat was at its moorings. The Stolls had not gone fishing. Usually they were away by nine. I took the jug from under my coat, and with fumbling hands began to wrap it up in the net and waterproof packing. I had made a botched job of it when the waiter came on to the balcony with my breakfast tray. He wished me good morning with his usual smile.

"I wonder," I said, "if you would do me a favour."

"You are welcome, sir," he replied.

"It concerns Mr. Stoll," I went on. "I believe he has chalet thirty-eight across the bay. He usually goes fishing every day, but I see his boat is still at the landing-stage."

"That is not surprising." The waiter smiled. "Mr. and Mrs. Stoll left this morning by car."

"I see. Do you know when they will be back?"

"They will not be back, sir. They have left for good. They are driving to the airport en route for Athens. The boat is probably vacant now if you wish to hire it."

He went down the steps into the garden, and the jar in its waterproof packing was still lying beside the breakfast tray.

The sun was already fierce upon my balcony. It was going to be a scorching day, too hot to paint. And anyway, I wasn't in the mood. The events of the night before had left me tired, jaded, with a curious sapped feeling due not so much to the intruder beyond my shutters as to those interminable dreams. I might be free of the Stolls themselves, but not of their legacy. I unwrapped it once again and turned it over in my hands. The leering, mocking face repelled me; its resemblance to the human Stoll was not pure fancy but compelling, sinister, doubtless his very reason for palming it off on me—I remembered the chuckle down the telephone—and if he possessed treasures of equal value to this rhyton, or even greater, then one object the less would not bother him. He would have a problem getting them through Customs, especially in Athens. The penalties were enormous for this sort of thing. Doubtless he had his contacts, knew what to do.

I stared at the dancing figures near the top of the jar, and once more I was struck by their likeness to the strutting Stoll on the shore of Spinalongha, his naked, hairy form, his protruding rump. Part man, part horse, a satyr . . . "Silenos, drunken tutor to the god Dionysus."

The jar was horrible, evil. Small wonder that my dreams had been distorted, utterly foreign to my nature. But not perhaps to Stoll's? Could it be that he, too, had realised its bestiality, but not until too late? The bar-tender had told me that it was only this year he had gone to pieces, taken to drink. There must be some link between his alcoholism and the finding of the jar. One thing was very evident, I must get rid of it—but how? If I took it to the management questions would be asked. They might not believe my story about its being dumped on my balcony the night before; they might suspect that I had taken it from some archaeological site, and then had second thoughts about trying to smuggle it out of the country or dispose of it somewhere on the island. So what? Drive along the coast and chuck it away, a rhyton centuries old and possibly priceless?

I wrapped it carefully in my jacket pocket and walked up the garden to the hotel. The bar was empty, the bar-tender behind his counter polishing glasses. I sat down on a stool in front of him and ordered a mineral water.

"No expedition today, sir?" he enquired.

"Not yet," I said. "I may go out later."

"A cool dip in the sea and a siesta on the balcony," he suggested, "and by the way, sir, I have something for you."

He bent down and brought out a small screw-topped bottle filled with what appeared to be bitter lemon.

"Left here last evening with Mr. Stoll's compliments," he said. "He waited for you in the bar until nearly midnight, but you never came. So I promised to hand it over when you did."

I looked at it suspiciously. "What is it?" I asked.

The bar-tender smiled. "Some of his chalet home-brew," he said. "It's quite harmless, he gave me a bottle for myself and my wife. She says it's nothing but lemonade. The real smelling stuff must have been thrown away. Try it." He had poured some into my mineral water before I could stop him.

Hesitant, wary, I dipped my finger into the glass and tasted it. It was like the barley-water my mother used to make when I was a child. And equally tasteless. And yet . . . it left a sort of aftermath on the palate and the tongue. Not as sweet as honey nor as sharp as grapes, but pleasant, like the smell of raisins under the sun, curiously blended with the ears of ripening corn.

"Oh well," I said, "here's to the improved health of Mr. Stoll," and I drank my medicine like a man.

"I know one thing," said the bar-tender, "I've lost my best customer. They went early this morning."

"Yes," I said, "so my waiter informed me."

"The best thing Mrs. Stoll could do would be to get him into hospital," the bar-tender continued. "Her husband's a sick man, and it's not just the drink."

"What do you mean?"

He tapped his forehead. "Something wrong up here," he said. "You could see for yourself how he acted. Something on his mind. Some sort of obsession. I rather doubt we shall see them again next year."

I sipped my mineral water, which was undoubtedly improved by the barley taste.

"What was his profession?" I asked.

"Mr. Stoll? Well, he told me he had been professor of classics in some American university, but you never could tell if he was speaking the truth or not. Mrs. Stoll paid the bills here, hired the boatman, arranged everything. Though he swore at her in public he seemed to depend on her. I sometimes wondered, though . . ."

He broke off.

"Wondered what?" I enquired.

"Well . . . she had a lot to put up with. I've seen her look at him sometimes, and it wasn't with love. Women of her age must seek some sort of satisfaction out of life. Perhaps she found it on the side while he indulged his passion for liquor and antiques. He had picked up quite a few items in Greece, and around the islands and here in Crete. It's not too difficult if you know the ropes."

He winked. I nodded, and ordered another mineral water. The warm atmosphere in the bar had given me a thirst.

"Are there any lesser known sites along the coast?" I asked. "I mean, places they might have gone ashore to from the boat?"

It may have been my fancy, but I thought he avoided my eye.

"I hardly know, sir," he said. "I dare say there are, but they would have custodians of some sort. I doubt if there are any places the authorities don't know about."

"What about wrecks?" I pursued. "Vessels that might have been sunk centuries ago, and are now lying on the sea bottom?"

He shrugged his shoulders. "There are always local rumours," he said casually, "stories that get handed down through generations. But it's mostly superstition. I've never believed in them myself, and I don't know anybody with education who does."

He was silent for a moment, polishing a glass. I wondered if I had said too much. "We all know small objects are discovered from time to time," he murmured, "and they can be of great value. They get smuggled out of the country, or if too much risk is involved they can be disposed of locally to experts and a good price paid. I have a cousin in the village connected with the local museum. He owns the café opposite the Bottomless Pool. Mr. Stoll used to patronise him. Papitos is the name. As a matter of fact, the boat hired by Mr. Stoll belongs to my cousin. He lets it out on hire to the visitors here at the hotel."

"I see."

"But there . . . you are not a collector, sir, and you're not interested in antiques."

"No," I said, "I am not a collector."

I got up from the stool and bade him good morning. I wondered if the small package in my pocket made a bulge.

I went out of the bar and strolled on to the terrace. Nagging curiosity made me wander down to the landing-stage below the Stolls' chalet. The chalet itself had evidently been swept and tidied, the balcony cleared, the shutters closed. No trace remained of the last occupants. Before the day was over, in all probability, it would be opened for some English family who would strew the place with bathing-suits.

The boat was at its moorings, and the Greek hand was swabbing down the sides. I looked out across the bay to my own chalet on the opposite side and saw it, for the first time, from Stoll's viewpoint. As he stood there, peering through his field-glasses, it seemed clearer to me than ever before that he must have taken me for an interloper, a spy—possibly, even, someone sent out from England to enquire into the true circumstances of Charles Gordon's death. Was the gift of the jar, the night before departure, a gesture of defiance? A bribe? Or a curse?

Then the Greek fellow on the boat stood up and faced towards me. It was not the regular boatman, but another one. I had not realised this before when his back was turned. The man who used to accompany the Stolls had been younger, dark and this was an older chap altogether. I remembered what the bar-tender had told me about the boat belonging to his cousin, Papitos, who owned the café in the village by the Bottomless Pool.

"Excuse me," I called, "are you the owner of the boat?"

The man climbed on to the landing-stage and stood before me.

"Nicolai Papitos is my brother," he said. "You want to go for trip round the bay? Plenty good fish outside. No wind today. Sea very calm."

"I don't want to fish," I told him. "I wouldn't mind an outing for an hour or so. How much does it cost?"

He gave me the sum in drachmae, and I did a quick reckoning and made it out to be not more than two pounds for the hour, though it would doubtless be double that sum to round the point and go along the coast as far as that spit of sand on the peninsula of Spinalongha. I took out my wallet to see if I had the necessary notes, or whether I should have to return to the reception desk and cash a travellers' cheque.

"You charge to hotel," he said quickly, evidently reading my thoughts. "The cost go on your bill."

This decided me. Damn it all, my extras had been moderate to date.

"Very well," I said, "I'll hire the boat for a couple of hours."

It was a curious sensation to be chug-chugging across the bay as the Stolls had done so many times, the line of chalets in my wake, the harbour astern on my right, and the blue waters of the open gulf ahead. I had no clear plan in mind. It was just that, for some inexplicable reason, I felt myself drawn towards that inlet near the shore where the boat had been anchored on the previous day. "The wreck was picked clean centuries ago . . ." Those had been Stoll's words. Was he lying? Or could it be that day after day, through the past weeks, that particular spot had been his hunting-ground, and his wife, diving, had brought the dripping treasure from its sea-bed to his grasping hands? We rounded the point, and inevitably, away from the sheltering arm that had hitherto encompassed us, the breeze appeared to freshen, the boat became more lively as the bows struck the short curling seas.

The long peninsula of Spinalongha lay ahead of us to the left, and I had some difficulty in explaining to my helmsman that I did not want him to steer into the comparative tranquillity of the waters bordering the salt-flats, but to continue along the more exposed outward shores of the peninsula bordering the open sea.

"You want to fish?" he shouted above the roar of the engine. "You find very good fish in there," pointing to my flats of yesterday.

"No, no," I shouted back, "farther on, along the coast."

He shrugged. He couldn't believe I had no desire to fish, and I wondered, when we reached our destination, what possible excuse I could make for heading the boat inshore and anchoring, unless—and this seemed plausible enough—I pleaded that the motion of the boat was proving too much for me.

The hills I had climbed yesterday swung into sight above the bows, and then, rounding a neck of land, the inlet itself, the ruined shepherd's hut close to the shore.

"In there," I pointed. "Anchor close to the shore."

He stared at me, puzzled, and shook his head. "No good," he shouted, "too many rocks."

"Nonsense," I yelled. "I saw some people from the hotel anchored here yesterday."

Suddenly he slowed the engine, so that my voice rang out foolishly on the air. The boat danced up and down in the troughs of the short seas.

"Not a good place to anchor," he repeated doggedly. "Wreck there, fouling the ground."

So there was a wreck . . . I felt a mounting excitement, and I was not to be put off.

"I don't know anything about that," I replied, with equal determination, "but this boat did anchor here, just by the inlet, I saw it myself."

He muttered something to himself, and made the sign of the cross.

"And if I lose the anchor?" he said. "What do I say to my brother Nicolai?"

He was nosing the boat gently, very gently, towards the inlet, and then, cursing under his breath, he went forward to the bows and threw the anchor overboard. He waited until it held, then returned and switched off the engine.

"If you want to go in close, you must take the dinghy," he said sulkily. "I blow it up for you, yes?"

He went forward once again, and dragged out one of those inflatable rubber affairs they use on air-sea rescue craft.

"Very well," I said, "I'll take the dinghy."

In point of fact, it suited my purpose better. I could paddle close inshore, and would not have him breathing over my shoulder. At the same time, I couldn't forbear a slight prick to his pride.

"The man in charge of the boat yesterday anchored further in without mishap," I told him.

My helmsman paused in the act of inflating the dinghy.

"If he like to risk my brother's boat that is his affair," he said shortly. "I have charge of it today. Other fellow not turn up for work this morning, so he lose his job. I do not want to lose mine."

I made no reply. If the other fellow had lost his job it was probably because he had pocketed too many tips from Stoll.

The dinghy inflated and was in the water; I climbed into it gingerly and began to paddle myself towards the shore. Luckily there was no run upon the spit of sand, and I was able to land successfully and pull the dinghy after me. I noticed that my helmsman was watching me with some interest from his safe anchorage, then, once he perceived that the dinghy was unlikely to come to harm, he turned his back and squatted in the bows of the boat, shoulders humped in protest, meditating, no doubt, upon the folly of English visitors.

My reason for landing was that I wanted to judge, from the shore, the exact spot where the boat had anchored yesterday. It was as I thought. Perhaps a hundred yards to the left of where we had anchored today, and closer in shore. The sea was smooth enough, I could navigate it perfectly in the rubber dinghy. I glanced towards the shepherd's hut, and saw my footprints of the day before. There were other footprints too. Fresh ones. The sand in front of the hut had been disturbed. It was as though something had lain there, and then been dragged to the water's edge where I stood now. The goatherd himself, perhaps, had visited the place with his flock earlier that morning.

I crossed over to the hut and looked inside. Curious . . . The little pile of rubble, odds and ends of pottery, had gone. The empty bottles still stood in the far corner, and three more had been added to their number, one of them half-full. It was warm inside the hut, and I was sweating. The sun had been beating down on my bare head for nearly an hour—like a fool I had left my hat back in the chalet, not having prepared myself for this expedition—and I was seized with an intolerable thirst. I had acted on impulse, and was paying for it now. It was, in retrospect, an idiotic thing to have done. I might become completely dehydrated, pass out with heat-stroke. The half-bottle of beer would be better than nothing.

I did not fancy drinking from it after the goatherd, if it was indeed he who had brought it here; these fellows were none too clean. Then I remembered the jar in my pocket. Well, it would at least serve a purpose. I pulled the package out of its wrappings and poured the beer into it. It was only after I had swallowed the first draught that I realised it wasn't beer at all. It was barley-water. It was the same home-brewed stuff that Stoll had left for me in the bar. Did the locals, then, drink it too? It was innocuous enough, I knew that; the bar-tender had tasted it himself, and so had his wife.

When I had finished the bottle I examined the jar once again. I don't know how it was, but somehow the leering face no longer seemed so lewd. It had a certain dignity that had escaped me before. The beard, for instance. The beard was shaped to perfection around the base—whoever had fashioned it was a master of his craft. I wondered whether Socrates had looked thus when he strolled in the Athenian agora with his pupils and discoursed on life. He could have done. And his pupils may not necessarily have been the young men whom Plato said they were, but of a tenderer age, like my lads at school, like those youngsters of eleven and twelve who had smiled upon me in my dreams last night.

I felt the scalloped ears, the rounded nose, the full soft lips of the tutor Silenos upon the jar, the eyes no longer protruding but questioning, appealing, and even the naked horsemen on the top had grown in grace. It seemed to me now they were not strutting in conceit but dancing with linked hands, filled with a gay abandon, a pleasing, wanton joy. It must have been my fear of the midnight intruder that had made me look upon the jar with such distaste.

I put it back in my pocket, and walked out of the hut and down the spit of beach to the rubber dinghy. Supposing I went to the fellow Papitos, who had connections with the local museum, and asked him to value the jar? Supposing it was worth hundreds, thousands, and he could dispose of it for me, or tell me of a contact in London? Stoll must be doing this all the time, and getting away with it. Or so the bar-tender had hinted . . . I climbed into the dinghy and began to paddle away from the shore, thinking of the difference between a man like Stoll, with all his wealth, and myself. There he was, a brute with a skin so thick you couldn't pierce it with a spear, and his shelves back at home in the States loaded with loot. Whereas I . . . Teaching small boys on an inadequate salary, and all for what? Moralists said that money made no difference to happiness, but they were wrong. If I had a quarter of the Stolls' wealth I could retire, live abroad, on a Greek island, perhaps, and winter in some studio in Athens or Rome. A whole new way of life would open up, and just at the right moment, too, before I touched middle-age.

I pulled out from the shore and made for the spot where I judged the boat to have anchored the day before. Then I let the dinghy rest, pulled in my paddles, and stared down into the water. The colour was pale green, translucent, yet surely fathoms deep, for as I looked down to the golden sands beneath, the sea-bed had all the tranquillity of another world, remote from the one I knew. A shoal of fish, silver-bright and gleaming, wriggled their way towards a tress of coral hair that might have graced Aphrodite, but was seaweed moving gently in whatever currents lapped the shore. Pebbles that on land would have been no more than rounded stones were brilliant here as jewels. The breeze that rippled the gulf beyond the anchored boat would never touch these depths, but only the surface of the water, and as the dinghy floated on, circling slowly without pull of wind or tide, I wondered whether it was the motion in itself that had drawn the unhearing Mrs. Stoll to underwater swimming. Treasure was the excuse, to satisfy her husband's greed, but down there, in the depths, she would escape from a way of life that must have been unbearable.

Then I looked up at the hills above the retreating spit of sand, and I saw something flash. It was a ray of sunlight upon glass, and the glass moved. Someone was watching me through field-glasses. I rested upon my paddles and stared. Two figures moved stealthily away over the brow of the hill, but I recognised them instantly. One was Mrs. Stoll, the other the Greek fellow who had acted as their crew. I glanced over my shoulder to the anchored boat. My helmsman was still staring out to sea. He had seen nothing.

The footprints outside the hut were now explained. Mrs. Stoll, the boatman in tow, had paid a final visit to the hut to clear the rubble, and now, their mission accomplished, they would continue their drive to the airport to catch the afternoon plane to Athens, their journey made several miles longer by the detour along the coast-road. And Stoll himself? Asleep, no doubt, at the back of the car upon the salt-flats, awaiting their return.

The sight of that woman once again gave me a profound distaste for my expedition. I wished I had not come. And my helmsman had spoken the truth: the dinghy was now floating above rock. A ridge must run out here from the shore in a single reef. The sand had darkened, changed in texture, become grey. I peered closer into the water, cupping my eyes with my hands, and suddenly I saw the vast encrusted anchor, the shells and barnacles of centuries upon its spikes, and as the dinghy drifted on, the bones of the long-buried craft itself appeared, broken, sparless, her decks, if decks there had been, long since dismembered or destroyed.

Stoll had been right: her bones had been picked clean. Nothing of any value could now remain upon that skeleton. No pitchers, no jars, no gleaming coins. A momentary breeze rippled the water, and when it became clear again and all was still I saw the second anchor by the skeleton bows, and a body, arms outstretched, legs imprisoned in the anchor's jaws. The motion of the water gave the body life, as though, in some desperate fashion, it still struggled for release, but, trapped as it was, escape would never come. The days and nights would follow, months and years, and slowly the flesh would dissolve, leaving the frame impaled upon the spikes.

The body was Stoll's, head, trunk, limbs grotesque, inhuman, as they swayed backwards and forwards at the bidding of the currents.

I looked up once more to the crest of the hill, but the two figures had long since vanished, and in an appalling flash of intuition a picture of what had happened became vivid: Stoll, strutting on the spit of sand, the half-bottle raised to his lips, and then they struck him down and dragged him to the water's edge, and it was his wife who towed him, drowning, to his final resting-place beneath the surface, there below me, impaled on the crusted anchor. I was sole witness to his fate, and no matter what lies she told to account for his disappearance I would remain silent; it was not my responsibility, guilt might increasingly haunt me, but I must never become involved.

I heard the sound of something choking beside me—I realise now it was myself, in horror and in fear—and I struck at the water with my paddles and started pulling away from the wreck back to the boat. As I did so my arm brushed against the jar in my pocket, and in sudden panic I dragged it forth and flung it overboard. It did not sink immediately but remained bobbing on the surface, then slowly filled with that green translucent sea, pale as the barley liquid laced with spruce and ivy. The eyes in the swollen face stared up at me, and they were not only those of Silenos the satyr tutor, and of the drowned Stoll, but my own as well, as I should see them one day reflected in a mirror. They seemed to hold all knowledge in their depths, and all despair.

The Most Obstinate
Customer in the World

GEORGES SIMENON

1   The 'Café des Ministères', or Joseph's Domain

The records of the police knew nothing like it; nobody had ever shown as much obstinacy or vanity in displaying himself from every angle, in posing as it were for hours on end—sixteen successive hours, to be exact—and in attracting, whether deliberately or not, the attention of dozens of people, to such a degree that Inspector Janvier, who had been called in, had gone up for a closer look. And yet when it came to reconstructing his appearance, the image remembered was an utterly vague and hazy one.

So much so that to some people—who were not particularly fanciful—this self-display seemed like a particularly cunning and original ruse.

However, it is essential to go over that day, 3 May, hour by hour; it was a warm, sunny day with that special thrill in the air that belongs to Paris in the spring; and from morning till night the honeyed scent of the chestnut trees on the Boulevard Saint-Germain drifted into the cool café.

It was at 8 a.m. as usual that Joseph opened the café doors. He was in shirt-sleeves and a waistcoat. The floor was covered with the sawdust he had sprinkled there at closing time on the previous evening, and chairs were piled high on the marble tables.

For the Café des Ministères, at the corner of the Boulevard Saint-Germain and the Rue des Saints-Pères, is one of the few old-fashioned cafés that still exist in Paris. It has not pandered to the vogue for bars serving quick drinks to casual customers, nor to the contemporary taste for gilt decorations, indirect lighting, pillars covered with looking-glass and little tables of some plastic material.

It is the typical café where regular customers have their own tables, their favourite corners, their games of draughts or chess, and where Joseph the waiter knows everyone by name: mostly head clerks or civil servants from the nearby Government offices.

And Joseph himself is quite a character. He has been a waiter for thirty years, and one cannot imagine him wearing a business suit like other people; one might not recognize him in the street if one met him in the suburb where he has built himself a little house.

Eight in the morning is cleaning-up time; the double door on to the Boulevard Saint-Germain is wide open; part of the pavement is in broad sunlight, but a cool, blue-hazed shadow prevails inside.

Joseph smokes a cigarette. This is the only moment in the day when he allows himself to smoke on the premises. He lights the gas under the percolator, which he then polishes till it gleams like a mirror. There is a whole series of almost ritual acts which are performed in an unchanging order: bottles of spirits and apéritifs to be lined up on the shelf, the sawdust to be swept up, the chairs to be set out round the tables . . .

At eight ten exactly, the man came in. Joseph was bending over his percolator and did not see him enter, which he subsequently regretted. Did the man hurry in as though he were escaping from somebody? Why did he choose the Café des Ministères, when on the opposite side of the street there is a café with a bar where, at this time of day, you can buy croissants and rolls, and which is swarming with people?

Joseph said, later:

"I turned round and I saw somebody standing in the middle of the café, a man wearing a grey hat and carrying a small suitcase."

Actually, although the café door was open, the place itself was not strictly speaking open yet; nobody ever came in so early, the coffee was not ready, the water was barely warm in the percolator and the chairs were still stacked on the tables.

"I can't serve you for another half-hour at least," Joseph had said.

He thought that would settle it. But the man, still clutching his case, picked up a chair from one of the tables and sat down, quite calmly, like someone who is not going to change his mind, and muttered:

"Never mind."

That in itself was enough to put Joseph in a bad temper. He's like those housewives who detest having someone in their way when they are turning out a room. Cleaning-up time is his own special time. And he grumbled between his teeth:

"I'm going to keep you waiting for your coffee!"

Until nine o'clock he carried on with his usual jobs, occasionally casting a furtive glance at his customer. A score of times he passed quite close to him, brushed up against him and even jostled him a little as he swept up the sawdust or removed chairs from tables.

Then, at two or three minutes past nine, he resigned himself to serving the man a cup of piping hot coffee with a small jug of milk and two lumps of sugar in a saucer.

"Have you any croissants?"

"You can get some across the street."

"Never mind."

Oddly enough, this stubborn customer, who must have been well aware that he was in the way, that this was not the moment to be settling down at the Café des Ministères, displayed a certain humility that was somehow endearing.

There was something else which Joseph was beginning to appreciate, used as he was to the various types of people who come to sit around in his café. Although he had been there for a whole hour, the man had not drawn a newspaper from his pocket nor asked for one, he had not found it necessary to consult the Bottin or the telephone directory, he had made no effort to enter into conversation with the waiter; he did not cross and uncross his legs, and he did not smoke.

It is excessively unusual to find anyone capable of sitting for an hour in a café without moving, without constantly checking the time, without displaying impatience in some way or another. If he was waiting for someone, he was waiting with remarkable placidity.

At ten o'clock, when the cleaning was finished, the man was still there. Another curious detail was that he had not chosen a seat by the windows, but at the far end of the room, close to the mahogany staircase that leads down to the lavatories. Joseph himself went down for a wash and brush-up. He had already turned the handle to let down the orange awning that shed a slight glow through the dark café.

Before going down he jingled some coins in his waistcoat pocket, hoping that his customer would take the hint, and make up his mind to pay and leave.

Nothing of the sort happened, and Joseph went down, changed his dickey and his collar, combed his hair and put on his short alpaca jacket.

When he came back the man was still sitting there in front of his empty cup. The cashier, Mademoiselle Berthe, appeared and settled down at her desk, took a few bits and pieces out of her bag and began to set out the telephone tokens in neat piles.

"I felt he was somebody very gentle, very respectable, and yet it seemed to me that his moustache was dyed like the Colonel's."

For the man had short, upturned moustaches, probably twisted with curling-tongs, and of a bluish black that suggested dye.

Another regular morning ritual is the delivery of ice. A huge fellow with a canvas sack over his shoulder brings in the opalescent blocks from which a few limpid drops are trickling, and sets them in the ice-box.

He, too, noticed the solitary customer, and later said of him:

"He reminded me of a seal."

Why a seal? That the delivery-man was never able to specify.

As for Joseph, still following a changeless time-table, he took down yesterday's newspapers from the long handles to which they were attached and replaced them with today's.

"Would you mind giving me one?"

The customer had actually spoken, in a low, almost timid voice.

"Which would you like? *Le Temps? Figaro? Les Débats?*"

"I don't mind."

This made Joseph think that the man was probably not a native Parisian. He couldn't have been a foreigner either, for he had no accent. More likely a visitor from the provinces. But there was no station near by. If he had got off a train before eight in the morning, why had he come half way across Paris with his suitcase to settle down in a café he did not know? For Joseph, who has an excellent memory for faces, was sure he had never seen the man before. Strangers who drop into the Café des Ministères are immediately made aware that they are not at home, and go away again.

Eleven o'clock; the time when the proprietor, Monsieur Monnet, comes down from his flat, newly shaved, fresh-complexioned, his grey hair sleekly brushed, wearing a grey suit and his everlasting patent-leather shoes. He could have retired from business a long time ago. He has set up cafés in the provinces for each of his children. If he stays here, it is because this corner of the Boulevard Saint-Germain is the only place in the world where he can bear to live and because his customers are his friends.

"Everything all right, Joseph?"

He immediately spotted the customer and his cup of coffee. A questioning look came into his eye. And the waiter whispered, behind the bar:

"He's been here since eight o'clock."

Monsieur Monnet walked to and fro past the stranger, rubbing his hands, which is a kind of invitation to open a conversation. Monsieur Monnet likes to chat with all his customers, to play cards or dominoes with them; he knows all their family problems and office gossip.

The man did not bat an eyelid.

"He looked to me very tired, like someone who has had a sleepless night on the train," Monsieur Monnet was later to declare.

When Maigret asked all three of them—Joseph, Mademoiselle Berthe and Monsieur Monnet—whether the man seemed to be watching for someone in the street, their answers were very different.

"No," said Monsieur Monnet.

"I got the impression he was expecting a lady," said the cashier.

And Joseph declared:

"Several times I caught him looking across to the bar over the way, but he always dropped his eyes immediately."

At eleven twenty he ordered a glass of Vichy. Some customers drink mineral waters; one knows them, one knows why: people like Monsieur Blanc from the War Ministry who are on a diet. Joseph noted automatically that this fellow neither smoked nor drank, which is pretty uncommon.

Then, for a couple of hours or so, they paid no more attention to him, because it was apéritif time; regular customers began to flock in, and the waiter knew beforehand what to serve each one of them, and which tables must be provided with cards.

"Waiter . . ."

One o'clock. The man was still there, having slipped his suitcase underneath the red velvet seat. Joseph pretended to think he was being asked for the bill, and after reckoning in an undertone, announced:

"Eight francs fifty."

"Can you let me have a sandwich?"

"I'm sorry, we don't serve them."

"You haven't any rolls either?"

"We don't serve any food."

It was not strictly true. Occasionally in the evening a party of bridge players who have not had time for dinner are provided with ham sandwiches. This, however, is exceptional.

The man nodded, murmuring:

"It doesn't matter."

This time Joseph was struck by the quivering of his lips, by the sad, resigned expression on his face.

"Can I bring you something else?"

"Another coffee, with plenty of milk."

Because he was hungry, and milk would at any rate provide a little nourishment. He had not asked for any other newspaper. He had had time to read his from the first line to the last, including the small ads.

The Colonel turned up and was annoyed to find the stranger sitting in his place; for the Colonel, who hated the slightest draught and who maintained that spring draughts are always the most treacherous, always liked to sit at the far end of the room.

Jules, the second waiter, who had only been three years in the profession and who would never look like a real café waiter, came on duty at half-past one, while Joseph went through the glazed door to eat the lunch sent down for him from the first floor.

Why did Jules think the stranger looked like one of those men who sell rugs and peanuts?

"I didn't think he looked straight. I thought he'd got a shifty look, and something soft and smarmy about his expression. If it had been up to me I'd have sent him off to the nearest *crémerie*."

Some customers noticed the man and were to notice him even more when they found him still there in the evening.

All this evidence came from amateur witnesses, so to speak. But it so happened that a professional observer also gave evidence, which proved as inconclusive as everyone else's.

For about ten years, at the start of his career, Joseph had been a waiter at the Brasserie Dauphine, a stone's throw from the Quai des Orfèvres, and a favourite haunt of most detectives of the Police Judiciaire. He had become a close friend of one of Maigret's best colleagues, Inspector Janvier, and he had married Janvier's sister-in-law, so that they were practically relatives.

At three o'clock in the afternoon, seeing his customer still in the same place, Joseph began to get really cross. He conjectured that if the fellow showed such obstinacy it must be not through love of the atmosphere of the Café des Ministères, but because he had some good reason not to leave it.

When he got off the train, Joseph argued, he must have felt himself being shadowed and come in for safety's sake to escape the police.

Joseph therefore rang up Police Headquarters and asked to speak to Janvier.

"I've got a queer sort of customer here who's been sitting in a corner since eight o'clock this morning and seems determined not to budge. He's had nothing to eat. Don't you think you'd better come over and have a look at him?"

Janvier, ever conscientious, collected the latest reports with photographs and descriptions of wanted persons, and came along to the Boulevard Saint-Germain.

By a strange chance, the café happened to be empty when he came in.

"Has he flown?" he asked Joseph.

But the waiter pointed to the basement. "He's just asked for a telephone token and gone to make a call."

This was a pity; a few minutes earlier it would have been possible, by contacting the switchboard, to find out to whom and about what he was telephoning. Janvier sat down and ordered a calvados. The man came upstairs again and went back to his place, as calm as ever, somewhat preoccupied but showing no signs of anxiety. It even seemed to Joseph, who was beginning to know him, that he was somewhat relaxed.

For twenty minutes Janvier scrutinized him from head to foot. He had plenty of time to compare that rather plump, flabby face with all the photographs of wanted persons. Finally he shrugged his shoulders.

"He's not on our lists," he told Joseph. "He looks to me like some poor devil who's been stood up by a woman. He must be an insurance agent or something of the sort."

Janvier even went on to joke:

"I shouldn't be surprised if he's a traveller for a firm of undertakers . . . In any case I'm not entitled to ask him to show his papers. There's no regulation to prevent him from staying in the café as long as he likes and doing without lunch."

Janvier stayed a little longer gossiping with Joseph and then went back to Police Headquarters, where he conferred with Maigret about an illegal gambling concern, but did not mention the man in the Café des Ministères.

In spite of the awning over the windows, rays of sunlight were now slanting into the café. By five o'clock, three tables were occupied by people playing *belote*. The proprietor himself was playing at one of them, just opposite the stranger, at whom he cast a glance from time to time.

By six o'clock the place was full. Joseph and Jules went from one table to another with their trays loaded with bottles and glasses, and the sharp odour of pernod conflicted with the over-sweet scent of the boulevard chestnut-trees.

At this point, each of the two waiters had his own sector. It so happened that the man's table was in Jules's sector, and Jules was less observant than his colleague. Moreover, he liked to slip behind the bar from time to time for a glass of white wine, so that from quite early on in the evening he tended to confuse things. All that he could say was that a woman had come.

"She was dark, nicely dressed, respectable-looking, not one of those women who come into a café in order to start a conversation with customers."

On the whole, in Jules's view, the sort of woman who only goes into a public place because she has arranged to meet her husband there. There were three or four tables still unoccupied. She had sat down at the one next to the stranger's.

"I'm sure they didn't speak to one another. She ordered a port. I think I recollect that besides her handbag—it was a brown or black leather bag—she was carrying a little parcel. I saw it on the table to begin with. When I brought her drink it wasn't there; she'd probably laid it down on the seat."

A pity! Joseph would have liked to have seen her. Mademoiselle Berthe, from the height of her pay-desk, had noticed the woman too.

"She looked quite a lady, hardly any make-up, in a blue suit with a white blouse, but I don't know why, I thought she wasn't a married woman."

Until dinner time, around eight o'clock, there was a constant coming and going. Then the room began to empty. By nine o'clock only six tables were occupied, four of them by chess players, two by bridge players who came regularly every evening for a game.

"What's certain," Joseph was later to assert, "is that the chap knows how to play bridge and chess. I'd even bet he's a good player. I could see that from the way he watched his neighbours and followed the games."

Had he been relatively carefree then, or was Jospeh mistaken?

At ten o'clock, only three tables were occupied. Men from Ministries tend to go to bed early. At half-past ten Jules went home, for his wife was expecting a baby, and he had arranged with his colleague to get off early.

The man was still there. Since eight ten in the morning he had drunk three coffees, a bottle of Vichy and one lemonade. He had not smoked. He had drunk no spirits. In the morning he had read *Le Temps*. In the afternoon he had bought an evening paper from a newsboy who had come into the café.

At 11 p.m. as usual, although two card games were still going on, Joseph began stacking the chairs on the tables and spreading sawdust on the floor.

Shortly afterwards, having finished his game, Monsieur Monnet shook hands with his companions—including the Colonel—and went up to bed, carrying the day's takings in a canvas bag in which Mademoiselle Berthe had put away banknotes and change.

As he left he glanced at the persistent customer about whom most of the regulars had been talking during the evening, and he said to Joseph:

"If he's a nuisance, don't hesitate to ring . . ."

For behind the counter there is an electric bell connected with his private rooms.

That, in short, was all. When Maigret began his enquiry next day he could elicit no further information.

Mademoiselle Berthe left at ten minutes to eleven to catch the last bus to Epinay, where she lived. She, too, had cast a final curious glance at the man.

"I can't say he struck me as being nervous. But he wasn't calm, either. If I'd met him in the street, for instance, I'd have been afraid of him, if you see what I mean? And if he'd got off the bus at Epinay at the same time as me I shouldn't have dared go home alone."

"Why?"

"He had a sort of inward look . . ."

"What do you mean by that?"

"He seemed to be indifferent to everything that was going on around him."

"Were the shutters closed?"

"No, Joseph only closes them at the last minute."

"From where you sit you could see the corner of the street and the café-bar over the way . . . Did you notice any suspicious comings and goings? Did anybody seem to be keeping a look-out for your customer?"

"I shouldn't have noticed . . . Although things are quiet enough on the Boulevard Saint-Germain side, people are on the go all the time along the Rue des Saints-Pères . . . And in the café-bar they're constantly going in and out."

"Did you see nobody as you left?"

"Nobody . . . Yes, though; there was a policeman at the corner of the street."

This was confirmed by the local police station. Unfortunately the officer on duty had been relieved shortly after.

Only two tables still occupied . . . A couple had come in for a drink after the pictures, regular customers, a doctor and his wife who lived three doors further down and who often dropped in at the Café des Ministères on their way home. They quickly paid and left.

The doctor commented later:

"We were sitting just in front of him, and I noticed that he looked ill."

"What sort of illness, in your opinion?"

"Liver trouble, undoubtedly."

"How old do you think he was?"

"It's hard to say, for I didn't pay as much attention as I now wish I had. To my mind, he was one of those men who look older than they are . . . You might say forty-five or more, because of those dyed moustaches."

"They were dyed, then?"

"I suppose so . . . But I've had patients of thirty-five who already had the same flabby colourless flesh, that lifeless air . . ."

"Couldn't he have looked lifeless because he hadn't eaten all day?"

"Maybe . . . But I stick to my diagnosis: a bad digestion, a bad liver, and I'd add bad bowels . . ."

The game at the last table was interminable. Three times it looked like ending, and three times the declarer failed to fulfil his contract. A five of clubs doubled and unexpectedly successful, owing to the nervousness of a player who set free dummy's long suit, finally brought the game to a close at ten minutes to twelve.

"Closing time, gentlemen," Joseph said politely, piling the last chairs on to the tables.

The card-players paid their bills, and the man still did not move. At that point, the waiter felt frightened, as he subsequently admitted. He almost asked the regulars to stay a few minutes longer, until he had got rid of the stranger.

He dared not do so, for the four card-players left together still discussing the game, and lingered for a moment's chat at the corner of the boulevard before finally separating.

"Eighteen francs seventy-five."

The two of them were alone together in the café, where Joseph had already switched off half the lights.

As he later confessed to Maigret:

"I'd noticed a siphon at the corner of the bar and if he'd made a move, I'd have broken it over his head . . ."

"You'd put the siphon there on purpose, hadn't you?"

That was obvious. Sixteen hours in the company of this enigmatic customer had reduced Joseph's nerves to shreds. He had come to think of the man as a sort of personal enemy, who was only there to do him an injury, who was waiting till they were alone to attack him and rob him.

And yet Joseph had made a mistake. As the customer, without rising from his seat, hunted deliberately in his pockets for money, the waiter, afraid of missing his bus, went to turn the handle that lowered the shutters. It is true that the door was still wide open, letting in the cool night air, and that there were still a number of people passing on the pavement of the Boulevard Saint-Germain.

"Here you are, waiter . . ."

Twenty-one francs. A two franc twenty-five tip after a whole day! The waiter nearly flung the money down on the table in a fury, and only his well-trained professional conscience prevented him.

"Perhaps you were a bit afraid of him, too," Maigret suggested.

"I don't know about that . . . At any rate I was in a hurry to get rid of him . . . Never in all my life has a customer made me as mad as that one did . . . If I could have foreseen, in the morning, that he was going to stay there all day!"

"Where were you, exactly, when he went out?"

"Let's see . . . For one thing, I had to remind him that he had a suitcase under the seat, for he was on the point of forgetting it."

"Did he seem annoyed at being reminded?"

"No . . ."

"Relieved?"

"Not that either . . . Indifferent . . . Talk about keeping calm! I've had customers of all sorts, but fancy sitting still for sixteen hours in front of a marble table without getting pins and needles in your legs!"

"So where were you?"

"Beside the cash-desk. I was paying the eighteen francs seventy-five into the till . . . You'll have noticed that there are two doors, one big double door opening on to the boulevard, and a smaller one opening on to the Rue des Saints-Pères. I nearly told him he was making a mistake when I saw him going out by the little door, then I shrugged my shoulders because, after all, I didn't care . . . Now I could get changed and shut up the place."

"In which hand was he holding his case?"

"I didn't notice."

"And did you notice whether he had one hand in his pocket?"

"I don't know . . . He wasn't wearing an overcoat . . . I couldn't see because the tables stacked with chairs hid him from me . . . He went out . . ."

"You were still in the same place?"

"Yes . . . Here, exactly . . . I was taking the check out of the till . . . With my other hand I was pulling the last counters out of my pocket . . . I heard a bang . . . Not much louder than what goes on all day, when cars backfire . . . But I understood all the same that it was not a car . . . I said to myself: 'Well, so he's got himself bumped off after all.'

"One thinks very fast on such occasions . . . I've often had to witness some rather nasty fights; it's part of my job . . . I've always been amazed how fast one's mind works . . .

"I blamed myself for it . . . For after all he was just a poor fellow who'd taken refuge here because he knew he'd get bumped off as soon as he stuck his nose outside the door . . .

"I felt guilty . . . He'd eaten nothing . . . Perhaps he hadn't any money to get a taxi and jump into it before being shot at by the chap who was waiting for him . . ."

"Did you rush out?"

"Well, to tell you the truth . . ." Joseph looked embarrassed. "I think I waited a few minutes to think it over . . . I've a wife and three kids, you understand? . . . First I pressed the electric bell that rings in the boss's room . . . Outside I heard people hurrying, voices . . . one woman was saying: 'Don't you get mixed up in it, Gaston . . .' Then a policeman's whistle.

"I went out. There were three people standing there in the Rue des Saints-Pères, a little way from the door."

"Eight metres away," Maigret specified after consulting the report.

"It's possible . . . I didn't measure . . . A man was crouching beside a figure lying on the ground . . . I only learnt later that it was a doctor on his way back from the theatre, who happens to be one of our customers . . . A good many doctors are customers of ours . . .

"He got up saying: 'He's had it . . . The bullet went in at the back of his neck and came out through the left eye.'

"The policeman arrived. I knew I was going to be questioned.

"Believe it or not, I dared not look on the ground . . . The thought of that left eye made me feel particularly sick . . . I didn't want to see my customer again in that state, with his eye out of his head . . .

"I kept thinking that it was somehow my fault, that I ought to have . . . But what exactly could I have done?

"I can still hear the voice of the policeman asking, with his notebook in his hand: 'Does anyone know him?'

"And I said automatically: 'I do . . . At least I believe I . . .'

"At last I did bend over him to have a look, and I swear to you, Monsieur Maigret, you who've known me such a long time, seeing how many thousands of glasses of beer and calvados I've served you with at the Brasserie Dauphine, I swear to you that I never had such a shock in my life.

"*It wasn't him!*

"It was a fellow I didn't know, that I'd never seen before, a tall thin chap, and on a lovely day like yesterday, on a night so mild you could sleep outside, he was wearing a fawn raincoat . . .

"It was a relief . . . Silly of me maybe, but I was glad not to have made that mistake . . . If my customer had been the victim instead of the murderer I'd have blamed myself for it all my life long . . .

"Since first thing that morning, you see, I'd felt there was something fishy about that fellow . . . I'd have sworn to it . . . That was why I rang up Janvier . . . Only Janvier, although he's practically my brother-in-law, he's a stickler for regulations . . . Suppose when I sent for him he'd asked to see the customer's papers . . . They surely weren't in order.

"An ordinary decent person doesn't spend a whole day in a café and end up shooting somebody on the pavement at midnight . . .

"He didn't take long to disappear, you'll notice. Nobody saw him after that shot.

"If it wasn't him who fired, he'd have stayed there . . . He'd not had time to go ten metres when I heard the shot . . .

"What I'm wondering is what the woman was up to, the one Jules served with a glass of port. For I've no doubt she came in on account of that fellow . . . We don't get many women on their own . . . We're not that sort of place."

"I understood they hadn't spoken to one another," Maigret objected.

"They wouldn't have needed to talk! . . . She had a small parcel when she came in; Jules noticed it, and Jules isn't a liar . . . He saw it on the table, then he didn't see it, and he assumed she'd laid it down on the seat . . . And Mademoiselle Berthe watched the lady going out, because she liked the look of her handbag and wished she had one like it. And Mademoiselle Berthe did not notice her carrying any parcel. That's the sort of thing that wouldn't escape a woman's eye, you'll admit.

"You can say what you like, I can't help feeling that I spent a whole day with a murderer and that I've probably had a narrow escape . . ."

2 The Man Who Drank White Wine and the Lady Who Ate Snails

Paris was blessed, next day, with one of those days such as spring brings only three or four times each year, when it deigns to make an effort; one of those days which one ought to enjoy without doing anything else, as one savours a sorbet; the sort of day one remembers from one's childhood. Everything was pleasant, light, heady, having a very special quality: the blue of the sky, the floating softness of the few clouds, the caressing breeze that met one suddenly at a street corner and that set the chestnuts quivering just enough to make one raise one's head and look at their clusters of honeyed flowers. A cat on a windowsill, a dog lying on the pavement, a cobbler in his leather apron standing in his doorway, an ordinary green and yellow bus sailing past, everything was precious that day, everything made one's heart rejoice, and that was no doubt why Maigret retained all his life a delightful memory of the crossroads of the Boulevard Saint-Germain and the Rue des Saints-Pères, and why, later on, he would often pause at a certain café to sit in the shade and drink a glass of beer which, unfortunately, seemed to have lost its flavour.

As for the case, it had quite unexpectedly become famous, less on account of the inexplicable obstinacy of the man who sat in the Café des Ministères or the shot fired at midnight than because of the motive for the crime.

At eight o'clock next morning, the Superintendent was in his office with all its windows wide open on to the blue and golden panorama of the Seine, and he was studying reports while smoking his pipe in greedy little puffs. It was thus that he made his first contact with the man from the Café des Ministères and with the one who had been killed in the Rue des Saints-Pères.

The local police had done a good job during the night. The police surgeon, Dr. Paul, had performed a post mortem at six that morning. The bullet, which had been recovered on the pavement—the case had also been found, almost at the corner of the Boulevard Saint-Germain, close to the wall—had already been submitted to the ballistics expert, Gastinne-Renette.

And now on Maigret's desk there lay the dead man's clothes, the contents of his pockets and a number of photographs taken on the spot by the representatives of the Records Department.

"Come into my office, will you, Janvier? I see from the report that you're somewhat involved in the case."

And so Maigret and Janvier were to be inseparable that day, as so often before.

The victim's clothes, in the first place: they were of good quality, less worn than appeared at first sight, but shockingly uncared for. The clothes of a man living alone, always wearing the same suit, which was never brushed and was even occasionally slept in. The shirt, which was new and had never been laundered, had been worn for a week at least, and the socks were as bad.

There were no identity papers in the pockets, no letters or documents making it possible to identify the stranger, but a collection of peculiar objects: a penknife with many blades, a corkscrew, a dirty handkerchief, a button off the man's coat, a key, an old pipe and a tobacco pouch; a wallet containing 2,350 francs and a photograph of a native hut in Africa, with half a dozen bare-bosomed black women staring at the camera; bits of string and a third class railway ticket from Juvisy to Paris, dated the previous day.

Finally, a child's printing set with an ink pad and rubber letters making up the words: I'LL GET YOU.

The pathologist's report included some interesting details. First, as regards the crime: the shot had been fired from behind, barely three metres away, and death had been instantaneous.

Secondly, the body bore a number of scars, including on the feet the marks left by "jiggers", those ticks peculiar to Central Africa which burrow into a man's toes and have to be dug out with a knife.

The liver was in a deplorable state, a real alcoholic's liver, and furthermore it was established that the man suffered from malaria.

"So there we are!" said Maigret, looking for his hat. "Off we go, Janvier old man."

They walked together to the scene of the crime; through the windows of the café, they saw Joseph doing his morning clean-up.

The Superintendent's first visit, however, was to the café across the street. The two establishments which faced one another at the corner of the Rue des Saints-Pères could not have been more different. Whereas Joseph's domain was old-fashioned and quiet, the other, which bore the name Chez Léon, was aggressively and vulgarly modern.

Needless to say, it included a long bar where two waiters in shirt-sleeves were kept busy serving cups of coffee and glasses of white wine, to be followed later by draughts of red and aniseed-flavored apéritifs.

There were pyramids of croissants, sandwiches, hard-boiled eggs . . . The *patron* and his wife took it in turns to preside over the tobacco-stall at the end of the counter; the room itself had pillars of red and gold mosaic, tables of some indeterminate substance with garish shimmering colours, and seats covered with embossed velvet of the crudest red.

Here, all doors open on to the street, there was a coming and going from morning till night. People came in and out, building workers in dusty overalls, deliverymen who left their carrier-tricycles by the curb for a moment, clerks and typists, people who were thirsty and others who wanted to use the telephone.

"One coffee! . . . Two beaujolais! . . . Three beers!"

The till never stopped working, and the waiters mopped their sweating brows with the cloths they used to wipe the counter. Glasses were plunged for an instant into the turbid water in the pewter bowls, then filled anew, without even being wiped dry, with red or white wine.

"Two dry white wines," ordered Maigret, who enjoyed all this morning hubbub.

And the white wine had that particular coarse tang only to be savoured in bistros of this kind.

"Tell me, waiter . . . Do you remember this man's face?"

The Records Office had done a good job; a sordid task, but a necessary and extremely tricky one. The photograph of a dead man is always difficult to recognize, particularly if the face has suffered some injury. So the gentlemen from the Identité Judiciaire make up the corpse's face and touch up the print so that it looks like the portrait of a living man.

"That's him, isn't it, Louis?"

And the other waiter, dishcloth in hand, came to have a look over the shoulder of his mate.

"That's him! . . . He was such a bloody nuisance all day yesterday that we can't fail to recognize him."

"Do you know what time he first came in here?"

"That's harder to say . . . You don't notice casual customers . . . But I remember that by ten o'clock in the morning this chap was all worked up . . . He couldn't keep still . . . He would come up to the bar, order a glass of the white, toss it off and pay . . . then he'd go outside. You thought you were rid of him and ten minutes later there he was again, sitting in the café and calling for another glass of white."

"Did he spend the whole day like that?"

"I really believe he did . . . At any rate, I saw him at least ten or fifteen times . . . Getting more and more edgy, looking at you in a funny way, and his fingers shaking like an old woman's when he held out the money . . . Didn't he break one of your glasses, Louis?"

"Yes . . . And he insisted on picking up all the bits out of the sawdust, saying: 'It was white wine . . . That's lucky, old man! And you see I need something to bring me luck today . . . Have you ever been to Gabon, young man?' "

"He talked about Gabon to me too," the other waiter broke in, "I can't remember in what connection . . . Oh yes, it was when he began eating hard-boiled eggs. He ate twelve or thirteen, one after the other . . . I was afraid he'd choke, particularly as he'd already had a lot to drink . . .

" 'Don't you worry kid,' he said. 'Once in Gabon I bet I'd eat thirty-six of them with as many glasses of beer, and I won the bet . . .' "

"Did he seem anxious?"

"Depends on what you mean by that. He kept going out and coming back. I thought at first he must be waiting for someone. He kept sniggering to himself as though he were telling himself funny stories. He got hold of an old chap who comes every afternoon for a couple of drinks, and he held him by his lapel for God knows how long . . ."

"Did you know he was armed?"

"How could I have guessed?"

"Because a man of that sort is quite capable of showing off his gun to everybody!"

He'd had one, in fact, a big revolver from which no shots had been fired and which had been found lying beside his body on the pavement.

"Another two glasses of white wine."

And Maigret was in such a cheerful humour that he could not resist the pleas of a little barefoot flower seller, a thin grimy little girl with the loveliest eyes in the world. He bought a bunch of violets from her and then, not knowing what to do with it, stuck it into his jacket pocket.

A good deal of drinking went on that day, it must be confessed. For Maigret and Janvier now had to cross the street and enter the Café des Ministères, with its dim light and its special flavour, and Joseph hurried up to greet them.

Here they were concerned to establish the appearance of the man with the little suitcase and the dyed moustache; a picture increasingly hazy, or rather one which gave the impression of a blurred photograph, or one on which several snapshots have been superimposed.

None of their witnesses agreed. Everyone had a different picture of the customer, and now there was even a fresh witness, the Colonel, who swore that the man had looked like somebody who was up to no good.

To some people he had seemed excited, to others amazingly calm. Maigret listened, nodded, filled his pipe with a meticulous forefinger, and lit it with little puffs, screwing up his eyes with delight at the lovely day that heaven had graciously granted to mankind.

"The woman . . ."

"You mean the young lady?"

For to Joseph, who had scarcely seen her, she had been a pretty young girl from a comfortable background.

"I'm sure she's not a working girl."

He could visualize her, rather, preparing dainty sweets and pastries in a bourgeois household. Mademoiselle Berthe, the cashier, on the other hand, expressed some doubts, saying:

"I shouldn't bank on her being an angel . . . But she's certainly worth two of him."

There were moments when Maigret felt a longing to stretch, such as one feels in the country when one's whole being is soaked in sunshine, and everything delighted him about the Boulevard Saint-Germain that morning: the buses stopping and starting, the ritual gesture of the conductor reaching for his bell as soon as the passengers were all on, the grating sound of brakes and gears, the waving shadow of chestnut-tree branches on the asphalt pavement.

"I bet she didn't go very far!" he muttered to Janvier, who was annoyed at not being able to give a more specific description of the man in spite of having looked so closely at him.

And they stood waiting for a while on the edge of the pavement. The two cafés, each at one corner of the street . . . A man in one of them, a man in the other . . . It seemed as though chance had set each of them in the appropriate atmosphere. Here, the little fellow with the moustache, who had not stirred all day except to make one telephone call, who had touched nothing but coffee, Vichy water and lemonade, and who had not even protested when Joseph had told him there was nothing to eat.

Across the street, amid the noisy throng of workmen, deliverymen, clerks, busy humble people, was a crazy fellow swilling white wine and devouring hard-boiled eggs, restlessly coming and going, buttonholing all and sundry to talk to them about Gabon.

"I bet there's a third café," said Maigret, looking across the boulevard.

He was wrong there. On the opposite pavement, just across from the Rue des Saints-Pères, at a place from which both corners of the street were visible, there was neither a café nor a bar but a restaurant with a narrow window and a long, low dining-room two steps below street level.

It was called À l'Escargot, and it was a typical homely restaurant with a light wooden rack against the wall in which regular customers kept their table napkins. There was a good smell of garlicky cooking and, this being a slack time, the *patronne* herself came out of her kitchen to welcome Maigret and Janvier.

"What can I do for you, gentlemen?"

The Superintendent introduced himself.

"I would like to know whether yesterday evening you had a lady customer who stayed an unusually long time in the restaurant."

The dining-room was empty. The tables were already laid, and tiny carafes of red or white wine stood on each of them.

"My husband looks after the cash-desk, and he's gone out to buy fruit. As for Jean, our waiter, he'll be here in a few minutes, for he comes on duty at eleven o'clock. Can I get you something meanwhile? We've got a nice little Corsican wine that my husband gets sent over specially."

Everybody was delightful that day. So was the little Corsican wine. And so was the low dining-room where the two men waited for Jean, while watching the people pass on the pavement outside and keeping an eye on the two cafés across the boulevard.

"Have you got an idea, Chief?"

"I've got several. But only one of them can be right, can it?"

Jean appeared. He was an elderly white-haired fellow who could have been recognized anywhere as a restaurant waiter. He dived into a cupboard for a change of clothes.

"Tell me, do you remember having a lady customer yesterday evening who behaved in a rather unusual way? . . . A girl with dark hair."

"A married lady," Jean corrected him. "At any rate I'm sure she was wearing a wedding ring; I noticed it because it was made of gold and copper alloy, and my wife and I have rings like that too . . ."

"Was she young?"

"I'd say about thirty . . . A very respectable person, hardly made up at all, and she spoke to one very politely . . ."

"What time did she come in?"

"That's just it! She came in about a quarter past six, while I was finishing laying the tables for dinner. Our customers, who are nearly all regulars" (he glanced towards the rack that held their napkins) "seldom come before seven o'clock . . . She seemed surprised when she came into the empty room and she seemed to draw back.

" 'Is it for dinner?' I asked her. Because sometimes people make a mistake and think we're a café.

" 'Come in,' I said. 'I can serve you in a quarter of an hour or so . . . Would you take something while you're waiting?'

"She ordered a glass of port . . ."

Maigret and Janvier exchanged a glance of satisfaction.

"She sat down beside the window. I had to ask her to move, because she had taken the table where the gentlemen from the Registry Office usually sit; they've been coming here for the past ten years.

"Actually she had to wait almost half an hour, because the snails weren't ready . . . She didn't seem impatient. I brought her a paper, but she didn't read it; she just sat peacefully looking out of the window."

Just like the gentleman with the dyed moustache! A quiet man, a quiet lady, and, at the other street corner, a crazy fellow in a state of nervous tension. Up till now, it was the crazy fellow who had been armed; it was he who had in his pocket a rubber stamp with the threatening words: I'LL GET YOU.

And it was he who had died, without having used his gun.

"She was a very nice lady. I thought she must be someone from the neighbourhood who had forgotten her key and was waiting for her husband to come so as to go home. That happens oftener than you'd think, you know."

"Did she eat a good dinner?"

"Let's see . . . A dozen snails . . . Then sweetbreads, cheese, strawberries and cream . . . I remember because there's an extra charge . . . She drank a small carafe of white wine and a coffee . . .

"She stayed very late. That's what made me think she must be expecting somebody. She wasn't quite the last to leave, but there were only two people left when she asked for the bill . . . It must have been soon after ten o'clock. We usually close at half-past ten . . ."

"You don't know in which direction she went off?"

"I hope she's not in any trouble?" asked old Jean, who seemed to have taken a fancy to his unusual customer. "Then I may as well tell you that when I left at a quarter to eleven and crossed the pavement, I was surprised to see her standing under one of the trees . . . It was the second tree on the left of the lamp-post."

"Did she still seem to be waiting for somebody?"

"I imagine so . . . She wasn't the sort of woman you might be thinking of . . . When she caught sight of me she looked away as if she was embarrassed."

"Tell me, was she carrying a handbag?"

"Why yes, of course . . ."

"Was it large or small? Did she open it in your presence?"

"Let's see . . . No, she didn't open it in my presence . . . She had put it on the window ledge, because her table was close to the window . . . It was a fairly large rectangular bag, of dark leather . . . There was an initial on it, made of silver or some other metal . . . I think it was an M."

"Well, Janvier, old man?"

"Well, Chief?"

If they went on having little drinks here, there and everywhere, they would end up by behaving like schoolboys on holiday, this wonderful spring day.

"Do you believe it was she who killed the chap?"

"We know that he was shot from behind, about three metres away."

"But the fellow from the Café des Ministères might have . . ."

"One minute, Janvier . . . Which of the two men, as far as we know, was on the look-out for the other?"

"The dead man . . ."

"Who wasn't yet dead . . . He was the one who was keeping watch . . . who was *certainly* armed . . . who was threatening the other. In the circumstances, unless he was dead drunk by midnight, it's hardly likely that the other man, coming out of the Café des Ministères, could have taken him unawares and shot him from behind, particularly at such close range. Whereas the woman . . ."

"What shall we do?"

To tell the truth, if Maigret had followed his instincts he would have lingered a little longer in the neighbourhood, he had taken such a sudden fancy to the atmosphere of the crossroads. He would have liked to go back to Joseph's, then to the bar over the way; to sniff around, have a few more drinks, study the same subject from different angles: the man with the waxed moustache, the other, riddled with drink and disease, and the woman, so respectable that she had won the heart of old Jean, dining off snails, sweetbreads and strawberries.

"I bet she's used to very simple, homely food and that she seldom eats out in restaurants."

"How can you tell that?"

"Because people who often eat out don't choose three dishes for which there's an extra charge, two of which one seldom cooks at home: snails and sweetbreads . . . Two dishes that don't go well together, and that suggest greediness."

"And do you think that a woman who's going to kill somebody is likely to bother about what she eats?"

"For one thing, Janvier my boy, nothing proves that she *knew* she was going to kill somebody that evening . . ."

"If she was the one who fired, she must have been armed . . . I saw what you meant by your questions about the handbag . . . I was expecting you to ask the waiter if it looked heavy."

"For another thing," went on Maigret imperturbably, "the most shocking dramas don't usually prevent people from minding what they eat . . . You must have noticed that as I have . . . There's been a death in a family, the house is topsy-turvy, everyone's weeping and groaning; you'd think life would never resume its normal course . . . All the same, a neighbour, or an aunt, or an old servant prepares a meal . . .

" 'I couldn't eat a thing,' the widow declares.

"The others encourage her, they force her to sit down to dinner. Eventually the whole family gets down to it, abandoning the deceased; very soon the whole family is enjoying the meal; and the widow is the one who demands salt and pepper because she finds the stew rather tasteless . . .

"Off we go, Janvier . . ."

"Where are we going?"

"To Juvisy . . ."

They really should have gone to the Gare de Lyon and taken the train. But to face that crowd, to wait at the booking office and then on the platform, to travel standing, maybe, or in a non-smokers' compartment, would have spoilt such a beautiful day.

The cash clerk at Police Headquarters could grumble if he liked; Maigret picked an open taxi and settled down in comfort.

"Take us to Juvisy and stop in front of the station."

And he spent the journey dozing luxuriously, with his eyes half closed and a thin thread of smoke issuing from the lips that held the stem of his pipe.

3   The Uncertain Identity of a Dead Woman

Many a time, when he was asked to talk about one of his cases, Maigret might have taken the opportunity to describe some enquiry in which he had played a brilliant role, literally forcing truth to emerge by dint of his obstinacy, his intuition and his understanding of human nature.

But the story that, in after time, he most enjoyed telling was that of the two cafés in the Boulevard Saint-Germain; true, it was not one of the cases that had earned him the most glory, but he could not help recalling it with a smile of pleasure.

And even so, when he was asked where the truth lay, he would add:

"It's up to you to choose which truth you prefer . . ."

For on one point at least, neither he nor anybody else ever discovered the whole truth.

It was half-past twelve when the taxi deposited Maigret and Janvier opposite Juvisy station, on the outskirts of Paris, and they first went into the Restaurant du Triage, a very ordinary sort of restaurant with a terrace surrounded by bay trees in green tubs.

One cannot enter a café without drinking something. They exchanged a glance; well, since they had been drinking white wine all morning, like the dead man in the Rue des Saints-Pères, they might as well go on.

"Tell me, *patron*, do you happen to know this fellow?"

The bruiser in shirt-sleeves who was officiating behind the zinc counter examined the faked photograph of the dead man, held it out at some distance from his short-sighted eyes, and called out:

"Julie! . . . Come here a minute . . . It's the chap from next door, isn't it?"

His wife, wiping her hands on her blue linen apron, carefully picked up the photograph.

"Sure, it's him! . . . But he's got a funny sort of look on this photo . . ."

Turning to the Superintendent, she went on:

"Only yesterday he kept us up till eleven o'clock while he put away one glass after another."

"Yesterday?" Maigret had a nasty shock.

"Wait, though . . . No, I mean the day before yesterday . . . Yesterday I was doing the washing and in the evening I went to the pictures."

"Can we eat here?"

"Of course you can eat . . . What would you like? *Fricandeau* of veal? Roast pork with lentils? . . . There's some nice *pâté de campagne* to start off with."

They lunched on the terrace, side by side with the taxi driver, whom they had kept. From time to time the *patron* came to have a chat with them.

"They'll tell you more at the place next door, where they take lodgers. We don't have rooms . . . It must be a month or two since your man came to stay there . . . When it comes to drinking, though, you'll find him all over the place . . . Only yesterday morning . . ."

"You're sure it was yesterday?"

"Positive . . . He came in at half-past six, just as I was opening the shutters, and he treated himself to two or three glasses of white wine for a pick-me-up . . . Then suddenly, as the Paris train was about to leave, he rushed off to the station."

The *patron* knew nothing about him except that he drank from morning till night, that he was always talking about Gabon, that he had the utmost contempt for anyone who had not lived in Africa and that he bore a grudge against somebody.

"Some people think themselves clever," he used to say. "But I'm going to get them in the end. Sure, there are plenty of swine about. Only some of them go too far."

Half an hour later, Maigret, still accompanied by Janvier, entered the Hôtel du Chemin de Fer, which boasted a restaurant exactly like the one they had just left except that the terrace was not surrounded by bay trees and the iron chairs were painted red instead of green.

The proprietor, at his bar, was reading a newspaper article aloud to his wife and the waiter. Maigret understood at once, when he saw the picture of the dead man splashed on the front page: the mid-morning papers had just reached Juvisy, and it was he himself who had sent the photographs to the press.

"Is that your lodger?"

A suspicious glance. "Yes . . . And what about it?"

"Nothing . . . I just wanted to know if it was your lodger."

"Good riddance, in any case!"

They had to order something, yet again, and you couldn't go on drinking white wine after lunch.

"Two calvados."

"You're from the police?"

"Yes . . ."

"I thought as much . . . I seem to know your face . . . Well?"

"I'd like to know your opinion."

"My opinion is that he's more likely to have bumped off someone else . . . Or to have got himself knocked out in a fight . . . Because when he was tight, and he was tight every evening, there was no holding him."

"Have you his registration?"

With great dignity, to show that he had nothing to conceal, the proprietor went to fetch his register and held it out to the Superintendent with a slightly disdainful air.

Ernest Combarieu, 47 years of age, born at Marsilly, near La Rochelle (Charente-Maritime), woodcutter. Last residence Libreville, Gabon.

"He stayed six weeks with you?"

"Six weeks too many!"

"Did he not pay?"

"He paid regularly, every week . . . But he was crazy . . . He'd stay two or three days in bed with fever, sending up for rum by way of medicine and drinking whole bottles of it, then he'd come down and for several days he'd do the round of all the bistros in the neighbourhood, sometimes forgetting to come home or else waking us up at three in the morning . . . Sometimes we had to undress him . . . He used to be sick on the stair carpet or on his rug."

"Had he any relatives in the district?"

The proprietor and his wife glanced at one another.

"He must have known somebody, but he would never tell us who. If it was a member of his family I can assure you he didn't love them, for he often used to say:

"'One day you'll hear tell of me and of a swine whom everyone thinks is a decent fellow, a phony who's the meanest thief in the world . . .'"

"Did you never find out whom he was talking about?"

"All that I know is that he was intolerable and that when he was drunk he used to pull out a big revolver from his pocket, aim at an imaginary target and shout: 'Bang, bang!' And then he'd burst out laughing and ask for another drink."

"You'll take a glass with us? . . . One more question . . . Do you know, somewhere in Juvisy, a gentleman of average height, stoutish without being fat, with a fine black moustache, who sometimes goes about carrying a little suitcase?"

"Does that say anything to you, love?" the *patron* asked his wife.

She searched her memory.

"No . . . Unless . . . But he's rather below average height and I don't call him stout . . ."

"Who are you talking about?"

"About Monsieur Auger, who lives in one of the new houses on the estate."

"Is he married?"

"Sure . . . Madame Auger is a pretty woman, very respectable and quiet, who practically never leaves Juvisy . . . I say! That reminds me . . ."

The three men watched her expectantly.

"That reminds me that yesterday, as I was doing my washing in the yard, I saw her going towards the station . . . I guessed she was taking the 4.37 train."

"She's dark, isn't she? And carries a black leather handbag?"

"I don't know what colour her handbag was, but she was wearing a blue suit and a white blouse."

"What is Monsieur Auger by profession?"

This time the *patronne* let her husband answer.

"He sells stamps . . . You'll see his name in the papers, in the small ads . . . *Stamps for collectors* . . . Packets of a thousand stamps for ten francs . . . packets of five hundred stamps . . . All sent by post, C.O.D."

"Does he travel much?"

"He goes to Paris from time to time, about his stamps I suppose, and he always takes his little suitcase . . . He's stopped here two or three times, when the train's been delayed . . . He drinks *café-crème* or Vichy water."

It was too easy. It was not an investigation but an outing, enlivened by the cheerful sunlight and by their ever-increasing consumption of white wine. And yet there was a glint in Maigret's eyes, as though he had guessed that behind this commonplace affair there lay one of the most extraordinary human mysteries that he had encountered in the whole of his career.

He had been given the Augers' address. It was a fair way off, in the plain, where alongside the river Seine some hundreds and thousands of little houses stood surrounded by little gardens, some of them of stone, some of red brick, some dressed with blue or yellow concrete.

He had been told that the Augers' house was called Mon Repos. They had to drive for a long way through streets that were too new, with rudimentary pavements along which someone had recently planted anaemic trees, as thin as skeletons, and where patches of waste ground lay between the houses.

They asked their way, and were frequently misdirected. Finally they reached their objective, and a curtain was twitched at the corner window of a small pink house with a bright red roof.

Next they had to find the bell.

"Shall I stay outside, Chief?"

"Perhaps it would be wiser . . . Yet I think it's going to be plain sailing . . . *Since there's somebody at home* . . ."

He was not mistaken. Eventually he found a tiny electric bell-push in the brand-new front door. He rang. He heard sounds, whispers. The door opened, and there stood before him, wearing probably the same blouse and skirt as on the previous evening, the young woman from the Café des Ministères and the Escargot.

"Superintendent Maigret from the Police Judiciaire," he introduced himself.

"I guessed it was the police . . . Come in."

They went up a few steps. The staircase seemed to be just out of the carpenter's hands, and so did all the woodwork; the plaster on the walls was barely dry.

"Will you be so kind . . ." She turned to a half-open door and made a sign to somebody whom Maigret could not see.

The corner room into which she ushered the Superintendent was a living-room with a divan, books, ornaments and brightly coloured silk cushions. On a small table there was the midday paper with the photograph of the dead man.

"Do sit down . . . I don't know if I may offer you anything?"

"Thank you, no."

"I should have known it's not allowed . . . My husband will be here directly . . . You needn't worry; he won't try to run away, and in any case he's done nothing wrong . . . Only he was unwell this morning . . . We came home by the first train . . . His heart's not too good

. . . He had an attack when we got home . . . He's just shaving and dressing now."

And the sound of running water could be heard from the bathroom, for the walls of the rooms were very thin.

The young woman was almost calm. She was rather pretty, with the quiet prettiness of a middle-class housewife.

"As you must have guessed, it was I who killed my brother-in-law. It was only just in time, for if I had not done so he would have killed my husband, and Raymond's life is surely worth more than his . . ."

"Raymond is your husband?"

"We've been married eight years . . . We've nothing to hide, Superintendent. Perhaps we should have gone last night to tell the police everything . . . Raymond wanted to do so, but knowing his weak heart I preferred to give him time to recover . . . I knew you'd be coming."

"You spoke, just now, of your brother-in-law?"

"Combarieu was my sister Marthe's husband . . . I think he used to be a decent fellow, but a bit crazy . . ."

"One minute . . . Do you mind if I smoke?"

"Please do. My husband doesn't smoke because of his heart, but I don't mind tobacco smoke."

"Where were you born?"

"At Melun . . . We were twin sisters, Marthe and I . . . My name's Isabelle . . . We were so much alike that when we were little our parents—they're dead now—used to give us different coloured hair-ribbons to tell us apart . . . And sometimes, for fun, we used to exchange ribbons . . ."

"Which of you was married first?"

"We were married on the same day . . . Combarieu was a clerk at the Préfecture offices at Melun . . . Auger was an insurance broker . . . They were acquaintances because, both being bachelors, they used to eat at the same restaurant . . . We met them together, my sister and I . . . After we were married we lived at Melun for several years, in the same street . . ."

"Combarieu still working at the Préfecture and your husband as an insurance broker?"

"Yes . . . But Auger was already thinking of the stamp business . . . He'd begun collecting himself, as a hobby . . . He realized there was money to be made from it."

"And Combarieu?"

"He was ambitious and restless . . . He was always short of money . . . He got to know a man who was just back from the Colonies and who gave him the idea of going there . . . At first he wanted my sister to go with him, but she refused, because of what she'd heard about the climate and its effect on a woman's health . . ."

"So he went out there alone?"

"Yes . . . He stayed away two years, and came back with his pockets full of money . . . He spent it faster than he'd made it . . . He'd already begun to drink . . . He claimed that my husband was a weakling, that a man could do something better with his life than sell insurance policies and postage stamps."

"Did he go back?"

"Yes, and he was less successful this time. We could sense that from his letters, although he was always inclined to boast . . . My sister Marthe, two winters ago, caught pneumonia and died of it . . . We wrote to tell her husband . . . Apparently he started drinking more heavily than ever . . . As for us, we came to settle here, for we'd been wanting for a long time to build something for ourselves and live nearer Paris. My husband had given up insurance, and the stamp business was doing well . . ."

She spoke slowly and calmly, weighing her words and listening to the sounds that issued from the bathroom.

"Five months ago my brother-in-law turned up without warning . . . He rang at our door one evening when he was drunk . . . He looked at me in a funny way and the first words he uttered, with a sneer, were: 'I guessed as much!'

"I didn't yet realize what he was thinking of. He was in a much worse state than the first time he'd come home . . . His health was poor, he was drinking far more and although he still had some money he was no longer a rich man.

"He started saying the queerest things to us. He would look at my husband and suddenly burst out: 'Admit that you're a rotten bastard!'

"He went off again . . . We don't know where to. Then he reappeared, drunk as usual. He greeted me with the remark: 'Well, Marthe my dear . . .'

" 'You know I'm not Marthe but Isabelle . . .'

"He laughed more wildly than ever. 'We'll see about that some day, won't we? As for your swine of a husband who sells stamps . . .'

"I don't know if you can understand what had happened . . . He wasn't exactly out of his mind . . . He drank too heavily . . . He had an obsession which we didn't guess for some while . . . We couldn't understand at first what he meant by his threatening manner, his sneering insinuations, or the notes that were now coming through the post for my husband saying: 'I'll get you.' "

"In a word," Maigret put in calmly, "your brother-in-law Combarieu had got it into his head, for one reason or another, that the woman who had died was not his own wife but Auger's."

It was an astonishing situation. Twin sisters so alike that their parents had to dress them differently to tell them apart. Combarieu, abroad, learning of his wife's death . . . And imagining, on his return, rightly or wrongly, that there had been a substitution, that the dead woman was Isabelle and that it was his own wife Marthe who, in his absence, had replaced her as Auger's.

Maigret's gaze darkened, and he drew more slowly on his pipe.

"For months now our life has been impossible . . . Threatening letters have come one after the other . . . Sometimes Combarieu bursts in at any hour of day or night, draws out his revolver, levels it at my husband and then says with a sneer: 'No, not yet, that would be too good!'

"He settled in the neighbourhood to torment us. He's as clever as a monkey. Even when he's drunk he knows perfectly well what he's doing . . ."

"He used to know," Maigret corrected her.

"I'm sorry." She blushed slightly. "He used to know, you're quite right . . . And I don't imagine he wanted to get caught . . . That was why we weren't too frightened here, because if he had killed Auger at Juvisy everyone would have pointed to him as the murderer . . .

"My husband dared not leave the place . . . Yesterday he simply had to go to Paris on business. I wanted to go with him, but he refused. He took the earliest train on purpose, hoping that Combarieu would still be sleeping off his drink and would not notice his departure.

"He was mistaken, and he rang me up in the afternoon to ask me to come to a café in the Boulevard Saint-Germain and bring him a revolver.

"I realized that he was at the end of his tether, and wanted to have done with it . . . I took him his Browning . . . He'd told me over the phone that he would stay in the café until it closed.

"I bought a second gun for myself . . . You must try and understand, Superintendent."

"In a word, you'd made up your mind to fire before he could shoot your husband . . ."

"I swear to you that when I pressed the trigger Combarieu had already raised his gun. That's all I have to say. I'll answer any questions you like to ask me."

"How does it happen that your handbag still bears the letter M?"

"Because it belonged to my sister . . . If Combarieu had been right, if we had practised the deception that he talked so much about, I suppose I'd have taken care to change the initial."

"So, it seems, you love a man enough to . . ."

"I love my husband . . ."

"I said: you love a man, whether or not he's your husband . . ."

"He is my husband."

"You love this man, Auger, enough to bring yourself to kill in order to save him or to prevent him from killing another man himself . . ."

She replied simply:

"Yes."

There was a sound outside the door.

"Come in," she said.

At long last Maigret saw the man of whom he had been given such varying descriptions, the café customer with the blue-black moustache, who, seen in his own home, and particularly after the declaration of love which the young woman had just made, appeared hopelessly commonplace, utterly mediocre.

He was looking around him anxiously. She smiled at him, saying:

"Sit down. I've told the Superintendent everything . . . *Your heart?*"

He felt his chest vaguely and murmured:

"It's all right . . ."

The jury of the Seine department acquitted Madame Auger as having acted in legitimate self-defence.

And each time Maigret told the story, he concluded with an ironical:

"*Is that everything?*"

"Does that imply you've got a mental reservation?"

"It implies nothing . . . Except that a man of the utmost banality can inspire a great love, a heroic passion . . . Even if he sells postage-stamps and has a weak heart . . ."

"But Combarieu?"

"What about him?"

"Was he mad when he imagined that his wife was not the woman who'd died but the one who gave herself out to be Isabelle?"

Maigret would shrug his shoulders and repeat, on a note of parody:

"*A great love! . . . A grand passion! . . .*"

And sometimes, when he was in a good humour and had been drinking a glass of old calvados, warmed in the hollow of his hand, he would add:

"A great love! . . . A grand passion! . . . It's not always the husband who inspires it, is it? . . . And sisters, in most families, have a tiresome habit of falling for the same man . . . Combarieu was a long way off . . ."

He would add, drawing deeply on his pipe:

"How can one distinguish between twins whom their own parents can't tell apart, parents whom we've not been able to question because they are dead . . . All the same, there never was such a fine day as that . . . And I can't remember ever drinking so much . . . Janvier, if he were to be indiscreet, might tell you how we found ourselves singing in chorus in the taxi that took us back to Paris, and when I got home Madame Maigret wondered how I came to have a bunch of violets in my pocket . . . That blessed Marthe! . . . Sorry, I mean: that blessed Isabelle!"

For Your Eyes Only

IAN FLEMING

The most beautiful bird in Jamaica, and some say the most beautiful bird in the world, is the streamertail or doctor hummingbird. The cock bird is about nine inches long, but seven inches of it are tail—two long black feathers that curve and cross each other and whose inner edges are in a form of scalloped design. The head and crest are black, the wings dark green, the long bill is scarlet, and the eyes, bright and confiding, are black. The body is emerald green, so dazzling that when the sun is on the breast you see the brightest green thing in nature. In Jamaica, birds that are loved are given nicknames. *Trochilus polytmus* is called "doctor bird" because his two black streamers remind people of the black tailcoat of the old-time physician.

Mrs. Havelock was particularly devoted to two families of these birds because she had been watching them sipping honey, fighting, nesting, and making love since she married and came to Content. She was now over fifty, so many generations of these two families had come and gone since the original two pairs had been nicknamed Pyramus and Thisbe and Daphnis and Chloe by her mother-in-law. But successive couples had kept the names, and Mrs. Havelock now sat at her elegant tea service on the broad, cool veranda and watched Pyramus, with a fierce "tee-tee-tee," dive-bomb Daphnis, who had finished up the honey on his own huge bush of Japanese hat and had sneaked in among the neighboring monkeyfiddle that was Pyramus's preserve. The two tiny black and green comets swirled away across the fine acres of lawn dotted with brilliant clumps of hibiscus and bougainvillea, until they were lost to sight in the citrus groves. They would soon be back. The running battle between the two families was a game. In this big, finely planted garden there was enough honey for all.

Mrs. Havelock put down her teacup and took a Patum Peperium sandwich. She said, "They really are the most dreadful show-offs."

Colonel Havelock looked over the top of his *Daily Gleaner*. "Who?"

"Pyramus and Daphnis."

"Oh, yes." Colonel Havelock thought the names idiotic. He said, "It looks to me as if Batista will be on the run soon. Castro's keeping up the pressure pretty well. Chap at Barclay's told me this morning that there's a lot of funk money coming over here already. Said that Belair's been sold to nominees. One hundred and fifty thousand pounds for a thousand acres of cattle-tick and a house the red ants'll have down by Christmas! Somebody's suddenly gone and bought that ghastly Blue Harbour hotel, and there's even talk that Jimmy Farquharson has found a buyer for his place—leaf-spot and Panama disease thrown in for good measure, I suppose."

"That'll be nice for Ursula. The poor dear can't stand it out here. But I can't say I like the idea of the whole island being bought up by these Cubans. But Tim, where do they get all the money from, anyway?"

"Rackets, union funds, government money—God knows. The place is riddled with crooks and gangsters. They must want to get their money out of Cuba and into something else quick. Jamaica's as good as anywhere else now we've got this convertibility with the dollar. Apparently the man who bought Belair just shoveled the money onto the floor of Aschenheim's office out of a suitcase. I suppose he'll keep the place for a year or two, and when the trouble's blown over or when Castro's got in and finished cleaning up he'll put it on the market again, take a reasonable loss, and move off somewhere else. Pity, in a way. Belair used to be a fine property. It could have been brought back if anyone in the family had cared."

"It was ten thousand acres in Bill's grandfather's day. It used to take the busher three days to ride the boundary."

"Fat lot Bill cares. I bet he's booked his passage to London already. That's one more of the old families gone. Soon won't be anyone left of that lot but us. Thank God Judy likes the place."

Mrs. Havelock said, "Yes, dear," calmingly and pinged the bell for the tea things to be cleared away. Agatha, a huge blue-black Negro woman wearing the old-fashioned white headcloth that has gone out in Jamaica except in the Hinterland, came out through the white and rose drawing room followed by Fayprince, a pretty young quadroon from Port Maria whom she was training as second housemaid. Mrs. Havelock said, "It's time we started bottling, Agatha. The guavas are early this year."

Agatha's face was impassive. She said, "Yes'm. But we done need more bottles."

"Why? It was only last year I got you two dozen of the best I could find at Henriques."

"Yes'm. Someone done mash five, six of dose."

"Oh, dear. How did that happen?"

"Couldn't say'm." Agatha picked up the big silver tray and waited, watching Mrs. Havelock's face.

Mrs. Havelock had not lived most of her life in Jamaica without learning that a mash is a mash and that one would not get anywhere hunting for a culprit. So she just said cheerfully, "Oh, all right, Agatha. I'll get some more when I go into Kingston."

"Yes'm." Agatha, followed by the young girl, went back into the house.

Mrs. Havelock picked up a piece of petit-point and began stitching, her fingers moving automatically. Her eyes went back to the big bushes of Japanese hat and monkeyfiddle. Yes, the two male birds were back. With gracefully cocked tails they moved among the flowers. The sun was low on the horizon, and every now and then there was a flash of almost piercingly beautiful green. A mockingbird, on the topmost branch of a frangipani, started on its evening repertoire. The tinkle of an early tree-frog announced the beginning of the short violet dusk.

Content, twenty thousand acres in the foothills of Candlefly Peak, one of the most easterly of the Blue Mountains in the county of Portland, had been given to an early Havelock by Oliver Cromwell as a reward for having been one of the signatories to King Charles's death warrant. Unlike so many other settlers of those and later times, the Havelocks had maintained the plantation through three centuries, through earthquakes and hurricanes and through boom and bust of cocoa, sugar, citrus, and copra. Now it was in bananas and cattle, and it was one of the richest and best-run of all the private estates in the island. The house, patched up or rebuilt after earthquake or hurricane, was a hybrid—a mahogany-pillared, two-storied central block on the old stone foundations, flanked by two single-storied wings with widely overhung, flat-pitched Jamaican roofs of silver cedar shingles. The Havelocks were now sitting on the deep veranda of the central block, facing the gently sloping garden, beyond which a vast tumbling jungle vista stretched away twenty miles to the sea.

Colonel Havelock put down his *Gleaner*. "I thought I heard a car."

Mrs. Havelock said firmly, "If it's those ghastly Feddens from Port Antonio, you've simply got to get rid of them. I can't stand any more of their moans about England. And last time they were both quite drunk when they left, and dinner was cold." She got up quickly. "I'm going to tell Agatha to say I've got a migraine."

Agatha came out through the drawing-room door. She looked fussed. She was followed closely by three men. She said hurriedly, "Gemmun from Kingston'm. To see de colonel."

The leading man slid past the housekeeper. He was still wearing his hat, a panama with a short, very upcurled brim. He took this off with his left hand and held it against his stomach. The rays of the sun glittered on hair-grease and on a mouthful of smiling white teeth. He went up to Colonel Havelock, his outstretched hand held straight in front of him. "Major Gonzales. From Havana. Pleased to meet you, Colonel."

The accent was the sham American of a Jamaican taxidriver. Colonel Havelock had got to his feet. He touched the outstretched hand briefly. He looked over the major's shoulder at the other two men, who had stationed themselves on either side of the door. They were both carrying that new holdall of the tropics, a Pan American overnight bag. The bags looked heavy. Now the two men bent down together and placed them beside their yellowish shoes. They straightened themselves. They wore flat white caps with transparent green visors that cast green shadows down to their cheekbones. Through the green shadows their intelligent animal eyes fixed themselves on the major, reading his behavior.

"They are my secretaries."

Colonel Havelock took a pipe out of his pocket and began to fill it. His direct blue eyes took in the sharp clothes, the natty shoes, the glistening fingernails of the major, and the blue jeans and calypso shirts of the other two. He wondered how he could get these men into his study and near the revolver in the top drawer of his desk. He said, "What can I do for you?" As he lit his pipe he watched the major's eyes and mouth through the smoke.

Major Gonzales spread his hands. The width of his smile remained constant. The liquid, almost golden eyes were amused, friendly. "It is a matter of business, Colonel. I represent a certain gentleman in Havana" —he made a throw-away gesture with his right hand. "A powerful gentleman. A very fine guy." Major Gonzales assumed an expression of sincerity. "You would like him, Colonel. He asked me to present his compliments and to inquire the price of your property."

Mrs. Havelock, who had been watching the scene with a polite half-smile on her lips, moved to stand beside her husband. She said kindly, so as not to embarrass the poor man, "What a shame, Major. All this way on these dusty roads! Your friend really should have written first, or asked anyone in Kingston or at Government House. You see, my husband's family have lived here for nearly three hundred years." She looked at him sweetly, apologetically. "I'm afraid there just isn't any question of selling Content. There never has been. I wonder where your important friend can possibly have got the idea from."

Major Gonzales bowed briefly. His smiling face turned back to Colonel Havelock. He said, as if Mrs. Havelock had not opened her mouth, "My gentleman is told this is one of the finest *estancias* in Jamaica. He is a most generous man. You may mention any sum that is reasonable."

Colonel Havelock said firmly, "You heard what Mrs. Havelock said. The property is not for sale."

Major Gonzales laughed. It sounded quite genuine laughter. He shook his head as if he were explaining something to a rather dense child. "You misunderstand me, Colonel. My gentleman desires this property and no other property in Jamaica. He has some funds, some extra funds, to invest. These funds are seeking a home in Jamaica. My gentleman wishes this to be their home."

Colonel Havelock said patiently, "I quite understand, Major. And I am so sorry you have wasted your time. Content will never be for sale in my lifetime. And now, if you'll forgive me. My wife and I always dine early, and you have a long way to go." He made a gesture to the left, along the veranda. "I think you'll find this is the quickest way to your car. Let me show you."

Colonel Havelock moved invitingly, but when Major Gonzales stayed where he was, he stopped. The blue eyes began to freeze.

There was perhaps one less tooth in Major Gonzales' smile, and his eyes had become watchful. But his manner was still jolly. He said cheerfully, "Just one moment, Colonel." He issued a curt order over his shoulder. Both the Havelocks noticed the jolly mask slip with the few sharp words through the teeth. For the first time Mrs. Havelock looked slightly uncertain. She moved still closer to her husband. The two men picked up their blue Pan American bags and stepped forward. Major Gonzales reached for the zipper on each of them in turn and pulled. The taut mouths sprang open. The bags were full to the brim with neat, solid wads of American money. Major Gonzales spread his arms. "All hundred-dollar bills. All genuine. Half a million dollars. That is, in your money, let us say, one hundred and eighty thousand pounds. A small fortune. There are many other good places to live in the world, Colonel. And perhaps my gentleman would add a further twenty thousand pounds to make the round sum. You would know in a week. All I need is half a sheet of paper with your signature. The lawyers can do the rest. Now, Colonel"—the smile was winning—"shall we say yes and shake hands on it? Then the bags stay here and we leave you to your dinner."

The Havelocks now looked at the major with the same expression—a mixture of anger and disgust. One could imagine Mrs. Havelock telling the story next day. "Such a common, greasy little man. And those filthy plastic bags full of money! Timmy was wonderful. He just told him to get out and take the dirty stuff away with him."

Colonel Havelock's mouth turned down with distaste. He said, "I thought I had made myself clear, Major. The property is not for sale at any price. And I do not share the popular thirst for American dollars. I must now ask you to leave." Colonel Havelock laid his cold pipe on the table as if he was preparing to roll up his sleeves.

For the first time Major Gonzales' smile lost its warmth. The mouth continued to grin, but it was now shaped in an angry grimace. The liquid golden eyes were suddenly brassy and hard. He said softly, "Colonel. It is I who have not made myself clear. Not you. My gentleman has instructed me to say that if you will not accept his most generous terms we must proceed to other measures."

Mrs. Havelock was suddenly afraid. She put her hand on Colonel Havelock's arm and pressed it hard. He put his hand over hers in reassurance. He said through tight lips, "Please leave us alone and go, Major. Otherwise I shall communicate with the police."

The pink tip of Major Gonzales' tongue came out and slowly licked along his lips. He said harshly, "So the property is not for sale in your lifetime, Colonel. Is that your last word?" His right hand went behind his back and he clicked his fingers softly, once. Behind him the gun hands of the two men slid through the openings of their gay shirts above the waistbands. The sharp animal eyes watched the major's fingers behind his back.

Mrs. Havelock's hand went up to her mouth. Colonel Havelock tried to say yes, but his mouth went dry. He swallowed noisily. He could not believe it. This mangy Cuban crook must be bluffing. He managed to say thickly, "Yes, it is."

Major Gonzales nodded curtly. "In that case, Colonel, my gentleman will carry on the negotiations with the next owner—with your daughter."

The fingers clicked. Major Gonzales stepped to one side to give a clear field of fire. The brown monkey-hands came out from under the gay shirts. The ugly sausage-shaped hunks of metal spat and thudded—again and again, even when the two bodies were on their way to the ground.

Major Gonzales bent down and verified where the bullets had hit. Then the three small men walked quickly back through the rose and white drawing room and across the dark carved mahogany hall and out through the elegant front door. They climbed unhurriedly into a black Ford Consul sedan with Jamaican number plates and, with Major Gonzales driving and the two gunmen sitting upright in the back seat, they drove off at an easy pace down the long avenue of royal palms. At the junction of the drive and the road to Port Antonio the cut telephone wires hung down through the trees like bright lianas. Major Gonzales slalomed the car carefully and expertly down the rough parochial road until he was on the metaled strip near the coast. Then he put on speed. Twenty minutes after the killing he came to the outer sprawl of the little banana port. There he ran the stolen car onto the grass verge beside the road, and the three men got out and walked the quarter of a mile through the sparsely lit main street to the banana wharves. The speed-boat was waiting, its exhaust bubbling. The three men got in, and the boat zoomed off across the still waters of what an American poetess has called the most beautiful harbor in the world. The anchor chain was already half up on the glittering fifty-ton Chris-Craft. She was flying the Stars and Stripes. The two graceful antennae of the deep-sea rods explained that these were tourists—from Kingston, perhaps, or from Montego Bay. The three men went on board, and the speedboat was swung in. Two canoes were circling, begging. Major Gonzales tossed a fifty-cent piece to each of them, and the stripped men dived. The twin Diesels awoke to a stuttering roar, and the Chris-Craft settled her stern down a fraction and made for the deep channel below the Titchfield Hotel. By dawn she would be back in Havana. The fishermen and wharfingers ashore watched her go, and went on with their argument as to which of the film stars holidaying in Jamaica this could have been.

Up on the broad veranda of Content the last rays of the sun glittered on the red stains. One of the doctor birds whirred over the balustrade and hovered close above Mrs. Havelock's heart, looking down. No, this was not for him. He flirted gaily off to his roosting-perch among the closing hibiscus.

There came the sound of someone in a small sports car making a racing change at the bend of the drive. If Mrs. Havelock had been alive she would have been getting ready to say, "Judy, I'm always telling you not to do that on the corner. It scatters gravel all over the lawn, and you know how it ruins Joshua's lawnmower."

It was a month later. In London, October had begun with a week of brilliant Indian summer, and the noise of the mowers came up from Regent's Park and in through the wide-open windows of M's office. They were motor-mowers, and James Bond reflected that one of the most beautiful noises of summer, the drowsy iron song of the old machines, was going forever from the world. Perhaps today children felt the same about the puff and chatter of the little two-stroke engines. At least the cut grass would smell the same.

Bond had time for these reflections because M seemed to be having difficulty in coming to the point. Bond had been asked if he had anything on at the moment, and he had replied happily that he hadn't and had waited for Pandora's box to be opened for him. He was mildly intrigued because M had addressed him as James and not by his number— 007. This was unusual during duty hours. It sounded as if there might be some personal angle to this assignment—as if it might be put to him more as a request than as an order. And it seemed to Bond that there was an extra small cleft of worry between the frosty, damnably clear gray eyes. And three minutes was certainly too long to spend getting a pipe going.

M swiveled his chair around square with the desk and flung the box of matches down so that it skidded across the red leather top toward Bond. Bond fielded it and skidded it politely back to the middle of the desk. M smiled briefly. He seemed to make up his mind. He said mildly, "James, has it ever occurred to you that every man in the fleet knows what to do except the commanding admiral?"

Bond frowned. He said, "It hadn't occurred to me, sir. But I see what you mean. The rest only have to carry out orders. The admiral has to decide on the orders. I suppose it's the same as saying that supreme command is the loneliest post there is."

M jerked his pipe sideways. "Same sort of idea. Someone's got to be tough. Someone's got to decide in the end. If you send a havering signal to the Admiralty you deserve to be put on the beach. Some people are religious—pass the decision on to God." M's eyes were defensive. "I used to try that sometimes in the Service, but He always passed the buck back again—told me to get on and make up my own mind. Good for one, I suppose, but tough. Trouble is, very few people keep touch after about forty. They've been knocked about by life—had troubles, tragedies, illnesses. These things soften you up." M looked sharply at Bond. "How's your coefficient of toughness, James? You haven't got to the dangerous age yet."

Bond didn't like personal questions. He didn't know what to answer, or what the truth was. He had not got a wife or children—had never suffered the tragedy of a personal loss. He had not had to stand up to blindness or a mortal disease. He had absolutely no idea how he would face these things that needed so much more toughness than he had ever had to show. He said hesitantly, "I suppose I can stand most things if I have to and if I think it's right, sir. I mean"—he did not like using such words—"if the cause is—er—sort of just, sir." He went on, feeling ashamed of himself for throwing the ball back at M, "Of course it's not easy to know what is just and what isn't. I suppose I assume that when I'm given an unpleasant job in the Service the cause is a just one."

"Dammit." M's eyes glittered impatiently. "That's just what I mean! You rely on *me*. You won't take any damned responsibility yourself." He thrust the stem of his pipe toward his chest. "I'm the one who has to do that. I'm the one who has to decide if a thing is right or not." The anger died out of the eyes. The grim mouth bent sourly. He said gloomily, "Oh, well, I suppose it's what I'm paid for. Somebody's got to drive the bloody train." M put his pipe back in his mouth and drew on it deeply to relieve his feelings.

Now Bond felt sorry for M. He had never before heard M use as strong a word as "bloody." Nor had M ever given a member of his staff any hint that he felt the weight of the burden he was carrying and had carried ever since he had thrown up the certain prospect of becoming Fifth Sea Lord in order to take over the Secret Service. M had got himself a problem. Bond wondered what it was. It would not be concerned with danger. If M could get the odds more or less right he would risk anything, anywhere in the world. It would not be political. M did not give a damn for the susceptibilities of any ministry and thought nothing of going behind their backs to get a personal ruling from the Prime Minister. It might be moral. It might be personal. Bond said, "Is there anything I can help over, sir?"

M looked briefly, thoughtfully at Bond, and then swiveled his chair so that he could not look out of the window at the high, summery clouds. He said abruptly, "Do you remember the Havelock case?"

"Only what I read in the papers, sir. Elderly couple in Jamaica. The daughter came home one night and found them full of bullets. There was some talk of gangsters from Havana. The housekeeper said three men had called in a car. She thought they might have been Cubans. It turned out the car had been stolen. A yacht had sailed from the local harbor that night. But as far as I remember, the police didn't get anywhere. That's all, sir. I haven't seen any signals passing on the case."

M said gruffly, "You wouldn't have. They've been personal to me. We weren't asked to handle the case. Just happens"—M cleared his throat; this private use of the Service was on his conscience—"I knew the Havelocks. Matter of fact I was best man at their wedding. Malta. Nineteen twenty-five."

"I see, sir. That's bad."

M said shortly, "Nice people. Anyway, I told Station C to look into it. They didn't get anywhere with the Batista people, but we've got a good man with the other side—with this chap Castro. And Castro's Intelligence people seem to have the government pretty well penetrated. I got the whole story a couple of weeks ago. It boils down to the fact that a man called Hammerstein, or von Hammerstein, had the couple killed. There are a lot of Germans well dug in in these banana republics. They're Nazis who got out of the net at the end of the war. This one's ex-Gestapo. He got a job as head of Batista's Counterintelligence. Made a packet of money out of extortion and blackmail and protection. He was set up for life until Castro's lot began to make headway. He was one of the first to start easing himself out. He cut one of his officers in on his loot, a man called Gonzales, and this man traveled around the Caribbean with a couple of gunmen to protect him and began salting away Hammerstein's money outside Cuba—put it in real estate and such under nominees. Only bought the best, but at top prices. Hammerstein could afford them. When money didn't work he'd use force—kidnap a child, burn down a few acres, anything to make the owner see reason. Well, this man Hammerstein heard of the Havelocks' property, one of the best in Jamaica, and he told Gonzales to go and get it. I suppose his orders were to kill the Havelocks if they wouldn't sell and then put pressure on the daughter. There's a daughter, by the way. Should be about twenty-five by now. Never seen her myself. Anyway, that's what happened. They killed the Havelocks. Then two weeks ago Batista sacked Hammerstein. May have got to hear about one of these jobs. I don't know. But anyway, Hammerstein cleared out and took his little team of three with him. Timed things pretty well, I should say. It looks as if Castro may get in this winter if he keeps the pressure up."

Bond said softly, "Where have they gone to?"

"America. Right up in the north of Vermont. Up against the Canadian border. Those sort of men like being close to frontiers. Place called Echo Lake. It's some kind of a millionaire's ranch he's rented. Looks pretty from the photographs. Tucked away in the mountains with this little lake in the grounds. He's certainly chosen himself somewhere where he won't be troubled with visitors."

"How did you get onto this, sir?"

"I sent a report of the whole case to Edgar Hoover. He knew of the man. I guessed he would. He's had a lot of trouble with this gunrunning from Miami to Castro. And he's been interested in Havana ever since the big American gangster money started following the casinos there. He said that Hammerstein and his party had come into the States on six-month visitors' visas. He was very helpful. Wanted to know if I'd got enough to build up a case on. Did I want these men extradited for trial in Jamaica? I talked it over here with the Attorney General and he said there wasn't a hope unless we could get the witnesses from Havana. There's no chance of that. It was only through Castro's Intelligence that we even know as much as we do. Officially the Cubans won't raise a finger. Next Hoover offered to have their visas revoked and get them on the move again. I thanked him and said no, and we left it at that."

M sat for a moment in silence. His pipe had died, and he relit it. He went on, "I decided to have a talk with our friends the Mounties. I got on to the Commissioner on the scrambler. He's never let me down yet. He strayed one of his frontier-patrol planes over the border and took a full aerial survey of this Echo Lake place. Said that if I wanted any other cooperation he'd provide it. And now"—M slowly swiveled his chair back square with the desk—"I've got to decide what to do next."

Now Bond realized why M was troubled, why he wanted someone else to make the decision. Because these had been friends of M. Because a personal element was involved, M had worked on the case by himself. And now it had come to the point when justice ought to be done and these people brought to book. But M was thinking, Is this justice, or is it revenge? No judge would take a murder case in which he had personally known the murdered person. M wanted someone else, Bond, to deliver judgment. There were no doubts in Bond's mind. He didn't know the Havelocks or care who they were. Hammerstein had operated the law of the jungle on two defenseless old people. Since no other law was available, the law of the jungle should be visited upon Hammerstein. In no other way could justice be done. If it was revenge, it was the revenge of the community.

Bond said, "I wouldn't hesitate for a minute, sir. If foreign gangsters find they can get away with this kind of thing they'll decide the English are as soft as some other people seem to think we are. This is a case for rough justice—an eye for an eye."

M went on looking at Bond. He gave no encouragement, made no comment.

Bond said, "These people can't be hung, sir. But they ought to be killed."

M's eyes ceased to focus on Bond. For a moment they were blank, looking inward. Then he slowly reached for the top drawer of his desk on the left-hand side, pulled it open, and extracted a thin file without the usual title across it and without the top-secret red star. He placed the file squarely in front of him, and his hand rummaged again in the open drawer. The hand brought out a rubber stamp and a red-ink pad. M opened the pad, stamped the rubber stamp on it, and then, carefully, so that it was properly aligned with the top right-hand corner of the docket, pressed it down on the gray cover.

M replaced the stamp and the ink pad in the drawer and closed the drawer. He turned the docket around and pushed it gently across the desk to Bond.

The red sans-serif letters, still damp, said: FOR YOUR EYES ONLY.

Bond said nothing. He nodded and picked up the docket and walked out of the room.

Two days later Bond took the Friday Comet to Montreal. He did not care for it. It flew too high and too fast and there were too many passengers. He regretted the days of the old Stratocruiser, that fine, lumbering old plane that took ten hours to cross the Atlantic. Then one had been able to have dinner in peace, sleep for seven hours in a comfortable bunk, and get up in time to wander down to the lower deck and have that ridiculous BOAC "country house" breakfast while the dawn came up and flooded the cabin with the first bright gold of the Western Hemisphere. Now it was all too quick. The stewards had to serve everything almost at the double, and then one had a bare two hours' snooze before the hundred-mile-long descent from forty thousand feet. Only eight hours after leaving London, Bond was driving a Hertz Plymouth and trying to remember to keep on the right of the road.

The headquarters of the Royal Canadian Mounted Police are in the Department of Justice alongside Parliament Buildings in Ottawa. Like most Canadian public buildings, the Department of Justice is a massive block of gray masonry built to look stodgily important and to withstand long and hard winters. Bond had been told to ask at the front desk for the Commissioner and to give his name as "Mr. James." He did so, and a young, fresh-faced RCMP corporal, who looked as if he did not like being kept indoors on a warm, sunny day, took him up in the lift to the third floor and handed him over to a sergeant in a large tidy office which contained two girl secretaries and a lot of heavy furniture. The sergeant spoke on an intercom, and there was a ten-minute delay during which Bond smoked and read a recruiting pamphlet which made the Mounties sound like a mixture between a dude ranch, Dick Tracy, and *Rose Marie*. When he was shown in through the connecting door a tall, youngish man in a dark blue suit, white shirt, and black tie turned away from the window and came toward him. "Mr. James?" The man smiled thinly. "I'm Colonel, let's say—er—Johns."

They shook hands. "Come along and sit down. The Commissioner's very sorry not to be here to welcome you himself. He has a bad cold—you know, one of those diplomatic ones." Colonel "Johns" looked amused. "Thought it might be best to take the day off. I'm just one of the help. I've been on one or two hunting trips myself, and the Commissioner fixed on me to handle this little holiday of yours." The colonel paused. "On me only. Right?"

Bond smiled. The Commissioner was glad to help but he was going to handle this with kid gloves. There would be no comeback on his office. Bond thought he must be a careful and very sensible man. He said, "I quite understand. My friends in London didn't want the Commissioner to bother himself personally with any of this. And I haven't seen the Commissioner or been anywhere near his headquarters. That being so, can we talk English for ten minutes or so—just between the two of us?"

Colonel Johns laughed. "Sure. I was told to make that little speech and then get down to business. You understand, Commander, that you and I are about to connive at various felonies, starting with obtaining a Canadian hunting license under false pretenses and being an accessory to a breach of the frontier laws, and going on down from there to more serious things. It wouldn't do anyone one bit of good to have any ricochets from this little plot. Get me?"

"That's how my friends feel too. When I go out of here, we'll forget each other, and if I end up in Sing Sing that's my worry. Well, now?"

Colonel Johns opened a drawer in the desk and took out a bulging file and opened it. The top document was a list. He put his pencil on the first item and looked across at Bond. He ran his eye over Bond's old black and white hound's-tooth tweed suit and white shirt and thin black tie. He said, "Clothes." He unclipped a plain sheet of paper from the file and slid it across the desk. "This is a list of what I reckon you'll need and the address of a big second-hand clothing store here in the city. Nothing fancy, nothing conspicuous—khaki shirt, dark brown jeans, good climbing-boots or shoes. See they're comfortable. And there's the address of a chemist for walnut stain. Buy a gallon and give yourself a bath in the stuff. There are plenty of browns in the hills at this time, and you won't want to be wearing parachute cloth or anything that smells of camouflage. Right? If you're picked up, you're an Englishman on a hunting trip in Canada who's lost his way and got across the border by mistake. Rifle. Went down myself and put it in the boot of your Plymouth while you were waiting. One of the new Savage 99Fs, Weatherby 6-by-62 'scope, five-shot repeater with twenty rounds of high-velocity .250-3,000. Lightest big-game lever action on the market. Only six and a half pounds. Belongs to a friend. Glad to have it back one day, but he won't miss it if it doesn't turn up. It's been tested and it's okay up to five hundred. Gun license"—Colonel Johns slid it over—"issued here in the city in your real name as that fits with your passport. Hunting license ditto, but small game only, vermin, as it isn't quite the deer season yet, also driving license to replace the provisional one I had waiting for you with the Hertz people. Haversack, compass—used ones, in the boot of your car. Oh, by the way"—Colonel Johns looked up from his list—"you carrying a personal gun?"

"Yes. Walther PPK in a Burns Martin holster."

"Right, give me the number. I've got a blank license here. If that gets back to me it's quite okay. I've got a story for it."

Bond took out his gun and read off the number. Colonel Johns filled in the form and pushed it over.

"Now then, maps. Here's a local Esso map that's all you need to get you to the area." Colonel Johns got up and walked round with the map to Bond and spread it out. "You take this Route 17 back to Montreal, get onto 37 over the bridge at Saint Anne's and then over the river again onto 7. Follow 7 on down to Pike River. Get on 52 to Stanbridge. Turn right in Stanbridge for Frelighsburg and leave the car in a garage there. Good roads all the way. Whole trip shouldn't take you more than five hours, including stops. Okay? Now this is where you've got to get things right. Make it that you get to Frelighsburg around three a.m. Garage hand'll be half asleep and you'll be able to get the gear out of the boot and move off without him noticing even if you were a double-headed Chinaman." Colonel Johns went back to his chair and took two more pieces of paper off the file. The first was a scrap of penciled map, the other a section of aerial photograph. He said, looking seriously at Bond, "Now, here are the only inflammable things you'll be carrying, and I've got to rely on you getting rid of them just as soon as they've been used, or at once if there's a chance of you getting into trouble. This"—he pushed the paper over—"is a rough sketch of an old smuggling route from Prohibition days. It's not used now or I wouldn't recommend it." Colonel Johns smiled sourly. "You might find some rough customers coming over in the opposite direction, and they're apt to shoot and not even ask questions afterwards—crooks, druggers, white-slavers—but nowadays they mostly travel up by Viscount. This route was used for runners between Franklin, just over the Derby Line, and Frelighsburg. You follow this path through the foothills, and you detour Franklin and get into the start of the Green Mountains. There it's all Vermont spruce and pine with a bit of maple, and you can stay inside that stuff for months and not see a soul. You get across country here, over a couple of highways, and you leave Enosburgh Falls to the west. Then you're over a steep range and down into the top of the valley you want. The cross is Echo Lake, and, judging from the photographs, I'd be inclined to come down on top of it from the east. Got it?"

"What's the distance? About ten miles?"

"Ten and a half. Take you about three hours from Frelighsburg if you don't lose your way, so you'll be in sight of the place around six and have about an hour's light to help you over the last stretch." Colonel Johns pushed over the square of aerial photograph. It was a central cut from the one Bond had seen in London. It showed a long, low range of well-kept buildings made of cut stone. The roofs were of slate, and there was a glimpse of graceful bow windows and a covered patio. A dust road ran past the front door, and on this side were garages and what appeared to be kennels. On the garden side was a stone-flagged terrace with a flowered border, and beyond this two or three acres of trim lawn stretched down to the edge of the small lake. The lake appeared to have been artificially created with a deep stone dam. There was a group of wrought-iron garden furniture where the dam wall left the bank, and, halfway along the wall, a diving board and a ladder to climb out of the lake. Beyond the lake the forest rose steeply up. It was from this side that Colonel Johns suggested an approach. There were no people in the photograph, but on the stone flags in front of the patio was a quantity of expensive-looking aluminum garden furniture and a central glass table with drinks. Bond remembered that the larger photograph had shown a tennis court in the garden and on the other side of the road the trim white fences and grazing horses of a stud farm. Echo Lake looked what it was—the luxurious retreat, in deep country, well away from atom-bomb targets, of a millionaire who liked privacy and could probably offset a lot of his running expenses against the stud farm and an occasional good let. It would be an admirable refuge for a man who had had ten steamy years of Caribbean politics and who needed a rest to recharge his batteries. The lake was also convenient for washing blood off hands.

Colonel Johns closed his now empty file and tore the typewritten list into small fragments and dropped them in the wastepaper basket. The two men got to their feet. Colonel Johns took Bond to the door and held out his hand. He said, "Well, I guess that's all. I'd give a lot to come with you. Talking about all this has reminded me of one or two sniping jobs at the end of the war. I was in the Army then. We were under Monty in Eighth Corps. On the left of the line in the Ardennes. It was much the same sort of country as you'll be using, only different trees. But you know how it is in these police jobs. Plenty of paper work and keep your nose clean for the pension. Well, so long and the best of luck. No doubt I'll read all about it in the papers"—he smiled—"whichever way it goes."

Bond thanked him and shook him by the hand. A last question occurred to him. He said, "By the way, is the Savage single pull or double? I won't have a chance of finding out and there may not be much time for experimenting when the target shows."

"Single pull, and it's a hair-trigger. Keep your finger off until you're sure you've got him. And keep outside three hundred if you can. I guess these men are pretty good themselves. Don't get too close." He reached for the door-handle. His other hand went to Bond's shoulder. "Our Commissioner's got a motto: 'Never send a man where you can send a bullet.' You might remember that. So long, Commander."

Bond spent the night and most of the next day at the Ko-Zee Motor Court outside Montreal. He paid in advance for three nights. He passed the day looking to his equipment and breaking in the soft ripple-rubber climbing-boots he had bought in Ottawa. He bought glucose tablets and some smoked ham and bread, from which he made himself sandwiches. He also bought a large aluminum flask and filled this with three-quarters Bourbon and one-quarter coffee. When darkness came he had dinner and a short sleep and then diluted the walnut stain and washed himself all over with the stuff even to the roots of his hair. He came out looking like a red Indian with blue-gray eyes. Just before midnight he quietly opened the side door into the automobile bay, got into the Plymouth, and drove off on the last lap south to Frelighsburg.

The man at the all-night garage was not as sleepy as Colonel Johns had said he would be.

"Going huntin', mister?"

You can get far in North America with laconic grunts. "Huh," "hun," and "hi!" in their various modulations, together with "sure," "guess so," "that so?" and "nuts!" will meet almost any contingency.

Bond, slinging the strap of his rifle over his shoulder, said, "Hun."

"Man got a fine beaver over by Highgate Springs Saturday."

Bond said indifferently, "That so?" paid for two nights, and walked out of the garage. He had stopped on the far side of the town, and now he had only to follow the highway for a hundred yards before he found the dirt track running off into the woods on his right. After half an hour the track petered out at a broken-down farmhouse. A chained dog set up a frenzied barking, but no light showed in the farmhouse, and Bond skirted it and at once found the path by the stream. He was to follow this for three miles. He lengthened his stride to get away from the dog. When the barking stopped there was silence, the deep velvet silence of woods on a still night. It was a warm night with a full yellow moon that threw enough light down through the thick spruce for Bond to follow the path without difficulty. The springy, cushioned soles of the climbing-boots were wonderful to walk on, and Bond got his second wind and knew he was making good time. At around four o'clock the trees began to thin, and he was soon walking through open fields with the scattered lights of Franklin on his right. He crossed a secondary, tarred road, and now there was a wider track through more woods and on his right the pale glitter of a lake. By five o'clock he had crossed the black rivers of U.S. Highways 108 and 120. On the latter was a sign saying: ENOSBURGH FALLS 1 MI. Now he was on the last lap—a small hunting trail that climbed steeply. Well away from the highway, he stopped and shifted his rifle and knapsack around, had a cigarette, and burned the sketch-map. Already there were a faint paling in the sky and small noises in the forest—the harsh, melancholy cry of a bird he did not know, and the rustlings of small animals. Bond visualized the house deep down in the little valley on the other side of the mountain ahead of him. He saw the blank curtained windows, the crumpled, sleeping faces of the four men, the dew on the lawn, and the widening rings of the early rise on the gunmetal surface of the lake. And here, on the other side of the mountain, was the executioner coming up through the trees. Bond closed his mind to the picture, trod the remains of his cigarette into the ground, and got going.

Is this a hill or a mountain? At what height does a hill become a mountain? Why don't they manufacture something out of the silver bark of birch trees? It looks so useful and valuable. The best things in America are chipmunks and oyster stew. In the evening darkness doesn't really fall, it rises. When you sit on top of a mountain and watch the sun go down behind the mountain opposite, the darkness rises up to you out of the valley. Will the birds one day lose their fear of man? It must be centuries since man has killed a small bird for food in these woods, yet they are still afraid. Who was this Ethan Allen who commanded the Green Mountain Boys of Vermont? Now, in American motels, they advertise Ethan Allen furniture as an attraction. Why? Did he make furniture? Army boots should have rubber soles like these.

With these and other random thoughts Bond steadily climbed upward and obstinately pushed away from him the thought of the four faces asleep on the white pillows.

The round peak was below the treeline, and Bond could see nothing of the valley below. He rested and then chose an oak tree and climbed up and out along a thick bough. Now he could see everything—the endless vista of the Green Mountains stretching in every direction as far as he could see, away to the east the golden ball of the sun just coming up in glory, and below, two thousand feet down a long easy slope of tree-tops broken once by a wide band of meadow, through a thin veil of mist, the lake, the lawns, and the house.

Bond lay along the branch and watched the band of pale early-morning sunshine creeping down into the valley. It took a quarter of an hour to reach the lake, and then seemed to flood at once over the glittering lawn and over the wet slate tiles of the roofs. Then the mist went quickly from the lake, and the target area, washed and bright and new, lay waiting like an empty stage.

Bond slipped the telescopic sight out of his pocket and went over the scene inch by inch. Then he examined the sloping ground below him and estimated ranges. From the edge of the meadow, which would be his only open field of fire unless he went down through the last belt of trees to the edge of the lake, it would be about five hundred yards to the terrace and the patio, and about three hundred to the diving board and the edge of the lake. What did these people do with their time? What was their routine? Did they ever swim? It was still warm enough. Well, there was all day. If by the end of it they had not come down to the lake, he would just have to take his chance at the patio and five hundred yards. But it would not be a good chance with a strange rifle. Ought he to get on down straight away to the edge of the meadow? It was a wide meadow, perhaps five hundred yards of going without cover. It would be as well to get that behind him before the house awoke. What time did these people get up in the morning?

As if to answer him, a white blind rolled up in one of the smaller windows to the left of the main block. Bond could distinctly hear the final snap of the spring roller. Echo Lake! Of course. Did the echo work both ways? Would he have to be careful of breaking branches and twigs? Probably not. The sounds in the valley would bounce upward off the surface of the water. But there must be no chances taken.

A thin column of smoke began to trickle up straight into the air from one of the left-hand chimneys. Bond thought of the bacon and eggs that would soon be frying. And the hot coffee. He eased himself back along the branch and down to the ground. He would have something to eat, smoke his last safe cigarette, and get on down to the firing-point.

The bread stuck in Bond's throat. Tension was building up in him. In his imagination he could already hear the deep bark of the Savage. He could see the black bullet lazily, like a slow flying bee, homing down into the valley toward a square of pink skin. There was a light smack as it hit. The skin dented, broke, and then closed up again, leaving a small hole with bruised edges. The bullet plowed on, unhurriedly, toward the pulsing heart—the tissues, the blood-vessels, parting obediently to let it through. Who was this man he was going to do this to? What had he ever done to Bond? Bond looked thoughtfully down at his trigger finger. He crooked it slowly, feeling in his imagination the cool curve of metal.

Almost automatically, his left hand reached out for the flask. He held it to his lips and tilted his head back. The coffee and whisky burned a small fire down his throat. He put the top back on the flask and waited for the warmth of the whisky to reach his stomach. Then he got slowly to his feet, stretched and yawned deeply, and picked up the rifle and slung it over his shoulder. He looked round carefully to mark the place for when he came back up the hill, and started slowly off down through the trees.

Now there was no trail and he had to pick his way slowly, watching the ground for dead branches. The trees were more mixed. Among the spruce and silver birch there was an occasional oak and beech and sycamore and, here and there, the blazing Bengal fire of a maple in autumn dress. Under the trees was a sparse undergrowth of their saplings and much dead wood from old hurricanes. Bond went carefully down, his feet making little sound among the leaves and moss-covered rocks, but soon the forest was aware of him and began to pass on the news. A large doe, with two Bambi-like young, saw him first and galloped off with an appalling clatter. A brilliant woodpecker with a scarlet head flew down ahead of him, screeching each time Bond caught up with it; and always there were the chipmunks, craning up on their hind feet, lifting their small muzzles from their teeth as they tried to catch his scent, and then scampering off to their rock holes with chatterings that seemed to fill the woods with fright. Bond willed them to have no fear, for the gun he carried was not meant for them, but with each alarm he wondered if, when he got to the edge of the meadow, he would see down on the lawn a man with glasses who had been watching the frightened birds fleeing the treetops.

But when he stopped behind a last broad oak and looked down across the long meadow to the final belt of trees and the lake and the house, nothing had changed. All the other blinds were still down, and the only movement was the thin plume of smoke.

It was eight o'clock. Bond gazed down across the meadow to the trees, looking for one which would suit his purpose. He found it—a big maple, blazing with russet and crimson. This would be right for his clothes, its trunk was thick enough, and it stood slightly back from the wall of spruce. From there, standing, he would be able to see all he needed of the lake and the house. Bond stood for a while, plotting his route down through the thick grass and goldenrod of the meadow. He would have to do it on his stomach, and slowly. A small breeze got up and combed the meadow. If only it would keep blowing and cover his passage!

Somewhere not far off, up to the left on the edge of the trees, a branch snapped. It snapped once decisively, and there was no further noise. Bond dropped to one knee, his ears pricked and his senses questing. He stayed like that for a full ten minutes, a motionless brown shadow against the wide trunk of the oak.

Animals and birds do not break twigs. Dead wood must carry a special danger signal for them. Birds never alight on twigs that will break under them, and even a large animal like a deer, with antlers and four hoofs to manipulate, moves quite silently in a forest unless it is in flight. Had these people after all got guards out? Gently Bond eased the rifle off his shoulder and put his thumb on the safe. Perhaps, if the people were still sleeping, a single shot, from high up in the woods, would pass for that of a hunter or a poacher. But then, between him and approximately where the twig had snapped, two deer broke cover and cantered unhurriedly across the meadow to the left. It was true that they stopped twice to look back, but each time they cropped a few mouthfuls of grass before moving on and into the distant fringe of the lower woods. They showed no fright and no haste. It was certainly they who had been the cause of the snapped branch. Bond breathed a sigh. So much for that. And now to get on across the meadow.

A five-hundred-yard crawl through tall, concealing grass is a long and wearisome business. It is hard on knees and hands and elbows, there is a vista of nothing but grass and flower-stalks, and the dust and small insects get into your eyes and nose and down your neck. Bond focused on placing his hands right and maintaining a slow, even speed. The breeze had kept up, and his wake through the grass would certainly not be noticeable from the house.

From above, it looked as if a big ground animal—a beaver perhaps, or a woodchuck—was on its way down the meadow. No, it would not be a beaver. They always move in pairs. And yet perhaps it might be a beaver—for now, from higher up on the meadow, something, somebody else, had entered the tall grass, and behind and above Bond a second wake was being cut in the deep sea of grass. It looked as if whatever it was would slowly catch up with Bond and the two wakes would converge just at the next treeline.

Bond crawled and slithered steadily on, stopping only to wipe the sweat and dust off his face and, from time to time, to make sure that he was on course for the maple. But when he was close enough for the treeline to hide him from the house, perhaps twenty feet from the maple, he stopped and lay for a while, massaging his knees and loosening his wrists for the last lap.

He had heard nothing to warn him, and when the soft, threatening whisper came from only feet away in the thick grass on his left, his head swiveled so sharply that the vertebrae of his neck made a crackling sound.

"Move an inch and I'll kill you." It had been a girl's voice, but a voice that fiercely meant what it said.

Bond, his heart thumping, stared up the shaft of the steel arrow whose blue-tempered triangular tip parted the grass stalks perhaps eighteen inches from his head.

The bow was held sideways, flat in the grass. The knuckles of the brown fingers that held the binding of the bow below the arrow-tip were white. Then there was the length of glinting steel and, behind the metal feathers, partly obscured by waving strands of grass, were grimly clamped lips below two fierce gray eyes against a background of sun-burned skin damp with sweat. That was all Bond could make out through the grass. Who the hell was this? One of the guards? Bond gathered saliva back into his dry mouth and began slowly to edge his right hand, his out-of-sight hand, round and up towards his waistband and his gun. He said softly, "Who the hell are you?"

The arrow-tip gestured threateningly. "Stop that right hand or I'll put this through your shoulder. Are you one of the guards?"

"No. Are you?"

"Don't be a fool. What are you doing here?" The tension in the voice had slackened, but it was still hard, suspicious. There was a trace of accent—what was it, Scots? Welsh?

It was time to get to level terms. There was something particularly deadly about the blue arrow-tip. Bond said easily, "Put away your bow and arrow, Robina. Then I'll tell you."

"You swear not to go for your gun?"

"All right. But for God's sake let's get out of the middle of this field." Without waiting, Bond rose on hands and knees and started to crawl again. Now he must get the initiative and hold it. Whoever this damned girl was, she would have to be disposed of quickly and discreetly before the shooting-match began. God, as if there wasn't enough to think of already!

Bond reached the trunk of the tree. He got carefully to his feet and took a quick look through the blazing leaves. Most of the blinds had gone up. Two slow-moving colored maids were laying a large breakfast table on the patio. He had been right. The field of vision over the tops of the trees that now fell sharply to the lake was perfect. Bond unslung his rifle and knapsack and sat down with his back against the trunk of the tree. The girl came out of the edge of the grass and stood up under the maple. She kept her distance. The arrow was still held in the bow, but the bow was unpulled. They looked warily at each other.

The girl looked like a beautiful unkempt dryad in ragged shirt and trousers. The shirt and trousers were olive green, crumpled and splashed with mud and stains and torn in places, and she had bound her pale blond hair with goldenrod to conceal its brightness for her crawl through the meadow. The beauty of her face was wild and rather animal, with a wide, sensuous mouth, high cheekbones, and silvery gray, disdainful eyes. There was the blood of scratches on her forearms and down one cheek, and a bruise had puffed and slightly blackened the same cheekbone. The metal feathers of a quiver full of arrows showed above her left shoulder. Apart from the bow, she carried nothing but a hunting-knife at her belt and, at her other hip, a small brown canvas bag that presumably carried her food. She looked like a beautiful, dangerous customer who knew wild country and forests and was not afraid of them. She would walk alone through life and have little use for civilization.

Bond thought she was wonderful. He smiled at her. He said softly, reassuringly, "I suppose you're Robina Hood. My name's James Bond." He reached for his flask and unscrewed the top and held it out. "Sit down and have a drink of this—firewater and coffee. And I've got some biltong. Or do you live on dew and berries?"

She came a little closer and sat down a yard from him. She sat like a red Indian, her knees splayed wide and her ankles tucked up high under her thighs. She reached for the flask and drank deeply with her head thrown back. She handed it back without comment. She did not smile. She said, "Thanks," grudgingly, and took her arrow and thrust it over her back to join the others in the quiver. She said, watching him closely, "I suppose you're a poacher. The deer-hunting season doesn't open for another three weeks. But you won't find any deer down here. They only come so low at night. You ought to be higher up during the day, much higher. If you like, I'll tell you where there are some. Quite a big herd. It's a bit late in the day, but you could still get to them. They're upwind from here, and you seem to know about stalking. You don't make much noise."

"Is that what you're doing here—hunting? Let's see your license."

Her shirt had buttoned-down breast pockets. Without protest she took out from one of them the white paper and handed it over.

The license had been issued in Burlington, Vermont. It had been issued in the name of Judy Havelock. There was a list of types of permit. "Non-resident hunting" and "Non-resident bow and arrow" had been ticked. The cost had been $18.50, payable to the Fish and Game Service, Montpelier, Vermont. Judy Havelock had given her age as twenty-five and her place of birth as Jamaica.

Bond thought, God Almighty! He handed the paper back. So that was the score! He said with sympathy and respect, "You're quite a girl, Judy. It's a long walk from Jamaica. And you were going to take him on with your bow and arrow. You know what they say in China: 'Before you set out on revenge, dig two graves.' Have you done that, or did you expect to get away with it?"

The girl was staring at him. "Who are you? What are you doing here? What do you know about it?"

Bond reflected. There was only one way out of this mess and that was to join forces with the girl. What a hell of a business! He said, resignedly, "I've told you my name. I've been sent out from London by, er, Scotland Yard. I know all about your troubles and I've come out here to pay off some of the score and see you're not bothered by these people. In London we think that the man in that house might start putting pressure on you, about your property, and there's no other way of stopping him."

The girl said bitterly, "I had a favorite pony, a Palomino. Three weeks ago they poisoned it. Then they shot my Alsatian. I'd raised it from a puppy. Then came a letter. It said, 'Death has many hands. One of these hands is now raised over you.' I was to put a notice in the paper, in the personal column, on a particular day. I was just to say, 'I will obey. Judy.' I went to the police. All they did was to offer me protection. It was people in Cuba, they thought. There was nothing else they could do about it. So I went to Cuba and stayed in the best hotel and gambled big in the casinos." She gave a little smile. "I wasn't dressed like this. I wore my best dresses and the family jewels. And people made up to me. I was nice to them. I had to be. And all the while I asked questions. I pretended I was out for thrills—that I wanted to see the underworld and some real gangsters, and so on. And in the end I found out about this man." She gestured down toward the house. "He had left Cuba. Batista had found out about him or something. And he had a lot of enemies. I was told plenty about him and in the end I met a man, a sort of high-up policeman, who told me the rest after I had"—she hesitated and avoided Bond's eyes—"after I had made up to him." She paused. She went on: "I left and went to America. I had read somewhere about Pinkerton's, the detective people. I went to them and paid to have them find this man's address." She turned her hands palms upward on her lap. Now her eyes were defiant. "That's all."

"How did you get here?"

"I flew up to Burlington. Then I walked. Four days. Up through the Green Mountains. I kept out of the way of people. I'm used to this sort of thing. Our house is in the mountains in Jamaica. They're much more

322   IAN FLEMING

difficult than these. And there are more people, peasants, about in them. Here no one ever seems to walk. They go by car."

"And what were you going to do then?"

"I'm going to shoot von Hammerstein and walk back to Burlington." The voice was as casual as if she had said she was going to pick a wild flower.

From down in the valley came the sound of voices. Bond got to his feet and took a quick look through the branches. Three men and two girls had come onto the patio. There were talk and laughter as they pulled out chairs and sat down at the table. One place was left empty at the head of the table between the two girls. Bond took out his telescopic sight and looked through it. The three men were very small and dark. One of them, who smiled all the time and whose clothes looked the cleanest and smartest, would be Gonzales. The other two were low peasant types. They sat together at the foot of the oblong table and took no part in the talk. The girls were swarthy brunettes. They looked like cheap Cuban whores. They wore bright bathing suits and a lot of gold jewelry, and laughed and chattered like pretty monkeys. The voices were almost clear enough to understand, but they were talking Spanish.

Bond felt the girl near him. She stood a yard behind him. Bond handed her the glass. He said, "The neat little man is called Major Gonzales. The two at the bottom of the table are gunmen. I don't know who the girls are. Von Hammerstein isn't there yet." She took a quick look through the glass and handed it back without comment. Bond wondered if she realized that she had been looking at the murderers of her father and mother.

The two girls had turned and were looking toward the door into the house. One of them called out something that might have been a greeting. A short, square, almost naked man came out into the sunshine. He walked silently past the table to the edge of the flagged terrace facing the lawn and proceeded to go through a five-minute program of physical drill.

Bond examined the man minutely. He was about five feet four with a boxer's shoulders and hips, but a stomach that was going to fat. A mat of black hair covered his breasts and shoulder-blades, and his arms and legs were thick with it. By contrast, there was not a hair on his face or head, and his skull was a glittering whitish yellow with a deep dent at the back that might have been a wound or the scar of a trepanning. The bone-structure of the face was that of the conventional Prussian officer —square, hard, and thrusting—but the eyes under the naked brows were close-set and piggish, and the large mouth had hideous lips, thick and wet and crimson. He wore nothing but a strip of black material, hardly larger than an athletic support-belt, round his stomach, and a large gold wristwatch on a gold bracelet. Bond handed the glass to the girl. He was relieved. Von Hammerstein looked just about as unpleasant as M's dossier said he was.

Bond watched the girl's face. The mouth looked grim, almost cruel, as she looked down on the man she had come to kill. What was he to do about her? He could see nothing but a vista of troubles from her presence. She might even interfere with his own plans and insist on playing some silly role with her bow and arrow. Bond made up his mind. He just could not afford to take chances. One short tap at the base of the skull and he would gag her and tie her up until it was all over. Bond reached softly for the butt of his automatic.

Nonchalantly the girl moved a few steps back. Just as nonchalantly she bent down, put the glass on the ground, and picked up her bow. She reached behind her for an arrow and fitted it casually into the bow. Then she looked up at Bond and said quietly, "Don't get any silly ideas. And keep your distance. I've got what's called wide-angled vision. I haven't come all the way here to be knocked on the head by a flatfooted London bobby. I can't miss with this at fifty yards, and I've killed birds on the wing at a hundred. I don't want to put an arrow through your leg, but I shall if you interfere."

Bond cursed his previous indecision. He said fiercely, "Don't be a silly bitch. Put that damned thing down. This is man's work. How in hell do you think you can take on four men with a bow and arrow?"

The girl's eyes blazed obstinately. She moved her right foot back into the shooting stance. She said through compressed, angry lips, "You go to hell. And keep out of this. It was my mother and father they killed. Not yours. I've already been here a day and a night. I know what they do and I know how to get von Hammerstein. I don't care about the others. They're nothing without him. Now then." She pulled the bow half taut. The arrow pointed at Bond's feet. "Either you do what I say or you're going to be sorry. And don't think I don't mean it. This is a private thing I've sworn to do and nobody's going to stop me." She tossed her head imperiously. "Well?"

Bond gloomily measured the situation. He looked the ridiculously beautiful wild girl up and down. This was good hard English stock spiced with the hot peppers of a tropical childhood. Dangerous mixture. She had keyed herself up to a state of controlled hysteria. He was quite certain that she would think nothing of putting him out of action. And he had absolutely no defense. Her weapon was silent, his would alert the whole neighborhood. Now the only hope would be to work with her. Give her part of the job, and he would do the rest. He said quietly,

"Now listen, Judy. If you insist on coming in on this thing we'd better do it together. Then perhaps we can bring it off and stay alive. This sort of thing is my profession. I was ordered to do it—by a close friend of your family, if you want to know. And I've got the right weapon. It's got at least five times the range of yours. I could take a good chance of killing him now, on the patio. But the odds aren't quite good enough. Some of them have got bathing-things on. They'll be coming down to the lake. Then I'm going to do it. You can give supporting fire." He ended lamely, "It'll be a great help."

"No." She shook her head decisively. "I'm sorry. You can give what you call supporting fire if you like. I don't care one way or the other. You're right about the swimming. Yesterday they were all down at the lake around eleven. It's just as warm today, and they'll be there again. I shall get him from the edge of the trees by the lake. I found a perfect place last night. The bodyguard men bring their guns with them—sort of tommy-gun things. They don't bathe. They sit around and keep guard. I know the moment to get von Hammerstein and I'll be well away from the lake before they take in what's happened. I tell you I've got it all planned. Now then. I can't hang around any more. I ought to have been in my place already. I'm sorry, but unless you say yes straight away there's no alternative." She raised the bow a few inches.

Bond thought, Damn this girl to hell. He said angrily, "All right then. But I can tell you that if we get out of this you're going to get such a spanking you won't be able to sit down for a week." He shrugged. He said with resignation, "Go ahead. I'll look after the others. If you get away all right, meet me here. If you don't, I'll come down and pick up the pieces."

The girl unstrung her bow. She said indifferently, "I'm glad you're seeing sense. These arrows are difficult to pull out. Don't worry about me. But keep out of sight and mind the sun doesn't catch that glass of yours." She gave Bond the brief, pitying, self-congratulatory smile of the woman who has had the last word, and turned and made off down through the trees.

Bond watched the lithe dark green figure until it had vanished among the tree-trunks, then he impatiently picked up the glass and went back to his vantage-point. To hell with her! It was time to clear the silly bitch out of his mind and concentrate on the job. Was there anything else he could have done—any other way of handling it? Now he was committed to wait for her to fire the first shot. That was bad. But if he fired first there was no knowing what the hotheaded bitch would do. Bond's mind luxuriated briefly in the thought of what he would do to the girl once all this was over. Then there was movement in front of the house, and he put the exciting thoughts aside and lifted his glass.

The breakfast things were being cleared away by the two maids. There was no sign of the girls or the gunmen. Von Hammerstein was lying back among the cushions of an outdoor couch, reading a newspaper and occasionally commenting to Major Gonzales, who sat astride an iron garden chair near his feet. Gonzales was smoking a cigar and from time to time he delicately raised a hand in front of his mouth, leaned sideways, and spat a bit of leaf out on the ground. Bond could not hear what von Hammerstein was saying, but his comments were in English and Gonzales answered in English. Bond glanced at his watch. It was ten-thirty. Since the scene seemed to be static, Bond sat down with his back to the tree and went over the Savage with minute care. At the same time he thought of what would shortly have to be done with it.

Bond did not like what he was going to do, and all the way from England he had had to keep on reminding himself what sort of men these were. The killing of the Havelocks had been a particularly dreadful killing. Von Hammerstein and his gunmen were particularly dreadful men whom many people around the world would probably be very glad to destroy, as this girl proposed to do, out of private revenge. But for Bond it was different. He had no personal motives against them. This was merely his job—as it was the job of a pest-control officer to kill rats. He was the public executioner appointed by M to represent the community. In a way, Bond argued to himself, these men were as much enemies of his country as were the agents of SMERSH or of other enemy Secret Services. They had declared and waged war against British people on British soil and they were currently planning another attack. Bond's mind hunted around for more arguments to bolster his resolve. They had killed the girl's pony and her dog with two casual sideswipes of the hand as if they had been flies. They—

A burst of automatic fire from the valley brought Bond to his feet. His rifle was up and taking aim as the second burst came. The harsh racket of noise was followed by laughter and hand-clapping. The kingfisher, a handful of tattered blue and gray feathers, thudded to the lawn and lay fluttering. Von Hammerstein, smoke still dribbling from the snout of his tommy-gun, walked a few steps and put the heel of his naked foot down and pivoted sharply. He took his heel away and wiped it on the grass beside the heap of feathers. The others stood round, laughing and applauding obsequiously. Von Hammerstein's red lips grinned with pleasure. He said something which included the words "crack shot." He handed the gun to one of the gunmen and wiped his hands down his fat backsides. He gave a sharp order to the girls, who ran off into the house; then, with the others following, he turned and ambled down the sloping lawn toward the lake. Now the girls came running back out of the house. Each one carried an empty champagne bottle. Chattering and laughing, they skipped down after the men.

Bond got himself ready. He clipped the telescopic sight onto the barrel of the Savage and took his stance against the trunk of the tree. He found a bump in the wood as a rest for his left hand, put his sights at 300, and took broad aim at the group of people by the lake. Then, holding the rifle loosely, he leaned against the trunk and watched the scene.

It was going to be some kind of shooting contest between the two gunmen. They snapped fresh magazines onto their guns and at Gonzales' orders stationed themselves on the flat stone wall of the dam, some twenty feet apart, on either side of the diving board. They stood with their backs to the lake and their guns at the ready.

Von Hammerstein took up his place on the grass verge, a champagne bottle swinging in each hand. The girls stood behind him, their hands over their ears. There was excited jabbering in Spanish, and laughter, in which the two gunmen did not join. Through the telescopic sight their faces looked sharp with concentration.

Von Hammerstein barked an order and there was silence. He swung both arms back and counted, "Uno . . . dos . . . tres." With the "tres" he hurled the champagne bottles high into the air over the lake.

The two men turned like marionettes, the guns clamped to their hips. As they completed the turn they fired. The thunder of the guns split the peaceful scene and racketed up from the water. Birds fled away from the trees, screeching, and some small branches cut by the bullets pattered down into the lake. The left-hand bottle disintegrated into dust; the right-hand one, hit by only a single bullet, split in two a fraction of a second later. The fragments of glass made small splashes over the middle of the lake. The gunman on the left had won. The smoke-clouds over the two of them joined and drifted away over the lawn. The echoes boomed softly into silence. The two gunmen walked along the wall to the grass, the rear one looking sullen, the leading one with a sly grin on his face. Von Hammerstein beckoned the two girls forward. They came reluctantly, dragging their feet and pouting. Von Hammerstein said something, asked a question of the winner. The man nodded at the girl on the left. She looked sullenly back at him. Gonzales and von Hammerstein laughed. Von Hammerstein reached out and patted the girl on the rump as if she were a cow. He said something in which Bond caught the words *"una noche."* The girl looked up at him and nodded obediently. The group broke up. The prize girl took a quick run and dived into the lake, perhaps to get away from the man who had won her favors, and the other girl followed her. They swam away across the lake, calling angrily to each other. Major Gonzales took off his coat and laid it on the grass and sat down on it. He was wearing a shoulder holster which showed the butt of a medium-caliber automatic. He watched von Hammerstein take off his watch and walk along the dam wall to the diving board. The gunmen stood back from the lake and also watched von Hammerstein and the two girls, who were now out in the middle of the little lake and were making for the far shore. The gunmen stood with their guns cradled in their arms, and occasionally one of them would glance round the garden or toward the house. Bond thought there was every reason why von Hammerstein had managed to stay alive so long. He was a man who took trouble to do so.

Von Hammerstein had reached the diving board. He walked along to the end and stood looking down at the water. Bond tensed himself and put up the safe. His eyes were fierce slits. It would be any minute now. His finger itched on the trigger-guard. What in hell was the girl waiting for?

Von Hammerstein had made up his mind. He flexed his knees slightly. The arms came back. Through the telescopic sight Bond could see the thick hair over his shoulder-blades tremble in a breeze that came to give a quick shiver to the surface of the lake. Now his arms were coming forward and there was a fraction of a second when his feet had left the board and he was still almost upright. In that fraction of a second there was a flash of silver against his back, and then von Hammerstein's body hit the water in a neat dive.

Gonzales was on his feet, looking uncertainly at the turbulence caused by the dive. His mouth was open, waiting. He did not know if he had seen something or not. The two gunmen were more certain. They had their guns at the ready. They crouched, looking from Gonzales to the trees behind the dam, waiting for an order.

Slowly the turbulence subsided and the ripples spread across the lake. The dive had gone deep.

Bond's mouth was dry. He licked his lips, searching the lake with his glass. There was a pink shimmer deep down. It wobbled slowly up. Von Hammerstein's body broke the surface. It lay head down, wallowing softly. A foot or so of steel shaft stuck up from below the left shoulder-blade, and the sun winked on the aluminum feathers.

Major Gonzales yelled an order, and the two tommy-guns roared and flamed. Bond could hear the crash of the bullets among the trees below him. The Savage shuddered against his shoulder and the right-hand man fell slowly forward on his face. Now the other man was running for the lake, his gun still firing from the hip in short bursts. Bond fired and missed and fired again. The man's legs buckled, but his momentum still carried him forward. He crashed into the water. The clenched finger went on firing the gun aimlessly up toward the blue sky until the water throttled the mechanism.

The seconds wasted on the extra shot had given Major Gonzales a chance. He had got behind the body of the first gunman and now he opened up on Bond with the tommy-gun. Whether he had seen Bond or was only firing at the flashes from the Savage, he was doing well. Bullets zwipped into the maple and slivers of wood spattered into Bond's face. Bond fired twice. The dead body of the gunman jerked. Too low! Bond reloaded and took fresh aim. A snapped branch fell across his rifle. He shook it free, but now Gonzales was up and running forward to the group of garden furniture. He hurled the iron table on its side and got behind it as two snap shots from Bond kicked chunks out of the lawn at his heels. With this solid cover his shooting became more accurate, and burst after burst, now from the right of the table and now from the left, crashed into the maple tree while Bond's single shots clanged against the white iron or whined off across the lawn. It was not easy to traverse the telescopic sight quickly from one side of the table to the other and Gonzales was cunning with his changes. Again and again his bullets thudded into the trunk beside and above Bond. Bond ducked and ran swiftly to the right. He would fire, standing, from the open meadow and catch Gonzales off-guard. But even as he ran, he saw Gonzales dart from behind the iron table. He also had decided to end the stalemate. He was running for the dam to get across and into the woods and come up after Bond. Bond stood and threw up his rifle. As he did so, Gonzales also saw him. He went down on one knee on the dam wall and sprayed a burst at Bond. Bond stood icily, hearing the bullets. The crossed hairs centered on Gonzales' chest. Bond squeezed the trigger. Gonzales rocked. He half got to his feet. He raised his arms and, with his gun still pumping bullets into the sky, dived clumsily face forward into the water.

Bond watched to see if the face would rise. It did not. Slowly he lowered his rifle and wiped the back of his arm across his face.

The echoes, the echoes of much death, rolled to and fro across the valley. Away to the right, in the trees beyond the lake, he caught a glimpse of the two girls running up toward the house. Soon they, if the maids had not already done so, would be on to the state troopers. It was time to get moving.

Bond walked back through the meadow to the lone maple. The girl was there. She stood up against the trunk of the tree with her back to him. Her head was cradled in her arms against the tree. Blood was running down the right arm and dripping to the ground, and there was a black stain high up on the sleeve of the dark green shirt. The bow and quiver of arrows lay at her feet. Her shoulders were shaking.

Bond came up behind her and put a protective arm across her shoulders. He said softly, "Take it easy, Judy. It's all over now. How bad's the arm?"

She said in a muffled voice, "It's nothing. Something hit me. But that was awful. I didn't—I didn't know it would be like that."

Bond pressed her arm reassuringly. "It had to be done. They'd have got you otherwise. Those were pro killers—the worst. But I told you this sort of thing was man's work. Now then, let's have a look at your arm. We've got to get going—over the border. The troopers'll be here before long."

She turned. The beautiful wild face was streaked with sweat and tears. Now the gray eyes were soft and obedient. She said, "It's nice of you to be like that. After the way I was. I was sort of—sort of wound up."

She held out her arm. Bond reached for the hunting knife at her belt and cut off her shirt sleeve at the shoulder. There was the bruised, bleeding gash of a bullet wound across the muscle. Bond took out his own khaki handkerchief, cut it into three lengths, and joined them together. He washed the wound clean with the coffee and whisky, and then took a thick slice of bread from his haversack and bound it over the wound. He cut her shirt sleeve into a sling and reached behind her neck to tie the knot. Her mouth was inches from his. The scent of her body had a warm animal tang. Bond kissed her once softly on the lips and once again, hard. He tied the knot. He looked into the gray eyes close to his. They looked surprised and happy. He kissed her again at each corner of the mouth, and the mouth slowly smiled. Bond stood away from her and smiled back. He softly picked up her right hand and slipped the wrist into the sling. She said docilely, "Where are you taking me?"

Bond said, "I'm taking you to London. There's this old man who will want to see you. But first we've got to get over into Canada, and I'll talk to a friend in Ottawa and get your passport straightened out. You'll have to get some clothes and things. It'll take a few days. We'll be staying in a place called the Ko-Zee Motor Court."

She looked at him. She was a different girl. She said softly, "That'll be nice. I've never stayed in a motel."

Bond bent down and picked up his rifle and knapsack and slung them over one shoulder. Then he hung her bow and quiver over the other, and turned and started up through the meadow.

She fell in behind and followed him, and as she walked she pulled the tired bits of goldenrod out of her hair and undid a ribbon and let the pale gold hair fall down to her shoulders.

CRIME SOLVING, STYLIZED PAST AND TRUE-LIFE PRESENT

ENGLAND AND AMERICA

The Image in the Mirror

DOROTHY SAYERS

The little man with the cowlick seemed so absorbed in the book that Wimsey had not the heart to claim his property, but, drawing up the other arm-chair and placing his drink within easy reach, did his best to entertain himself with the Dunlop Book, which graced, as usual, one of the tables in the lounge.

The little man read on, his elbows squared upon the arms of his chair, his ruffled red head bent anxiously over the text. He breathed heavily, and when he came to the turn of the page, he set the thick volume down on his knee and used both hands for his task. Not what is called "a great reader," Wimsey decided.

When he reached the end of the story, he turned laboriously back, and read one passage over again with attention. Then he laid the book, still open, upon the table, and in so doing caught Wimsey's eye.

"I beg your pardon, sir," he said in his rather thin Cockney voice, "is this your book?"

"It doesn't matter at all," said Wimsey graciously, "I know it by heart. I only brought it along with me because it's handy for reading a few pages when you're stuck in a place like this for the night. You can always take it up and find something entertaining."

"This chap Wells," pursued the red-haired man, "he's what you'd call a very clever writer, isn't he? It's wonderful how he makes it all so real, and yet some of the things he says, you wouldn't hardly think they could be really possible. Take this story now; would you say, sir, a thing like that could actually happen to a person, as it might be you—or me?"

Wimsey twisted his head round so as to get a view of the page.

"*The Plattner Experiment*," he said, "that's the one about the school-master who was blown into the fourth dimension and came back with

his right and left sides reversed. Well, no, I don't suppose such a thing
would really occur in real life, though of course it's very fascinating to
play with the idea of a fourth dimension."

"Well——" He paused and looked up shyly at Wimsey. "I don't
rightly understand about this fourth dimension. I didn't know there was
such a place, but he makes it all very clear no doubt to them that know
science. But this right-and-left business, now, I know that's a fact. By
experience, if you'll believe me."

Wimsey extended his cigarette-case. The little man made an instinctive motion towards it with his left hand and then seemed to check himself and stretched his right across.

"There, you see. I'm always left-handed when I don't think about it.
Same as this Plattner. I fight against it, but it doesn't seem any use. But
I wouldn't mind that—it's a small thing and plenty of people are left-
handed and think nothing of it. No. It's the dretful anxiety of not knowing what I mayn't be doing when I'm in this fourth dimension or whatever it is."

He sighed deeply.

"I'm worried, that's what I am, worried to death."

"Suppose you tell me about it," said Wimsey.

"I don't like telling people about it, because they might think I had a
slate loose. But it's fairly getting on my nerves. Every morning when I
wake up I wonder what I've been doing in the night and whether it's the
day of the month it ought to be. I can't get any peace till I see the
morning paper, and even then I can't be sure. . . .

"Well, I'll tell you, if you won't take it as a bore or a liberty. It
all began——" He broke off and glanced nervously about the room.
"There's nobody to see. If you wouldn't mind, sir, putting your hand
just here a minute——"

He unbuttoned his rather regrettable double-breasted waistcoat, and
laid a hand on the part of his anatomy usually considered to indicate
the site of the heart.

"By all means," said Wimsey, doing as he was requested.

"Do you feel anything?"

"I don't know that I do," said Wimsey. "What ought I to feel? A
swelling or anything? If you mean your pulse, the wrist is a better
place."

"Oh, you can feel it *there,* all right," said the little man. "Just try the
other side of the chest, sir."

Wimsey obediently moved his hand across.

"I seem to detect a little flutter," he said after a pause.

"You do? Well, you wouldn't expect to find it that side and not the other, would you? Well, that's where it is. I've got my heart on the right side, that's what I wanted you to feel for yourself."

"Did it get displaced in an illness?" asked Wimsey sympathetically.

"In a manner of speaking. But that's not all. My liver's got round the wrong side, too, and my organs. I've had a doctor see it, and he told me I was all reversed. I've got my appendix on my left side—that is, I had till they took it away. If we was private, now, I could show you the scar. It was a great surprise to the surgeon when they told him about me. He said afterwards it made it quite awkward for him, coming left-handed to the operation, as you might say."

"It's unusual, certainly," said Wimsey, "but I believe such cases do occur sometimes."

"Not the way it occurred to me. It happened in an air-raid."

"In an air-raid?" said Wimsey, aghast.

"Yes—and if that was all it had done to me I'd put up with it and be thankful. Eighteen I was then, and I'd just been called up. Previous to that I'd been working in the packing department at Crichton's—you've heard of them, I expect—Crichton's for Admirable Advertising, with offices in Holborn. My mother was living in Brixton, and I'd come up to town on leave from the training-camp. I'd been seeing one or two of my old pals, and I thought I'd finish the evening by going to see a film at the Stoll. It was after supper—I had just time to get in to the last house, so I cut across from Leicester Square through Covent Garden Market. Well, I was getting along when wallop! A bomb came down it seemed to me right under my feet, and everything went black for a bit."

"That was the raid that blew up Oldham's, I suppose."

"Yes, it was January 28th, 1918. Well, as I say, everything went right out. Next thing as I knew, I was walking in some place in broad daylight, with green grass all round me, and trees, and water to the side of me, and knowing no more about how I got there than the man in the moon."

"Good Lord!" said Wimsey. "And was it the fourth dimension, do you think?"

"Well, no, it wasn't. It was Hyde Park, as I come to see when I had my wits about me. I was along the bank of the Serpentine and there was a seat with some women sitting on it, and children playing about."

"Had the explosion damaged you?"

"Nothing to see or feel, except that I had a big bruise on one hip and shoulder as if I'd been chucked up against something. I was fairly staggered. The air-raid had gone right out of my mind, don't you see, and I couldn't imagine how I came there, and why I wasn't at Crichton's. I looked at my watch, but that had stopped. I was feeling hungry. I felt in my pocket and found some money there, but it wasn't as much as I should have had—not by a long way. But I felt I must have a bit of something, so I got out of the Park by the Marble Arch gate, and went into a Lyons. I ordered two poached on toast and a pot of tea, and while I was waiting I took up a paper that somebody had left on the seat. Well, that finished me. The last thing I remembered was starting off to see that film on the 28th—and here was the date on the paper—January 30th! I'd lost a whole day and two nights somewhere!"

"Shock," suggested Wimsey. The little man took the suggestion and put his own meaning on it.

"Shock? I should think it was. I was scared out of my life. The girl who brought my eggs must have thought I was barmy. I asked her what day of the week it was, and she said 'Friday.' There wasn't any mistake.

"Well, I don't want to make this bit too long, because that's not the end by a long chalk. I got my meal down somehow, and went to see a doctor. He asked me what I remembered doing last, and I told him about the film, and he asked whether I was out in the air-raid. Well, then it came back to me, and I remembered the bomb falling, but nothing more. He said I'd had a nervous shock and lost my memory a bit, and that it often happened and I wasn't to worry. And then he said he'd look me over to see if I'd got hurt at all. So he started in with his stethoscope, and all of a sudden he said to me:

" 'Why, you keep your heart on the wrong side, my lad!'

" 'Do I?' said I. 'That's the first I've heard of it.'

"Well, he looked me over pretty thoroughly, and then he told me what I've told you, that I was all reversed inside, and he asked a lot of questions about my family. I told him I was an only child and my father was dead—killed by a motor-lorry, he was, when I was a kid of ten—and I lived with my mother in Brixton and all that. And he said I was an unusual case, but there was nothing to worry about. Bar being wrong side round I was sound as a bell, and he told me to go home and take things quietly for a day or two.

"Well, I did, and I felt all right, and I thought that was the end of it, though I'd overstayed my leave and had a bit of a job explaining myself to the R.T.O. It wasn't till several months afterwards the draft was called up, and I went along for my farewell leave. I was having a cup of coffee in the Mirror Hall at the Strand Corner House—you know it, down the steps?"

Wimsey nodded.

"All the big looking-glasses all round. I happened to look into the one near me, and I saw a young lady smiling at me as if she knew me. I saw her reflection, that is, if you understand me. Well, I couldn't make it out, for I had never seen her before, and I didn't take any notice, thinking she'd mistook me for somebody else. Besides, though I wasn't so very old then, I thought I knew her sort, and my mother had always brought me up strict. I looked away and went on with my coffee, and all of a sudden a voice said quite close to me:

" 'Hullo, Ginger—aren't you going to say good evening?'

"I looked up and there she was. Pretty, too, if she hadn't been painted up so much.

" 'I'm afraid,' I said, rather stiff, 'you have the advantage of me, miss.'

" 'Oh, Ginger,' says she, 'Mr. Duckworthy, and after Wednesday night!' A kind of mocking way she had of speaking.

"I hadn't thought so much of her calling me Ginger, because that's what any girl would say to a fellow with my sort of hair, but when she got my name off so pat, I tell you it did give me a turn.

" 'You seem to think we're acquainted, miss,' said I.

" 'Well, I should rather say so, shouldn't you?' said she.

"There! I needn't go into it all. From what she said I found out she thought she'd met me one night and taken me home with her. And what frightened me most of all, she said it had happened on the night of the big raid.

" 'It *was* you,' she said, staring into my face a little puzzled-like. 'Of course it was you. I knew you in a minute when I saw your face in the glass.'

"Of course, I couldn't say that it hadn't been. I knew no more of what I'd been and done that night than the babe unborn. But it upset me cruelly, because I was an innocent sort of lad in those days and hadn't ever gone with girls, and it seemed to me if I'd done a thing like that I ought to know about it. It seemed to me I'd been doing wrong and not getting full value for my money either.

"I made some excuse to get rid of her, and I wondered what else I'd been doing. She couldn't tell me farther than the morning of the 29th, and it worried me a bit wondering if I'd done any other queer things."

"It must have," said Wimsey, and put his finger on the bell. When the waiter arrived, he ordered drinks for two and disposed himself to listen to the rest of Mr. Duckworthy's adventures.

"I didn't think much about it, though," went on the little man; "we went abroad, and I saw my first corpse and dodged my first shell and had my first dose of trenches, and I hadn't much time for what they call introspection.

"The next queer thing that happened was in the C.C.S. at Ypres. I'd got a blighty one near Caudry in September during the advance from

Cambrai—half buried, I was, in a mine explosion and laid out unconscious near twenty-four hours it must have been. When I came to, I was wandering about somewhere behind the lines with a nasty hole in my shoulder. Somebody had bandaged it up for me, but I hadn't any recollection of that. I walked a long way, not knowing where I was, till at last I fetched up in an aid-post. They fixed me up and sent me down the line to a base hospital. I was pretty feverish, and the next thing I knew, I was in bed with a nurse looking after me. The bloke in the next bed to mine was asleep. I got talking to a chap in the next bed beyond him, and he told me where I was, when all of a sudden the other man woke up and says:

" 'My God,' he says, 'you dirty ginger-haired swine, it's you, is it? What have you done with them vallables?'

"I tell you, I was struck all of a heap. Never seen the man in my life. But he went on at me and made such a row, the nurse came running in to see what was up. All the men were sitting up in bed listening—you never saw anything like it.

"The upshot was, as soon as I could understand what this fellow was driving at, that he'd been sharing a shell-hole with a chap that he said was me, and that this chap and he had talked together a bit and then, when he was weak and helpless, the chap had looted his money and watch and revolver and what not and gone off with them. A nasty, dirty trick, and I couldn't blame him for making a row about it, if true. But I said and stood to it, it wasn't me, but some other fellow of the same name. He said he recognised me—said he and this other chap had been together a whole day, and he knew every feature in his face and couldn't be mistaken. However, it seemed this bloke had said he belonged to the Blankshires, and I was able to show my papers and prove I belonged to the Buffs, and eventually the bloke apologised and said he must have made a mistake. He died, anyhow, a few days after, and we all agreed he must have been wandering a bit. The two divisions were fighting side by side in that dust-up and it was possible for them to get mixed up. I tried afterwards to find out whether by any chance I had a double in the Blankshires, but they sent me back home, and before I was fit again the Armistice was signed, and I didn't take any more trouble.

"I went back to my old job after the war, and things seemed to settle down a bit. I got engaged when I was twenty-one to a regular good girl, and I thought everything in the garden was lovely. And then, one day— up it all went! My mother was dead then, and I was living by myself in lodgings. Well, one day I got a letter from my intended, saying that she had seen me down at Southend on the Sunday, and that was enough for her. All was over between us.

"Now, it was most unfortunate that I'd had to put off seeing her that week-end, owing to an attack of influenza. It's a cruel thing to be ill all alone in lodgings, and nobody to look after you. You might die there all on your own and nobody the wiser. Just an unfurnished room I had, you see, and no attendance, and not a soul came near me, though I was pretty bad. But my young lady she said as she had seen me down at Southend with another young woman, and she would take no excuse. Of course, I said, what was *she* doing down at Southend without me, any-how, and that tore it. She sent me back the ring, and the episode, as they say, was closed.

"But the thing that troubled me was, I was getting that shaky in my mind, how did I know I hadn't been to Southend without knowing it? I thought I'd been half sick and half asleep in my lodgings, but it was misty-like to me. And knowing the things I had done other times—well, there! I hadn't any clear recollection one way or another, except fever-dreams. I had a vague recollection of wandering and walking some-where for hours together. Delirious, I thought I was, but it might have been sleep-walking for all I knew. I hadn't a leg to stand on by way of evidence. I felt it very hard, losing my intended like that, but I could have got over that if it hadn't been for the fear of myself and my brain giving way or something.

"You may think this is all foolishness and I was just being mixed up with some other fellow of the same name that happened to be very like me. But now I'll tell you something.

"Terrible dreams I got to having about that time. There was one thing as always haunted me—a thing that had frightened me as a little chap. My mother, though she was a good, strict woman, liked to go to a cinema now and again. Of course, in those days they weren't like what they are now, and I expect we should think those old pictures pretty crude if we was to see them, but we thought a lot of them at that time. When I was about seven or eight I should think, she took me with her to see a thing—I remember the name now—*The Student of Prague,* it was called. I've forgotten the story, but it was a costume piece, about a young fellow at the university who sold himself to the devil, and one day his reflection came stalking out of the mirror on its own, and went about committing dreadful crimes, so that everybody thought it was him. At least, I think it was that, but I forget the details, it's so long ago. But what I shan't forget in a hurry is the fright it gave me to see that dretful figure come out of the mirror. It was that ghastly to see it, I cried and yelled, and after a time mother had to take me out. For

months and years after that I used to dream of it. I'd dream I was looking in a great long glass, same as the student in the picture, and after a
bit I'd see my reflection smiling at me and I'd walk up to the mirror
holding out my left hand, it might be, and seeing myself walking to meet
me with its right hand out. And just as it came up to me, it would suddenly—that was the awful moment—turn its back on me and walk away
into the mirror again, grinning over its shoulder, and suddenly I'd know
that *it* was the real person and *I* was only the reflection, and I'd make a
dash after it into the mirror, and then everything would go grey and
misty round me and with the horror of it I'd wake up all of a perspi-
ration."

"Uncommonly disagreeable," said Wimsey. "That legend of the *Dop-
pelgänger,* it's one of the oldest and the most widespread and never fails
to terrify me. When *I* was a kid, my nurse had a trick that frightened
me. If we'd been out, and she was asked if we'd met anybody, she used
to say, 'Oh, no—we saw nobody nicer than ourselves.' I used to toddle
after her in terror of coming round a corner and seeing a horrid and
similar pair pouncing out at us. Of course I'd have rather died than tell
a soul how the thing terrified me. Rum little beasts, kids."

The little man nodded thoughtfully.

"Well," he went on, "about that time the nightmare came back. At
first it was only at intervals, you know, but it grew on me. At last it
started coming every night. I hadn't hardly closed my eyes before there
was the long mirror and the thing coming grinning along, always with
its hand out as if it meant to catch hold of me and pull me through the
glass. Sometimes I'd wake up with the shock, but sometimes the dream
went on, and I'd be stumbling for hours through a queer sort of world—
all mist and half-lights, and the walls would be all crooked like they are
in that picture of 'Dr. Caligari.' Lunatic, that's what it was. Many's the
time I've sat up all night for fear of going to sleep. I didn't know, you
see. I used to lock the bedroom door and hide the key for fear—you see,
I didn't know what I might be doing. But then I read in a book that
sleepwalkers can remember the places where they've hidden things
when they were awake. So that was no use."

"Why didn't you get someone to share the room with you?"

"Well, I did." He hesitated. "I got a woman—she was a good kid.
The dream went away then. I had blessed peace for three years. I was
fond of that girl. Damned fond of her. Then she died."

He gulped down the last of his whisky and blinked.

"Influenza, it was. Pneumonia. It kind of broke me up. Pretty she
was, too. . . .

"After that, I was alone again. I felt bad about it. I couldn't—I didn't like—but the dreams came back. Worse. I dreamed about doing things—well! That doesn't matter now.

"And one day it came in broad daylight. . . .

"I was going along Holborn at lunch-time. I was still at Crichton's. Head of the packing department I was then, and doing pretty well. It was a wet beast of a day, I remember—dark and drizzling. I wanted a hair-cut. There's a barber shop on the south side, about half way along —one of those places where you go down a passage and there's a door at the end with a mirror and the name written across it in gold letters. You know what I mean.

"I went in there. There was a light in the passage, so I could see quite plainly. As I got up to the mirror I could see my reflection coming to meet me, and all of a sudden the awful dream-feeling came over me. I told myself it was all nonsense and put my hand out to the door-handle—my left hand, because the handle was that side and I was still apt to be left-handed when I didn't think about it.

"The reflection, of course, put out its right hand—that was all right, of course—and I saw my own figure in my old squash hat and burberry —but the face—oh, my God! It was grinning at me—and then just like in the dream, it suddenly turned its back and walked away from me, look-ing over its shoulder——

"I had my hand on the door, and it opened, and I felt myself stum-bling and falling over the threshold.

"After that, I don't remember anything more. I woke up in my own bed and there was a doctor with me. He told me I had fainted in the street, and they'd found some letters on me with my address and taken me home.

"I told the doctor all about it, and he said I was in a highly nervous condition and ought to find a change of work and get out in the open air more.

"They were very decent to me at Crichton's. They put me on to inspecting their outdoor publicity. You know. One goes round from town to town inspecting the hoardings and seeing what posters are dam-aged or badly placed and reporting on them. They gave me a Morgan to run about in. I'm on that job now.

"The dreams are better. But I still have them. Only a few nights ago it came to me. One of the worst I've ever had. Fighting and strangling in a black, misty place. I'd tracked the devil—my other self—and got him down. I can feel my fingers on his throat now—killing myself.

"That was in London. I'm always worse in London. Then I came up here. . . .

"You see why that book interested me. The fourth dimension . . .

it's not a thing I ever heard of, but this man Wells seems to know all about it. You're educated now. Daresay you've been to college and all that. What do you think about it, eh?"

"I should think, you know," said Wimsey, "it was more likely your doctor was right. Nerves and all that."

"Yes, but that doesn't account for me having got twisted round the way I am, now, does it? Legends, you talked of. Well, there's some people think those medeeval johnnies knew quite a lot. I don't say I believe in devils and all that. But maybe some of them may have been afflicted, same as me. It stands to reason they wouldn't talk such a lot about it if they hadn't felt it, if you see what I mean. But what I'd like to know is, can't I get back any way? I tell you, it's a weight on my mind. I never know, you see."

"I shouldn't worry too much, if I were you," said Wimsey. "I'd stick to the fresh-air life. And I'd get married. Then you'd have a check on your movements, don't you see. And the dreams might go again."

"Yes. Yes. I've thought of that. But—did you read about that man the other day? Strangled his wife in his sleep, that's what he did. Now, supposing I—that would be a terrible thing to happen to a man, wouldn't it? Those dreams. . . ."

He shook his head and stared thoughtfully into the fire. Wimsey, after a short interval of silence, got up and went out into the bar. The landlady and the waiter and the barmaid were there, their heads close together over the evening paper. They were talking animatedly, but stopped abruptly at the sound of Wimsey's footsteps.

Ten minutes later, Wimsey returned to the lounge. The little man had gone. Taking up his motoring-coat, which he had flung on a chair, Wimsey went upstairs to his bedroom. He undressed slowly and thoughtfully, put on his pyjamas and dressing-gown, and then, pulling a copy of the *Evening News* from his motoring-coat pocket, he studied a front-page item attentively for some time. Presently he appeared to come to some decision, for he got up and opened his door cautiously. The passage was empty and dark. Wimsey switched on a torch and walked quietly along, watching the floor. Opposite one of the doors he stopped, contemplating a pair of shoes which stood waiting to be cleaned. Then he softly tried the door. It was locked. He tapped cautiously.

A red head emerged.

"May I come in a moment?" said Wimsey, in a whisper.

The little man stepped back, and Wimsey followed him in.

"What's up?" said Mr. Duckworthy.

"I want to talk to you," said Wimsey. "Get back into bed, because it may take some time."

The little man looked at him, scared, but did as he was told. Wimsey gathered the folds of his dressing-gown closely about him, screwed his monocle more firmly into his eye, and sat down on the edge of the bed. He looked at Mr. Duckworthy a few minutes without speaking, and then said:

"Look here. You've told me a queerish story tonight. For some reason I believe you. Possibly it only shows what a silly ass I am, but I was born like that, so it's past praying for. Nice, trusting nature and so on. Have you seen the paper this evening?"

He pushed the *Evening News* into Mr. Duckworthy's hand and bent the monocle on him more glassily than ever.

On the front page was a photograph. Underneath was a panel in bold type, boxed for greater emphasis:

"The police at Scotland Yard are anxious to get into touch with the original of this photograph, which was found in the handbag of Miss Jessie Haynes, whose dead body was found strangled on Barnes Common last Thursday morning. The photograph bears on the back the words 'J. H. with love from R. D.' Anybody recognising the photograph is asked to communicate immediately with Scotland Yard or any police station."

Mr. Duckworthy looked, and grew so white that Wimsey thought he was going to faint.

"Well?" said Wimsey.

"Oh, God, sir! Oh, God! It's come at last." He whimpered and pushed the paper away, shuddering. "I've always known something of this would happen. But as sure as I'm born I knew nothing about it."

"It's you all right, I suppose?"

"The photograph's me all right. Though how it came there I *don't* know. I haven't had one taken for donkey's years, on my oath I haven't —except once in a staff group at Crichton's. But I tell you, sir, honest-to-God, there's times when I don't know what I'm doing, and that's a fact."

Wimsey examined the portrait feature by feature.

"Your nose, now—it has a slight twist—if you'll excuse my referring to it—to the right, and so it has in the photograph. The left eyelid droops a little. That's correct, too. The forehead here seems to have a distinct bulge on the left side—unless that's an accident in the printing."

"No!" Mr. Duckworthy swept his tousled cowlick aside. "It's very conspicuous—unsightly, I always think, so I wear the hair over it."

With the ginger lock pushed back, his resemblance to the photograph was more startling than before.

"My mouth's crooked, too."

"So it is. Slants up to the left. Very attractive, a one-sided smile, I always think—on a face of your type, that is. I have known such things to look positively sinister."

Mr. Duckworthy smiled a faint, crooked smile.

"Do you know this girl, Jessie Haynes?"

"Not in my right senses, I don't, sir. Never heard of her—except, of course, that I read about the murder in the papers. Strangled—oh, my God!" He pushed his hands out in front of him and stared woefully at them.

"What can I do? If I was to get away——"

"You can't. They've recognised you down in the bar. The police will probably be here in a few minutes. No"—as Duckworthy made an attempt to get out of bed—"don't do that. It's no good, and it would only get you into worse trouble. Keep quiet and answer one or two questions. First of all, do you know who I am? No, how should you? My name's Wimsey—Lord Peter Wimsey——"

"The detective?"

"If you like to call it that. Now, listen. Where was it you lived at Brixton?"

The little man gave the address.

"Your mother's dead. Any other relatives?"

"There was an aunt. She came from somewhere in Surrey, I think. Aunt Susan, I used to call her. I haven't seen her since I was a kid."

"Married?"

"Yes—oh, yes—Mrs. Susan Brown."

"Right. Were you left-handed as a child?"

"Well, yes, I was, at first. But mother broke me of it."

"And the tendency came back after the air-raid. And were you ever ill as a child? To have the doctor, I mean?"

"I had measles once, when I was about four."

"Remember the doctor's name?"

"They took me to the hospital."

"Oh, of course. Do you remember the name of the barber in Holborn?"

This question came so unexpectedly as to stagger the wits of Mr. Duckworthy, but after a while he said he thought it was Biggs or Briggs.

Wimsey sat thoughtfully for a moment, and then said:

"I think that's all. Except—oh, yes! What is your Christian name?"

"Robert."

"And you assure me that, so far as you know, you had no hand in this business?"

"That," said the little man, "that I swear to. As far as I know, you know. Oh, my Lord! If only it was possible to prove an alibi! That's my only chance. But I'm so afraid, you see, that I *may* have done it. Do you think—do you think they would hang me for that?"

"Not if you could prove you knew nothing about it," said Wimsey. He did not add that, even so, his acquaintance might probably pass the rest of his life at Broadmoor.

"And you know," said Mr. Duckworthy, "if I'm to go about all my life killing people without knowing it, it would be much better that they should hang me and done with it. It's a terrible thing to think of."

"Yes, but you may not have done it, you know."

"I hope not, I'm sure," said Mr. Duckworthy. "I say—what's that?"

"The police, I fancy," said Wimsey lightly. He stood up as a knock came at the door, and said heartily, "Come in!"

The landlord, who entered first, seemed rather taken aback by Wimsey's presence.

"Come right in," said Wimsey hospitably. "Come in, sergeant; come in, officer. What can we do for you?"

"Don't," said the landlord, "don't make a row if you can help it."

The police sergeant paid no attention to either of them, but stalked across to the bed and confronted the shrinking Mr. Duckworthy.

"It's the man all right," said he. "Now, Mr. Duckworthy, you'll excuse this late visit, but as you may have seen by the papers, we've been looking for a person answering your description, and there's no time like the present. We want——"

"I didn't do it," cried Mr. Duckworthy wildly. "I know nothing about it——"

The officer pulled out his note-book and wrote: "He said before any question was asked him, 'I didn't do it.'"

"You seem to know all about it," said the sergeant.

"Of course he does," said Wimsey; "we've been having a little informal chat about it."

"You have, have you? And who might you be—sir?" The last word appeared to be screwed out of the sergeant forcibly by the action of the monocle.

"I'm so sorry," said Wimsey, "I haven't a card on me at the moment. I am Lord Peter Wimsey."

"Oh, indeed," said the sergeant. "And may I ask, my lord, what you know about this here?"

"You may, and I may answer if I like, you know. I know nothing at all about the murder. About Mr. Duckworthy I know what he has told me and no more. I dare say he will tell you, too, if you ask him nicely. But no third degree, you know, sergeant. No Savidgery."

Baulked by this painful reminder, the sergeant said, in a voice of annoyance:

"It's my duty to ask him what he knows about this."

"I quite agree," said Wimsey. "As a good citizen, it's his duty to answer you. But it's a gloomy time of night, don't you think? Why not wait till the morning? Mr. Duckworthy won't run away."

"I'm not so sure of that."

"Oh, but I am. I will undertake to produce him whenever you want him. Won't that do? You're not charging him with anything, I suppose?"

"Not yet," said the sergeant.

"Splendid. Then it's all quite friendly and pleasant, isn't it? How about a drink?"

The sergeant refused this kindly offer with some gruffness in his manner.

"On the waggon?" inquired Wimsey sympathetically. "Bad luck. Kidneys? Or liver, eh?"

The sergeant made no reply.

"Well, we are charmed to have had the pleasure of seeing you," pursued Wimsey. "You'll look us up in the morning, won't you? I've got to get back to town fairly early, but I'll drop in at the police-station on my way. You will find Mr. Duckworthy in the lounge, here. It will be more comfortable for you than at your place. Must you be going? Well, good night, all."

Later, Wimsey returned to Mr. Duckworthy, after seeing the police off the premises.

"Listen," he said, "I'm going up to town to do what I can. I'll send you up a solicitor first thing in the morning. Tell him what you've told me, and tell the police what he tells you to tell them and no more. Remember, they can't force you to say anything or to go down to the police-station unless they charge you. If they do charge you, go quietly and say nothing. And whatever you do, don't run away, because if you do, you're done for."

Wimsey arrived in town the following afternoon, and walked down Holborn, looking for a barber's shop. He found it without much difficulty. It lay, as Mr. Duckworthy had described it, at the end of a narrow passage, and it had a long mirror in the door, with the name Briggs scrawled across it in gold letters. Wimsey stared at his own reflection distastefully.

"Check number one," said he, mechanically setting his tie to rights. "Have I been led up the garden? Or is it a case of fourth dimensional mystery? 'The animals went in four by four, *vive la compagnie!* The camel he got stuck in the door.' There is something intensely unpleasant about making a camel of one's self. It goes for days without a drink and its table-manners are objectionable. But there is no doubt that this door is made of looking-glass. Was it always so, I wonder? On, Wimsey, on. I cannot bear to be shaved again. Perhaps a hair-cut might be managed."

He pushed the door open, keeping a stern eye on his reflection to see that it played him no trick.

Of his conversation with the barber, which was lively and varied, only one passage is deserving of record.

"It's some time since I was in here," said Wimsey. "Keep it short behind the ears. Been re-decorated, haven't you?"

"Yes, sir. Looks quite smart, doesn't it?"

"The mirror on the outside of the door—that's new, too, isn't it?"

"Oh, no, sir. That's been there ever since we took over."

"Has it! Then it's longer ago than I thought. Was it there three years ago?"

"Oh, yes, sir. Ten years Mr. Briggs has been here, sir."

"And the mirror too?"

"Oh, yes, sir."

"Then it's my memory that's wrong. Senile decay setting in. 'All, all are gone, the old familiar landmarks.' No, thanks, if I go grey I'll go grey decently. I don't want any hair-tonics to-day, thank you. No, nor even an electric comb. I've had shocks enough."

It worried him, though. So much so that when he emerged, he walked back a few yards along the street, and was suddenly struck by seeing the glass door of a tea-shop. It also lay at the end of a dark passage and had a gold name written across it. The name was "The BRIDGET Tea-shop," but the door was of plain glass. Wimsey looked at it for a few moments and then went in. He did not approach the tea-tables, but accosted the cashier, who sat at a little glass desk inside the door.

Here he went straight to the point and asked whether the young lady remembered the circumstance of a man's having fainted in the doorway some years previously.

The cashier could not say; she had only been there three months, but she thought one of the waitresses might remember. The waitress was produced, and after some consideration, thought she did recollect something of the sort. Wimsey thanked her, said he was a journalist—which seemed to be accepted as an excuse for eccentric questions—parted with half a crown, and withdrew.

His next visit was to Carmelite House. Wimsey had friends in every newspaper office in Fleet Street, and made his way without difficulty to the room where photographs are filed for reference. The original of the "J. D." portrait was produced for his inspection.

"One of yours?" he asked.

"Oh, no. Sent out by Scotland Yard. Why? Anything wrong with it?"

"Nothing. I wanted the name of the original photographer, that's all."

"Oh! Well, you'll have to ask them there. Nothing more I can do for you?"

"Nothing, thanks."

Scotland Yard was easy. Chief-Inspector Parker was Wimsey's closest friend. An inquiry of him soon furnished the photographer's name, which was inscribed at the foot of the print. Wimsey voyaged off at once in search of the establishment, where his name readily secured an interview with the proprietor.

As he had expected, Scotland Yard had been there before him. All information at the disposal of the firm had already been given. It amounted to very little. The photograph had been taken a couple of years previously, and nothing particular was remembered about the sitter. It was a small establishment, doing a rapid business in cheap portraits, and with no pretensions to artistic refinements.

Wimsey asked to see the original negative, which, after some search, was produced.

Wimsey looked it over, laid it down, and pulled from his pocket the copy of the *Evening News* in which the print had appeared.

"Look at this," he said.

The proprietor looked, then looked back at the negative.

"Well, I'm dashed," he said. "That's funny."

"It was done in the enlarging lantern, I take it," said Wimsey.

"Yes. It must have been put in the wrong way round. Now, fancy that happening. You know, sir, we often have to work against time, and I suppose—but it's very careless. I shall have to inquire into it."

"Get me a print of it right way round," said Wimsey.

"Yes, sir, certainly, sir. At once."

"And send one to Scotland Yard."

"Yes, sir. Queer it should have been just this particular one, isn't it, sir? I wonder the party didn't notice. But we generally take three or four positions, and he might not remember, you know."

"You'd better see if you've got any other positions and let me have them too."

"I've done that already, sir, but there are none. No doubt this one was selected and the others destroyed. We don't keep all the rejected negatives, you know, sir. We haven't the space to file them. But I'll get three prints off at once."

"Do," said Wimsey. "The sooner the better. Quick-dry them. And don't do any work on the prints."

"No, sir. You shall have them in an hour or two, sir. But it's astonishing to me that the party didn't complain."

"It's not astonishing," said Wimsey. "He probably thought it the best likeness of the lot. And so it would be—to him. Don't you see—that's the only view he could ever take of his own face. That photograph, with the left and right sides reversed, is the face he sees in the mirror every day— the only face he can really recognise as his. 'Wad the gods the giftie gie us,' and all that."

"Well, that's quite true, sir. And I'm much obliged to you for pointing the mistake out."

Wimsey reiterated the need for haste, and departed. A brief visit to Somerset House followed; after which he called it a day and went home.

Inquiry in Brixton, in and about the address mentioned by Mr. Duckworthy, eventually put Wimsey on to the track of persons who had known him and his mother. An aged lady who had kept a small greengrocery in the same street for the last forty years remembered all about them. She had the encyclopædic memory of the almost illiterate, and was positive as to the date of their arrival.

"Thirty-two years ago, if we lives another month," she said. "Michaelmas it was they come. She was a nice-looking young woman, too, and my daughter, as was expecting her first, took a lot of interest in the sweet little boy."

"The boy was not born here?"

"Why, no, sir. Born somewheres on the south side, he was, but I remember she never rightly said where—only that it was round about the New Cut. She was one of the quiet sort and kep' herself to herself. Never one to talk, she wasn't. Why even to my daughter, as might 'ave good reason for bein' interested, she wouldn't say much about 'ow she got through 'er bad time. Chlorryform she said she 'ad, I know, and she disremembered about it, bit it's my belief it 'ad gone 'ard with 'er and she didn't care to think overmuch about it. 'Er 'usband—a nice man 'e was, too—'e says to me, 'Don't remind 'er of it, Mrs. 'Arbottle, don't remind 'er of it.' Whether she was frightened or whether she was 'urt by it I don't know, but she didn't 'ave no more children. 'Lor!' I says to 'er time and again, 'you'll get used to it, my dear, when you've 'ad nine of 'em same as me,' and she smiled, but she never 'ad no more, none the more for that."

"I suppose it does take some getting used to," said Wimsey, "but nine of them don't seem to have hurt *you,* Mrs. Harbottle, if I may say so. You look extremely flourishing."

"I keeps my 'ealth, sir, I am glad to say, though stouter than I used to be. Nine of them does 'ave a kind of spreading action on the figure. You wouldn't believe, sir, to look at me now, as I 'ad a eighteen-inch waist when I was a girl. Many's the time me pore mother broke the laces on me, with 'er knee in me back and me 'oldin' on to the bedpost."

"One must suffer to be beautiful," said Wimsey politely. "How old was the baby, then, when Mrs. Duckworthy came to live in Brixton?"

"Three weeks old, 'e was, sir—a darling dear—and a lot of 'air on 'is 'ead. Black 'air it was then, but it turned into the brightest red you ever see—like them carrots there. It wasn't so pretty as 'is ma's, though much the same colour. He didn't favour 'er in the face, neither, nor yet 'is dad. She said 'e took after some of 'er side of the family."

"Did you ever see any of the rest of the family?"

"Only 'er sister, Mrs. Susan Brown. A big, stern, 'ard-faced woman she was—not like 'er sister. Lived at Evesham she did, as well I remembers, for I was gettin' my grass from there at the time. I never sees a bunch o' grass now but what I think of Mrs. Susan Brown. Stiff, she was, with a small 'ead, very like a stick o' grass."

Wimsey thanked Mrs. Harbottle in a suitable manner and took the next train to Evesham. He was beginning to wonder where the chase might lead him, but discovered, much to his relief, that Mrs. Susan Brown was well known in the town, being a pillar of the Methodist Chapel and a person well respected.

She was upright still, with smooth, dark hair parted in the middle and drawn tightly back—a woman broad in the base and narrow in the shoulder—not, indeed, unlike the stick of asparagus to which Mrs. Harbottle had compared her. She received Wimsey with stern civility, but disclaimed all knowledge of her nephew's movements. The hint that he was in a position of some embarrassment, and even danger, did not appear to surprise her.

"There was bad blood in him," she said. "My sister Hetty was softer by half than she ought to have been."

"Ah!" said Wimsey. "Well, we can't all be people of strong character, though it must be a source of great satisfaction to those that are. I don't want to be a trouble to you, madam, and I know I'm given to twaddling rather, being a trifle on the soft side myself—so I'll get to the point. I see by the register at Somerset House that your nephew, Robert Duckworthy, was born in Southwark, the son of Alfred and Hester Duckworthy. Wonderful system they have there. But of course—being only human—it breaks down now and again—doesn't it?"

She folded her wrinkled hands over one another on the edge of the table, and he saw a kind of shadow flicker over her sharp dark eyes.

"If I'm not bothering you too much—in what name was the other registered?"

The hands trembled a little, but she said steadily:

"I do not understand you."

"I'm frightfully sorry. Never was good at explaining myself. There were twin boys born, weren't there? Under what name did they register the other? I'm so sorry to be a nuisance, but it's really rather important."

"What makes you suppose that there were twins?"

"Oh, I don't suppose it. I wouldn't have bothered you for a supposition. I know there was a twin brother. What became—at least, I do know more or less what became of him——"

"It died," she said hurriedly.

"I hate to seem contradictory," said Wimsey. "Most unattractive behaviour. But it didn't die, you know. In fact, it's alive now. It's only the name I want to know, you know."

"And why should I tell you anything, young man?"

"Because," said Wimsey, "if you will pardon the mention of anything so disagreeable to a refined taste, there's been a murder committed and your nephew Robert is suspected. As a matter of fact, I happen to know that the murder was done by the brother. That's why I want to get hold of him, don't you see. It would be such a relief to my mind—I am naturally nice-minded—if you would help me to find him. Because, if not, I shall have to go to the police, and then you might be subpœna'd as a witness, and I shouldn't like—I really shouldn't like—to see you in the witness-box at a murder trial. So much unpleasant publicity, don't you know. Whereas, if we can lay hands on the brother quickly, you and Robert need never come into it at all."

Mrs. Brown sat in grim thought for a few minutes.

"Very well," she said, "I will tell you."

"Of course," said Wimsey to Chief-Inspector Parker a few days later, "the whole thing was quite obvious when one had heard about the reversal of friend Duckworthy's interior economy."

"No doubt, no doubt," said Parker. "Nothing could be simpler. But all the same, you are aching to tell me how you deduced it and I am willing to be instructed. Are all twins wrong-sided? And are all wrong-sided people twins?"

"Yes. No. Or rather, no, yes. Dissimilar twins and some kinds of similar twins may both be quite normal. But the kind of similar twins that result from the splitting of a single cell *may* come out as looking-glass twins. It depends on the line of fission in the original cell. You can do it artificially with tadpoles and a bit of horsehair."

"I will make a note to do it at once," said Parker gravely.

"In fact, I've read somewhere that a person with a reversed inside practically always turns out to be one of a pair of similar twins. So you see, while poor old R. D. was burbling on about the *Student of Prague* and the fourth dimension, I was expecting the twin-brother.

"Apparently what happened was this. There were three sisters of the name of Dart—Susan, Hester and Emily. Susan married a man called Brown; Hester married a man called Duckworthy; Emily was unmarried. By one of those cheery little ironies of which life is so full, the only sister who had a baby, or who was apparently capable of having babies, was the unmarried Emily. By way of compensation, she overdid it and had twins.

"When this catastrophe was about to occur, Emily (deserted, of course, by the father) confided in her sisters, the parents being dead. Susan was a tartar—besides, she had married above her station and was climbing steadily on a ladder of good works. She delivered herself of a few texts and washed her hands of the business. Hester was a kind-hearted soul. She offered to adopt the infant, when produced, and bring it up as her own. Well, the baby came, and, as I said before, it was twins.

"That was a bit too much for Duckworthy. He had agreed to one baby, but twins were more than he had bargained for. Hester was allowed to pick her twin, and, being a kindly soul, she picked the weaklier-looking one, which was our Robert—the mirror-image twin. Emily had to keep the other, and, as soon as she was strong enough, decamped with him to Australia, after which she was no more heard of.

"Emily's twin was registered in her own name of Dart and baptised Richard. Robert and Richard were two pretty men. Robert was registered as Hester Duckworthy's own child—there were no tiresome rules in those days requiring notification of births by doctors and midwives, so one could do as one liked about these matters. The Duckworthys, complete with baby, moved to Brixton, where Robert was looked upon as being a perfectly genuine little Duckworthy.

"Apparently Emily died in Australia, and Richard, then a boy of fifteen, worked his passage home to London. He does not seem to have been a nice little boy. Two years afterwards, his path crossed that of Brother Robert and produced the episode of the air-raid night.

"Hester may have known about the wrong-sidedness of Robert, or she may not. Anyway, he wasn't told. I imagine that the shock of the explosion caused him to revert more strongly to his natural left-handed tendency. It also seems to have induced a new tendency to amnesia under similar shock-conditions. The whole thing preyed on his mind, and he became more and more vague and somnambulant.

"I rather think that Richard may have discovered the existence of his double and turned it to account. That explains the central incident of the mirror. I think Robert must have mistaken the glass door of the tea-shop for the door of the barber's shop. It really was Richard who came to meet him, and who retired again so hurriedly for fear of being seen and noted. Circumstances played into his hands, of course—but these meetings do take place, and the fact that they were both wearing soft hats and burberries is not astonishing on a dark, wet day.

"And then there is the photograph. No doubt the original mistake was the photographer's, but I shouldn't be surprised if Richard welcomed it and chose that particular print on that account. Though that would mean, of course, that he knew about the wrong-sidedness of Robert. I don't know how he could have done that, but he may have had opportunities for inquiry. It was known in the Army, and the rumours may have got round. But I won't press that point.

"There's one rather queer thing, and that is that Robert should have had that dream about strangling, on the very night, as far as one could make out, that Richard was engaged in doing away with Jessie Haynes. They say that similar twins are always in close sympathy with one another—that each knows what the other is thinking about, for instance, and contracts the same illness on the same day and all that. Richard was the stronger twin of the two, and perhaps he dominated Robert more than Robert did him. I'm sure I don't know. Daresay it's all bosh. The point is that you've found him all right."

"Yes. Once we'd got the clue there was no difficulty."

"Well, let's toddle round to the Cri and have one."

Wimsey got up and set his tie to rights before the glass.

"All the same," he said, "there's something queer about mirrors. Uncanny, a bit, don't you think so?"

The Prognosis for This Patient Is Horrible

BERTON ROUECHÉ

At around two o'clock on the afternoon of Tuesday, September 12, 1978, an eleven-month-old boy named Chad Shelton, the only child of Bruce Shelton, a television repairman, and his wife, Sallie Betten Shelton, was admitted to Immanuel Medical Center, in Omaha, Nebraska, for evaluation of persistent vomiting. Chad, his parents told the admitting physician, had been vomiting off and on for two days—since early Sunday evening. They added that they, too, had become sick Sunday evening, with severe abdominal cramps, diarrhea, and vomiting, but had now pretty well recovered.

The determination of the cause of an ailing infant's illness can be a serious diagnostic challenge. The diagnostician, being unable to elicit any account of how the patient feels or where he hurts, can make a judgment only on the observable and measurable signs of abnormality. The admitting physician at Immanuel Medical Center noted and recorded that Chad was "irritable," that his "right tympanic membrane was red," and that his tonsils were red and somewhat swollen. On the basis of these rudimentary findings, together with the information provided by the Sheltons, he recorded three tentative diagnoses: gastroenteritis, otitis media (inflammation of the middle ear), and tonsillitis. He also, as is usual in such ambiguous cases, sought the opinion of a consultant. The consulting physician's observations were entered on Chad Shelton's chart the following day. He observed that the patient was "somnolent through the evening, and this morning was noted to be poorly responsive." He noted what appeared to be multiple "bruises." Preliminary laboratory tests were generally normal, with two striking exceptions. One showed abnormal liver function. The other was the blood-platelet count. Platelets are protoplasms intricately involved in the salvational coagulation of blood that normally follows trauma. A normal platelet count ranges from a hundred and fifty thousand to three hundred thousand and upward. Chad's platelet count was nineteen thousand. That would seem to explain the "bruises." They were hemorrhages. The consultant noted his preliminary impression: "This may be a Reye's syndrome." Reye's syndrome, an entity of recent recognition, is a disease of still uncertain origin that largely afflicts young children and is characterized by vomiting, central-nervous-system damage, and liver damage. The production of platelets is a function of the bone marrow, and a low platelet count may reflect defective production or disordered distribution. The latter can be the result of a rush of platelets to a damaged organ—for example, the liver. The consultant recommended that more definitive tests be made and that the patient be transferred to the intensive-care unit of Children's Memorial Hospital.

Chad was admitted to Children's Hospital late that afternoon. He arrived there in a coma. It was noted on his chart that "within an hour after admission, the child's respiratory status began to deteriorate and it was necessary to place him on a ventilator. . . . A repeat platelet count at 4:30 P.M. revealed a platelet count of 18,000 [and] support was begun with platelets and whole blood. . . . During the evening and early morning hours, bleeding problems became increasingly difficult to control. The child's condition continued to deteriorate, and he was pronounced dead at 4:30 A.M. the morning of September 14th." An autopsy was performed. It revealed an "essentially complete necrosis of the child's hepatic [liver] cells, with very little fatty infiltration." The opinion of the pathologist was that "this pattern is more consistent with a toxic ingestion of an unknown agent rather than Reye's syndrome or other infectious etiologies." The final diagnosis reflected his opinion. It read, "1. Severe acute hepatic necrosis secondary to a toxic ingestion of an unknown agent. 2. Disseminated intravascular coagulation. 3. Cerebral hemorrhage secondary to #2. 4. Cerebral edema secondary to #1 and #2. 5. Terminal renal failure."

That was the beginning, but only the beginning. Shortly before noon that day—Thursday, September 14th, the day of Chad Shelton's death—a man named Duane N. Johnson, aged twenty-four and a trucker by trade, was admitted to Immanuel Medical Center by way of the emergency room. He was brought to the hospital by ambulance from the office of his family physician. He had collapsed in the waiting room there, and when he reached the hospital he was comatose. His wife, Sandra Betten Johnson, accompanied him. She told the admitting physician that her husband had become ill on Sunday evening. He had had an attack of chills, then diarrhea, then vomiting. He vomited several times on Monday and again on Tuesday. Yesterday, Wednesday, he had a severe nosebleed. This morning, he felt even worse—he was still vomiting, his head ached, light hurt his eyes, he was exhausted—and he arranged to see their doctor. Mrs. Johnson was frightened and confused. Her husband had never been sick a day in his life. Now he was lying there unconscious. And not only that. Sherrie, their three-year-old daughter, was also sick. Not as sick as Duane, but she had complained of stomach pains, and she had vomited several times. The last few days had been a nightmare. Mrs. Johnson didn't know what was happening. Her sister Sallie and her husband had also been sick this week—sick to their stomachs, like Sherrie. And only last night—early this morning—Chad, her sister's little baby, had died at Children's Hospital. They said he might have been poisoned. The admitting physician pricked up his ears. Chad? Was her nephew named Shelton? That's right—Chad Shelton. Did the doctor know about him? The doctor said he did. He said it was he who had admitted him to the hospital here on Tuesday. The doctor stopped and reflected. He reminded himself that Chad had suffered multiple hemorrhages. And Johnson had had a nosebleed. He asked himself if there might be some connection here. And Mrs. Johnson had said that their daughter was sick. He asked Mrs. Johnson to bring her daughter around to the hospital. He thought he ought to take a careful look at her.

Johnson remained comatose. The results of the admitting physician's preliminary examination were both unrevealing and alarming. The pupil of Johnson's right eye was "dilated and fixed," he wrote in his report. "Left pupil was pinpoint. Evidence of some conjunctival hemorrhage bilaterally. There was some blood in the pharynx." The physician again felt that a second opinion would be helpful. The consultant's findings, refined by a series of laboratory tests, fully justified the admitting physician's alarm. He noted on Johnson's chart, "There is no motor movement. There is no response to painful stimuli. . . . He is on a respirator. He has had an intracranial hemorrhage. . . . A CAT scan shows an intracerebral hematoma." Johnson's platelet count was a mere six thousand. An S.G.O.T. test was performed. This is a test that determines the concentration in the blood of an enzyme whose excessive presence is indicative of liver damage. A normal S.G.O.T. count is from five to eighteen units. Johnson's count was nine hundred and ten. The consultant concluded his report, "The patient, I think, has essentially gone into . . . a neurological situation from which he cannot be retrieved." Nevertheless, in the hope of retrieval, Johnson was transferred late that day to another hospital, Bishop Clarkson Memorial Hospital, where a technical procedure not available at Immanuel Medical Center could be performed. He was examined at Clarkson by a second consultant. It is usual for a physician confronted by a hopeless or near-hopeless case to note on the patient's chart some easy euphemism like "The prognosis is guarded." Johnson's condition jolted the consultant at Clarkson into the open. He concluded his report, "The prognosis for this patient is horrible."

Meanwhile, as requested by the physician who had admitted her husband that morning, Sandra Johnson returned to Immanuel Medical Center with her daughter, Sherrie. Sherrie was still in pain, still vomiting. She was admitted there at around two o'clock in the afternoon. The preliminary physical examination revealed a scattering of small intradermal hemorrhages on her eyelids and on her lower legs. Her liver was found to be tender and somewhat enlarged. Her platelet count was thirteen thousand. Her S.G.O.T. was seven hundred and two. An exchange blood transfusion was ordered. Following that, in the late afternoon, Sherrie was moved to Children's Hospital and placed in the intensive-care unit there.

Mrs. Johnson saw Sherrie settled at Children's Hospital. There was nothing more that she could do. She then visited her comatose husband at Clarkson Memorial Hospital. There was nothing that she could do there, either. She went home. But at least she did not go home to an empty house. Her second sister, Susan Betten Conley, was then staying with the Johnsons. The two distraught young women talked—about Duane, about Sherrie, about Chad. It was hard for them to believe that this was happening. Nothing in this terrible day seemed quite real. They later drove over to the Sheltons' house. The Sheltons were not as well recovered from their gastrointestinal troubles as they had tried to persuade themselves. Chad's pathetic illness and then his shattering death had distracted them from their own illness. Now they realized that they were far from well. Sallie Shelton, especially, felt poorly. She had abdominal pain, diarrhea, and nausea. Shelton and the three sisters talked. It was suggested that maybe Sallie should be hospitalized. Susan and Sandra left. They felt even more bewildered after talking with their sister and brother-in-law. They couldn't understand why they themselves were not sick—why they alone of the two families, the two households, were well. Sandra drove back to Children's Hospital. Sherrie was asleep, and her condition was described as stable. Sandra drove on to Clarkson Memorial. Her husband was still in a coma. There had been no improvement in his condition. He was almost certainly dying. She settled down to an all-night vigil.

Sallie Shelton spent a restless night. She awoke the next morning—Friday, September 15th—feeling very definitely ill. As she and her husband were dressing, the telephone rang. It was Sandra Johnson. Duane was dead. He had died about an hour ago, without recovering any degree of consciousness. That decided the Sheltons. They drove to Clarkson Memorial Hospital. Mrs. Shelton was examined in the emergency room. Her son's death and its cryptic nature were remembered. She was admitted for observation and testing. Then, as a precaution, it was decided to also admit her husband. The indicated tests revealed that Bruce Shelton's S.G.O.T. was mildly elevated (a hundred and twenty-five units) and his platelet count was a hundred and twenty-three thousand, or a little low. Sallie Shelton's condition was found to be more serious. She was still nauseated, still diarrheic, she had a headache, she was running a fever, and she was noticeably lethargic. Her S.G.O.T. level was eighty-five, and although her initial platelet count was a hundred and sixteen thousand, only a little lower than her husband's, subsequent evaluations showed an ominous downward trend.

Later that day, with Mrs. Johnson's permission, an autopsy was performed on Duane Johnson. The immediate cause of death was found to have been a cerebral hemorrhage. The pathologist's report also noted an almost total lack of platelets, and massive liver damage "of unknown etiology."

A memorandum dated September 18, 1978, from J. Lyle Conrad, director of the Field Services Division, Bureau of Epidemiology, Center for Disease Control, in Atlanta, reads:

On September 15, 1978, Alan Kendal, Ph.D., Respiratory Virology Branch, Virology Division, Bureau of Laboratories, C.D.C., received a call from Paul A. Stoesz, M.D., State Epidemiologist, Nebraska, concerning two recent deaths in a group of families in Omaha, Nebraska. . . . Dr. Stoesz related that 2 people, an 11-month-old child and a 30-year-old [sic] man, had died within the past 2 days of an illness characterized by vomiting and diarrhea. Clinical information on the child indicated a death from hepatic failure. No information was available on the cause of death in the man, although an autopsy was being performed. . . . Both toxic and infectious etiologies are being considered as possible causes for these deaths.

Dr. Stoesz, on behalf of Henry D. Smith, M.D., Director of Health, Nebraska State Department of Health, and Warren Jacobson, M.D., Director, Douglas County Health Department, invited

C.D.C. to assist in an investigation of the situation. . . . After further discussions about potential etiologies for the outbreak, Dr. Conrad then contacted . . . John P. M. Lofgren, M.D., E.I.S. [Epidemic Intelligence Service] Officer in Jefferson City, Missouri. . . . Dr. Lofgren departed for Omaha the evening of September 15.

"Yes," Dr. Lofgren says. "I got Dr. Conrad's call at about three o'clock in the afternoon. Omaha and Jefferson City are not that close together, but apparently I was the nearest E.I.S. officer to the scene. Anyway, I got the call and went home and packed and took off. I drove the rest of the day and part of the night. I got to Omaha—to a motel room that the doctors there had reserved for me—at about 2 A.M. There was a message waiting for me. There was to be a big meeting the next morning in the conference room at Clarkson Memorial Hospital, and one of the local doctors would pick me up. Which he did. At the meeting, there were about thirty people—the attending physicians, house officers and medical students involved in the case, lab people and pathologists, hospital social workers, the staff of the county health department, and the state epidemiologist and his staff. We settled down to work in good order. We had the two autopsy reports and the charts on the three surviving patients. It was a strange case, and very wide open. But there were a few conclusions that we could be comfortable with. It seemed clear that we were dealing with a disease that was not epidemic, that was limited to just the Johnson and the Shelton families. Then we defined the disease. Our case definition required these symptoms: vomiting, an increased S.G.O.T., and a decrease in platelets.

"The state and county epidemiologists had made a good beginning. A setting had begun to take shape. The Johnson home seemed to be the site of the trouble. The outbreak had its origin there on the afternoon of Sunday, September 10th, sometime between three and four o'clock. The two families had not been together in about a week until then. But that afternoon the three Sheltons—Bruce, Sallie, and the baby, Chad—dropped in on the Johnsons and Susan Conley. They visited about an hour. At about three-fifteen, Sandra Johnson went to the refrigerator and took out a white plastic pitcher of lemonade. She added ice and filled some glasses. Bruce Shelton took a couple of swallows from his glass and then poured about three-quarters of an inch in a glass for little Chad, and Sallie Shelton finished off the rest. Sandra didn't like lemonade, and she drank none. Neither did her sister Susan. Duane Johnson and the little girl, Sherrie, both drank some of the lemonade. It was suggested that Duane might have drunk two glasses. The Sheltons left to make another call and then started home. On the way home, Bruce and Sallie began to feel sick to the stomach. A few minutes after they got home—at about six o'clock—Sallie vomited. That made her feel a little better. Then, at about seven o'clock, Bruce vomited, and then little Chad. Then Sallie vomited again, and she and her husband vomited again and again during the next four hours. But Chad vomited only that once that night. The two Johnsons—Duane and his daughter, Sherrie— had much the same experience. The investigation had shown that Sandra Johnson had made the lemonade. She had made it a day or two before Sunday—maybe as early as the previous Thursday. But she had made it as she always did—a packaged mix with water and sugar. It was uncertain whether all the lemonade was drunk or whether some was left and thrown out. In any event, the pitcher was empty. The fatal lemonade was gone.

"I say 'fatal' because, as unlikely as lemonade sounds as a cause of poisoning, we were satisfied that the outbreak was an outbreak of poisoning, and that the lemonade was the vehicle. There had been some toxic material in it. The onset of illness was compatible with poisoning by some organic poison. The incubation period was all wrong for an infectious disease. Much too short. Later, after the meeting, I went out to the Johnson house and had a look around. It was a lower-middle-class house on low ground and in bad repair. The plumbing was poor. The house had already been carefully searched, and I was provided with samples of everything that could be even remotely connected with the trouble. One of these possibilities was some firecrackers. Firecrackers contain yellow phosphorus, and its taste could have been masked by the lemonade. There was no indication of how the phosphorus might have got into the lemonade. So that's where we stood. We had a clear clinical syndrome and a likely vehicle. But we didn't have any idea of what the toxic agent might have been. The answer, if we were going to get one, would seem to be up to the laboratory people. John Wiley, the Douglas County epidemiologist, was very helpful. We arranged for samples of everything found in the Johnson house that could be analyzed and sent them off to C.D.C. We also sent off blood and urine samples taken from all the patients, and frozen liver, brain, lung, kidney, and spleen specimens from Duane Johnson. That was about the end of my role in the investigation. I went back to Jefferson City and wrote up my report."

The samples gathered for Dr. Lofgren by Mr. Wiley and his staff were received at C.D.C.—at the Toxicology Branch of the Bureau of Laboratories—in three installments, on September 20th, 21st, and 25th. It was a comprehensive and a very considerable collection. It numbered thirty-four items, including a packet of twenty firecrackers. Animal experiments were at once begun. A group of laboratory rats were fed (by gavage) various materials found in the Johnson kitchen—tap water, sugar, lemonade mix. Other rats were injected with material taken from the several patients. The plastic pitcher in which the lemonade had been made was treated with a citric-acid solution in the hope of extracting some minuscule remains of the lemonade, and the solution was fed to another group of rats. The firecrackers were anatomized. They were found to contain only an insignificant quantity of yellow phosphorus. The laboratory animals were sacrificed at intervals during the next week or so, and their kidneys, livers, and other organs and tissues were examined for eloquent pathological changes. None were found. Liver tissue obtained from Johnson at autopsy was further analyzed for the presence of selenium, a substance that in large concentrations has a toxic affinity for the liver, and for arsenic. The results were essentially normal. Urine samples taken from Bruce and Sallie Shelton at the peak of their illness were analyzed for evidence of a dangerous herbicide called paraquat. The results again were negative.

The toxicological examination of the various samples and specimens relating to the Omaha outbreak was monitored and its results were evaluated by a research medical officer in the Toxicology Branch of C.D.C. named Renate D. Kimbrough. Dr. Kimbrough, a native of Germany and a graduate in medicine of the University of Göttingen, is the wife of a research chemist and the mother of three children. She is also a pathologist and a toxicologist of national distinction. She found the laboratory results, for all their negativity, both useful and interesting.

"One thing was particularly noteworthy," Dr. Kimbrough says. "The liver was the only affected organ. That eliminated a good many possible poisons. Most toxic chemicals that cause severe liver damage also cause damage to other parts of the body. As a matter of fact, it is unusual to find only liver damage—to find the liver destroyed and none of the other organs affected. There were also other limiting factors to consider. One was that the poison had to be something that was easily soluble in water —in lemonade. Another was that it had to be more or less tasteless and odorless. There was no indication that the Johnson lemonade had either a funny taste or a funny smell. Well, those factors eliminated a number of other compounds. In fact, they narrowed the field to a group of readily modifiable hydrocarbons called alkylating agents. This was not an area in which I felt very much at home, but I knew someone who did. I knew an expert. I put in a call to Ronald C. Shank. Dr. Shank is associate professor of toxicology in the Department of Community and

Environmental Medicine at the University of California at Irvine. I told him my story and what I needed. Could he give me a list of water-soluble alkylating agents? No problem. He gave me a list of eight—methyl methane sulfonate; dimethyl sulfate; dimethylnitrosamine; N-methyl-N'-nitro-N-nitrosoguanidine; 1, 2 dimethylhydrazine; methyl chloride; methyl bromide; and methyl iodide. Then I went to work. It was another process of evaluation and elimination. I ruled out methyl chloride, methyl bromide, and methyl iodide almost at once. They are all weak alkylating agents, and they are lethal only in very large amounts—amounts too large to go undetected in a glass of lemonade. Moreover, the initial impact of those agents is on the brain, so the initial effect is mental confusion. That had not been noted in any of the Omaha cases. I could also rule out 1, 2 dimethylhydrazine. It causes severe damage to the red blood cells, and no such damage was noted in any of the Omaha reports. Then I eliminated methyl methane sulfonate. The kind of liver damage it produces is quite different from that observed in Duane Johnson and Chad Shelton. The same was true of dimethyl sulfate and N-methyl-N'-nitro-N-nitrosoguanidine. And the latter, again, is lethal only in very large amounts. That left dimethylnitrosamine.

"I think I knew almost at once that dimethylnitrosamine was the answer. It perfectly met all the required criteria. It is a liquid, and it is well miscible with water. It is largely odorless and tasteless. It is extremely toxic in very small amounts. The lethal dose for a medium-sized adult is less than two grams, and for a small child about one-third of a gram. A third of a gram is about seven drops, or less than half a teaspoonful. And dimethylnitrosamine is peculiarly liver-specific. It attacks the liver and only the liver, and the lesions it causes are quite distinctive. I studied the textbook lesions caused by dimethylnitrosamine. Then I examined under the microscope the liver specimens taken at autopsy from Duane Johnson and Chad Shelton. The Johnson and Shelton lesions were identical with the textbook examples. Now, let me move ahead for a moment. I was satisfied that the poison involved was dimethylnitrosamine, but I wanted to be more than that. I wanted to be absolutely sure. This was not an accidental poisoning. Everyone involved in the matter was certain that the poison had been deliberately added to the lemonade. It was a case of murder. Well, I called Dr. Shank again. Dimethylnitrosamine is very rapidly metabolized and excreted—within a couple of days of ingestion. So there was no possibility of turning up any trace of it in the liver samples. Its presence in the liver, however, causes certain chemical changes that can be measured by a high-pressure liquid-chromatography procedure that was recently developed by Dr. Shank. I asked him if he would perform his test on a group of liver tissues. This was to be, of course, a blind test. I supplied Dr. Shank with eight coded vials of material. They consisted of liver tissue taken from Duane Johnson, kidney tissue taken from him, and six liver and kidney specimens taken from cases in our storage file—three of them from alleged cases of methyl-bromide poisoning and three from cases of Reye's syndrome. Dr. Shank reported that one specimen of the eight was positive for dimethylnitrosamine. That was the coded sample of liver tissue taken from Duane Johnson. And that was definitive.

"But all this, as I say, came later. Much later—in August of 1979. So now let's go back to where we were—to October of 1978. I was reasonably satisfied that dimethylnitrosamine was the poison involved, and I acted on that assumption. The next question was: How did it get in the lemonade? And where did it come from? It certainly didn't come from the corner drugstore. Dimethylnitrosamine is not an everyday compound, and its uses are rather limited. It was originally developed in England, as a solvent for use in the automobile industry, and it may have some other highly specialized industrial uses, but it is also known to be a powerful carcinogen. That quality has given it a certain vogue in cancer research. It is widely used to induce cancer in laboratory animals. I thought about that, and I thought about Omaha. Omaha is not a great industrial center; it is a great insurance center. And it is something of a medical center. It has Creighton University School of Medicine and the University of Nebraska Medical School, and it has the Eppley Institute—the Eppley Institute for cancer research.

"I had talked with John Wiley, the Douglas County epidemiologist, a time or two in the course of the investigation. So now I called him again. I told him what I had in mind. I don't believe I actually singled out dimethylnitrosamine. I think I simply said that I was convinced that the poison involved was an alkylating agent, and that it might very well be one used in cancer research. I suggested that it might be a good idea to check and see if anybody connected with the Johnson or Shelton families had any connection with the Eppley Institute. He said he would. And he did. And there was a connection—a very direct, a very real connection."

The criminal investigation of the deaths of Chad Shelton and Duane Johnson was directed by Samuel W. Cooper, the Deputy Douglas County Attorney, together with Lieutenant Foster Burchard, of the Homicide Division of the Omaha Police Department. Much of the field work, and most of the most productive work, was done by a detective in Lieutenant Burchard's command named Kenneth G. Miller.

"It was a strange case," Cooper says. "Our investigation was the third phase of three quite distinct phases. There was first the medical investigation, then Renate Kimbrough's toxicological investigation, and then our homicide investigation. And even our phase was unusual. It was never, from our point of view, a simple case of whodunit. By the time we came into the picture, it had been established that the murder weapon was a toxic substance. So it was more a case of how-he-dunit. It took us a good long time to build up a provable case, but we had both the who and the how, and even the why, in only a matter of days. That was where Ken Miller came in. Miller had been working closely with John Wiley at the Health Department, and Wiley told him about his conversation with Dr. Kimbrough and her suggestion about a possible link between the families involved and the Eppley Institute. Miller was smart enough to take her suggestion seriously. He went back to his office and ran the Johnsons and the Sheltons through the computer file we have on victims of some sort of criminal act. And almost at once he found a lead. It involved the Johnsons—Duane and Sandra—and Sandra's mother and brother. One night in June of 1975, Duane and Sandra—they weren't the Johnsons yet, they were only going together—and her mother and brother went to the movies. Afterward, they were standing together out in front of the Betten house, talking, when a car drove up and a man jumped out and opened fire with a shotgun. One of the pellets hit Sandra's mother, and Sandra's brother was nicked a couple of times, but neither was really hurt. The man drove off, but there was no big mystery about the attack. The man had been a high-school sweetheart of Sandra's. He was jealous and crazed, furious that she had dropped him for another man, and his intended victim may have been Duane Johnson. His name was Steven Roy Harper, and he was a rather familiar type. Good student, quiet, never drank, smoked, or used drugs. The records showed that Harper was arrested, pleaded no contest to a charge of shooting with intent to kill, and was sentenced to one to five years in prison. That was on December 6, 1976. He was paroled on November 16, 1977. Ken Miller absorbed all that and then moved on to the Eppley Institute. It was almost too much. Harper had worked at the Eppley Institute. He had found a job there a few months after his release, and his job was one that put him in the vicinity of various chemical compounds, including alkylating agents, including dimethylnitrosamine. He had held the job for about five months, until August 18, 1978, when he resigned to take a better-paying job as a construction worker. That was the bare bones of our investigation. There was, of course, a great deal more—a lot of legwork, a lot of interviewing of Sandra Johnson and others, a lot of detail. Harper had been in Omaha at the time of the lemonade party, but now he was on a construction job in Beaumont, Texas. Miller and a couple of other detectives and I flew down to Beaumont with a warrant. We arranged for the F.B.I. to pick Harper up, and we took him into custody."

That was on Friday, October 13th, less than a month after the deaths of Chad Shelton and Duane Johnson. After his arrest, Harper made an informal declaration to a homicide detective in Cooper's entourage named Greg Thompson. Thompson's transcript of it reads, in its essentials:

Harper states that he is still in love with Sandra Johnson, that his life has been miserable for the past four years, and everything built up in him until it came to this point. While working in the Gene Eppley Cancer Care Center [sic], he took a chemical which he called DMNA [dimethylnitrosamine], a carcinogen. . . .

Harper stated that he remembers driving up by the Johnson house, looking and seeing that no one was there, drove past it and parked down the street, around the corner. Harper then got out and walked back up the street, around the corner to the Johnson house, walked all the way around the Johnson house, looking for a way to get in. Harper states that he thought he went in the side door, but he may have went in the window, he can't really remember. Or maybe he just left by the side door. He remembers going into the house, opening up the refrigerator, taking the small vial, which he described to be between two (2) and three (3) inches long and maybe a half-inch (½) diameter, pouring it into the lemonade in the refrigerator. . . . Harper then left the residence.

Harper denied in his statement to Thompson that he had poisoned the lemonade with murderous intent. He told Thompson that "he didn't believe that it [the dimethylnitrosamine] was toxic, that it would only cause cancer." If such was his intention, he may have been not entirely unsuccessful. Of the three surviving victims of his poisoned lemonade, Bruce and Sallie Shelton were discharged from the hospital as fully recovered—he after four days of treatment, she after a stay of sixteen days. Sandra Johnson's daughter, Sherrie, was less fortunate. She was hospitalized for three weeks and then was followed for several months as an outpatient. The most recent record of her condition noted "continuous hepatosplenomegaly [enlargement of the liver and spleen] and elevated liver enzymes, and a liver biopsy obtained three months after exposure showed chronic active hepatitis." A liver so damaged is often eventually hospitable to the development of cancer.

Harper was returned to Omaha. His case was presented at a preliminary judicial hearing, after which the presiding judge charged him with two counts of murder in the first degree and three counts of poisoning. On October 5, 1979, after a three-week trial in which Cooper served as prosecuting attorney and Dr. Kimbrough appeared as a key witness for the state, Harper was found guilty on all five counts and sentenced to die in the electric chair.

AN INTERNATIONAL
TOUR DE FORCE

WITH A
CAST FROM
THREE CONTINENTS
ON A
SNOWBOUND TRAIN

Murder on the Orient Express

AGATHA CHRISTIE

PART I—The Facts

1. *An Important Passenger on the Taurus Express*

It was five o'clock on a winter's morning in Syria. Alongside the platform at Aleppo stood the train grandly designated in railway guides as the Taurus Express. It consisted of a kitchen and dining-car, a sleeping-car and two local coaches.

By the step leading up into the sleeping-car stood a young French lieutenant, resplendent in uniform, conversing with a small man, muffled up to the ears, of whom nothing was visible but a pink-tipped nose and the two points of an upward curled moustache.

It was freezingly cold, and this job of seeing off a distinguished stranger was not one to be envied, but Lieutenant Dubosc performed his part manfully. Graceful phrases fell from his lips in polished French. Not that he knew what it was all about. There had been rumours, of course, as there always were in such cases. The General—*his* General's—temper had grown worse and worse. And then there had come this Belgian stranger—all the way from England, it seemed. There had been a week—a week of curious tensity. And then certain things had happened. A very distinguished officer had committed suicide, another had resigned—anxious faces had suddenly lost their anxiety, certain military precautions were relaxed. And the General—Lieutenant Dubosc's own particular General—had suddenly looked ten years younger.

Dubosc had overheard part of a conversation between him and the stranger. "You have saved us, *mon cher*," said the General emotionally, his great white moustache trembling as he spoke. "You have saved the honour of the French Army—you have averted much bloodshed! How can I thank you for acceding to my request? To have come so far——"

To which the stranger (by name M. Hercule Poirot) had made a fitting reply including the phrase, "But indeed do I not remember that once you saved my life?" And then the General had made another fitting reply to that disclaiming any merit for that past service, and with more mention of France, of Belgium, of glory, of honour and of such kindred things they had embraced each other heartily and the conversation had ended.

As to what it had all been about, Lieutenant Dubosc was still in the dark, but to him had been delegated the duty of seeing off M. Poirot by the Taurus Express, and he was carrying it out with all the zeal and ardour befitting a young officer with a promising career ahead of him.

"To-day is Sunday," said Lieutenant Dubosc. "To-morrow, Monday evening, you will be in Stamboul."

It was not the first time he had made this observation. Conversations on the platform, before the departure of a train, are apt to be somewhat repetitive in character.

"That is so," agreed M. Poirot.

"And you intend to remain there a few days, I think?"

"*Mais oui*. Stamboul, it is a city I have never visited. It would be a pity to pass through—*comme ça*." He snapped his fingers descriptively. "Nothing presses—I shall remain there as a tourist for a few days."

"La Sainte Sophie, it is very fine," said Lieutenant Dubosc, who had never seen it.

A cold wind came whistling down the platform. Both men shivered. Lieutenant Dubosc managed to cast a surreptitious glance at his watch. Five minutes to five—only five minutes more!

Fancying that the other man had noticed his surreptitious glance, he hastened once more into speech.

"There are few people travelling this time of year," he said, glancing up at the windows of the sleeping-car above them.

"That is so," agreed M. Poirot.

"Let us hope you will not be snowed up in the Taurus!"

"That happens?"

"It has occurred, yes. Not this year, as yet."

"Let us hope, then," said M. Poirot. "The weather reports from Europe, they are bad."

"Very bad. In the Balkans there is much snow."

"In Germany too, I have heard."

"*Eh bien*," said Lieutenant Dubosc hastily as another pause seemed to be about to occur. "To-morrow evening at seven-forty you will be in Constantinople."

"Yes," said M. Poirot, and went on desperately, "La Sainte Sophie, I have heard it is very fine."

"Magnificent, I believe."

Above their heads the blind of one of the sleeping-car compartments was pushed aside and a young woman looked out.

Mary Debenham had had little sleep since she left Baghdad on the preceding Thursday. Neither in the train to Kirkuk, nor in the Rest House at Mosul, nor last night on the train had she slept properly. Now, weary of lying wakeful in the hot stuffiness of her overheated compartment, she got up and peered out.

This must be Aleppo. Nothing to see, of course. Just a long, poor-lighted platform with loud furious altercations in Arabic going on somewhere. Two men below her window were talking French. One was a French officer, the other was a little man with enormous moustaches. She smiled faintly. She had never seen anyone quite so heavily muffled up. It must be very cold outside. That was why they heated the train so terribly. She tried to force the window down lower, but it would not go.

The Wagon Lit conductor had come up to the two men. The train was about to depart, he said. Monsieur had better mount. The little man removed his hat. What an egg-shaped head he had. In spite of her pre-occupations Mary Debenham smiled. A ridiculous-looking little man. The sort of little man one could never take seriously.

Lieutenant Dubosc was saying his parting speech. He had thought it out beforehand and had kept it till the last minute. It was a very beauti-ful, polished speech.

Not to be outdone, M. Poirot replied in kind.

"En voiture, Monsieur," said the Wagon Lit conductor.

With an air of infinite reluctance M. Poirot climbed aboard the train. The conductor climbed after him. M. Poirot waved his hand. Lieutenant Dubosc came to the salute. The train, with a terrific jerk, moved slowly forward.

"Enfin!" murmured M. Hercule Poirot.

"Brrrrr," said Lieutenant Dubosc, realising to the full how cold he was. . . .

"Voilà, Monsieur." The conductor displayed to Poirot with a dramatic gesture the beauty of his sleeping compartment and the neat arrange-ment of his luggage. "The little valise of Monsieur, I have placed it *here.*"

His outstretched hand was suggestive. Hercule Poirot placed in it a folded note.

"*Merci, Monsieur.*" The conductor became brisk and businesslike. "I have the tickets of Monsieur. I will also take the passport, please. Monsieur breaks his journey in Stamboul, I understand?"

M. Poirot assented.

"There are not many people travelling, I imagine?" he said.

"No, Monsieur. I have only two other passengers—both English. A Colonel from India, and a young English lady from Baghdad. Monsieur requires anything?"

Monsieur demanded a small bottle of Perrier.

Five o'clock in the morning is an awkward time to board a train. There was still two hours before dawn. Conscious of an inadequate night's sleep, and of a delicate mission successfully accomplished, M. Poirot curled up in a corner and fell asleep.

When he awoke it was half-past nine, and he sallied forth to the restaurant-car in search of hot coffee.

There was only one occupant at the moment, obviously the young English lady referred to by the conductor. She was tall, slim and dark—perhaps twenty-eight years of age. There was a kind of cool efficiency in the way she was eating her breakfast and in the way she called to the attendant to bring her more coffee, which bespoke a knowledge of the world and of travelling. She wore a dark-coloured travelling dress of some thin material eminently suitable for the heated atmosphere of the train.

M. Hercule Poirot, having nothing better to do, amused himself by studying her without appearing to do so.

She was, he judged, the kind of young woman who could take care of herself with perfect ease wherever she went. She had poise and efficiency. He rather liked the severe regularity of her features and the delicate pallor of her skin. He liked the burnished black head with its neat waves of hair, and her eyes, cool, impersonal and grey. But she was, he decided, just a little too efficient to be what he called "*jolie femme.*"

Presently another person entered the restaurant-car. This was a tall man of between forty and fifty, lean of figure, brown of skin, with hair slightly grizzled round the temples.

"The colonel from India," said Poirot to himself.

The newcomer gave a little bow to the girl.

"Morning, Miss Debenham."

"Good-morning, Colonel Arbuthnot."

The Colonel was standing with a hand on the chair opposite her.

"Any objection?" he asked.

"Of course not. Sit down."

"Well, you know, breakfast isn't always a chatty meal."

"I should hope not. But I don't bite."

The Colonel sat down.

"Boy," he called in peremptory fashion.

He gave an order for eggs and coffee.

His eyes rested for a moment on Hercule Poirot, but they passed on indifferently. Poirot, reading the English mind correctly, knew that he had said to himself, "Only some damned foreigner."

True to their nationality, the two English people were not chatty. They exchanged a few brief remarks, and presently the girl rose and went back to her compartment.

At lunch time the other two again shared a table and again they both completely ignored the third passenger. Their conversation was more animated than at breakfast. Colonel Arbuthnot talked of the Punjab, and occasionally asked the girl a few questions about Baghdad where it became clear that she had been in a post as governess. In the course of conversation they discovered some mutual friends which had the immediate effect of making them more friendly and less stiff. They discussed old Tommy Somebody and Jerry Someone Else. The Colonel inquired whether she was going straight through to England or whether she was stopping in Stamboul.

"No, I'm going straight on."

"Isn't that rather a pity?"

"I came out this way two years ago and spent three days in Stamboul then."

"Oh, I see. Well, I may say I'm very glad you are going right through, because I am."

He made a kind of clumsy little bow, flushing a little as he did so.

"He is susceptible, our Colonel," thought Hercule Poirot to himself with some amusement. "The train, it is as dangerous as a sea voyage!"

Miss Debenham said evenly that that would be very nice. Her manner was slightly repressive.

The Colonel, Hercule Poirot noticed, accompanied her back to her compartment. Later they passed through the magnificent scenery of the Taurus. As they looked down toward the Cilician Gates, standing in the corridor side by side, a sigh came suddenly from the girl. Poirot was standing near them and heard her murmur:

"It's so beautiful! I wish—I wish——"

"Yes?"

"I wish I could enjoy it!"

Arbuthnot did not answer. The square line of his jaw seemed a little sterner and grimmer.

"I wish to Heaven you were out of all this," he said.

"Hush, please. Hush."

"Oh! it's all right." He shot a slightly annoyed glance in Poirot's direction. Then he went on: "But I don't like the idea of your being a governess—at the beck and call of tyrannical mothers and their tiresome brats."

She laughed with just a hint of uncontrol in the sound.

"Oh! you mustn't think that. The downtrodden governess is quite an exploded myth. I can assure you that it's the parents who are afraid of being bullied by *me*."

They said no more. Arbuthnot was, perhaps, ashamed of his outburst.

"Rather an odd little comedy that I watch here," said Poirot to himself thoughtfully.

He was to remember that thought of his later.

They arrived at Konya that night about half-past eleven. The two English travellers got out to stretch their legs, pacing up and down the snowy platform.

M. Poirot was content to watch the teeming activity of the station through a window pane. After about ten minutes, however, he decided that a breath of air would not perhaps be a bad thing, after all. He made careful preparations, wrapping himself in several coats and mufflers and encasing his neat boots in goloshes. Thus attired he descended gingerly to the platform and began to pace its length. He walked out beyond the engine.

It was the voices which gave him the clue to the two indistinct figures standing in the shadow of a traffic van. Arbuthnot was speaking.

"Mary——"

The girl interrupted him.

"Not now. Not now. When it's all over. When it's behind us— *then*——"

Discreetly M. Poirot turned away. He wondered.

He would hardly have recognised the cool, efficient voice of Miss Debenham. . . .

"Curious," he said to himself.

The next day he wondered whether, perhaps, they had quarrelled. They spoke little to each other. The girl, he thought, looked anxious. There were dark circles under her eyes.

It was about half-past two in the afternoon when the train came to a halt. Heads were poked out of windows. A little knot of men were clustered by the side of the line looking and pointing at something under the dining-car.

Poirot leaned out and spoke to the Wagon Lit conductor who was hurrying past. The man answered and Poirot drew back his head and, turning, almost collided with Mary Debenham who was standing just behind him.

"What is the matter?" she asked rather breathlessly in French. "Why are we stopping?"

"It is nothing, Mademoiselle. It is something that has caught fire under the dining-car. Nothing serious. It is put out. They are now repairing the damage. There is no danger, I assure you."

She made a little abrupt gesture, as though she were waving the idea of danger aside as something completely unimportant.

"Yes, yes, I understand that. But the *time!*"

"The time?"

"Yes, this will delay us."

"It is possible—yes," agreed Poirot.

"But we can't afford delay! The train is due in at 6:55 and one has to cross the Bosphorus and catch the Simplon Orient Express the other side at nine o'clock. If there is an hour or two of delay we shall miss the connection."

"It is possible, yes," he admitted.

He looked at her curiously. The hand that held the window bar was not quite steady, her lips too were trembling.

"Does it matter to you very much, Mademoiselle?" he asked.

"Yes. Yes, it does. I—I must catch that train."

She turned away from him and went down the corridor to join Colonel Arbuthnot.

Her anxiety, however, was needless. Ten minutes later the train started again. It arrived at Haydapassar only five minutes late, having made up time on the journey.

The Bosphorus was rough and M. Poirot did not enjoy the crossing. He was separated from his travelling companions on the boat, and did not see them again.

On arrival at the Galata Bridge he drove straight to the Tokatlian Hotel.

2. *The Tokatlian Hotel*

At the Tokatlian, Hercule Poirot asked for a room with bath. Then he stepped over to the concierge's desk and inquired for letters.

There were three waiting for him and a telegram. His eyebrows rose a little at the sight of the telegram. It was unexpected.

He opened it in his usual neat, unhurried fashion. The printed words stood out clearly.

Development you predicted in Kassner Case has come unexpectedly please return immediately.

"*Voilà ce qui est embêtant,*" murmured Poirot vexedly. He glanced up at the clock.

"I shall have to go on to-night," he said to the concierge. "At what time does the Simplon Orient leave?"

"At nine o'clock, Monsieur."

"Can you get me a sleeper?"

"Assuredly, Monsieur. There is no difficulty this time of year. The trains are almost empty. First-class or second?"

"First."

"*Très bien, Monsieur.* How far are you going?"

"To London."

"*Bien, Monsieur.* I will get you a ticket to London and reserve your sleeping-car accommodation in the Stamboul-Calais coach."

Poirot glanced at the clock again. It was ten minutes to eight.

"I have time to dine?"

"But assuredly, Monsieur."

The little Belgian nodded. He went over and cancelled his room order and crossed the hall to the restaurant.

As he was giving his order to the waiter a hand was placed on his shoulder.

"Ah! *mon vieux,* but this is an unexpected pleasure," said a voice behind him.

The speaker was a short, stout elderly man, his hair cut *en brosse.* He was smiling delightedly.

Poirot sprang up.

"M. Bouc."

"M. Poirot."

M. Bouc was a Belgian, a director of the Compagnie Internationale des Wagons Lits, and his acquaintance with the former star of the Belgian Police Force dated back many years.

"You find yourself far from home, *mon cher,*" said M. Bouc.

"A little affair in Syria."

"Ah! And you return home—when?"

"To-night."

"Splendid! I, too. That is to say, I go as far as Lausanne, where I have affairs. You travel on the Simplon Orient, I presume?"

"Yes. I have just asked them to get me a sleeper. It was my intention to remain here some days, but I have received a telegram recalling me to England on important business."

"Ah!" sighed M. Bouc. *"Les affaires—les affaires!* But you—you are at the top of the tree nowadays, *mon vieux!"*

"Some little success I have had, perhaps." Hercule Poirot tried to look modest but failed signally.

Bouc laughed.

"We will meet later," he said.

Hercule Poirot addressed himself to the task of keeping his moustaches out of the soup.

That difficult task accomplished, he glanced round him whilst waiting for the next course. There were only about half a dozen people in the restaurant, and of those half-dozen there were only two that interested Hercule Poirot.

These two sat at a table not far away. The younger was a likeable-looking young man of thirty, clearly an American. It was, however, not he but his companion who had attracted the little detective's attention.

He was a man of between sixty and seventy. From a little distance he had the bland aspect of a philanthropist. His slightly bald head, his domed forehead, the smiling mouth that displayed a very white set of false teeth, all seemed to speak of a benevolent personality. Only the eyes belied this assumption. They were small, deep set and crafty. Not only that. As the man, making some remark to his young companion, glanced across the room, his gaze stopped on Poirot for a moment, and just for that second there was a strange malevolence, and unnatural tensity in the glance.

Then he rose.

"Pay the bill, Hector," he said.

His voice was slightly husky in tone. It had a queer, soft, dangerous quality.

When Poirot rejoined his friend in the lounge, the other two men were just leaving the hotel. Their luggage was being brought down. The younger was supervising the process. Presently he opened the glass door and said:

"Quite ready now, Mr. Ratchett."

The elder man grunted an assent and passed out.

"Eh bien," said Poirot. "What do you think of those two?"

"They are American," said M. Bouc.

"Assuredly they are Americans. I meant what did you think of their personalities?"

"The young man seemed quite agreeable."

"And the other?"

"To tell you the truth, my friend, I did not care for him. He produced on me an unpleasant impression. And you?"

Hercule Poirot was a moment before replying.

"When he passed me in the restaurant," he said at last, "I had a curious impression. It was as though a wild animal—an animal savage, but savage! you understand—had passed me by."

"And yet he looked altogether of the most respectable."

"*Précisément!* The body—the cage—is everything of the most respectable—but through the bars, the wild animal looks out."

"You are fanciful, *mon vieux,*" said M. Bouc.

"It may be so. But I could not rid myself of the impression that evil had passed me by very close."

"That respectable American gentleman?"

"That respectable American gentleman."

"Well," said M. Bouc cheerfully. "It may be so. There is much evil in the world."

At that moment the door opened and the concierge came towards them. He looked concerned and apologetic.

"It is extraordinary, Monsieur," he said to Poirot. "There is not one first-class sleeping berth to be had on the train."

"*Comment?*" cried M. Bouc. "At this time of year? Ah, without doubt there is some party of journalists—of politicians——?"

"I don't know, sir," said the concierge, turning to him respectfully. "But that's how it is."

"Well, well," M. Bouc turned to Poirot. "Have no fear, my friend. We will arrange something. There is always one compartment—the No. 16, which is not engaged. The conductor sees to that!" He smiled, then glanced up at the clock. "Come," he said, "it is time we started."

At the station M. Bouc was greeted with respectful *empressement* by the brown-uniformed Wagon Lit conductor.

"Good-evening, Monsieur. Your compartment is the No. 1."

He called to the porters and they wheeled their load half-way along the carriage on which the tin plates proclaimed its destination:

ISTANBUL TRIESTE CALAIS

"You are full up to-night, I hear?"

"It is incredible, Monsieur. All the world elects to travel to-night!"

"All the same, you must find room for this gentleman here. He is a friend of mine. He can have the No. 16."

"It is taken, Monsieur."

"What? The No. 16?"

A glance of understanding passed between them, and the conductor smiled. He was a tall, sallow man of middle age.

"But yes, Monsieur. As I told you, we are full—full—everywhere."

"But what passes itself?" demanded M. Bouc angrily. "There is a conference somewhere? It is a party?"

"No, Monsieur. It is only chance. It just happens that many people have elected to travel to-night."

M. Bouc made a clicking sound of annoyance.

"At Belgrade," he said, "there will be the slip coach from Athens. There will also be the Bucharest-Paris coach—but we do not reach Belgrade until to-morrow evening. The problem is for to-night. There is no second-class berth free?"

"There *is* a second-class berth, Monsieur——"

"Well, then——"

"But it is a lady's berth. There is already a German woman in the compartment—a lady's-maid."

"*Là là*, that is awkward," said M. Bouc.

"Do not distress yourself, my friend," said Poirot. "I must travel in an ordinary carriage."

"Not at all. Not at all." He turned once more to the conductor. "Everyone has arrived?"

"It is true," said the man, "that there is one passenger who has not yet arrived."

He spoke slowly with hesitation.

"But speak then?"

"No. 7 berth—a second-class. The gentleman has not yet come, and it is four minutes to nine."

"Who is it?"

"An Englishman." The conductor consulted his list. "A M. Harris."

"A name of good omen," said Poirot. "I read my Dickens. M. Harris, he will not arrive."

"Put Monsieur's luggage in No. 7," said M. Bouc. "If this M. Harris arrives we will tell him that he is too late—that berths cannot be retained so long—we will arrange the matter one way or another. What do I care for a M. Harris?"

"As Monsieur pleases," said the conductor.

He spoke to Poirot's porter, directing him where to go.

Then he stood aside the steps to let Poirot enter the train.

"Tout à fait au bout, Monsieur," he called. "The end compartment but one."

Poirot passed along the corridor, a somewhat slow progress, as most of the people travelling were standing beside their carriages.

His polite *"Pardons"* were uttered with the regularity of clockwork. At last he reached the compartment indicated. Inside it, reaching up to a suitcase, was the tall young American of the Tokatlian.

He frowned as Poirot entered.

"Excuse me," he said. "I think you've made a mistake." Then, laboriously in French, *"Je crois que vous avez un erreur."*

Poirot replied in English.

"You are Mr. Harris?"

"No, my name is MacQueen. I——"

But at that moment the voice of the Wagon Lit conductor spoke from over Poirot's shoulder. An apologetic, rather breathless voice.

"There is no other berth on the train, Monsieur. The gentleman has to come in here."

He was hauling up the corridor window as he spoke and began to lift in Poirot's luggage.

Poirot noticed the apology in his tone with some amusement. Doubtless the man had been promised a good tip if he could keep the compartment for the sole use of the other traveller. However, even the most munificent of tips lose their effect when a director of the company is on board and issues his orders.

The conductor emerged from the compartment, having swung the suitcases up on to the racks.

"Voilà, Monsieur," he said. "All is arranged. Yours is the upper berth, the number 7. We start in one minute."

He hurried off down the corridor. Poirot re-entered the compartment.

"A phenomenon I have seldom seen," he said cheerfully. "A Wagon Lit conductor himself puts up the luggage! It is unheard of!"

His fellow traveller smiled. He had evidently got over his annoyance —had probably decided that it was no good to take the matter other than philosophically.

"The train's remarkably full," he said.

A whistle blew, there was a long, melancholy cry from the engine. Both men stepped out into the corridor.

Outside a voice shouted.

"En voiture."

"We're off," said MacQueen.

But they were not quite off. The whistle blew again.

"I say, sir," said the young man suddenly, "if you'd rather have the lower berth—easier, and all that—well, that's all right by me."

A likeable young fellow.

"No, no," protested Poirot. "I would not deprive you——"

"That's all right——"

"You are too amiable——"

Polite protests on both sides.

"It is for one night only," explained Poirot. "At Belgrade——"

"Oh, I see. You're getting out at Belgrade——"

"Not exactly. You see——"

There was a sudden jerk. Both men swung round to the window, looking out at the long, lighted platform as it slid slowly past them.

The Orient Express had started on its three-days' journey across Europe.

3. Poirot Refuses a Case

M. Hercule Poirot was a little late in entering the luncheon-car on the following day. He had risen early, breakfasted almost alone, and had spent the morning going over the notes of the case that was recalling him to London. He had seen little of his travelling companion.

M. Bouc, who was already seated, gesticulated a greeting and summoned his friend to the empty place opposite him. Poirot sat down and soon found himself in the favoured position of the table which was served first and with the choicest morsels. The food, too, was unusually good.

It was not till they were eating a delicate cream cheese that M. Bouc allowed his attention to wander to matters other than nourishment. He was at the stage of a meal when one becomes philosophic.

"Ah!" he sighed. "If I had but the pen of a Balzac! I would depict this scene."

He waved a hand.

"It is an idea, that," said Poirot.

"Ah, you agree? It has not been done, I think? And yet—it lends itself to romance, my friend. All around us are people of all classes, of all nationalities, of all ages. For three days these people, these strangers to one another, are brought together. They sleep and eat under one roof, they cannot get away from each other. At the end of three days they part, they go their several ways, never, perhaps, to see each other again."

"And yet," said Poirot, "suppose an accident——"

"Ah no, my friend——"

"From your point of view it would be regrettable, I agree. But nevertheless let us just for one moment suppose it. Then, perhaps, all these here are linked together—by death."

"Some more wine," said M. Bouc, hastily pouring it out. "You are morbid, *mon cher*. It is, perhaps, the digestion."

"It is true," agreed Poirot, "that the food in Syria was not, perhaps, quite suited to my stomach."

He sipped his wine. Then, leaning back, he ran his eye thoughtfully round the dining-car. There were thirteen people seated there and, as M. Bouc had said, of all classes and nationalities. He began to study them.

At the table opposite them were three men. They were, he guessed, single travellers graded and placed there by the unerring judgment of the restaurant attendants. A big, swarthy Italian was picking his teeth with gusto. Opposite him a spare, neat Englishman had the expressionless disapproving face of the well-trained servant. Next to the Englishman was a big American in a loud suit—possibly a commercial traveller.

"You've got to put it over *big*," he was saying in a loud nasal voice.

The Italian removed his toothpick to gesticulate with it freely.

"Sure," he said. "That whatta I say alla de time."

The Englishman looked out of the window and coughed.

Poirot's eye passed on.

At a small table, sitting very upright, was one of the ugliest old ladies he had ever seen. It was an ugliness of distinction—it fascinated rather than repelled. She sat very upright. Round her neck was a collar of very large pearls which, improbable though it seemed, were real. Her hands were covered with rings. Her sable coat was pushed back on her shoulders. A very small expensive black toque was hideously unbecoming to the yellow, toad-like face beneath it.

She was speaking now to the restaurant attendant in a clear, courteous but completely autocratic tone.

"You will be sufficiently amiable to place in my compartment a bottle of mineral water and a large glass of orange juice. You will arrange that I shall have chicken cooked without sauces for dinner this evening —also some boiled fish."

The attendant replied respectfully that it should be done.

She gave a slight gracious nod of the head and rose. Her glance caught Poirot's and swept over him with the nonchalance of the uninterested aristocrat.

"That is Princess Dragomiroff," said M. Bouc in a low tone. "She is a Russian. Her husband realised all this money before the Revolution and invested it abroad. She is extremely rich. A cosmopolitan."

Poirot nodded. He had heard of Princess Dragomiroff.

"She is a personality," said M. Bouc. "Ugly as sin, but she makes herself felt. You agree?"

Poirot agreed.

At another of the large tables Mary Debenham was sitting with two other women. One of them was a tall middle-aged woman in a plaid blouse and tweed skirt. She had a mass of faded yellow hair unbecomingly arranged in a large bun, wore glasses, and had a long, mild, amiable face rather like a sheep. She was listening to the third woman, a stout, pleasant-faced, elderly woman who was talking in a slow clear monotone which showed no signs of pausing for breath or coming to a stop.

". . . And so my daughter said, 'Why,' she said, 'you just can't apply Amurrican methods in this country. It's just natural to the folks here to be indolent,' she said. 'They just haven't got any hustle in them.' But all the same you'd be surprised to know what our college there is doing. They've gotten a fine staff of teachers. I guess there's nothing like education. We've got to apply our Western ideals and teach the East to recognise them. My daughter says——"

The train plunged into a tunnel. The calm monotonous voice was drowned.

At the next table, a small one, sat Colonel Arbuthnot—alone. His gaze was fixed upon the back of Mary Debenham's head. They were not sitting together. Yet it could easily have been managed. Why?

Perhaps, Poirot thought, Mary Debenham had demurred. A governess learns to be careful. Appearances are important. A girl with her living to get has to be discreet.

His glance shifted to the other side of the carriage. At the far end, against the wall, was a middle-aged woman dressed in black with a broad expressionless face. German or Scandinavian, he thought. Probably a German lady's-maid.

After her came a couple leaning forward and talking animatedly together. The man wore English clothes of loose tweed—but he was not English. Though only the back of his head was visible to Poirot, the shape of it and the set of the shoulders betrayed him. A big man, well made. He turned his head suddenly and Poirot saw his profile. A very handsome man of thirty odd with a big fair moustache.

The woman opposite him was a mere girl—twenty at a guess. A tight-fitting little black coat and skirt, white satin blouse, small chic black toque perched at the fashionable outrageous angle. She had a beautiful foreign-looking face, dead white skin, large brown eyes, jet-black hair. She was smoking a cigarette in a long holder. Her manicured hands had deep red nails. She wore one large emerald set in platinum. There was coquetry in her glance and voice.

"*Elle est jolie—et chic,*" murmured Poirot. "Husband and wife—eh?" M. Bouc nodded.

"Hungarian Embassy, I believe," he said. "A handsome couple."

There were only two more lunchers—Poirot's fellow traveller Mac-Queen and his employer Mr. Ratchett. The latter sat facing Poirot, and for the second time Poirot studied that unprepossessing face, noting the false benevolence of the brow and the small, cruel eyes.

Doubtless M. Bouc saw a change in his friend's expression.

"It is at your wild animal you look?" he asked.

Poirot nodded.

As his coffee was brought to him, M. Bouc rose to his feet. Having started before Poirot, he had finished some time ago.

"I return to my compartment," he said. "Come along presently and converse with me."

"With pleasure."

Poirot sipped his coffee and ordered a liqueur. The attendant was passing from table to table with his box of money, accepting payment for bills. The elderly American lady's voice rose shrill and plaintive.

"My daughter said, 'Take a book of food tickets and you'll have no trouble—no trouble at all.' Now, that isn't so. Seems they have to have a ten per cent. tip, and then there's that bottle of mineral water—and a queer sort of water too. They hadn't got any Evian or Vichy, which seems queer to me."

"It is—they must—how you say—serve the water of the country," explained the sheep-faced lady.

"Well, it seems queer to me." She looked distastefully at the heap of small change on the table in front of her. "Look at all this peculiar stuff he's given me. Dinars or something. Just a lot of rubbish, it looks. My daughter said——"

Mary Debenham pushed back her chair and left with a slight bow to the other two. Colonel Arbuthnot got up and followed her. Gathering up her despised money, the American lady followed suit, followed by the lady like a sheep. The Hungarians had already departed. The restaurant-car was empty save for Poirot and Ratchett and MacQueen.

Ratchett spoke to his companion, who got up and left the car. Then he rose himself, but instead of following MacQueen he dropped unexpectedly into the seat opposite Poirot.

"Can you oblige me with a light?" he said. His voice was soft—faintly nasal. "My name is Ratchett."

Poirot bowed slightly. He slipped his hand into his pocket and produced a matchbox which he handed to the other man, who took it but did not strike a light.

"I think," he went on, "that I have the pleasure of speaking to M. Hercule Poirot. Is that so?"

Poirot bowed again.

"You have been correctly informed, Monsieur."

The detective was conscious of those strange shrewd eyes summing him up before the other spoke again.

"In my country," he said, "we come to the point quickly. Mr. Poirot, I want you to take on a job for me."

Hercule Poirot's eyebrows went up a trifle.

"My *clientèle,* Monsieur, is limited nowadays. I undertake very few cases."

"Why, naturally, I understand that. But this, Mr. Poirot, means big money." He repeated again in his soft, persuasive voice, "Big money."

Hercule Poirot was silent a minute or two, then he said:

"What is it you wish me to do for you, M.—er—Ratchett?"

"Mr. Poirot, I am a rich man—a very rich man. Men in that position have enemies. I have an enemy."

"Only one enemy?"

"Just what do you mean by that question?" asked Ratchett sharply.

"Monsieur, in my experience when a man is in a position to have, as you say, enemies, then it does not usually resolve itself into one enemy only."

Ratchett seemed relieved by Poirot's answer. He said quickly:

"Why, yes, I appreciate that point. Enemy or enemies—it doesn't matter. What does matter is my safety."

"Safety?"

"My life has been threatened, Mr. Poirot. Now, I'm a man who can take pretty good care of himself." From the pocket of his coat his hand brought a small automatic into sight for a moment. He continued grimly. "I don't think I'm the kind of man to be caught napping. But as I look at it I might as well make assurance doubly sure. I fancy you're the man for my money, Mr. Poirot. And remember—*big* money."

Poirot looked at him thoughtfully for some minutes. His face was completely expressionless. The other could have had no clue as to what thoughts were passing in that mind.

"I regret, Monsieur," he said at length. "I cannot oblige you."

The other looked at him shrewdly.

"Name your figure, then," he said.

Poirot shook his head.

"You do not understand, Monsieur. I have been very fortunate in my profession. I have made enough money to satisfy both my needs and my caprices. I take now only such cases as—interest me."

"You've got a pretty good nerve," said Ratchett. "Will twenty thousand dollars tempt you?"

"It will not."

"If you're holding out for more, you won't get it. I know what a thing's worth to me."

"I also—M. Ratchett."

"What's wrong with my proposition?"

Poirot rose.

"If you will forgive me for being personal—I do not like your face, M. Ratchett," he said.

And with that he left the restaurant-car.

4. A Cry in the Night

The Simplon Orient Express arrived at Belgrade at a quarter to nine that evening. It was not due to depart again until 9:15, so Poirot descended to the platform. He did not, however, remain there long. The cold was bitter and though the platform itself was protected, heavy snow was falling outside. He returned to his compartment. The conductor, who was on the platform stamping his feet and waving his arms to keep warm, spoke to him.

"Your valises have been moved, Monsieur, to the compartment No. 1, the compartment of M. Bouc."

"But where is M. Bouc, then?"

"He has moved into the coach from Athens which has just been put on."

Poirot went in search of his friend. M. Bouc waved his protestations aside.

"It is nothing. It is nothing. It is more convenient like this. You are going through to England, so it is better that you should stay in the through coach to Calais. Me, I am very well here. It is most peaceful. This coach is empty save for myself and one little Greek doctor. Ah! my friend, what a night! They say there has not been so much snow for years. Let us hope we shall not be held up. I am not too happy about it, I can tell you."

At 9:15 punctually the train pulled out of the station, and shortly afterwards Poirot got up, said good-night to his friend and made his way along the corridor back into his own coach which was in front next to the dining-car.

On this, the second day of the journey, barriers were breaking down. Colonel Arbuthnot was standing at the door of his compartment talking to MacQueen.

MacQueen broke off something he was saying when he saw Poirot. He looked very surprised.

"Why," he cried, "I thought you'd left us. You said you were getting off at Belgrade."

"You misunderstood me," said Poirot, smiling. "I remember now, the train started from Stamboul just as we were talking about it."

"But, man, your baggage—it's gone."

"It has been moved into another compartment—that is all."

"Oh, I see."

He resumed his conversation with Arbuthnot and Poirot passed on down the corridor.

Two doors from his own compartment, the elderly American lady, Mrs. Hubbard, was standing talking to the sheep-like lady who was a Swede. Mrs. Hubbard was pressing a magazine on the other.

"No, do take it, my dear," she said. "I've got plenty other things to read. My, isn't the cold something frightful?" She nodded amicably to Poirot.

"You are most kind," said the Swedish lady.

"Not at all. I hope you'll sleep well and that your head will be better in the morning."

"It is the cold only. I make myself a cup of tea."

"Have you got some aspirin? Are you sure, now? I've got plenty. Well, good-night, my dear."

She turned to Poirot conversationally as the other woman departed.

"Poor creature, she's a Swede. As far as I can make out, she's a kind of missionary—a teaching one. A nice creature, but doesn't talk much English. She was *most* interested in what I told her about my daughter."

Poirot, by now, knew all about Mrs. Hubbard's daughter. Everyone on the train who could understand English did! How she and her husband were on the staff of a big American college in Smyrna and how this was Mrs. Hubbard's first journey to the East, and what she thought of the Turks and their slipshod ways and the condition of their roads.

The door next to them opened and the thin, pale manservant stepped out. Inside Poirot caught a glimpse of Mr. Ratchett sitting up in bed.

He saw Poirot and his face changed, darkening with anger. Then the door was shut.

Mrs. Hubbard drew Poirot a little aside.

"You know, I'm dead scared of that man. Oh, not the valet—the other—his master. Master, indeed! There's something *wrong* about that man. My daughter always says I'm very intuitive. 'When Momma gets a hunch, she's dead right,' that's what my daughter says. And I've got a hunch about that man. He's next door to me, and I don't like it. I put my grips against the communicating door last night. I thought I heard him trying the handle. Do you know, I shouldn't be a bit surprised if that man turns out to be a murderer—one of these train robbers you read about. I dare say I'm foolish, but there it is. I'm downright scared of the man! My daughter said I'd have an easy journey, but somehow I don't feel happy about it. It may be foolish, but I feel anything might happen. Anything at all. And how that nice young fellow can bear to be his secretary I can't think."

Colonel Arbuthnot and MacQueen were coming towards them down the corridor.

"Come into my carriage," MacQueen was saying. "It isn't made up for the night yet. Now what I want to get right about your policy in India is this——"

The men passed and went on down the corridor to MacQueen's carriage.

Mrs. Hubbard said good-night to Poirot.

"I guess I'll go right to bed and read," she said. "Good-night."

"Good-night, Madame."

Poirot passed into his own compartment, which was the next one beyond Ratchett's. He undressed and got into bed, read for about half an hour and then turned out the light.

He awoke some hours later, and awoke with a start. He knew what it was that had wakened him—a loud groan, almost a cry, somewhere close at hand. At the same moment the ting of a bell sounded sharply.

Poirot sat up and switched on the light. He noticed that the train was at a standstill—presumably at a station.

That cry had startled him. He remembered that it was Ratchett who had the next compartment. He got out of bed and opened the door just as the Wagon Lit conductor came hurrying along the corridor and knocked on Ratchett's door. Poirot kept his door open a crack and watched. The conductor tapped a second time. A bell rang and a light showed over another door farther down. The conductor glanced over his shoulder.

At the same moment a voice from within the next-door compartment called out:

"*Ce n'est rien. Je me suis trompé.*"

"*Bien, Monsieur.*" The conductor scurried off again, to knock at the door where the light was showing.

Poirot returned to bed, his mind relieved, and switched off the light. He glanced at his watch. It was just twenty-three minutes to one.

5. The Crime

He found it difficult to go to sleep again at once. For one thing, he missed the motion of the train. If it *was* a station outside it was curiously quiet. By contrast, the noises on the train seemed unusually loud. He could hear Ratchett moving about next door—a click as he pulled down the washbasin, the sound of the tap running, a splashing noise, then another click as the basin shut to again. Footsteps passed up the corridor outside, the shuffling footsteps of someone in bedroom slippers.

Hercule Poirot lay awake staring at the ceiling. Why was the station outside so silent? His throat felt dry. He had forgotten to ask for his usual bottle of mineral water. He looked at his watch again. Just after a quarter-past one. He would ring for the conductor and ask him for some mineral water. His finger went out to the bell, but he paused as in the stillness he heard a ting. The man couldn't answer every bell at once.

Ting . . . ting . . . ting. . . .

It sounded again and again. Where was the man? Somebody was getting impatient.

Ting. . . .

Whoever it was was keeping their finger solidly on the push.

Suddenly with a rush, his footsteps echoing up the aisle, the man came. He knocked at a door not far from Poirot's own.

Then came voices—the conductor's, deferential, apologetic, and a woman's—insistent and voluble.

Mrs. Hubbard!

Poirot smiled to himself.

The altercation—if it was one—went on for some time. Its proportions were ninety per cent. of Mrs. Hubbard's to a soothing ten per cent. of the conductor's. Finally the matter seemed to be adjusted. Poirot heard distinctly:

"Bonne nuit, Madame," and a closing door.

He pressed his own finger on the bell.

The conductor arrived promptly. He looked hot and worried.

"De l'eau minerale, s'il vous plait."

"Bien, Monsieur." Perhaps a twinkle in Poirot's eye led him to unburden himself.

"La dame Americaine——"

"Yes?"

He wiped his forehead.

"Imagine to yourself the time I have had with her! She insists—but *insists*—that there is a man in her compartment! Figure to yourself, Monsieur. In a space of this size." He swept a hand round. "Where would he conceal himself? I argue with her. I point out that it is impossible. She insists. She woke up and there was a man there. And how, I ask, did he get out and leave the door bolted behind him? But she will not listen to reason. As though, there were not enough to worry us already. This snow——"

"Snow?"

"But yes, Monsieur. Monsieur has not noticed? The train has stopped. We have run into a snowdrift. Heaven knows how long we shall be here. I remember once being snowed up for seven days."

"Where are we?"

"Between Vincovci and Brod."

"Là, là," said Poirot vexedly.

The man withdrew and returned with the water.

"Bon soir, Monsieur."

Poirot drank a glass of water and composed himself to sleep.

He was just dropping off when something again woke him. This time it was as though something heavy had fallen with a thud against the door.

He sprang up, opened it and looked out. Nothing. But to his right some way down the corridor a woman wrapped in a scarlet kimono was retreating from him. At the other end, sitting on his little seat, the conductor was entering up figures on large sheets of paper. Everything was deathly quiet.

"Decidedly I suffer from the nerves," said Poirot and retired to bed again. This time he slept till morning.

When he awoke the train was still at a standstill. He raised a blind and looked out. Heavy banks of snow surrounded the train.

He glanced at his watch and saw that it was past nine o'clock.

At a quarter to ten, neat, spruce, and dandified as ever, he made his way to the restaurant-car, where a chorus of woe was going on.

Any barriers there might have been between the passengers had now quite broken down. All were united by a common misfortune. Mrs. Hubbard was loudest in her lamentations.

"My daughter said it would be the easiest way in the world. Just sit in the train until I got to Parrus. And now we may be here for days and days," she wailed. "And my boat sails day after to-morrow. How am I going to catch it now? Why, I can't even wire to cancel my passage. I feel too mad to talk about it."

The Italian said that he had urgent business himself in Milan. The large American said that that was "too bad, Ma'am," and soothingly expressed a hope that the train might make up time.

"My sister—her children wait me," said the Swedish lady and wept. "I get no word to them. What they think? They will say bad things have happen to me."

"How long shall we be here?" demanded Mary Debenham. "Doesn't anybody *know?*"

Her voice sounded impatient, but Poirot noted that there were no signs of that almost feverish anxiety which she had displayed during the check to the Taurus Express.

Mrs. Hubbard was off again.

"There isn't anybody knows a thing on this train. And nobody's trying to do anything. Just a pack of useless foreigners. Why, if this were at home, there'd be someone at least *trying* to do something."

Arbuthnot turned to Poirot and spoke in careful British French.

"Vous êtes un directeur de la ligne, je crois, Monsieur. Vous pouvez nous dire——"

Smiling, Poirot corrected him.

"No, no," he said in English. "It is not I. You confound me with my friend M. Bouc."

"Oh! I'm sorry."

"Not at all. It is most natural. I am now in the compartment that he had formerly."

M. Bouc was not present in the restaurant-car. Poirot looked about to notice who else was absent.

Princess Dragomiroff was missing and the Hungarian couple. Also Ratchett, his valet, and the German lady's-maid.

The Swedish lady wiped her eyes.

"I am foolish," she said. "I am baby to cry. All for the best, whatever happen."

This Christian spirit, however, was far from being shared.

"That's all very well," said MacQueen restlessly. "We may be here for days."

"What is this country anyway?" demanded Mrs. Hubbard tearfully. On being told it was Yugo-Slavia she said:

"Oh! one of these Balkan things. What can you expect?"

"You are the only patient one, Mademoiselle," said Poirot to Miss Debenham.

She shrugged her shoulders slightly.

"What can one do?"

"You are a philosopher, Mademoiselle."

"That implies a detached attitude. I think my attitude is more selfish. I have learned to save myself useless emotion."

She was not even looking at him. Her gaze went past him, out of the window to where the snow lay in heavy masses.

"You are a strong character, Mademoiselle," said Poirot gently. "You are, I think, the strongest character amongst us."

"Oh, no. No, indeed. I know one far far stronger than I am."

"And that is——?"

She seemed suddenly to come to herself, to realise that she was talking to a stranger and a foreigner with whom, until this morning, she had only exchanged half a dozen sentences.

She laughed a polite but estranging laugh.

"Well—that old lady, for instance. You have probably noticed her. A very ugly old lady, but rather fascinating. She has only to lift a little finger and ask for something in a polite voice—and the whole train runs."

"It runs also for my friend M. Bouc," said Poirot. "But that is because he is a director of the line, not because he has a masterful character."

Mary Debenham smiled.

The morning wore away. Several people, Poirot amongst them, remained in the dining-car. The communal life was felt, at the moment, to pass the time better. He heard a good deal more about Mrs. Hubbard's daughter and he heard the lifelong habits of Mr. Hubbard, deceased, from his rising in the morning and commencing breakfast with a cereal to his final rest at night in the bed-socks that Mrs. Hubbard herself had been in the habit of knitting for him.

It was when he was listening to a confused account of the missionary aims of the Swedish lady that one of the Wagon Lit conductors came into the car and stood at his elbow.

"Pardon, Monsieur."

"Yes?"

"The compliments of M. Bouc, and he would be glad if you would be so kind as to come to him for a few minutes."

Poirot rose, uttered excuses to the Swedish lady and followed the man out of the dining-car.

It was not his own conductor, but a big fair man.

He followed his guide down the corridor of his own carriage and along the corridor of the next one. The man tapped at a door, then stood aside to let Poirot enter.

The compartment was not M. Bouc's own. It was a second-class one —chosen presumably because of its slightly larger size. It certainly gave the impression of being crowded.

M. Bouc himself was sitting on the small seat in the opposite corner. In the corner next the window facing him was a small, dark man looking out at the snow. Standing up and quite preventing Poirot from advancing any farther was a big man in blue uniform (the *chef de train*) and his own Wagon Lit conductor.

"Ah, my good friend," cried M. Bouc. "Come in. We have need of you."

The little man in the window shifted along the seat, Poirot squeezed past the other two men and sat down facing his friend.

The expression on M. Bouc's face gave him, as he would have expressed it, furiously to think. It was clear that something out of the common had happened.

"What has occurred?" he asked.

"You may well ask that. First this snow—this stoppage. And now——"

He paused—and a sort of strangled gasp came from the Wagon Lit conductor.

"And now what?"

"*And now a passenger lies dead in his berth—stabbed.*"

M. Bouc spoke with a kind of calm desperation.

"An American. A man called—called—" he consulted some notes in front of him, "Ratchett—that is right—Ratchett?"

"Yes, Monsieur," the Wagon Lit man gulped.

Poirot looked at him. He was as white as chalk.

"You had better let that man sit down," he said. "He may faint otherwise."

The *chef de train* moved slightly and the Wagon Lit man sank down in the corner and buried his face in his hands.

"Brr!" said Poirot. "This is serious!"

"Certainly it is serious. To begin with, a murder—that by itself is a calamity of the first water. But not only that, the circumstances are unusual. Here we are, brought to a standstill. We may be here for hours—and not only hours—days! Another circumstance. Passing through most countries we have the police of that country on the train. But in Yugo-Slavia—no. You comprehend?"

"It is a position of great difficulty," said Poirot.

"There is worse to come. Dr. Constantine—I forgot, I have not introduced you—Dr. Constantine, M. Poirot."

The little dark man bowed and Poirot returned it.

"Dr. Constantine is of the opinion that death occurred at about 1 a.m."

"It is difficult to say exactly in these matters," said the doctor, "but I think I can say definitely that death occurred between midnight and two in the morning."

"When was this M. Ratchett last seen alive?" asked Poirot.

"He is known to have been alive at about twenty minutes to one, when he spoke to the conductor," said M. Bouc.

"That is quite correct," said Poirot. "I myself heard what passed. That is the last thing known?"

"Yes."

Poirot turned toward the doctor, who continued:

"The window of M. Ratchett's compartment was found wide open, leading one to suppose that the murderer escaped that way. But in my opinion that open window is a blind. Anyone departing that way would have left distinct traces in the snow. There were none."

"The crime was discovered—when?" asked Poirot.

"Michel!"

The Wagon Lit conductor sat up. His face still looked pale and frightened.

"Tell this gentleman exactly what occurred," ordered M. Bouc.

The man spoke somewhat jerkily.

"The valet of this M. Ratchett, he tapped several times at the door this morning. There was no answer. Then, half an hour ago, the restaurant-car attendant came. He wanted to know if Monsieur was taking *déjeuner*. It was eleven o'clock, you comprehend.

"I open the door for him with my key. But there is a chain, too, and that is fastened. There is no answer and it is very still in there, and cold —but cold. With the window open and snow drifting in. I thought the gentleman had had a fit, perhaps. I got the *chef de train*. We broke the chain and went in. He was—Ah! *c'était terrible!*"

He buried his face in his hands again.

"The door was locked and chained on the inside," said Poirot thoughtfully. "It was not suicide—eh?"

The Greek doctor gave a sardonic laugh.

"Does a man who commits suicide stab himself in ten—twelve—fifteen places?" he asked.

Poirot's eyes opened.

"That is great ferocity," he said.

"It is a woman," said the *chef de train,* speaking for the first time. "Depend upon it, it was a woman. Only a woman would stab like that."

Dr. Constantine screwed up his face thoughtfully.

"She must have been a very strong woman," he said. "It is not my desire to speak technically—that is only confusing—but I can assure you that one or two of the blows were delivered with such force as to drive them through hard belts of bone and muscle."

"It was not, clearly, a scientific crime," said Poirot.

"It was most unscientific," said Dr. Constantine. "The blows seem to have been delivered haphazard and at random. Some have glanced off, doing hardly any damage. It is as though somebody had shut their eyes and then in a frenzy struck blindly again and again."

"C'est une femme," said the *chef de train* again. "Women are like that. When they are enraged they have great strength." He nodded so sagely that everyone suspected a personal experience of his own.

"I have, perhaps, something to contribute to your store of knowledge," said Poirot. "M. Ratchett spoke to me yesterday. He told me, as far as I was able to understand him, that he was in danger of his life."

" 'Bumped off'—that is the American expression, is it not?" said M. Bouc. "Then it is not a woman. It is a 'gangster' or a 'gunman.' "

The *chef de train* looked pained at his theory having come to naught.

"If so," said Poirot, "it seems to have been done very amateurishly." His tone expressed professional disapproval.

"There is a large American on the train," said M. Bouc, pursuing his idea—"a common-looking man with terrible clothes. He chews the gum which I believe is not done in good circles. You know whom I mean?"

The Wagon Lit conductor to whom he had appealed nodded.

"Oui, Monsieur, the No. 16. But it cannot have been he. I should have seen him enter or leave the compartment."

"You might not. You might not. But we will go into that presently. The question is, what to do?" He looked at Poirot.

Poirot looked back at him.

"Come, my friend," said M. Bouc. "You comprehend what I am about to ask of you. I know your powers. Take command of this investigation! No, no, do not refuse. See, to us it is serious—I speak for the Compagnie Internationale des Wagons Lits. By the time the Yugo-Slavian police arrive, how simple if we can present them with the solution! Otherwise delays, annoyances, a million and one inconveniences.

Perhaps, who knows, serious annoyance to innocent persons. Instead—*you* solve the mystery! We say, 'A murder has occurred—*this* is the criminal!'"

"And suppose I do not solve it?"

"Ah! *mon cher*." M. Bouc's voice became positively caressing. "I know your reputation. I know something of your methods. This is the ideal case for you. To look up the antecedents of all these people, to discover their bona fides—all that takes time and endless inconvenience. But have I not heard you say often that to solve a case a man has only to lie back in his chair and think? Do that. Interview the passengers on the train, view the body, examine what clues there are and then—well, I have faith in you! I am assured that it is no idle boast of yours. Lie back and think—use (as I have heard you say so often) the little grey cells of the mind—and you will *know!*"

He leaned forward, looking affectionately at his friend.

"Your faith touches me, my friend," said Poirot emotionally. "As you say, this cannot be a difficult case. I myself, last night—but we will not speak of that now. In truth, this problem intrigues me. I was reflecting, not half an hour ago, that many hours of boredom lay ahead whilst we are stuck here. And now—a problem lies ready to my hand."

"You accept then?" said M. Bouc eagerly.

"*C'est entendu.* You place the matter in my hands."

"Good—we are all at your service."

"To begin with, I should like a plan of the Istanbul-Calais coach, with a note of the people who occupied the several compartments, and I should also like to see their passports and their tickets."

"Michel will get you those."

The Wagon Lit conductor left the compartment.

"What other passengers are there on the train?" asked Poirot.

"In this coach Dr. Constantine and I are the only travellers. In the coach from Bucharest is an old gentleman with a lame leg. He is well known to the conductor. Beyond that are the ordinary carriages, but these do not concern us, since they were locked after dinner had been served last night. Forward of the Istanbul-Calais coach there is only the dining-car."

"Then it seems," said Poirot slowly, "as though we must look for our murderer in the Istanbul-Calais coach." He turned to the doctor. "That is what you were hinting, I think?"

The Greek nodded.

"At half an hour after midnight we ran into the snowdrift. No one can have left the train since then."

M. Bouc said solemnly:

"The murderer is with us—on the train now. . . ."

6. A Woman?

"First of all," said Poirot, "I should like a word or two with young M. MacQueen. He may be able to give us valuable information."

"Certainly," said M. Bouc.

He turned to the *chef de train*.

"Get M. MacQueen to come here."

The *chef de train* left the carriage.

The conductor returned with a bundle of passports and tickets. M. Bouc took them from him.

"Thank you, Michel. It would be best now, I think, if you were to go back to your post. We will take your evidence formally later."

"Very good, Monsieur."

Michel in his turn left the carriage.

"After we have seen young MacQueen," said Poirot, "perhaps M. le docteur will come with me to the dead man's carriage."

"Certainly."

"After we have finished there——"

But at this moment the *chef de train* returned with Hector Mac-Queen.

M. Bouc rose.

"We are a little cramped here," he said pleasantly. "Take my seat, M. MacQueen. M. Poirot will sit opposite you—so."

He turned to the *chef de train*.

"Clear all the people out of the restaurant-car," he said, "and let it be left free for M. Poirot. You will conduct your interviews there, *mon cher?*"

"It would be the most convenient, yes," agreed Poirot.

MacQueen had stood looking from one to the other, not quite following the rapid flow of French.

"Qu'est ce qu'il y a?" he began laboriously. *"Pourquoi——?"*

With a vigorous gesture Poirot motioned him to the seat in the corner. He took it and began once more.

"Pourquoi——?" then, checking himself and relapsing into his own tongue, "What's up on the train? Has anything happened?"

He looked from one man to another.

Poirot nodded.

"Exactly. Something has happened. Prepare yourself for a shock. *Your employer, M. Ratchett, is dead!*"

MacQueen's mouth pursed itself in a whistle. Except that his eyes grew a shade brighter, he showed no signs of shock or distress.

"So they got him after all," he said.

"What exactly do you mean by that phrase, M. MacQueen?"

MacQueen hesitated.

"You are assuming," said Poirot, "that M. Ratchett was murdered?"

"Wasn't he?" This time MacQueen did show surprise. "Why, yes," he said slowly. "That's just what I did think. Do you mean he just died in his sleep? Why, the old man was as tough as—as tough——"

He stopped, at a loss for a simile.

"No, no," said Poirot. "Your assumption was quite right. M. Ratchett was murdered. Stabbed. But I should like to know why you were so sure it *was* murder, and not just—death."

MacQueen hesitated.

"I must get this clear," he said. "Who exactly are you? And where do you come in?"

"I represent the Compagnie Internationale des Wagons Lits." He paused, then added, "I am a detective. My name is Hercule Poirot."

If he expected an effect he did not get one. MacQueen said merely, "Oh, yes?" and waited for him to go on.

"You know the name, perhaps."

"Why, it does seem kind of familiar—only I always thought it was a woman's dressmaker."

Hercule Poirot looked at him with distaste.

"It is incredible!" he said.

"What's incredible?"

"Nothing. Let us advance with the matter in hand. I want you to tell me, M. MacQueen, all that you know about the dead man. You were not related to him?"

"No. I am—was—his secretary."

"For how long have you held that post?"

"Just over a year."

"Please give me all the information you can."

"Well, I met Mr. Ratchett just over a year ago when I was in Persia——"

Poirot interrupted.

"What were you doing there?"

"I had come over from New York to look into an oil concession. I don't suppose you want to hear all about that. My friends and I had been let in rather badly over it. Mr. Ratchett was in the same hotel. He had just had a row with his secretary. He offered me the job and I took it. I was at a loose end, and glad to find a well-paid job ready made, as it were."

"And since then?"

"We've travelled about. Mr. Ratchett wanted to see the world. He was hampered by knowing no languages. I acted more as a courier than a secretary. It was a pleasant life."

"Now tell me as much as you can about your employer."

The young man shrugged his shoulders. A perplexed expression passed over his face.

"That's not so easy."

"What was his full name?"

"Samuel Edward Ratchett."

"He was an American citizen?"

"Yes."

"What part of America did he come from?"

"I don't know."

"Well, tell me what you do know."

"The actual truth is, Mr. Poirot, that I know nothing at all! Mr. Ratchett never spoke of himself, or of his life in America."

"Why do you think that was?"

"I don't know. I imagined that he might have been ashamed of his beginnings. Some men are."

"Does that strike you as a satisfactory solution?"

"Frankly, it doesn't."

"Has he any relations?"

"He never mentioned any."

Poirot pressed the point.

"You must have formed *some* theory, M. MacQueen."

"Well, yes, I did. For one thing, I don't believe Ratchett was his real name. I think he left America definitely in order to escape someone or something. I think he was successful—until a few weeks ago."

"And then?"

"He began to get letters—threatening letters."

"Did you see them?"

"Yes. It was my business to attend to his correspondence. The first letter came a fortnight ago."

"Were these letters destroyed?"

"No, I think I've got a couple still in my files—one I know Ratchett tore up in a rage. Shall I get them for you?"

"If you would be so good."

MacQueen left the compartment. He returned a few minutes later and laid down two sheets of rather dirty notepaper before Poirot.

The first letter ran as follows:

Thought you'd double-cross us and get away with it, did you? Not on your life. We're out to GET you, Ratchett, and we WILL get you!

There was no signature.

With no comment beyond raised eyebrows, Poirot picked up the second letter.

We're going to take you for a ride, Ratchett. Some time soon. We're going to GET you, see?

Poirot laid the letter down.

"The style is monotonous!" he said. "More so than the handwriting."

MacQueen stared at him.

"You would not observe," said Poirot pleasantly. "It requires the eye of one used to such things. This letter was not written by one person, M. MacQueen. Two or more persons wrote it—each writing a letter of a word at a time. Also, the letters are printed. That makes the task of identifying the handwriting much more difficult."

He paused, then said:

"Did you know that M. Ratchett had applied for help to me?"

"To *you?*"

MacQueen's astonished tone told Poirot quite certainly that the young man had not known of it. He nodded.

"Yes. He was alarmed. Tell me, how did he act when he received the first letter?"

MacQueen hesitated.

"It's difficult to say. He—he—passed it off with a laugh in that quiet way of his. But somehow"—he gave a slight shiver—"I felt that there was a good deal going on underneath the quietness."

Poirot nodded. Then he asked an unexpected question.

"M. MacQueen, will you tell me, quite honestly, exactly how you regarded your employer? Did you like him?"

Hector MacQueen took a moment or two before replying.

"No," he said at last. "I did not."

"Why?"

"I can't exactly say. He was always quite pleasant in his manner." He paused, then said, "I'll tell you the truth, Mr. Poirot. I disliked and distrusted him. He was, I am sure, a cruel and a dangerous man. I must admit, though, that I have no reasons to advance for my opinion."

"Thank you, M. MacQueen. One further question—when did you last see M. Ratchett alive?"

"Last evening about"—he thought for a minute—"ten o'clock, I should say. I went into his compartment to take down some memoranda from him."

"On what subject?"

"Some tiles and antique pottery that he bought in Persia. What was delivered was not what he had purchased. There has been a long, vexatious correspondence on the subject."

"And that was the last time M. Ratchett was seen alive?"

"Yes, I suppose so."

"Do you know when M. Ratchett received the last threatening letter?"

"On the morning of the day we left Constantinople."

"There is one more question I must ask you, M. MacQueen: were you on good terms with your employer?"

The young man's eyes twinkled suddenly.

"This is where I'm supposed to go all goosefleshy down the back. In the words of a best seller, 'You've nothing on me.' Ratchett and I were on perfectly good terms."

"Perhaps, M. MacQueen, you will give me your full name and your address in America."

MacQueen gave his name—Hector Willard MacQueen, and an address in New York.

Poirot leaned back against the cushions.

"That is all for the present, M. MacQueen," he said. "I should be obliged if you would keep the matter of M. Ratchett's death to yourself for a little time."

"His valet, Masterman, will have to know."

"He probably knows already," said Poirot dryly. "If so, try to get him to hold his tongue."

"That oughtn't to be difficult. He's a Britisher, and does what he calls 'Keeps himself to himself.' He's a low opinion of Americans and no opinion at all of any other nationality."

"Thank you, M. MacQueen."

The American left the carriage.

"Well?" demanded M. Bouc. "You believe what he says, this young man?"

"He seems honest and straightforward. He did not pretend to any affection for his employer as he probably would have done had he been involved in any way. It is true M. Ratchett did not tell him that he had tried to enlist my services and failed, but I do not think that is really a suspicious circumstance. I fancy M. Ratchett was a gentleman who kept his own counsel on every possible occasion."

"So you pronounce one person at least innocent of the crime," said M. Bouc jovially.

Poirot cast on him a look of reproach.

"Me, I suspect everybody till the last minute," he said. "All the same, I must admit that I cannot see this sober, long-headed MacQueen losing his head and stabbing his victim twelve or fourteen times. It is not in accord with his psychology—not at all."

"No," said M. Bouc thoughtfully. "That is the act of a man driven almost crazy with a frenzied hate—it suggests more the Latin temperament. Or else it suggests, as our friend the *chef de train* insisted, a woman."

7. *The Body*

Followed by Dr. Constantine, Poirot made his way to the next coach and the compartment occupied by the murdered man. The conductor came and unlocked the door for them with his key.

The two men passed inside. Poirot turned inquiringly to his companion.

"How much has been disarranged in this compartment?"

"Nothing has been touched. I was careful not to move the body in making my examination."

Poirot nodded. He looked round him.

The first thing that struck the senses was the intense cold. The window was pushed down as far as it would go and the blind was drawn up.

"Brrr," observed Poirot.

The other smiled appreciatively.

"I did not like to close it," he said.

Poirot examined the window carefully.

"You are right," he announced. "Nobody left the carriage this way. Possibly the open window was intended to suggest the fact, but, if so, the snow has defeated the murderer's object."

He examined the frame of the window carefully. Taking a small case from his pocket he blew a little powder over it.

"No fingerprints at all," he said. "That means it has been wiped.

Well, if there had been fingerprints it would have told us very little. They would have been those of M. Ratchett or his valet or the conductor. Criminals do not make mistakes of that kind nowadays.

"And that being so," he added cheerfully, "we might as well shut the window. Positively it is the cold storage in here!"

He suited the action to the word and then turned his attention for the first time to the motionless figure lying in the bunk.

Ratchett lay on his back. His pyjama jacket, stained with rusty patches, had been unbuttoned and thrown back.

"I had to see the nature of the wounds, you see," explained the doctor.

Poirot nodded. He bent over the body. Finally he straightened himself with a slight grimace.

"It is not pretty," he said. "Someone must have stood there and stabbed him again and again. How many wounds are there exactly?"

"I make it twelve. One or two are so slight as to be practically scratches. On the other hand, at least three would be capable of causing death."

Something in the doctor's tone caught Poirot's attention. He looked at him sharply. The little Greek was standing staring down at the body with a puzzled frown.

"Something strikes you as odd, does it not?" he asked gently. "Speak, my friend. There is something here that puzzles you?"

"You are right," acknowledged the other.

"What is it?"

"You see these two wounds—here and here." He pointed. "They are deep, each cut must have severed blood-vessels—and yet—the edges do not gape. They have not bled as one would have expected."

"Which suggests?"

"That the man was already dead—some little time dead—when they were delivered. But that is surely absurd."

"It would seem so," said Poirot thoughtfully. "Unless our murderer figured to himself that he had not accomplished his job properly and came back to make quite sure; but that is manifestly absurd! Anything else?"

"Well, just one thing."

"And that?"

"You see this wound here—under the right arm—near the right shoulder. Take this pencil of mine. Could you deliver such a blow?"

Poirot raised his hand.

"*Précisément,*" he said. "I see. With the *right* hand it is exceedingly difficult—almost impossible. One would have to strike backhanded, as it were. But if the blow were struck with the *left* hand——"

"Exactly, M. Poirot. That blow was almost certainly struck with the *left* hand."

"So that our murderer is left-handed? No, it is more difficult than that, is it not?"

"As you say, M. Poirot. Some of these other blows are just as obviously right-handed."

"Two people. We are back at two people again," murmured the detective. He asked abruptly:

"Was the electric light on?"

"It is difficult to say. You see it is turned off by the conductor every morning about ten o'clock."

"The switches will tell us," said Poirot.

He examined the switch of the top light and also the roll back bedhead light. The former was turned off. The latter was closed.

"*Eh bien,*" he said thoughtfully. "We have here a hypothesis of the First and Second Murderer, as the great Shakespeare would put it. The First Murderer stabbed his victim and left the compartment, turning off the light. The Second Murderer came in in the dark, did not see that his or her work had been done and stabbed at least twice at a dead body. *Que pensez-vous de ça?*"

"Magnificent," said the little doctor with enthusiasm.

The other's eyes twinkled.

"You think so? I am glad. It sounded to me a little like the nonsense."

"What other explanation can there be?"

"That is just what I am asking myself. Have we here a coincidence or what? Are there any other inconsistencies, such as would point to two people being concerned?"

"I think I can say yes. Some of these blows, as I have already said, point to a weakness—a lack of strength, or a lack of determination. They are feeble glancing blows. But this one here—and this one——" Again he pointed. "Great strength was needed for those blows. They have penetrated the muscle."

"They were, in your opinion, delivered by a man."

"Most certainly."

"They could not have been delivered by a woman?"

"A young, vigorous athletic woman might have struck them, especially if she were in the grip of a strong emotion, but it is in my opinion highly unlikely."

Poirot was silent a moment or two.

The other said anxiously:

"You understand my point?"

"Perfectly," said Poirot. "The matter begins to clear itself up wonderfully! The murderer was a man of great strength, he was feeble, it was a woman, it was a right-handed person, it was a left-handed person—*Ah! c'est rigolo, tout ça!*"

He spoke with sudden anger.

"And the victim—what does he do in all this? Does he cry out? Does he struggle? Does he defend himself?"

He slipped his hand under the pillow and drew out the automatic pistol which Ratchett had shown him the day before.

"Fully loaded, you see," he said.

They looked round them. Ratchett's day clothing was hanging from the hooks on the wall. On the small table formed by the lid of the washing basin were various objects—false teeth in a glass of water; another glass, empty; a bottle of mineral water, a large flask and an ashtray containing the butt of a cigar and some charred fragments of paper; also two burnt matches.

The doctor picked up the empty glass and sniffed it.

"Here is the explanation of the victim's inertia," he said quietly.

"Drugged?"

"Yes."

Poirot nodded. He picked up the two matches and scrutinised them carefully.

"You have a clue then?" demanded the little doctor eagerly.

"Those two matches are of a different shape," said Poirot. "One is flatter than the other. You see?"

"It is the kind you get on the train," said the doctor, "in paper covers."

Poirot was feeling in the pockets of Ratchett's clothing. Presently he pulled out a box of matches. He compared them carefully.

"The rounder one is a match struck by M. Ratchett," he said. "Let us see if he had also the flatter kind."

But a further search showed no other matches.

Poirot's eyes were darting about the compartment. They were bright and sharp like a bird's. One felt that nothing could escape their scrutiny.

With a little exclamation he bent and picked up something from the floor.

It was a small square of cambric, very dainty. In the corner was an embroidered initial—H.

"A woman's handkerchief," said the doctor. "Our friend the *chef de train* was right. There is a woman concerned in this."

"And most conveniently she leaves her handkerchief behind!" said Poirot. "Exactly as it happens in the books and on the films—and to make things even easier for us it is marked with an initial."

"What a stroke of luck for us!" exclaimed the doctor.

"Is it not?" said Poirot.

Something in his tone surprised the doctor.

But before he could ask for elucidation, Poirot had made another dive on to the floor.

This time he held out on the palm of his hand—a pipe-cleaner.

"It is perhaps the property of M. Ratchett?" suggested the doctor.

"There was no pipe in any of his pockets, and no tobacco or tobacco pouch."

"Then it is a clue."

"Oh! decidedly. And again dropped most conveniently. A masculine clue this time, you note! One cannot complain of having no clues in this case. There are clues here in abundance. By the way, what have you done with the weapon?"

"There was no sign of any weapon. The murderer must have taken it away with him."

"I wonder why," mused Poirot.

"Ah!" The doctor had been delicately exploring the pyjama pockets of the dead man.

"I overlooked this," he said. "I unbuttoned the jacket and threw it straight back."

From the breast pocket he brought out a gold watch. The case was dented savagely, and the hands pointed to a quarter-past one.

"You see?" cried Constantine eagerly. "This gives us the hour of the crime. It agrees with my calculations. Between midnight and two in the morning is what I said, and probably about one o'clock, though it is difficult to be exact in these matters. *Eh bien,* here is confirmation. A quarter-past one. That was the hour of the crime."

"It is possible, yes. It is certainly possible."

The doctor looked at him curiously.

"You will pardon me, M. Poirot, but I do not quite understand you."

"I do not understand myself," said Poirot. "I understand nothing at all, and, as you perceive, it worries me."

He sighed and bent over the little table, examining the charred fragment of paper. He murmured to himself.

"What I need at this moment is an old-fashioned woman's hatbox."

Dr. Constantine was at a loss to know what to make of this singular remark. In any case, Poirot gave him no time for questions. Opening the door into the corridor, he called for the conductor.

The man arrived at a run.

"How many women are there in this coach?"

The conductor counted on his fingers.

"One, two, three—six, Monsieur. The old American lady, a Swedish lady, the young English lady, the Countess Andrenyi and Madame la Princesse Dragomiroff and her maid."

Poirot considered.

"They all have hatboxes, yes?"

"Yes, Monsieur."

"Then bring me—let me see—yes, the Swedish lady's and that of the lady's-maid. Those two are the only hope. You will tell them it is a customs regulation—something—anything that occurs to you."

"That will be all right, Monsieur. Neither lady is in her compartment at the moment."

"Then be quick."

The conductor departed. He returned with the two hatboxes. Poirot opened that of the lady's-maid and tossed it aside. Then he opened the Swedish lady's and uttered an exclamation of satisfaction. Removing the hats carefully, he disclosed round humps of wire netting.

"Ah, here is what we need. About fifteen years ago hatboxes were made like this. You skewered through the hat with a hatpin on to this hump of wire-netting."

As he spoke he was skilfully removing two of the attachments. Then he repacked the hatbox and told the conductor to return them both where they belonged.

When the door was shut once more he turned to his companion.

"See you, my dear doctor, me, I am not one to rely upon the expert procedure. It is the psychology I seek, not the fingerprint or the cigarette ash. But in this case I would welcome a little scientific assistance. This compartment is full of clues, but can I be sure that those clues are really what they seem to be?"

"I do not quite understand you, M. Poirot."

"Well, to give you an example—we find a woman's handkerchief. Did a woman drop it? Or did a man, committing the crime, say to himself 'I will make this look like a woman's crime. I will stab my enemy an unnecessary number of times, making some of the blows feeble and ineffective, and I will drop this handkerchief where no one can miss it. That is one possibility. Then there is another. Did a woman kill him and did she deliberately drop a pipe-cleaner to make it look like a man's work? Or are we seriously to suppose that two people—a man and a woman—were separately concerned, and that each was so careless as to drop a clue to their identity? It is a little too much of a coincidence, that!"

"But where does the hatbox come in?" asked the doctor, still puzzled.

"Ah! I'm coming to that. As I say, these clues, the watch stopped at a quarter-past one, the handkerchief, the pipe cleaner, they may be genuine, or they may be fake. As to that I cannot yet tell. But there is *one* clue here which I believe—though again I may be wrong—has *not* been faked. I mean this flat match, M. le docteur. *I believe that that match was used by the murderer, not by M. Ratchett*. It was used to burn an incriminating paper of some kind. Possibly a note. If so, there was something in that note, some mistake, some error, that left a possible clue to the assailant. I am going to endeavour to resurrect what that something was."

He went out of the compartment and returned a few moments later with a small spirit stove and a pair of curling tongs.

"I use them for the moustaches," he said, referring to the latter.

The doctor watched him with great interest. He flattened out the two humps of wire, and with great care wriggled the charred scrap of paper on to one of them. He clapped the other on top of it and then, holding both pieces together with the tongs, held the whole thing over the flame of the spirit lamp.

"It is a very makeshift affair, this," he said over his shoulder. "Let us hope that it will answer its purpose."

The doctor watched the proceedings attentively. The metal began to glow. Suddenly he saw faint indication of letters. Words formed themselves slowly—words of fire.

It was a very tiny scrap. Only three words and a part of another showed.

-member little Daisy Armstrong.

"Ah!" Poirot gave a sharp exclamation.

"It tells you something?" asked the doctor.

Poirot's eyes were shining. He laid down the tongs carefully.

"Yes," he said. "*I know the dead man's real name. I know why he had to leave America.*"

"What was his name?"

"Cassetti."

"Cassetti." Constantine knitted his brows. "It brings back to me something. Some years ago. I cannot remember. . . . It was a case in America, was it not?"

"Yes," said Poirot. "A case in America."

Further than that Poirot was not disposed to be communicative. He looked round him as he went on:

"We will go into all that presently. Let us first make sure that we have seen all there is to be seen here."

Quickly and deftly he went once more through the pockets of the dead man's clothes but found nothing there of interest. He tried the communicating door which led through to the next compartment, but it was bolted on the other side.

"There is one thing that I do not understand," said Dr. Constantine, "if the murderer did not escape through the window, and if this communicating door was bolted on the other side, and if the door into the corridor was not only locked on the inside but chained, how then did the murderer leave the compartment?"

"That is what the audience says when a person bound hand and foot is shut into a cabinet—and disappears."

"You mean——?"

"I mean," explained Poirot, "that if the murderer intended us to believe that he had escaped by way of the window he would naturally make it appear that the other two exits were impossible. Like the 'disappearing person' in the cabinet—it is a trick. It is our business to find out how the trick is done."

He locked the communicating door on their side.

"In case," he said, "the excellent Mrs. Hubbard should take it into her head to acquire first-hand details of the crime to write to her daughter."

He looked round once more.

"There is nothing more to do here, I think. Let us rejoin M. Bouc."

8. The Armstrong Kidnapping Case

They found M. Bouc finishing an omelet.

"I thought it best to have lunch served immediately in the restaurant-car," he said. "Afterwards it will be cleared and M. Poirot can conduct his examination of the passengers there. In the meantime I have ordered them to bring us three some food here."

"An excellent idea," said Poirot.

Neither of the other two men was hungry, and the meal was soon eaten, but not till they were sipping their coffee did M. Bouc mention the subject that was occupying all their minds.

"*Eh bien?*" he asked.

"*Eh bien,* I have discovered the identity of the victim. I know why it was imperative he should leave America."

"Who was he?"

"Do you remember reading of the Armstrong baby? This is the man who murdered little Daisy Armstrong—Cassetti."

"I recall it now. A shocking affair—though I cannot remember the details."

"Colonel Armstrong was an Englishman—a V.C. He was half American, as his mother was a daughter of W. K. Van der Halt, the Wall Street millionaire. He married the daughter of Linda Arden, the most famous tragic American actress of her day. They lived in America and had one child—a girl—whom they idolised. When she was three years old she was kidnapped, and an impossibly high sum demanded as the price of her return. I will not weary you with all the intricacies that followed. I will come to the moment, when, after having paid over the enormous sum of two hundred thousand dollars, the child's dead body was discovered, it having been dead at least a fortnight. Public indignation rose to fever point. And there was worse to follow. Mrs. Armstrong was expecting another child. Following the shock of the discovery, she gave birth to a dead child born prematurely, and herself died. Her brokenhearted husband shot himself."

"*Mon Dieu,* what a tragedy. I remember now," said M. Bouc. "There was also another death, if I remember rightly?"

"Yes—an unfortunate French or Swiss nursemaid. The police were convinced that she had some knowledge of the crime. They refused to believe her hysterical denials. Finally, in a fit of despair, the poor girl threw herself from a window and was killed. It was proved afterwards that she was absolutely innocent of any complicity in the crime."

"It is not good to think of," said M. Bouc.

"About six months later, this man Cassetti was arrested as the head of the gang who had kidnapped the child. They had used the same methods in the past. If the police seemed likely to get on their trail, they had killed their prisoner, hidden the body, and continued to extract as much money as possible before the crime was discovered.

"Now, I will make clear to you this, my friend. Cassetti was the man! But by means of the enormous wealth he had piled up and by the secret hold he had over various persons, he was acquitted on some technical inaccuracy. Notwithstanding that, he would have been lynched by the populace had he not been clever enough to give them the slip. It is now clear to me what happened. He changed his name and left America. Since then he has been a gentleman of leisure, travelling abroad and living on his *rentes*."

"*Ah! quel animal!*" M. Bouc's tone was redolent of heartfelt disgust. "I cannot regret that he is dead—not at all!"

"I agree with you."

"*Tout de même,* it is not necessary that he should be killed on the Orient Express. There are other places."

Poirot smiled a little. He realised that M. Bouc was biased in the matter.

"The question we have now to ask ourselves is this," he said. "Is this murder the work of some rival gang whom Cassetti had double-crossed in the past, or is it an act of private vengeance?"

He explained his discovery of the few words on the charred fragment of paper.

"If I am right in my assumption, then the letter was burnt by the murderer. Why? Because it mentioned the word 'Armstrong,' which is the clue to the mystery."

"Are there any members of the Armstrong family living?"

"That, unfortunately, I do not know. I think I remember reading of a younger sister of Mrs. Armstrong's."

Poirot went on to relate the joint conclusions of himself and Dr. Constantine. M. Bouc brightened at the mention of the broken watch.

"That seems to give us the time of the crime very exactly."

"Yes," said Poirot. "It is very convenient."

There was an indescribable something in his tone that made both the other two look at him curiously.

"You say that you yourself heard Ratchett speak to the conductor at twenty minutes to one?"

Poirot related just what had occurred.

"Well," said M. Bouc, "that proves at least that Cassetti—or Ratchett, as I shall continue to call him—was certainly alive at twenty minutes to one."

"Twenty-three minutes to one, to be precise."

"Then at twelve thirty-seven, to put it formally, M. Ratchett was alive. That is *one* fact, at least."

Poirot did not reply. He sat looking thoughtfully in front of him.

There was a tap on the door, and the restaurant attendant entered.

"The restaurant-car is free now, Monsieur," he said.

"We will go there," said M. Bouc, rising.

"I may accompany you?" asked Constantine.

AGATHA CHRISTIE

"Certainly, my dear doctor. Unless M. Poirot has any objection?"

"Not at all. Not at all," said Poirot.

After a little politeness in the matter of procedure, *"Après vous, Monsieur." "Mais non, après vous,"* they left the compartment.

PART II—The Evidence

1. The Evidence of the Wagon Lit Conductor

In the restaurant-car all was in readiness.

Poirot and M. Bouc sat together on one side of a table. The doctor sat across the aisle.

On the table in front of Poirot was a plan of the Istanbul-Calais coach with the names of the passengers marked in in red ink.

The passports and tickets were in a pile at one side. There was writing paper, ink, pen and pencils.

"Excellent," said Poirot. "We can open our Court of Inquiry without more ado. First, I think, we should take the evidence of the Wagon Lit conductor. You probably know something about the man. What character has he? Is he a man in whose word you would place reliance?"

"I should say so most assuredly. Pierre Michel has been employed by the company for over fifteen years. He is a Frenchman—lives near Calais. Thoroughly respectable and honest. Not, perhaps, remarkable for brains."

Poirot nodded comprehendingly.

"Good," he said. "Let us see him."

Pierre Michel had recovered some of his assurance, but he was still extremely nervous.

"I hope Monsieur will not think that there has been any negligence on my part," he said anxiously, his eyes going from Poirot to M. Bouc. "It is a terrible thing that has happened. I hope Monsieur does not think that it reflects on me in any way?"

Having soothed the man's fears, Poirot began his questions. He first elicited Michel's name and address, his length of service, and the length of time he had been on this particular route. These particulars he already knew, but the routine questions served to put the man at his ease.

"And now," went on Poirot, "let us come to the events of last night. M. Ratchett retired to bed—when?"

"Almost immediately after dinner, Monsieur. Actually before we left Belgrade. So he did on the previous night. He had directed me to make up the bed while he was at dinner, and I did so."

"Did anybody go into his compartment afterwards?"

"His valet, Monsieur, and the young American gentleman his secretary."

"Anyone else?"

"No, Monsieur, not that I know of."

"Good. And that is the last you saw or heard of him?"

"No, Monsieur. You forget, he rang his bell about twenty to one—soon after we had stopped."

"What happened exactly?"

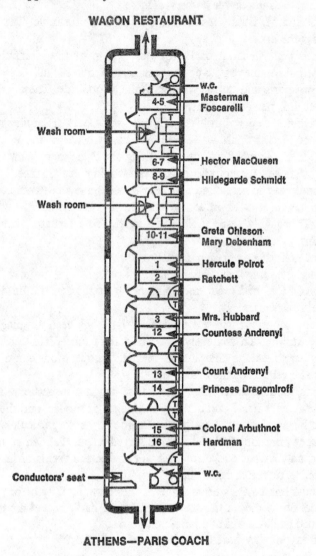

"I knocked at the door, but he called out and said he had made a mistake."

"In English or in French?"

"In French."

"What were his words exactly?"

"Ce n'est rien. Je me suis trompé."

"Quite right," said Poirot. "That is what I heard. And then you went away?"

"Yes, Monsieur."

"Did you go back to your seat?"

"No, Monsieur, I went first to answer another bell that had just rung."

"Now, Michel, I am going to ask you an important question. Where were you at a quarter-past one?"

"I, Monsieur? I was at my little seat at the end—facing up the corridor."

"You are sure?"

"Mais oui—at least——"

"Yes?"

"I went into the next coach, the Athens coach, to speak to my colleague there. We spoke about the snow. That was at some time soon after one o'clock. I cannot say exactly."

"And you returned—when?"

"One of my bells rang, Monsieur—I remember—I told you. It was the American lady. She had rung several times."

"I recollect," said Poirot. "And after that?"

"After that, Monsieur? I answered your bell and brought you some mineral water. Then, about half an hour later, I made up the bed in one of the other compartments—that of the young American gentleman, M. Ratchett's secretary."

"Was M. MacQueen alone in his compartment when you went to make up his bed?"

"The English Colonel from No. 15 was with him. They had been sitting talking."

"What did the Colonel do when he left M. MacQueen?"

"He went back to his own compartments."

"No. 15—that is quite close to your seat, is it not?"

"Yes, Monsieur, it is the second compartment from that end of the corridor."

"His bed was already made up?"

"Yes, Monsieur. I had made it up while he was at dinner."

"What time was all this?"

"I could not say exactly, Monsieur. Not later than two o'clock, certainly."

"And after that?"

"After that, Monsieur, I sat in my seat till morning."

"You did not go again into the Athens coach?"

"No, Monsieur."

"Perhaps you slept?"

"I do not think so, Monsieur. The train being at a standstill prevented me from dozing off as I usually do."

"Did you see any of the passengers moving up or down the corridor?"

The man reflected.

"One of the ladies went to the toilet at the far end, I think."

"Which lady?"

"I do not know, Monsieur. It was far down the corridor, and she had her back to me. She had on a kimono of scarlet with dragons on it."

Poirot nodded.

"And after that?"

"Nothing, Monsieur, until the morning."

"You are sure?"

"Ah, pardon, you yourself, Monsieur, opened your door and looked out for a second."

"Good, my friend," said Poirot. "I wondered whether you would remember that. By the way, I was awakened by what sounded like something heavy falling against my door. Have you any idea what that could have been?"

The man stared at him.

"There was nothing, Monsieur. Nothing, I am positive of it."

"Then I must have had the *cauchemar*," said Poirot philosophically.

"Unless," said M. Bouc, "it was something in the compartment next door that you heard."

Poirot took no notice of the suggestion. Perhaps he did not wish to before the Wagon Lit conductor.

"Let us pass to another point," he said. "Supposing that last night an assassin joined the train. Is it quite certain that he could not have left it after committing the crime?"

Pierre Michel shook his head.

"Nor that he can be concealed on it somewhere?"

"It has been well searched," said M. Bouc. "Abandon that idea, my friend."

"Besides," said Michel, "no one could get on to the sleeping-car without my seeing them."

"When was the last stop?"

"Vincovci."

"What time was that?"

"We should have left there at 11:58. But owing to the weather we were twenty minutes late."

"Someone might have come along from the ordinary part of the train?"

"No, Monsieur. After the service of dinner the door between the ordinary carriages and the sleeping-cars is locked."

"Did you yourself descend from the train at Vincovci?"

"Yes, Monsieur. I got down on to the platform as usual and stood by the step up into the train. The other conductors did the same."

"What about the forward door? The one near the restaurant-car?"

"It is always fastened on the inside."

"It is not so fastened now."

The man looked surprised, then his face cleared.

"Doubtless one of the passengers has opened it to look out on the snow."

"Probably," said Poirot.

He tapped thoughtfully on the table for a minute or two.

"Monsieur does not blame me?" said the man timidly.

Poirot smiled on him kindly.

"You have had the evil chance, my friend," he said. "Ah! One other point while I remember it. You said that another bell rang just as you were knocking at M. Ratchett's door. In fact, I heard it myself. Whose was it?"

"It was the bell of Madame la Princesse Dragomiroff. She desired me to summon her maid."

"And you did so?"

"Yes, Monsieur."

Poirot studied the plan in front of him thoughtfully. Then he inclined his head.

"That is all," he said, "for the moment."

"Thank you, Monsieur."

The man rose. He looked at M. Bouc.

"Do not distress yourself," said the latter kindly. "I cannot see that there has been any negligence on your part."

Gratified, Pierre Michel left the compartment.

2. The Evidence of the Secretary

For a minute or two Poirot remained lost in thought.

"I think," he said at last, "that it would be well to have a further word with M. MacQueen, in view of what we now know."

The young American appeared promptly.

"Well," he said, "how are things going?"

"Not too badly. Since our last conversation I have learnt something—the identity of M. Ratchett."

Hector MacQueen leaned forward interestedly.

"Yes?" he said.

"Ratchett, as you suspected, was merely an alias. Ratchett was Cassetti, the man who ran the celebrated kidnapping stunts—including the famous affair of little Daisy Armstrong."

An expression of utter astonishment appeared on MacQueen's face; then it darkened.

"The damned skunk!" he exclaimed.

"You had no idea of this, M. MacQueen?"

"No, sir," said the young American decidedly. "If I had I'd have cut off my right hand before it had a chance to do secretarial work for him!"

"You feel strongly about the matter, M. MacQueen?"

"I have a particular reason for doing so. My father was the district attorney who handled the case, M. Poirot. I saw Mrs. Armstrong more than once—she was a lovely woman. So gentle and heartbroken." His face darkened. "If ever a man deserved what he got, Ratchett or Cassetti is the man. I'm rejoiced at his end. Such a man wasn't fit to live!"

"You almost feel as though you would have been willing to do the good deed yourself?"

"I do. I——" He paused, then flushed rather guiltily. "Seems I'm kind of incriminating myself."

"I should be more inclined to suspect you, M. MacQueen, if you displayed an inordinate sorrow at your employer's decease."

"I don't think I could do that, even to save myself from the chair," said MacQueen grimly.

Then he added:

"If I'm not being unduly curious, just how did you figure this out? Cassetti's identity, I mean."

"By a fragment of a letter found in his compartment."

"But surely—I mean—that was rather careless of the old man?"

"That depends," said Poirot, "on the point of view."

The young man seemed to find this remark rather baffling. He stared at Poirot as though trying to make him out.

"The task before me," said Poirot, "is to make sure of the movements of everyone on the train. No offence need be taken, you understand? It is only a matter of routine."

"Sure. Get right on with it and let me clear my character if I can."

"I need hardly ask you the number of your compartment," said Poirot, smiling, "since I shared it with you for a night. It is the second-class compartment Nos. 6 and 7, and after my departure you had it to yourself."

"That's right."

"Now, M. MacQueen, I want you to describe your movements last night from the time of leaving the dining-car."

"That's quite easy. I went back to my compartment, read a bit, got out on the platform at Belgrade, decided it was too cold, and got in again. I talked for a while to a young English lady who is in the compartment next to mine. Then I fell into conversation with that Englishman, Colonel Arbuthnot—as a matter of fact I think you passed us as we were talking. Then I went in to Mr. Ratchett and, as I told you, took down some memoranda of letters he wanted written. I said good-night to him and left him. Colonel Arbuthnot was still standing in the corridor. His compartment was already made up for the night, so I suggested that he should come along to mine. I ordered a couple of drinks and we got right down to it. Discussed world politics and the Government of India and our own troubles with the financial situation and the Wall Street crisis. I don't as a rule cotton to Britishers—they're a stiff-necked lot—but I liked this one."

"Do you know what time it was when he left you?"

"Pretty late. Getting on for two o'clock, I should say."

"You noticed that the train had stopped?"

"Oh, yes. We wondered a bit. Looked out and saw the snow lying very thick, but we didn't think it was serious."

"What happened when Colonel Arbuthnot finally said good-night?"

"He went along to his compartment and I called to the conductor to make up my bed."

"Where were you whilst he was making it?"

"Standing just outside the door in the corridor smoking a cigarette."

"And then?"

"And then I went to bed and slept till morning."

"During the evening did you leave the train at all?"

"Arbuthnot and I thought we'd get out at—what was the name of the place?—Vincovci to stretch our legs a bit. But it was bitterly cold—a blizzard on. We soon hopped back again."

"By which door did you leave the train?"

"By the one nearest to our compartment."

"The one next to the dining-car?"

"Yes."

"Do you remember if it was bolted?"

MacQueen considered.

"Why, yes, I seem to remember it was. At least there was a kind of bar that fitted across the handle. Is that what you mean?"

"Yes. On getting back into the train did you replace that bar?"

"Why, no—I don't think I did. I got in last. No, I don't seem to remember doing so."

He added suddenly:

"Is that an important point?"

"It may be. Now, I presume, Monsieur, that while you and Colonel Arbuthnot were sitting talking the door of your compartment into the corridor was open?"

Hector MacQueen nodded.

"I want you, if you can, to tell me if anyone passed along that corridor *after* the train left Vincovci until the time you parted company for the night."

MacQueen drew his brows together.

"I think the conductor passed along once," he said, "coming from the direction of the dining-car. And a woman passed the other way, going towards it."

"Which woman?"

"I couldn't say. I didn't really notice. You see, I was just arguing a point with Arbuthnot. I just seem to remember a glimpse of some scarlet silk affair passing the door. I didn't look, and anyway I wouldn't have seen the person's face. As you know, my carriage faces the dining-car end of the train, so a woman going along the corridor in that direction would have her back to me as soon as she'd passed."

Poirot nodded.

"She was going to the toilet, I presume?"

"I suppose so."

"And you saw her return?"

"Well, no, now that you mention it, I didn't notice her returning, but I suppose she must have done so."

"One more question. Do you smoke a pipe, M. MacQueen?"

"No, sir, I do not."

Poirot paused a moment.

"I think that is all at present. I should now like to see the valet of M. Ratchett. By the way, did both you and he always travel second-class?"

"He did. But I usually went first—if possible in the adjoining compartment to Mr. Ratchett. Then he had most of his baggage put in my compartment and yet could get at both it and me easily whenever he chose. But on this occasion all the first-class berths were booked except the one which he took."

"I comprehend. Thank you, M. MacQueen."

3. The Evidence of the Valet

The American was succeeded by the pale Englishman with the inexpressive face whom Poirot had already noticed on the day before. He stood waiting very correctly. Poirot motioned to him to sit down.

"You are, I understand, the valet of M. Ratchett?"

"Yes, sir."

"Your name?"

"Edward Henry Masterman."

"Your age?"

"Thirty-nine."

"And your home address?"

"21 Friar Street, Clerkenwell."

"You have heard that your master has been murdered?"

"Yes, sir. A very shocking occurrence."

"Will you now tell me, please, at what hour you last saw M. Ratchett?"

The valet considered.

"It must have been about nine o'clock, sir, last night. That or a little after."

"Tell me in your own words exactly what happened."

"I went in to Mr. Ratchett as usual, sir, and attended to his wants."

"What were your duties exactly?"

"To fold or hang up his clothes, sir. Put his dental plate in water and see that he had everything he wanted for the night."

"Was his manner much the same as usual?"

The valet considered a moment.

"Well, sir, I think he was upset."

"In what way—upset?"

"Over a letter he'd been reading. He asked me if it was I who had put it in his compartment. Of course I told him I hadn't done any such thing, but he swore at me and found fault with everything I did."

"Was that unusual?"

"Oh, no, sir, he lost his temper easily—as I say, it just depended what had happened to upset him."

"Did your master ever take a sleeping draught?"

Dr. Constantine leaned forward a little.

"Always when travelling by train, sir. He said he couldn't sleep otherwise."

"Do you know what drug he was in the habit of taking?"

"I couldn't say, I'm sure, sir. There was no name on the bottle. Just *'The Sleeping Draught to be taken at bedtime.'*"

"Did he take it last night?"

"Yes, sir. I poured it into a glass and put it on top of the toilet table ready for him."

"You didn't actually see him drink it?"

"No, sir."

"What happened next?"

"I asked if there was anything further, and asked what time M. Ratchett would like to be called in the morning. He said he didn't want to be disturbed till he rang."

"Was that usual?"

"Quite usual, sir. He used to ring the bell for the conductor and then send him for me when he was ready to get up."

"Was he usually an early or a late riser?"

"It depended, sir, on his mood. Sometimes he'd get up for breakfast, sometimes he wouldn't get up till just on lunch time."

"So that you weren't alarmed when the morning wore on and no summons came?"

"No, sir."

"Did you know that your master had enemies?"

"Yes, sir."

The man spoke quite unemotionally.

"How did you know?"

"I had heard him discussing some letters, sir, with Mr. MacQueen."

"Had you an affection for your employer, Masterman?"

Masterman's face became, if possible, even more inexpressive than it was normally.

"I should hardly like to say that, sir. He was a generous employer."

"But you didn't like him?"

"Shall we put it that I don't care very much for Americans, sir."

"Have you ever been in America?"

"No, sir."

"Do you remember reading in the paper of the Armstrong kidnapping case?"

A little colour came into the man's cheeks.

"Yes, indeed, sir. A little baby girl, wasn't it? A very shocking affair."

"Did you know that your employer, M. Ratchett, was the principal instigator in that affair?"

"No, indeed, sir." The valet's tone held positive warmth and feeling for the first time. "I can hardly believe it, sir."

"Nevertheless, it is true. Now, to pass to your own movements last night. A matter of routine, you understand. What did you do after leaving your master?"

"I told Mr. MacQueen, sir, that the master wanted him. Then I went to my own compartment and read."

"Your compartment was——?"

"The end second-class one, sir. Next to the dining-car."

Poirot was looking at his plan.

"I see—and you had which berth?"

"The lower one, sir."

"That is No. 4?"

"Yes, sir."

"Is there anyone in with you?"

"Yes, sir. A big Italian fellow."

"Does he speak English?"

"Well, a kind of English, sir." The valet's tone was deprecating. "He's been in America—Chicago—I understand."

"Do you and he talk together much?"

"No, sir. I prefer to read."

Poirot smiled. He could visualise the scene—the large voluble Italian, and the snub direct administered by the gentleman's gentleman.

"And what, may I ask, are you reading?" he inquired.

"At present, sir, I am reading *Love's Captive*, by Mrs. Arabella Richardson."

"A good story?"

"I find it highly enjoyable, sir."

"Well, let us continue. You returned to your compartment and read *Love's Captive* till—when?"

"At about ten-thirty, sir, this Italian wanted to go to bed. So the conductor came and made the beds up."

"And then you went to bed and to sleep?"

"I went to bed, sir, but I didn't sleep."

"Why didn't you sleep?"

"I had the toothache, sir."

"Oh, *là là*—that is painful."

"Most painful, sir."

"Did you do anything for it?"

"I applied a little oil of cloves, sir, which relieved the pain a little, but I was still not able to get to sleep. I turned the light on above my head and continued to read—to take my mind off it, as it were."

"And did you not go to sleep at all?"

"Yes, sir, I dropped off about four in the morning."

"And your companion?"

"The Italian fellow? Oh, he just snored."

"He did not leave the compartment at all during the night?"

"No, sir."

"Did you?"

"No, sir."

"Did you hear anything during the night?"

"I don't think so, sir. Nothing unusual, I mean. The train being at a standstill made it all very quiet."

Poirot was silent a moment or two, then he said:

"Well, I think there is very little more to be said. You cannot throw any light upon the tragedy?"

"I'm afraid not. I'm sorry, sir."

"As far as you know, was there any quarrel or bad blood between your master and M. MacQueen?"

"Oh, no, sir. Mr. MacQueen was a very pleasant gentleman."

"Where were you in service before you came to M. Ratchett?"

"With Sir Henry Tomlinson, sir, in Grosvenor Square."

"Why did you leave him?"

"He was going to East Africa, sir, and did not require my services any longer. But I am sure he will speak for me, sir. I was with him some years."

"And you have been with M. Ratchett—how long?"

"Just over nine months, sir."

"Thank you, Masterman. By the way, are you a pipe smoker?"

"No, sir. I only smoke cigarettes—gaspers, sir."

"Thank you. That will do."

Poirot gave him a nod of dismissal.

The valet hesitated a moment.

"You'll excuse me, sir, but the elderly American lady is in what I might describe as a state, sir. She's saying she knows all about the murderer. She's in a very excitable condition, sir."

"In that case," said Poirot, smiling, "we had better see her next."

"Shall I tell her, sir? She's been demanding to see someone in authority for a long time. The conductor's been trying to pacify her."

"Send her to us, my friend," said Poirot. "We will listen to her story now."

4. The Evidence of the American Lady

Mrs. Hubbard arrived in the dining-car in such a state of breathless excitement that she was hardly able to articulate her words.

"Now just tell me this. Who's in authority here? I've got some vurry important information, *vurry* important, indeed, and I just want to tell it to someone in authority as soon as may be. If you gentlemen——"

Her wavering glance fluctuated between the three men. Poirot leaned forward.

"Tell it to me, Madame," he said. "But, first, pray be seated."

Mrs. Hubbard plumped heavily down on to the seat opposite to him.

"What I've got to tell you is just this. There was a murder on the train last night, and the murderer was *right there in my compartment!*"

She paused to give dramatic emphasis to her words.

"You are sure of this, Madame?"

"Of course I'm sure! The idea! I know what I'm talking about. I'll tell you just everything there is to tell. I'd gotten into bed and gone to sleep, and suddenly I woke up—all in the dark, it was—and I knew there was a man in my compartment. I was just so scared I couldn't scream, if you know what I mean. I just lay there and thought, 'Mercy, I'm going to be killed.' I just can't describe to you how I felt. These nasty trains, I thought, and all the outrages I'd read of. And I thought, 'Well, anyway, he won't get my jewellery,' because, you see, I'd put that in a stocking and hidden it under my pillow—which isn't so mighty comfortable, by the way, kinder bumpy, if you know what I mean. But that's neither here nor there. Where was I?"

"You realised, Madame, that there was a man in your compartment."

"Yes, well, I just lay there with my eyes closed, and I thought whatever should I do, and I thought, 'Well, I'm just thankful that my daughter doesn't know the plight I'm in.' And then, somehow, I got my wits about me and I felt about with my hand and I pressed the bell for the conductor. I pressed it and I pressed it, but nothing happened, and I can tell you I thought my heart was going to stop beating. 'Mercy,' I said to myself, 'maybe they've murdered every single soul on the train.' It was at a standstill, anyhow, and a nasty quiet feel in the air. But I just went on pressing that bell, and oh! the relief when I heard footsteps coming running down the corridor and a knock on the door. 'Come in,' I screamed, and I switched on the lights at the same time. And, would you believe it, there wasn't a soul there."

This seemed to Mrs. Hubbard to be a dramatic climax rather than an anti-climax.

"And what happened next, Madame?"

"Why, I told the man what had happened, and he didn't seem to believe me. Seemed to imagine I'd dreamt the whole thing. I made him look under the seat, though he said there wasn't room for a man to squeeze himself in there. It was plain enough the man had got away, but there *had* been a man there and it just made me mad the way the conductor tried to soothe me down! I'm not one to imagine things, Mr.—— I don't think I know your name?"

"Poirot, Madame, and this is M. Bouc, a director of the company, and Dr. Constantine."

Mrs. Hubbard murmured:

"Pleased to meet you, I'm sure," to all three of them in an abstracted manner, and then plunged once more into her recital.

"Now I'm just not going to pretend I was as bright as I might have been. I got it into my head that it was the man from next door—the poor fellow who's been killed. I told the conductor to look at the door between the compartments, and sure enough it wasn't bolted. Well, I soon saw to that. I told him to bolt it then and there, and after he'd gone out I got up and put a suitcase against it to make sure."

"What time was this, Mrs. Hubbard?"

"Well, I'm sure I can't tell you. I never looked to see. I was so upset."

"And what is your theory now?"

"Why, I should say it was just as plain as plain could be. The man in my compartment was the murderer. Who else could he be?"

"And you think he went back into the adjoining compartment?"

"How do I know where he went? I had my eyes tight shut."

"He must have slipped out through the door into the corridor."

"Well, I couldn't say. You see, I had my eyes tight shut."

Mrs. Hubbard sighed convulsively.

"Mercy, I was scared! If my daughter only knew——"

"You do not think, Madame, that what you heard was the noise of someone moving about next door—in the murdered man's compartment?"

"No, I do not, Mr.—what is it?—Poirot. The man was *right there in the same compartment with me*. And, what's more, I've got proof of it."

Triumphantly she hauled a large handbag into view and proceeded to burrow in its interior.

She took out in turn two large clean handkerchiefs, a pair of horn-rimmed glasses, a bottle of aspirin, a packet of Glauber's salts, a celluloid tube of bright green peppermints, a bunch of keys, a pair of scissors, a book of American Express cheques, a snapshot of an extraordinarily plain-looking child, some letters, five strings of pseudo Oriental beads and a small metal object—a button.

"You see this button? Well, it's not one of *my* buttons. It's not off anything I've got. I found it this morning when I got up."

As she placed it on the table, M. Bouc leaned forward and gave an exclamation.

"But this is a button from the tunic of a Wagon Lit attendant!"

"There may be a natural explanation for that," said Poirot.

He turned gently to the lady.

"This button, Madame, may have dropped from the conductor's uniform, either when he searched your cabin, or when he was making the bed up last night."

"I just don't know what's the matter with all you people. Seems as though you don't do anything but make objections. Now listen here. I was reading a magazine last night before I went to sleep. Before I turned the light out I placed that magazine on a little case that was standing on the floor near the window. Have you got that?"

They assured her that they had.

"Very well, then. The conductor looked under the seat from near the door and then he came in and bolted the door between me and the next compartment, but he never went up near the window. Well, this morning that button was lying right on top of the magazine. What do you call that, I should like to know?"

"That, Madame, I call evidence," said Poirot.

The answer seemed to appease the lady.

"It makes me madder than a hornet to be disbelieved," she explained.

"You have given us most interesting and valuable evidence," said Poirot soothingly. "Now, may I ask you a few questions?"

"Why, willingly."

"How was it, since you were nervous of this man Ratchett, that you hadn't already bolted the door between the compartments?"

"I had," returned Mrs. Hubbard promptly.

"Oh, you had?"

"Well, as a matter of fact, I asked that Swedish creature—a pleasant soul—if it was bolted, and she said it was."

"How was it you couldn't see for yourself?"

"Because I was in bed and my sponge-bag was hanging on the door handle."

"What time was it when you asked her to do this for you?"

"Now let me think. It must have been round about half-past ten or a quarter to eleven. She'd come along to see if I'd got an aspirin. I told her where to find it, and she got it out of my grip."

"You yourself were in bed?"

"Yes."

Suddenly she laughed.

"Poor soul—she was in quite a taking. You see, she'd opened the door of the next compartment by mistake."

"M. Ratchett's?"

"Yes. You know how difficult it is as you come along the train and all the doors are shut. She opened his by mistake. She was very distressed about it. He'd laughed, it seemed, and I fancy he may have said something not quite nice. Poor thing, she was all in a flutter. 'Oh! I make mistake,' she said. 'I ashamed make mistake. Not nice man,' she said. 'He say, "You too old." '"

Dr. Constantine sniggered and Mrs. Hubbard immediately froze him with a glance.

"He wasn't a nice kind of man," she said, "to say a thing like that to a lady. It's not right to laugh at such things."

Dr. Constantine hastily apologised.

"Did you hear any noise from M. Ratchett's compartment after that?" asked Poirot.

"Well—not exactly."

"What do you mean by that, Madame?"

"Well——" She paused. "He snored."

"Ah! he snored, did he?"

"Terribly. The night before it quite kept me awake."

"You didn't hear him snore after you had had the scare about a man being in your compartment?"

"Why, Mr. Poirot, how could I? He was dead."

"Ah, yes, truly," said Poirot. He appeared confused.

"Do you remember the affair of the Armstrong kidnapping, Mrs. Hubbard?" he asked.

"Yes, indeed I do. And how the wretch that did it escaped scot free! My, I'd have liked to get my hands on him."

"He has not escaped. He is dead. He died last night."

"You don't mean——?" Mrs. Hubbard half rose from her chair in excitement.

"But yes, I do. Ratchett was the man."

"*Well!* Well, to think of that! I must write and tell my daughter. Now, didn't I tell you last night that that man had an evil face? I was right, you see. My daughter always says: 'When Momma's got a hunch, you can bet your bottom dollar it's O.K.'"

"Were you acquainted with any of the Armstrong family, Mrs. Hubbard?"

"No. They moved in a very exclusive circle. But I've always heard that Mrs. Armstrong was a perfectly lovely woman and that her husband worshipped her."

"Well, Mrs. Hubbard, you have helped us very much—very much indeed. Perhaps you will give me your full name?"

"Why, certainly. Caroline Martha Hubbard."

"Will you write your address down here?"

Mrs. Hubbard did so, without ceasing to speak.

"I just can't get over it. Cassetti—on this train. I had a hunch about that man, didn't I, Mr. Poirot?"

"Yes, indeed, Madame. By the way, have you a scarlet silk dressing-gown?"

"Mercy, what an odd question! Why, no. I've got two dressing-gowns with me—a pink flannel one that's kind of cosy for on board ship, and one my daughter gave me as a present—a kind of local affair in purple silk. But what in creation do you want to know about my dressing-gowns for?"

"Well, you see, Madame, someone in a scarlet kimono entered either your or Mr. Ratchett's compartment last night. It is, as you said just now, very difficult when all the doors are shut to know which compartment is which."

"Well, no one in a scarlet dressing-gown came into my compartment."

"Then she must have gone into M. Ratchett's."

Mrs. Hubbard pursed her lips together and said grimly:

"That wouldn't surprise me any."

Poirot leaned forward.

"So you heard a woman's voice next door?"

"I don't know how you guessed that, Mr. Poirot. I don't really. But—well—as a matter of fact, I *did*."

"But when I asked you just now if you heard anything next door, you only said you heard Mr. Ratchett snoring."

"Well that was true enough. He *did* snore part of the time. As for the other——" Mrs. Hubbard got rather pink. "It isn't a very nice thing to speak about."

"What time was it when you heard a woman's voice?"

"I can't tell you. I just woke up for a minute and heard a woman talking, and it was plain enough where she was. So I just thought, 'Well, that's the kind of man he is. Well, I'm not surprised,' and then I went to sleep again, and I'm sure I should never have mentioned anything of the kind to three strange gentlemen if you hadn't dragged it out of me."

"Was it before the scare about the man in your compartment, or after?"

"Why, that's like what you said just now! He wouldn't have had a woman talking to him if he were dead, would he?"

"*Pardon*. You must think me very stupid, Madame."

"I guess even you get kinder muddled now and then. I just can't get over it being that monster Cassetti. What my daughter will say——"

Poirot managed adroitly to help the good lady to restore the contents of her handbag and he then shepherded her towards the door.

At the last moment he said:

"You have dropped your handkerchief, Madame."

Mrs. Hubbard looked at the little scrap of cambric he held out to her.

"That's not mine, Mr. Poirot. I've got mine right here."

"*Pardon*. I thought as it had the initial H on it——"

"Well, now, that's curious, but it's certainly not mine. Mine are marked C.M.H., and they're sensible things—not expensive Paris fallals. What good is a handkerchief like that to anybody's nose?"

Neither of the three men seemed to have an answer to this question, and Mrs. Hubbard sailed out triumphantly.

5. The Evidence of the Swedish Lady

M. Bouc was handling the button Mrs. Hubbard had left behind her.

"This button. I cannot understand it. Does it mean that, after all,

Pierre Michel is involved in some way?" he said. He paused, then continued, as Poirot did not reply. "What have you to say, my friend?"

"That button, it suggests possibilities," said Poirot thoughtfully. "Let us interview next the Swedish lady before we discuss the evidence we have heard."

He sorted through the pile of passports in front of him.

"Ah! here we are. Greta Ohlsson, age forty-nine."

M. Bouc gave directions to the restaurant attendant, and presently the lady with the yellowish-grey bun of hair and the long mild sheeplike face was ushered in. She peered short-sightedly at Poirot through her glasses, but was quite calm.

It transpired that she understood and spoke French, so that the conversation took place in that language. Poirot first asked her the questions to which he already knew the answers—her name, age, and address. He then asked her her occupation.

She was, she told him, matron in a missionary school near Stamboul. She was a trained nurse.

"You know, of course, of what took place last night, Mademoiselle?"

"Naturally. It is very dreadful. And the American lady tells me that the murderer was actually in her compartment."

"I heard, Mademoiselle, that you were the last person to see the murdered man alive?"

"I do not know. It may be so. I opened the door of his compartment by mistake. I was much ashamed. It was a most awkward mistake."

"You actually saw him?"

"Yes. He was reading a book. I apologised quickly and withdrew."

"Did he say anything to you?"

A slight flush showed on the worthy lady's cheek.

"He laughed and said a few words. I—I did not quite catch them."

"And what did you do after that, Mademoiselle?" asked Poirot, passing from the subject tactfully.

"I went in to the American lady, Mrs. Hubbard. I asked her for some aspirin and she gave it to me."

"Did she ask you whether the communicating door between her compartment and that of M. Ratchett was bolted?"

"Yes."

"And was it?"

"Yes."

"And after that?"

"After that I go back to my own compartment, I take the aspirin and lie down."

"What time was all this?"

"When I got into bed it was five minutes to eleven, because I look at my watch before I wind it up."

"Did you go to sleep quickly?"

"Not very quickly. My head got better, but I lay awake some time."

"Had the train come to a stop before you went to sleep?"

"I do not think so. We stopped, I think, at a station, just as I was getting drowsy."

"That would be Vincovci. Now your compartment, Mademoiselle, is this one?" He indicated it on the plan.

"That is so, yes."

"You had the upper or the lower berth?"

"The lower berth, No. 10."

"And you had a companion?"

"Yes, a young English lady. Very nice, very amiable. She had travelled from Baghdad."

"After the train left Vincovci, did she leave the compartment?"

"No, I am sure she did not."

"Why are you sure if you were asleep?"

"I sleep very lightly. I am used to waking at a sound. I am sure if she had come down from the berth above I should have awakened."

"Did you yourself leave the compartment?"

"Not until this morning."

"Have you a scarlet silk kimono, Mademoiselle?"

"No, indeed. I have a good comfortable dressing-gown of Jaeger material."

"And the lady with you, Miss Debenham? What colour is her dressing-gown?"

"A pale mauve abba such as you buy in the East."

Poirot nodded. Then he said in a friendly tone:

"Why are you taking this journey? A holiday?"

"Yes, I am going home for a holiday. But first I go to Lausanne to stay with a sister for a week or so."

"Perhaps you will be so amiable as to write me down the name and address of your sister?"

"With pleasure."

She took the paper and pencil he gave her and wrote down the name and address as requested.

"Have you ever been in America, Mademoiselle?"

"No. Very nearly once. I was to go with an invalid lady, but it was cancelled at the last moment. I much regretted. They are very good, the Americans. They give much money to found schools and hospitals. They are very practical."

"Do you remember hearing of the Armstrong kidnapping case?"

"No, what was that?"

Poirot explained.

Greta Ohlsson was indignant. Her yellow bun of hair quivered with her emotion.

"That there are in the world such evil men! It tries one's faith. The poor mother. My heart aches for her."

The amiable Swede departed, her kindly face flushed, her eyes suffused with tears.

Poirot was writing busily on a sheet of paper.

"What is it you write there, my friend?" asked M. Bouc.

"*Mon cher,* it is my habit to be neat and orderly. I make here a little table of chronological events."

He finished writing and passed the paper to M. Bouc.

	9:15	Train leaves Belgrade.
about	9:40	Valet leaves Ratchett with sleeping draught beside him.
about	10:00	MacQueen leaves Ratchett.
about	10:40	Greta Ohlsson sees Ratchett (last seen alive). N.B.—He was awake reading a book.
	12:10	Train leaves Vincovci (late).
	12:30	Train runs into a snowdrift.
	12:37	Ratchett's bell rings. Conductor answers it. Ratchett says, *"Ce n'est rien. Je me suis trompé."*
about	1:17	Mrs. Hubbard thinks man is in her carriage. Rings for conductor.

M. Bouc nodded approval.

"That is very clear," he said.

"There is nothing there that strikes you as at all odd?"

"No, it seems all quite clear and above board. It seems quite plain that the crime was committed at 1:15. The evidence of the watch shows us that, and Mrs. Hubbard's story fits in. For my mind, I will make a guess at the identity of the murderer. I say, my friend, that it is the big Italian. He comes from America—from Chicago—and remember an Italian's weapon is the knife, and he stabs not once but several times."

"That is true."

"Without a doubt, that is the solution of the mystery. Doubtless he and this Ratchett were in this kidnapping business together. Cassetti is an Italian name. In some way Ratchett did on him what they call the double-cross. The Italian tracks him down, sends him warning letters first, and finally revenges himself upon him in a brutal way. It is all quite simple."

Poirot shook his head doubtfully.

"It is hardly as simple as that, I fear," he murmured.

"Me, I am convinced it is the truth," said M. Bouc, becoming more and more enamoured of his theory.

"And what about the valet with the toothache who swears that the Italian never left the compartment?"

"That is the difficulty."

Poirot twinkled.

"Yes, it is annoying, that. Unlucky for your theory, and extremely lucky for our Italian friend that M. Ratchett's valet should have had the toothache."

"It will be explained," said M. Bouc with magnificent certainty.

Poirot shook his head again.

"No, it is hardly so simple as that," he murmured again.

6. *The Evidence of the Russian Princess*

"Let us hear what Pierre Michel has to say about this button," he said.

The Wagon Lit conductor was recalled. He looked at them inquiringly.

M. Bouc cleared his throat.

"Michel," he said. "Here is a button from your tunic. It was found in the American lady's compartment. What have you to say for yourself about it?"

The conductor's hand went automatically to his tunic.

"I have lost no button, Monsieur," he said. "There must be some mistake."

"That is very odd."

"I cannot account for it, Monsieur."

The man seemed astonished, but not in any way guilty or confused.

M. Bouc said meaningly:

"Owing to the circumstances in which it was found, it seems fairly certain that this button was dropped by the man who was in Mrs. Hubbard's compartment last night when she rang the bell."

"But, Monsieur, there was no one there. The lady must have imagined it."

"She did not imagine it, Michel. The assassin of M. Ratchett passed that way—*and dropped that button*."

As the significance of M. Bouc's word became plain to him, Pierre Michel flew into a violent state of agitation.

"It is not true, Monsieur, it is not true!" he cried. "You are accusing me of the crime. Me? I am innocent. I am absolutely innocent. Why should I want to kill a Monsieur whom I have never seen before?"

"Where were you when Mrs. Hubbard's bell rang?"

"I told you, Monsieur, in the next coach, talking to my colleague."

"We will send for him."

"Do so, Monsieur, I implore you, do so."

The conductor of the next coach was summoned. He immediately confirmed Pierre Michel's statement. He added that the conductor from the Bucharest coach had also been there. The three of them had been discussing the situation caused by the snow. They had been talking some ten minutes when Michel fancied he heard a bell. As he opened the doors connecting the two coaches, they had all heard it plainly. A bell ringing repeatedly. Michel had run post-haste to answer it.

"So you see, Monsieur, I am not guilty," cried Michel anxiously.

"And this button from a Wagon Lit tunic—how do you explain it?"

"I cannot, Monsieur. It is a mystery to me. All my buttons are intact."

Both of the other conductors also declared that they had not lost a button. Also that they had not been inside Mrs. Hubbard's compartment at any time.

"Calm yourself, Michel," said M. Bouc, "and cast your mind back to the moment when you ran to answer Mrs. Hubbard's bell. Did you meet anyone at all in the corridor?"

"No, Monsieur."

"Did you see anyone going away from you down the corridor in the other direction?"

"Again, no, Monsieur."

"Odd," said M. Bouc.

"Not so very," said Poirot. "It is a question of time. Mrs. Hubbard wakes to find someone in her compartment. For a minute or two she lies paralysed, her eyes shut. Probably it was then that the man slipped out into the corridor. Then she starts ringing the bell. But the conductor does not come at once. It is only the third or fourth peal that he hears. I should say myself that there was ample time——"

"For what? For what, *mon cher?* Remember that there are thick drifts of snow all round the train."

"There are two courses open to our mysterious assassin," said Poirot slowly. "He could retreat into either of the toilets or he could disappear into one of the compartments."

"But they were all occupied."

"Yes."

"You mean that he could retreat into his *own* compartment?"

Poirot nodded.

"It fits, it fits," murmured M. Bouc. "During that ten minutes' absence of the conductor, the murderer comes from his own compartment, goes into Ratchett's, kills him, locks and chains the door on the inside, goes out through Mrs. Hubbard's compartment and is back safely in his own compartment by the time the conductor arrives."

Poirot murmured:

"It is not quite so simple as that, my friend. Our friend the doctor here will tell you so."

With a gesture M. Bouc signified that the three conductors might depart.

"We have still to see eight passengers," said Poirot. "Five first-class passengers—Princess Dragomiroff, Count and Countess Andrenyi, Colonel Arbuthnot and Mr. Hardman. Three second-class passengers—Miss Debenham, Antonio Foscarella and the lady's-maid, Fräulein Schmidt."

"Who will you see first—the Italian?"

"How you harp on your Italian! No, we will start at the top of the tree. Perhaps Madame la Princesse will be so good as to spare us a few moments of her time. Convey that message to her, Michel."

"Oui, Monsieur," said the conductor, who was just leaving the car.

"Tell her we can wait on her in her compartment if she does not wish to put herself to the trouble of coming here," called M. Bouc.

But Princess Dragomiroff declined to take this course. She appeared in the dining-car, inclined her head slightly and sat down opposite Poirot.

Her small, toad-like face looked even yellower than the day before. She was certainly ugly, and yet, like the toad, she had eyes like jewels, dark and imperious, revealing latent energy and an intellectual force that could be felt at once.

Her voice was deep, very distinct, with a slight grating quality in it.

She cut short a flowery phrase of apology from M. Bouc.

"You need not offer apologies, Messieurs. I understand a murder has taken place. Naturally, you must interview all the passengers. I shall be glad to give all the assistance in my power."

"You are most amiable, Madame," said Poirot.

"Not at all. It is my duty. What do you wish to know?"

"Your full Christian names and address, Madame. Perhaps you would prefer to write them yourself?"

Poirot proffered a sheet of paper and pencil, but the Princess waved them aside.

"You can write it," she said. "There is nothing difficult—Natalia Dragomiroff, 17 Avenue Kleber, Paris."

"You are travelling home from Constantinople, Madame?"

"Yes, I have been staying at the Austrian Embassy. My maid is with me."

"Would you be so good as to give me a brief account of your movements last night from dinner onwards?"

"Willingly. I directed the conductor to make up my bed whilst I was in the dining-car. I retired to bed immediately after dinner. I read until the hour of eleven, when I turned out my light. I was unable to sleep owing to certain rheumatic pains from which I suffer. At about a quarter to one I rang for my maid. She massaged me and then read aloud till I felt sleepy. I cannot say exactly when she left me. It may have been half an hour, it may have been later."

"The train had stopped then?"

"The train had stopped."

"You heard nothing—nothing unusual during the time, Madame?"

"I heard nothing unusual."

"What is your maid's name?"

"Hildegarde Schmidt."

"She has been with you long?"

"Fifteen years."

"You consider her trustworthy?"

"Absolutely. Her people come from an estate of my late husband's in Germany."

"You have been in America, I presume, Madame?"

The abrupt change of subject made the old lady raise her eyebrows. "Many times."

"Were you at any time acquainted with a family of the name of Armstrong—a family in which a tragedy occurred?"

With some emotion in her voice the old lady said:

"You speak of friends of mine, Monsieur."

"You knew Colonel Armstrong well, then?"

"I knew him slightly; but his wife, Sonia Armstrong, was my goddaughter. I was on terms of friendship with her mother, the actress, Linda Arden. Linda Arden was a great genius, one of the greatest tragic actresses in the world. As Lady Macbeth, as Magda, there was no one to touch her. I was not only an admirer of her art, I was a personal friend."

"She is dead?"

"No, no, she is alive, but she lives in complete retirement. Her health is very delicate, she has to lie on a sofa most of the time."

"There was, I think, a second daughter?"

"Yes, much younger than Mrs. Armstrong."

"And she is alive?"

"Certainly."

"Where is she?"

The old woman bent an acute glance at him.

"I must ask you the reason of these questions. What have they to do with the matter in hand—the murder on this train?"

"They are connected in this way, Madame: the man who was murdered was the man responsible for the kidnapping and murder of Mrs. Armstrong's child."

"Ah!"

The straight brows drew together. Princess Dragomiroff drew herself a little more erect.

"In my view, then, this murder is an entirely admirable happening! You will pardon my slightly biased point of view."

"It is most natural, Madame. And now to return to the question you did not answer. Where is the younger daughter of Linda Arden, the sister of Mrs. Armstrong?"

"I honestly cannot tell you, Monsieur. I have lost touch with the younger generation. I believe she married an Englishman some years ago and went to England, but at the moment I cannot recollect the name."

She paused a minute and then said:

"Is there anything further you want to ask me, gentlemen?"

"Only one thing, Madame, a somewhat personal question. The colour of your dressing-gown."

She raised her eyebrows slightly.

"I must suppose you have a reason for such a question. My dressing-gown is of blue satin."

"There is nothing more, Madame. I am much obliged to you for answering my questions so promptly."

She made a slight gesture with her heavily-beringed hand.

Then, as she rose, and the others rose with her, she stopped.

"You will excuse me, Monsieur," she said, "but may I ask your name? Your face is somehow familiar to me."

"My name, Madame, is Hercule Poirot—at your service."

She was silent a minute, then:

"Hercule Poirot," she said. "Yes. I remember now. This is Destiny."

She walked away, very erect, a little stiff in her movements.

"Voilà une grande dame," said M. Bouc. "What do you think of her, my friend?"

But Hercule Poirot merely shook his head.

"I am wondering," he said, "what she meant by Destiny."

7. The Evidence of Count and Countess Andrenyi

Count and Countess Andrenyi were next summoned. The Count, however, entered the dining-car alone.

There was no doubt that he was a fine-looking man seen face to face. He was at least six feet in height, with broad shoulders and slender hips. He was dressed in very well-cut English tweeds, and might have been taken for an Englishman had it not been for the length of his moustache and something in the line of the cheek-bone.

"Well, Messieurs," he said, "what can I do for you?"

"You understand, Monsieur," said Poirot, "that in view of what has occurred I am obliged to put certain questions to all the passengers."

"Perfectly, perfectly," said the Count easily. "I quite understand your position. Not, I fear, that my wife and I can do much to assist you. We were asleep and heard nothing at all."

"Are you aware of the identity of the deceased, Monsieur?"

"I understand it was the big American—a man with a decidedly unpleasant face. He sat at that table at meal times."

He indicated with a nod of his head the table at which Ratchett and MacQueen had sat.

"Yes, yes, Monsieur, you are perfectly correct. I meant did you know the name of the man?"

"No." The Count looked thoroughly puzzled by Poirot's queries.

"If you want to know his name," he said, "surely it is on his passport?"

"The name on his passport is Ratchett," said Poirot. "But that, Monsieur, is not his real name. He is the man Cassetti, who was responsible for a celebrated kidnapping outrage in America."

He watched the Count closely as he spoke, but the latter seemed quite unaffected by the piece of news. He merely opened his eyes a little.

"Ah!" he said. "That certainly should throw light upon the matter. An extraordinary country, America."

"You have been there, perhaps, Monsieur le Comte?"

"I was in Washington for a year."

"You knew, perhaps, the Armstrong family?"

"Armstrong—Armstrong—it is difficult to recall—one met so many."
He smiled, shrugged his shoulders.

"But to come back to the matter in hand, gentlemen," he said. "What more can I do to assist you?"

"You retired to rest—when, Monsieur le Comte?"

Hercule Poirot's eyes stole to his plan. Count and Countess Andrenyi occupied compartments No. 12 and 13 adjoining.

"We had one compartment made up for the night whilst we were in the dining-car. On returning we sat in the other for a while——"

"What number would that be?"

"No. 13. We played picquet together. About eleven o'clock my wife retired for the night. The conductor made up my compartment and I also went to bed. I slept soundly until morning."

"Did you notice the stopping of the train?"

"I was not aware of it till this morning."

"And your wife?"

The Count smiled.

"My wife always takes a sleeping draught when travelling by train. She took her usual dose of trional."

He paused.

"I am sorry I am not able to assist you in any way."

Poirot passed him a sheet of paper and a pen.

"Thank you, Monsieur le Comte. It is a formality, but will you just let me have your name and address?"

The Count wrote slowly and carefully.

"It is just as well I should write this for you," he said pleasantly. "The spelling of my country estate is a little difficult for those unacquainted with the language."

He passed the paper across to Poirot and rose.

"It will be quite unnecessary for my wife to come here," he said. "She can tell you nothing more than I have."

A little gleam came into Poirot's eye.

"Doubtless, doubtless," he said. "But all the same I think I should like to have just one little word with Madame la Comtesse."

"I assure you it is quite unnecessary."

His voice rang out authoritatively.

Poirot blinked gently at him.

"It will be a mere formality," he said. "But you understand, it is necessary for my report."

"As you please."

The Count gave way grudgingly. He made a short, foreign bow and left the dining-car.

Poirot reached out a hand to a passport. It set out the Count's name and titles. He passed on to the further information—*accompanied by wife*. Christian name Elena Maria; maiden name Goldenberg; age twenty. A spot of grease had been dropped some time by a careless official on it.

"A diplomatic passport," said M. Bouc. "We must be careful, my friend, to give no offence. These people can have nothing to do with the murder."

"Be easy, *mon vieux*, I will be most tactful. A mere formality."

His voice dropped as the Countess Andrenyi entered the dining-car. She looked timid and extremely charming.

"You wish to see me, Messieurs?"

"A mere formality, Madame la Comtesse." Poirot rose gallantly, bowed her into the seat opposite him. "It is only to ask you if you saw or heard anything last night that may throw light upon this matter."

"Nothing at all, Monsieur. I was asleep."

"You did not hear, for instance, a commotion going on in the compartment next to yours? The American lady who occupies it had quite an attack of hysterics and rang for the conductor."

"I heard nothing, Monsieur. You see, I had taken a sleeping draught."

"Ah! I comprehend. Well, I need not detain you further." Then, as she rose swiftly, "Just one little minute—these particulars, your maiden name, age and so on, they are correct?"

"Quite correct, Monsieur."

"Perhaps you will sign this memorandum to that effect, then."

She signed quickly, a graceful slanting handwriting.

Elena Andrenyi.

"Did you accompany your husband to America, Madame?"

"No, Monsieur." She smiled, flushed a little. "We were not married then; we have only been married a year."

"Ah yes, thank you, Madame. By the way, does your husband smoke?"

She stared at him as she stood poised for departure.

"Yes."

"A pipe?"

"No. Cigarettes and cigars."

"Ah! Thank you."

She lingered; her eyes watched him curiously. Lovely eyes they were, dark and almond shaped, with very long black lashes that swept the exquisite pallor of her cheeks. Her lips, very scarlet, in the foreign fashion, were parted just a little. She looked exotic and beautiful.

"Why did you ask me that?"

"Madame," Poirot waved an airy hand, "detectives have to ask all sorts of questions. For instance, perhaps you will tell me the colour of your dressing-gown?"

She stared at him. Then she laughed.

"It is corn-coloured chiffon. Is that really important?"

"Very important, Madame."

She asked curiously:

"Are you really a detective, then?"

"At your service, Madame."

"I thought there were no detectives on the train when it passed through Yugo-Slavia—not until one got to Italy."

"I am not a Yugo-Slavian detective, Madame. I am an international detective."

"You belong to the League of Nations?"

"I belong to the world, Madame," said Poirot dramatically. He went on, "I work mainly in London. You speak English?" he added in that language.

"I speak a leetle, yes."

Her accent was charming.

Poirot bowed once more.

"We will not detain you further, Madame. You see, it was not so very terrible."

She smiled, inclined her head and departed.

"*Elle est jolie femme*," said M. Bouc appreciatively.

He sighed.

"Well, that did not advance us much."

"No," said Poirot. "Two people who saw nothing and heard nothing."

"Shall we now see the Italian?"

Poirot did not reply for a moment. He was studying a grease spot on a Hungarian diplomatic passport.

8. *The Evidence of Colonel Arbuthnot*

Poirot roused himself with a slight start. His eyes twinkled a little as they met the eager ones of M. Bouc.

"Ah! my dear old friend," he said. "You see, I have become what they call the snob! The first-class, I feel it should be attended to before the second-class. Next, I think, we will interview the good-looking Colonel Arbuthnot."

Finding the Colonel's French to be of a severely limited description, Poirot conducted his interrogation in English.

Arbuthnot's name, age, home address and exact military standing were all ascertained. Poirot proceeded:

"It is that you come home from India on what is called the leave—what we call *en permission?*"

Colonel Arbuthnot, uninterested in what a pack of foreigners called anything, replied with true British brevity:

"Yes."

"But you do not come home on the P. & O. boat?"

"No."

"Why not?"

"I chose to come by the overland route for reasons of my own."

"And that," his manner seemed to say, "is one for you, you interfering little jackanapes."

"You came straight through from India?"

The Colonel replied dryly:

"I stopped for one night to see Ur of the Chaldees and for three days in Baghdad with the A.O.C., who happens to be an old friend of mine."

"You stopped three days in Baghdad. I understand that the young English lady, Miss Debenham, also comes from Baghdad. Perhaps you met her there?"

"No, I did not. I first met Miss Debenham when she and I shared the railway convoy car from Kirkuk to Nissibin."

Poirot leaned forward. He became persuasive and a little more foreign than he need have been.

"Monsieur, I am about to appeal to you. You and Miss Debenham are the only two English people on the train. It is necessary that I should ask you each your opinion of the other."

"Highly irregular," said Colonel Arbuthnot coldly.

"Not so. You see, this crime, it was most probably committed by a woman. The man was stabbed no less than twelve times. Even the *chef de train* said at once, 'It is a woman.' Well, then, what is my first task? To give all the women travelling on the Stamboul-Calais coach what Americans call the 'once over.' But to judge of an Englishwoman is difficult. They are very reserved, the English. So I appeal to you, Monsieur, in the interests of justice. What sort of a person is this Miss Debenham? What do you know about her?"

"Miss Debenham," said the Colonel with some warmth, "is a lady."

"Ah!" said Poirot with every appearance of being much gratified.

"So you do not think that she is likely to be implicated in this crime?"

"The idea is absurd," said Arbuthnot. "The man was a perfect stranger—she had never seen him before."

"Did she tell you so?"

"She did. She commented at once upon his somewhat unpleasant appearance. If a woman *is* concerned, as you seem to think (to my mind without any evidence but mere assumption), I can assure you that Miss Debenham could not possibly be indicated."

"You feel warmly in the matter," said Poirot with a smile.

Colonel Arbuthnot gave him a cold stare.

"I really don't know what you mean," he said.

The stare seemed to abash Poirot. He dropped his eyes and began fiddling with the papers in front of him.

"All this is by the way," he said. "Let us be practical and come to facts. This crime, we have reason to believe, took place at a quarter-past one last night. It is part of the necessary routine to ask everyone on the train what he or she was doing at that time."

"Quite so. At a quarter-past one, to the best of my belief, I was talking to the young American fellow—secretary to the dead man."

"Ah! Were you in his compartment, or was he in yours?"

"I was in his."

"That is the young man of the name of MacQueen?"

"Yes."

"He was a friend or acquaintance of yours?"

"No, I never saw him before this journey. We fell into casual conversation yesterday and both became interested. I don't as a rule like Americans—haven't any use for 'em——"

Poirot smiled, remembering MacQueen's strictures on "Britishers."

"——But I liked this young fellow. He'd got hold of some tomfool idiotic ideas about the situation in India; that's the worst of Americans—they're so sentimental and idealistic. Well, he was interested in what I had to tell him. I've had nearly thirty years experience of the country. And I was interested in what he had to tell me about the financial situation in America. Then we got down to world politics in general. I was quite surprised to look at my watch and find it was a quarter to two."

"That is the time you broke up this conversation?"

"Yes."

"What did you do then?"

"Walked along to my own compartment and turned in."

"Your bed was made up ready?"

"Yes."

"That is the compartment—let me see—No. 15—the one next but one to the end away from the dining-car?"

"Yes."

"Where was the conductor when you went to your compartment?"

"Sitting at the end at a little table. As a matter of fact, MacQueen called him just as I went to my own compartment."

"Why did he call him?"

"To make up his bed, I suppose. The compartment hadn't been made up for the night."

"Now, Colonel Arbuthnot, I want you to think carefully. During the time you were talking to Mr. MacQueen did anyone pass along the corridor outside the door?"

"A good many people, I should think. I wasn't paying attention."

"Ah! but I am referring to—let us say the last hour and a half of your conversation. You got out at Vincovci, didn't you?"

"Yes, but only for about a minute. There was a blizzard on. The cold was something frightful. Made one quite thankful to get back to the fug, though as a rule I think the way these trains are overheated is something scandalous."

M. Bouc sighed.

"It is very difficult to please everybody," he said. "The English, they open everything—then others, they come along and shut everything. It is very difficult."

Neither Poirot nor Colonel Arbuthnot paid any attention to him.

"Now, Monsieur, cast your mind back," said Poirot encouragingly. "It was cold outside. You have returned to the train. You sit down again, you smoke—perhaps a cigarette, perhaps a pipe——"

He paused for the fraction of a second.

"A pipe for me. MacQueen smoked cigarettes."

"The train starts again. You smoke your pipe. You discuss the state of Europe—of the world. It is late now. Most people have retired for the night. Does anyone pass the door—think?"

Arbuthnot frowned in the effort of remembrance.

"Difficult to say," he said. "You see, I wasn't paying any attention."

"But you have the soldier's observation for detail. You notice without noticing, so to speak."

The Colonel thought again, but shook his head.

"I couldn't say. I don't remember anyone passing except the conductor. Wait a minute—and there was a woman, I think."

"You saw her? Was she old—young?"

"Didn't see her. Wasn't looking that way. Just a rustle and a sort of smell of scent."

"Scent? A *good* scent?"

"Well, rather fruity, if you know what I mean. I mean you'd smell it a hundred yards away. But mind you," the Colonel went on hastily, "this may have been earlier in the evening. You see, as you said just now, it was just one of those things you notice without noticing, so to speak. Some time that evening I said to myself, 'Woman—scent—got it on pretty thick.' But *when* it was I can't be sure, except that—why, yes, it must have been after Vincovci."

"Why?"

"Because I remember—sniffing, you know—just when I was talking about the utter washout Stalin's Five Year Plan was turning out. I know the idea—woman—brought the idea of the position of women in Russia into my mind. And I know we hadn't got on to Russia until pretty near the end of our talk."

"You can't pin it down more definitely than that?"

"N-no. It must have been roughly within the last half-hour."

"It was after the train had stopped?"

The other nodded.

"Yes, I'm almost sure it was."

"Did you ever know a Colonel Armstrong?"

"Armstrong—Armstrong—I've known two or three Armstrongs. There was Tommy Armstrong in the 60th—you don't mean him? And Selby Armstrong—he was killed on the Somme."

"I mean the Colonel Armstrong who married an American wife and whose only child was kidnapped and killed."

"Ah, yes, I remember reading about that—shocking affair. I don't think I actually ever came across the fellow, though, of course, I knew of him. Toby Armstrong. Nice fellow. Everybody liked him. He had a very distinguished career. Got the V.C."

"The man who was killed last night was the man responsible for the murder of Colonel Armstrong's child."

Arbuthnot's face grew rather grim.

"Then in my opinion the swine deserved what he got. Though I would have preferred to have seen him properly hanged—or electrocuted, I suppose, over there."

"In fact, Colonel Arbuthnot, you prefer law and order to private vengeance?"

"Well, you can't go about having blood feuds and stabbing each other like Corsicans or the Mafia," said the Colonel. "Say what you like, trial by jury is a sound system."

Poirot looked at him thoughtfully for a minute or two.

"Yes," he said. "I am sure that would be your view. Well, Colonel

Arbuthnot, I do not think there is anything more I have to ask you. There is nothing you yourself can recall last night that in any way struck you—or shall we say strikes you now looking back—as suspicious?"

Arbuthnot considered for a moment or two.

"No," he said. "Nothing at all. Unless——" He hesitated.

"But yes, continue, I pray of you."

"Well, it's nothing really," said the Colonel slowly. "But you said *anything*."

"Yes, yes. Go on."

"Oh, it's nothing. A mere detail. But as I got back to my compartment I noticed that the door of the one beyond mine—the end one, you know——"

"Yes, No. 16."

"Well, the door of it was not quite closed. And the fellow inside peered out in a furtive sort of way. Then he pulled the door to quickly. Of course, I know there's nothing in that—but it just struck me as a bit odd. I mean, it's quite usual to open a door and stick your head out if you want to see anything. But it was the furtive way he did it that caught my attention."

"Ye-es," said Poirot doubtfully.

"I told you there was nothing to it," said Arbuthnot apologetically. "But you know what it is—early hours of the morning—everything very still—the thing had a sinister look—like a detective story. All nonsense, really."

He rose.

"Well, if you don't want me any more—"

"Thank you, Colonel Arbuthnot, there is nothing else."

The soldier hesitated for a minute. His first natural distaste for being questioned by "foreigners" had evaporated.

"About Miss Debenham," he said rather awkwardly. "You can take it from me that she's all right. She's a *pukka sahib*."

Flushing a little, he withdrew.

"What," asked Dr. Constantine with interest, "does a *pukka sahib* mean?"

"It means," said Poirot, "that Miss Debenham's father and brothers were at the same kind of school as Colonel Arbuthnot."

"Oh!" said Dr. Constantine, disappointed. "Then it has nothing to do with the crime at all."

"Exactly," said Poirot.

He fell into a reverie, beating a light tattoo on the table. Then he looked up.

"Colonel Arbuthnot smokes a pipe," he said. "In the compartment of M. Ratchett I found a pipe-cleaner. M. Ratchett smoked only cigars."

"You think——?"

"He is the only man so far who admits to smoking a pipe. And he knew of Colonel Armstrong—perhaps actually did know him though he won't admit it."

"So you think it possible——?"

Poirot shook his head violently.

"That is just it—it is *im*possible—quite impossible—that an honourable, slightly stupid, upright Englishman should stab an enemy twelve times with a knife! Do you not feel, my friends, how impossible it is?"

"That is the psychology," said M. Bouc.

"And one must respect the psychology. This crime has a signature and it is certainly not the signature of Colonel Arbuthnot. But now to our next interview."

This time M. Bouc did not mention the Italian. But he thought of him.

9. The Evidence of Mr. Hardman

The last of the first-class passengers to be interviewed—Mr. Hardman—was the big flamboyant American who had shared a table with the Italian and the valet.

He wore a somewhat loud check suit, a pink shirt, a flashy tiepin, and was rolling something round his tongue as he entered the dining-car. He had a big, fleshy, coarse-featured face, with a good-humoured expression.

"Morning, gentlemen," he said. "What can I do for you?"

"You have heard of this murder, Mr.—er—Hardman?"

"Sure."

He shifted the chewing gum deftly.

"We are of necessity interviewing all the passengers on the train."

"That's all right by me. Guess that's the only way to tackle the job."

Poirot consulted the passport lying in front of him.

"You are Cyrus Bethman Hardman, United States subject, forty-one years of age, travelling salesman for typewriting ribbons?"

"O.K., that's me."

"You are travelling from Stamboul to Paris?"

"That's so."

"Reason?"

"Business."

"Do you always travel first-class, Mr. Hardman?"

"Yes, sir. The firm pays my travelling expenses."

He winked.

"Now, Mr. Hardman, we come to the events of last night."

The American nodded.

"What can you tell us about the matter?"

"Exactly nothing at all."

"Ah, that is a pity. Perhaps, Mr. Hardman, you will tell us exactly what you did last night, from dinner onwards?"

For the first time the American did not seem ready with his reply. At last he said:

"Excuse me, gentlemen, but just who are you? Put me wise."

"This is M. Bouc, a director of the Compagnie des Wagons Lits. This gentleman is the doctor who examined the body."

"And you yourself?"

"I am Hercule Poirot. I am engaged by the company to investigate this matter."

"I've heard of you," said Mr. Hardman. He reflected a minute or two longer. "Guess I'd better come clean."

"It will certainly be advisable for you to tell us all you know," said Poirot dryly.

"You'd have said a mouthful if there was anything I *did* know. But I don't. I know nothing at all—just as I said. But I *ought* to know something. That's what makes me sore. I *ought* to."

"Please explain, Mr. Hardman."

Mr. Hardman sighed, removed the chewing gum, and dived into a pocket. At the same time his whole personality seemed to undergo a change. He became less of a stage character and more of a real person. The resonant nasal tones of his voice became modified.

"That passport's a bit of bluff," he said. "That's who I really am."

Poirot scrutinised the card flipped across to him. M. Bouc peered over his shoulder.

MR. CYRUS B. HARDMAN,
McNeil's Detective Agency
New York

Poirot knew the name. It was one of the best known and most reputable private detective agencies in New York.

"Now, Mr. Hardman," he said, "let us hear the meaning of this."

"Sure. Things came about this way. I'd come over to Europe trailing a couple of crooks—nothing to do with this business. The chase ended in Stamboul. I wired the Chief and got his instructions to return, and I would have been making my tracks back to little old New York when I got this."

He pushed across a letter.

The heading at the top was the Tokatlian Hotel.

Dear Sir,—You have been pointed out to me as an operative of the McNeil Detective Agency. Kindly report to my suite at four o'clock this afternoon.

It was signed "S. E. Ratchett."

"*Eh bien?*"

"I reported at the time stated and Mr. Ratchett put me wise to the situation. He showed me a couple of letters he'd got."

"He was alarmed?"

"Pretended not to be, but he was rattled all right. He put up a proposition to me. I was to travel by the same train as he did to Parrus and see that nobody got him. Well, gentlemen, I *did* travel by the same train and, in spite of me, somebody *did* get him. I certainly feel sore about it. It doesn't look any too good for me."

"Did he give you any indication of the line you were to take?"

"Sure. He had it all taped out. It was his idea that I should travel in the compartment alongside his—well, that was blown upon straight away. The only place I could get was berth No. 16, and I had a bit of a job getting that. I guess the conductor likes to keep that compartment up his sleeve. But that's neither here nor there. When I looked all round the situation, it seemed to me that No. 16 was a pretty good strategic position. There was only the dining-car in front of the Stamboul sleeping-car, the door on to the platform at the front end was barred at night. The only way a thug could come was through the rear end door to the platform or along the train from the rear—in either case he'd have to pass right by my compartment."

"You had no idea, I suppose, of the identity of the possible assailant."

"Well, I knew what he looked like. Mr. Ratchett described him to me."

"What?"

All three men leaned forward eagerly.

Hardman went on:

"A small man, dark, with a womanish kind of voice—that's what the old man said. Said, too, that he didn't think it would be the first night out. More likely the second or third."

"He knew something," said M. Bouc.

"He certainly knew more than he told his secretary," said Poirot thoughtfully. "Did he tell you anything about this enemy of his? Did he, for instance, say *why* his life was threatened?"

"No, he was kinder reticent about that part of it. Just said the fellow was out for his blood and meant to get it."

"A small man—dark—with a womanish voice," said Poirot thoughtfully.

Then, fixing a sharp glance on Hardman, he said:

"You know who he really was, of course?"

"Which, mister?"

"Ratchett. You recognised him?"

"I don't get you."

"Ratchett was Cassetti, the Armstrong murderer."

Mr. Hardman gave way to a prolonged whistle.

"That certainly is some surprise!" he said. "Yes, *sir!* No, I didn't recognise him. I was away out West when that case came on. I suppose I saw photos of him in the papers, but I wouldn't recognise my own mother when a press photographer had done with her. Well, I don't doubt that a few people had it in for Cassetti all right."

"Do you know of anyone connected with the Armstrong case who answers to that description—small, dark, womanish voice?"

Hardman reflected a minute or two.

"It's hard to say. Pretty nearly everyone to do with that case is dead."

"There was the girl who threw herself out of the window, remember."

"Sure. That's a good point, that. She was a foreigner of some kind. Maybe she had some wop relations. But you've got to remember that there were other cases besides the Armstrong case. Cassetti had been running this kidnapping stunt some time. You can't concentrate on that only."

"*Ah,* but we have reason to believe that this crime is connected with the Armstrong case."

Mr. Hardman cocked an inquiring eye. Poirot did not respond. The American shook his head.

"I can't call to mind anybody answering that description in the Armstrong case," he said slowly. "But of course I wasn't in it and didn't know much about it."

"Well, continue your narrative, M. Hardman."

"There's very little to tell. I got my sleep in the daytime and stayed awake on the watch at night. Nothing suspicious happened the first night. Last night was the same, as far as I was concerned. I had my door a little ajar and watched. No stranger passed."

"You are sure of that, M. Hardman?"

"I'm plumb certain. Nobody got on that train from outside and nobody came along the train from the rear carriages. I'll take my oath on that."

"Could you see the conductor from your position?"

"Sure. He sits on that little seat almost flush with my door."

"Did he leave that seat at all after the train stopped at Vincovci?"

"That was the last station? Why, yes, he answered a couple of bells—that would be just after the train came to a halt for good. Then, after that, he went past me into the rear coach—was there about a quarter of an hour. There was a bell ringing like mad and he came back running. I stepped out into the corridor to see what it was all about—felt a mite nervous, you understand—but it was only the American dame. She was raising hell about something or other. I grinned. Then he went on to another compartment and came back and got a bottle of mineral water for someone. After that he settled down in his seat till he went up to the far end to make somebody's bed up. I don't think he stirred after that until about five o'clock this morning."

"Did he doze off at all?"

"That I can't say. He may have done."

Poirot nodded. Automatically his hands straightened the papers on the table. He picked up the official card once more.

"Be so good as just to initial this," he said.

The other complied.

"There is no one, I suppose, who can confirm your story of your identity, M. Hardman?"

"On this train? Well, not exactly. Unless it might be young Mac-Queen. I know him well enough—seen him in his father's office in New York—but that's not to say he'll remember me from a crowd of other operatives. No, Mr. Poirot, you'll have to wait and cable New York when the snow lets up. But it's O.K., I'm not telling the tale. Well, so long, gentlemen. Pleased to have met you, Mr. Poirot."

Poirot proffered his cigarette case.

"But perhaps you prefer a pipe?"

"Not me."

He helped himself, then strode briskly off.

The three men looked at each other.

"You think he is genuine?" asked Dr. Constantine.

"Yes, yes. I know the type. Besides, it is a story that would be very easily disproved."

"He has given us a piece of very interesting evidence," said M. Bouc.

"Yes, indeed."

"A small man, dark, with a high-pitched voice," said M. Bouc thoughtfully.

"A description which applies to no one on the train," said Poirot.

10. The Evidence of the Italian

"And now," said Poirot with a twinkle in his eye, "we will delight the heart of M. Bouc and see the Italian."

Antonio Foscarelli came into the dining-car with a swift, cat-like tread. His face beamed. It was a typical Italian face, sunny looking and swarthy.

He spoke French well and fluently, with only a slight accent.

"Your name is Antonio Foscarelli?"

"Yes, Monsieur."

"You are, I see, a naturalised American subject?"

The American grinned.

"Yes, Monsieur. It is better for my business."

"You are an agent for Ford motor cars?"

"Yes, you see——"

A voluble exposition followed. At the end of it, anything that the three men did not know about Foscarelli's business methods, his journeys, his income, and his opinion of the United States and most European countries seemed a negligible factor. This was not a man who had to have information dragged from him. It gushed out.

His good-natured childish face beamed with satisfaction as, with a last eloquent gesture, he paused and wiped his forehead with a handkerchief.

"So you see," he said, "I do big business. I am up to date. I understand salesmanship!"

"You have been in the United States, then, for the last ten years on and off?"

"Yes, Monsieur. Ah! well do I remember the day I first took the boat—to go to America, so far away! My mother, my little sister——"

Poirot cut short the flood of reminiscence.

"During your sojourn in the United States did you ever come across the deceased?"

"Never. But I know the type. Oh, yes." He snapped his fingers expressively. "It is very respectable, very well dressed, but underneath it is all wrong. Out of my experience I should say he was the big crook. I give you my opinion for what it is worth."

"Your opinion is quite right," said Poirot dryly. "Ratchett was Cassetti, the kidnapper."

"What did I tell you? I have learned to be very acute—to read the face. It is necessary. Only in America do they teach you the proper way to sell."

"You remember the Armstrong case?"

"I do not quite remember. The name, yes? It was a little girl—a baby —was it not?"

"Yes, a very tragic affair."

The Italian seemed the first person to demur to this view.

"Ah, well, these things they happen," he said philosophically, "in a great civilisation such as America——"

Poirot cut him short.

"Did you ever come across any members of the Armstrong family?"

"No, I do not think so. It is difficult to say. I will give you some figures. Last year alone I sold——"

"Monsieur, pray confine yourself to the point."

The Italian's hands flung themselves out in a gesture of apology.

"A thousand pardons."

"Tell me, if you please, your exact movements last night from dinner onwards."

"With pleasure. I stay here as long as I can. It is more amusing. I talk to the American gentleman at my table. He sells typewriter ribbons. Then I go back to my compartment. It is empty. The miserable John Bull who shares it with me is away attending to his master. At last he comes back—very long face as usual. He will not talk—says yes and no. A miserable race, the English—not sympathetic. He sits in the corner, very stiff, reading a book. Then the conductor comes and makes our beds."

"Nos. 4 and 5," murmured Poirot.

"Exactly—the end compartment. Mine is the upper berth. I get up there. I smoke and read. The little Englishman has, I think, the toothache. He gets out a little bottle of stuff that smells very strong. He lies in bed and groans. Presently I sleep. Whenever I wake I hear him groaning."

"Do you know if he left the carriage at all during the night?"

"I do not think so. That, I should hear. The light from the corridor—

one wakes up automatically thinking it is the Customs examination at some frontier."

"Did he ever speak of his master? Ever express any animus against him?"

"I tell you he did not speak. He was not sympathetic. A fish."

"You smoke, you say—a pipe, cigarettes, cigars?"

"Cigarettes only."

Poirot proffered him one which he accepted.

"Have you ever been in Chicago?" inquired M. Bouc.

"Oh, yes—a fine city—but I know best New York, Washington, Detroit. You have been to the States? No? You should go, it——"

Poirot pushed a sheet of paper across to him.

"If you will sign this, and put your permanent address, please."

The Italian wrote with a flourish. Then he rose—his smile was as engaging as ever.

"That is all? You do not require me further? Good-day to you, Messieurs. I wish we could get out of the snow. I have an appointment in Milan——" He shook his head sadly. "I shall lose the business."

He departed.

Poirot looked at his friend.

"He has been a long time in America," said M. Bouc, "and he is an Italian, and Italians use the knife! And they are great liars! I do not like Italians."

"*Ça se voit,*" said Poirot with a smile. "Well, it may be that you are right, but I will point out to you, my friend, that there is absolutely no evidence against the man."

"And what about the psychology? Do not Italians stab?"

"Assuredly," said Poirot. "Especially in the heat of a quarrel. But this—this is a different kind of crime. I have the little idea, my friend, that this is a crime very carefully planned and staged. It is a far-sighted, long-headed crime. It is not—how shall I express it?—a *Latin* crime. It is a crime that shows traces of a cool, resourceful, deliberate brain—I think an Anglo-Saxon brain."

He picked up the last two passports.

"Let us now," he said, "see Miss Mary Debenham."

11. The Evidence of Miss Debenham

When Mary Debenham entered the dining-car she confirmed Poirot's previous estimate of her.

Very neatly dressed in a little black suit with a French grey shirt, the smooth waves of her dark head were neat and unruffled. Her manner was as calm and unruffled as her hair.

She sat down opposite Poirot and M. Bouc and looked at them inquiringly.

"Your name is Mary Hermione Debenham, and you are twenty-six years of age?" began Poirot.

"Yes."

"English?"

"Yes."

"Will you be so kind, Mademoiselle, as to write down your permanent address on this piece of paper?"

She complied. Her writing was clear and legible.

"And now, Mademoiselle, what have you to tell us of the affair last night?"

"I am afraid I have nothing to tell you. I went to bed and slept."

"Does it distress you very much, Mademoiselle, that a crime has been committed on this train?"

The question was clearly unexpected. Her grey eyes widened a little.

"I don't quite understand you."

"It was a perfectly simple question that I asked you, Mademoiselle. I will repeat it. Are you very much distressed that a crime should have been committed on this train?"

"I have not really thought about it from that point of view. No, I cannot say that I am at all distressed."

"A crime—it is all in the day's work to you, eh?"

"It is naturally an unpleasant thing to have happen," said Mary Debenham quietly.

"You are very Anglo-Saxon, Mademoiselle. *Vous n'éprouvez pas d'emotion.*"

She smiled a little.

"I am afraid I cannot have hysterics to prove my sensibility. After all, people die every day."

"They die, yes. But murder is a little more rare."

"Oh, certainly."

"You were not acquainted with the dead man?"

"I saw him for the first time when lunching here yesterday."

"And how did he strike you?"

"I hardly noticed him."

"He did not impress you as an evil personality?"

She shrugged her shoulders slightly.

"Really, I cannot say I thought about it."

Poirot looked at her keenly.

"You are, I think, a little bit contemptuous of the way I prosecute my inquiries," he said with a twinkle. "Not so, you think, would an English inquiry be conducted. There everything would be cut and dried—it would be all kept to the facts—a well-ordered business. But I, Mademoiselle, have my little originalities. I look first at my witness, I sum up his or her character, and I frame my questions accordingly. Just a little minute ago I am asking questions of a gentleman who wants to tell me all his ideas on every subject. Well, him I keep strictly to the point. I want him to answer yes or no, this or that. And then you come. I see at once that you will be orderly and methodical. You will confine yourself to the matter in hand. Your answers will be brief and to the point. And because, Mademoiselle, human nature is perverse, I ask of you quite different questions. I ask what you *feel,* what you *thought.* It does not please you this method?"

"If you will forgive my saying so, it seems somewhat of a waste of time. Whether or not I liked Mr. Ratchett's face does not seem likely to be helpful in finding out who killed him."

"Do you know who the man Ratchett really was, Mademoiselle?"

She nodded.

"Mrs. Hubbard has been telling everyone."

"And what do you think of the Armstrong affair?"

"It was quite abominable," said the girl crisply.

Poirot looked at her thoughtfully.

"You are travelling from Baghdad, I believe, Miss Debenham?"

"Yes."

"To London?"

"Yes."

"What have you been doing in Baghdad?"

"I have been acting as governess to two children."

"Are you returning to your post after your holiday?"

"I am not sure."

"Why is that?"

"Baghdad is rather out of things. I think I should prefer a post in London if I can hear of a suitable one."

"I see. I thought, perhaps, you might be going to be married."

Miss Debenham did not reply. She raised her eyes and looked Poirot full in the face. The glance said plainly, "You are impertinent."

"What is your opinion of the lady who shares your compartment—Miss Ohlsson?"

"She seems a pleasant, simple creature."

"What colour is her dressing-gown?"

Mary Debenham stared.

"A kind of brownish colour—natural wool."

"Ah! I may mention without indiscretion, I hope, that I noticed the colour of your dressing-gown on the way from Aleppo to Stamboul. A pale mauve, I believe."

"Yes, that is right."

"Have you any other dressing-gown, Mademoiselle? A scarlet dressing-gown, for example?"

"No, that is not mine."

Poirot leant forward. He was like a cat pouncing on a mouse.

"Whose, then?"

The girl drew back a little, startled.

"I don't know. What do you mean?"

"You do not say, 'No, I have no such thing.' You say, 'That is not mine'—meaning that such a thing *does* belong to someone else."

She nodded.

"Somebody else on this train?"

"Yes."

"Whose is it?"

"I told you just now. I don't know. I woke up this morning about five o'clock with the feeling that the train had been standing still for a long time. I opened the door and looked out into the corridor, thinking we might be at a station. I saw someone in a scarlet kimono some way down the corridor."

"And you don't know who it was? Was she fair or dark or grey-haired?"

"I can't say. She had on a shingle cap and I only saw the back of her head."

"And in build?"

"Tallish and slim, I should judge, but it's difficult to say. The kimono was embroidered with dragons."

"Yes, yes, that is right, dragons."

He was silent a minute. He murmured to himself:

"I cannot understand. I cannot understand. None of this makes sense."

Then, looking up, he said:

"I need not keep you further, Mademoiselle."

"Oh!" She seemed rather taken aback, but rose promptly.

In the doorway, however, she hesitated a minute and then came back.

"The Swedish lady—Miss Ohlsson, is it?—seems rather worried. She says you told her she was the last person to see this man alive. She thinks, I believe, that you suspect her on that account. Can't I tell her that she has made a mistake? Really, you know, she is the kind of creature who wouldn't hurt a fly."

She smiled a little as she spoke.

"What time was it that she went to fetch the aspirin from Mrs. Hubbard?"

"Just after half-past ten."

"She was away—how long?"

"About five minutes."

"Did she leave the compartment again during the night?"

"No."

Poirot turned to the doctor.

"Could Ratchett have been killed as early as that?"

The doctor shook his head.

"Then I think you can reassure your friend, Mademoiselle."

"Thank you." She smiled suddenly at him, a smile that invited sympathy. "She's like a sheep, you know. She gets anxious and bleats."

She turned and went out.

12. The Evidence of the German Lady's-Maid

M. Bouc was looking at his friend curiously.

"I do not quite understand you, *mon vieux*. You were trying to do—what?"

"I was searching for a flaw, my friend."

"A flaw?"

"Yes—in the armour of a young lady's self-possession. I wished to shake her *sang-froid*. Did I succeed? I do not know. But I know this—she did not expect me to tackle the matter as I did."

"You suspect her," said M. Bouc slowly. "But why? She seems a very charming young lady—the last person in the world to be mixed up in a crime of this kind."

"I agree," said Constantine. "She is cold. She has not emotions. She would not stab a man; she would sue him in the law courts."

Poirot sighed.

"You must, both of you, get rid of your obsession that this is an unpremeditated and sudden crime. As for the reason why I suspect Miss Debenham, there are two. One is because of something that I overheard, and that you do not as yet know."

He retailed to them the curious interchange of phrases he had overheard on the journey from Aleppo.

"That is curious, certainly," said M. Bouc when he had finished. "It needs explaining. If it means what you suspect it means, then they are both of them in it together—she and the stiff Englishman."

Poirot nodded.

"And that is just what is not borne out by the facts," he said. "See you, if they were both in this together, what should we expect to find—that each of them would provide an alibi for the other. Is not that so? But no—that does not happen. Miss Debenham's alibi is provided by a Swedish woman whom she has never seen before, and Colonel Arbuthnot's alibi is vouched for by MacQueen, the dead man's secretary. No, that solution of the puzzle is too easy."

"You said there was another reason for your suspicions of her," M. Bouc reminded him.

Poirot smiled.

"Ah! but that is only psychological. I ask myself, is it possible for Miss Debenham to have planned this crime? Behind this business, I am convinced, there is a cool, intelligent, resourceful brain. Miss Debenham answers to that description."

M. Bouc shook his head.

"I think you are wrong, my friend. I do not see that young English girl as a criminal."

"Ah, well," said Poirot, picking up the last passport, "to the final name on our list. Hildegarde Schmidt, lady's-maid."

Summoned by the attendant, Hildegarde Schmidt came into the restaurant-car and stood waiting respectfully.

Poirot motioned her to sit down.

She did so, folding her hands and waiting placidly till he questioned her. She seemed a placid creature altogether—eminently respectable—perhaps not over intelligent.

Poirot's methods with Hildegarde Schmidt were a complete contrast to his handling of Mary Debenham.

He was at his kindest and most genial, setting the woman at her ease. Then, having got her to write down her name and address, he slid gently into his questions.

The interview took place in German.

"We want to know as much as possible about what happened last night," he said. "We know that you cannot give us much information bearing on the crime itself, but you may have seen or heard something that, while conveying nothing to you, may be valuable to us. You understand?"

She did not seem to. Her broad, kindly face remained set in its expression of placid stupidity as she answered:

"I do not know anything, Monsieur."

"Well, for instance, you know that your mistress sent for you last night?"

"That, yes."

"Do you remember the time?"

"I do not, Monsieur. I was asleep, you see, when the attendant came and told me."

"Yes, yes. Was it usual for you to be sent for in this way?"

"It was not unusual, Monsieur. The gracious lady often required attention at night. She did not sleep well."

"*Eh bien*, then, you received the summons and you got up. Did you put on a dressing-gown?"

"No, Monsieur, I put on a few clothes. I would not like to go in to her Excellency in my dressing-gown."

"And yet it is a very nice dressing-gown—scarlet, is it not?"

She stared at him.

"It is a dark-blue flannel dressing-gown, Monsieur."

"Ah! continue. A little pleasantry on my part, that is all. So you went along to Madame la Princesse. And what did you do when you got there?"

"I gave her massage, Monsieur, and then I read aloud. I do not read aloud very well, but her Excellency says that is all the better. So it sends her better to sleep. When she became sleepy, Monsieur, she told me to go, so I closed the book and I returned to my own compartment."

"Do you know what time that was?"

"No, Monsieur."

"Well, how long had you been with Madame la Princesse?"

"About half an hour, Monsieur."

"Good, continue."

"First, I fetched her Excellency an extra rug from my compartment. It was very cold in spite of the heating. I arranged the rug over her and she wished me good-night. I poured her out some mineral water. Then I turned out the light and left her."

"And then?"

"There is nothing more, Monsieur. I returned to my carriage and went to sleep."

"And you met no one in the corridor?"

"No, Monsieur."

"You did not, for instance, see a lady in a scarlet kimono with dragons on it?"

Her mild eyes bulged at him.

"No, indeed, Monsieur. There was nobody about except the attendant. Everyone was asleep."

"But you did see the conductor?"

"Yes, Monsieur."

"What was he doing?"

"He came out of one of the compartments, Monsieur."

"What?" M. Bouc leaned forward. "Which one?"

Hildegarde Schmidt looked frightened again and Poirot cast a reproachful glance at his friend.

"Naturally," he said. "The conductor often has to answer bells at night. Do you remember which compartment it was?"

"It was about the middle of the coach, Monsieur. Two or three doors from Madame la Princesse."

"Ah! tell us, if you please, exactly where this was and what happened."

"He nearly ran into me, Monsieur. It was when I was returning from my compartment to that of the Princess with the rug."

"And he came out of a compartment and almost collided with you? In which direction was he going?"

"Towards me, Monsieur. He apologised and passed on down the corridor towards the dining-car. A bell began ringing, but I do not think he answered it."

She paused and then said:

"I do not understand. How is it——?"

Poirot spoke reassuringly.

"It is just a question of times," he said. "All a matter of routine. This poor conductor, he seems to have had a busy night—first waking you and then answering bells."

"It was not the same conductor who woke me, Monsieur. It was another one."

"Ah, another one! Had you seen him before?"

"No, Monsieur."

"Ah! Do you think you would recognise him if you saw him?"

"I think so, Monsieur."

Poirot murmured something in M. Bouc's ear. The latter got up and went to the door to give an order.

Poirot was continuing his questions in an easy friendly manner.

"Have you ever been to America, Frau Schmidt?"

"Never, Monsieur. It must be a fine country."

"You have heard, perhaps, of who this man who was killed really was—that he was responsible for the death of a little child."

"Yes, I have heard, Monsieur. It was abominable—wicked. The good

God should not allow such things. We are not so wicked as that in Germany."

Tears had come into the woman's eyes. Her strong motherly soul was moved.

"It was an abominable crime," said Poirot gravely.

He drew a scrap of cambric from his pocket and handed it to her.

"Is this your handkerchief, Frau Schmidt?"

There was a moment's silence as the woman examined it. She looked up after a minute. The colour had mounted a little in her face.

"Ah! no, indeed. It is not mine, Monsieur."

"It has the initial H, you see. That is why I thought it was yours."

"Ah! Monsieur, it is a lady's handkerchief, that. A very expensive handkerchief. Embroidered by hand. It comes from Paris, I should say."

"It is not yours and you do not know whose it is?"

"I? Oh, no, Monsieur."

Of the three listening, only Poirot caught the nuance of hesitation in the reply.

M. Bouc whispered in his ear. Poirot nodded and said to the woman:

"The three sleeping-car attendants are coming in. Will you be so kind as to tell me which is the one you met last night as you were going with the rug to the Princess?"

The three men entered. Pierre Michel, the big blond conductor of the Athens-Paris coach, and the stout burly conductor of the Bucharest one.

Hildegarde Schmidt looked at them and immediately shook her head.

"No, Monsieur," she said. "None of these is the man I saw last night."

"But these are the only conductors on the train. You must be mistaken."

"I am quite sure, Monsieur. These are all tall, big men. The one I saw was small and dark. He had a little moustache. His voice when he said 'Pardon' was weak like a woman's. Indeed, I remember him very well, Monsieur."

13. Summary of the Passengers' Evidence

"A small dark man with a womanish voice," said M. Bouc.

The three conductors and Hildegarde Schmidt had been dismissed. M. Bouc made a despairing gesture.

"But I understand nothing—but nothing of all this! The enemy that this Ratchett spoke of, he was then on the train after all? But where is he now? How can he have vanished into thin air? My head, it whirls. Say something, then, my friend, I implore you. Show me how the impossible can be possible!"

"It is a good phrase that," said Poirot. "The impossible cannot have happened, therefore the impossible must be possible in spite of appearances."

"Explain to me then, quickly, what actually happened on the train last night."

"I am not a magician, *mon cher*. I am, like you, a very puzzled man. This affair advances in a very strange manner."

"It does not advance at all. It stays where it was."

Poirot shook his head.

"No, that is not true. We are more advanced. We know certain things. We have heard the evidence of the passengers."

"And what has that told us? Nothing at all."

"I would not say that, my friend."

"I exaggerate, perhaps. The American, Hardman, and the German maid—yes, they have added something to our knowledge. That is to say, they have made the whole business more unintelligible than it was."

"No, no, no," said Poirot soothingly.

M. Bouc turned upon him.

"Speak, then, let us hear the wisdom of Hercule Poirot."

"Did I not tell you that I was, like you, a very puzzled man? But at least we can face our problem. We can arrange such facts as we have with order and method."

"Pray continue, Monsieur," said Dr. Constantine.

Poirot cleared his throat and straightened a piece of blotting-paper.

"Let us review the case as it stands at this moment. First, there are certain indisputable facts. This man Ratchett, or Cassetti, was stabbed in twelve places and died last night. That is fact one."

"I grant it to you—I grant it, *mon vieux*," said M. Bouc with a gesture of irony.

Hercule Poirot was not at all put out. He continued calmly:

"I will pass over for the moment certain rather peculiar appearances which Dr. Constantine and I have already discussed together. I will come to them presently. The next fact of importance, to my mind, is the *time* of the crime."

"That, again, is one of the few things we do know," said M. Bouc. "The crime was committed at a quarter-past one this morning. Everything goes to show that that was so."

"Not *everything*. You exaggerate. There is, certainly, a fair amount of evidence to support that view."

"I am glad you admit that at least."

Poirot went on calmly, unperturbed by the interruption.

"We have before us three possibilities:

"One: That the crime was committed, as you say, at a quarter-past one. This is supported by the evidence of the German woman, Hildegarde Schmidt. It agrees with the evidence of Dr. Constantine.

"Possibility two: The crime was committed later and the evidence of the watch was deliberately faked.

"Possibility three: The crime was committed earlier and the evidence faked for the same reason as above.

"Now, if we accept possibility one as the most likely to have occurred and the one supported by most evidence, we must also accept certain facts arising from it. To begin with, if the crime was committed at a quarter-past one, the murderer cannot have left the train, and the question arises: Where is he? And *who* is he?

"To begin with, let us examine the evidence carefully. We first hear of the existence of this man—the small dark man with a womanish voice —from the man Hardman. He says that Ratchett told him of this person and employed him to watch out for the man. There is no *evidence* to support this—we have only Hardman's word for it. Let us next examine the question: Is Hardman the person he pretends to be—an operative of a New York detective agency?

"What to my mind is so interesting in this case is that we have none of the facilities afforded to the police. We cannot investigate the bona fides of any of these people. We have to rely solely on deduction. That, to me, makes the matter very much more interesting. There is no routine work. It is a matter of the intellect. I ask myself, 'Can we accept Hardman's account of himself?' I make my decision and I answer, 'Yes.' I am of the opinion that we *can* accept Hardman's account of himself."

"You rely on the intuition—what the Americans call the hunch?" said Dr. Constantine.

"Not at all. I regard the probabilities. Hardman is travelling with a false passport—that will at once make him an object of suspicion. The first thing that the police will do when they do arrive upon the scene is to detain Hardman and cable as to whether his account of himself is true. In the case of many of the passengers, to establish their bona fides will be difficult; in most cases it will probably not be attempted, especially since there seems nothing in the way of suspicion attaching to them. But in Hardman's case it is simple. Either he is the person he represents himself to be or he is not. Therefore I say that all will prove to be in order."

"You acquit him of suspicion?"

"Not at all. You misunderstand me. For all I know, any American detective might have his own private reasons for wishing to murder Ratchett. No, what I am saying is that I think we *can* accept Hardman's own account of *himself*. This story, then, that he tells of Ratchett's seeking him out and employing him, is not unlikely and is most probably, though not of course certainly, true. If we are going to accept it as true, we must see if there is any confirmation of it. We find it in rather an unlikely place—in the evidence of Hildegarde Schmidt. Her description of the man she saw in Wagon Lit uniform tallies exactly. Is there any further confirmation of these two stories? There is. There is the button found in her compartment by Mrs. Hubbard. And there is also another corroborating statement which you may not have noticed."

"What is that?"

"The fact that both Colonel Arbuthnot and Hector MacQueen mention that the conductor passed their carriage. They attached no importance to the fact, but, Messieurs, *Pierre Michel has declared that he did not leave his seat except on certain specified occasions,* none of which would take him down to the far end of the coach past the compartment in which Arbuthnot and MacQueen were sitting.

"Therefore this story, the story of a small dark man with a womanish voice dressed in Wagon Lit uniform, rests on the testimony—direct or indirect—of four witnesses."

"One small point," said Dr. Constantine. "If Hildegarde Schmidt's story is true, how is it that the real conductor did not mention having seen her when he came to answer Mrs. Hubbard's bell?"

"That is explained, I think. When he arrived to answer Mrs. Hubbard, the maid was in with her mistress. When she finally returned to her own compartment, the conductor was in with Mrs. Hubbard."

M. Bouc had been waiting with difficulty until they had finished.

"Yes, yes, my friend," he said impatiently to Poirot. "But whilst I admire your caution, your method of advancing a step at a time, I submit that you have not yet touched the point at issue. We are all agreed that this person exists. The point is—*where did he go?*"

Poirot shook his head reprovingly.

"You are in error. You are inclined to put the cart before the horse. Before I ask myself, *'Where did this man vanish to?'* I ask myself, *'Did such a man really exist?'* Because, you see, if the man were an invention —a fabrication—how much easier to make him disappear! So I try to establish first that there really *is* such a flesh and blood person."

"And having arrived at the fact that there is—*eh bien*—where is he now?"

"There are only two answers to that, *mon cher*. Either he is still hidden on the train in a place of such extraordinary ingenuity that we cannot even think of it, or else he is, as one might say, *two persons*. That is, he is both himself—the man feared by M. Ratchett—and a passenger on the train so well disguised that M. Ratchett did not recognise him."

"It is an idea, that," said M. Bouc, his face lighting up. Then it clouded over again. "But there is one objection——"

Poirot took the words out of his mouth.

"The height of the man. It is that you would say? With the exception of M. Ratchett's valet, all the passengers are big men—the Italian, Colonel Arbuthnot, Hector MacQueen, Count Andrenyi. Well, that leaves us the valet—not a very likely supposition. But there is another possibility. Remember the 'womanish' voice. That gives us a choice of alternatives. The man may be disguised as a woman, or, alternatively, he may actually *be* a woman. A tall woman dressed in man's clothes would look small."

"But surely Ratchett would have known——"

"Perhaps he *did* know. Perhaps, already, this woman had attempted his life wearing men's clothes the better to accomplish her purpose. Ratchett may have guessed that she would use the same trick again, so he tells Hardman to look for a man. But he mentions, however, a womanish voice."

"It is a possibility," said M. Bouc. "But——"

"Listen, my friend, I think that I should now tell you of certain inconsistencies noticed by Dr. Constantine."

He retailed at length the conclusions that he and the doctor had arrived at together from the nature of the dead man's wounds. M. Bouc groaned and held his head again.

"I know," said Poirot sympathetically. "I know exactly how you feel. The head spins, does it not?"

"The whole thing is a fantasy," cried M. Bouc.

"Exactly. It is absurd—improbable—it cannot be. So I myself have said. And yet, my friend, *there it is!* One cannot escape from the facts."

"It is madness!"

"Is it not? It is so mad, my friend, that sometimes I am haunted by the sensation that really it must be very simple. . . .

"But that is only one of my 'little ideas'. . . ."

"Two murderers," groaned M. Bouc. "And on the Orient Express." The thought almost made him weep.

"And now let us make the fantasy more fantastic," said Poirot cheerfully. "Last night on the train there are two mysterious strangers. There is the Wagon Lit attendant answering to the description given us by M. Hardman, and seen by Hildegarde Schmidt, Colonel Arbuthnot and M. MacQueen. There is also a woman in a red kimono—a tall, slim woman —seen by Pierre Michel, by Miss Debenham, by M. MacQueen and by myself—and smelt, I may say, by Colonel Arbuthnot! Who was she? No one on the train admits to having a scarlet kimono. She, too, has vanished. Was she one and the same with the spurious Wagon Lit attendant? Or was she some quite distinct personality? Where are they, these two? And, incidentally, where is the Wagon Lit uniform and the scarlet kimono?"

"Ah! that is something definite." M. Bouc sprang up eagerly. "We must search all the passengers' luggage. Yes, that will be something."

Poirot rose also.

"I will make a prophecy," he said.

"You know where they are?"

"I have a little idea."

"Where, then?"

"You will find the scarlet kimono in the baggage of one of the men and you will find the uniform of the Wagon Lit conductor in the baggage of Hildegarde Schmidt."

"Hildegarde Schmidt? You think——?"

"Not what you are thinking. I will put it like this. If Hildegarde Schmidt is guilty, the uniform *might* be found in her baggage—but if she is innocent it *certainly* will be."

"But how——" began M. Bouc and stopped.

"What is this noise that approaches?" he cried. "It resembles a locomotive in motion."

The noise drew nearer. It consisted of shrill cries and protests in a woman's voice. The door at the end of the dining-car flew open. Mrs. Hubbard burst in.

"It's too horrible," she cried. "It's just too horrible. In my sponge-bag. My sponge-bag. A great knife—all over blood."

And, suddenly toppling forward, she fainted heavily on M. Bouc's shoulder.

14. *The Evidence of the Weapon*

With more vigour than chivalry, M. Bouc deposited the fainting lady with her head on the table. Dr. Constantine yelled for one of the restaurant attendants, who came at a run.

"Keep her head so," said the doctor. "If she revives give her a little cognac. You understand?"

Then he hurried off after the other two. His interest lay wholly in the crime—swooning middle-aged ladies did not interest him at all.

It is possible that Mrs. Hubbard revived rather quicker with these methods than she might otherwise have done. A few minutes later she was sitting up, sipping cognac from a glass proffered by the attendant, and talking once more.

"I just can't say how terrible it was. I don't suppose anybody on this train can understand my feelings. I've always been vurry, vurry sensitive ever since a child. The mere sight of blood—ugh—why even now I come over queer when I think about it."

The attendant proffered the glass again.

"Encore un peu, Madame."

"D'you think I'd better? I'm a lifelong teetotaller. I just never touch spirits or wine at any time. All my family are abstainers. Still, perhaps as this is only medical——"

She sipped once more.

In the meantime Poirot and M. Bouc, closely followed by Dr. Constantine, had hurried out of the restaurant-car and along the corridor of the Stamboul coach towards Mrs. Hubbard's compartment.

Every traveller on the train seemed to be congregated outside the door. The conductor, a harassed look on his face, was keeping them back.

"Mais il n'y a rien à voir," he said, and repeated the sentiment in several other languages.

"Let me pass, if you please," said M. Bouc.

Squeezing his rotundity past the obstructing passengers, he entered the compartment, Poirot close behind him.

"I am glad you have come, Monsieur," said the conductor with a sigh of relief. "Everyone has been trying to enter. The American lady—such screams as she gave—*ma foi!* I thought she too had been murdered! I came at a run and there she was screaming like a mad woman, and she cried out that she must fetch you and she departed, screeching at the top of her voice and telling everybody whose carriage she passed what had occurred."

He added, with a gesture of the hand:

"*It* is in there, Monsieur. I have not touched it."

Hanging on the handle of the door that gave access to the next compartment was a large-size checked rubber sponge-bag. Below it on the floor, just where it had fallen from Mrs. Hubbard's hand, was a straight-bladed dagger—a cheap affair, sham Oriental, with an embossed hilt and a tapering blade. The blade was stained with patches of what looked like rust.

Poirot picked it up delicately.

"Yes," he murmured. "There is no mistake. Here is our missing weapon all right—eh, *docteur?*"

The doctor examined it.

"You need not be so careful," said Poirot. "There will be no finger-prints on it save those of Mrs. Hubbard."

Constantine's examination did not take long.

"It is the weapon all right," he said. "It would account for any of the wounds."

"I implore you, my friend, do not say that."

The doctor looked astonished.

"Already we are heavily overburdened by coincidence. Two people decide to stab M. Ratchett last night. It is too much of a good thing that each of them should select an identical weapon."

"As to that, the coincidence is not, perhaps, so great as it seems," said the doctor. "Thousands of these sham Eastern daggers are made and shipped to the bazaars of Constantinople."

"You console me a little, but only a little," said Poirot.

He looked thoughtfully at the door in front of him, then, lifting off the sponge-bag, he tried the handle. The door did not budge. About a foot above the handle was the door bolt. Poirot drew it back and tried again, but still the door remained fast.

"We locked it from the other side, you remember," said the doctor.

"That is true," said Poirot absently. He seemed to be thinking about something else. His brow was furrowed as though in perplexity.

"It agrees, does it not?" said M. Bouc. "The man passes through this carriage. As he shuts the communicating door behind him he feels the sponge-bag. A thought comes to him and he quickly slips the blood-stained knife inside. Then, all unwitting that he has awakened Mrs. Hubbard, he slips out through the other door into the corridor."

"As you say," murmured Poirot. "That is how it must have happened."

But the puzzled look did not leave his face.

"But what is it?" demanded M. Bouc. "There is something, is there not, that does not satisfy you?"

Poirot darted a quick look at him.

"The same point does not strike you? No, evidently not. Well, it is a small matter."

The conductor looked into the carriage.

"The American lady is coming back."

Dr. Constantine looked rather guilty. He had, he felt, treated Mrs. Hubbard rather cavalierly. But she had no reproaches for him. Her energies were concentrated on another matter.

"I'm just going to say one thing right out," she said breathlessly as she arrived in the doorway. "I'm not going on any longer in this compartment! Why, I wouldn't sleep in it to-night if you paid me a million dollars."

"But, Madame——"

"I know what you are going to say, and I'm telling you right now that I won't do any such thing! Why, I'd rather sit up all night in the corridor."

She began to cry.

"Oh! if my daughter could only know—if she could see me now, why——"

Poirot interrupted firmly.

"You misunderstand, Madame. Your demand is most reasonable. Your baggage shall be changed at once to another compartment."

Mrs. Hubbard lowered her handkerchief.

"Is that so? Oh, I feel better right away. But surely it's all full up, unless one of the gentlemen——"

M. Bouc spoke.

"Your baggage, Madame, shall be moved out of this coach altogether. You shall have a compartment in the next coach which was put on at Belgrade."

"Why, that's splendid. I'm not an out of the way nervous woman, but to sleep in that compartment next door to a dead man——" She shivered. "It would drive me plumb crazy."

"Michel," called M. Bouc. "Move this baggage into a vacant compartment in the Athens-Paris coach."

"Yes, Monsieur—the same one as this—the No. 3?"

"No," said Poirot before his friend could reply. "I think it would be better for Madame to have a different number altogether. The No. 12, for instance."

"*Bien, Monsieur.*"

The conductor seized the luggage. Mrs. Hubbard turned gratefully to Poirot.

"That's vurry kind and delicate of you. I appreciate it, I assure you."

"Do not mention it, Madame. We will come with you and see you comfortably installed."

Mrs. Hubbard was escorted by the three men to her new home. She looked round her happily.

"This is fine."

"It suits you, Madame? It is, you see, exactly like the compartment you have left."

"That's so—only it faces the other way. But that doesn't matter, for these trains go first one way and then the other. I said to my daughter, 'I want a carriage facing the engine,' and she said, 'Why, Momma, that'll be no good to you, for if you go to sleep one way, when you wake up the train's going the other.' And it was quite true what she said. Why, last evening we went into Belgrade one way and out the other."

"At any rate, Madame, you are quite happy and contented now?"

"Well, no, I wouldn't say that. Here we are stuck in a snowdrift and nobody doing anything about it, and my boat sailing the day after to-morrow."

"Madame," said M. Bouc, "we are all in the same case—every one of us."

"Well, that's true," admitted Mrs. Hubbard. "But nobody else has had a murderer walking right through their compartment in the middle of the night."

"What still puzzles me, Madame," said Poirot, "is how the man got into your compartment if the communicating door was bolted as you say. You are sure that it *was* bolted?"

"Why, the Swedish lady tried it before my eyes."

"Let us just reconstruct that little scene. You were lying in your bunk —so—and you could not see for yourself, you say?"

"No, because of the sponge-bag. Oh, my, I shall have to get a new sponge-bag. It makes me feel sick in my stomach to look at this one."

Poirot picked up the sponge-bag and hung it on the handle of the communicating door into the next carriage.

"*Précisément*—I see," he said. "The bolt is just underneath the han-dle—the sponge-bag masks it. You could not see from where you were lying whether the bolt were turned or not."

"Why, that's just what I've been telling you!"

"And the Swedish lady, Miss Ohlsson, stood so, between you and the door. She tried it and told you it was bolted."

"That's so."

"All the same, Madame, she may have made an error. You see what I mean." Poirot seemed anxious to explain. "The bolt is just a projection of metal—so. Turned to the right the door is locked, left straight, it is not. Possibly she merely tried the door, and as it was locked on the other side she may have assumed that it was locked on your side."

"Well, I guess that would be rather stupid of her."

"Madame, the most kind, the most amiable are not always the cleverest."

"That's so, of course."

"By the way, Madame, did you travel out to Smyrna this way?"

"No. I sailed right to Stamboul, and a friend of my daughter's—Mr. Johnson (a perfectly lovely man; I'd like to have you know him)—met me and showed me all round Stamboul, which I found a very disappointing city—all tumbling down. And as for those mosques and putting on those great shuffling things over your shoes—where was I?"

"You were saying that Mr. Johnson met you."

"That's so, and he saw me on board a French Messagerie boat for Smyrna, and my daughter's husband was waiting right on the quay. What he'll say when he hears about all this! My daughter said this would be just the safest, easiest way imaginable. 'You just sit in your carriage,' she said, 'and you get right to Parrus and there the American Express will meet you.' And, oh dear, what am I to do about cancelling my steamship passage? I ought to let them know. I can't possibly make it now. This is just too terrible——"

Mrs. Hubbard showed signs of tears once more.

Poirot, who had been fidgeting slightly, seized his opportunity.

"You have had a shock, Madame. The restaurant attendant shall be instructed to bring you along some tea and some biscuits."

"I don't know that I'm so set on tea," said Mrs. Hubbard tearfully. "That's more an English habit."

"Coffee, then, Madame. You need some stimulant."

"That cognac's made my head feel mighty funny. I think I would like some coffee."

"Excellent. You must revive your forces."

"My, what a funny expression."

"But first, Madame, a little matter of routine. You permit that I make a search of your baggage?"

"Whatever for?"

"We are about to commence a search of all the passengers' luggage. I do not want to remind you of an unpleasant experience, but your sponge-bag—remember."

"Mercy! Perhaps you'd better! I just couldn't bear to get any more surprises of that kind."

The examination was quickly over. Mrs. Hubbard was travelling with the minimum of luggage—a hatbox, a cheap suitcase, and a well-burdened travelling bag. The contents of all three were simple and straightforward, and the examination would not have taken more than a couple of minutes had not Mrs. Hubbard delayed matters by insisting on due attention being paid to photographs of "My daughter" and two rather ugly children—"My daughter's children. Aren't they cunning?"

15. The Evidence of the Passengers' Luggage

Having delivered himself of various polite insincerities, and having told Mrs. Hubbard that he would order coffee to be brought to her, Poirot was able to take his leave accompanied by his two friends.

"Well, we have made a start and drawn a blank," observed M. Bouc. "Whom shall we tackle next?"

"It would be simplest, I think, just to proceed along the train carriage by carriage. That means that we start with No. 16—the amiable M. Hardman."

Mr. Hardman, who was smoking a cigar, welcomed them affably.

"Come right in, gentlemen—that is, if it's humanly possible. It's just a mite cramped in here for a party."

M. Bouc explained the object of their visit, and the big detective nodded comprehendingly.

"That's O.K. To tell the truth, I've been wondering you didn't get down to it sooner. Here are my keys, gentlemen, and if you like to search my pockets too, why, you're welcome. Shall I reach the grips down for you?"

"The conductor will do that. Michel!"

The contents of Mr. Hardman's two "grips" were soon examined and passed. They contained perhaps an undue proportion of spiritous liquor. Mr. Hardman winked.

"It's not often they search your grips at the frontiers—not if you fix the conductor. I handed out a wad of Turkish notes right away, and there's been no trouble so far."

"And at Paris?"

Mr. Hardman winked again.

"By the time I get to Paris," he said, "what's left over of this little lot will go into a bottle labelled hairwash."

"You are not a believer in Prohibition, M. Hardman," said M. Bouc with a smile.

"Well," said Hardman, "I can't say Prohibition has ever worried me any."

"Ah!" said M. Bouc. "The speakeasy." He pronounced the word with care, savouring it.

"Your American terms are so quaint, so expressive," he said.

"Me, I would much like to go to America," said Poirot.

"You'd learn a few go-ahead methods over there," said Hardman. "Europe wants waking up. She's half asleep."

"It is true that America is the country of progress," agreed Poirot. "There is much that I admire about Americans. Only—I am perhaps old-fashioned—but me, I find the American woman less charming than my own countrywomen. The French or Belgian girl, coquettish, charming—I think there is no one to touch her."

Hardman turned away to peer out at the snow for a minute.

"Perhaps you're right, M. Poirot," he said. "But I guess every nation likes its own girls best."

He blinked as though the snow hurt his eyes.

"Kind of dazzling, isn't it?" he remarked. "Say, gentlemen, this business is getting on my nerves. Murder and the snow and all, and nothing *doing*. Just hanging about and killing time. I'd like to get busy after someone or something."

"The true Western spirit of hustle," said Poirot with a smile.

The conductor replaced the bags and they moved on to the next compartment. Colonel Arbuthnot was sitting in a corner smoking a pipe and reading a magazine.

Poirot explained their errand. The Colonel made no demur. He had two heavy leather suitcases.

"The rest of my kit has gone by long sea," he explained.

Like most Army men, the Colonel was a neat packer. The examination of his baggage took only a few minutes. Poirot noted a packet of pipe-cleaners.

"You always use the same kind?" he asked.

"Usually. If I can get 'em."

"Ah!" Poirot nodded.

These pipe-cleaners were identical with the one he had found on the floor of the dead man's compartment.

Dr. Constantine remarked as much when they were out in the corridor again.

"*Tout de même,*" murmured Poirot, "I can hardly believe it. It is not *dans son caractère,* and when you have said that you have said every-thing."

The door of the next compartment was closed. It was that occupied by Princess Dragomiroff. They knocked on the door and the Princess's deep voice called, *"Entrez."*

M. Bouc was spokesman. He was very deferential and polite as he explained their errand.

The Princess listened to him in silence, her small toad-like face quite impassive.

"If it is necessary, Messieurs," she said quietly when he had finished, "that is all there is to it. My maid has the keys. She will attend to it with you."

"Does your maid always carry your keys, Madame?" asked Poirot.

"Certainly, Monsieur."

"And if during the night at one of the frontiers the Customs officials should require a piece of luggage to be opened?"

The old lady shrugged her shoulders.

"It is very unlikely. But in such a case this conductor would fetch her."

"You trust her, then, implicitly, Madame?"

"I have told you so already," said the Princess quietly. "I do not em-ploy people whom I do not trust."

"Yes," said Poirot thoughtfully. "Trust is indeed something in these days. It is, perhaps, better to have a homely woman whom one can trust than a more *chic* maid—for example, some smart Parisienne."

He saw the dark intelligent eyes come slowly round and fasten them-selves upon his face.

"What exactly are you implying, M. Poirot?"

"Nothing, Madame. I? Nothing."

"But yet. You think, do you not, that I should have a smart French-woman to attend to my toilet?"

"It would be, perhaps, more usual, Madame."

She shook her head.

"Schmidt is devoted to me." Her voice dwelt lingeringly on the words. "Devotion—*c'est impayable.*"

The German woman had arrived with the keys. The Princess spoke to her in her own language, telling her to open the valises and help the gentlemen in their search. She herself remained in the corridor looking out at the snow and Poirot remained with her, leaving M. Bouc to the task of searching the luggage.

She regarded him with a grim smile.

"Well, Monsieur, do you not wish to see what my valises contain?"

He shook his head.

"Madame, it is a formality, that is all."

"Are you so sure?"

"In your case, yes."

"And yet I knew and loved Sonia Armstrong. What do you think, then? That I would not soil my hands with killing such *canaille* as that man Cassetti? Well, perhaps you are right."

She was silent a minute or two, then she said:

"With such a man as that, do you know what I should have liked to have done? I should have liked to call to my servants: 'Flog this man to death and fling him out on the rubbish heap.' That is the way things were done when I was young, Monsieur."

Still he did not speak, just listened attentively.

She looked at him with a sudden impetuosity.

"You do not say anything, M. Poirot. What is it that you are thinking, I wonder?"

He looked at her with a very direct glance.

"I think, Madame, that your strength is in your will—not in your arm."

She glanced down at her thin, black-clad arms ending in those claw-like yellow hands with the rings on the fingers.

"It is true," she said. "I have no strength in these—none. I do not know if I am sorry or glad."

Then she turned abruptly back towards her carriage, where the maid was busily packing up the cases.

The Princess cut short M. Bouc's apologies.

"There is not need for you to apologise, Monsieur," she said. "A murder has been committed. Certain actions have to be performed. That is all there is to it."

"*Vous êtes bien amiable, Madame.*"

She inclined her head slightly as they departed.

The doors of the next two carriages were shut. M. Bouc paused and scratched his head.

"*Diable!*" he said. "This may be awkward. These are diplomatic passports. Their baggage is exempt."

"From Customs examination, yes. But a murder is different."

"I know. All the same—we do not want to have complications——"

"Do not distress yourself, my friend. The Count and Countess will be reasonable. See how amiable Princess Dragomiroff was about it."

"She is truly *grande dame*. These two are also of the same position, but the Count impressed me as a man of somewhat truculent disposition. He was not pleased when you insisted on questioning his wife.

And this will annoy him still further. Suppose—eh—we omit them. After all, they can have nothing to do with the matter. Why should I stir up needless trouble for myself."

"I do not agree with you," said Poirot. "I feel sure that Count Andrenyi will be reasonable. At any rate, let us make the attempt."

And, before M. Bouc could reply, he rapped sharply on the door of No. 13.

A voice from within cried, *"Entrez."*

The Count was sitting in the corner near the door reading a newspaper. The Countess was curled up in the opposite corner near the window. There was a pillow behind her head, and she seemed to have been asleep.

"Pardon, Monsieur le Comte," began Poirot. "Pray forgive this intrusion. It is that we are making a search of all the baggage on the train. In most cases a mere formality. But it has to be done. M. Bouc suggests that, as you have a diplomatic passport, you might reasonably claim to be exempt from such a search."

The Count considered for a moment.

"Thank you," he said. "But I do not think that I care for an exception to be made in my case. I should prefer that our baggage should be examined like that of the other passengers."

He turned to his wife.

"You do not object, I hope, Elena?"

"Not at all," said the Countess without hesitation.

A rapid and somewhat perfunctory search followed. Poirot seemed to be trying to mask an embarrassment in making various small pointless remarks, such as:

"Here is a label all wet on your suitcase, Madame," as he lifted down a blue morocco case with initials on it and a coronet.

The Countess did not reply to this observation. She seemed, indeed, rather bored by the whole proceeding, remaining curled up in her corner, staring dreamily out through the window whilst the men searched her luggage in the compartment next door.

Poirot finished his search by opening the little cupboard above the wash-basin and taking a rapid glance at its contents—a sponge, face cream, powder and a small bottle labelled trional.

Then, with polite remarks on either side, the search party withdrew. Mrs. Hubbard's compartment, that of the dead man, and Poirot's own came next.

They now came to the second-class carriages. The first one, Nos. 10, 11, was occupied by Mary Debenham, who was reading a book, and

Greta Ohlsson, who was fast asleep but woke with a start at their entrance.

Poirot repeated his formula. The Swedish lady seemed agitated, Mary Debenham calmly indifferent.

Poirot addressed himself to the Swedish lady.

"If you permit, Mademoiselle, we will examine your baggage first, and then perhaps you would be so good as to see how the American lady is getting on. We have moved her into one of the carriages in the next coach, but she is still very upset as the result of her discovery. I have ordered coffee to be sent to her, but I think she is of those to whom someone to talk to is a necessity of the first water."

The good lady was instantly sympathetic. She would go immediately. It must have been indeed a terrible shock to the nerves, and already the poor lady was upset by the journey and leaving her daughter. Ah, yes, certainly she would go at once—her case was not locked—and she would take with her some sal ammoniac.

She bustled off. Her possessions were soon examined. They were meagre in the extreme. She had evidently not yet noticed the missing wires from the hatbox.

Miss Debenham had put her book down. She was watching Poirot. When he asked her, she handed over her keys. Then, as he lifted down a case and opened it, she said:

"Why did you send her away, M. Poirot?"

"I, Mademoiselle? Why, to minister to the American lady."

"An excellent pretext—but a pretext all the same."

"I don't understand you, Mademoiselle."

"I think you understand me very well."

She smiled.

"You wanted to get me alone. Wasn't that it?"

"You are putting words into my mouth, Mademoiselle."

"And ideas into your head? No, I don't think so. The ideas are already there. That is right, isn't it?"

"Mademoiselle, we have a proverb——"

"*Qui s'excuse s'accuse;* is that what you were going to say? You must give me the credit for a certain amount of observation and common sense. For some reason or other you have got it into your head that I know something about this sordid business—this murder of a man I never saw before."

"You are imagining things, Mademoiselle."

"No, I am not imagining things at all. But it seems to me that a lot of time is wasted by not speaking the truth—by beating about the bush instead of coming straight out with things."

"And you do not like the waste of time. No, you like to come straight to the point. You like the direct method. *Eh bien,* I will give it to you, the direct method. I will ask you the meaning of certain words that I overheard on the journey from Syria. I had got out of the train to do what the English call 'stretch the legs' at the station of Konya. Your voice and the Colonel's, Mademoiselle, they came to me out of the night. You said to him, *'Not now. Not now. When it's all over. When it's behind us.'* What did you mean by those words, Mademoiselle?"

She said very quietly:

"Do you think I meant—murder?"

"It is I who am asking you, Mademoiselle."

She sighed—was lost a minute in thought. Then, as though rousing herself, she said:

"Those words had a meaning, Monsieur, but not one that I can tell you. I can only give you my solemn word of honour that I had never set eyes on this man Ratchett in my life until I saw him on this train."

"And—you refuse to explain those words?"

"Yes—if you like to put it that way—I refuse. They had to do with—with a task I had undertaken."

"A task that is now ended?"

"What do you mean?"

"It is ended, is it not?"

"Why should you think so?"

"Listen, Mademoiselle, I will recall to you another incident. There was a delay to the train on the day we were to reach Stamboul. You were very agitated, Mademoiselle. You, so calm, so self-controlled. You lost that calm."

"I did not want to miss my connection."

"So you said. But, Mademoiselle, the Orient Express leaves Stamboul every day of the week. Even if you had missed the connection it would only have been a matter of twenty-four hours' delay."

Miss Debenham for the first time showed signs of losing her temper.

"You do not seem to realise that one may have friends awaiting one's arrival in London, and that a day's delay upsets arrangements and causes a lot of annoyance."

"Ah, it is like that? There are friends awaiting your arrival? You do not want to cause them inconvenience?"

"Naturally."

"And yet—it is curious——"

"What is curious?"

"On this train—again we have a delay. And this time a more serious delay, since there is no possibility of sending a telegram to your friends or of getting them on the long—the long——"

"The long distance? The telephone, you mean."

"Ah, yes, the portmanteau call, as you say in England."

Mary Debenham smiled a little in spite of herself.

"Trunk call," she corrected. "Yes, as you say, it is extremely annoying not to be able to get any word through, either by telephone or telegraph."

"And yet, Mademoiselle, *this* time your manner is quite different. You no longer betray the impatience. You are calm and philosophical."

Mary Debenham flushed and bit her lips. She no longer felt inclined to smile.

"You do not answer, Mademoiselle?"

"I am sorry. I did not know that there was anything to answer."

"The explanation of your change of attitude, Mademoiselle."

"Don't you think that you are making rather a fuss about nothing, M. Poirot?"

Poirot spread out his hands in an apologetic gesture.

"It is perhaps a fault with us detectives. We expect the behaviour to be always consistent. We do not allow for changes of mood."

Mary Debenham made no reply.

"You know Colonel Arbuthnot well, Mademoiselle?"

He fancied that she was relieved by the change of subject.

"I met him for the first time on this journey."

"Have you any reason to suspect that he may have known this man Ratchett?"

She shook her head decisively.

"I am quite sure he didn't."

"Why are you sure?"

"By the way he spoke."

"And yet, Mademoiselle, we found a pipe-cleaner on the floor of the dead man's compartment. And Colonel Arbuthnot is the only man on the train who smokes a pipe."

He watched her narrowly, but she displayed neither surprise nor emotion, merely said:

"Nonsense. It's absurd. Colonel Arbuthnot is the last man in the world to be mixed up in a crime—especially a theatrical kind of crime like this."

It was so much what Poirot himself thought that he found himself on the point of agreeing with her. He said instead:

"I must remind you that you do not know him very well, Mademoiselle."

She shrugged her shoulders.

"I know the type well enough."

He said very gently:

"You still refuse to tell me the meaning of those words—'When it's behind us'?"

She said coldly:

"I have nothing more to say."

"It does not matter," said Hercule Poirot. "I shall find out."

He bowed and left the compartment, closing the door after him.

"Was that wise, my friend?" asked M. Bouc. "You have put her on her guard—and through her you have put the Colonel on his guard also."

"*Mon ami,* if you wish to catch a rabbit you put a ferret into the hole, and if the rabbit is there he runs. That is all I have done."

They entered the compartment of Hildegarde Schmidt.

The woman was standing in readiness, her face respectful but unemotional.

Poirot took a quick glance through the contents of the small case on the seat. Then he motioned to the attendant to get down the bigger suitcase from the rack.

"The keys?" he said.

"It is not locked, Monsieur."

Poirot undid the hasps and lifted the lid.

"Aha!" he said, and turning to M. Bouc, "You remember what I said? Look here a little moment!"

On the top of the suitcase was a hastily rolled up brown Wagon Lit uniform.

The stolidity of the German woman underwent a sudden change.

"Ach!" she cried. "That is not mine. I did not put it there. I have never looked in that case since we left Stamboul. Indeed, indeed, it is true."

She looked from one to another pleadingly.

Poirot took her gently by the arm and soothed her.

"No, no, all is well. We believe you. Do not be agitated. I am as sure you did not hide the uniform there as I am sure that you are a good cook. See. You are a good cook, are you not?"

Bewildered, the woman smiled in spite of herself.

"Yes, indeed, all my ladies have said so. I——"

She stopped, her mouth open, looking frightened again.

"No, no," said Poirot. "I assure you all is well. See, I will tell you how this happened. This man, the man you saw in Wagon Lit uniform, comes out of the dead man's compartment. He collides with you. That is bad luck for him. He has hoped that no one will see him. What to do next? He must get rid of his uniform. It is now not a safeguard, but a danger."

His glance went to M. Bouc and Dr. Constantine, who were listening attentively.

"There is the snow, you see. The snow which confuses all his plans. Where can he hide these clothes? All the compartments are full. No, he passes one where the door is open and shows it to be unoccupied. It must be the one belonging to the woman with whom he has just collided. He slips in, removes the uniform and jams it hurriedly into a suitcase on the rack. It may be some time before it is discovered."

"And then?" said M. Bouc.

"That we must discuss," said Poirot with a warning glance.

He held up the tunic. A button, the third down, was missing. Poirot slipped his hand into the pocket and took out a conductor's pass key, used to unlock the doors of the compartments.

"Here is the explanation of how our man was able to pass through locked doors," said M. Bouc. "Your questions to Mrs. Hubbard were unnecessary. Locked or not locked, the man could easily get through the communicating door. After all, if a Wagon Lit uniform, why not a Wagon Lit key?"

"Why not, indeed," said Poirot.

"We might have known it, really. You remember Michel said that the door into the corridor of Mrs. Hubbard's compartment was locked when he came in answer to her bell."

"That is so, Monsieur," said the conductor. "That is why I thought the lady must have been dreaming."

"But now it is easy," continued M. Bouc. "Doubtless he meant to relock the communicating door also, but perhaps he heard some movement from the bed and it startled him."

"We have now," said Poirot, "only to find the scarlet kimono."

"True. And these last two compartments are occupied by men."

"We will search all the same."

"Oh! assuredly. Besides, I remember what you said."

Hector MacQueen acquiesced willingly in the search.

"I'd just as soon you did," he said with a rueful smile. "I feel I'm just definitely the most suspicious character on the train. You've only got to find a will in which the old man left me all his money, and that'll just about fix things."

M. Bouc bent a suspicious glance upon him.

"That's just my fun," said MacQueen hastily. "He'd never have left me a cent, really. I was just useful to him—languages and so on. You're apt to be done down, you know, if you don't speak anything but good American. I'm no linguist myself, but I know what I call shopping and hotel snappy bits in French and German and Italian."

His voice was a little louder than usual. It was as though he was slightly uneasy at the search in spite of his willingness.

Poirot emerged.

"Nothing," he said. "Not even a compromising bequest!"

MacQueen sighed.

"Well, that's a load off my mind," he said humorously.

They moved on to the last compartment. The examination of the luggage of the big Italian and of the valet yielded no result.

The three men stood at the end of the coach looking at each other.

"What next?" asked M. Bouc.

"We will go back to the dining-car," said Poirot. "We know now all that we can know. We have the evidence of the passengers, the evidence of their baggage, the evidence of our eyes. We can expect no further help. It must be our part now to use our brains."

He felt in his pocket for his cigarette case. It was empty.

"I will join you in a moment," he said. "I shall need the cigarettes. This is a very difficult, a very curious affair. Who wore that scarlet kimono? Where is it now? I wish I knew. There is something in this case—some factor—that escapes me! It is difficult because it has been made difficult. But we will discuss it. Pardon me a moment."

He went hurriedly along the corridor to his own compartment. He had, he knew, a further supply of cigarettes in one of his valises.

He got it down and snapped back the lock.

Then he sat back on his heels and stared.

Neatly folded on the top of the case was a thin scarlet silk kimono embroidered with dragons.

"So," he murmured. "It is like that. A defiance. Very well. I take it up."

PART III—Hercule Poirot Sits Back and Thinks

1. Which of Them?

M. Bouc and Dr. Constantine were talking together when Poirot entered the dining-car. M. Bouc was looking depressed.

"*Le voilà*," said the latter when he saw Poirot.

Then he added as his friend sat down:

"If you solve this case, *mon cher*, I shall indeed believe in miracles!"

"It worries you, this case?"

"Naturally it worries me. I cannot make head or tail of it."

"I agree," said the doctor.

He looked at Poirot with interest.

"To be frank," he said, "I cannot see what you are going to do next."

"No?" said Poirot thoughtfully.

He took out his cigarette case and lit one of his tiny cigarettes. His eyes were dreamy.

"That, to me, is the interest of this case," he said. "We are cut off from all the normal routes of procedure. Are these people whose evidence we have taken speaking the truth or lying? We have no means of finding out—except such means as we can devise ourselves. It is an exercise, this, of the brain."

"That is all very fine," said M. Bouc. "But what have you to go upon?"

"I told you just now. We have the evidence of the passengers and the evidence of our own eyes."

"Pretty evidence—that of the passengers! It told us just nothing at all."

Poirot shook his head.

"I do not agree, my friend. The evidence of the passengers gave us several points of interest."

"Indeed," said M. Bouc sceptically. "I did not observe it."

"That is because you did not listen."

"Well, tell me—what did I miss?"

"I will just take one instance—the first evidence we heard—that of the young MacQueen. He uttered, to my mind, one very significant phrase."

"About the letters?"

"No, not about the letters. As far as I can remember, his words were: *'We travelled about. Mr. Ratchett wanted to see the world. He was hampered by knowing no languages. I acted more as a courier than a secretary.'*"

He looked from the doctor's face to that of M. Bouc.

"What? You still do not see? That is inexcusable—for you had a second chance again just now when he said, *'You're apt to be done down if you speak nothing but good American.'*"

"You mean——?" M. Bouc still looked puzzled.

"Ah, it is that you want it given to you in words of one syllable. Well, here it is! *M. Ratchett spoke no French.* Yet, when the conductor came in answer to his bell last night, it was a voice speaking in *French* that told him that it was a mistake and that he was not wanted. It was moreover, a perfectly idiomatic phrase that was used, not one that a man knowing only a few words of French would have selected. *'Ce n'est rien. Je me suis trompé.'*"

"It is true," cried Constantine excitedly. "We should have seen that! I remember your laying stress on the words when you repeated them to us. Now I understand your reluctance to rely upon the evidence of the dented watch. Already at twenty-three minutes to one, Ratchett was dead——"

"And it was his murderer speaking!" finished M. Bouc impressively.

Poirot raised a deprecating hand.

"Let us not go too fast. And do not let us assume more than we actually know. It is safe, I think, to say that at that time, twenty-three minutes to one, *some other person* was in Ratchett's compartment and that that person was either French, or could speak the French language fluently."

"You are very cautious, *mon vieux.*"

"One should advance only a step at a time. We have no actual *evidence* that Ratchett was dead at that time."

"There is the cry that awakened you."

"Yes, that is true."

"In one way," said M. Bouc thoughtfully, "this discovery does not affect things very much. You heard someone moving about next door. That someone was not Ratchett, but the other man. Doubtless he is washing blood from his hands, clearing up after the crime, burning the incriminating letter. Then he waits till all is still, and when he thinks it is safe and the coast is clear he locks and chains Ratchett's door on the inside, unlocks the communicating door through into Mrs. Hubbard's compartment and slips out that way. In fact it is exactly as we thought— *with the difference that Ratchett was killed about half an hour earlier,* and the watch put on to a quarter-past one to create an alibi."

"Not such a famous alibi," said Poirot. "The hands of the watch pointed to 1:15—the exact time when the intruder actually left the scene of the crime."

"True," said M. Bouc, a little confused. "What, then, does the watch convey to you?"

"If the hands were altered—I say *if*—then the time at which they were set *must* have a significance. The natural reaction would be to suspect anyone who had a reliable alibi for the time indicated—in this case 1:15."

"Yes, yes," said the doctor. "That reasoning is good."

"We must also pay a little attention to the time the intruder *entered* the compartment. When had he an opportunity of doing so? Unless we are to assume the complicity of the real conductor, there was only one time when he could have done so—during the time the train stopped at Vincovci. After the train left Vincovci the conductor was sitting facing the corridor and whereas any one of the passengers would pay little attention to a Wagon Lit attendant, the *one* person who would notice an impostor would be the real conductor. But during the halt at Vincovci the conductor is out on the platform. The coast is clear."

"And, by our former reasoning, it *must* be one of the passengers," said M. Bouc. "We come back to where we were. Which of them?"

Poirot smiled.

"I have made a list," he said. "If you like to see it, it will, perhaps, refresh your memory."

The doctor and M. Bouc pored over the list together. It was written out neatly in a methodical manner in the order in which the passengers had been interviewed.

HECTOR MACQUEEN—American subject
Berth No. 6. Second Class
Motive: Possibly arising out of association with dead man?
Alibi: From midnight to 2 a.m. (Midnight to 1:30 vouched for by Col. Arbuthnot and 1:15 to 2 vouched for by conductor.)
Evidence against him: None.
Circumstances: None.

CONDUCTOR—PIERRE MICHEL—French subject

Motive: None.

Alibi: From midnight to 2 a.m. (Seen by H. P. in corridor at same time as voice spoke from Ratchett's compartment at 12:37. From 1 a.m. to 1:16 vouched for by other two conductors.)

Evidence against him: None.

Suspicious circumstances: The Wagon Lit uniform found is a point in his favour since it seems to have been intended to throw suspicion on him.

EDWARD MASTERMAN—English subject

Berth No. 4. Second Class

Motive: Possibly arising out of connection with deceased, whose valet he was.

Alibi: From midnight to 2 a.m. (Vouched for by Antonio Foscarelli.)

Evidence against him or suspicious circumstances: None, except that he is the only man the right height or size to have worn the Wagon Lit uniform. On the other hand, it is unlikely that he speaks French well.

MRS. HUBBARD—American subject

Berth No. 3. First Class

Motive: None.

Alibi: From midnight to 2 a.m.—None.

Evidence against her or suspicious circumstances: Story of man in her compartment is substantiated by the evidence of the woman Schmidt.

GRETA OHLSSON—Swedish subject

Berth No. 10. Second Class

Motive: None.

Alibi: From midnight to 2 a.m. (Vouched for by Mary Debenham.) Note.—Was last to see Ratchett alive.

PRINCESS DRAGOMIROFF—Naturalised French subject

Motive: Was intimately acquainted with Armstrong family, and godmother to Sonia Armstrong.

Alibi: From midnight to 2 a.m. (Vouched for by conductor and maid.)

Evidence against her or suspicious circumstances: None.

COUNT ANDRENYI—Hungarian subject
Diplomatic passport
Berth No. 13. First Class
Motive: None.
Alibi: Midnight to 2 a.m. (Vouched for by conductor—this does not cover period from 1 to 1:15.)

COUNTESS ANDRENYI—As above
Berth No. 12
Motive: None.
Alibi: Midnight to 2 a.m. Took trional and slept. (Vouched for by husband. Trional bottle in her cupboard.)

COLONEL ARBUTHNOT—British subject
Berth No. 15. First Class
Motive: None.
Alibi: Midnight to 2 a.m. Talked with MacQueen till 1:30. Went to own compartment and did not leave it. (Substantiated by MacQueen and conductor.)
Evidence against him or suspicious circumstances: Pipe-cleaner.

CYRUS HARDMAN—American subject
Berth No. 16. Second Class
Motive: None known.
Alibi: Midnight to 2 a.m. Did not leave compartment. (Substantiated by MacQueen and conductor.)
Evidence against him or suspicious circumstances: None.

ANTONIO FOSCARELLI—American subject
(Italian birth)
Berth No. 5. Second Class
Motive: None known.
Alibi: Midnight to 2 a.m. (Vouched for by Edward Masterman.)
Evidence against him or suspicious circumstances: None, except that weapon used might be said to suit his temperament. (Vide B. Bouc.)

MARY DEBENHAM—British subject
Berth No. 11. Second Class
Motive: None.
Alibi: Midnight to 2 a.m. (Vouched for by Greta Ohlsson.)

Evidence against her or suspicious circumstances: Conversation overheard by H. P. and her refusal to explain same.

HILDEGARDE SCHMIDT—German subject

Berth No. 8. Second Class

Motive: None.

Alibi: Midnight to 2 a.m. (Vouched for by conductor and her mistress.) Went to bed. Was aroused by conductor at 12:38 approx. and went to mistress.

Note: The evidence of the passengers is supported by the statement of the conductor that no one entered or left Mr. Ratchett's compartment between the hours of midnight to 1 o'clock (when he himself went into the next coach) and from 1:15 to 2 o'clock.

"That document, you understand," said Poirot, "is a mere précis of the evidence we heard, arranged that way for convenience."

With a grimace M. Bouc handed it back.

"It is not illuminating," he said.

"Perhaps you may find this more to your taste," said Poirot with a slight smile as he handed him a second sheet of paper.

2. *Ten Questions*

On the paper was written:

Things needing explanation

1. The handkerchief marked with the initial H. Whose is it?
2. The pipe-cleaner. Was it dropped by Colonel Arbuthnot? Or by someone else?
3. Who wore the scarlet kimono?
4. Who was the man or woman masquerading in Wagon Lit uniform?
5. Why do the hands of the watch point to 1:15?
6. Was the murder committed at that time?
7. Was it earlier?
8. Was it later?
9. Can we be sure that Ratchett was stabbed by more than one person?

10.   What other explanation of his wounds can there be?

"Well, let us see what we can do," said M. Bouc, brightening a little at this challenge to his wits. "The handkerchief to begin with. Let us by all means be orderly and methodical."

"Assuredly," said Poirot, nodding his head in a satisfied fashion.

M. Bouc continued somewhat didactically.

"The initial H is connected with three people—Mrs. Hubbard, Miss Debenham, whose second name is Hermione, and the maid Hildegarde Schmidt."

"Ah! And of those three?"

"It is difficult to say. But I *think* I should vote for Miss Debenham. For all one knows, she may be called by her second name and not her first. Also there is already some suspicion attaching to her. That conversation you overheard, *mon cher,* was certainly a little curious, and so is her refusal to explain it."

"As for me, I plump for the American," said Dr. Constantine. "It is a very expensive handkerchief that, and Americans, as all the world knows, do not care what they pay."

"So you both eliminate the maid?" asked Poirot.

"Yes. As she herself said, it is the handkerchief of a member of the upper classes."

"And the second question—the pipe-cleaner. Did Colonel Arbuthnot drop it, or somebody else?"

"That is more difficult. The English, they do not stab. You are right there. I incline to the view that someone else dropped the pipe-cleaner—and did so to incriminate the long-legged Englishman."

"As you said, M. Poirot," put in the doctor, "*two* clues is too much carelessness. I agree with M. Bouc. The handkerchief was a genuine oversight—hence no one will admit that it is theirs. The pipe-cleaner is a faked one. In support of that theory, you notice that Colonel Arbuthnot shows no embarrassment and admits freely to smoking a pipe and using that type of cleaner."

"You reason well," said Poirot.

"Question No. 3—who wore the scarlet kimono?" went on M. Bouc. "As to that I will confess I have not the slightest idea. Have you any views on the subject, Dr. Constantine?"

"None."

"Then we confess ourselves beaten there. The next question has, at any rate, possibilities. Who was the man or woman masquerading in Wagon Lit uniform? Well, one can say with certainty a number of people whom it could *not* be. Hardman, Colonel Arbuthnot, Foscarelli, Count Andrenyi and Hector MacQueen are all too tall. Mrs. Hubbard, Hildegarde Schmidt and Greta Ohlsson are too broad. That leaves the valet, Miss Debenham, Princess Dragomiroff and Countess Andrenyi—and none of them sounds likely! Greta Ohlsson in one case and Antonio Foscarelli in the other both swear that Miss Debenham and the valet never left their compartments. Hildegarde Schmidt swears to the Princess being in hers, and Count Andrenyi has told us that his wife took a sleeping draught. Therefore it seems impossible that it can be anybody—which is absurd!"

"As our old friend Euclid says," murmured Poirot.

"It must be one of those four," said Dr. Constantine. "Unless it is someone from outside who has found a hiding-place—and that, we agreed, was impossible."

M. Bouc had passed on to the next question on the list.

"No. 5—why do the hands of the broken watch point to 1:15? I can see two explanations of that. Either it was done by the murderer to establish an alibi and afterwards he was prevented from leaving the compartment when he meant to do so by hearing people moving about, or else—wait—I have an idea coming——"

The other two waited respectfully while M. Bouc struggled in mental agony.

"I have it," he said at last. "It was *not* the Wagon Lit murderer who tampered with the watch! It was the person we have called the Second Murderer—the left-handed person—in other words the woman in the scarlet kimono. She arrives later and moves back the hands of the watch in order to make an alibi for herself."

"Bravo," said Dr. Constantine. "It is well imagined, that."

"In fact," said Poirot, "she stabbed him in the dark, not realising that he was dead already, but somehow deduced that he had a watch in his pyjama pocket, took it out, put back the hands blindly and gave it the requisite dent."

M. Bouc looked at him coldly.

"Have you anything better to suggest yourself?" he asked.

"At the moment—no," admitted Poirot.

"All the same," he went on, "I do not think you have either of you appreciated the most interesting point about that watch."

"Does question No. 6 deal with it?" asked the doctor. "To that question—was the murder committed at that time—1:15—I answer, 'No.'"

"I agree," said M. Bouc. " 'Was it earlier?' is the next question. I say yes. You, too, doctor?"

The doctor nodded.

"Yes, but the question 'Was it later?' can also be answered in the affirmative. I agree with your theory, M. Bouc, and so, I think, does M. Poirot, although he does not wish to commit himself. The First Murderer came earlier than 1:15, the Second Murderer came *after* 1:15. And as regards the question of left-handedness, ought we not to take steps to ascertain which of the passengers is left-handed?"

"I have not completely neglected that point," said Poirot. "You may have noticed that I made each passenger write either a signature or an address. That is not conclusive, because some people do certain actions with the right hand and others with the left. Some write right-handed, but play golf left-handed. Still, it is something. Every person questioned took the pen in their right hand—with the exception of Princess Drago-miroff, who refused to write."

"Princess Dragomiroff, impossible," said M. Bouc.

"I doubt if she would have had the strength to inflict that particular left-handed blow," said Dr. Constantine dubiously. "That particular wound had been inflicted with considerable force."

"More force than a woman could use?"

"No, I would not say that. But I think more force than an elderly woman could display, and Princess Dragomiroff's physique is particularly frail."

"It might be a question of the influence of mind over body," said Poirot. "Princess Dragomiroff has great personality and immense will power. But let us pass from that for the moment."

"To questions Nos. 9 and 10. Can we be sure that Ratchett was stabbed by more than one person, and what other explanation of the wounds can there be? In my opinion, medically speaking, there can *be no other* explanation of those wounds. To suggest that one man struck first feebly and then with violence, first with the right hand and then with the left, and after an interval of perhaps half an hour inflicted fresh wounds on a dead body—well, it does not make sense."

"No," said Poirot. "It does not make sense. And you think that two murderers do make sense?"

"As you yourself have said, what other explanation can there be?"

Poirot stared straight ahead of him.

"That is what I ask myself," he said. "That is what I never cease to ask myself."

He leaned back in his seat.

"From now on, it is all here." He tapped himself on the forehead. "We have thrashed it all out. The facts are all in front of us—neatly arranged with order and method. The passengers have sat here, one by one, giving their evidence. We know all that can be known—*from out-side.* . . ."

He gave an affectionate smile at M. Bouc.

"It has been a little joke between us, has it not—this business of sit-ting back and *thinking* out the truth? Well, I am about to put my theory into practice—here before your eyes. You two must do the same. Let us all three close our eyes and think. . . ."

"One or more of those passengers killed Ratchett. *Which of them?*"

3. Certain Suggestive Points

It was quite a quarter of an hour before anyone spoke.

M. Bouc and Dr. Constantine had started by trying to obey Poirot's instructions. They had endeavoured to see through a maze of conflicting particulars to a clear and outstanding solution.

M. Bouc's thoughts had run something as follows:

"Assuredly I must think. But as far as that goes I have already thought. . . . Poirot obviously thinks this English girl is mixed up in the matter. I cannot help feeling that that is most unlikely. . . . The English are extremely cold. Probably it is because they have no figures. . . . But that is not the point. I suppose the English valet is not lying when he said the other never left the compartment? But why should he? It is not easy to bribe the English, they are so unapproach-able. The whole thing is most unfortunate. I wonder when we shall get out of this. There must be *some* rescue work in progress. They are so slow in these countries . . . it is hours before anyone thinks of doing anything. And the police of these countries, they will be most trying to deal with—puffed up with importance, touchy, on their dignity. They will make a grand affair of all this. It is not often that such a chance comes their way. It will be in all the newspapers. . . ."

And from there on M. Bouc's thoughts went along a well-worn course which they had already traversed some hundred times.

Dr. Constantine's thoughts ran thus:

"He is queer, this little man. A genius? Or a crank? Will he solve this mystery? Impossible. I can see no way out of it. It is all too confus-ing. . . . Everyone is lying, perhaps. . . . But even then that does not help one. If they are all lying it is just as confusing as if they were speaking the truth. Odd about those wounds. I cannot understand it. . . . It would be easier to understand if he had been shot—after all, the term gunman must mean that they shoot with a gun. A curious country, America. I should like to go there. It is so progressive. When I get home I must get hold of Demetrius Zagone—he has been to America, he has all the modern ideas. . . . I wonder what Zia is doing at this moment. If my wife ever finds out——"

His thoughts went on to entirely private matters.

Hercule Poirot sat very still.

One might have thought he was asleep.

And then, suddenly, after a quarter of an hour's complete immobility, his eyebrows began to move slowly up his forehead. A little sigh escaped him. He murmured beneath his breath:

"But, after all, why not? And if so—why, if so, that would explain everything."

His eyes opened. They were green like a cat's. He said softly:

"*Eh bien.* I have thought. And you?"

Lost in their reflections, both men started violently.

"I have thought also," said M. Bouc just a shade guilty. "But I have arrived at no conclusion. The elucidation of crime is your *métier,* not mine, my friend."

"I, too, have reflected with great earnestness," said the doctor unblushingly, recalling his thoughts from certain pornographic details. "I thought of many possible theories, but not one that really satisfies me."

Poirot nodded amiably. His nod seemed to say:

"Quite right. That is the proper thing to say. You have given me the cue I expected."

He sat very upright, threw out his chest, caressed his moustache and spoke in the manner of a practised speaker addressing a public meeting.

"My friends, I have reviewed the facts in my mind, and have also gone over to myself the evidence of the passengers—with this result. I see, nebulously as yet, a certain explanation that would cover the facts as we know them. It is a very curious explanation, and I cannot be sure as yet that it is the true one. To find out definitely, I shall have to make certain experiments.

"I would like first to mention certain points which appear to me suggestive. Let us start with a remark made to me by M. Bouc in this very place on the occasion of our first lunch together on the train. He commented on the fact that we were surrounded by people of all classes, of all ages, of all nationalities. That is a fact somewhat rare at this time of year. The Athens-Paris and the Bucharest-Paris coaches, for instance, are almost empty. Remember also one passenger who failed to turn up. It is, I think, significant. Then there are some minor points that strike me as suggestive—for instance, the position of Mrs. Hubbard's sponge-bag, the name of Mrs. Armstrong's mother, the detective methods of M. Hardman, the suggestion of M. MacQueen that Ratchett himself destroyed the charred note we found, Princess Dragomiroff's Christian name, and a grease spot on a Hungarian passport."

The two men stared at him.

"Do they suggest anything to you, those points?" asked Poirot.

"Not a thing," said M. Bouc frankly.

"And M. le docteur?"

"I do not understand in the least of what you are talking."

M. Bouc, meanwhile, seizing upon the one tangible thing his friend had mentioned, was sorting through the passports. With a grunt he picked up that of Count and Countess Andrenyi and opened it.

"Is this what you mean? This dirty mark?"

"Yes. It is a fairly fresh grease spot. You notice where it occurs?"

"At the beginning of the description of the Count's wife—her Christian name, to be exact. But I confess that I still do not see the point."

"I am going to approach it from another angle. Let us go back to the handkerchief found at the scene of the crime. As we have stated not long ago—three people are associated with the letter H. Mrs. Hubbard, Miss Debenham and the maid, Hildegarde Schmidt. Now let us regard that handkerchief from another point of view. It is, my friends, an extremely expensive handkerchief—an *object de luxe,* hand made, embroidered in Paris. Which of the passengers, apart from the initial, was likely to own such a handkerchief? Not Mrs. Hubbard, a worthy woman with no pretensions to reckless extravagance in dress. Not Miss Debenham; that class of Englishwoman has a dainty linen handkerchief, but not an expensive wisp of cambric costing perhaps two hundred francs. And certainly not the maid. But there *are* two women on the train who would be likely to own such a handkerchief. Let us see if we can connect them in any way with the letter H. The two women I refer to are Princess Dragomiroff——"

"Whose Christian name is Natalia," put in M. Bouc ironically.

"Exactly. And her Christian name, as I said just now, is decidedly suggestive. The other woman is Countess Andrenyi. And at once something strikes us——"

"*You!*"

"*Me,* then. Her Christian name on her passport is disfigured by a blob of grease. Just an accident, anyone would say. But consider that Christian name. Elena. Suppose that, instead of Elena, it were *Helena.* That capital H could be turned into a capital E and then run over the small e next to it quite easily—and then a spot of grease dropped to cover up the alteration."

"Helena," cried M. Bouc. "It is an idea, that."

"Certainly it is an idea! I look about for any confirmation, however slight, of my idea—and I find it. One of the luggage labels on the Countess's baggage is slightly damp. It is one that happens to run over the first initial on top of the case. That label has been soaked off and put on again in a different place."

"You begin to convince me," said M. Bouc. "But the Countess Andrenyi—surely——"

"Ah, now, *mon vieux,* you must turn yourself round and approach an entirely different angle of the case. How was this murder intended to appear to everybody? Do not forget that the snow has upset all the murderer's original plan. Let us imagine, for a little minute, that there is no snow, that the train proceeded on its normal course. What, then, would have happened?

"The murder, let us say, would still have been discovered in all probability at the Italian frontier early this morning. Much of the same evidence would have been given to the Italian police. The threatening letters would have been produced by M. MacQueen, M. Hardman would have told his story, Mrs. Hubbard would have been eager to tell how a man passed through her compartment, the button would have been found. I imagine that two things only would have been different. The man would have passed through Mrs. Hubbard's compartment just before one o'clock—and the Wagon Lit uniform would have been found cast off in one of the toilets."

"You mean?"

"I mean that the murder was *planned to look like an outside job.* The assassin would have been presumed to have left the train at Brod, where the train is timed to arrive at 12:58. Somebody would probably have passed a strange Wagon Lit conductor in the corridor. The uniform would be left in a conspicuous place so as to show clearly just how the trick had been played. No suspicion would have been attached to the passengers. That, my friends, was how the affair was intended to appear to the outside world.

"But the accident to the train changes everything. Doubtless we have here the reason why the man remained in the compartment with his victim so long. He was waiting for the train to go on. But at last he realised *that the train was not going on.* Different plans would have to be made. The murderer would now be *known* to be still on the train."

"Yes, yes," said M. Bouc impatiently. "I see all that. But where does the handkerchief come in?"

"I am returning to it by a somewhat circuitous route. To begin with, you must realise that the threatening letters were in the nature of a blind. They might have been lifted bodily out of an indifferently written American crime novel. They are not *real*. They are, in fact, simply intended for the police. What we have to ask ourselves is, 'Did they deceive Ratchett?' On the face of it, the answer seems to be, 'No.' His instructions to Hardman seem to point to a definite 'private' enemy of the identity of whom he was well aware. That is if we accept Hardman's story as true. But Ratchett certainly received *one* letter of a very different character—the one containing a reference to the Armstrong baby, a fragment of which we found in his compartment. In case Ratchett had not realised it sooner, this was to make sure that he understood the reason of the threats against his life. That letter, as I have said all along, was *not* intended to be found. The murderer's first care was to destroy it. This, then, was the second hitch in his plans. The first was the snow, the second was our reconstruction of that fragment.

"That note being destroyed so carefully can only mean one thing. *There must be on the train someone so intimately connected with the Armstrong family that the finding of that note would immediately direct suspicion upon that person.*

"Now we come to the other two clues that we found. I pass over the pipe-cleaner. We have already said a good deal about that. Let us pass on to the handkerchief. Taken at its simplest, it is a clue which directly incriminates someone whose initial is H, and it was dropped there unwittingly by that person."

"Exactly," said Dr. Constantine. "She finds out that she has dropped the handkerchief and immediately takes steps to conceal her Christian name."

"How fast you go. You arrive at a conclusion much sooner than I would permit myself to do."

"Is there any other alternative?"

"Certainly there is. Suppose, for instance, that you have committed a crime and wish to cast a suspicion for it on someone else. Well, there is on the train a certain person connected intimately with the Armstrong family—a woman. Suppose, then, that you leave there a handkerchief belonging to that woman. . . . She will be questioned, her connection with the Armstrong family will be brought out—*et voilà.* Motive—*and* an incriminating article of evidence."

"But in such a case," objected the doctor, "the person indicated being innocent, would not take steps to conceal her identity."

"Ah, really? That is what you think? That is truly the opinion of the police court. But I know human nature, my friend, and I tell you that, suddenly confronted with the possibility of being tried for murder, the most innocent person will lose their head and do the most absurd things. No, no, the grease spot and the changed label do not prove guilt —they only prove that the Countess Andrenyi is anxious for some reason to conceal her identity."

"What do you think her connection with the Armstrong family can be? She has never been in America, she says."

"Exactly, and she speaks broken English, and she has a very foreign appearance which she exaggerates. But it should not be difficult to guess who she is. I mentioned just now the name of Mrs. Armstrong's mother. It was Linda Arden, and she was a very celebrated actress—among other things a Shakespearean actress. Think of *As You Like It*—the Forest of Arden and Rosalind. It was there she got the inspiration for her acting name. Linda Arden, the name by which she was known all over the world, was not her real name. It may have been Goldenberg—she quite likely had central European blood in her veins—a strain of Jewish, perhaps. Many nationalities drift to America. I suggest to you, gentlemen, that that young sister of Mrs. Armstrong's, little more than a child at the time of the tragedy, was Helena Goldenberg, the younger daughter of Linda Arden, and she married Count Andrenyi when he was an attaché in Washington."

"But Princess Dragomiroff says that she married an Englishman."

"Whose name she cannot remember! I ask you, my friends—is that really likely? Princess Dragomiroff loved Linda Arden as great ladies do love great artists. She was godmother to one of her daughters. Would she forget so quickly the married name of the other daughter? It is not likely. No, I think we can safely say that Princess Dragomiroff was lying. She knew Helena was on the train, she had seen her. She realised at once, as soon as she heard who Ratchett really was, that Helena would be suspected. And so, when we question her as to the sister she promptly lies—is vague, cannot remember, but 'thinks Helena married an Englishman'—a suggestion as far away from the truth as possible."

One of the restaurant attendants came through the door at the end and approached them. He addressed M. Bouc.

"The dinner, Monsieur, shall I serve it? It is ready some little time."

M. Bouc looked at Poirot. The latter nodded.

"By all means, let dinner be served."

The attendant vanished through the doors at the other end. His bell could be heard ringing and his voice upraised:

"*Premier Service. Le dîner est servi. Premier dîner*—First Service."

4. The Grease Spot on a Hungarian Passport

Poirot shared a table with M. Bouc and the doctor.

The company assembled in the restaurant-car was a very subdued one. They spoke little. Even the loquacious Mrs. Hubbard was unnaturally quiet. She murmured as she sat:

"I don't feel as though I've got the heart to eat anything," and then partook of everything offered her, encouraged by the Swedish lady, who seemed to regard her as a special charge.

Before the meal was served Poirot had caught the chief attendant by the sleeve and murmured something to him. Constantine had a pretty good guess what the instructions had been, as he noticed that the Count and Countess Andrenyi were always served last and that at the end of the meal there was a delay in making out their bill. It therefore came about that the Count and Countess were the last left in the restaurant-car.

When they rose at length and moved in the direction of the door, Poirot sprang up and followed them.

"Pardon, Madame, you have dropped your handkerchief."

He was holding out to her the tiny monogrammed square.

She took it, glanced at it, then handed it back to him.

"You are mistaken, Monsieur, that is not my handkerchief."

"Not your handkerchief? Are you sure?"

"Perfectly sure, Monsieur."

"And yet, Madame, it has your initial—the initial H."

The Count made a sudden movement. Poirot ignored him. His eyes were fixed on the Countess's face.

Looking steadily at him she replied:

"I do not understand, Monsieur. My initials are E. A."

"I think not. Your name is Helena—not Elena. Helena Goldenberg, the younger daughter of Linda Arden—Helena Goldenberg, the sister of Mrs. Armstrong."

There was a dead silence for a minute or two. Both the Count and Countess had gone deadly white. Poirot said in a gentler tone:

"It is of no use denying. That is the truth, is it not?"

The Count burst out furiously:

"I demand, Monsieur, by what right you——"

She interrupted him, putting up a small hand towards his mouth.

"No, Rudolph. Let me speak. It is useless to deny what this gentleman says. We had better sit down and talk the matter out."

Her voice had changed. It still had the southern richness of tone, but it had become suddenly more clear cut and incisive. It was, for the first time, a definitely American voice.

The Count was silenced. He obeyed the gesture of her hand, and they both sat down opposite Poirot.

"Your statement, Monsieur, is quite true," said the Countess. "I am Helena Goldenberg, the younger sister of Mrs. Armstrong."

"You did not acquaint me with that fact this morning, Madame la Comtesse."

"No."

"In fact, all that your husband and you told me was a tissue of lies."

"Monsieur," cried the Count angrily.

"Do not be angry, Rudolph. M. Poirot puts the fact rather brutally, but what he says is undeniable."

"I am glad you admit the fact so freely, Madame. Will you now tell me your reasons for so doing and also for altering your Christian name on your passport."

"That was my doing entirely," put in the Count.

Helena said quietly:

"Surely, M. Poirot, you can guess my reason—our reason. This man who was killed is the man who murdered my baby niece, who killed my sister, who broke my brother-in-law's heart. Three of the people I loved best and who made up my home—my world!"

Her voice rang out passionately. She was a true daughter of that mother, the emotional force of whose acting had moved huge audiences to tears.

She went on more quietly.

"Of all the people on the train, I alone had probably the best motive for killing him."

"And you did not kill him, Madame?"

"I swear to you, M. Poirot, and my husband knows and will swear also—that, much as I may have been tempted to do so, I never lifted a hand against that man."

"I too, gentlemen," said the Count. "I give you my word of honour that last night Helena never left her compartment. She took a sleeping draught exactly as I said. She is utterly and entirely innocent."

Poirot looked from one to the other of them.

"On my word of honour," repeated the Count.

Poirot shook his head slightly.

"And yet you took it upon yourself to alter the name in the passport?"

"Monsieur Poirot," the Count spoke earnestly and passionately. "Consider my position. Do you think I could stand the thought of my wife dragged through a sordid police case. She was innocent, I knew it, but what she said was true—because of her connection with the Armstrong family she would have been immediately suspected. She would have been questioned—arrested, perhaps. Since some evil chance had taken us on the same train as this man Ratchett, there was, I felt sure, but one thing for it. I admit, Monsieur, that I lied to you—all, that is, save in one thing. My wife never left her compartment last night."

He spoke with an earnestness that it was hard to gainsay.

"I do not say that I disbelieve you, Monsieur," said Poirot slowly. "Your family is, I know, a proud and ancient one. It would be bitter indeed for you to have your wife dragged into an unpleasant police case. With that I can sympathise. But how, then, do you explain the presence of your wife's handkerchief actually in the dead man's compartment?"

"That handkerchief is not mine, Monsieur," said the Countess.

"In spite of the initial H?"

"In spite of the initial. I have handkerchiefs not unlike that, but not one that is exactly of that pattern. I know, of course, that I cannot hope to make you believe me, but I assure you that it is so. That handkerchief is not mine."

"It may have been placed there by someone in order to incriminate you?"

She smiled a little.

"You are enticing me to admit that, after all, it is mine? But indeed, M. Poirot, it isn't."

She spoke with great earnestness.

"Then why, if the handkerchief was not yours, did you alter the name in the passport?"

The Count answered this.

"Because we heard that a handkerchief had been found with the initial H on it. We talked the matter over together before we came to be interviewed. I pointed out to Helena that if it were seen that her Christian name began with an H she would immediately be subjected to much more rigorous questioning. And the thing was so simple—to alter Helena to Elena was easily done."

"You have, M. le Comte, the makings of a very fine criminal," remarked Poirot dryly. "A great natural ingenuity, and an apparently remorseless determination to mislead justice."

"Oh, no, no." The girl leaned forward. "M. Poirot, he's explained to you how it was." She broke from French into English. "I was scared—absolutely dead scared, you understand. It had been so awful—that time—and to have it all raked up again. And to be suspected and perhaps thrown into prison. I was just scared stiff, M. Poirot. Can't you understand at all?"

Her voice was lovely—deep—rich—pleading, the voice of the daughter of Linda Arden the actress.

Poirot looked gravely at her.

"If I am to believe you, Madame—and I do not say that I will *not* believe you—then you must help me."

"Help you?"

"Yes. The reason for the murder lies in the past—in that tragedy which broke up your home and saddened your young life. Take me back into the past, Madame, that I may find there the link that explains the whole thing."

"What can there be to tell you? They are all dead." She repeated mournfully, "All dead—all dead—Robert, Sonia—darling, darling Daisy. She was so sweet—so happy—she had such lovely curls. We were all just crazy about her."

"There was another victim, Madame. An indirect victim, you might say."

"Poor Susanne? Yes, I had forgotten about her. The police questioned her. They were convinced she had something to do with it. Perhaps she had—but if so, only innocently. She had, I believe, chatted idly with someone, giving information as to the time of Daisy's outings. The poor thing got terribly wrought up—she thought she was being held responsible." She shuddered. "She threw herself out of the window. Oh, it was horrible."

She buried her face in her hands.

"What nationality was she, Madame?"

"She was French."

"What was her last name?"

"It's absurd, but I can't remember—we all called her Susanne. A pretty laughing girl. She was devoted to Daisy."

"She was the nursery-maid, was she not?"

"Yes."

"Who was the nurse?"

"She was a trained hospital nurse. Stengelberg her name was. She, too, was devoted to Daisy—and to my sister."

"Now, Madame, I want you to think carefully before you answer this question. Have you, since you were on this train, seen anyone that you recognised?"

She stared at him.

"I? No, no one at all."

"What about Princess Dragomiroff?"

"Oh, her? I know her, of course. I thought you meant anyone—anyone from—from that time."

"So I did, Madame. Now think carefully. Some years have passed, remember. The person might have altered their appearance."

Helena pondered deeply. Then she said:

"No—I am sure—there is no one."

"You yourself—you were a young girl at the time—did you have no one to superintend your studies or to look after you?"

"Oh, yes, I had a dragon—a sort of governess to me and secretary to Sonia combined. She was English or rather Scotch—a big, red-haired woman."

"What was her name?"

"Miss Freebody."

"Young or old?"

"She seemed frightfully old to me. I suppose she couldn't have been more than forty. Susanne, of course, used to look after my clothes and maid me."

"And there were no other inmates of the house?"

"Only servants."

"And you are certain—quite certain, Madame—that you have recognised no one on the train?"

She replied earnestly:

"No one, Monsieur. No one at all."

5. The Christian Name of Princess Dragomiroff

When the Count and Countess had departed, Poirot looked across at the other two.

"You see," he said, "we make progress."

"Excellent work," said M. Bouc cordially. "For my part, I should never have dreamed of suspecting Count and Countess Andrenyi. I will admit I thought them quite *hors de combat*. I suppose there is no doubt that she committed the crime? It is rather sad. Still, they will not guillotine her. There are extenuating circumstances. A few years' imprisonment—that will be all."

"In fact you are quite certain of her guilt."

"My dear friend, surely there is no doubt of it? I thought your reassuring manner was only to smooth things over till we are dug out of the snow and the police take charge."

"You do not believe the Count's positive assertion—on his word of honour—that his wife is innocent?"

"*Mon cher*—naturally—what else *could* he say? He adores his wife. He wants to save her! He tells his lie very well—quite in the grand Seigneur manner, but what else than a lie could it be?"

"Well, you know, I had the preposterous idea that it might be the truth."

"No, no. The handkerchief, remember. The handkerchief clinches the matter."

"Oh, I am not so sure about the handkerchief. You remember, I always told you that there were two possibilities as to the ownership of the handkerchief."

"All the same——"

M. Bouc broke off. The door at the end had opened, and Princess Dragomiroff entered the dining-car. She came straight to them and all three men rose to their feet.

She spoke to Poirot, ignoring the others.

"I believe, Monsieur," she said, "that you have a handkerchief of mine."

Poirot shot a glance of triumph at the other two.

"Is this it, Madame?"

He produced the little square of fine cambric.

"That is it. It has my initial in the corner."

"But, Madame la Princesse, that is the letter H," said M. Bouc. "Your Christian name—pardon me—is Natalia."

She gave him a cold stare.

"That is correct, Monsieur. My handkerchiefs are always initialled in the Russian characters. H is N in Russian."

M. Bouc was somewhat taken aback. There was something about this indomitable old lady which made him feel flustered and uncomfortable.

"You did not tell us that this handkerchief was yours at the inquiry this morning."

"You did not ask me," said the Princess dryly.

"Pray be seated, Madame," said Poirot.

She sighed.

"I may as well, I suppose."

She sat down.

"You need not make a long business of this, Messieurs. Your next question will be—how did my handkerchief come to be lying by a murdered man's body? My reply to that is that I have no idea."

"You have really no idea?"

"None whatever."

"You will excuse me, Madame, but how much can we rely upon the truthfulness of your replies?"

Poirot said the words very softly. Princess Dragomiroff answered contemptuously.

"I suppose you mean because I did not tell you that Helena Andrenyi was Mrs. Armstrong's sister?"

"In fact you deliberately lied to us in the matter."

"Certainly. I would do the same again. Her mother was my friend. I believe, Messieurs, in loyalty—to one's friends and one's family and one's caste."

"You do not believe in doing your utmost to further the ends of justice?"

"In this case I consider that justice—strict justice—has been done."

Poirot leaned forward.

"You see my difficulty, Madame. In this matter of the handkerchief, even, am I to believe you? Or are you shielding your friend's daughter?"

"Oh! I see what you mean." Her face broke into a grim smile. "Well, Messieurs, this statement of mine can be easily proved. I will give you the address of the people in Paris who make my handkerchiefs. You have only to show them the one in question and they will inform you that it was made to my order over a year ago. The handkerchief is mine, Messieurs."

She rose.

"Have you anything further you wish to ask me?"

"Your maid, Madame, did she recognise this handkerchief when we showed it to her this morning?"

"She must have done so. She saw it and said nothing? Ah, well, that shows that she too can be loyal."

With a slight inclination of her head she passed out of the dining-car.

"So that was it," murmured Poirot softly. "I noticed just a trifling hesitation when I asked the maid if she knew to whom the handkerchief belonged. She was uncertain whether or not to admit that it was her mistress's. But how does that fit in with that strange central idea of mine? Yes, it might well be."

"Ah!" said M. Bouc with a characteristic gesture—"she is a terrible old lady, that!"

"Could she have murdered Ratchett?" asked Poirot of the doctor.

He shook his head.

"Those blows—the ones delivered with great force penetrating the muscle—never, never could anyone with so frail a physique inflict them."

"But the feebler ones?"

"The feebler ones, yes."

"I am thinking," said Poirot, "of the incident this morning when I said to her that the strength was in her will rather than in her arm. It was in the nature of a trap, that remark. I wanted to see if she would look down at her right or her left arm. She did neither. She looked at them both. But she made a strange reply. She said, 'No, I have no strength in these. I do not know whether to be sorry or glad.' A curious remark that. It confirms me in my belief about the crime."

"It did not settle the point about the left-handedness."

"No. By the way, did you notice that Count Andrenyi keeps his handkerchief in his right-hand breast pocket?"

M. Bouc shook his head. His mind reverted to the astonishing revelations of the last half-hour. He murmured:

"Lies—and again lies—it amazes me, the amount of lies we had told to us this morning."

"There are more still to discover," said Poirot cheerfully.

"You think so?"

"I shall be very disappointed if it is not so."

"Such duplicity is terrible," said M. Bouc. "But it seems to please you," he added reproachfully.

"It has this advantage," said Poirot. "If you confront anyone who has lied with the truth, they usually admit it—often out of sheer surprise. It is only necessary to guess *right* to produce your effect.

"That is the only way to conduct this case. I select each passenger in turn, consider their evidence and say to myself, '*If* so and so is lying, on what point are they lying and what is the *reason* for the lie?' And I answer *if* they are lying—*if*, you mark—it could only be for such a reason and on such a point. We have done that once very successfully with Countess Andrenyi. We shall now proceed to try the same method on several other persons."

"And supposing, my friend, that your guess happens to be wrong?"

"Then one person, at any rate, will be completely freed from suspicion."

"Ah! A process of elimination."

"Exactly."

"And who do we tackle next?"

"We are going to tackle that *pukka sahib*, Colonel Arbuthnot."

6. A Second Interview with Colonel Arbuthnot

Colonel Arbuthnot was clearly annoyed at being summoned to the dining-car for a second interview. His face wore a most forbidding expression as he sat down and said:

"Well?"

"All my apologies for troubling you a second time," said Poirot. "But there is still some information that I think you might be able to give us."

"Indeed? I hardly think so."

"To begin with, you see this pipe-cleaner?"

"Yes."

"Is it one of yours?"

"Don't know. I don't put a private mark on them, you know."

"Are you aware, Colonel Arbuthnot, that you are the only man amongst the passengers in the Stamboul-Calais carriage who smokes a pipe?"

"In that case it probably is one of mine."

"Do you know where it was found?"

"Not the least idea."

"It was found by the body of the murdered man."

Colonel Arbuthnot raised his eyebrows.

"Can you tell us, Colonel Arbuthnot, how it is likely to have got there?"

"If you mean did I drop it there myself, no, I didn't."

"Did you go into M. Ratchett's compartment at any time?"

"I never even spoke to the man."

"You never spoke to him and you did not murder him?"

The Colonel's eyebrows went up again sardonically.

"If I had, I should hardly be likely to acquaint you with the fact. As a matter of fact I *didn't* murder the fellow."

"Ah, well," murmured Poirot. "It is of no consequence."

"I beg your pardon?"

"I said that it was of no consequence."

"Oh!" Arbuthnot looked taken aback. He eyed Poirot uneasily.

"Because, you see," continued the little man, "the pipe-cleaner, it is of no importance. I can myself think of eleven other excellent explanations of its presence."

Arbuthnot stared at him.

"What I really wished to see you about was quite another matter," went on Poirot. "Miss Debenham may have told you, perhaps, that I overheard some words spoken to you at the station of Konya?"

Arbuthnot did not reply.

"She said, *'Not now. When it's all over. When it's behind us.'* Do you know to what those words referred?"

"I am sorry, M. Poirot, but I must refuse to answer that question."

"*Pourquoi?*"

The Colonel said stiffly:

"I suggest that you should ask Miss Debenham herself for the meaning of those words."

"I have done so."

"And she refused to tell you?"

"Yes."

"Then I should think it would have been perfectly plain—even to you—that my lips are sealed."

"You will not give away a lady's secret?"

"You can put it that way, if you like."

"Miss Debenham told me that they referred to a private matter of her own."

"Then why not accept her word for it?"

"Because, Colonel Arbuthnot, Miss Debenham is what one might call a highly suspicious character."

"Nonsense," said the Colonel with warmth.

"It is not nonsense."

"You have nothing whatever against her."

"Not the fact that Miss Debenham was companion governess in the Armstrong household at the time of the kidnapping of little Daisy Armstrong?"

There was a minute's dead silence.

Poirot nodded his head gently.

"You see," he said, "we know more than you think. If Miss Debenham is innocent, why did she conceal that fact? Why did she tell me that she had never been in America?"

The Colonel cleared his throat.

"Aren't you possibly making a mistake?"

"I am making no mistake. Why did Miss Debenham lie to me?"

Colonel Arbuthnot shrugged his shoulders.

"You had better ask her. I still think that you are wrong."

Poirot raised his voice and called. One of the restaurant attendants came from the far end of the car.

"Go and ask the English lady in No. 11 if she will be good enough to come here."

"Bien, Monsieur."

The man departed. The four men sat in silence. Colonel Arbuthnot's face looked as though it were carved out of wood; it was rigid and impassive.

The man returned.

"The lady is just coming, Monsieur."

"Thank you."

A minute or two later Mary Debenham entered the dining-car.

7. *The Identity of Mary Debenham*

She wore no hat. Her head was thrown back as though in defiance. The sweep of her hair back from her face, the curve of her nostril suggested the figurehead of a ship plunging gallantly into a rough sea. In that moment she was beautiful.

Her eyes went to Arbuthnot for a minute—just a minute.

She said to Poirot:

"You wished to see me?"

"I wished to ask you, Mademoiselle, why you lied to us this morning?"

"Lied to you? I don't know what you mean."

"You concealed the fact that at the time of the Armstrong tragedy you were actually living in the house. You told me that you had never been in America."

He saw her flinch for a moment and then recover herself.

"Yes," she said. "That is true."

"No, Mademoiselle, it was false."

"You misunderstood me. I mean that it is true that I lied to you."

"Ah, you admit it?"

Her lips curved into a smile.

"Certainly. Since you have found me out."

"You are at least frank, Mademoiselle."

"There does not seem anything else for me to be."

"Well, of course, that is true. And now, Mademoiselle, may I ask you the reason for these evasions?"

"I should have thought the reason leapt to the eye, M. Poirot."

"It does not leap to mine, Mademoiselle."

She said in a quiet, even voice with a trace of hardness in it:

"I have my living to get."

"You mean——?"

She raised her eyes and looked him full in the face.

"How much do you know, M. Poirot, of the fight to get and keep decent employment? Do you think that a girl who had been detained in connection with a murder case, whose name and perhaps photographs were reproduced in the English papers—do you think that any nice ordinary middle-class Englishwoman would want to engage that girl as governess to her daughters?"

"I do not see why not—if no blame attached to you."

"Oh, blame—it is not blame—it is publicity! So far, M. Poirot, I have succeeded in life. I have had well-paid, pleasant posts. I was not going to risk the position I had attained when no good end could have been served."

"I will venture to suggest, Mademoiselle, that I would have been the best judge of that, not you."

She shrugged her shoulders.

"For instance, you could have helped me in the matter of identification."

"What do you mean?"

"Is it possible, Mademoiselle, that you did not recognise in the Countess Andrenyi Mrs. Armstrong's young sister whom you taught in New York?"

"Countess Andrenyi? No." She shook her head. "It may seem extraordinary to you, but I did not recognise her. She was not grown up, you see, when I knew her. That was over three years ago. It is true that the Countess reminded me of someone—it puzzled me. But she looks so foreign—I never connected her with the little American schoolgirl. It is true that I only glanced at her casually when coming into the restaurant-car. I noticed her clothes more than her face—" she smiled faintly—"women do! And then—well, I had my own preoccupations."

"You will not tell me your secret, Mademoiselle?"

Poirot's voice was very gentle and persuasive.

She said in a low voice:

"I can't—I can't."

And suddenly, without warning, she broke down, dropping her face down upon her outstretched arms and crying as though her heart would break.

The Colonel sprang up and stood awkwardly beside her.

"I—look here——"

He stopped and, turning round, scowled fiercely at Poirot.

"I'll break every bone in your damned body, you dirty little whipper-snapper," he said.

"Monsieur," protested M. Bouc.

Arbuthnot had turned back to the girl.

"Mary—for God's sake——"

She sprang up.

"It's nothing. I'm all right. You don't need me any more, do you, M. Poirot? If you do, you must come and find me. Oh, what an idiot—what an idiot I'm making of myself!"

She hurried out of the car. Arbuthnot, before following her, turned once more on Poirot.

"Miss Debenham's got nothing to do with this business—nothing, do you hear? And if she's worried and interfered with, you'll have me to deal with."

He strode out.

"I like to see an angry Englishman," said Poirot. "They are very amusing. The more emotional they feel the less command they have of language."

But M. Bouc was not interested in the emotional reactions of Englishmen. He was overcome by admiration of his friend.

"Mon cher, vous êtes épatant," he cried. "Another miraculous guess. *C'est formidable."*

"It is incredible how you think of these things," said Dr. Constantine admiringly.

"Oh, I claim no credit this time. It was not a guess. Countess Andrenyi practically told me."

"Comment? Surely not?"

"You remember I asked her about her governess or companion? I had already decided in my mind that *if* Mary Debenham were mixed up in the matter, she must have figured in the household in some such capacity."

"Yes, but the Countess Andrenyi described a totally different person."

"Exactly. A tall, middle-aged woman with red hair—in fact, the exact opposite in every respect of Miss Debenham, so much so as to be quite remarkable. But then she had to invent a name quickly, and there it was that the unconscious association of ideas gave her away. She said Miss Freebody, you remember."

"Yes?"

"Eh bien, you may not know it, but there is a shop in London that was called, until recently, Debenham & Freebody. With the name Debenham running in her head, the Countess clutches at another name

quickly, and the first that comes is Freebody. Naturally I understood immediately."

"That is yet another lie. Why did she do it?"

"Possibly more loyalty. It makes things a little difficult."

"*Ma foi*," said M. Bouc with violence. "But does everybody on this train tell lies?"

"That," said Poirot, "is what we are about to find out."

8. Further Surprising Revelations

"Nothing would surprise me now," said M. Bouc. "Nothing! Even if everybody in the train proved to have been in the Armstrong household I should not express surprise."

"That is a very profound remark," said Poirot. "Would you like to see what your favourite suspect, the Italian, has to say for himself?"

"You are going to make another of these famous guesses of yours?"

"Precisely."

"It is really a *most* extraordinary case," said Constantine.

"No, it is most natural."

M. Bouc flung up his arms in comic despair.

"If this is what you call natural, *mon ami*——"

Words failed him.

Poirot had by this time requested the dining-car attendant to fetch Antonio Foscarelli.

The big Italian had a wary look in his eye as he came in. He shot nervous glances from side to side like a trapped animal.

"What do you want?" he said. "I have nothing to tell you—nothing, do you hear! *Per Dio*——" He struck his hand on the table.

"Yes, you have something more to tell us," said Poirot firmly. "The truth!"

"The truth?" He shot an uneasy glance at Poirot. All the assurance and geniality had gone out of his manner.

"*Mais oui*. It may be that I know it already. But it will be a point in your favour if it comes from you spontaneously."

"You talk like the American police. 'Come clean,' that is what they say—'come clean.' "

"Ah! so you have had experience of the New York police?"

"No, no, never. They could not prove a thing against me—but it was not for want of trying."

Poirot said quietly:

"That was in the Armstrong case, was it not? You were the chauffeur?"

His eyes met those of the Italian. The bluster went out of the big man. He was like a pricked balloon.

"Since you know—why ask me?"

"Why did you lie this morning?"

"Business reasons. Besides, I do not trust the Yugo-Slav police. They hate the Italians. They would not have given me justice."

"Perhaps it is exactly justice that they *would* have given you!"

"No, no, I had nothing to do with this business last night. I never left my carriage. The long-faced Englishman, he can tell you so. It was not I who killed this pig—this Ratchett. You cannot prove anything against me."

Poirot was writing something on a sheet of paper. He looked up and said quietly:

"Very good. You can go."

Foscarelli lingered uneasily.

"You realise that it was not I—that I could have had nothing to do with it?"

"I said that you could go."

"It is a conspiracy. You are going to frame me? All for a pig of a man who should have gone to the chair! It was an infamy that he did not. If it had been me—if I had been arrested——"

"But it was not you. You had nothing to do with the kidnapping of the child."

"What is that you are saying? Why, that little one—she was the delight of the house. Tonio, she called me. And she would sit in the car and pretend to hold the wheel. All the household worshipped her! Even the police came to understand that. Ah, the beautiful little one."

His voice had softened. The tears came into his eyes. Then he wheeled round abruptly on his heel and strode out of the dining-car.

"Pietro," called Poirot.

The dining-car attendant came at a run.

"The No. 10—the Swedish lady."

"*Bien, Monsieur.*"

"Another?" cried M. Bouc. "Ah, no—it is not possible. I tell you it is not possible."

"*Mon cher,* we have to know. Even if in the end everybody on the train proves to have a motive for killing Ratchett, we have to know. Once we know, we can settle once for all where the guilt lies."

"My head is spinning," groaned M. Bouc.

Greta Ohlsson was ushered in sympathetically by the attendant. She was weeping bitterly.

She collapsed on the seat facing Poirot and wept steadily into a large handkerchief.

"Now do not distress yourself, Mademoiselle. Do not distress yourself." Poirot patted her on the shoulder. "Just a few little words of truth, that is all. You were the nurse who was in charge of little Daisy Armstrong?"

"It is true—it is true," wept the wretched woman. "Ah, she was an angel—a little sweet, trustful angel. She knew nothing but kindness and love—and she was taken away by that wicked man—cruelly treated—and her poor mother—and the other little one who never lived at all. You cannot understand—you cannot know—if you had been there as I was—if you had seen the whole terrible tragedy—I ought to have told you the truth about myself this morning. But I was afraid. I did so rejoice that that evil man was dead—that he could not any more kill or torture little children. Ah! I cannot speak—I have no words. . . ."

She wept with more vehemence than ever.

Poirot continued to pat her gently on the shoulder.

"There—there—I comprehend—I comprehend everything—everything, I tell you. I will ask you no more questions. It is enough that you have admitted what I know to be the truth. I understand, I tell you."

By now inarticulate with sobs, Greta Ohlsson rose and groped her way blindly towards the door. As she reached it she collided with a man coming in.

It was the valet—Masterman.

He came straight up to Poirot and spoke in his usual, quiet, unemotional voice.

"I hope I'm not intruding, sir. I thought it best to come along at once, sir, and tell you the truth. I was Colonel Armstrong's batman in the war, sir, and afterwards I was his valet in New York. I'm afraid I concealed that fact this morning. It was very wrong of me, sir, and I thought I'd better come and make a clean breast of it. But I hope, sir, that you're not suspecting Tonio in any way. Old Tonio, sir, wouldn't hurt a fly. And I can swear positively that he never left the carriage all last night. So, you see, sir, he couldn't have done it. Tonio may be a foreigner, sir, but he's a very gentle creature—not like those nasty murdering Italians one reads about."

He stopped.

Poirot looked steadily at him.

"Is that all you have to say?"

"That is all, sir."

He paused, then, as Poirot did not speak, he made an apologetic little bow, and after a momentary hesitation left the dining-car in the same quiet, unobtrusive fashion as he had come.

"This," said Dr. Constantine, "is more wildly improbable than any *roman policier* I have ever read."

"I agree," said M. Bouc. "Of the twelve passengers in that coach, nine have been proved to have had a connection with the Armstrong case. What next, I ask you? Or, should I say, who next?"

"I can almost give you the answer to your question," said Poirot. "Here comes our American sleuth, M. Hardman."

"Is he, too, coming to confess?"

Before Poirot could reply, the American had reached their table. He cocked an alert eye at them and, sitting down, he drawled out:

"Just exactly what's up on this train? It seems bughouse to me."

Poirot twinkled at him:

"Are you quite sure, M. Hardman, that you yourself were not the gardener at the Armstrong home?"

"They didn't have a garden," replied Mr. Hardman literally.

"Or the butler?"

"Haven't got the fancy manner for a place like that. No, I never had any connection with the Armstrong house—but I'm beginning to believe I'm about the only one on this train who hadn't! Can you beat it—that's what I say? Can you beat it?"

"It is certainly a little surprising," said Poirot mildly.

"*C'est rigolo,*" burst from M. Bouc.

"Have you any ideas of your own about the crime, M. Hardman?" inquired Poirot.

"No, sir. It's got me beat. I don't know how to figure it out. They can't all be in it; but which one is the guilty party is beyond me. How did you get wise to all this, that's what I want to know?"

"I just guessed."

"Then, believe me, you're a pretty slick guesser. Yes, I'll tell the world you're a slick guesser."

Mr. Hardman leaned back and looked at Poirot admiringly.

"You'll excuse me," he said, "but no one would believe it to look at you. I take off my hat to you. I do, indeed."

"You are too kind, M. Hardman."

"Not at all. I've got to hand it to you."

"All the same," said Poirot, "the problem is not yet quite solved. Can we say with authority that we know who killed M. Ratchett?"

"Count me out," said Mr. Hardman. "I'm not saying anything at all. I'm just full of natural admiration. What about the other two you've not had a guess at yet? The old American dame and the lady's-maid? I suppose we can take it that they're the only innocent parties on the train?"

"Unless," said Poirot, smiling, "we can fit them into our little collection as—shall we say?—housekeeper and cook in the Armstrong household."

"Well, nothing in the world would surprise me now," said Mr. Hardman with quiet resignation. "Bughouse—that's what this business is—bughouse!"

"Ah, *mon cher*, that would be indeed stretching coincidence a little too far," said M. Bouc. "They cannot all be in it."

Poirot looked at him.

"You do not understand," he said. "You do not understand at all. Tell me," he said, "do you know who killed Ratchett?"

"Do you?" countered M. Bouc.

Poirot nodded.

"Oh, yes," he said. "I have known for some time. It is so clear that I wonder you have not seen it also." He looked at Hardman and asked, "And you?"

The detective shook his head. He stared at Poirot curiously.

"I don't know," he said. "I don't know at all. Which of them was it?"

Poirot was silent a minute. Then he said:

"If you will be so good, M. Hardman, assemble everyone here. There are two possible solutions of this case. I want to lay them both before you all."

9. Poirot Propounds Two Solutions

The passengers came crowding into the restaurant-car and took their seats round the tables. They all bore more or less the same expression, one of expectancy mingled with apprehension. The Swedish lady was still weeping and Mrs. Hubbard was comforting her.

"Now you must just take a hold on yourself, my dear. Everything's going to be perfectly all right. You mustn't lose your grip on yourself. If one of us is a nasty murderer we know quite well it isn't you. Why, anyone would be crazy even to think of such a thing. You sit here and I'll stay right by you; and don't you worry any."

Her voice died away as Poirot stood up.

The Wagon Lit conductor was hovering in the doorway.

"You permit that I stay, Monsieur?"

"Certainly, Michel."

Poirot cleared his throat.

"Messieurs et Mesdames, I will speak in English, since I think all of you know a little of that language. We are here to investigate the death of Samuel Edward Ratchett—alias Cassetti. There are two possible solutions of the crime. I shall put them both before you, and I shall ask M. Bouc and Dr. Constantine here to judge which solution is the right one.

"Now you all know the facts of the case. Mr. Ratchett was found stabbed this morning. He was last known to be alive at 12:37 last night, when he spoke to the Wagon Lit conductor through the door. A watch in his pyjama pocket was found to be badly dented and it had stopped at a quarter-past one. Dr. Constantine, who examined the body when found, puts the time of death as having occurred between midnight and two in the morning. At half an hour after midnight, as you all know, the train ran into a snowdrift. After that time *it was impossible for anyone to leave the train*.

"The evidence of Mr. Hardman, who is a member of a New York detective agency" (several heads turned to look at Mr. Hardman) "shows that no one could have passed his compartment (No. 16 at the extreme end) without being seen by him. We are therefore forced to the conclusion that the murderer is to be found among the occupants of one particular coach—the Stamboul-Calais coach.

"That, I will say, *was* our theory."

"*Comment?*" ejaculated M. Bouc, startled.

"But I will put before you an alternative theory. It is very simple. Mr. Ratchett had a certain enemy whom he feared. He gave Mr. Hardman a description of this enemy and told him that the attempt, if made at all, would most probably be made on the second night out from Stamboul.

"Now I put it to you, ladies and gentlemen, that Mr. Ratchett knew a good deal more than he told. The enemy, as Mr. Ratchett expected, joined the train at *Belgrade, or possibly at Vincovci,* by the door left open by Colonel Arbuthnot and Mr. MacQueen who had just descended to the platform. He was provided with a suit of Wagon Lit uniform, which he wore over his ordinary clothes, and a pass key which enabled him to gain access to Mr. Ratchett's compartment in spite of the door being locked. Mr. Ratchett was under the influence of a sleeping draught. This man stabbed him with great ferocity and left the compartment through the communicating door leading to Mrs. Hubbard's compartment—"

"That's so," said Mrs. Hubbard, nodding her head.

"He thrust the dagger he had used into Mrs. Hubbard's sponge-bag in passing. Without knowing it, he lost a button of his uniform. Then he slipped out of the compartment and along the corridor. He hastily thrust the uniform into a suitcase in an empty compartment, and a few minutes later, dressed in ordinary clothes, he left the train just before it started off. Again using the same means of egress—the door near the dining-car."

Everybody gasped.

"What about that watch?" demanded Mr. Hardman.

"There you have the explanation of the whole thing. *Mr. Ratchett had omitted to put his watch back an hour as he should have done* at Tzaribrod. His watch still registered Eastern European time, which is one hour *ahead* of Central European time. It was a quarter-past *twelve* when Mr. Ratchett was stabbed—not a quarter-past one."

"But it is absurd, that explanation," cried M. Bouc. "What of the voice that spoke from the compartment at twenty-three minutes to one. It was either the voice of Ratchett—or else of his murderer."

"Not necessarily. It might have been—well—a third person. One who had gone in to speak to Ratchett and found him dead. He rang the bell to summon the conductor, then, as you express it, the wind rose in him —he was afraid of being accused of the crime and he spoke pretending to be Ratchett."

"*C'est possible,*" admitted M. Bouc grudgingly.

Poirot stared at Mrs. Hubbard.

"Yes, Madame, you were going to say——?"

"Well, I don't quite know what I was going to say. Do you think I forgot to put my watch back too?"

"No, Madame. I think you heard the man pass through—but unconsciously; later you had a nightmare of a man being in your compartment and woke up with a start and rang for the conductor."

"Well, I suppose that's possible," admitted Mrs. Hubbard.

Princess Dragomiroff was looking at Poirot with a very direct glance.

"How do you explain the evidence of my maid, Monsieur?"

"Very simply, Madame. Your maid recognised the handkerchief I showed her as yours. She somewhat clumsily tried to shield you. She did encounter the man—but earlier—while the train was at Vincovci station. She pretended to have seen him at a later hour with a confused idea of giving you a watertight *alibi.*"

The Princess bowed her head.

"You have thought of everything, Monsieur. I—I admire you."

There was a silence.

Then everyone jumped as Dr. Constantine suddenly hit the table a blow with his fist.

"But no," he said. "No, no, and again no! That is an explanation that will not hold water. It is deficient in a dozen minor points. The crime was not committed so—M. Poirot must know that perfectly well."

Poirot turned a curious glance on him.

"I see," he said, "that I shall have to give you my second solution. But do not abandon this one too abruptly. You may agree with it later."

He turned back again to face the others.

"There is another possible solution of the crime. This is how I arrived at it.

"When I had heard all the evidence, I leaned back and shut my eyes and began to *think*. Certain points presented themselves to me as worthy of attention. I enumerated these points to my two colleagues. Some I had already elucidated—such as a grease-spot on a passport, etc. I will run over the points that remain. The first and most important is a remark made to me by M. Bouc in the restaurant-car at lunch on the first day after leaving Stamboul—to the effect that the company assembled was interesting because it was so varied—representing as it did all classes and nationalities.

"I agreed with him, but when this particular point came into my mind, I tried to imagine whether such an assembly were ever likely to be collected under any other conditions. And the answer I made to myself was—only in America. In America there might be a household composed of just such varied nationalities—an Italian chauffeur, an English governess, a Swedish nurse, a French lady's-maid and so on. That led me to my scheme of 'guessing'—that is, casting each person for a certain part in the Armstrong drama much as a producer casts a play. Well, that gave me an extremely interesting and satisfactory result.

"I had also examined in my own mind each separate person's evidence with some curious results. Take first the evidence of Mr. MacQueen. My first interview with him was entirely satisfactory. But in my second he made rather a curious remark. I had described to him the finding of a note mentioning the Armstrong case. He said, 'But surely——' and then paused and went on, 'I mean—that was rather careless of the old man.'

"Now I could feel that that was not what he had started out to say. *Supposing what he had meant to say was, 'But surely that was burnt!'* In which case, *MacQueen knew of the note and of its destruction*—in other words, he was either the murderer or an accomplice of the murderer. Very good.

"Then the valet. He said his master was in the habit of taking a sleeping draught when travelling by train. That might be true, but *would Ratchett have taken one last night?* The automatic under his pillow gave the lie to that statement. Ratchett intended to be on the alert last night. Whatever narcotic was administered to him must have been done so without his knowledge. By whom? Obviously by MacQueen or the valet.

"Now we come to the evidence of Mr. Hardman. I believed all that he told me about his own identity, but when it came to the actual methods he had employed to guard Mr. Ratchett, his story was neither more nor less than absurd. The only way effectively to have protected Ratchett was to have passed the night actually in his compartment or in some spot where he could watch the door. The only thing that his evidence *did* show plainly was that no one *in any other part of the train could possibly have murdered Ratchett*. It drew a clear circle round the Stamboul-Calais carriage. That seemed to me a rather curious and inexplicable fact, and I put it aside to think over.

"You probably have all heard by now of the few words I overheard between Miss Debenham and Colonel Arbuthnot. The interesting thing to my mind was the fact that Colonel Arbuthnot called her *Mary* and was clearly on terms of intimacy with her. But the Colonel was only supposed to have met her a few days previously—and I know Englishmen of the Colonel's type. Even if he had fallen in love with the young lady at first sight, he would have advanced slowly and with decorum—not rushing things. Therefore I concluded that Colonel Arbuthnot and Miss Debenham were in reality well acquainted, and were for some reason pretending to be strangers. Another small point was Miss Debenham's easy familiarity with the term 'long distance' for a telephone call. Yet Miss Debenham had told me that she had never been in the States.

"To pass to another witness. Mrs. Hubbard had told us that lying in bed she was unable to see whether the communicating door was bolted or not, and so asked Miss Ohlsson to see for her. Now, though her statement would have been perfectly true if she had been occupying compartments Nos. 2, 4, 12, or any *even* number—where the bolt is directly under the handle of the door—in the *uneven* numbers, such as compartment No. 3, the bolt is well *above* the handle and could not therefore be masked by the sponge-bag in the least. I was forced to the conclusion that Mrs. Hubbard was inventing an incident that had never occurred.

"And here let me say just a word or two about *times*. To my mind, the really interesting point about the dented watch was the place where it was found—in Ratchett's pyjama pocket, a singularly uncomfortable and unlikely place to keep one's watch, especially as there is a watch 'hook' provided just by the head of the bed. I felt sure, therefore, that the watch had been deliberately placed in the pocket and faked. The crime, then, was not committed at a quarter-past one.

"Was it, then, committed earlier? To be exact, at twenty-three minutes to one? My friend M. Bouc advanced as an argument in favour of it the loud cry which awoke me from sleep. But if Ratchett were heavily drugged *he could not have cried out*. If he had been capable of crying out he would have been capable of making some kind of a struggle to defend himself, and there were no signs of any such struggle.

"I remembered that MacQueen had called attention, not once but twice (and the second time in a very blatant manner), to the fact that Ratchett could speak no French. I came to the conclusion that the whole business at twenty-three minutes to one was a comedy played for my benefit! Anyone might see through the watch business—it is a common enough device in detective stories. They assumed that I *should* see through it and that, pluming myself on my own cleverness, I would go on to assume that since Ratchett spoke no French the voice I heard at twenty-three minutes to one could not be his, and that Ratchett must be already dead. But I am convinced that at twenty-three minutes to one Ratchett was still lying in his drugged sleep.

"But the device has succeeded! I have opened my door and looked out. I have actually heard the French phrase used. If I am so unbelievably dense as not to realise the significance of that phrase, it must be brought to my attention. If necessary MacQueen can come right out in the open. He can say, 'Excuse me, M. Poirot, *that can't have been Mr. Ratchett speaking*. He can't speak French.'

"Now when was the real time of the crime? And who killed him?

"In my opinion, and this is only an opinion, Ratchett was killed at some time very close upon two o'clock, the latest hour the doctor gives us as possible.

"As to who killed him——"

He paused, looking at his audience. He could not complain of any lack of attention. Every eye was fixed upon him. In the stillness you could have heard a pin drop.

He went on slowly:

"I was particularly struck by the extraordinary difficulty of proving a case against any one person on the train and on the rather curious coincidence that in each case the testimony giving an alibi came from what I might describe as an 'unlikely' person. Thus Mr. MacQueen and Colonel Arbuthnot provided alibis for each other—two persons between whom it seemed most unlikely there should be any prior acquaintanceship. The same thing happened with the English valet and the Italian, with the Swedish lady and the English girl. I said to myself, 'This is extraordinary—they cannot *all* be in it!'

"And then, Messieurs, I saw light. They were *all* in it. For so many people connected with the Armstrong case to be travelling by the same train by a coincidence was not only unlikely, it was *impossible*. It must be not chance, but *design*. I remembered a remark of Colonel Arbuthnot's about trial by jury. A jury is composed of twelve people—there were twelve passengers—Ratchett was stabbed twelve times. And the thing that had worried me all along—the extraordinary crowd travelling in the Stamboul-Calais coach at a slack time of year was explained.

"Ratchett had escaped justice in America. There was no question as to his guilt. I visualised a self-appointed jury of twelve people who condemned him to death and were forced by the exigencies of the case to be their own executioners. And immediately, on that assumption, the whole case fell into beautiful shining order.

"I saw it as a perfect mosaic, each person playing his or her allotted part. It was so arranged that if suspicion should fall on any one person, the evidence of one or more of the others would clear the accused person and confuse the issue. Hardman's evidence was necessary in case some outsider should be suspected of the crime and be unable to prove an alibi. The passengers in the Stamboul carriage were in no danger. Every minute detail of their evidence was worked out beforehand. The whole thing was a very cleverly-planned jig-saw puzzle, so arranged that every fresh piece of knowledge that came to light made the solution of the whole more difficult. As my friend M. Bouc remarked, the case seemed fantastically impossible! That was exactly the impression intended to be conveyed.

"Did this solution explain everything? Yes, it did. The nature of the wounds—each inflicted by a different person. The artificial threatening letters—artificial since they were unreal, written only to be produced as evidence. (Doubtless there were real letters, warning Ratchett of his fate, which MacQueen destroyed, substituting for them these others.) Then Hardman's story of being called in by Ratchett—a lie, of course, from beginning to end—the description of the mythical 'small dark man with a womanish voice,' a convenient description, since it had the merit of not incriminating any of the actual Wagon Lit conductors and would apply equally well to a man or a woman.

"The idea of stabbing is at first sight a curious one, but on reflection nothing would fit the circumstances so well. A dagger was a weapon that could be used by everyone—strong or weak—and it made no noise. I fancy, though I may be wrong, that each person in turn entered Ratchett's darkened compartment through that of Mrs. Hubbard—and struck! They themselves would never know which blow actually killed him.

"The final letter which Ratchett had probably found on his pillow was carefully burnt. With no clue pointing to the Armstrong case, there would be absolutely no reason for suspecting any of the passengers on the train. It would be put down as an outside job, and the 'small dark man with the womanish voice' would actually have been seen by one or more of the passengers leaving the train at Brod.

"I do not know exactly what happened when the conspirators discovered that that part of their plan was impossible owing to the accident to the train. There was, I imagine, a hasty consultation, and then they decided to go through with it. It was true that now one and all of the passengers were bound to come under suspicion, but that possibility had already been foreseen and provided for. The only additional thing to be done was to confuse the issue even further. Two so-called 'clues' were dropped in the dead man's compartment—one incriminating Colonel Arbuthnot (who had the strongest alibi and whose connection with the Armstrong family was probably the hardest to prove) and the second clue, the handkerchief, incriminating Princess Dragomiroff, who by virtue of her social position, her particularly frail physique and the alibi given her by her maid and the conductor, was practically in an unassailable position. Further to confuse the issue, a 'red herring' was drawn across the trail—the mythical woman in the red kimono. Again I am to bear witness to this woman's existence. There is a heavy bang at my door. I get up and look out—and see the scarlet kimono disappearing in the distance. A judicious selection of people—the conductor, Miss Debenham and MacQueen—will also have seen her. It was, I think, someone with a sense of humour who thoughtfully placed the scarlet kimono on the top of my suitcase whilst I was interviewing people in the dining-car. Where the garment came from in the first place I do not know. I suspect it is the property of Countess Andrenyi, since her luggage contained only a chiffon negligée so elaborate as to be more a tea gown than a dressing-gown.

"When MacQueen first learned that the letter which had been so carefully burnt had in part escaped destruction, and that the word Armstrong was exactly the word remaining, he must at once have communicated his news to the others. It was at this minute that the position of Countess Andrenyi became acute and her husband immediately took steps to alter the passport. It was their second piece of bad luck!

"They one and all agreed to deny utterly any connection with the Armstrong family. They knew I had no immediate means of finding out the truth, and they did not believe that I should go into the matter unless my suspicions were aroused against one particular person.

"Now there was one further point to consider. Allowing that my theory of the crime was the correct one, and I believe that it *must* be the correct one, then obviously the Wagon Lit conductor himself must be privy to the plot. But if so, that gave us thirteen persons, not twelve. Instead of the usual formula, 'Of so many people one is guilty,' I was faced with the problem that of thirteen persons one and one only was innocent. Which was that person?

"I came to a very odd conclusion. I came to the conclusion that the person who had taken no part in the crime was the person who would be considered the most likely to do so. I refer to Countess Andrenyi. I was impressed by the earnestness of her husband when he swore to me solemnly on his honour that his wife never left her compartment that night. I decided that Count Andrenyi took, so to speak, his wife's place.

"If so, then Pierre Michel was definitely one of the twelve. But how could one explain his complicity? He was a decent man who had been many years in the employ of the Company—not the kind of man who could be bribed to assist in a crime. Then Pierre Michel must be involved in the Armstrong case. But that seemed very improbable. Then I remembered that the dead nursery-maid was French. Supposing that that unfortunate girl had been Pierre Michel's daughter. That would explain everything—it would also explain the place chosen for the staging of the crime. Were there any others whose part in the drama was not clear? Colonel Arbuthnot I put down as a friend of the Armstrongs. They had probably been through the war together. The maid, Hildegarde Schmidt, I could guess her place in the Armstrong household. I am, perhaps, overgreedy, but I sense a good cook instinctively. I laid a trap for her—she fell into it. I said I knew she was a good cook. She answered, 'Yes, indeed, all my ladies have said so.' But if you are employed as a *lady's-maid* your employers seldom have a chance of learning whether or not you are a good cook.

"Then there was Hardman. He seemed quite definitely not to belong to the Armstrong household. I could only imagine that he had been in love with the French girl. I spoke to him of the charm of foreign women —and again I obtained the reaction I was looking for. Sudden tears came into his eyes, which he pretended were dazzled by the snow.

"There remains Mrs. Hubbard. Now Mrs. Hubbard, let me say, played the most important part in the drama. By occupying the compartment communicating with that of Ratchett she was more open to suspicion than anyone else. In the nature of things she could not have an alibi to fall back upon. To play the part she played—the perfectly natural, slightly ridiculous American fond mother—an artist was needed. But there *was* an artist connected with the Armstrong family—Mrs. Armstrong's mother—Linda Arden, the actress. . . ."

He stopped.

Then, in a soft rich dreamy voice, quite unlike the one she had used all the journey, Mrs. Hubbard said:

"I always fancied myself in comedy parts."

She went on still dreamily:

"That slip about the sponge-bag was silly. It shows you should always rehearse properly. We tried it on the way out—I was in an even number compartment then, I suppose. I never thought of the bolts being in different places."

She shifted her position a little and looked straight at Poirot.

"You know all about it, M. Poirot. You're a very wonderful man. But even you can't quite imagine what it was like—that awful day in New York. I was just crazy with grief—so were the servants—and Colonel Arbuthnot was there, too. He was John Armstrong's best friend."

"He saved my life in the war," said Arbuthnot.

"We decided then and there—perhaps we were mad—I don't know—that the sentence of death that Cassetti had escaped had got to be carried out. There were twelve of us—or rather eleven—Susanne's father was over in France, of course. First we thought we'd draw lots as to who should do it, but in the end we decided on this way. It was the chauffeur, Antonio, who suggested it. Mary worked out all the details later with Hector MacQueen. He'd always adored Sonia—my daughter—and it was he who explained to us exactly how Cassetti's money had managed to get him off.

"It took a long time to perfect our plan. We had first to track Ratchett down. Hardman managed that in the end. Then we had to try to get Masterman and Hector into his employment—or at any rate one of them. Well, we managed that. Then we had a consultation with Susanne's father. Colonel Arbuthnot was very keen on having twelve of us. He seemed to think it made it more in order. He didn't like the stabbing idea much, but he agreed that it did solve most of our difficulties. Well, Susanne's father was willing. Susanne was his only child. We knew from Hector that Ratchett would be coming back from the East sooner or later by the Orient Express. With Pierre Michel actually working on that train, the chance was too good to be missed. Besides, it would be a good way of not incriminating any outsiders.

"My daughter's husband had to know, of course, and he insisted on coming on the train with her. Hector wangled it so that Ratchett selected the right day for travelling when Michel would be on duty. We N2 meant to engage every carriage in the Stamboul-Calais coach, but unfortunately there was one carriage we couldn't get. It was reserved long beforehand for a director of the company. Mr. Harris, of course, was a myth. But it would have been awkward to have any stranger in Hector's compartment. And then, at the last minute, *you* came. . . ."

She stopped.

"Well," she said. "You know everything now, M. Poirot. What are you going to do about it? If it must all come out, can't you lay the blame upon me and me only? I would have stabbed that man twelve times willingly. It wasn't only that he was responsible for my daughter's death and her child's, and that of the other child who might have been alive and happy now. It was more than that. There had been other children before Daisy—there might be others in the future. Society had condemned him; we were only carrying out the sentence. But it's unnecessary to bring all these others into it. All these good faithful souls—and poor Michel—and Mary and Colonel Arbuthnot—they love each other. . . ."

Her voice was wonderful echoing through the crowded space—that deep, emotional, heart-stirring voice that had thrilled many a New York audience.

Poirot looked at his friend.

"You are a director of the company, M. Bouc," he said. "What do you say?"

M. Bouc cleared his throat.

"In my opinion, M. Poirot," he said, "the first theory you put forward was the correct one—decidedly so. I suggest that that is the solution we offer to the Yugo-Slavian police when they arrive. You agree, Doctor?"

"Certainly I agree," said Dr. Constantine. "As regards the medical evidence, I think—er—that I made one or two fantastic suggestions."

"Then," said Poirot, "having placed my solution before you, I have the honour to retire from the case. . . ."